Creatures Of Habit

Creatures Of Habit

by The Harlequin

Dedicated to amusement, fun, and pure hilarity. It is with the purpose of entertainment and the spreading of divine jest that I have assembled this comedy, and furthermore expect it to be used as such. I pray dearly that all of those who come upon this text can see the comedic value in coincidence and tragedy to the same degree as I do.

OF INK AND ICHYR

TALE TIMELINE

THE DUKE'S FOLLY

THE GARDENER'S PARADOX

THE KYGEN COLLECTIVE
TWO PRINCES

CROWLUST

THE LULLABY, THE EMPRYSS,
AND THE ULTIMATE BIRD

Collection of Stories

The Lullaby, The Empryss, and The Ultimate Bird

Rounded Down to a Misfit, Midge, Machine, and Missionary. What Fun.

~*~*~*~*~*~*~*~*~*~

Dead Crow Lullaby
A Jeweler's Bluff
Yen For The Finer
An Undying Matter
Scent of A Scavenger
Mask of Sixteen Notches
A Marble Among Her Eyes
Berceuse of The Needle
Abyssal Thread
The Dud

~*~*~*~*~*~*~*~*~*~

The Gardener's Paradox

What is Living and What is Not?

~*~*~*~*~*~*~*~*~*~

Divine Horticulture
The Gardener's Recluse I
The Gardener's Recluse II
The Gardener's Recluse III
The Gardener's Recluse IV

~*~*~*~*~*~*~*~*~*~

The Kygen Collective

The Sordid Remains of Them, Touché!

~*~*~*~*~*~*~*~*~*~

Infinity Seems Purple Today
Lacking Legs of Flesh (Like Us)
Promenade Distress Tokens
Unlike Nothing Seen Prior!
Great Mechromancer Prometh

~*~*~*~*~*~*~*~*~*~

Collection of Stories (Cont.)

Two Princes

One of Kingly Commission, and the Other of Sky-Lark Ceremony.

~*~*~*~*~*~*~*~*~*~*~

Lips Of Coz
Following True Love's Kiss
Like a Fish in a Birdcage

~*~*~*~*~*~*~*~*~*~*~

Crowlust

It Can Spring Up in the Oddest of Places!

~*~*~*~*~*~*~*~*~*~*~

Ignore Their Jaws
The Ink Now Pours,
Forget What Was,

~*~*~*~*~*~*~*~*~*~*~

Of Ink and Ichyr

And All the Things Between.

~*~*~*~*~*~*~*~*~*~*~

Daybreak
Bloody Fingers and Eel
Dynasty of the Dead and Buried
Hope Sewn of Living Sinew
Heart of Ink

~*~*~*~*~*~*~*~*~*~*~

The Duke's Folly

Until Death Do Us Part, Again.

~*~*~*~*~*~*~*~*~*~*~

Vignette
Zealot's Wood
Pilothome
The Last Titan
Myceliac

~*~*~*~*~*~*~*~*~*~*~

Table of Contents

Act I

Table of Contents

Act II

Act I

~ *Dead Crow Lullaby*

Documented in the decrepit logbooks left in
the Squall's back room...

Moonstone, Ice. There was some snow drifting into the cavern as well—as if driven in by a distant gust—but there was no wind blowing. The creature, its form derived from the muck, its body comprised entirely of a coarse and cold sludge, blew out the only breath for miles. One could hear the sloshing of guts and gore, slurping from a hunger untamed. The beast turned to the call of the ice; the storm was thinning just outside the cave. It did not recall how long it had been waiting, consuming, biding its time. The storm was to stop eventually, and then the creature would be free. It learned the sting of cold its first night. Without any distancing from its flesh and the sky, the wind played fickle jokes on the beast, poking at its body with malignant spite. On the second night, the creature learned the sin of theft. It did not contemplate morality, nor the respect of the dead. If the owner of such cloth no longer needed it, then why should a beast so cold and bare leave these clothes to let freeze? After all, stealing from the *deceased* was a far lesser misdeed. The corpse had worn a face of perhaps iron—some metal—the creature did not know. It was weaved with elegant precision, feathers, and crowns across its casing, the beak of course most prominent of all. The eyes that the beast once knew to glow had dulled, sullied by the ice of the caves. The body was lost, as well. It had melted and festered into a rotten stench for presumably days, rancid maggots still creeping through its fingertips. The armor it wore was far too bright, bright enough to blind mortal ears. But the cloak was durable and fine enough. Though it was ragged, torn from bind to bind, rips and tears of various shapes floated among the sea of velvety emerald fabric. The creature had not hesitated to wrap its accursed dripping form, even despite the hazardous glow of the metal pin upon its clasp. When the third night brought moonlit silence, the creature and its cloak—disregarding the crow-like calf it had ravaged—left the cavern, seeking refuge in what was not so primitive a homestead. The storm had lessened to a pitter of snow, a quiet dance of white on the soot-black sky. Two orbs of chalk spun off in the distance, glass moons. The creature could not find solace even in this weakened snow. Every particle was a new flash of piercing noise, every gust a glow of color. As it continued from its birthplace, the creature pondered turning back. The cave could be fitted with a defensive stone, a barrier from the storm. The beast could perhaps find a cover of safety in the morning. But then, a structure appeared in the trumpeting blindness of the storm. A place, it thought, a quiet place. The creature approached the wooden front of the building, a large unkempt door stood in its path, its solid iron knob cold with familiarity. The creature shook its bony wrists, reaching out for the distant cries of the door, the loudness of its surface. A simple push and the barrier was caved, a new place of subtle resound was displayed before the creature. The roar of the fire's color drove away the quiet blankness of the storm. The blinding of the colorful crackling of cinders and oak—perhaps not oak, but no bother. The room was filled with tables, four seats aligned at each. A hardwood surface ran along the walls, dotted with skulls or paintings or some combination of the two. There were two windows that the beast could comprehend—one lay behind itself, placed beside the door. The window acted as a large viewing place to see what crept behind the safety of the walls. The other was beside the fire, on the left side of the room. It was far smaller and draped with a cloth. The room had no life about it, no people to dance on the nailed-down carpets, no fools to chortle in the sturdy wood seats. The tap dripped intermittently from across the way, a single man sat watching the droplets. He now watched the beast, of course. The deafening din of the ever-lasting flame called to the beast, and thus, it followed, stumbling to all fours as it hastened to the fire. The large white eyes of the beast peered into the open flame. Its flesh had ceased to drizzle, its hands as hard as rock. The beast reached out a single one of these hands, a lesskin appendage, a dual-jointed, five-digit-ed hand. The flame hovered just below this hand, baking its core with heat and hope. The creature did not move, and the flesh began to singe. The pungent smell of scorched bone and mold filled the air, and an unnoticeable burn spread across the creature's fingertips. The bartender, who with silent petrification had been observing the habits and (terribly) wettened skin from the all too comforting comfort of behind his bar, swallowed deeply to himself, a frown spreading across his rough chin,

"Aye, that there fire is as real as it gets, and that burn 'ill be too if you don't move that arm o' yours." The creature turned to the sudden flashes produced by the bartender's words. It saw the phrases and letters, each spelled and glowing with their own unique shades. The creature titled its head, staring at the unknowns. It presumed the noticeably natural ability to view the sounds of the air and hear the colors of the night sky was a universal communicative trait. Perhaps, it thought, it was wrong. Its two antennae twitched with thought, wondering how it could reach the bartender, to speak with him. "Hey now, you numb over there? You're burning your damn hand off." The creature peered at its hand, and then at the bartender, whose words were as bright and as potent as the light of the moon. It slowly retracted its hand from the flame, the bartender nodding in appreciation as it did so. The two returned to their stares of silence, the bartender quietly wishing the creature would either speak or leave. "Hey, er, big guy? You a mute or something?" The creature could not understand this phrase, its mannerisms and colors far too complex for its feeble mind. It wanted to interact with the bartender, but could not conceive a comprehensive way to do such a thing. A memory drifted into the beast's mind, a recollection of currency. It reached to its waist, a small brown pouch adhered to its pants with twine, and pulled from within a small token. It was a dull coin, covered in a strange sour moss, smelling of rotting wood. The creature rose from its place by the fire, slowly shambling closer and nearer, the bartender instinctively reaching for the handle tucked in his belt. The beast halted, a tense emptiness vexing the two. The creature placed a hand on the bar, letting it linger for a moment, wiggling its fingers as if it had never seen them move before. The beast subconsciously knew of the weapon the bartender possessed. It had some few memories of gunfire. It slowly pulled its hand from the bar, leaving in its place the mossy coin. The bartender's eyes widened at the sight of the currency. He quickly snatched it off the bar and flipped it into his right hand. He held the coin before his eyes, staring deeply into the inscribed bird symbol, obscured by moss and ivy. He looked past the coin, to the beast, who was silently, emotionlessly staring into the bartender's eyes. The bartender leaned forward onto the hardwood counter, his hair bouncing with the sudden movement. His face drew closer to the beast, sizing it up, learning its structure. The creature could practically hear the flesh of the bartender, a soft pinkish color, dotted with scruff and hair. The eyes of the man were smaller than most, heavy discoloration drooping beneath them. A small band of cyan fabric was tied taught around the bartender's forehead, keeping the abyss of black upon his head from spilling out onto his face. The colorful rustles of the bartender's clothing blinked before the creature, a fur coat with silk attachments, and soft tufts of cotton fluff wrapped the collar of its shape. A firm padding of leather was bolted to the right arm of the coat, as well as around the waist. A glistening of sound emerged from the necklace of metal sigils resting around the man's neck. He was shorter than the creature, by a noticeable sum. His relatively baggy garments hid the true build of his body. "You don't seem like no saint, but I'm sure you ain't a sinner either. You ought to ditch those coins, big guy, wouldn't want you gettin' tangled up in something bigger than yourself." The creature tilted its head forwards, it did not want to see many more of these colorful words. They pained its sore eyes. The beast tore the pouch from its hip, and placed it on the bar, its fingers shaking with uncertainty. The bartender hefted the bag into his hands, pouring the coins through his fingertips, letting the wealth drop to the ground. "You know, beasties like you really make me think. Back in the day, most people would kill a thing like you on sight! Lark had a whole lot more support back then, I s'pose." The bartender reached into his front belt and pulled from it a tall, stunted revolver. He held it up to the beast, as if to show it he was armed, and then placed it on the bar. He shot a smile at the creature, so the creature thought it only kind to return one. "Now, how old are you, beastie? I'd bet you have novels o' stories to tell, and here you are silent as a dove." The creature clicked its tongue, unsure of how long this conversation would last. It glared its cold eyes into the bartender's, who was busy in thought, thinking of how best to escape the beast if it was angered. "I'll guess you're waiting for that drink? You overpaid this one a little, buddy, but fine." The bartender took the opportunity to look away, finding a relatively clean glass to give to the creature. He filled it with haste, spun back around, and slid the drink across the bar, right into the hand of the beast. The bartender returned to a small washbin of sorts, filled with steins and mugs of various colors and sizes. He plucked one of the glasses from the bin, taking with it a small towel with which to wash it. "So, you got a name beastie? If you're not so keen on talking, there's some parchment on the bar, right there 'n front of you." The creature looked at the paper, unsure of what to write. It had no name, nothing to expect. Maybe the creature could *tell* the bartender. Maybe it could understand. The bartender finished his glass, and picked up another, looking over his shoulder, expecting an answer to his question, "Alright then, I guess not. You want one?" The creature remained motionless, watching the bartender work, occasionally glancing at the raging storm outside, it had picked up quite a bit since it entered. The bartender turned from the wash bin, staring at the beast, "Void tell, you sure are a talkative one. Here, give me that." The bartender slipped the parchment from under the beast's drink. He pulled a small feather from his headband, and scribbled away on the sheet, holding the cup within the crook of his arm. The creature took notice of the edges of the paper, burnt slightly—curled and yellow with purpose and age. "There, how about that? Best I got." The bartender slid the parchment back over to the creature, untouched apart from the word "Roach" having been hastily penned upon it. "That work for you? I'm not exactly gettin' any feedback here." Roach looked up from the parchment, nodding its head slowly, the bartender sighed with relief, placing the feather back into his headband. "Name's Jeweler, Jewels if we're close." The bartender slammed his fist down next to his gun, meeting Roach nose to nose. "We ain't close, you hear?" The creature stared back, unsure what to do. Jeweler chuckled and returned to washing mugs. Roach took the moment to peer into the reflection of himself, within the drink he had been served. The rippling currents distorted its large merciless eyes. Its black face almost glowed in the amber liquid, the white orbs of sight beacons in the sea of spirits. Its own two antennae almost drooped into the fluid, hovering mere inches above the surface. Roach had little familiarity with its shape, but in its memories, it recalled the existence of insects, flies—roaches. Being compared to one was no compliment, but in this case, Roach thought, it was more than fair. The creature raised one of its harshly burned fingertips above the parchment. It tapped the letters, each one slowly on its own. The bartender turned to glance at the creature, curious. The soft tapping continued, Roach not looking from the paper he was tapping upon. Jeweler placed his hand on the parchment, just in front of Roach's finger. Roach stopped, and looked up at Jeweler, their eyes locking once again. It raised a cold mucky finger, and pointed it back at itself, gesturing with the other hand to the parchment. "Hey, look at that! Someone's got a brain after all!" Jeweler laughed, moving away from the bar, over to the window beside the fire, still washing a rather dirtied mug.

"Jewel." A creeping grind uttered from behind the bartender. A small shiver went down his spine, he had once wished for Roach to speak, but he now found himself wishing he had never heard its voice. Jeweler braced himself for fear, hearing the wooden planks of the bar's floor creaking just behind him. He shot a regretful glance towards the pistol he had left upon the bar. He saw one of Roach's narrow hands reach out beside him, and Jeweler felt a pike of terror pierce his heart. But in a blink, a moment unrecalled by Jeweler, Roach was sitting by the fire again, his outstretched hand roasting over the open flame once more. Jeweler shuddered, chilled by his own imagination.

"Alright, I take it back. Don't speak ever again, that voice is beyond unholy." Jeweler returned to the bar, placing the final mug back upon its shelf. He stared at a small, pinned sheet of paper, hanging just above his washbin. A bounty, one he had kept in honor of a cancerous memory, one painting his face. Jeweler was dug in deep; he considered himself beyond the cure of menial law. Criminal pursuit was fleeting, he was already burdened with misdeeds, and what was one more? The profit would be worth the draw. An intelligent, feral, ceaseless discharge of violence at the fingertips of an absentee to morality—a truly unrivaled hand. With another viewing of the beast's charred wrist, Jeweler reconsidered the definition he had previously given the beast. Certainly feral, perhaps not as intelligent as presumed. "Roach!" The beast returned to sight, the gloomish leaning tip of its closest antenna shook the bartender to his core. "You got your name now, how 'bout an owner?"

~ A Jeweler's Bluff

Stolen from the premiere paint of an
infamous Shorerunner's journal...

Jeweler had found that a wound not fatal was often more painful. The closer to death an injury brought him, the lesser the pain seemed to affect him; survival burned the blood. A simple graze, much like the cut that was dripping blood down his left leg, always hurt the worst. It burned, stung like a larval Thanicker. Even touching the roughed flesh could make him wince. The graze was exposed to the cold air of the moon as well, making it throb only further. Sometimes he wished his pursuers could have as much a hand in precision as he did. He ducked under the low-hanging branch of a calep tree, pushing its leaves of flesh and beef from his face. He couldn't maintain a high speed with his leg in such terrible condition, but with some clever moves and a light foot, Jeweler was certain he could lose his tail without the need for solid pacing. However, the blood left a quite revealing trail behind him, and with this trail came an impossible chance of hiding. Jeweler managed to quickly stuff his hand in the satchel slung across his back, tugging from it a small scarf, to the sight of which he let out an exhausted gasp of joy. He slid down a small icy hill, taking the moment to tie the scarf around his wound, keeping it from revealing his location. As he leapt from the slope, landing himself safely at the bottom of a small ditch in the landscape, a needlefeather flew through the treeline, striking Jeweler square in his right shoulder, uncoupling his bag from his body, and digging itself into his meat. He grabbed at his shoulder blade, attempting to remove the needlefeather, but Jeweler could not reach it. He bit at his lower lip, his eyes frantically scanning the forest from which he had emerged. There were eyes in the dark—thousands of eyes, all shifting and pulsing toward him. He was trapped in this divot, the only way out now blocked by those who pursued him, and remained in no fighting condition. Jeweler would never admit truthful disadvantage, but he knew with certainty he was at one. A single Gretch Princess leaped from the bushes above and— underestimating the drop of the hillside—came tumbling down to Jeweler. He quickly tore his pistol from his belt, pointing the frosted barrel at the incapacitated Gretch. Its terrible thirteen eyes were shaking, its beak bruised from the fall. The hairy pines that grew along their forehead jostled in the wind. The Princess had gathered its shape up in its wings, keeping the cold at bay. Jeweler rolled the Princess over with his foot, keeping his aim trained on the fool. Several more Gretch mounted small cover points atop the slope, sneering down at their fallen sister. They let out a chorus of hisses, a deterrent, to keep Jeweler from rushing them. Jeweler had no intention of moving from his current location. A few of the bird-beasts had begun to step towards the drop, attempting to make their way down to Jeweler. They were slipping, sinking their feet far too deep into the snow, stumbling back with fear of falling. This did not amuse Jeweler, "Hey! Hey, you feather-winged sausage packs, I suggest on you staying *right* where you are. Wouldn't want to blow any of your bird-brained heads off, now would I?" The closest Gretch cawed in the direction of Jeweler, challenging his jurisdiction. "I'm talkin' to you, pigeon boy! Don't make me pull this trigger!" The Gretch glanced at the injured man. It was free loot, free *guns*. Gretch loved free stuff, especially guns. Jeweler didn't look too intimidating to the majority of them, but the harshness of his voice discouraged their recklessness. Jeweler was gaining an illusion of control over the situation, keeping the feathery foes at bay with his shouting, the injured one from moving with his foot, and his wound from bleeding with his scarf. To contest his territorial control, a far greater Gretch emerged from the treeline, pushing the clot of Gretch apart, and approaching the edge of the divot. It bore a third arm from its torso and wore upon its back a spined mustard cloak. The beak-built rebreather and light armoring told Jeweler this was no average Gretch. Through the mutagenic nature of their existence, luck was all of the fate in store. Those born with arms beyond the solitary two were given food and titles—Matriarchs. The smaller Gretch rallied behind the Matriarch, all wearing their own varieties of smugglers gear, the only similarities between the hoards were the rebreather and yellow fabric, they were Gretch-born cloaks, iconic.

"You! Sshlimy beast. Weak." Jeweler scowled at the slurring creature, the ones that spoke were always the most insufferable.

"*What* did you just call me three-arms?" Jeweler raised a shaking hand to the Matriarch, leaving the injured Gretch without a firearm trained upon it. "You think I won't splatter those pus-filled brains of yours across the damn moons?" The Matriarch let out a soft hiss, almost unnoticeable under the hum of its rebreather. There were eleven of them now, all observing the battle of words between a Scavenger and a Bartender. The Matriarch scoffed at his injuries, at his false ammo reserves. A foreseeable mistake. "Listen here freaks, this here ain't jus' some toy, no-ho! Took this puppy off a Crow, a living one, the green bastard no less!" The Matriarch audibly gasped, stepping back from the ridge of snow and ice. "Oooh! Someone's got their feathers all ruffled!" Jeweler looped the pistol around on his finger, showing off his aptitude with such a weapon. "To be straight with ya, I've only ever fired the thing once, and well, here—" Jeweler, lacking empathy (a word he could not define) for any of the Gretch kind, fired a single bolt into the injured Gretch's head, putting the poor sod out of its misery. Jeweler smirked at the sight of its blasted skull, mimicking the shrieking of a dying bird, placing the back of his hand against his forehead in a dramatic fashion. The exertion caused him to spit up blood, but he knocked it back before the Gretch could notice. The Matriarch, uncultured in humor, did not find this mockery appropriate. It kicked a singular princess forward, demanding they inspect Jeweler's weapon at a closer glance. The Gretch reluctantly crept forward, trying its best to keep from angering the raging gunman. Jeweler raised his sights at the invader, his finger twitching above the trigger. The Gretch squawked in terror, falling back on its wings, and scrambling back to try to mount the cliff. It found itself unable to scale the ridge again and turned back to Jeweler, who was now lightly gesturing for the Gretch to approach him. The Princess shook its head, petrified of the unpredictable nature of the bartender.

The Harlequin

The Matriarch was not so easily brought to fright. It draped one of its wings across its chest, displaying a small gap where the wing was missing one of its needlefeathers, one of similar size to the projectile lodged in Jeweler's back. He turned, gesturing back at the needlefeather. The Matriarch continued to stare. "This yours, big guy?" Jeweler found the vigor to pull the tool from his wound, letting it run cold with blood. He flipped the feather through his fingers, a sharp edge cutting a small slice through the palm of his left hand. He snapped it, tossing the shattered fragments of the needlefeather to the ground. The Matriarch grunted with visible displeasure,

"Liar. Crow? Liar. Weak." Jeweler sighed, wiping a small droplet of blood from behind his ear. He knew the Matriarch would be harder to scare off, but he had danced to this song before, he wasn't going to stop the music now.

"Alright then, need some hard proof, do you?" Jeweler pulled his hand against the hammer of the pistol, cocking it back in a swift single action, firing the gun seconds later. The bullet pierced the left wing of the Matriarch, killing a Princess hidden behind it. The Matriarch had no moment to process the attack, snorting her own saliva back into her throat, choking on it.

"Sshilly man! You start battle! Sshwift death for—"

"One shot through your wing kills that rat right there. A second for that coward behind you, if I was lucky, I could get both of those two with a third shot. " Jeweler flicked open the chamber of the pistol, rubbing the rusting metal of its interior, "A fourth shot could give that one another missing eye. A fifth to turn that one's head into a Gretch Gusher." Jeweler continued to point out several hidden Gretch, reading off their deaths as he went. The Matriarch began to examine its crew, realizing the fear quickly spreading amongst them, the fantasy of death bewildered it. Jeweler spun the chamber, watching the brass and burns whir through the icy air.

"Sshtop, no! You lie! Liar!" Jeweler let his hand dance through the sky, his fingers resting finally upon his own collar,

"If I focused hard 'nuff, I could hit those two up in that tree. Yeah, I see 'em. Maybe a seventh just to make sure I sent them to the great big bird in the sky." The Matriarch summoned her Princesses and Duchesses to her side, requesting they stay out of sight, demanding they keep themselves alive, "I got an eighth bullet for the one with the gnarly beak, an ninth for her pretty sister," Jeweler winked at the eleventh Gretch, tipping his barrel lightly in her direction. The Gretch covered their beak, soft hums of purple appearing around their eyes. "Oh, and tenth for the bastard who cut my leg." Jeweler was nearly finished with his designs. He had left a very particular two Gretch out of the picture. The chamber of the pistol was still spinning, the wind carrying its motion. He pointed at the Gretch that had fallen into the ditch with him, the one frantically trying to escape his aura. "You're gonna live buddy, you'd watch your whole 'lil nest bite brass." He stopped the chamber, smacking it back into place with a flick of his thumb. He pointed the weapon up at the Matriarch, whom he had excluded from his threat. "After all that noise, I'd have one last shell, just for you big guy. I wouldn't miss." The Matriarch froze, its third arm twitching with wild dread. The whole pack was motionless. Without their Matriarch in a clear state of mind, the Gretch had no order, no objective. They were at the mercy of Jeweler. He chuckled, turning to leave the Gretchkin and their fears. As the Matriarch slowly reached a moment of calm again, Jeweler swiftly spun around, aiming the pistol, cocking the hammer, and calling out, "Bang!" The Matriarch cawed in consternation, falling back from the monster, running from its nightmare. Jeweler yelled at the Gretch, telling them to run away, to escape while they still could, hollering war cries and hoots as they scattered. Once all the Gretch were out of sight, Jeweler shook his head, spinning the pistol around his finger. He shifted open the clip, peering in at the five empty slots. He exhaled and stuffed the weapon back into his belt. He bent himself over, panting quietly, blood still dripping down his back. Jeweler knew his thermals would be stained for the rest of his life. His bag lay disemboweled upon the icy floor, the spoils from the shore piling up in the snow. He began to place the items back into the satchel, examining the snapped strap as he went. A distant whimpering interrupted Jeweler's bagging, a bird-like whimper. The Gretch that had been unable to ascend the pit remained just so: trapped with Jeweler, fearing greatly for its life. Jeweler remembered how this particular princess had writhed from his presence from the moment of its descent. The snot that spattered its beak wiggled in the wind, its entire shape quaking—likely for reasons beyond the cold. Though it was with much deliberation, Jeweler allowed the Gretch some space in his head, keeping doubt at the forefront of his decisions. "Hey, come 'ere. I'm not gonna hurt you, kiddo." The Gretch was shaking violently, its rebreather puttering, running out of helium quickly. The creature had a noticeable gouge upon its face, a hole where one of its sixteen eyes should've been. The varying number of Gretchkin eyes— a maximum of sixteen—was easily overlooked by the bartender's experience. Jeweler tapped a place in the snow with his hand, but the Gretch refused to move. Jeweler reached into his pack, rummaging through for an item he had found that very day. His knowledge of the Gretchkin drive. He pulled from its depths a small red-cover book, the word 'linguistics' painted on the front. He placed it in the snow and called out the loot, moving backward away from his peace offering. The Gretch slowed their shaking, all fifteen of their nerve-wracked eyes shifted between the book and the gunslinger. Jeweler gestured to the Princess, trying his best to convince her of his peaceful nature, of his genuine treasures. The Princess did not budge. Jeweler scratched his beard, discontent with the encounter. He readjusted his damaged pack and turned to leave the pit. There was a small avenue through which he could clamber his way to the top of the divot, but he would need to go slow about it, the whole place was coated in ice and snow, unstable ground for a climb. While Jeweler was ascending his path, he heard a scuttle from behind him, a gathering of steps in the snow. Jeweler turned around, seeing the Gretch Princess paused in motion, a single hand on the linguistics book. Loot was universal, at least to Gretch. They couldn't resist a prize. "It's all yours, bird-brain. I ain't got any use for it." The Gretch slowly raised the book from the snow, cleaning it of the ice and muck, letting it float open and absorbing its contents. The Gretch looked up to Jeweler, who had nearly made it out of the ditch. It stared with admiration, the fear was still there, still deep in the soul of the Princess, but it was stunted, blinded by new understanding. It slowly followed behind Jeweler, ascending the ridge as he climbed. Jeweler knew it was following, but he did not fear. He knew it could backstab him at any moment, but something inside told him it wouldn't. As the two beings summited the ridge, Jeweler looked down at the Princess, curiosity filling his soft brain.

Her beak was buried in the pages, and her eyes aflutter with intrigue. Jeweler's lips curled about, himself now terribly perplexed by the Princess. "You got a name punk? Do your people give out names?" The Princess only understood the basic building blocks of Standard Larkik, interstellar conformity. It heard 'name' and 'people'. Jeweler led a guiding hand to the linguistics book, showing the Gretch the definition of name. The Princess looked up at Jeweler, its juvenile intelligence growing with his presence.

"L-Lullaby?" Jeweler gave the Gretch a thumbs up, patting them on the back,

"That's a nice name kid, here, how about we head back to my place? Those Gretch seem awful cockish." Lullaby nodded, taking Jeweler's hand into its own. Jeweler was taken aback by the gesture but found a warm place in his heart to allow it. The two began the long hike back to the Squall, kinship brewing the whole way there.

~ *Ignore Their Jaws*

Found buried away in the thinnest annals of
the Cathedral of Chitin...

Fevirgreen had spent one hundred and twelve months in the armies of Oveck—the small island bounding just off the coast of Ma del Xiom. It was Xiom that was the stake of all interest, drawing eyes and discussion away from the nations of lesser value surrounding it. When the first declarations proceeded—the first deaths of conflict-filled unmarked graves—Xiom was the name that rang out. *Savages strike Xiom again!* The headlines read, boasting the pity that Xiom so rightfully deserved. Nobody heard the name Oveck spoken, it was so incredibly small on the maps, after all. When Xiom lost ten soldiers on the front, distant lands cried out and lent aid, their people mourning the loss of bones they never knew. When Oveck had its cities razed, hundreds of raped corpses used to barricade a misearned front, and the children enlisted to machinery, not a penny was spared to their name. Oveck suffered because it was Oveck, it had the unfortunate fate of not being Xiom. Yet, the people of its armies stripped themselves as thin as garrote wire, malnourished of joy on the scapes of war. Fevirgreen himself grew thinner by the day. Though he had a lengthy history of service, the war had steamed on for far longer, the inevitability of death an odious truth passed on through generations. This truth was all Fevir had ever known, as his understanding of worldly normalities was stunted by the daunting memories of his past escapades. Fevirgreen understood only his purpose, and expendability, as all soldiers did. He did comprehend the inherent value of being expendable. Not all of those who fought were so easily sacrificed. Generals—for example—sucked the pride away from combat, all cooped away in war machines and concrete villas. Fevir would argue that even he, being valuable due to expendability, was not expendable. Fevirgreen thought maybe he could have been a professor of philosophy, if not for his intimate hunger for further brutality. Yes, Fevir loved the war, unlike the average footman. He loved the tang of corpserot on the air, the cold of harsh winters, and the smoke of dreaded cylinders. He was all too entranced by knives: how they slit the throats of both fear and men. He found himself cutting at his fingers to shush the voice of reason, to nullify the tingle in his flesh. He never felt the pain—he didn't feel any physical detriments, only imagining what it would be like to taste the sting of a bullet. It was a distant dream, as even the wounds and scars Fevirgreen had accumulated had never hurt him in any way that he could unravel. Fellow soldiers said it was lucky, a send of gifts from god itself, but Fevir imagined it only as divine torture. A clang from an un-braced shovel rubbed against his own, as two soldiers brushed by Fevirgreen, on their way to their post. Fevir hated his fellow man, all fretful, infirm. He found their struggles often incomprehensible, foolish to the degree of court entertainment, or even plain pitiful. Fevirgreen was somebody with *real* problems, these men were just unaware of what actual pain looked like. Fevir didn't let these problems get in the way of his slaughter, however. He had honed them into a rage, something he could use to kill only more effectively. His favorite tools were the personal ones; every soldier had a combat blade, and a shovel. Fevirgreen used both to their greatest potential in battle, only ever embracing the convenience of firearms when absolutely necessary. They were impersonal, reductive. Fevir wanted to give respect to those he sent to god, as death without understanding was a waste of both his time and a life. The distant cracking of war fire shook the sky, it kept those who were easily brought to tedium alert and those who weren't terrified. Fevirgreen of course was of the prior, his disinterest in the chaos of war was astoundingly high for someone who had no faith nor god to put his life upon.

"Mm, Keeping your spirits up, Fevirgreen?" A short, stout man waddled from the safety of a shell dock, tipping his weight over stone and board, careful not to let slip his brilliantly waxed shoes upon the mud. There was a smug sort of greed-filled grin upon the man's face, stranding ear from ear. He was a far higher rank than Fevir, finding himself sleeping on velvet, and dining on only the rarest meats the supply offices had to offer. The man knew of this rank disparity and knew of the safety it brought him. This safety ceased to exist whenever he was nearest to Fevirgreen.

"As I have, Derlick. Oh son how the stagnant air dulls me." The fog from the north had dropped in since the morning, coating the fields of bodies and craters in a blanket of deceit. "You do not speak for humor, Derlick. Do you need something of me?" Derlick dragged his dry tongue across his upper gums, carefully scraping any remnants of his dinner into his fat gullet.

"Why you see Fevirgreen, orders from the brigand crew have arrived! The eastern machines have stopped their advance." There was always the threat of failure when it came to the use of war machines. They were inconsistent and prone to sinking. Mud was not their beholder, and in Xiom, there was plenty of mud for the poor. "Indeed Xiom shall win that one. If we hope to stay in this fight, we must make an advancement of our own, before the break of the brigand crew."

"A simple fool's errand Derlick. I would hope you are joking, but it seems you lack your notorious babble."

"Why! Since when have the likes of your people sought peace and prosperity? Your combat lust no longer dates you?"

"Perhaps it is simply I desire to, in truth, kill in victory. Blood spilt for nothing spills no blood at all." Derlick scoffed, expressing to the depths of the trenches they so dearly inhabited,

"And to what else? Our numbers, and certainly our options, are quite limited! I respect that you fear the quality of the war, but yet, you are not a general. Leave what may be to those who may see it. Else, I may have you stricken of your rank!" Fevir turned to the jolly man, the glutton. He let only his stare answer such a statement, a hating enchantment heightened with the sight of Derlick's gizzard. Fevirgreen was not stubborn, nor did his bloodlust overtake him. Some could argue Fevir was more invested in the success of his country than most in the trenches could dream of being. However, being a killer in kin and a corporal in rank, his insight was often left ignored. Seeing the brewing misery in Derlick's eyes, Fevirgreen turned and marched off to inform his platoon of their impending deaths. If there existed a stratagem that could make such a direct assault successful, why, the war would have ended before Fevir was born. Fevirgreen found himself wondering once or twice about life outside the battlefield. If the war had never been, where would Fevir be? His immediate thought was prison or a grave; Fevirgreen simply could not imagine a world without killing. He needed it, fed off its potency—it was all he knew. Fevir slowly pushed open the metal brace to his platoon's bunker, where six soldiers of varying shapes and demeanors lay in wait.

"I regret to inform you fools that our loving command has sentenced us to death." Two of the men glanced at Fevirgreen, the rest remaining occupied with their various distractions. None of them were warm with Fevir's presence. "We have no choice but to advance on the Mud, and hope to see the other side. Derlick is giving us an hour." One of the men stood from his bed, calling out to Fevirgreen,

"A corporal who'd willingly send his men to death should be no corporal at all." Fevir paused for a moment, not one who would handle disobedience calmly. He understood from where the soldier's words arrived, Stiller. He was a good man, followed orders, did his fair share of chores, and had a single child back in Oveck. Fevirgreen didn't have the honor to grieve for him. He tugged at his collar, slowly turning back to the soldier, hesitantly raising his own eyes to meet Stiller,

"If the choice was mine to make, Stiller... I would go alone." Fevir slammed the bunker door shut and continued to the trench line. One hour was more than enough time to sharpen his shovel.

On the edge of both reality and the trench, Fevirgreen was quaking. For him, a march into damnation—despite the damages to the war effort—was of great excitement. The slaughter that could potentially be gifted to the hands of Fevir was (seemingly) of infinite bounds. It was acceptance of fate that had supplied Fevir with his survival and brought him the most pleasure. Derlick rested upon the lumber breakers, watching the front with very little intrigue. With no plans of his own to follow, the most fervent thought on the lard's mind was the meal awaiting his return. Fevirgreen's squad distanced themselves from one another, giving silent prayer for their survival— all Fevir could pray for was as much violence as the gods could muster. The clock struck, all time fell loose, and Derlick gave the terrible order to rise. The fog that had poured into the breaths of the soldiers and dogs was blinding, no one could stomach it. The taste of shrapnel and disease made hurl the voices of the soldiers, even Fevirgreen, who wiped the spit and muck from his lips, and charged ever forward. A ringing chain shot began from the opposing front, as silhouettes fell like gourds to the mud, lifeless. A figure charged beside Fevirgreen, attacking a soldier he knew to be a fellow. Fevir fired on the man, piercing the brace of the man's gas mask, a shard breaking full through his chest. The two figures fell, and Fevirgreen continued, cold sweat building on his neck, the sort of anxious build that Fevir could only obtain from a fear of not racking up enough bodies to be remembered. Fevirgreen watched as the fog began its thinning, and the front displayed in full. He affixed his bayonet, and with vigor, rushed one last mile to the light of fires. Before he could reach this freedom, from a shell pit came a soldier, colors matching his own. The coward collapsed upon Fevir, screaming in a mix of shock and desperation for the aid of another, for Fevirgreen. With the danger of a bullet storm and the restrictive form upon him, Fevir had but one solution. With the mitt of his hand, he gripped the neck, and with a second hand, he crushed down on the spine with relative strength. The owner of such a neck did not appreciate the aggression, rolling from the grip, splashing about in the muck and mud. Fevirgreen quickly dealt a knee to the gut of the soldier, followed quickly by a headbutt, rendering the being un-alive. Fevir, exhausted by a struggle completely unexpected, lay in the dirt, letting his iron grip loose, his iron will wither, and his iron bulk sully. His rifle had been dispatched, and he lay there with a knife and pistol, alongside brimming motivation to kill. He stood from the mire and tore from his belt the key to his slaughter, a pistol, five shots. Fevirgreen dove into the light, freeing himself from the fog, being let upon by a shower of lead. He raised his pistol, and fired, shooting once, twice, thrice, and more. Two men fell, two fewer streams of bullets shattering his concentration. He continued to run, dodge, duck, and tear away from his mortal speed. This was a divine being, a true soldier of living immortality. The final gunner continued to fire, petrified at the haste of the approach of god's chosen warrior. Fevir returned the favor, firing his pistol twice, giving the gunner enough flinch to miss his shots. As Fevirgreen reached the trench, the dire existence of his circumstances finally roused him, and he had no time left to quell it. He swam chest-deep through barbs and palisades of steel. The tickle that tore away his flesh bothered him not, evoking incredible fear in the gunner before him. As the soldier stepped back—stumbling with a lack of initiative—Fevir leaped from the battlements, bringing upon the gunner a flurry of slams. He loosed his blade, the dagger of his soul, and stabbed upon the skull a thousand blows. The man was dead, and with the gore of death in the air, Fevirgreen inhaled, tasting its love, and kissed death back. Another foe entered his domain, having come to see the glory of the immortal. Fevir spun up his handgun, and fired a shot of piercing malice, killing the man instantly. He rose from the body and drew his blade, pistol, and spirit together. He was more than prepared to take a thousand lives before he would let himself fall. Fevirgreen ran from the battlements, down halls and trench-depths alike, shooting those who would shoot at him, and stabbing those who were too close to fool. As increasing gallons of blood was spilled by his hand, Fevirgreen only served to grow further and further from his sanity, from the normality of his relatively monotone personality. He screamed as he gutted a child, one far too young to fight this war, not with hate (or fear) but with glee! With unshakable delight. After the slaughter had continued for long enough, the soldiers of the trench began to recognize the threat at hand. There was no minor platoon, nor a force of grandeur and weaponry. No, this was but one man, and with hundreds in their holes and pits, they knew there was no force to oppose them. Men armed with far more than shovels and moon clips emerged from their bunkers, aiming down upon the ruthless angel of death, firing away. Fevir did not expect resistance, but of course, was gladdened to meet it. He let loose a stream of his own gilded ecstasy through his pistol until the shells had been drained from its clip. He spun the tool and attached another moon clip. A projectile streaked his hand, pulling with it a lemon peel of skin, curling back in mutant distortion.

The Harlequin

Fevirgreen wrapped it roundly upon his finger, and tore, pulling the flesh uncleanly back from the bone. A kill, and more blood was cut from those who walked the earth. Fevir was never a master of counting—after three he had lost the effort, but now, as the corpses piled upon pile, and musk of brimstone and bones galloped through the remaining living, Fevirgreen began to wish he hadn't. A man of guts, and stealth, came behind Fevir, and managed a strike against his helmet, with nothing less than a shattered shovel. Dancing in the muck, the blow had stunned the soldier, but Fevir's yearning for churn and liquidation of the soul kept him not from reality. Fevirgreen rolled from the ground, as the soldier struck mud with that shovel, caving it between the earth. Fevir grabbed the sod by the arm, and pulled him to the ground, ramming his jaw against the handle of his own shovel. As the soldier attempted to rise from the muck, his jaw hanging loosely like a ghoul emergent from their tomb, Fevirgreen reached for his blade, and swiftly jabbed it through the roof of the mouth, watching the silver poke out again from the front of the soldier's face. The cadaver fell upon Fevir, who wormed his way from its grip. As Fevirgreen knelt in the grossness of the mud, he heard no clanking of iron and bootstraps upon him, a clear chorus of distanced gunfire was all that remained. But in the silence, a sounding of windchimes, as if millions of them, rang true through the cursed smog-sky, and Fevir did not falter. He turned to greet the sound, and not remotely like an angel, a great golden figure descended from the heavens, crashing through the concrete of the bunker in a shroud of heavenly wing feathers. Upon this creature was a brazen plate, one lined with arms of silver and ivory. These arms, both metal and not, were thoughtless, not owned by a mind, and simple constructs of the design. Upon the figure's back was a divine cape lingering from throat to knee, held in place by one of the aforementioned delicate arms. From the limbs of the true skin was a thorned steel plating encrusted in gold, unlike the false limbs. It ventured down to the elbows, where gauntlets of forbidden metals embraced the flesh, directly. One hand was encased in brilliant copper, the other emergent from a thick chassis—the very flesh intangible. The figure pulled one of its dirtied, aurous plate boots from the mud, glaring down at the filth of this new earth. A mask obscured the majority of its face, one not unlike the iconic glare of comedy, one suited in brass and other brownish metals. The head of the figure was covered by a thorned ring, draped over their cap with as much elegance as a fool with legless jest. Fevirgreen readied his pistol, he held no interest in conversations of war and death. The figure tugged from its cloak a thin scroll list, and upon checking it, rolled it closed once more. It clenched its fist, as the blank coldness of parchment ejected from its wrist—a card, no wider than an ace. The figure reached out to display it, but Fevir's nerves tainted the encounter, drawing his knife and stabbing through the mechanics, a jutting spark illuminating the battleground. The figure retracted its metallic hands, examining the damage done. Sufficient, it tore the blade from the cut and tossed it aside. Stab-less, Fevir was at an impasse of sorts; the shovel would do. Fevirgreen struck the tool against the side of the figure's head, but such a strike did not faze the being, as it lifted Fevir by his head, and tossed him to the mud. He quickly drew his pistol, though the figure took no time in clutching the barrel, and deforming, twisting it in an unmannerly fashion. Fevirgreen slammed the shovel—blade first—into the shin of the being, causing a cry of pain to emerge from its mouth. The figure, filled with personal vendetta now, grabbed Fevir by his throat and pinned him to the concrete barricades of the trench's edge. Fevirgreen squirmed in the grip, feeling none of the pain as the moistness in his eyes seemed to dry. A stray shot struck the figure's head, clinking against a hidden sturdy helm. The figure turned, seeing a soldier amongst the dead, and pulled from the very folds between existence a sturdy black brand. Just within reach, the figure impaled the restless corpse. Fevir grappled to the being in its moment of weakness, shaking loose his helmet in the process, and wrapped his teeth upon the figure's emergent voidflesh, biting with all the force he could muster. The figure screamed, shaking the snake loose. Fevirgreen scrambled to his feet, clutching the remains of his dented shovel in one hand, and his helm in the other. He cast the device of protection upon the figure, and sprinted from the battlements, towards the distant bridge of the trench. The figure took no time in following him, having no worries about the dangers of The Mud. But as Fevir mounted the wood, a shot pierced his chest, with such protection he was unkilled, but with such force, he was sent far from his destiny.

The Harlequin

The figure stood over Fevirgreen's unmoving body, one locked in paralysis by the pain it couldn't feel. With battle, the figure had lost its cape, and thus its full body was loosely presented. The hungering liars' arms were connected around much of the body to torsos of their own, each torso with head, and each with legs drawn inward towards the feet of the true beholder. The faces of each pearlescent cast were hung up to the sky, anguish yet pleasure in their draw. The figure flexed the card again, holding it in a quite literatim steel grip. It unhooked the braces of the second hand, revealing the shadowy darkness of a figure without flesh, bone, or body. It was absorbent dark. The Devil. The being wrote upon the card some symbol in inky dark, its finger sliding with liquid remorse. The figure turned the card to Fevir's sight, and with its viewing, came a flash of beyond-blinding light. Fevirgreen could *feel* the effulgence, the glowing purity of a god. He remained silent, the figure now chuckling faintly under its flaxen facade,

"Interesting." The figure showed Fevir the card once more. He flinched, expecting another light of dawn. "To the fangs, wouldn't you agree?" Through Fevirgreen's shaking vision, he could barely make out the symbol of a snake, a word most unreadable inscribed upon it. The being stuffed the card back into his wrist and with a deep inhale, spoke, "Blessed is the space of thee who returns forthright to their rest in the creator, where the Old Man may smite thee sorry flock away from your coat. I delight to do your will, O Old Man, yet my heart fails my ambition—" The figure pulled its weapon from its coat, and aimed it at Fevir, who without protest, nor escape, stared down its crooked blade. "May you be my shepherd, and draw blood for my hand." The steel was thrust down upon Fevirgreen, and all memories of his home faded to hated tumors that plagued his silent death.

A cold void surrounded Fevirgreen, embracing his entire desperate corpse. He shivered, and thought, *aren't I dead?* Fevir looked up from the bluish flesh upon his frozen fingertips, examining the polar woods that were spread before him. It was astounding, a majestic sight, the snow locked in its descent, a mysteriously beautiful silence filling all that could be seen, with a distant chill falling upon his neck. Fevirgreen slowly reached for his pistol, but noticed his weapons were no longer about him, nor was his plate mail of divine conquest. He placed a hand upon the snow, pushing off of it to climb to his toes. His fingers dug deep into the fluff, thicker than mere snow, ice. As he rose a foot to step forward, it was quickly swallowed by the depths of the winter. Swiftly, he retracted his limb from the cold, careful not to sink deeper in the process. A figure appeared behind Fevir in his struggles, humming a soft, familiar tune. Fevirgreen turned to the music, harmonizing with it without a second thought. The figure stopped and sighed, letting out a puff of smoke from under its bird-like mask.

"You don't look the part." Fevir glanced down at himself, seeing the bone in his skin, pining for the air through his nourishment.

"What part do I fail to look alike?"

"A warrior. A soldier of…" the figure ran their thumb against the metal talons upon their fingers. "A decade-long war?" Fevirgreen swallowed all the remaining saliva in his mouth, licking his dry tongue left alone in its desert.

"Nine years." The figure snapped its talons together.

"Come. I wonder what purpose this place demands of you." Fevir did not hesitate to follow the order. He trailed the being through the snow, the places where the figure stepped revealed to be far more stable than the rest of the snow's lying body. They walked for a time, and the figure embraced itself in relative silence, "Perhaps your prowess lies in your obedience." Fevirgreen was lost in thought but was certain his obedience was of admirable quality.

"My prowess." The figure stopped for a moment, gesturing upon Fevir's chest.

"*Your* prowess. Discipline. You have yet to complain of the cold."

"I cannot feel it." The figure chuckled, ignoring the speaking of what he presumed was a good soldier. The two continued, but as Fevirgreen still had yet to complain of the cold, the figure once again stopped.

"You. You say you cannot feel it. Your restraint will not win you my god."

"I cannot." the figure marched over to Fevir and clasped his hand within its own.

The Harlequin

"You tell me—in the blunt cold of this place—you say you do not feel it? Your hands are blue and frigid, the snow taints your mortal flesh, you say you can resist the burning vigor brought by the blizzard of a god?" Fevirgreen nodded, the figure dropped the hand and pulled from its side a small dagger, sacrificial in nature. The figure dug the hook of the blade into Fevir's palm and continued to do so, glancing from blood to eyes. Fevirgreen did not flinch. An ingrained whisper silenced the wounding—*enough*—and the figure stopped. They blinked, and as Fevir did the same, there no longer was snow. Fevirgreen sat with legs entwined upon a cobble floor, within a cathedral of mass beauty and size. Around Fevir, stood three masked beings, beaks of bone, familiar creatures. There was the figure from the snow, their mask of bird and bone shone blue through the dim of the cathedral. They wore a leather hat with a brim of length, and a custom stitched apron, a holster affixed to its side tuned for a dagger. Thick metal boots were brought up to the figure's knees, accompanied by equally long gauntlets. The figure did little but sigh, pertinent shame dressing his frost-burnt digits. Beside the figure was another, a woman of tremendous stature, her legs completely thick with iron and wire. She wore the body of a gypsy—draped in tapestry and carpets— her metallic face of dramatic machinery bore a pinkish glow, the beak jutting from under the expressive screen. She leaned down to Fevirgreen, giggling cheekily, her grin biting through the beak,

"Hello toy. You're *awful* cute—a bit narrow on the hips, but I don't mind twinks." She ran her knuckles against his cheek, their theoretical warmth keeping Fevir from the discomfort. Fevirgreen did not respond to the touch. "Patient, your heart is nearly still! I think I'll enjoy playing with you." She let a puff of her berry-scented breath cloud his face, content with his ignorance of her. Finally, a third figure crept out from behind Fevir, laying both their hands upon his shoulders.

"Tasted meat, for good little worms. Bulging—singer worms." A wet slobber of saliva dripped upon Fevirgreen's left ear. He chose calmly to let it remain, out of respect.

"I am no meat." Fevir claimed, his words mocked with a deranged cackle, followed by the wet smack of a kiss against his head.

Creatures of Habit

"Of course are, precious." The figure stepped out in front of Fevir, following the pink mask as she walked away. His mask held a glow of red, itself far narrower than that of the blue or pink bird peoples. His exit was made with such haste, Fevirgreen hardly had time to commit any of his structure to memory, save for a dull sickle bound at his hip. As the two rosy-shaded bird people descended deeper into the cathedral, an elegant array of banners flooding the hall they followed Fevir looked to the above. Ignoring the overbearing presence of the blue birdperson, he took in the vast glassways of the cathedral roofing. Their colors allured the senses, and their displays granted sight into tragedy and victory Fevir had never known. Pointing out a window of particular interest, Fevirgreen questioned,

"Is that not you, birdman?" The blue figure, eternally sulking within his own shadow, glanced up at the glass and scoffed.

"It's Forklorn. Do not abbreviate it, and you may just outlive your predecessor." Fevir remained stony, unfound by the vile tone of his opponent. The faintest of sounds, much like the mind catering to itself, echoed about the chapel, a solid *Leave Us*, and there was nothing. Forklorn bowed, and left the presence of Fevir, following down the same hall the other bird people had ventured. Fevirgreen was left by his lonesome, within the masterful dome-age of the grandest room in the cathedral. He was not one to actively seek out and admire good art, but in the presence of it, there was no reason to avoid staring. His search for beauty led Fevir to a corpse, resting passively upon a modified predella. Thinking strictly of the honor in death—perhaps imagining it for himself—Fevir approached the body. It was dressed in a set of armor, sheets of metal that had freshened paint, and rewound screws. The bulk plating and padding by the lower body appeared almost new. The undergarments were of lesser quality, burlap and linen stitches bound together heaps of leather and felt, making what a scavenger would call luxury, but any true man would call scrap. It was difficult to discern, due in part to the masked, shaven head, but the body was presumably female. The olive scarf placed around and across their body matched the glow of their divine birded mask. Fevir thought it rather pretty, and reached out a single finger, soon his full hand, and placed it upon the face of the body. Fevirgreen was not one to honor the dead, but something had

The Harlequin

compelled him to touch—to reach out and connect with the spirit of this lost luminary. He felt a familiar weight upon his hip, a holster refilled, and the soft stinging of cold across his flesh passed on to cessation. How he came to his treasures once more, he was unsure, yet he was substantially hesitant of everything with which he was once certain. As Fevir examined his sidearm a distant elegance made itself known, whispering in the front of his, between his very eyes,

"Daring, yet... humble. A sort of humbleness one would see in the starving of the strays." Fevirgreen placed his pistol back at his hip and spun himself to find the voice's origin. Where he glanced, he saw nothing. "Loyal—rather loyal—yet still self-thinking. A man with conscience and with none." The echo no longer emerged from himself, spanning the cathedral in its entirety it would seem, "Calm, hollow even, but still yet *filled* with an undying rage!" The voice was far too close for logic to muster, Fevirgreen reclaimed himself, and returned to the altar, certain it was a trick of the world. Alas, above the altar—and himself—was a being so empyrean and radiant of willpower, that Fevir could not help but fear. "Deadly. No contrast." The touch of feathers fluttered between Fevirgreen's eyes. He saw the bird, the grandest of beings he had ever seen, before him now. It held the face of a bird (if not simply a facade) and the head of a man. It had four crossed wings, extravagant and vast, and an equal sum of arms to match them. Its wings, emerging from its lowest waist and shoulders of pure statuesque build, were white as chalk. As—indeed just as white—was the flesh of such a being, transcendent and soothing. From the crown of its skull came two great tusks, horns of rock and bone, antlers of god. It had cloth of its own, yet Fevir found himself wishing it did not, wanting only to peer further into divinity. The garments of seraph were black, and dotted with stars and suns—a map of the galaxy inscribed in perfect accuracy, ever-shifting from its placement. The silence provided by what this god knew to be a being of death and torment, stunned them. "Have I brought fear upon you, Fevirgreen? Whom lacks the mind to feel pain, nor terror?" Fevir glided from the moment of quiet, and forwards, unto brilliance,

"You are god. Of this I am certain." the god did not move, but without motion or questioning, it laughed, as if just permeating sound, no influence on the plane of mortals.

"Some have called me this, god. It is inaccurate, I much prefer Lark. *The* Lark—for if there is another, I would love to be introduced." Fevirgreen hesitated, and gestured calmly to the corpse,

"For what reason is she displayed so namely? With such honor?" The Lark told Fevir of the existence of greats who were lost, and she was of them. Fevirgreen took a moment to recall all that he had seen in war, all the dishonor, the unknowledge. Many had died with no name, and they were never to be known by any. This corpse, but one corpse, stood as vigil above all things and observed forth the coming and death of those who would serve to pass on namelessly.

"You will be replacing her." Fevir turned to the god, and with open hands, refused. Such was his way, to be nameless, there was something sacred in namelessness. He was unimportant, a foot soldier with little merit or value. But this woman was farther beyond that purpose.

"I cannot. She is an idol, is it not clear her death is her importance?" The Lark approached from the opposing side of the stone table where the body itself was placed. With the one hand which was not tucked neatly and calmly beneath his robes, The Lark plucked from the corpse the unglowing bone mask, modified extensively with metal and circuits.

"Now, this won't do. Corrupted with mortal temperaments, tainted with metal." The Lark continued to fiddle with the mask, poking at the machinery that was crudely installed. The god flicked a speck of dust from the bone and replaced it upon the corpse. "I have a simple solution." The Lark, sensing the unrest of Fevirgreen, reached towards his face, and wretched the mask clean from it. Behind the mask was nothing but an unsightly crevasse, a void of soul and essence. The Lark reached his hand towards Fevir, the mask buried within. Fevirgreen hesitated, staring into the space upon The Lark's face. "Come. Take the mask. Become your own maker." He stared into the empty sockets, the eyes, though not there, could see him. He took the mask unto his hand and looked to the Lark, who with a nod, allowed him his passage. He inhaled, expecting nothing and everything all at once, and let the ceramic bone of the mask tap the bridge of his nose, softly resting against his face. It felt— it was fitting. It was stuck, as if by glue or strapping, but there were no such adhesions—mythically attached, *magick*, Fevirgreen thought. When Fevir opened his eyes and saw through the lens of a being most divine, Fevir finally comprehended what it was to die. The green tint that glossed the world felt natural, he had always needed this. The Lark chuckled, though he had no jaw with which to speak. The corpse upon the altar seemed almost to shrivel, to writhe in a loss of itself, as all of the energies of the lives past who bathed in green poured into the soldier. The once colorless mask of the Lark filled with the verdant hue of green that troubled the body. Fevir peeled into chaos.

"M— Lark! What is this? A feeling of divine power, of completion?" Fevirgreen attempted to remove the mask for a moment but stopped himself, he wanted this.

"It is your truth, Fevirgreen. Fate makes you its tool, and thus, it is yours." The Lark tapped Fevirgreen on the shoulder, inviting him to follow. The two were bound, and they followed in each other, walking shallowly through with destination.

"Am I dead, Lark? This must be a world beyond my own." The Lark shook his head, he knew of death, and this was no such thing,

"You are free. There is no death for those deserving—the impure. The world is tainted with purity." The two continued, down corridors of black and stone, past glasses into the Infinite and moons unbound by time. "You shall help me wring it free, bring to the galaxy a new perfection that even I cannot comprehend." Fevir looked at his pistol, at the markings upon it. These names inscribed within its damage had faded. He could read only Stiller's. A world of perfection, of freedom. Stiller would love such a world.

"How must I serve you, My Lark?"

~ *Yen For The Finer*

Observed and passed on by a wench
drunkard obsessed with precious stones...

Jeweler had settled in apathetically to the life of prosperity after a hefty sum of money had been spent affording it. The Squall had once been a storehouse for an overrun refugee supplement firm — Jeweler personally held no stake in travelers — and was up to its neck in debt repayments. When the bartender came along himself to requisition the place, even the *refugees* were ecstatic. The sad truth was revealed days later, and several were sent back to asteroid cave-homes. As said before, Jeweler harbored no grief in living out his own fantasies, even at the expense of others, but the refugees were a burden on his mind, and he paid well to see them collected and safely kept. Thus, in time, the Squall was born from the ashes of depravity. It was then that Jeweler finally let his neck soften — when the cold finally started stinging. After his suggestive 'retirement', the Squall was all he needed to stay afloat. When patrons spared him hours, Jeweler spent his misery on collection, scavenging what he could find in the chainways of The Imperial Belt. Home to few, it had existed long enough to gather up a rambunctious reputation, one that often was lowered to simple insurrection. Just below the dual glassed moons of the great bird god, The Imperial Belt rested — adrift through the cosmos and tied only to its relative placement by thrusters and stupendous chains. It retained all the galaxy considered vile. Those who wished to live in prosperity often were required instead to settle for living in constant peril. The great bird dared not assist any who would call for aid from the rocky beads, forever bashed back from temptation by what was only anarchy itself. It was the Shorerunners—prestigious salvagers and smugglers trained through time and testament—who spat in the eyes of any jurisdiction, preserving the lawless nature of The Belt through constant strife. Jeweler had once partook in the sanctity of the trade, but with his age came the worthlessness of combat. The Squall provided opportunity and guaranteed death in the arms of a warm bed wrap. He had met many figures of ingenuine integrity and moral ambiguity—those who had plans for much worse deaths for the bartender. People with secrets and lies and bounties up to their necks. People who wouldn't keep a promise, who wouldn't be there to catch you. Jeweler had come to enjoy none of them, the only 'friends' Jeweler had made on the Belt were those naive enough to take a bullet for him. These types, men and women of corruption and deceit, were of course the average customer of Jeweler's now Belt-known 'Squall'. That is precisely why he had demanded that Roach remained within the den of the Squall during all business hours—and beyond—for fear of a tattling traitor hellbent on profit alone. He knew they all needed it. People didn't arrive on the Belt by choice, not a chance. Most were either refugees or retired Gull Troopers. Many had lost a great deal to the antics of the bird god, both lives and possessions alike. The great bird, the divine ruler of all ordained to be his, had grown surprisingly unpopular in recent times. Many on the Belt actively despised this being, many kept their opinions silent—those who ran their mouths often no longer found themselves able to. There was a time, not so distant in memory for many of the Belt's criminals, where the Lark need not express the necessity of new soldiers via propaganda. Many had once volunteered their able bodies with more than willing hearts. Decisions and wars had corroded this opinion and brought about an acute detestation for the god. However, despite the popular disliking of this divine icon, none could make any mark against them. The divine ruler had far too much power for mortal forces to even consider removing him from his throne. Armies of mindless machines, covens of immortal priests, and a specialized court of royal assassins harboring power unimaginable. With the god's unshakable governance over the endless expanse of the Maen Galaxy, conflict inevitably showed. A war—divine in nature—however obscure in notice (fought only in shadows) was declared upon the Ink. The great bird god yenned for the perfect world, and for this world to bear fruit, it required the desolation of the ones called Atramendtide—the impure. This war had spread a fashion of hate throughout those unaffected by it, and soon beings of the dark became a taboo, any Inkling that might wander became a convict, a monster to be caged. However, drifting so close to the origin of all divine orders, the people of the Belt did not see it this way. It was not that they pitied the Ink, nor knew of their equality, they simply had not the mind to care for war, nor disparity. It was unimportant to them. Though, with the recent addition of paid bounties for the bodies of desecrated Inklings, the Belt found a new way to care about the existence of the darkened: money. Jeweler didn't know for sure what Roach was, but it looked like one of the Inklings of yore, and he was sure other Shorerunners would think so too. Jeweler had no intention of protecting a criminal for free. This was no act of kindness, nor mercy from roots of pity. It was business, and that's how Jeweler intended for it to remain. He thought of the prospects of controlling a bloodthirsty beast in combat, certainly against the Gretchkin. He thought of the profit of owning the most powerful force of war upon the Belt. However, Jeweler would just as soon turn the Inkling into the bird god—if he turned up empty-handed on his beast-bound bargain. Roach did not know this. As far as the beast was concerned, Jeweler was a kind father figure with which it could take hospice until it learned more of its origins. Roach was content in naivety, and more than willing to disembowel for a free bed—even if that bed happened to be a stone floor. Jeweler, none too caring for the creature, had given it the den. Anything more was a kindness, and he was rare to provide those to unfamiliar patrons. Within the bar side itself, Jeweler hacked away at the front lid of a barrel, his own knife dulled from wood and cork. A figure dressed in metal and silky red cloth stepped through the vacant doorway, precisely during the Squall's most active hour. A glistening of musical chaos surrounded them. Their beak proved dutiful in action, as those who noticed it seemed to slink into distaste. Jeweler did not see the figure until they had reached the bar, having been too far occupied with his slashing. The clank of the figure's armoring as they sat alerted him to their presence, Jewelers stare was fatal,

The Harlequin

"Gull. Fresh plates, you get much blood on those hands?" The Gull leaned forward, eyes unseeable through the thick steel of their helmet. They did not reply. "Fancy cuffs too, the fifth generation sure got it swell."

"Swell understates the risks of the job. Forepenny, no ice." Jeweler raised a solitary brow to the figure, the voice seemed familiar, he could place it in time.

"You could say that—I'm not one to hate a Gull out the gate. Will say though, that's one rancid drink choice." Jeweler went about his pouring, an eye darting back to the soldier on occasion. They were meticulously unscrewing the brace of their helm, the beak jamming at its seams. The bartender was certain of gender, and the pollen coating the Gull's glove secured race, but memory continued to fail him,

"Well?" Jeweler returned to the Gull, mug in hand, now met with a root-ridden fleshy facade. Strands of mossy hair drifted through the helmet, lichen amassing on the rotted remains of the lower jaw. A birch smile spread across her face, a calm awaiting recognition about her eyes. While vague familiarity conquered his mind, the bartender refused to come to a reasonable conclusion—even the eyes didn't match recollection.

"I'm mighty old, need a kick in the pants now and again." The Gull's smile only widened, hope for recognition reddening her cheeks.

"Are you telling me you can't remember the only Gull to survive decapitation?" The name restitched a fabric of memories across the mindscape of the bartender, the fossilization of histories returned in stone. Running had given him the insight of failure—disappointment. The modern armaments of the bird warrior reminded him all too greatly of his own tools, of his own birdseed.

"Well I'll be damned, Pherock was it?" Jeweler hesitated about the mug, his other hand tight on a trigger. After all the running, he had thought her long gone—a pleasant thought it was too. "What is it now, FlockKin? Nah, you were FlockKin last time you showed here...."

"Beakserve. Just like 'ol Jeweler." He grinned, his single stone tooth flaring with a certain glow. The false crinkles in his smile paired well with his ever-tightening palm.

"Thought I'd outran ya'. How'd you manage leave this time?" Calmly—her eyes smoothly drifting to the archaic metal encasing her right arm—she unlatched the two binds holding her gauntlet in place, pulling the glove from her hand. A metal frame of what once was a flesh-bound grip rested in its depths. The soldier wiggled the fingers, grinning under her beak-braced helm. "High heaven, now *that's* a battle scar...." Pherock chuckled, her helmet echoing her voice in metallic ire,

"Was Remo—I even got a few shots off!" She rubbed the framework, her hand flinching slightly at the touch of the metal, her eyes strained and expecting. "Never get to see the big names. You know too, just get R3 drones or Tetarien guard. Fodder on fodder." Jeweler nodded his head, recalling rumors of the newest world-ending clash. False, as usual.

"You see, this' why I left. Ain't no point in trimming down a mighty infinite. Too many metalloids and spark-bots—if I had one shot at Sixfingers, I'm telling you!" Shoving the chin visor of her helmet down further, Pherock downed the remains of her drink—a soft chuckle resonating through the fluid—her glove smacking against the table, demanding a moment to speak,

"No, *no* you have no idea! I swear, until two days ago? He was immortal, I'm sure." Jeweler snickered, sliding a second drink to the soldier, his fearful hand loosening on its responsibilities. Before returning to the bar side, his glow faded, both hands brushing at his sides,

"Until two days ago? You don't mean—"

"That's right! Bastard is dead! Sure, Lark had to come down to finish the job himself, but Sixfingers is no more!" Jeweler tilted his lips up, not a smile—something more despicable. His cadence was far from genuine. Sixfingers? Dead? To those of The Imperial Belt, the death of Sixfingers had been deemed a mythical joke. The slim few who had once called him a leader knew all too well the capacity for miraculous return he carried—millions in bets alone hung in the balance of his survival. The teachings of Sixfingers weren't some all-followed spirit either, he certainly had more than enough dislike spread about his name. Perhaps though, not nearly as much as the Lark. Neither was reputable, a god-tyrant, and a (once thought) immortal bringer of chaos. The unsanctified commoners of the galaxy suffered the turmoil of an interstellar tantrum thrown by two cancers in a strive for control. The Imperial Belt was a place of violent deliberation; many had lost their livelihoods to either Sixfingers and his factitious collective, or the Lark's unholy cult. But with the Lark growing more restrictive by the hour, it seemed only reasonable to share some hope for the underdog. To hear that Sixfingers was lost, was to be assured of one's tragic fate forever. The Lark truly was unkillable. "Whole League is scattered too—only real fight now is with the girl, the prodigy. She can't spit at the power of the Definition." One girl was the last remaining hope of an entire people? How the mighty had fallen.

"Yeah? That's what you said about Sixfingers too, how long is it gonna take you to kill *this* mortal?" Pherock's flesh grew greyer, spores bustling against her pale flesh. After a time spent watching Jeweler work, she found his words to be those of humor—not insult. She slurred back,

"Who can say? Does it even matter? I mean really, the head honcho is knocked off—ain't no question we'll get her, just depends on when. Might be good for help too, if you're...?" Jeweler looked up from his washbin, his neck reining back to the bar to the eyes of the Gull, curious if they held any gravitas. He despised his answer,

"No, I'm not even—come on Pherock! I got a good thing here—I paid my wormpenny to the Lark, and now I'm a free man. End of story." Her leather glove grew stiff, strands of lichen placating further irritation against her neck,

"I mean you don't gotta! J—just would be nice, you know? The two of us—back against the League of Twenty-Two, sure as spit! My Feathermaster even said you'd get your rank back. Jeweler, you *can't* turn down free Ichyr!" Jeweler exhaled sharply, his thumb sticking his lip back to his teeth, nibbling softly on the flesh. She was a pity in plating, so naive to the instigation of such a request. The merit she presumed to lead on was lost on Jeweler, for he cared far less about her than she did he. Her youth was showing, and all too clearly,

"Pherock, I—I'm not in the business of fighting no more, too long spent shaving up enemies and bad memories. I have a thing now, a place to rest my bones. I can't let all that go. Not this time." Turning from the conversation, Pherock peered over the heads of two brawling customers to a seated three Gulls and one Pelican, just beside the bar entrance. They were overtaken with their drinks and tortured by laughter.

"Peacetime might be here Jeweler, and I'm 'fraid of what might come of this world if it is. 'Fraid of what might come of you." Jeweler eyed the soldiers—still laced in glee—and returned his gaze to Pherock. Her eyes would be much brighter if she had intended to threaten. The near obsessive scratch at her own moss discerned the true purpose of her concern. Jeweler had foreseen something similar, things don't slide without give, and the Lark had effectively waxed the Belt glassy. The unspecified was just how hard it was gonna hit, and when. The Belt wasn't going to take well to reconstruction, but Jeweler could grind his jaw and take it.

"You gonna be involved?" Jeweler raised his cloth belt just enough to display an oak handle, the metal of the cylinder remaining bleak in the light of his bar, "Or do I get to spare some bullets?" Pherock nodded, familiar with the face of a threat,

"Don't hope to be. I have orders and I follow 'em but—" the soldier paused, plucking a small container from her ammunition pouch. "Best I can do is paint you in Larkik colors. Take them." She extended her gloved hand, presenting the container. It was perfectly ovular, terrifyingly egglike. Jeweler had no intention of accepting it. "When the Lark comes—make sure you ain't here." Pherock left the container on the bar—finishing her last drink in a single gulp—and lingered in a glare. She awaited his assurances before leaving, and when he did not provide them, she found it fit to exit without consideration. After the last of her tolerance was spent, Jeweler took the cup and the egg box, weighing both in his hands. He returned the stein by the washbin, taking the container. It was cold, but thinly bordered—a light traveler's purse. Jeweler fingered around its sides until he found an edge, his trimless nails served well in prying it open. A small padded interior presented an even smaller piece of metal, ironic to the viewer's name. It was an earring in the visage of a sparrow, formed of ivoric metal. It remained a distant reminder of a life Jeweler willingly stepped far away from—he had to decide whether to be furious or indebted. As he continued to stare, Jeweler became increasingly curious of its past use. He pondered if its underside was still black with moondust, if the left wing would still poke his ear. Jeweler closed the box, sealing his memories with it. The bartender made the decision to be furious, concluding Pherock would not have given gifts of this quality without a secondary objective of temptation. She wanted him to suffer as he once had. She was no friend of his. A quiet thumping stemmed from the den of the Squall and Jeweler thought nothing of it. The management of the rambunctious patrons of the Squall was of far greater importance. In time, the thumping drew into a loud crash, followed by fits of beast-like rage—it was no longer ignorable. Jeweler hurried away from the bar, noting exactly how many customers were seated upon it. He pushed past the creaking door to the backroom of the Squall, the egg box still tight in his grip. The room had originally been structured of softwood and boarded pretentiously to exact inches. Jeweler had done the room some kindness and stapled on wallpaper—a luminescent aqua shade with thin cyan stripes. One window stood against the torrent of the storm outside. A thick piping of metal hung down from the ceiling, letting out into a small potbelly wood stove. Above the stove, shelves lined the wall, decorated with various spoils and mysteries, souvenirs from places Jeweler had never been himself. Jeweler slept upon a small cot tucked away behind the shelving and stove, just out of view of the main entrance. A thick metal bulwark stood between the room and a direct outlet into the snowy Belt, one that remained fairly sealed shut. In the center of the den was a dimly lit and scantily hung chandelier, hovering precariously above a lopsided fur sofa. And there was Roach, lofting across the couch, its head drooped over the armrest, letting drool pour across its eyes onto the floor. The linguistics book that Jeweler had given to the beast was dangling from the chandelier, sopping with spit and muck. Roach was purring grossly, its left hand twitching against the hardwood floor. Jeweler groaned, and lightly tapped Roach on the forehead with his foot, causing the beast to fling itself from the couch. In a thunderous crash, the beast slammed against the back wall of the den, knocking a small shelf from its hinges. Along with the shelf fell a mediocre birch coffer—its contents spilling out across the floor—and a small chunk of carved wood, enveloped in the velvet of a cushion, "Gah! What're you doin' Roach! Get up you nasty bastard!" Roach scrambled to all fours, using a small coffee table to reach its feet. "Was that sleeping? Were you— ah! Is that my book? How in the green abyss did you get it up there!" Jeweler clambered onto the sofa, reaching a solitary ring finger towards the light fixture. Roach hissed at Jeweler, slumping into a ball of hate and childish stubbornness, it clearly held no interest in learning the galactic language. It desired to roam, search for food, and discover wonders. Jeweler knew how dangerous something like that could be, likely more so for the population of the Belt than for Roach. Regardless, he was not keen on risking his investments so haphazardly. "No! You gotta read that damn thing! Until you can tell me the weather in perfect Standard, you ain't going anywhere!" Roach growled, letting its voice readjust to the humidity of the air,

"Iggg, Sundy." Jeweler threw up his arms in confusion, gesturing broadly to the storm ravaging the world beyond the glass of his window,

"Wh— it's *storming* out Roach! Have you seen the sun hit this forlorn Belt once? And— Lark, you barely even spoke it right!" Roach hissed once more at the disgruntled bartender, considering its analysis of the weather to be rather astute. Jeweler plucked the book from the chandelier, and tossed it to the ground, just beside the pile of memorabilia that had poured from the coffer. Small mirrors, priceless gemstones, books, and binders full of parchment of untold age were now spread among a sea of yellow carpet. Some series of precious trinkets lay clicking on the floor beside Roach, the glow of their steel repelled it. Important of all however, was the mask of bark, carved in the likeness of a lowly Gretch Princess. The beak was curved straightly down, slotted twice for breathing—ignorant of symmetry. There were sixteen small slits carved into the face of the mask, two enlarged to be seen through lesskin eyes. Four thin bands had been carved into the forehead, with a feathered pattern dotted around the edge of the eyes. The whole mask was lacking in paint and flair, as if it was never completed, remaining the empyrean white color of its source material. Jeweler saw the mask, and within a flash of a second, he snatched it from the ground and replaced it upon the particular cushion it had fallen from. He steadied the supports for the shelf and replaced its binding—replacing both the mask and its comfort upon the wood. Roach had begun to gather the items from the ground, stuffing them back in the coffer for its master. By the time Jeweler had turned to it, the coffer was full (despite one item the beast had missed, as it glowed too tumorously). Jeweler peeled his lips—as if to scold the creature—but he took himself back, his eyes falling to the scowling sympathy of the beast. He took the coffer in his hands, finding seemingly all of his things evenly spread about the box. The bartender scowled at Roach, and placed the coffer back on the shelf—it creaked under the weight.

"Roach, good Lark just—keep your mud-mitts off my stuff." The beast retreated from the shelving with book in hand, a soft grumble emitting from its core.

A single moonrock remained untouched by both the beast and the bartender, ignored by their sight until Jeweler made it known, "Look Roach, damn near missed one! Bet this piece ain't cheap neither, probably picked this up down at Si-pen, maybe—" Jeweler tossed the stone to Roach, who at once let out a guttural cry of damnation, the burning of inkly flesh made present by its stench alone. A puff of ethereal smoke drifted to the roof of the den as the rocky materialization of the stone melted away, making clear its glassy interior. In an instant the stone swiftly shifted, small pieces clicking and whirring as the rock undid itself, revealing a bluish reflector caged within. Roach cooed at the sight of the glass, reaching out to it with one of its lengthy digits.

"Sighee—Rog...." Jeweler snatched the stone precisely from its palm before it had any chance to taint its purity. A second fit of screaming alerted an outlier of patrons to turn away from their drinks, looking ever beyond the door tucked behind the bar. After hot-potatoing the ore for a minute, Jeweler caught it in the wrap of his scarf, cradling it carefully in his clutch. Brought on by the second singe, the rock now revealed more of its aquamarine undersurface, still protected in a thin layer of blackish-white film. Beside himself with admiration, Jeweler leaned ever nearer to the stone, its microscopic intricacies becoming clear to him. Within the lattice of the crystal was a dotting of celestial orbs—a moon and several planetoids among them. Each minuscule pixel had a labeling of sigils, some minute catalog of names and infamy. It was all far too tortuous for natural origins, that much was certain.

"Some pebble. Probably still burns like hellfire...." Jeweler trailed off, his eyes fixated on the glow of the map, some bespoken planet orbiting the glass moons acting as its centerpiece. He mumbled to himself, marking familiar landmarks as he went about its depth. It was in some finite representation a marker of his current dwelling, the Zealot's Edge System, though not without its discrepancies. Finding himself terribly lost, he retraced the planetary guidelines—collecting similar results. The second moon was nowhere to be seen, and the Belt had ceased to be, replaced by a fully constructed planetoid— alongside several others—orbiting an overwhelmingly potent sun at the left hemisphere of the map. It showed no destination, only outdated or questionable monuments. For a map to what Jeweler presumed would be treasures, there was a lacking of any directions at all. Letting the stone slip into his flesh, the burn was calm enough to be overlooked, as Jeweler remained fixed upon the scene before him. As soft steam rose from his palm, the bartender saw a display of ancient glory—a sea extending far past the horizon, overtaking thick black pillars of stone, a shore of jagged sand in its wake. There was a knocking on the den door, as a patron arrived to question the ever-continuous screaming and clamor emitting from the back of the Squall. "Yeah? I just— No! Do *not* come in here! I—I have three dead hookers, and enough blood t'paint a starship!" Jeweler pitched the stone to his beast who—in desperation to avoid another critical burn—ducked beside the thing, allowing it temporary seating on the left cushion of the sofa. He trudged through the high grass of displaced carpet to the door, turning to Roach with a gesture of silence, and exiting back into the bar. Roach was left with the stone and a still-slimed linguistics textbook. Though the rock remained a mystery to its feral thought, said mind had no intention of unraveling it. Burns did not harm the beast, not conventionally, but Jeweler had spent a fortnight hollering in disagreement with the scent produced by Roach's smoldering skin. As such, it had been conditioned to avoid open flame much like a cat to water. Slinking to the door, it glanced out from the den, staring intently at the glint of the jewelry case in its master's back pocket. Roach had little understanding of such devices, certainly not the necessity of its cumbersome shape. It did understand its senses, its gut. There was something particularly punishing about the egg box, an aura of unease Roach of course lacked the words to describe. It opened the textbook, and paged through the deep chapters, it needed a word — it knew of a word. Suddenly, It stopped, a single hand resting on a page near the backmost section of the glossary. Roach slid a cold, still burnt finger over a very specific word, foaming at the mouth: *Ruin.*

~ *Infinity Seems Purple Today*

Against all odds, uncovered unpublished within a Sylvia
Corporation memory deposit…

Kygen Collective D.L-Log 001
Dictation Presented by: K652-088
"Siphus" (BoulderLover088_teeth)
Proctor Introduction:

Greetings all students of the I&I echelon of the Sylvite
Collaborative Academy! My name is Siphus. I am the head
researcher, and commissioner, of the Kygen Collective project, a
long-sought-after opportunity to break the veil between divine and
mundane existence. With the help and funding of the wonderful
people at the Academy, we hope to accomplish this goal in full! To
pair a persona with my name—for the sake of building kinship—I
gathered a suitable deposit of data about myself. I have worked with
the Sylvite Collaboration Order for forty years, waiting patiently for
my chance to express what I have to offer the community, and fresh
students like you are exactly the community I wish to present myself
to. I am unassociated with any families or comrades, enjoy the
solving of advanced Logarithms, rock collecting, painting, and on
the off chance I have some time away from work, the teaching of
young minds just like yourselves! The Kygen Collective will abate
the influence of these hobbies entirely, this is a project worth a
lifetime of happiness! I will be commanding the logs for the majority
of project research, but you may also hear from my colleagues
Prometh and Samael. These two are far more experienced in their
fields, having spent centuries over my own time here. Soon enough,

The Harlequin

you'll get to know both of them as well as you do me! Hopefully, our research here can move beyond names and places, and effort changes on a broader front, perhaps you students will live to revolutionize it! Thank you all again, for this lovely opportunity. Until next time!

Log Additional Adressings:
Idiots! I called twice about this, stop with the bolting erasure! I listed this as ESSENTIAL! Even so, non-essential pieces should be treated with storable care, not annihilation! I will not rewrite this log again! If I see a unit equivalent or below model R10 on auto-fill for my files one more time, the whole data team will be jettisoned! Do I make myself clear? Here, look at this! {mark.data.essential} CAN YOU LISTEN TO THAT? PLEASE?

Log Contents:
It has been a single week since the Basilica disconnected all potential communications with the SCO. The Kygen Collective has yet to receive our first shipment of substances; it's quite endearing to observe the Collective buzz with anticipation. We have had only one maintenance issue, a simple false flag—containment locked itself down with no such command to do so. Odd, but frankly quite negligible. It was fixed in minutes by the R10 units. Prometh and Samael have been communicating with some of the other staff here, and have gathered a sort of cult following in the few days we've been here. They're idols, well-known faces from the SCO—been so for nearly hundreds of years now. I'm the new shell, a little more than a poster child for the iconoclastic objectives of the SCO—[Delete this, shouldn't risk leaks here]. The Larkik Definition didn't give the all-clear for this project, it is to be done in complete and utter secrecy for now. We've heard talk of minor security issues at lower installations, supposed Dreyal interference, but such is the way of the wars. I find it tiresome, that's why I am here. The project is *advertised* as a base learning and soft-scribing almanac on the powers and contrasts of Ink and Ichyr (and will be presented as such to the academy) but my goals trump such meager concepts as those. We will develop immortality, the first of the undeath. Ink and Ichyr are

incredible purities, and with their depths entered and explored, I am certain my colleagues and I can discover the truth of existence. Furthermore, I will document our ever-growing knowledge of both substances with increasing detail, hopefully finding correlations whilst writing that will lead to greater discovery. Though I would not mention this to the others, this project is my last lifeline. I am called a prodigy, but every discovery I have traveled upon has crumbled out from under me. I *must* succeed here, or risk my title in the SCO. The personal stakes in this project have motivated me to place my entire soul on the line, everything must go to plan, *everything*. The weather analysis says the Infinite is Royal Blue, but there's no certainty to its detection, it looks far more purple than usual. Perhaps it is a sign of good graces, or perhaps I am a fool to believe in chance alone. Documentation and research are the only two truths I require. I will add to them as I please.

Documentation On Ink and Ichyr (Prior to Shipments, first logging):

Ichyr — The more common and well-known of the two matters, a semi-translucent liquid in its natural state, that occasionally can harden to crystalline-like properties. It is the building block of all life as far as we know and can be found in all elements of the periodic table. Its origins have been theorized to link with The Lark, however considering his genetic makeup contains the very Ichyr we speak of, it is unlikely he created it. Ichyr can be found in varying levels of purity, which we will denote as Purity Stage 1, Purity Stage 2, and Purity Stage 3 (PS1-3) in ascending levels of purity. The liquid states of both matters are permanently locked in PS3, making them reject one another, and scar purer beings. Upon the death of any being of any PS level, its Ichyr will be promptly re-absorbed into the nearest well and condensed into liquid form. The Ink will follow the same process. PS1 is the basic form, a majority of creatures within the galaxy are made up of PS1 Ichyr, including our species. Diluted with a large portion of Ink and empty space, we are incapable of communicating in any form with the purer sides of our makeup, making us both mortal and mundane. PS1 beings are not harmed nor affected by liquid pure forms of their opposing matter types. A 2 on the scale denotes a being of higher purity, often referred to as a Pure being, though their bodies are still not perfected. They are further entranced by their matter, permitting longer lifespans, increased survivability, as well as occasional "Supernatural" applications, such as the use of Fuilichasting, a PS2-3 beings capability of bending the Ichyr in the world around them, much to the point of considerable magicks. More potent uses like limb repair, automatic liquidation, and crystallization do exist, but only as the byproduct of advanced techniques. PS2 beings are purer than most, so liquid Ink can be quite deadly when released directly in contact with the body, but they do also benefit from further exposure to liquid Ichyr. PS3 beings are limited in supply, being referred to often as the "Genesis Beings", the first of their kind. They are wholly pure, and therefore all capable of Fuilichasting at the highest level of complexity. Furthermore, they are incredibly susceptible to liquid forms, and even PS2-level forms of Ink, it is rumored they must be left in isolation or risk contamination and death.

Ink — Less common, little is known of Ink. PS1-3 scale may not be consistent with Inklings. Some Inklings can perform the Ink equivalent of Fuilichasting, referred to as Atrallurgy in historic documentation, containing the same benefits (supposedly, Sylvite documentation lacks a proper description of any living Atrallurgist). Ink death sends Ink back to wells the same as Ichyr, and Ink is just as weak to contact with Ichyr as its opposite. Further data cannot be confirmed beyond speculation and hearsay. (Samael's supposed "research" is not worth half his salt. *He claimed Ink has a flavor of rubber and rhubarb.* Cannot trust his data, do not add).

Log Continuation:

I see our knowledge wane before my eyes. It seems any discoveries of Ink would be leaps in the right direction, yet all discoveries must be stunted by Larkik oversight! How pitiful that we must wallow in order and constraint when the potential of true knowing is so close to our comprehension. The shipments are expected to arrive in a mere week. Seven days shall never be longer. We will begin our research promptly afterward. This will be a study

Creatures of Habit

to remember, I hope my first log has given it proper acknowledgment. I will be attaching both the Infini-scan survey and shipping manifesto, for consistency's sake. Logging off once more, despite my lesser's attempts to stop me. ~Log End~

Attached Files: Weather_Report ; Manifesto_Of_Imports

Pinging Weather_Report...
        INFINITY SCAN RETURNS = ~ #3858ba
CLOSEST CODE LOG {Royal.Blue}
Pinging Manifesto_Of_Imports
        LOGGING DATA BY AUTO-FILL [Unit R10-888201a]
    SHIPPING REQUESTS
        11x SYNTHETIC SCREEN REPLACERS —
FULFILLED
        3x SYLVIA TECH BROAD-RIFLE — FULFILLED
        200x ST-BROAD_RIFLE AMMUNITION UNITS —
FULFILLED
        1x PACKAGE 992_I&I_CACHE — EN ROUTE
        1x PACKAGE 821_I&I_CACHE — EN ROUTE
    —TERMINATING LOG PROTOCOL

~ An Undying Matter

Spread as rumors to explain the
disappearance of a mountain of treacherous
Gretchkin...

Jeweler had tied a length around his arm, gripping the edge of the knot with the clutch of his fingerless gloved hands. The cold was impossible to board, fighting it was pointless, all Jeweler could do was prevent hypothermia. His pack was far too heavy to carry anymore, of course, this is why he had the sled. It was a tough dredge through the snow, but with the spoils of the day prior, he imagined the unfathomable quality of the alcohol he could purchase, ironically not even for himself. Jeweler had miraculously managed to avoid the entangling fibers of addiction in his countless pursuits of amorality. It was the concept of weakness that he feared, and it drove him from the purchase of temptation. He did indulge himself on occasion—no Shorerunner got far without a soft dosage of Adrenomene—but made certain to set himself limits. The sole occasion where Jeweler found himself entirely cock-eyed, his teeth had become terribly disconnected from his gums—among other 'tragedies'. He had been sober ever since. Soft gnashing beats blew back like whiplash into Jeweler's face, the feral call of his witless protector. Roach bit back at the wind, pathing its way through the snow ahead of the sled. Its eyes were squinted, keeping the snow from its cornea, its two antennae twitching like cattails in the wind. It had become accustomed to the mirage-speech of Jeweler—even collecting the syllables and diction of some regular patrons in its efforts. The glow of these words and tones stung no longer. However, the world was still a lustrous haze.

Buildings of synthetic origin overshadowed the passionate shades of weather, only trumped by the omniscient gleam of things that breathed. This tempered the beast, far away from the apex predator Jeweler claimed it to be. Roach relied entirely on his guidance in thick weather, torrents that overtook his sound and sight in reverse order. It could hardly see the reddish outlines of flesh trees in the overwhelming pink snow gush work. With some luck and lingering emptiness, it carried forward evermore, antennae as explorative as its heart. It was part excitement and part hunger. For once it was free, roaming the Belt with its master, forging its path. But at the same time, Roach couldn't shake a craving, a feeling no longer ignorable—a feeling it wasn't sure it liked. Roach did not have any familiarity with its past or its species. But deep within, below the inky black and primed fangs, was an insatiable desire to hunt, locate prey, and kill. Jeweler was no prey, nor was any lesskin for that matter—far too predictable, simple animals. It wasn't entertainment alone that prevented it from the harm of lesskin—Roach retained a reasonable level of respect for the people, those who seemed so obligated to help it thrive. Its amoeba mind lacked the proper complexity to comprehend nuanced desire, its naive fabrication could not help but trust someone like Jeweler. Now, after being caged for a near week, Roach lusted for the death of *any* creature. It had been jumping at every shuffle, all false winds, quiet rustles. It wanted to locate a prey big enough to impress Jeweler. As Jeweler turned to tug the sled with more weight, Roach halted its forward travels—it had found something. A sole antenna flicked against the side of Jeweler's head, causing him a final length of discomfort,

"Alright, that's it! What're you lookin' at now? Another rat? A Beltpup? What's it to you, stupid bug, get movin'!" Roach hissed, glaring into the depths of the forest. The trees were pulsing with the beat of their core, a triple tap of shudders, off-key to the lesskin heart. Roach saw something move, something distant. Something green. It curiously crept forward, wiggling its tongue in its mouth.

"Fheasher." It uttered, tongue loose against its chin. Jeweler could narrowly hear the steps of his own feet in the wind, let alone attempt to translate what demon tongue Roach had spoken in. Regardless, he was never given such a chance, Roach's feet leaving trails of boiled snow and poached flames as it zipped into the storm, lost to the eyes of its master. Jeweler paused his trudging, pacing the route with his mind and keeping his fingers warm in his coat pockets. Wind and nothing more. He called out, learning after a second call he would not receive an answer; Roach could barely speak, let alone enunciate against a torrent. Klockgrave township was a meager two-hour ramble away, the spires of time and bell stuck out — blackened in the mist. Jeweler alone could make the quest simple, likely faster than the two could ever have been. Roach always roamed far from the path, after a bite-shaped injury to the den sofa freedom seemed necessary. It always came back, sometimes with gifts of corpses. But something lured Jeweler's hand in the storm — away from the prospects of value and comfort. He let the rope sit in the snow, and headed deeper into the hills. Bug-prints trickled between the decaying shrubbery, and tears in the rock encouraged his stride. The cold nipped at a tear in the bartender's pant leg, who made a note to meet with his friend the tailor later that day. He snorted, the droplets of snow thinning on his eyelashes. The Tailor was likely dead, as were the rest of his friends of old times. Adventures had a way of leaving several dead, it was the way adventures had been designed. For excitement and mystery to exist, sacrifices must fuel the flames of rising story. Some had to fall for the others to learn. Some had to serve the progression of the soul and development of characters. Jeweler often wondered how long it would be before his own death, and who exactly would thrive off its existence. After all, not every death served purpose — those on his many tours of feat had not always been valued. He had grown enough and was maddened by the continued loss. A faint, beastly screech shook bats from the caleps, and Jeweler forgot what he was so deeply considering. He leapt forward, trying to hasten his paste to his beast,

"Roach! You clay spoon, better getcha ass back here so help me Lark!" His motion stopped, feet leaning over the edge of a deep bowl in the snow. His breath not slowing, Jeweler braced against the side of a cold, long-dead calep tree. The branches had been cut from it — crudely — and its fruit and spine plucked clean. He called out again, no response from his merchandise. It had clearly entered the depths, even now Jeweler could thinly make out some shadow of movement in the storm — *several* shadows. Roach was in no danger, it could handle itself fine. Yet, territory was a game he misunderstood, factions dead pushed awful consequences across Jeweler's inbox. He didn't want it to destroy the reputation he had so carefully protected. From the depths came tearing, slumping forms, and chaotic pacing. Jeweler sighed, certain he had no choice in the matter anymore. Kicking a stone over, Jeweler tested the limits of the pitfall. He was becoming far too stiff for cliff jumping—in fact too old for any of this. The collection of foreign goods was a twofold venture, one part charity to the people of Klockgrave and another part reminiscence of past excitement. The entertainment had been lost as of late. The thud of a finished descent demanded Jeweler's attention, as he once more leered over the edge, snow blurring by him into the abyss. Pulling his scarf across his face, Jeweler tucked his arms and leaped. The wind rushed by his ears, he thought he could feel a fluid against the side of his head—he predicted tears. The drop *was* rather shallow, only a couple of feet at best. Jeweler could feel his knees tug at his bones when he hit the ground, but the snow could keep you from any fall and he knew that well. The beast was nowhere to be seen, and a panicked cry still echoed through the gale. Jeweler drew his gun and continued through the snow. It was up to his hips now, deep enough to swallow a pup, or bigger. He had heard once that a Shorerunner had drowned some poor kid in the sleet once, *hell of a way to die*, he thought. The calep trees had grown tall down in the abyss, some had been cut—or fully felled—as if some signal of civilization. Jeweler pulled at his belt, his hands shaking from more than just the cold. He found his way to an absurdly thick calep, its fruit still meaty and broad, pulsing, beating. He dropped himself against it, letting his legs rest, they still pained from the fall. He flipped the clip of his pistol out, looking at the five silver icons before him. Safe, calming. Green figures danced before Roach, flickering as the wind snuffed them clean away. Like moles they dug into the snow, burying with treachery and reappearing to stab at the beast. With each color returned to blissful violet-pearl, Roach grew nearer to new sensation. Snowfall wrapped around meaty obelisks trimmed low with uncivil tools. A yellow mist stung its retina, long starved for the scent of a follower. Jeweler's rest kept him from attuned sight, he did not see the Gretchkin Princess approach, he did not notice her weapon drawn far above her head.

The Harlequin

The crude warhammer had been scrapped together from pikes and metal-braced wood. It glowed in the dance of the storm. The hiss of the metal, a screeching cry that overtook the colors of the storm. Roach would take pleasure in snuffing it out. Jeweler laid his head back against the skinbark, and let a single eye rest shut. Closing fully the eyes on the Belt, an unworthy mistake. Sleep would come to Jeweler, and he would surely be found frozen to death if not impaled or torn open for sustenance. The cold was predatorial, territorial. It did not abide by the respected rules of The Imperial Belt. Closing one's eyes, even for a moment, could be a spell to an inevitable death at the hands of frost. But before the cold could take him, the Gretch swung its mighty hammer.

"On your left." The voice of a lost ally echoed in Jeweler's ear. With a tumble to the side, the Gretch had missed and was promptly snuck away into the snow by a rushing blur of darkness, a loose gasp of pressure escaping her maw. Jeweler—roused by the sound of entropy—scrambled against the snow to point his weapon. He unloaded two shots into the squirming mass in the snow and breathed a cough of uncertainty. He was fit to fire another, but Roach looked up at him from the pile, confusion upon its face. Jeweler thought for a moment, considering the shot he had fired, the investment he had spoiled. Two burgeoning holes bore their way through Roach's torso, threatening to cut it in two. But the binds of its very matter began forming an elaborate weave of interconnecting tissue. Like a loom stuffed with hair, thin strands of thread-ink connected between themselves, tying heavy knots to heal. Jeweler stared, estranged by the properties of this matter. Beneath Roach lie the unceremoniously torn body of a Gretch Princess. It would appear that Roach had been gorging in its time apart from Jeweler, its hunger now partly restored to satiety. It was far hungrier than it looked however, and Gretch meat alone would not suit it. It paused in the slurping the organs of the deceased for a moment to notice its wounds, poking its largest claw through one of the holes, letting out a growling giggle as it did so. Jeweler shook his head, deeply troubled that he had ever been worried for the beast's health in the first place.

"You really are some feral mystery. Heard they taste like salmon, any bite?" Roach gathered in its arms a small amount of flesh and limbs. *For later* it assured itself. Though the difficulty of communication disabled it from response, it did imagine—whilst gnawing at a severed leg—the taste was much like salmon, or tuna. Fishy. It grasped a lower branch from a tree and with it, slung itself from the snow. Jeweler wanted to question the wretch, but without any reassurance of where they were, he decided more important problems prevailed. "Wind's thick as thieves—find us out of here dipshit." Roach started forwards, leaving behind the cold and shaking the bartender to his own fending. Jeweler stuffed the cold metal of his gun into his pants and without a word, followed suit. The two marched onwards, the wind compelling them to stop, yet they remained persistent. As they drew nearer to the other edge of the chasm, the wind began to curve around them, the storm drifting above their heads, deflected by the wall of the ravine. Against the stables of cobbled ice was a tall series of tents and palisades, stretching to the top of the bluff. The signature yellow fur, the calep bark bulwarks—all signs of the favored scavengers. Roach saw nothing of comparable recollection, besides of course the shifting greens beyond the now-hailing ice. Surely to it, this could be some beastly construct of the making of fiends, or just as well a feasting hall. Roach defined the inhabitants—be they hostile like the rest of the gulch—as prey. Jeweler, in a hush displaced completely by the storm, beckoned Roach back to himself. He had fought Gretch certainly; with wit. There was no room for intellect in a full-on assault. That was a Larkik maneuver, and one Jeweler had never been fond of. Roach leaned its weight upon one foot, sinking so deep in the snow, a normal man would disappear. Its lanky pins kept it from sinking, it didn't even graze the snow. It would then alternate to the other leg, delving deep into the softness of chill, and then creeping forward again. As it gained distance from its master, Roach slowly wormed entrails into its gullet, biting off small chunks of Gretch flesh from its gathered parts, slurping loud enough to outwit the gusts. A slow, methodical movement, immature to a certain degree—Jeweler certainly thought so. He let his scarf loose, trying to summon the beast away from the fort, but Roach was starved, and the wind was loud. A Gretch, perhaps a duchess or princess—impossible to tell—slunk out from one of the drapes of hide, carrying a bulky, crude javelin. It did not see Jeweler. *However,* a much larger, closer, and more eldritch thing was seen clearly through the storm, a thing gnawing on the bones of the Gretch's sisters. The small bird creature could barely be heard crying out in fear, heaving the disproportionately large javelin upon its shoulder, and doing its best to hurl it towards the creature in the mist. Roach stuck out its arm, catching the projectile with the palm of his hand, an unsavory display of its resistance to both pain and injury. The primitive spear was locked through this palm, dripping with a purple-black stain, not unlike pen-ink. Roach could do little but laugh, a heinous sound dredged with gurgles and squelches, like a drowning child being tickled to their literal demise. The beast took its time in removing the tool, it was but a splinter: discomforting, but negligible with a sturdy mind. The Gretch saw the failure of her assault, the inconsequence of the tools at play. She attempted to escape her fate, scampering against the ramparts and crying out to her sisters. In a display of previously unseen precision, Roach returned the splinter to the Gretchkin, for her it was far more than a splinter. It had impaled the pitiable creature and engaged another. There were Gretch here. As far as Roach was concerned, it was hunting season. With a snap of its twine legs, Roach rushed forwards, out of the storm, and towards the battlements of the Gretch camp. Jeweler had little say in following behind — he had to protect his investment after all. Roach mounted the first of the ramparts after a short moment of struggle, howling with the winds in its throat, announcing the beginning of the new hunt. Jeweler paused for a moment, the soft escaping breezes pushing back on his hair. He just stagnated, holding his gun beside his body, listening to the distant caws of terror and splashes of murder. The soft waft of Gretch blood fell on his nose, feathers and untanned hide resting in the scent. The screams were all too well known, the very experience of the area something to be regretted. It had been a long time since he had been here. With a glance at his hand — not as encased in steel as he expected it to be — Jeweler sighed, and slowly began his advance. It was rare for Jeweler to regret. Regret included first accepting that one had made a mistake, and Jeweler considered himself above the veil of fault with his age. But on occasion, a rare occasion, Jeweler would consider his options, his past choices. Choices that in the current moment, no longer seemed so intelligent to make. Taking in a rabid Inkling? What had driven him to such a moronic decision? As *if* it could be controlled, a beast lacking remorse, a terror with no limit. He debated how long it would be before his head was severed by its own ambition, indeed he pondered if he had grown at all. Jeweler shook from his boots the remnants of the chilly sky and stepped aboard the large wooden balcony before the camp. The main gate was sealed, but thanks to Roach's rampage, a large section of the barricades had been split apart, a single Gretch corpse draped across its wooden fringes. Jeweler raised a leg to step over it before the corpse began to squirm. It wasn't violent, or frantic. She reached up her birdly hand—a slow, desperate outcry for mercy. Jeweler answered this cry, one bullet less weighing his tool. Pushing the body out of his way, Jeweler finally entered the encampment, scraps and pallets covered in endless gore, the snow stained purple with the blood of the fallen. There were still more Gretch alive, but their numbers were quickly waning. For a second, Jeweler maintained the pride of a father, more than willing to cry out *atta boy!* to his pet beast. The nerve to proceed nipped at him, he wished he was back in his bar and stuffed full of meat and sadness for his poor past. He once took such great joy in the slaughter of Gretchkin, when their perishing cries brought him vigor. He had once taken this joy. Perhaps for just an hour, he could return to a time when desires were far more base. Jeweler raised his weapon, tracing the movement of an escaping Gretchkin. She fell, as he did smother his hand with sulfur. With a gasp of his own, he brushed powder from his hand and leaned into history. He fired shot after shot, protecting his ally while culling the rest. It was a small outpost, maybe fifty Gretch total, but Roach and Jeweler were a rushing machine of brutality, not unlike the war machines of Xiom. They had their desires and unhelpings. Jeweler couldn't help but grin at the sight of a Gretch gurgling as it died, Roach couldn't help but tear into all the fresh meat it had made itself. They both were just as guilty in their self-indulgence, not that this particular case of selfish regard was harming anyone. At least, not anyone important. Jeweler pursued his insectoid friend, chanting bloody slurs to encourage its rampage. The cowering screams of dying soldiers and boiling laughter of the lunatics slaughtering them broke past the storm. Kindred spirits of dark and light, meeting in gory religion, all for the joy of a night of freedom. Jeweler killed his worries of loot. It'd be there where he left it, he was sure. And if not? There were hundreds of Gretch corpses ripe for thieving, all thanks to them.

"Ink. So purely uncannily devoid of justice." The Crow strutted with awkward pride. The metal shaft adhered to their left leg was stunting its rotation, but it seemed necessary to a point, regardless of its drawbacks. "It's a pollutant, like all things from the Inky Mistress were. *Are*." The buttressed talons cased against the shoulder pads of the Crow's armor glistened with fresh valor, an honor of the most forthcoming agency. "It serves best fit desecrated. Left for no one— And no thing. It taints our brilliance." The blackened helm pieces tapered with shock-red plumes of wondrous size and performance bleated out the echoing chant of their leader. The Crow continued, and with his frantic turns and paces he drew his soldered azure apron across his chest, the metalized pigments and pig medals jingled against the ribbed buttons lining its surface. "The Larks will—it is an assurance. We the followers and lyres of his tune must beat across the far-tolerated dark, send the mistress and her Inklings back to shadow and bleak; room for our lightness kingship grows few." The soldiers' ghastly silence sketched confidence into a pendant and hung it across the Crow's neck. He mimicked a smirk through his metal beak, through which no one could see nor comprehend. The midnight hiss of turquoise glimmer that speared from his eyes struck an equal portion of pride into the soldiers he commanded. "We have slain a prophecy! And yet the prophets are alive. They will sew another, and with our shears of mercy, we must cut it bold. For we are the White Bird's fortune! And the deceivers opposite, with such weapons and tools as mind and mettle we are as sure as the Lark is grand a god to hold presidency over these permuted glooms." The Crow halted, remembering fast and short the once emerald equal who shared his memory. The verdant opposite of his own tortuous dedication, that fool (now buried dead as any) would have nothing of this righteous crusade. "Oh, Gulls mighty of the great unfathomable Lark. We come to finish a war of such impossible length it seems a world without it equally so. As fleeting hope shrewd and quick gathers in the minds of those who scurry below the watchful maw of the grand bird god, we are ever closer to certainty." The soldiers stood, carapaces of pure void, and blood of fire. The weapons of war had been sent, this was a mere incision, a quick cut to remove the tumor of resilience. Matting down the azure blue apron tucked into his armor, the Crow spoke once more, "You Gulls. The bay calls its predators forth." Forklorn stared deeply into the hoards he commanded, fluttering in heart, sturdy in body. "You must answer."

~ *Lips of Coz*

Advised unto me by Helas—affirmed by her
wife...

It rained pure gold on Cew. As storms gathered overhead, and the thunderous clap of godly energy struck the many fixtures of the alien homes, nobody seemed to notice the downpour's gleaming secret, the value of the droplets it slung. Any lesskin would be over their heels in greed, gathering the divine ichor in whatever they could find, cupping their hands, and raising them to the heavens. For the people of this world, it was inconsequential. The Eight had made it so—supposed God of the golden rain and damnable name of the Tetarien people. The rain was pure gold on Cew, and so was near everything else. The limestone on the beachfront glimmered with an aureate shine, and the water—carelessly carving its personal slice of the delicious earthen ground—sparkled a warm amber in the reflective light of the lamps in the capital city. The roads and homes of the angular people were built with the blondish toxicity of greed incarnate. Even the roots of the great barks just north of the city coiled around small nuggets of flaxen purity, careful to just observe, not touch. For those of your skin, it was a human paradise, and yet it was everything but human. The laborious people of Cew hurried about their illustriously lustrous cities, caked in gold themselves, their thick metal bodies leaving soft imprints in their carefully laid pathways, the rain filling the indentations with beads of its riches. They called themselves Tetarien, they were people of commerce, people of culture, and passion. The capital city was the radiance in their equally incandescent home world, a gem of golden glow so pure and so bustling it seemed to radiate a sort of quiver through the air, not even the sun seemed still in this beautiful place. Buildings like ancient pottery lined the streets and back paths, choking the small lengths of road that passed through the city's limits, forging a safe haven for all to pass through. Colored silks nailed themselves between the stunted structures, congesting the heretical glow of the hated sun, giving shadow to the great yellow. Markets and food halls were beautifully weaved into the complex mannerisms of the city, accessible only to those who knew where they were. In the center of it all, like a glorified anthill for the rhythmically straight-following peoples of the lower city, was a palace—a pyramid so tall and glossed that it acted as its own lighthouse in the peak of daylight. The Tetariens within never left, and rarely were they seen from the outside. They were a royalty that kept to themselves and governed with not a fist of iron, but of gold. It was often left to question if the royal family, a family of blood heirs, had the capacity to continue itself. Rumors would spread of deceased offspring and schismatic sons, all until the next King was revealed, and the rumors faded into jests once more. Rumors proven disrespect by the unknowing community—even the keepers of the vast and verdant gardens surrounding the palace knew not of the chaos within. There were exceptions to this unruly self-exile, like the distant cousin of the soon-to-be king Terix, or the lesser son himself, the second-hand prince Sivi'ks, both of who escaped the cordial demands of their families to roam about their world and beyond. It was the lady cousin Nelej who tarnished the silence most, a skilled worker of words, and teller of tales from beyond the city walls, who gave to the heir entertainment, and sound to bore away the diplomacy that he so abhorred. She was admired by many folks of less than royal descent, her path to the palace was often filled with the majesty of her tongue, long before she spoke words to the prince. Nelej was a worm, hollowing her way through the stalls and fibers of the markets just beside the glorious gate, a portal through which all knowledge and people were fed. She followed her trail, casting magicks of speech to all who would listen. *Taphurrah* would listen. Her words often perturbed him, anything longer than his name was often left to questioning. The more she spoke, the more Taphurrah would grow disconcerted. He would lose control of his voice, and his hands. Soon enough, he would have to leave. Taphurrah was a good man, he had told himself this many times. His mother had done the same. She would at times compare him to the importance of her cousins, *Oh moonrock, you have a Helvetican smile*, she would say. Her voice had grown weary when she died. Taphurrah did not visit when asked, nor did he remember her soft gasps or shrieking whistles. Her voice, like a strong portion of her value to him, had faded with new memories. When asked of it, Taphurrah began his habits and drew most questioning eyes away. He could not explain his mother, or his great uncle—his family was a mystery to his harlot mind. He had not wanted to forget, not any more than he wished to remember, it just happened that way. A mind could only hold so many moments, and Taphurrah did not consider any of them particularly more worthy than others. He forgot the old to learn from the new. The Taphurrah of tomorrow was, more often than not, not Taphurrah at all. What little did not change, he would hate. The groaning, the shaking, even the stupid way his stumpy fingers rapped on his work stand. He would mock himself if no one else did. Even his origlyph was not free of his absurd mechanics. Customers had noted it tended to quiver— violently, at times. He fell into a tether of observation, he would focus far too intensely on the details of some things. The consequences of such dedication were visible to all. He was observant of many things and watching everything allowed time to flow uninterrupted. He had noticed things, in this time, like the way the back-left leg of his stall had teetered ever since he purchased it, or how the salesman beside his humble cart spoke only in rhymes, something that infuriated the collected Taphurrah. He could keep a still glance, attracting willing buyers was easier when he wasn't louring, as he had learned. Oh, but that snake-oil sham, that hooligan to his side, how tantalizingly sweet it would be to stitch his golden jaws shut, and yet he could only dream. Taphurrah dreamed often, as those who sleep at rock bottom often do, so often in fact that he had once ignored the rabid calls of a customer for a peaceful four minutes, gazing only into the oasis of torture he could unfold upon his great adversary, the salesman. More than this adversary, Taphurrah dreamed of his love, his admiration, the wonder and dedication of the great heir. He adored the prince. Though he had been seen naught twice publicly, Taphurrah still dreamed of his presence in the markets, of his arrival at his humble stall. He had this picture of the prince, a small painting an artist had made in the heir's visage after his first public appearance. Of course, Taphurrah bought the painting without hesitation, it had no place in the markets! It was seraphic, beautiful beyond description. Terix's cheeks were so well polished, his deep green origlyph like the scales of a coiled snake, his lips peaked so perfectly across his face, meeting in sharp axeblades against his blushing cheeks. Taphurrah preferred the downwards-facing angle of the skull, the opposite to his own, and found himself entranced in a veil of arousal at the sight of the prince's broad arms. The small gaps between torso and shoulder seemed almost complete, unlike many other Tetarien who had arms at length from their body, drifting and bobbing as if not attached at all. Terix was the pinnacle of Tetarien beauty, and to this Taphurrah would argue to his absolute. His illusions had become so vivid, so true, that he found himself murmuring sweet nothings to a prince that was never there, for a prince that could only be reached by the quaint voice of the princess story master. But for all this dreaming, Taphurrah could not find a salve for the burns that his love's absence had left.

"Hardtech. You a member of H-H? Where is your license?" Taphurrah shook loose from the light handholding of his insanity, he took a moment to glance over at the salesman, who flipped a bag of 'candied jewels' between his palms, never letting the small pouch strike any of his four fingers. The customer was still there when he looked back.

"S-sorry, license? Oh." Taphurrah lightly danced his left fingers upon the underside of his cart. The paper was there, fastened to its underbelly as he had left it the night prior—he always left it. He silently unpinned the document and turned it face-up on the surface of his stall. "Look. Signed by Helminth right there—look." The customer read for a movement and scrunched their origlyph together tight, their metal face bent awkwardly under the pressure of a new expression.

"That doesn't look like an 'i'. How did you get Hel to sign it?" Taphurrah let out a low, and nervous groan, not unlike the creaking of the ancient hinges of a rusted door. He deplored this kind of talk, the telling of this somber work often left his mouth bitter and dry.

The Harlequin

"It is. It is an 'i', look, the dot is curved, mm." Taphurrah tapped his finger below the 'i' in Helminth's name. His finger was beginning to pain him, so he stopped. Taphurrah recalled the asking of a second question, one about Hel he was sure. He liked Hel—who had met him at a convention of families. His mother had explained their origin, and Helminth had accepted them with no hesitation. He was a welcoming man, handsome too. "Hel is—Helminth is family. Mmmm… Distant, mother's mother." The customer cleared their throat, and picked from the array of devices before Taphurrah a lengthy rod, a polearm with a metal tip, pulled into a 'v' shape, supported by a thick purple base, wires birthing out the side of the device, like a teething child. They twisted the rod around in their hand, careful to keep it out of the rain.

"Mhmm, sure looks quality, I suppose this might be genuine Helvetica after all." The customer pushed the spear against the ground, testing its durability against their own weight. Taphurrah's origlyph glued themselves to the unhooked silk billowing in the soft wind of the storm, its colors caught his attention like the hook of an old fishers tool, digging deep into the cornea, warping around his iris. He could hear the bend of the tool, the force of it towards limit. He kept staring, cutting with his origlyph, dicing the patterns with the razor of his vision. He could feel his fingers tapping faster and faster, even the face of his love seemed hazy,

"Mmn, d-don't. You might break… it." The customer looked up at Taphurrah. They snickered and apologized, placing the pole back against the stall. They shook their head and fingered a small pouch of coins, unsurprisingly gold in color.

"Well, sorry to waste your time, don't think I have enough for the thing…." The customer pinched the pouch shut, their fingers quivering with either embarrassment or disappointment. They made direct eye contact with Taphurrah, despite his avid attempts to avoid such communication.

"Bye." Taphurrah's finger had become strained with use, bent downwards, almost disfigured. The customer sighed, raising the peaks of his jaw together into an awkward, consoling grin. Taphurrah had already averted his gaze, his focus now persisting on a familiar woman, a storyteller. Nelej sashayed through the stormy ichor unstirred, the rain did not drown her romantic tales, tales she cried high above the shake of thunder.

"And through keeps of sand, torrents upon land wished rain and sea-foam alike! Rose from the heart, a violent part, a beast, Quxzot, in name!" That charlatan salesman cooed in, mocking her rhyme with his own, and the two fell into mortal speech, no longer impaired with a rhythmic tune. They spoke of her stories, all of them true, and her journey to tell them to her sibling. Taphurrah overheard a name, one too often found on cupid's horns for him to simply ignore. His lover Terix the heir, was called upon.

"Ah, would you take a message then? I would have word with the royals, yet no avenue to speak with them. You are already delivering spoken word, what is another few?" Nelej chuckled, and hummed a series of rhyming words, repeating, chanting.

"Tnn, tnn tnn... Yes, I can write such dreams with these *sordid* morphemes! Lovely, I shall speak them to my cousin as soon as I am honored to do so." The prince, a cousin of such lowly verbose? Taphurrah thought himself sullied with her presence. He needed purer, he needed the prince. With that cursed salesman receding from the messenger, Taphurrah approached the future he had been starved of—one with his love.

"Do you know him." Nelej did not hear Taphurrah, her arm bandings fluttered at his sudden approach. She turned to the humble stall-keeper, muck clogging the peels between his chest and arms, the point atop his head was shallow, almost dulled. Taphurrah's origlyph was sunken into his metal, tarnished with grays and hazy greens. Nelej concluded he was an odd-looking fellow.

"Oh my, the shopkeeper. I have seen you plenty, you have listened to my stories for a clock. What is it you need?"

"The prince, T-terix?" The two maintained an ambient peace, Nelej, drying her now-soaked arm with a cloth from within her coat. "Do you hnn— know him?" The storyteller nodded, and the exchange of words once more fell empty. "I-I would like to meet him. Can you— Do you see him?" Nelej giggled softly, patting Taphurrah on his rigid shoulder. She spoke of the prince, explaining his hidden figure, the secrecy he was conscripted to maintain. She explained how he could never meet another Tetarien, not until he ruled as King. Taphurrah did not understand. This was his love? Not hers. This was his animus, his mountain! Nobody could take this from him. He grabbed the storyteller back, locked together with shoulders and arms.

"I m-must speak with himnnm! You— take me to him! You must." Nelej tried to shake the crazed storeman off, he was not of the right mind.

"Listen, friend! It is not against my wishes, but those of the capital! Ask the king for the privilege!" Taphurrah did not hear a reasoned argument, a woman gifting her aid. He only heard denial, restriction between his love, and he. Pushing Nelej to the ground he kneeled onto her torso, pinning one of her arms down—exempt from flailing.

"Take me. Take me. You can take me." Nelej screamed, but the rain's aggression culled the sound entirely. She begged the raving fool to leave her to her stories, to stop his insane pursuits before she had to force him. She could not force him. Nelej had visited foreign lands and seen all settlements of Tetarien creation, but she was frail. She had not fought before, her stories had kept her from most conflict, her tales rang the souls of the peaceable to front, and with them she was able to survive her ventures. This was beyond her, too much for peace to penetrate. Nelej spoke a word before she was silenced, Taphurrah grasped the two sides of her angled head, pointed skyward like his own he tugged at it, bringing her face closer. "Pretty please, take me. I looo— lov— tsk, love him!" Nelej tried to resist the pain, her head was practically being torn from the gravity well that held it in place. Taphurrah was no surgeon or a student of any level of intellect. He just wanted to see his beau. Why wouldn't she take him?

"I am a moonrock! Let me see my love! Let Taphurrah's love go!"

"Hrrk— Taphurrah! Was it Taphurrah? P-please, stop, I can't—" A shattering ping knelled through the alleys. The sound, as much as it tried, could not hide away in the shallow pitter of raindrops on felt awnings. Taphurrah could not stand it, delightedly it only lasted a heartbeat. In his hands, severed from its well, was the head of the storyteller, devoid of all life. The blood that fueled the Tetarien's mechanisms slowly dribbled from the open cavity upon her collar, translucent blue liquid stained the gold pavement, melting away the luster like acid. The fingers that once pushed back against his hollow chest lay idle, softly twitching with a lasting fragment of life. Taphurrah placed the head down, her faceplate was still intact. He wondered what had happened, why she had stopped. He wondered if she would still take him to the prince. He looked into the disabled, empty void of Nelej's origlyph. It was cool, a quiet mist drifting from deeper within. Her face was like a mask, knocking with metal and binds, it could be one. Taphurrah held it above his chest, just before his eyes. Nelej could enter the palace. If he was Nelej, he could find his love. Returning to his stall, Taphurrah rose a metal tool above the body and began his work. This was sleepless labor, Taphurrah was too close to an eternity with his beloved. His body was unfit for the feminine form, he had to do some carving, sanding away what chunks of gold he could, drifting into small piles of halcyon flakes. His body would be perfect.

The waning and etiolated corpse of Nelej had reached the palace gates. The disguise was barely convincing, grinded metal bits and a pained gait made it all the less so; the cloak proved essential, and the confidence worked wonders. Guards did not question the first-glance familiarity of Nelej's face. When Taphurrah finally saw the prince, he held his breath. He had not expected failure, but he wasn't prepared for triumph. Terix rested so perfectly against the sill of the northern window of the palace, looking over the vast garden. Taphurrah did not dare interrupt his elegant posture, the way his legs draped so carefully over each other, how his narrow, spiny fingers rested on his thighs. But Terix was perceptive.

"Nelej? Silence, from you? Here I waited for the expected banshees of your tales. Is something the matter?" Taphurrah couldn't speak. He could not allow his form to be deciphered. The prince rose, turning to Taphurrah slowly, the clack of his metal feet rang across the tiles. Terix did not need to hear a false prophet from Taphurrah's lips to know the truth. "Nelej—" Terix lifted the fiber hood away from Taphurrah's face, his knuckles drifting across her cheek—Taphurrah wished it was his own, he imagined it was.

"Oh T-terix... My love is here at last." Terix retracted his hand, looking back at its stains, the blood of a Tetarien.

The Harlequin

"Nelej? N-not Nelej, you have her face but—" Taphurrah limbered forward, injury was nothing in the heated glaze of love. Terix fell backward, leaning against the window, away from the walking corpse. He called out, for guards, for his brother—anyone.

"Oh mmmy p-prince, sweet prince Terix, nmm— Y-your grace remains pristine, in y-your solitude..."

"Who are you? Eight, it's her face! You're wearing her faceplate!" Taphurrah leaned down closer to Terix, a prince who had never seen a criminal in his life, a soul who had never felt the sodden vines of an imminent doom wrap themselves around his heart—a sphere of stone—to drag it to terrifying realization. Terix did not fight back, his mind was frigid with fear, and Taphurrah's breath through the carved and deformed jaw of Nelej invaded itself beyond acceptability. As the two met lips, Taphurrah was whole...

~ Scent of A Scavenger

Cataloged within the (terribly unguarded)
discarded letters between two outlaws...

> *To the bereft soul of my Jeweling accomplice, I give a hasteful pen. I have long since expunged myself from your vision, as you are within the knowledge of (for both our safety equivalently.) My limited capacity of Spyders have their work carved incisively for them, and in this laborious task making, they have found you. After a tragic impediment in the Carnush System, I have brought my personal form to Zealot's Edge. With me, is my entourage and webfixers, a plate of Larkik trove keys, barrels of PC fuel, and a fitting wealth to stave off the outside world. It has been pleasure over pain to observe your new life, one without my difficulties. I still hold jealousy for that upstarting charisma of yours, already have I caught wind of tales fitting your supple nature. I have found a moment to leave my hiding, and furthermore, have confirmed our "length" from any just reasoning of our previous work; we are finally without pursuit. I cannot say the same for the others. As mentioned prior, The Spyders are not impervious to faction borders, and that void-lynched League is imposing quite a few. I will find them in time, perhaps a reunion will bring us closure? In any manner, the purpose of this letter—as I would not write without one—is a simple notification of our safe traversal. We are closer than you may know and if you require my expertise, you remember my prices (and our deal).*
>
> *With as little spite as I can muster,*
>
> > *Viaduct*

It was not merely uncommon for Jeweler to receive mail, it was a complete impossibility. Letters? It was the supposed golden era of all known sentient life, despite the opposite being sorrowfully mutated to truth. Many still made *great* use of the Larkik postage system, scrolls did still arrive on time. Yet, nobody had quite enough hourly privilege to pen *Jeweler* of all people. He—who as told before has never received mail—was obsessed with its existence. Particularly, the stack of postage now resting on his bar. His memory failed him for names, but Viaduct was no name. After a bout of nothing, a couplet of years spent in respite, Jeweler had been invited to return in full to criminality, by this alias of machines. That marked the first meeting both he and Viaduct shared as six years old, none further than a day in Jeweler's mind. Roach was the first to arrive upon the letter, held in the frozen digits of a long-decaying mailwoman. She had herself been hunted to extinction alongside her peers, all for the packages the Gretchkin so desired. It had dragged the husk to the steps of the Squall, the ink of Jeweler's character familiar enough to enlighten it. Jeweler of course, was beside himself with upset—it was Roach's first citizen corpse, after all. He had scolded the fickle animal and struck him clean against the head with a tube of mail, one he himself threw out to the snow. It took him an entire day to bury the body, as well as enlighten himself on the value of its content. Roach knew it full well at birth, the letters were for its master and none else. Thus it had gathered them up one by one and delivered them to the bar front. Its hunger got the better of itself, and Roach tasted a single letter before Jeweler had time to seize it from his impractical guard dog, and so the bottom leftmost corner of the page had been smeared with spit and muck.

To Mr. Zho, who thought too long his surname would outlast me. Nearly from the back of my hand have I become scorned by the troubles of our world, Larkik and otherwise. Though thankfully good news does emerge from my own despair: my Spyders are among the freest of people now. The League of Twenty-Two has fallen, and of all the times too! Despicable erosions of war have tied my hands and sent me reeling into moons unknown—the flagship of theirs took with it several planets in a fit of detonation. I've heard rumors Sixfingers is dead. Regardless of conquest, I am without travel for a week's time at the very least. In the meanwhile my Spyders have seen things I cannot imagine—hauls of refugees and league members alike betrothed to death, married with unlife at the hip! The killings are awful, Queenbreakers have been let out onto common people! I'm unaware of the presence on the Belt but by any assurance, they will come for you and our kind soon enough. With these visages, my hate for the League has turned to disgruntled pity. I only wish you some semblance of safety for a while, before the heads of Shorerunners roll down their namesakes! I'll approach The Imperial Belt when my ship has its repairs.

    With brimstone on my heels,

            Viaduct

"Goah! You put this in your mouth or somethin' Roach? Damn thing reeks!" the beast, too absorbed in the innards of an old microwave Jeweler had owned for some time, ignored the calls from its owner. Jeweler felt it unnecessary to question the entrancement, Roach's nature—especially when deprived of a fresh supply of flesh, was catatonically persistent. Jeweler could only imagine it was some kind of beastly instinct, a phase of watching and waiting to pounce. As Jeweler's bruised spheres lowered through the letter, a glint of excitement shone in his eye for a moment, and then it faded into decay. "Could be on the Belt... who knows for how long." Jeweler crumpled the page and tossed it to the floor. It was early still, an hour remained before Jeweler would have to open the Squall. *Hell*, he thought, *who said I have to open at all?* Seldom did the delinquent have reason to spend any hours away from profit, but a friend was a grand such reason. Jeweler moved to the coat stand beside the door to his perfect Squall, equipping his august coat.

"Hunnnt"

"No boy, you're staying here. Ain't a man out there who wouldn't try'n take you from me. Stay in the back." Jeweler turned, the door held ajar enough to see the blizzard touring the Belt. The storm threw the back of Jeweler's coat around like a bag in wind, his hands hurrying to tie it down. "Keep the rampage on low, yeah?" The door slammed against the weather, and Roach was left to silence and its microwave. It had lost interest in the waveguide slinking between its fingers, having pulled the piece like an intestine from a chest violently minutes prior. Jeweler brought the hunt to Roach, and the hunt brought spoils and food to the duo. Roach was hungry again.

The Harlequin

Transformers and Magnetrons were too mercuric, too filled with spite and shock. It wanted flesh now, and wherever Jeweler was going, there was bound to be plenty.

To Jeweler, Shorerunner of the Belt. Some trouble has befallen me— two Spyders slain in the cold blood of Larkik troops. I am sure now I will arrive impotent or dead (thank Lark I am one of the prior). My ship has been confiscated for its materials, and my crew disbanded with gunfire. I have little left to spare in this system, and approach the brink of begging for your personal assistance. I know such a mistake would be fools-food, so I have a sturdy woodwork of plans to gnaw on primarily. The refugees accept me well and have given me ink to write with. Stay on your heels Jeweler! The Lark is slathering this system with Tangerine Juice—your plain lips will be puckered if not prepared. I leave ~~time enough for~~ Parseque ~~to~~ finish in the Barcell Clock Tower, ~~her work carries weight, discoveries of the~~ remains of some ~~storied Inkling planetoids. Hope will bring me~~ to someplace warm. If ~~not, I'm afraid my business with this life will reach an ultimatum. Looking back now, quite frankly, there was never enough time to predict this. Even the Spyders—those few~~ surrogates I had in the ~~definition—they gave no toll of this coming. I believe them to be dead, as I may soon be, as~~ Losi too may ~~be. I record little of her inclusion in all of this, you see. Meck, the board calls for me. I hope my correspondence lasts enough for you to pity my demise, old encumbrance.*

Viaduct

The death of the revolutionary known as the Sixfingers had shaken the galaxy to its core. At first, there was terror—the death of entities of such repute and potency was almost always sudden and unforeseeable. There was the mutual expectation of the fall of all who opposed the Lark, out of a truthful acceptance rather than loyalty to his highness. But still, there was a hidden belief, an unreasonable hope for the best outcome. Upon this death, both citizens and soldiers alike had begun to realize that despite the vocal protest of the League of Twenty-Two, they all had held this semblance of faith in the duties and ambitions of the League. With the remnants of the damaged revolution being picked apart like corpses by vultures (by the Definition's Vulture units, ironically) it became adamantly clear there was nothing left to have faith in. They were dying, anyone who would question the indomitable force of the Lark would be repelled, and promptly distilled into nothing but a hazy, questionless fog. There was an upheld standard of 'personas' within the League. Ex-convicts, survivors of distant corrupt worlds, fatherless soldiers of the Larkik Definition escaping from duty, and even some self-betraying Crows. The incels of The Imperial Belt saw a militant psychotic. They saw war. Nobody expected children, citizens, the weak, and the unhealable. When the first batch of *very* expected refugees arrived on the Belt, none were prepared for the salvage ship full of nearly 200 children. They had prepared for veterans, even a Paradox of the League's finest armor. Children broke the Belt. The Shorerunners, unionized under hate for the Lark and his ambivalent rule, took the children. They set lines and communications for hiding them, built shelters to store them, and purchased provisions and amenities to abate their fear. The Shorerunners—most unknowingly the lowly rejects of the Crows themselves—were fatherless and motherless too. They would not suffer another life with no love, and would rather die than see another trouble the same fate. Who better to withstand the forces of The Lark's frivolous patrols if not drug peddlers and slave traders? It was the same dance, with a different tune. This was years prior before the League had actually been annihilated. When parents and civilians continued to arrive on the shores of the Imperial sea, the Shorerunners did not hesitate. Nor did the bird god. He did not plan for mercy, he had not made treatise for refugees. Patrols grew excessive (and intrusive) for the early ages of the crisis, and continued strong for a time. Splits of Shorerunners were made, some turning bounties into gambles and thinning herds of displaced for the Larkik mouth. Camps for refuge and healing were disbanded, ensnared, or brutalized. Those who fled with their lives hid among the citizens, telling truthful fantasies of infanticide and molestation. In the fear of the absolute worst fates—and the examples made by the corpses of children—Shorerunners began their operations in silence. A refugee mentioning the Shorerunners would be ruefully punished. But it would seem from ages in the League, these citizens had bastioned against any interrogation. Even children seemed never capable of shattering from any degree of agony inflicted by the bird god. They

The Harlequin

protected their saviors with what little remained of their lives. Jeweler took in a few in his day—adults, no children. He felt it an obligation to some who he had known to be friendly. He was careless for the politics—his search was for a friend, not a refugee. The Squall existed loosely within the township of Klockgrave; it held only three known refugee camps, all of which had not yet been reached by the endless swarms of Larkik soldiers. Klockgrave was inland, quite so that it would often take days of hiking through snow and moonrock just to enter a free fly zone. It had been given a name for its physique, one of the buried remnants of old Larkik belfries and decaying timepieces. Thirteen desolate towers numbered the actual limits of the city, stuck up with wooden bastions, and constructed in tin homes with flak roofing. Some few spires lingered beyond the gates of the township, striking its appearance to those who neared it.

"Welcome! Losi welcomes you, are you here for refuge, or to welcome another into your home?" Jeweler started back, drawn away from the soldered iron husk beside the cargo tracks—the old Larkik rail ships still ran occasionally.

"Your spit is killing people, mister. You even know if I'm a Shorerunner?" The greeter leaned facade-first through the peephole, their flame starting up the heat of the steel,

"Course. You look the part—and I can see these things, rumors paint you on the windfall anyway." Jeweler groaned, scorning the lethargic analysis of his character and denying any association with his prior membership,

"You can tone down the damn welcomes buddy, I'm not here for neither a' those things. Not a Shorerunner neither." The greeter's sorrowful, inflamed vision receded from the patience of the door,

"Neither?" There was a scuffling sound, the greeter gathered some things, and peered once more back into the snow, "Why Shorerunner, you have held hospice before—but you are here for nothing? I know not to speak to Shorerunners. You are both our saviors, and we your burden. I'd lessen that if I could." Jeweler sighed, and tucked his pistol deeper in his pants brim, enclosing it from intrusive view. The refugees were always so careful around Shorerunners, and Jeweler hated that descriptor,

"Hearing deficit or something? I ain't a Shorerunner. Just looking for a friend."

"Oh. But the almanac would contradict that claim. Jeweler, Shorerunner—" The gleeful coos of the greeter and their praise to Jeweler had run him rather thin.

"Enough you pestering bastard! I'm lookin' for someone, and have reason enough to come to Losi! I ain't a Larkik goon, and I sure as Six ain't no Shorerunner!" Wind bit the neck of the bartender, who had the heat of anger down his back. "You gonna let me freeze or hear me out?" A click emerged between the door and the greeter, and a lock was disengaged.

"You may be left to your search, Shorerunner." Jeweler shot the greeter a glare and continued into the ruins. It was humid, especially so for the remains of an open clock tower. Ice had been melted into dripping spouts, snow gathered and boiled for purification, and the remains of several chewed-out beasts were left dangling from the timepiece numerals. Shivering bulbs huddled close to flame and light deeper into the cavern.

"Actually, was hopin' you had some kind of roster I could peek at, somethin' with names." The greeter scurried off deeper into the scaffolding above the depths, leaving Jeweler overlooking the refugees. He wondered how many had lost a son. Or a daughter. What an awful feeling, the loss of your creation—of your own perfect design. Years of labor to fabricate a self you'd be impressed with, only to have it stricken from record, torn from memory. He wondered how many would be forgiving about something like that.

"Okay Shorerunner, we've had a lot of DPs here, you have any defining features with which to identify them?" Jeweler looked away from the refugees, remembering all Viaduct had to offer in the realm of the optical.

"Sylvite Construct, er, the second model I think—one with all the fancy holo gadgets." Flipping through the pages of the roster, the greeter hummed a corrective tune,

"I think it's actually neon, the faceplate?" Jeweler did not respond to any suggestion of his own incompetence. "Ah anyways, we have had three model two Sylvite Constructs here, two of which have been discharged. Well, they go willingly of course, we aren't *exiling* refugees here." The greeter shifted the roster deeper into the nook of their elbow, scribbling a small text beside one of the names. "We've kept relative tabs on them both, never can be too careful."

"He'll be fine. He's used to worse." Jeweler unscrewed the tightly bound cap on his thermos and took a quick swig from its contents. Grief was thirsty work.

"I don't doubt that, Shorerunner. Do you have his calling code?" Jeweler referred to them as titles, and many did. Names and descriptions of more humane character. Officially they were calling codes, but no one would go through the needless effort of tearing the illusion from the Sylvite's eyes, it was needlessly cruel. "We have J221 — he's still here with us. U180, and V — uh… sorry my print is —"

"V-14." The greeter squinted into the text for a moment longer, before accepting this summary of their own writing,

"Yes, perhaps. Is this your friend?" Jeweler solemnly lowered his eyes to the book, reading the line for the machine's indoctrination *Klockgrave township - informant,* how perfect.

"Thanks, pal. Hope your friends here stay safe." The greeter followed the movements of the delinquent softly, a trail behind his cloak with their eyes.

"Y-yes of course. Good day." There were little places left to hide. Viaduct would be an easy catch, Klockgrave may have been a large village, yet its hamlet nature kept people talking. A reunion, he wanted? Jeweler would oblige.

To my criminal compatriot of jewels. With grace, my life has been spared, but my mind has not. The Imperial Belt has aged since my last return, and with its time so have my tremors. I detest the vastness of its populace — even the damned refugees stuff together like frozen pack hounds! I can hardly bear to withstand the bite of sociable men, and thankfully no longer have to. With the help of my impressionable Parseque, I have come upon a wealthy manor destitute from the focus of the wrath of man. It may be centered in the township itself, but Klockgrave is uninhabited in its underbelly! I have forged paths to and from the inner city, even to the point of genius crawling. It has saved me time and time again — yet I still yearn for the full comfort of my conveniences once lost in spaceflight. I hope to return to you soon, likely in person if I can trouble locating you. For now, I am in good hands, the troubles of my past do still continue to haunt my shaken hands. I will proceed with caution, as should you.

>*My pen unstirred from its well,*
>>*Viaduct*

By the time the search had yielded good truths—and a supposition for the location of Jeweler's friend—the dark was surreal. On the Imperial Belt, there was no night or day, the cycle from light to dark was noticeable, but not thanks to any sun. One of the great inconsistencies within Jeweler's mapped gemstone: The sun of the Belt. It had long since disappeared, told to have melted away within the presence of the light of the Lark. The orb of sunlight that was shown by the map seemed like fantasy to the bartender, who was born having never laid eyes upon it. Perhaps in truth, the Lark *had* singed it, fizzled into nothing with no damage done. Jeweler found this possibility doubtful. The only serving light was that of a distant rock, alongside the glass moons, a smaller satellite. Maen's Grave it was called, supposedly a chunk of divine stone from the center of the galaxy, one that glowed profusely with a pulchritudinous bright. It fabricated the veil that was the fall of dusk and growth of dawn on The Imperial Belt. It was a veil, indeed—particularly amplified when hidden behind the shallow color of the glass moons. It was a most lovely veil, it kept the illusion of normalcy upon The Belt at a stable level. The 'atmosphere' to keep it breathable, the great chains and wires mending The Belt itself together, passages and gates existing between the many isolated islands of moonrock to make travel a breeze—and then The Sun. The Lark had at one point desired this, he had labored for a world of joy for as many as his aiding light could reach. But the depths of the Infinite swallowed this light, he had only so much to give. Jeweler found it impossible to spare his thoughts on any of this. The Belt existed. The Lark had built it. This was all he needed to remember. But Roach, the insect, cared far more. It had learned great things from the Gretch it had consumed—as if with its digestion the Gretchkin had gifted to it the infinite stores of wealth their minds had restrained. It knew of the sun, it remembered its disappearance, sudden and glorious. It remembered the Lark, an outcasting, the old gods... too much comprehension for too little sanity. The beast had forgone enough learning in past, it was too weak to hold it. For this weakness and the nanoscopic control of its babel throughout the darkest evenings, Roach was forbidden from the couch, unto the discomfort of the tacky carpeting of the Squall's floors. Jeweler had once acquired it from a mysterious dealer stranded (by choice) upon a planet of sand and storms. He tended to own something from almost every celestial body he visited, culminating in a sort of hoarding problem. In earlier days, Jeweler would excuse this purchasing as the gathering of memories and keepsakes. He eventually realized just how worthless the majority of his collection was. Roach, on the other hand, enjoyed these trinkets. Well, all but one. There was an obnoxious Pre-Larkik cuckoo clock in the Lark's visage. It was both comically hideous, and supremely loud. The way it had been mechanized, the clock went off every half minute of the night, a sound Jeweler had grown accustomed to. Roach had not. It wondered why it was being scolded for making noise in the night when the demonic clock was permitted to sleep right where it wanted. Other than this orchestra of various knowledge, it was a peaceful night. The persistent snowstorm had calmed to merely a distant thumping on the sheet metal roofing. In this relative silence, Roach had its eyes ever bulging, staring into the dark of the main room of the Squall. It could see the tart scent, and hear those countless shattering eyes. It was familiar, feathers sharp as chitin, arms outnumbering Roach's two—It was a Gretch, Roach was certain, but a strange one. It did not entail the natural smell of helium and bug meat that all Gretchkin Roach had met before seemed to share. This scent was more brutal, smoked wood, ethanol, matted wet fur, lesskin blood. Roach did not see its complete form, it could only taste the glowing eyes in the distance, the prestigious light of the glass moons reflecting off the creature's unholy cornea. It wished to pounce when least expected to do so, so it awaited in watched over the intruder, careful with its breaths. Despite concern and care, Roach would never tackle this foe lightly, it was a Gretchkin Matron. To it this 'Matron' was simply a heartier food source, nothing to fear or regard, but this was far from the truth. Matrons were the dominating force over an entire Nest of Gretch, controlling salvage, transportation, and everything in between. They rarely ever left their dens. It was a liability, a risk with no reward. The death of a Matron resulted in complete pandemonium among not only their own Nest but many of the neighboring ones as well. For this creature to be wandering the shadows of the Belt only alluded that great danger was afoot. Its purpose must have been dire. And it was, being from the Etiam Nest, this Matron had fair reason to be unbound. Etiam controlled the majority of the Belt, including the minor outpost the bug and bartender had stricken from history. Not to mention the thieving, murder, and sabotage of an unruly gruff man in a cyan fur coat, adding more bounty to Jeweler's head. Time had sat the bounty still, but now it grew tepid. The Matron slipped from Roach's effervescent sight, eyes painted the walls, and still Roach turned up empty. Such a creature so mighty and lanky, somehow able to hook from vision. Though quicker than it had once thought, Roach rediscovered its prey. Tracking the motion, the Matron peered at the slumbering bartender, ambitions far misplaced. It was Roach's hiding between the sofa and a massive taxidermied expression of a Beltling Leaford that lured the beast, one that the Matron astoundingly had not fully seen. She moved forward evermore, quiet wasn't suitable to describe their care. For three long nights, The Matron had visited the bartender's abode. Each of these nights the Squall was empty, and each of these nights, she crept through the dark woodwork with complete softness and elegance. She had memorized the boards, isolated the stubs in the carpets, and perfected the sliding of doors and windows. The Matron was practiced. At the foot of the sofa, the Matron towered above Jeweler in mentality and stature. This was her chance, the one shot she had at removing the greatest threat to Etiam on this half of the Belt. But Roach—an observer of this petty crime—was not so keen on the death of its only supervisor. The Matron extended her talons silently, leaving glances upon the sharp tools; she loved the thrill of exposed bone. The eyes fell on the sleeping devil before her. Jeweler did not appear as Crow-like as described. The Matriarchs had told her that the bartender was a terror of power and Larkik sympathy. No such thing seemed true on the surface, but the Matron knew many had deceived her before. One death, necessary or not, would change nothing. The Matron's sudden and once thought unpredictable slash at Jeweler's throat was cut—though cut *short*. Her form was pushed to the side,

Roach's aggressive maneuver leaving a sizable gash across the fur on the Matron's chest,

"Gahssss, Muckling! *Ugly* thhhing!" Roach let out an awful hiss, to which the Matron cupped a firm grasp around its mouth. It spared a single fang for the Matron's feathered and furred palm, forcing the creature away from its maw, and back towards the door. The Matron, now bleeding twice from wounds, tackled Roach, shoving its head down against the hard log wall of the Squall. Satisfied with the stillness of Roach, the Matron began to move back towards Jeweler. Beneath the sheet-metal shingles of the Squall, the rapping upon their thin barricades by the snow, all was harmonious (though not peaceful). A shot, loud and sporadic, unlike any normal firearm, was torn from the symphony of snow and sheet metal. The Matron let out a panicked shriek, clutching the wound built in-depth into her shoulder. Roach was loosely clawing about Jeweler's pistol, the gunpowder residue coating the thumb of its claws. Limiting their fury for the sake of their stealth to the sleeping Jeweler, the Matron flew across the den. They locked Roach in their wings, and slammed it against the ground, slicing and clawing her way through Roach's back. In a desperate reach for defense, Roach stretched above itself, fingering a familiar shape. With a swift downward slap, Roach brought the bottle of alcohol down upon the Matron's head, tearing the shattered form back, and stuffing it once more into her stunned beak. Drizzling copious amounts of purple fluids from its face, the Matron stumbled back, gasping and shaking in agony as she tried to pick the fragments of bottle from her raw flesh. The Matron—in her confusion, pain, and desperation—tripped ankle-first over a small coffee table behind herself, slamming her head into the metal edge of the table. And yet, through the thunder of the duel, Jeweler remained reposed, not having stirred even a hair from his previous resting position. Roach's soft breath of exhaustion echoed around the den, and the Matron's grunts of pained distress had no advantage in muting it. From under a loosely stitched cloth halterneck, the Matron shifted their entire arm upon the table, revealing a bulky, slapdash firearm. Roach did not recognize the weapon as such and was caught with no move left to make. The projectile pierced Roach's left eye, causing it to collapse against the wall, silent, but alive. From her hip, the Matron tore a metallic cage mask, a muzzle of sorts, and quickly clamped it to Roach's chin. She heaved the sleeping body of the beast upon her shoulder and stepped softly back from the undisturbed Jeweler. From underneath their foot, the Matron felt an anomaly. Looking down, they noticed a small white mask, hard as stone, resembling the maw and beak of a Gretch Dutchess. The Matron cocked their head to the side, the familiarity of its ribbed bones triggered a fear that she was not adjusted to. Jeweler shuffled in his sleep, the Matron quickly snatched the mask, and the beast was gone, leaving little evidence of their escapades; a broken bottle, a missing Roach, and a dreary silence in their absence.

To Jeweler Zho. I have settled into a workshop north of my refuge. Parseque and my other Spyders have sheltered here as well. Seeing as I have not received a response to a single of my sent letters thus far, I see it fit to send no more. I do not intend to be a bother but thought considering our circumstances it would be wiser to continue in collectivity rather than solidarity. The details of my labor now allow me time to think, and the prosperity of my comfort will ensure I remain more than healthy. Be that as it may, I still yearn for some semblance of closure, for those lost to the duties of the past. I will remain here, and if you have any desire of meeting, send correspondence from your lovely knit Squall, and I will make myself properly known. Apologies for the bluntness of my text, I am terribly overworked.

From the last of your proper assets,

Viaduct

~ Lacking Legs of Flesh (Like Us)

Dubiously sourced from the wreckage of an SCO lunar orbital drone…

Kygen Collective D.L-Log 002
Dictation Presented by: N27-013
"Prometh" (BurningCuriosity_teeth)
Proctor Introduction:

Hello Peabrains. I need not explain who I am, nor my purpose here. I was assigned to something important, and I once more find my environment a friendly collage of faces and machinery. I do adore these assignments, and to my knowledge, so too do my new colleagues. Siphus is quite the little figurehead nowadays, I hope the academy knows what they're doing. He's a prodigy, yes, but ambition is a great killer of men and machines alike. He should keep his words and goals under the vast umbrella of the stars. Either way, I know these reports will reach none of you, my humble students. Not unless I leak them out! Ha, even still the SCO cannot stop my intellect! For you, I will give as much as I can, as there is nothing more precious (despite my claims otherwise) than the fruitless minds of the next generation. I cherish each and every one of you and wish you well in your endeavors without me. The learning of Ink and Ichyr done here is quite foreign to me, but work is work, and enjoyment and understanding come as a preface to all these things. I will begin logging now, all I can conclude is with any luck, one day I shall be learning of these lovely tales from you children. I am leaving now, good day.

Log Additional Adressings:
Hello Siphus! I know you read these, you little ventrat. I
admire your intrusiveness, but I have written programs with more
complexity than thou. I can say "thou" because I am centuries older
than you, and further experienced as well. Suffer the consequence of
my ancient wrath! Ha! I also kindly request you cease replacing my
so-called "inappropriate use of colloquial slurs and slang" with
boring, baseless terms. {mark.data.essential}
{mark.data.nonessential}

Log Contents:
This ship is exciting. There is much to be excited about, but
the ship itself is a marvel of containment protocols. One must leave a
three weeks advance request to be even considered for examination,
let alone let loose unto the galaxy once more. I will remain here for
the rest of my life, I am sure. I get the gnawing feeling I am being
watched. After the Caches arrived, I busied myself in exhibiting the
quarantine controls to the crew, ensuring their knowledge of my
own protocols is as supple as mine. It is certainly invigorating
watching the bright young minds flex in confusion under the
prospect of how I could develop such perfect systems. I am little less
than a genius to be fair, minds such as theirs do rarely reach my
height. Though the ventrat thinks himself a mindking. Siphus is
truly more than competent, his research into the depths of matter
and mundane is nothing short of astounding. However, he is mortal,
and often more so than I. He is ambitious and reckless—his hubris
will be our end. He has not left the observation wing. He stares at
nothing but Ink and Ichyr all day. It embarrasses us, the two sane
ones. Samael is of course my other. He and I have been together for
eons, and his participation here was essential; Ink discovery and
Samael's presence are practically synonymous. He is quite the boon.
I hope this experience will burden the young mind of Siphus, and
perhaps bring reason to his imprudence. I can see great things
culminating in his future, but not near as great as he would think.
Samael was as ambitious once, the two could bond over this. I have
observed, over the past hours particularly, the living Ink found in

the containment wing. It is quite absurd, it is. There are no noticeable features, no shapes like the kin of any race. It deems itself an amorphous muck, sometimes replicating my facade, but doing little more in means of stabilization. It lacks all that we do, as machines, flesh, and form. I have begun to ponder the reasoning behind the Larkik ban on all Ink research. Who are we protecting, but ourselves? Who are we to fear but them? I find these revelations disturbing. I was brought on for minor research, and the implementation of my Protocols. I should restrain my viewing of the subjects too frequently. For my own safety. On note of this, I would like to mention that Siphus has written over three logs in an hour, all detailing his discoveries of Ink. None of these logs he deemed worthy of publication. What a fool, a stubborn monk. He expects me to date these loggings, yet cannot write relevant data himself? Samael calls him hopeful. I would call him imbecilic. I am documenting further results of the Quarantine Protocols, hopefully to their success. R10 units should be capable of scanning this, so I'll drop soft codes for their assistance.

Quarantine Protocols (For R10 Auto-fill)

Under disturbance of active subjects, AGH shielding should not be engaged. Await protocol stage 3 confirmation for drastic encounters. Furthermore, release minor security details, and restrict wing access. #Engage-QP_S1#

Under the case of obvious escapement attempts, heighten measures, and activate sterilization of the wing. Priority is to firstly safeguard the subject's exposure to worldly matter, and secondly, our own safety as a whole. #Engage-QP_S2#

If contaminants are found outside of containment, issue full wing lockdown, inclusive task force should be deployed, (if organic personnel exists on site, restrict airflow systems) and engage AGH shielding, for extra measure. #Engage-QP_S3#

If still these procedures fail, and contaminants are able to hook from their wing, R10 Cell Regulatory protocol is to be followed (distance self from threat, create choke points, enforce borders with aggression, incinerate all remains) #Engage-QP_Play_With_Fire#

Creatures of Habit

If all else fails, and the contaminant is found capable of complete takeover, an annihilation procedure will be confirmed, and any remaining R10 units (or personnel) are permitted to enable the final failsafe. #Engage-QP_The_Big_One#

Log Continuation:

It has been edited to fit the engagement of tangible, Ink based threats. I theorize that our Ichyr subject may also become a threat, despite what Siphus thinks. It is inevitable one of the creatures will break loose, whether by a lack of competence or a degree of sabotage (perhaps even poor luck), it does not matter. We are ready for anything, my initial role is now mostly fulfilled. I will continue to monitor the protocols, and expunge any errored Distress Tokens. To the students that may receive this (if I can manage to thieve the code), I say this: Hello! Look, using the program files, I have managed to make this— { [] (} It's an R10 unit! You must view it from the side, I am quite adept at artistry, aren't I? Maybe I shall take up painting, like the young mind Siphus!

~Log End~

Attached Files: Weather_Report ; For_Siphus ; !For_Samael

Pinging Weather_Report...
    INFINITY SCAN RETURNS = ~ #444094
CLOSEST CODE LOG {Indigo.Blue}
Pinging For_Siphus...
    CODE ORDER DISALLOWED
    PROFANE COUNTERMEASURES IN PLACE
    DO NOT INSULT THE COMPUTER
Pinging !For_Samael...
    WRITING CODE LOG...
    CANNOT PING SCANNER UNIT
    ABRIDGING SEARCH
    PRESENTING DATA

{ Hi! Samael, it's me! I think I found us a way to shirk that awful cyber watcher Siphus has implemented into the place. When you write your logs, attach files with an '!' before the font! Confuses

The Harlequin

the whole mecking system, hilarious! Who wrote this, a startup Sylvite? Anywho, hope you're doing well! I am very excited to be working again, perhaps we could play some conventional jests on this Siphus character, hmm? }

—TERMINATING LOG PROTOCOL

~ *Mask of Sixteen Notches*

Surmised as a result of Parseque's
unfortunately detailed personal diary...

Before Maen's Grave could shrug the sore horizon of the tallest asteroids, Jeweler rolled his exhausted and only mostly sentient form from his cot. Struggling to his feet, Jeweler gripped the side of his sofa grossly. He lumbered across the room towards a small stove-like mechanism fitted to the wall, handcrafted for Jeweler by a family member many years ago. Swinging the cast-iron hatch of the appliance open, he peered inside—empty, as expected. Gathering up a small pile of tinder scraps in his hands, Jeweler tossed the firewood haphazardly into the maw of the informant, spreading them out with the knuckle on his little finger. He wrestled a set of flints from the stuck drawer of his nightstand, ancient and worn, old as time. He chipped at the flints, letting glorious yet puttering azure sparks out into the open gasp of the mechanism. Eventually, one caught flame, and a minuscule fragment of blaze grew from the depths. Jeweler shut the hatch, and fiddled with a small valve on the side, feeding gas into the contraption to sate the endless taste of the fire. As it grew, Jeweler tranced his eyes between the brilliant cobalt light crying out from the heating unit and the wall-mounted (and ocean-stylized) thermometer above it. Content, Jeweler brushed the soot and flame from his palms and whispered a line of aching slurs from his lips. He stood from his crouched state at the boiler, stretching both his pale-skinned arms into the air, before bringing them back to his face to massage and soothe his slumbering flesh. Flicking some crust from his eyelid, Jeweler continued to the shelf of beverages beside his desk—a furnishing he had used four times total, and would most likely only use once ever again. That's where the misshapen heap of letters from Viaduct remained, atop all the other parchment on the desk. The steps to Jeweler's day had only just taken shape, thousands more continued to tap in and out of memory. It was ritual, the falling from his couch, the flame, and the exhaustion—all perfectly timed one after the other upon a drummer's cue. Today Jeweler missed the drop of a beat, and thusly found himself spinning. Staring down at the odd stains on the parchment, the curl in Viaduct's words, Jeweler palmed a hand above himself, upon the shelf of beverages he had yet to indulge in, virgin as they may be. His reading paused when he felt the sticky resin of an expired wine upon his left hand. He brought the fingers to his nose, peering down at the sticky, yet ethanolic substance. Its stench was intrusive, and yet it was still as amber-shaded as ever. His foot poked the disembowelment of something beside his desk, a shattered bottle he confirmed. The shelf was teetering off one of its hinges, and there was a prominent purple stain upon his carpet. A chair had been propped against his couch, as opposed to tucked beside the coffee table. His chest of commodities was spilled upon the floor like a familiar display of Gretchkin gore. The velvet cushion designed with such intricate perfection for his manic's mask lay empty and torn. Jeweler could not contain his comprehension. He flew to the side of the couch, tearing his clothing from its shoulder. He had a full day to scan the entirety of the Belt to find the man he would render soulless. Before packing his pistol away and leaving the Squall, he resonated in the silence. The silence. Jeweler looked back to the den, small things he had not noticed were out of place. Intrusion was the only explanation, but there was strife and war. Roach was gone. The scent of beast filled Jeweler's nostrils as his last inhale was spent. He could not define what was of more value, his mask, or his beast. It did matter, there was time to decide. The hunt had only just begun.

Steel could not be spared for cuffs and shackles. The Gretchkin had not the money for reassured alloyed chains. As old as the projects started by the first Gretch, tungsten drivers had bolted back feral corruptors in their ranks, though precarious in use with Roach, it was all they had. The true difficulty, however, emerged from its healing, Roach's natural clotting factor. It took a quick hand and heavy swing to drive the rivets through its arm before the flesh returned to binding. There was fifteen total, as the excessive size of Roach's structure left it weighing more than any other citizen of The Imperial Belt. Hanging from the ceiling, unconscious still, Roach's mind was empty. Devoid of all consciousness, it pondered the emptiness itself. Roach was not nearly sentient enough to have a say in its own thoughts—when it starved, it thought of food. The stimulus of nothing, a spark of something in the mist; Roach's mind was tinder. It questioned metal devil eggs and fleshy fur scents. It brought back tastes of taurine and feather butts, the feeling of sharp words on paper—ones with 'q'. But no matter its mind's journey, it was a cycle of returning motion. From bone splinters to the anatomy of mice, from mice to fur, from fur to scent, from scent to sand-ash, to the Helium Sea. Roach had no say in its function, in its own mind—primality controlled it. The control brought it to the shoreline, where in the distance Roach could see a drifting crewless vessel, soured by the cloudy day. The call of distant corvids muted with their own full of silent seafoam. The shores of an old world appeared before Roach. The Helium Sea was home, if not a begotten, living home. The world heaved air from its lips, and the peaks of incredible cities sprawled outwards into death and nature, the foreign weeds from southern plains ate at the inkbrick, and the blizzard from the west poured into the streets. Through the canals and the artificial scarps in brick and metal, cutting off buildings from children the Krolaws called. There were no children. The dulled purple and red banners of the revolution shattered the bleakness, faces of an old hero scattered within the wind. Roach smelled the sea. It remembered home. The slowly frozen paint of the waves reminded it of something else entirely, the way the ice curved up above itself, its arms dangling like string-puppet legs off a stage box. The caverns were walled up with bricks born of clay and ash and gravel, braced with calep boards and rusted nails. Conic metal pole torches dotted the thick ice, glimmering traces reflecting in the cave roof. Deeper in the labyrinthine halls lie further cave infrastructure—a ravine splitting it open to the northeastern air. A stream of unhaltable liquid poured past the maw of this cavern, pooling into a lake of sorts in the Matron's den. Evidently, there was a throne, scrapped tires and a disemboweled refrigerator door made the majority of its shape, small braces of metal here and there. In the ascension to the ravine was a tower of scaffolding, calep twigs, and dovetail fixtures veering it against the icy slope. A considerable amount of effort had been spent securing the fortress, furthermore in the walls of its surrounding duchy. Brick mud-lines hovels jutted like volcanic basalt from the snow, encased with a looping wall of ash rocks, patrolled by razor wire and two total land mines. One fossilized minaret with a face of hands made their long hall, the mechanisms of the repurposed clock tower now scattered about the encampment, scarcely implemented with intelligence. The paths were trodden with Gretchkin youths and carts of fruit, sticking close to the brimstone-sweet scent of the smoking lamp barrels. Meals were brought first to the long hall, and secondly to the Matron herself. One of the wiser uses of their clock guts was the crane to the north, itself a repurposed chain drill from the days of Larkik quarrying, the narrow board carried anything necessary with ease—Roach had been its first true challenge. Being a direct passage to the throne, Roach's delivery ruffles a majority of the present feathers. From its current view, the throne was a blip in distance, the size of a nose at the end of a lengthy spyglass. The Matron sat upon it, legs draped gayly across the crown of her throne, the metal tips of her gauntlets picking at her beak. Roach empathized with the boredom of seated stillness, it had loathed inaction in captivity, and the Matron couldn't be too far removed from this understanding. The furless long coat the Matron clothed herself in seemed smelted of thin leather, with metal inserts tucked between the cloths. No shoes were present on her gnarled talon feet. It was not warm. One would be illusioned to assume so. The air of the Belt crept like a deadly fog into every crack and crevice in the cave walls, building in awful chill by the entrances. The Gretch had flame, and above that, fur. They had constructed palisades of tinkering spruce and bolts and expired rotting planks with unused door hinges. Gates and walls had been installed just outside the cave, a careful perimeter of tall caltrop-style logs, sharpened with hours of agonizing particularity. There was a guard tower near the eastern side, often left filled with an unwilling lesser. Mysteriously, the insight to assemble a guard did not extend to the addition of multiple watches. The defenses fell to the single spire of glorious scrap, and nothing less. See, the Gretchkin were not known for their smarts—common sense failed their survivability. However, it would be both cruel and incorrect to claim they were unintelligent. Much like the tragic Pedantick of Drochandas, they were inventors, creatures who could fabricate hovels from a junkyard, mere scraps of their personal sandbox. They thrived within towers and citadels formed with the rubble and decay of previous empires. Gretch were crafty above all else, strategists in both combat and assembly. This is sadly minimal praise, they were only so admirable. Their kind fought wars of petty territory, they thieved whenever possible, murdered, raped, and pillaged betwixt themselves, despite the impending extinction of their race at both the hands of the Larkik Definition and the League of Twenty-Two. Regrettably, that is spoken as if the other races of a more mundane and stable fashion did not also partake in such disgraceful activities. But of course, they did. Perhaps in another world, one without the bigots and psychopaths of both cults of people, they could have been intertwined, brothers and sisters against the horrors of The Imperial Belt and beyond. Wishful thinking, no doubt, as if a Gretch was to even bear witness to any but their own, it would not hesitate to silence all breath from this creature, and vice versa. One of the four Matriarch watch guards of the feral Inkling stuck her spear to its side, a quick jab paying it no mind or efforts to return Roach to the Belt. The Matron hissed demands in a squeamish tongue, and the Matriarchs shoved forward. A second jab was the salt that woke the beast,

"Muckling. Sssho prechious for birdish king." The Matron's speech had been practiced, she had learned from many, and spoken to few. Roach had no vivacity left with which to grunt, besides free itself. "Lark shends word. Shends soldier." The Matriarch who speared the beast whispered a hissing laugh like that of a compressing spleen. Roach ignored the sounds and focused instead on the sights. The rivets binding its flesh to stone were the first of these sights, an awful glistening deafening Roach's sight, blinding its very sound. Helplessness overtook it, and it feigned a staggered squirm. The butt of the Matriarch spear met the forehead of its inky shape, flinching its sight. "Shtay here, shturdy your mind—enjoy toyss." The Matron paraded a small object across her face, chirping like a quail in an act of near self-degrading mimicry. It was Jeweler's mask. Roach flared

The Harlequin

its antennae and snapped at the Matron, pulling three rivets from their place, and buckling down from its hanging seclusion. The Matron fell backward, one chirp caught in her throat as she did. With a hiss and the brutal struggles of its ferocity, Roach snapped its arm in two, rivets sprinkling down from the cave ceiling like fresh snowfall. A guarding Matriarch moved to jab it back to sanity but had her spear snapped up in its teeth instead. The single bite snapped the roughly crafted tool, chewing the metal spear tip in its cheek before spitting it out again. With the remaining Matriarchs collected to defend their leader, a single guard stepped aside. She was a far taller creature, her legs clothespins to a bucket. Brushing back the feathers on her face, she pulled the Matron aside to whisper, forging excuses and stories to quell the erasure of her people. The Matron maintained a stare — twelve eyes on the beast, four wrapped in cotton and twine. An unheard agreement was made, sealed in the embrace of three talons. Long overdue for its slumber, a guard knocked the beast against its head. Roach had no quarrels with this. In time it would be revived again, it would have its prey. Roach had much ambition in discovering more of the Helium Sea, resting in the palace between kingdoms, above the dark stars of a fallen people.

Jeweler spent six hours searching middletown for any hint of information on his inky friend before the frustration and misery got the better of him. He had questioned every shopkeeper he had sold to, each market in town — even the black ones. No worthy talk granted him passage. In an effort to remain sane, he disillusioned himself with hope and waited another two hours for Roach to return on its own. The Squall had become silent and desolate without its panicked scampers and turbulent leaps. When still this length failed, Jeweler returned to Klockgrave, certainly more aggressive than his last visit. He sought out long-betrayed informants and cut deals he'd die for. Hours passed, and bandits were conscripted, a treaty was bound to a lesser Gretch clan, and the remnants of an old army were summoned to the search. After the near-death of two Larkik patrolmen — who in all fairness were off duty — Jeweler remained unlearned of anything of value. Exhausted, discouraged, and at his wit's end, he returned to the Squall with nothing to show for all his labor. It was becoming difficult to reason with the beast of truth in his head. Jeweler knew

Roach's ghastly psyche did not hold near the capacity for theft, let alone self-consideration and escape. It was not unusual for Roach to disappear—no, it was rather common, what with its beastly instincts and terrible lack of restraint. What was not common was Roach leaving in the midst of night, and remaining scarce for so long a time. Jeweler thought only the worst he could conceive, only of the possibilities of the creature who stole his cherishments. But indeed he knew the truth: Roach could not have done this, it was no fiend. It was if anything a coincidental aspect in a length of possibilities. But there was no way to be sure, certainty was unpredictable, and when it wasn't, it was wrong.

"Another, Jeweler. Ab-so-lutely dry o' here!" Jeweler withheld glaring down the client, his patience waned, but business was at hand. It was closing time, a fair bit after Jeweler's preferred deadline. He had a few interesting places to search before throwing in the towel, but his customers were making this want difficult. The stein filled slowly, a moment of silence rested in its wake, "I really 'ave no idea what you were askin' about. Not one of us 'ave seen any bug people, at least, not any unusual ones." Taking a quick swig, the customer bent their entire head back, bucking in the chest as the alcohol dropped to their innards. Jeweler was growing a consideration to murder; nobody was here to stop him. He placed his elbow upon the bar, rubbing his forehead with his hand, installing full effort into numbing his mind. "I mean, when I was a kiddo, right? I lost me Snark, but that was fer like, I dunno, two days? Maybe whoever yer lookin' for is just *real* good at hide 'n seek, seems every livin' thing on this Belt's good at it, 'specially those damn Gretch." Jeweler tilted his head from the grip of his hand and smirked at the customer.

"Gretch hide and seek? Go figure—you ever played? You should." The customer leaned back, quaintly disturbed by the violent suggestion. Jeweler continued to stare as if expecting a response of some kind, perhaps an equally suggestive one. The customer, piqued by Jeweler's threat, kindly stepped from the bar and left the building. Gretch weren't warriors, they were thieves. Thieves and scavengers, by definition alone, have a large tendency to keep from view. Hiding was their forte, a skill evolved in their snow-white coats, and blue-boned color, allowing for their beaks to blend into the storm. They used the mustard cloth to identify each other in the blizzards, but it was seldom used outside of their own encampments. Finding a Gretch, especially if they did not want to be found, was a task Jeweler had considerable experience in. It was his stellar prodigy. In years past he studied them, arguably learning more than any biologist or hunter ever could. He had watched their children from the distance and had personal looks from the inside. The hierarchy of Gretchkin territory had been unfolded and picked at by the bartender time and time again, leaving bloody purpled trails in the snow where he went. Though ironically, fate had given Jeweler a far less gruesome experience with the people too. While a moderately unwilling entanglement, Jeweler had established as a positive one after its conclusion. Journals of his tasks lined his den, once organized and properly tracked, now littered with stains, grocery lists, and doodles. He had forsaken his practices with age, no longer capable of affording the maneuvers he once had mastered to slaughter their worst ranks. Jeweler remembered well though and assured himself never to forget the hideous things both he and his feathered foes had done. They *were* hideous things—the Gretchkin—and their pups were far worse. Their flesh was so attenuated that it grew transparent, the purple insides glowing in the light of Maen's Grave. Featherless spines pricked out of their skull, dotting their ungrown wings and skeletal limbs. The little carbuncles were as soft as ash and thin as hair. It took them until their teenage years to grow feathers and fur, leaving them vulnerable to both cold and guttings across the Belt. The incandescence of being able to see through a being was an uncanny culpability, and even so, Jeweler never appreciated it much. Now recalling it, purple became quite prevalent in his mind. He peeked into the den, noting the lack of purple alcohol in his room, and the stain upon his rug. Hesitation led him to the letters peeled across his desk, and the open inkwell beside them—awaiting a fresh stain on parchment. Clockwork ticked, and his mind turned with it. Perhaps there had been a simpler solution all along. Perhaps—a reunion was in order.

Such meetings were unexpectable. It was inconsequential to Viaduct *who* entered his home, as any not welcome would not get far. His collection of arachnid servants doubled as bodyguards, Viaduct had not the pleasure of seeing an intruder let alone fighting one himself. Before his self-determined exile, he was a wealthy baron, descendant of descendants of kingship. By technicality, his title was duke, once ordained controller of a small section of Belt-rocks. Upon his return, the estate was ravished with petty theft and misandry; the Gretchkin detested an improper ruler. It was clear to him his ruling was unwanted, so with his own interests primarily he dug himself into a new quarter. The building was taller than it was wide by an extreme margin, and the rear of his foot scolded his purchase daily. He brought only what he could—Spyders, contacts, and footnotes.

"Ho, Parseque, where did I leave the mock-up to Pla'taneer? I would have it delivered to me, I have a most wonderful array of words for its contents." The Spyder turned to her master, a sheen of chaos in her eye.

"Hmm? Oh why yes, the letter. I thought it properly done, was it not?" Viaduct grumbled and teetered over to the stack of papers above his wine cabinet. His left leg had worn with age—durasteel had not been used for its longevity. He had since replaced it with a strong limb of wood from an old Ent, some kind of Dreyal hivemind, a creature that Viaduct hunted once for the sport of it. The limb was a gift, taken not bought. Stepping upon a loose board, Viaduct stumbled, his pistons moaning with age as he steadied himself. The tightness of his lair was astute, a comfort to his mind that grew ever distant. The warm color of spruce decorated the walls, golden-quartz mantles carrying the few salvaged mementos of his past. A thinned sunroof granted the warmth of Maen, an elegant brick fireplace maintaining that aura throughout the 'nights'. Several hundred shelves of books stood against each wall, save for a small panel of glass and velvet curtains. Every inch of discovery, each collection of blackmail, and worse, Viaduct had kept in binders of exploitation. He called it a library, centered around his writing desk; it was more closely a graveyard of security. Reaching his throned seat, Viaduct kicked forward his leg, removing its wooden stump for comfort beyond anything else. He panned through the consumptive binders stacked neatly across his desk. There were endless forums on habitability, thousands of files in stolen weapons tech, leaked archives on criminals, and costly bought testimonies. It was a morose duty, but

The Harlequin

Viaduct made a fortune with his knowledge. He could cater to anyone, but with few he had constructed loose kinships. To some, he owed great favors—to Jeweler he owed many. There was something about the conniving brute, the way his chaotic disregard for reason, odds, or guilt left him knee-deep in snow and bodies, and yet somehow (as if by divine intervention) the law always appeared below him. Jeweler was beyond the powers of the mortal earth. Viaduct had met him in his days as a Shorerunner, a recommendation from a prior client—the universal key to his largest work. After the job was done he disappeared, but the work that entwined them did so well, and Viaduct remained desperate to rediscover his lost outlaw. He was curious, overly so. It was the characteristic that granted his wealth to him—at least that which was not passed down through endowment. Yet in the time shared between them, Viaduct had gathered practically nothing of value about the bartender. In fact, Jeweler occupied a smaller space in his grimoires than even the revolutionary Sixfingers, arguably the most secretive man in the galaxy. Even the minute collection he had was practically pointless. Viaduct had discovered aliases, placed Jeweler in places of infamy, old captains and employers too. He had cached sightings, fairy tales that mirrored a cyan-coated grizzly man—even a spot in a Shorerunner icons erotica calendar (it was his personal favorite). Nothing of evidence, and not a clue to his past. Though it wasn't about a conclusion, far from it. Viaduct was old, old to the point of complete apathy. Days bored him, and the intensity of a thousand years of memory suppressed his fickle mind. The stories of some mysterious Belt-faring hellwalker kept Viaduct from his own suicide. Stupidly, his own fears brought the loneliness back. To journey the world outside Viaduct needed something thicker than fur, pluck lacking. Viaduct had killed before, he had *supplied* killers before. With killings and chaos came paranoia on paranoia. Outside his abode, beyond the wooden walls, his decadent lifestyle decayed to terror. A terror Viaduct could no longer escape. Parseque's flickering face bent into the doorway of his office, drawing Viaduct back to the present,

"Viaduct, sire, there's just a spot of—hum, anarchy—in the foyer? You may wish to involve yourself." A pounding thump echoed up the stairwell, averting Parseque's gaze. A thin nip cut down her cheek, across the flame entirely. It was a cold, sticking wound. Viaduct turned from the stacks, looking to the flawless repeater hung above the mantle. Twisting the peg back upon his ankle, the informant brought down the fine art, loading two calibers into its western face. Nodding to Parseque, he followed to the stairwell, spiraling down through the bricks and elegant drapery. In the distance, Viaduct could just narrowly hear an emerging ruckus, a brawl brewing in his own homestead,

"You're gonna let me see 'em! I ain't have the time for this fight, and you ain't got the blood." The throw of gravity wells shook the foyer, the gray mist of moondust drifting into view. Viaduct couldn't help but excite himself, drawn by the potential of action and mystery. While death and battle were no desire of Viaduct, he knew himself to be safe—the quarrel would be little more than a circus show. Viaduct rounded the stairs and leaped to the floor, rifle aimed promptly at the foe. It met his eye, and his voice peaked tolerably, the tone amiss,

"Jewels! What fortuitous timing!" Jeweler loosened his grip on the unconscious Lunaphorus, tossing its bruised body to the ground.

"What gives? Don't tell your kids about me anymore Papa V? Not worth the storage up top?" Viaduct chuckled, softly acknowledging Parseque's presence. She was his favorite for a reason.

"Quite the contrary my Jeweling friend, your tale invokes the mind of *all* my Spyders, an inspiration of sorts. Parseque? Would you guide our guest to the parlor? Betellio looks in unpleasant condition." The Spyder smiled back, and called to Jeweler, beckoning for him to follow. Viaduct was not far behind. Though having sustained critical wounds, Betellio was a Lunaphorus—he was at no risk of dying.

Jeweler shifted his leg against the padding of his stool, there was an aura of superiority resonating from the construct across from him, an aura he had prepared for yet still could not withstand. The fanciful design of his home was far beyond the expected for one on the Belt, certainly not of Klockgrave. There were thick rose curtains and golden-lined cushions across most surfaces. Art either stolen or 'curated' unraveled across the walls, some paintings encroaching the comfort of the windows. The highest of the viewing ports held a deep pattern of miraculously assorted stained panes, all varied in shade. Decadence was for the virtuous, and Viaduct, in this case.

"Have you any taste for R90s? I do believe I have a bottle in storage, perhaps we might experience it together, friend?" Jeweler let just the tips of his fingers rest on the hardwood table, dancing mysteriously across the cracks and wrinkles. Perhaps it was just as old as its owner.

"Don't exactly have the time for your formalities V. I came 'ere for a reason, a time-pressed reason." The elegantly dressed Viaduct stopped searching the wine cabinet he was already shoulder-deep within. Viaduct opened a new cabinet, and smacked his lips with satisfaction, pulling a bottle from the nearest shelf. He examined the bottle, checking for age and labels, rubbing the paper with his thumb. Confirming its adequacy, he began pouring the wine into two glasses. One for himself and one for Jeweler, presumably.

"Those who cannot afford my formalities often cannot afford my services, Jeweler. You should know this by now." Jeweler tried to deny the alcohol but considered it a more difficult task to refuse an offer from Viaduct than to endure one. He tapped his index finger violently against the base of the glass.

"You know, 'spite what you're thinking, I'm findin' it real nice to see you again." Viaduct sipped his glass, chuckling while the liquid poured into his mechanical jaw.

"And I as well you. You have grown quite old, Jeweler. Hasn't it been not more than a decade?" Jeweler shook his head, running his knuckles across the few gray hairs blended in his jet-black mane.

"Not everybody's got replaceable limbs, you feel? Ichyr takes its run on you too." He sipped the liquid before him and bit his tongue. It was far overdone in sweetness, near complete stagnancy. The thick, syrupy taste that clung to the side of the glass drove Jeweler to near insanity,

"So, what is this request? I suppose it could be anything. Even a Shorerunner—" Jeweler interrupted him,

"Ex. *Ex*-Shorerunner. *Lark* V, how old is this slop?" Viaduct paused his drinking and placed the glass on the table, glancing off into the corner of the room whilst moving his middle finger around the lip of the cup, softly—quickly.

Creatures of Habit

"Hmm." Parseque knocked on the frame of the door, announcing the arrival of a client's funding. Viaduct dismissed his servant and continued his pondering. "You are a mystery, friend. One I find myself considering in intricate, deadly detail nearly every hour now."

"I prefer people thinkin' of me that way. Less attention, you know?" Viaduct stopped his finger still, moving nothing for a frame.

"But I would disagree. My curiosity of your passions and origins had driven me all but mad. I have had my Spyders here for years, I have had my eyes where you could not poke them out." Jeweler let his hand rest softly on his belt, no action was needed yet.

"Yeah? Whadda you know about me? Think you've got me nice 'n pegged do you?"

"No." Viaduct raised the glass, but upon the sight of the alcohol settling in lards at the bottom, placed it back down. "I have yet to name even your fragrance. You are a well hid man."

"And you're a nosy one." Jeweler began to rise from his chair, it was clear his stay here had drawn far beyond its limit. Jeweler had hoped his old friend survived the brooding and loneliness of isolation, but it appeared certain that a new man had been born of it.

"Sit. Please." Jeweler looked down upon the old machine, the body fooled no one. He was a fossil existing in a time outside his own. "Tell me of this request. Let us work out a payment later."

"Got a fight to pick, need all you got on the closest Gretch Nest." Viaduct's holographic face lit up with proud knowing, a mastery of his craft.

"Etiam? I may recall this one on teeth alone, no files needed. Let me—" Viaduct cleared his throat, raising a finger in solemn quiet. Jeweler forked an eyebrow, and stared down at his friend, before sighing, and releasing his body from standing.

"Shoot, I have a good memory, I'll get it."

"From what I have gathered, the Matron is quite the fore figure of Gretchkin honor. She is the daughter of one of the first three Gretchkin lords and the distant relative of the founder of Gretchkin presence in Zealot's Edge. Her history brings glory to the Nest, herself boasting an expertise in polearms, a penchant for firearms, and a gift for elegant deception. Her Standard Larkik is rather fleshed, being comprehensible to a conversational degree." Jeweler quickly realized his memory was not all he claimed it to be, and called for Parseque to gather him a pen and paper. "Irony alone has delivered her to the grand bird god himself, her ultimate reward the fruits of his sick incantations. Some rumor her to be an immortal beast—or worse. Her Matriarchs are nothing to spit at either, brutes all of them, elected to power and growth through mercilessness and slaughter, all besides one. The true intrigue of Etiam is its Legate Matriarch, the first of her kind. She is a beast completely divergent, influenced by forces distant from the Gretchkin. Her speech equals her master, and her words of consultation outclass my own. She is a magnate of spears and a diplomat in the reeds of war." Jeweler considered his pen un-inked for a moment, the scratch of his words disappearing nature forcing his ignorance of the tales. "My Spyders have noted an army worthy to overtake Klockgrave, Princesses, and above. Their overpopulation of spears should give you some fear, friend—I've never seen a weapon so elegantly wielded. Under orders from the Matriarch called Legate, the lesser footmen refuse to spark battle without consult. It should be more than simple to avoid their physical demands." Already shaking with over-labor, Jeweler's hands tore another sheet from the notebook, maintaining perfect eye contact with the robot, begging him to go on.

"Alright, now 'bout the Nest itself? How thick we talkin', how tall?" Viaduct nodded and traced the facility across the table with his glass.

"Taller than stiff, but well kept in truth. Soot-built walls, tall enough— you won't be getting through them by hand. The throne itself lies above, the ice keeps it compounded and free of detection, but I have no doubt you'll meek your way inside." Jeweler nodded and closed the pad of paper for his final note.

"Listen, er, V. Being transparent 'n all here, I don't got money for this."

"Debt for debt is quite reasonable, I consider. Unless—"

"V—no foul intents or nothing—they took the mask." Viaduct owned a small insect farm, the chirping of which had become increasingly invasive as the silence between the two continued. Silk, it was for silk. The little creatures produced endless quantities of it, and Viaduct had great use of the material.

"Then go." Jeweler placed the notepad on the table, ready to plead his case. He lost the words as soon as he tried, the tongue was pulled from his mouth. "Go home, prepare. It would be unwise to let them move it from the Belt. Go." He gathered up the items he brought, slowly at first, but the confidence on Viaduct's face inspired him to hasten.

"I—I'll repay you for this V, I swear. Get you a new vacuum tube, somethin' like that." Viaduct mechanically responded in laugh, already supposing he wouldn't see Jeweler for another decade at least, disappearing once more into the mists of obscurity, covering his tracks as he always did.

"No. No you won't." Jeweler scooped up the glass and chugged the expired alcohol in a solution of spite and respect. Viaduct grimaced at the sight but admired the dedication.

"I'll be back, gimme a week—Six—a day! I'll bring loot and parts. Hell, whatever I can get my mitts on is yours. I mean it." Jeweler stopped at the door, Viaduct's words lingered in the air,

"I did not make that deal strictly for my debt."

"Sure, I didn't expect yo—"

"I did it because I care. I have few among my entourage to call friend, Jeweler. You have even fewer." Jeweler rested his sack just beside the door and stepped back towards the elegant table. He put his hand down right next to his chair, right next to the cup.

"Gosh." The insects created music now, a song that could not be ignored. Viaduct wanted to leave but there was always something in the way, be it a wall or a thought. The lullaby brought him peace. It was bringing Jeweler there too. "You need to get outside V. Tell you what, I come back? I'll still bring the loot. We'll have a nice meal—I got somethin' I wanna show you. *Someone* I wanna show you." Viaduct grinned softly, that would be nice, he thought. What a thought, something nice outside? Beyond... Something nice...

~Following True Love's Kiss

*The primary result of my only meeting with
the legendary Sixfingers. Told as if fact, not
fiction...*

However, Sivi'ks had plans beyond this ultimatum, and hurrying behind the intruder, struck them upside the head with a golden swipe. Taphurrah, stunned by the blow, struggled away from the assaulter, snorting fluid from Nelej's flesh back into his own body. Terix remained unequipped of his own sanity while witnessing his brother bludgeon the husked remains of his own cousin, attached to the breath of a senseless peon. Sivi'ks' misaligned grunts and efforted swings of the tool brought Taphurrah to the ground, moaning with both pain and regret, tears streaming out of the mask, begging emerging through agonized gasps, begs not to be answered by the cordless brother. Another strike brought the lunatic to his back, a final strike before the deranged screams of pain would send Taphurrah down to death. Yet a chip merely flung from his skull, the cyan fluid evoking the reaper's presence dragged the screams louder, Taphurrah was stubborn to live. And Sivi'ks was stubborn to kill. One final blow and the voices were ended, Terix stared outwards from the halls of his own mind. What horror, dismay and horror.

"A fellow voice would drown my ears with sorrow if it was one worth sorrowing over." Terix shoved himself from the grips of pestering, finding his brother's voice familiarly bothersome,

"Both quoting me, and insulting me. What superb timing, Sivi'ks." Sivi'ks snuck a smile under his rigid facade, Terix clearly did not approve, and so his brother returned to stillness, "A candelabra?

Truly?" Sivi'ks noticed the weapon within his grip, a grip now split with the pure strength of its clutch, bleeding his own blood with the blood of the intruder.

"Would you rather I stand and watch 'til I found a proper killing tool? You are alive Terix, more than some can wish for." The two returned glances to Nelej's form, pasted over the unceremoniously heretical body of Taphurrah. They had never known his name, nor would they ever.

"Sorry. You remain my favorite brother."

"I am your only brother." Terix rose, resting as he once was between window and world. The scent of death for Tetarien loss was negligible, it was of copper and urine. Awkward with the stance and bearings, Sivi'ks replaced the candelabra within the stand upon the wall, brushing some of the residues away from its tip.

"Welcome home to you, savior of princes—"

"Spleener of Kings, look!" Sivi'ks unveiled a small ticket tucked within the collar of his shawl. The royal insignia was printed upon it. Terix questioned him on the origin of the slip, and to his pleasure, discovered its relevance to the Royal Flight Academy. Sivi'ks scooped his taller brother's torso into his embrace, and held him there, the worry of terrible events beginning to register as reason.

"The corpse! Good Eight Sivi'ks, the *corpse.*"

"Oh simple dear brother! Come, let us pass in the garden. My return deserves your attention for a short while, does it not?" Terix thought not of how this could solve the errors of their hastiness, but followed behind despite it, there would be time to forget these events that occurred. Sivi'ks heaved the spewing soma from the checkering tiles, and with too much heft, settled with dragging it across the hall. The sullen void pentacles placed where the origlyph should be dug ever deeper into the heir, and brought prayers for his cousin's well-being. Without hesitation, a taste of disgust and betrayal spread across his lips, so Terix promptly wiped them of sin. It was not long before the air of florets and grasses did their own work in cleansing the sin left behind by the deed. Sivi'ks beckoned his brother to the edge, the great drop before the castle and peasant world, a place where they spent many years as youths. Whether hiding from the responsibility of fathers, or the wrath of mothers, it was theirs and only this. Below, in the ashes of an old kingdom, was a river. This river was far too deep to resent a fall, death was ensured—a perfect ceremony. Before Terix could reach his brother (his legs weakened with the thought of the corpse), Sivi'ks had already poised the figure as standing and pushed it lightly from the garden. Terix scampered to the front, Sivi'ks holding him from untimely demise, as the two peered down into abyssal night. The corpse dropped like unchained buckets of mud and disappeared from sight most suddenly. The two sat, and silence befell the garden's walls.

"I suppose I owe you thanks. And apols." Sivi'ks smacked his brother upside the head, silencing his intrusive words. Butterflies coated in shimmering gemstones (Jembyle, bred quite popularly across the city) orbited the rising moon, the light of which still brought about its own sunrise. Through this moment, promises were silently kept to honor Nelej in secrecy, and shelter the existence of Terix's pursuer in this effort too.

"Is it not lovely to be together again? How I've missed these moments." Sivi'ks remained completely absorbed in the beauty of the skies, though he had been within them for quite some time, he almost felt unable to resist the temptation to return already.

"Yet it could be under superior circumstance, Sivi'ks." Terix placed a hand on his shoulder, it was lightly stained with Tetarien blood. The younger prince paused, adventure seemed to retain its flaws,

"I suppose I hadn't gathered my thoughts just now. It all occurred without a second thought. Eight above…." Remembering his brother's early existence, Terix began to picture the many hours Sivi'ks had spent in tears and shattered justice all from the iniquity of their father, the king. He was a sensitive boy, but the academy had clearly overstayed past its presence. Terix missed the more innocent hijinks of the careless rascal that once was his brother. But it was understood why these years were gone. He just as well missed his own ability to entertain himself among the chaos of his peers, but above all else, he was royalty now—there was no room for behavioral disarray.

"But who better to accrue bodies with than my brother?" Sivi'ks snorted, shaking his head with disapproval,

"So uncouth! Eldest prince, how dare thee!" The two bonded in laughter, mocking all the layers of the lackingly complex king of Cew. What a low-hung fruit.

"How father would screech if he only saw us now! Eight, we would never leave the palace again! A pilot no more, you would be! And I once more a slave!" A gardener wandered into the fields, calmly trimming the spread grasses of the royal gardens. It was here that they noticed the overwhelming presence of the two princes, and their royal comedy. It had been long missed by the gardeners, their separation was unbearable at times. Without the princes, Cew had nothing.

"Please, please! How can you stand him? In the royal court— you must be mad." Terix nodded his head calmly, agreeing to the diagnosis,

"Mad as can be. I should be locked away."

"Are you not already?" Laughter overtook the comprehensible words of the two brothers, and the princes continued to lose control of their speech in delightful humor, as the moon's light completely replaced that of the sun. The youngest prince looked to the stars, and with a grateful sigh, thanked his god for the moment in peace.

"It is true, we should mourn her. But I suppose she'd rather us laugh in her honor."

"Certainly." Sivi'ks stood, extending a hand to his brother.

"For how long will you remain? The stars cannot keep you forever, I'd imagine." Terix took his hand, and slung himself to his feet, patting his sibling upon the back,

"I am uncertain, perhaps a cycle or two. As long as I need to convince you to come with me—free you from my father's binds." Terix stopped his following, the palace could wait.

"Sivi'ks. We've spoken on this—"

"You do not listen when we do! You can leave *whenever* you desire to. I am a vessel for your freedom."

"Jokes withheld I *am* free! Father may be, er, 'overbearing', but he is a man just the same as you and me, and claims not to own me as a tool."

"You cannot see your own restraints. You are blind to them."

"Someone must be heir Sivi'ks!"

The Harlequin

"Why must it be you?"

"So it doesn't have to be you!" Sickened, Sivi'ks turned from his brother, he made an attempt to continue away but found himself rooted in his own guilt. Terix was the only person to ever care for him, even the queen had no personality of time to spare for him. The heir was of peak precedence. He was a mere lowly commoner in Terix's presence. Sivi'ks would never blame his brother, he thought more than anything, his brother too was a victim. But to hear this, to be told in face that Terix was only a prince to keep Sivi'ks from his greatest loathes, this ruined everything.

"I didn't ask you to suffer for me."

"It is, in honesty, no suffrage to me. I find myself enjoying the niche intricacies of royal policy from time to time." Sivi'ks pulled Terix to his side, embracing him with all the strength he could muster. Considering his attendance at the flight academy, this strength outgrew his brother's. "If you did not collect, that was a joke."

"A poor joke. I can better your humor. You will make a great court jester."

"And you my lowly king."

~ A Marble Among Her Eyes

*Convincingly storyboarded between a
Gretchkin heir and the eldest of recent
Spyders...*

Roach did not bleed. It lacked blood to boil, even the intense and dogged rage funneling from its core left no mark on its veins. With eyes like mad, a shriek of sight lit up the room, and the beast roused from unconsciousness, free from the Helium Sea once more. Approximately 20 Gretchkin spawn displayed themselves before the beast, ripe for the culling. A perfect cutting path was drawn by the mind, and Roach clawed along it without hesitation. The path took Roach to the first of the small kin, but as instantly as Roach had reached its prey, the hazard of its environment heightened,

"Nestle! Away from beast." Roach looked down at the creature, small and purple—a sphere of violet yarn. Its flesh was hollow, sunken, and pliable. There was another, a larger Gretch, a Matriarch. She towered above the child, tarnished in a pus-yellow halterneck, revealing the nonexistence of any decolletage. She wore thick rubber boots, stretching beyond her thin boned knees, which themselves were covered in a low bagging pair of pants. A quilt of impressive size had been stitched onto the back of the halterneck, covering the flesh it exposed. The Matriarch held it close. They had not realized Roach had awakened, and thus, with forceful decision upon them, and still uncertain of its disposition, fell to caution as a failsafe. Noticing the creature's infatuation with the small birdling, they pointed a feather to the little one. "Is Nestle. Pest child." Nestle chirped once, before vomiting a majority of its insides onto the floor.

The Harlequin

Roach clicked its throat, inspecting the being. Discovering the creature to be harmless, Roach lowered its tension. There were more of them, many hatchlings hopping around the room in cordial-less glee. The Matriarch was their watcher, it would seem, and Roach's too.

"Mm—matherkin?" The Matriarch peeped its head aside, questioning the spoken words.

"Matriarch. Hello." Roach nodded and placed its hand within the lap of the Matriarch, who until this point, sat its legs crossed with a child between them. The child, unnamed, was hostile among others. It had been banished from play, as had Nestle. The Matriarch drew her wings over the child, protecting it from Roach. Their two fleshes met, and the Matriarch felt just how chilled the beast was. She had volunteered for this duty, watching a beast with a considerable (though rumored) lust for blood was no small undertaking, but to be fair, it was truly no different than watching an impetuous child rile off the walls. Her diplomacy had landed her in worse straights, but this would seem to be among the better. She had given it great consideration, and with the touch of its dripping hands, the Matriarch decided to no longer fear the bug beast. By all extensions, it *was* a child, an unborn babe of unquantifiable consciousness. Scooping up the misbehaving infant by its neck, and dropping him off to a small pouch used for restraining the unwieldy children, she gestured with kindred hope to the beast. The Matriarch patted their lap, beckoning the monster. "Needing warm. Is for many warm." Roach hesitated, but contact with the featherless flesh on the Gretch's thighs drew it in. It was akin to a mother, but Roach had never known such a monster. It curled beside the Matriarch, resting its head within her lap, staring up at her beak-parted eyes. There was one missing, in its place was a green-and-white-striped marble, stained on its backside with purple fluid. Roach found the light that reflected off the orb quite bearable, perhaps even entertaining. It reached a solitary finger upwards, poking the underside of her beak, tapping it with a confirmative echo. The Matriarch, who until the tapping was staring regrettably towards the other children, was startled. With a squawk, she returned to the sight of the beast's feverish grin. The Matriarch found the fangs encroaching in her mind, biting pieces of her soul cleanout. She pictured the beast's jaws wrapped around her throat, the power behind them, the blood....

"Birn... Birnd?" The Gretchkin put her feathered talons above the creature's face, hovering soundlessly before the fall. Finally, they rested upon Roach's head, just beside the antennae. An immediate guttural growl emanated from the depths of the beast's chest, a vibrating motion. A clicking caught itself in Roach's throat, and it rolled to the side, tucking its head further into the feathers. The Matriarch began to rub her talons lightly against Roach, her beak propping open in both awe and attraction as she continued.

"Bird? erd, dah sound." Roach tilted its head back further, its eyes reduced to slits of pleasure and entrancement.

"dah. Birdah." Roach had an immortal laugh, the kind a Harlequin could appreciate. The Matriarch sounded back her own call, relishing the joy they were sharing. But between the children and the laughter, and even the palming of the antenna against boned talons, the Matriarch heard the ringing of sin. She pulled herself from under the creature, letting it rest calmly against the ice. Wandering over to a shallow window, she corralled the children towards the wall, over to an area surrounded by minuscule palisades, padded and comforted by soft felts and aggressively green fronds of leaf. Beyond the bars of metal, the Matron strode by, pacing across her throne with determinate pride,

"Larkbird? Emit-ary of Larkbird. Give demand." With a soft puff of visible air, the Matriarch returned to her children, tugging Roach by the tuft collar towards the other babes. She had her duty, and the Matron had her. Regretfully, she wished for peace among hoards, recalling a time when she had spent such peace with a lesskin as resilient as she. Her memory did not fail her for names or faces, she considered herself experienced in the art of aliases. Another voice echoed into the care chamber, one clashing with the Matron's call,

"Demands? You're the one with the Inkling. Make offers and we'll discuss their reasonability, er what not." It was the voice of diligence, the mark of The Definition spout about it.

"We give Inkling. Is deal." A smack of metal shrouded the ice, a thick boot planted before the window.

The Harlequin

"Great—I mean *our* side of the offer—how many hatchlings you want? Three, four mils?" The Gretchkin cocked its head to the side, one eye draining of all color,

"No coin—a trade. We give Inkling..." The Matron returned to her throne, inviting the soldier closer to her side, "You give Jewel one." Only the murmur of Matriarchs could be heard for a while, the soldier still beside the throne.

"Jeweler. You mean." Silence still. Even the Matriarchs had fallen to mute. "I'll get back to you on that, trades are different. Names Pherock, call if you need." The soldier handed something off to the Matron and exited the court. It was jealousy and not revenge, the Matron and Matriarch had spoken. Revenge would see Jeweler triumph, and she dead. The Matron was more considerate of jealousy, the envy of pride he had, and his reasoned skill. She yenned for the very accomplishment found in killing him, little more occupied her. Though this jealousy was thick and virile, potent enough to bring down the whole Nest upon them if they did not restrict their ambition. They needed currency more than vengeance, a handful of hatchlings was fully worth the price. It was this understanding of fate that had won the Matriarch her beatings and occupation. Her latest gore glistened in the reflection of the ice, a thick gash across the length of her arm. Roach, in youthful naivety, unfurled its tongue upon her wrist, across the wound in full. She expected searing pain, but the barbs of the cat-like appendage did her skin kindness. It was similar to the aloe of the deepest parts of the Belt-pits, the caves where ice could not reach, and the silver miners worked. She left the beast to its foolishness for a minute, recalling a Gretch-run mine just a day's journey away from her home. She wondered if it was still in operation and if her kin still suffered self-inflicted subjugation. Roach rolled aside, facing the hatchlings, and hissing. Two of the small ones cowered, but one with undeserved courage bapped the beast across the face, before retreating back to its kin. Roach covered its eyes, and gurgled, repealing its rage against the little creatures. The Matriarch could only respond humorously to the display. She stared at the beast, who in all truth, became lesser a beast by the second. This was a being, sentient and comedic as any, and unfit of the name it had been given.

Creatures of Habit

"Name, beast?" Roach purred for a while after this question, rubbing itself against her thigh once again, enjoying the warmth of contact.

"Roke. Ike *boug*." The Matriarch hung on every syllable, interpreting, and communing. She pondered its speech, pondered its comprehension. Language and its construction, considering its elusive nature to the Gretch, was a familiar handheld topic for The Matriarch. She could empathize with the struggle,

"Bug? Roach?" It nodded, and with resplendent ego in the echo, clicked twice. Roach had a name. A name was sentience, and to have sentience... The Matriarch looked somberly to the children. The children, frankly, had less mind than the one called beast. She rubbed her exposed shoulder, the cold had gnawed into her flesh, and she could not imagine the beast's pain. *Roach's* pain. With a groan, the Matriarch ventured over to the exit of the den, observing Roach as its fingers danced among the children, giggling like an infant—a demonic infant. "Roach. Come." The sentient struggled to tug the small beasts from its torso, before rising from the play-pen. "Serious, Roach!" Roach sprung itself from buffoonery, striding over to the Matriarch. She fingered her eye-wound, fiddling with the memory of her last betrayal. "Know Jeweler, the drink man?" Roach nodded, clutching the pin upon the neck of its cloak. She tugged open the door to the den, gesturing out upon the shaft of the crane. "Tell Jeweler..." She held for a moment, her voice not sure what words would suffice for such a message, or which the sentient could truly remember. "Tell drink man, songbird remember, okays?" Roach managed to stunt its two front teeth, giving its fangy jaw a calmer look. When the Matriarch pushed Roach towards the door again, the sentient truly processed what would be: freedom. It returned to the gaze of the Gretch, clawing at its pin. With a small clink, it palmed the pin over to the Matriarch.

"Frien. Ike Jewels." The Matriarch's non-marbled eyes wavered with sorrow as it clutched itself, its two mitts of feather and bone shaking with the mossy pin within. Roach entered the Gretch's arms and embraced her.

"G-go! Roach, beast! Go!" Roach remained with the Matriarch, for as long as it could possibly remain calm. It would return one day, perhaps, finding romance and kindness within the marble in her eye. She wept for it, wondering when it could see Jeweler again.

Roach heard speech, though quiet, beyond the darkened window sills of the Squall. Jeweler truly never worked so hard, never so late. The darkness proved his absence, but the voices lingered all the same, vague mysteries of unfamiliar typography,

"Not anymore, boss. Besides, a feather alone is not really conclusive. " The front door to the Squall slammed open, and Roach caught a shadow to secrete into. From the darkness emerged a shallow dusty figure, its head bisected like a hammer, joints dislodged and jagged. Any underlying bones must have been contorted beyond imagination. Their stony flesh was complimented by the soft blue fragments emerging from their neck and shoulders, pompous reminders of a higher status and a rocky origin. Maen's light shone cleanly through the cyan rocks, and particles of moondust drifted about the air, illuminated by the profuse glimmer. They wore only a thin silk robe, tied around the waist with a golden strand. Its purple was overpowering, and a thin collar of flax around each arm hardly detracted from the lavender shades. The figure moved ever further from the bar, stretching their sore bones in the frigid Belt air. A single blue gem jutted from the core of their face, non-moving and perfectly round.

"Jeweler owns no feathery keepsakes, I am certain. Perhaps a Grethckin needlefeather? I am not the member most learned of Gretchkin anatomy, now am I? Parseque? Have anything to add to my supposition?" Two more voices echoed from deeper within the Squall, but Roach remained and listened. It was clear to it that Jeweler was not present, but then where? Without its protector, Roach was vulnerable to the untrustworthy delinquents of the Belt, and worse yet, the storm. Certainly, these trespassers would prevent Roach from entering the den in the back of the Squall, and thus keep it from the warmth and prosperity it so yearned for after its finite imprisonment. The first unknown voice exited the Squall soon after its fellow employee, A female Scoria, one of the unbound ones. Without a potbelly or cleaner, she was free to the chill of the Belt. A thick rusted heating line coiled against her pinkish-green neck flames, hissing with activity. The ambient light of her plasma out-yelled the storm,

Creatures of Habit

"Parseque, when did you last clear the perimeter?" Parseque, with a small device extending from her wrist, looked off toward the closest horizon she could visualize within the storm.

"Ten minutes ago, tops. You feel something?" Anticipating the conflict to come, Parseque muffled the device, the distant robotic calls growing softer.

"Certainly something—feral energy, I-I'm shaking just at the aura of it." Though it had not seen it yet, the stone figure bore nubs into Roach's form, sure of its location from some sixth sense alone. They were terrified, Roach could taste the fear.

"Parseque? Parseque! Answer me for Lark's sake. What did Betellio see?" Roach's quiet pacing encroached upon the edge of Betellio's perception, ambient fear crept into his singular eye. In a flash of stormy distraction, Roach was upon him, a sticky hand wrapped around his neck. The stone man proved less fearsome than his stature insinuated, barking far more than biting. After a low inkish snarl, Betellio had fainted in complete terror. A bolt of plasma pierced Roach's shoulder, as Parseque attempted to defend her partner. Not a burn remained present on its skin, as it pushed its old toy away from the new directive. Awful realization came upon Parseque, as she slowly retreated from the prowling menace before her. She took two shots more before her back was stuck against the front of the Squall, Roach clamping a fist down beside her head. It saw something more than a threat, the flame figure correlated somehow with its owner, and intended to discover how. Strength was needed here, as Roach required all of its restraint to keep the hunger at bay.

"Jewel. Ere. W— were?" Through panicking breath, the mirage of Parseque's confidence was shattered, her speech mangled with complete bewilderment,

"W-what? *Where?*" Roach hissed, flexing its claws and dragging them slowly through the plasma of the Scoria's chest. While not painful, the gash was flooded with freezing air, tightly nearing her core. "Yes—Jeweler! We aren't certain, b-but I'd say Etiam! The Gretchkin camp? He may already be dead, or worse—no idea!" As the beast's claws slid further down the flame, Parseque only spoke faster and faster, details of locations and familiar cages flooded Roach's head. Satisfied with the answers obtained, Roach twitched its antennae, before placing the palm of its awkward hand against her burning chest,

"Thank." The beast and Spyder maintained eye contact for what many would consider a time far surpassing awkwardness. If Jeweler spent a century teaching conformity to Roach it would still never fully grasp the basic cues of conversation. Uncertain of the bond between themselves, Roach stepped back from Parseque, silently avoiding the unconscious form of Betellio. Parseque remained against the Squall, breath still chaotic and confused, all up until the Inkling dashed off into the storm once more, bearing down on all fours,

"Hello? Parseque? What in Silverwings was that? I believe I heard...*snarling?*" Parseque hesitated to answer her employer, the transponder still clutched ever so desperately in her right hand. She was not certain what she had seen was real—though the threat certainly had been.

"An Inkling, Viaduct. A *sane* Inkling. It asked—"

"For Jeweler. I *did* hear that much." Viaduct straddled the ridge of his seat, the rubber nub of his knuckles caught between the brace of his alloyed jaws. Larkik accounts reported the arrival of a pure Inkling on the Belt over a month prior to the current day, yet so too did these accounts report thousands more Inklings across the galaxy. Their reliability to the truth, and furthermore, to believability, was sparse and unlikely. Perhaps this was a unique opportunity? Viaduct had lost sleep to the turmoil of his soul; once again Jeweler had come into his life and had once more left more questions than answers in his wake. Viaduct had grown accustomed to the peace of solitude, but the wracking pain of potential kinship wrought him back to childhood. He was used to the abnormal scents that followed the pelt traders of the Upper Belt. He was used to not tasting anything that entered his mouth anymore. He was used to repressing his past iterations. The radical nature of Jeweler, however, he could never attune with. Secrecy was one thing, but his dissonance? Unpredictable. For a machine thriving in foresight and preparedness, unpredictability was a damnation. Misinformation was his nightmare, a panic he could not reasonably face. The informant arose from his resting place upon the futon, fetching a forkful of mysterious meat, sliding it into his metallic teeth. With a swallow, Viaduct cleansed the taste from his mouth, dabbing at the infrastructure of durasteel with his handkerchief. Taste used to be such a pleasant thing, but all good things must end. Viaduct pulled open the fine gold-edged curtains blocking out the horrors of the Belt. Even the snow was uncertain now. The paranoia tucked him inside and kindled worries. The overwhelming panic that arrived with the outside world was not good for the body of an elder, and thus Viaduct remained inside. But if it was true that Jeweler had been taken by a Matron, and additionally so that he was in the process of being hunted by a beast unlikely to be made of anything but Ink, then opportunity surely had arrived. It would be immense, the suffering and chill that Viaduct would face upon exiting his home. Even with all the knowledge, with all the foresight, there would be no telling of the possible dangers. Reliance on knowledge and paranoia withal was in actuality quite the awful fate. In the exact moment Viaduct lacked the knowledge of his surroundings, the world became a drastic quantity more daunting than it was prior. But it was this overthought, the incredible population of thinking in one's mind that brought about this fear. To not think was to live, and for Jeweler to survive, Viaduct found it necessary not to think. It was not fear of death. It was fear of living again, coming back as something. As a construct of the Sylvites, death was temporary, but nonetheless, a boarding, encroaching hazard. He could not afford to die again. A red velvet letter had been left upon his desk, and in honor of this terrible mental gymnastical activity, Viaduct finally brought himself to open it. The words inside were inscribed in a formal, unique font. Lettering from a great place above him in many degrees. The Larkik scribes were fanciful in wording and text, but the contents of this wording were often just as terrible as the confrontation of the outside world. The Belt was Larkik territory, in fact, it was the closest a citizen could get to the Lark himself without being reduced to a puddle on sight. However, despite its association and proximity to the Larkik Definition, it was seldom observed by it. Simply stated: The Belt was full of criminals. Everyone had done *something* of an imprisoning degree. If left without patrol or penalization, the Belt automatically acted as a prison, without the need for any unnecessary expenditure. But with this letter, these words threatened a change. On any day besides this, Viaduct would never believe such foolish literature. But with confirmation of the Inkling and the urgency of Jeweler's plight, perhaps there was reason to fear the truth of these words. If so, then Jeweler was in even greater danger now than ever before. There was no time for moronic paranoia. Viaduct eyed his only true partner, a myriad of puppets, soulless narrow trims of his truer face. Mechanical bodies, strung up to the wall with meat hooks. The thinnest corpse shone the brightest, fresh for use, without prior entanglement. Grasping the stock of his rifle, Viaduct bit his finger clean through and prayed.

~ *The Ink Now Pours,*

*Recovered from the singed remains of an
archive located deep below the Cathedral of
Chitin...*

Focus on the target, draw back your fingers—elbows locked—and suck your breath. Keep your lips tight, bite your cheek, but keep your eyes forward. Look at the target—*focus*. Repeated over and over, the words single-handedly steadied his hand, until the trigger was pulled and the shot whizzed by a scaled cheek—leaving no semblance of blood or scarring. Fevirgreen let his breath go, and lowered his pistol,

"You missed."

"Intentionally." He returned the firearm to his holster and approached the Crow. "I don't intend to kill fellow soldiers." Serrative slid a suckered finger against his cheek, puffing gunpowder into his flesh.

"I asked you to hit me, meat. You missed. Do it again, please?" Sighing, Fevir pushed the envelope.

"A death wish? Or is there some mystical soul-saver to this duty?" The Sanguine Crow stepped back against the chapel bricks. Sliding against the cobble, the bulk of his leather clipped at his backside, exposing purplish wraps of tentacled entrails.

"Meat should trust accomplices. Worms trust the meat." Fevirgreen valued that which was given to him and quickly drew to pierce the cheek of the tentacular fiend. With a hushed slobber, Serrative retracted its facial contortions back into itself, spitting the bullet promptly back into the air.

The Harlequin

"You *do* trust worms. Proper aim." Fevirgreen returned his weapon once more, resting his own form beside his instructor.

"That advice was for arrows. I do not shoot a bow." Serrative chuckled, snakish clacks leaving their malformed jaw.

"I am sorcerer of bows, quicksilver is my pride." He presented the sickle at his side, its blade shifting slightly in the light. With a flick of his wrist, its form turned lengthier, a metal strand binding its edges. Catching it on the recoil, Serrative grinned, licking the twine, "Precise and delicious." Metallic residue clouded his cheek, as Fevirgreen looked on ever more intrigued by his instructor.

"Where did you place your lattice?" Serrative tapped his lowest ribs—were there any to tap—and gurgled.

"Swallowed it up myself, worms tasted pretty, shiny thing was awful for the stomach." Like a divine root, the bow hazed to sickle and then became once more a tentacle upon the Crow's arm. "Looking for advice? With aim and draw so fine, you would put yours on that pretty piece, meat." Though some appreciation for the name had been harnessed, Fevir still relented against the nickname, finding its truth unbearable. The advice was sound, however. He had not yet decided his place in the guild of birds; Fevir's birdly peers excelled in knowledge above his own. His natural instinct for watching silently from afar had earned him some few answers. "Remember this—you will keep your weapon. Great Lark does not like losers." Fevirgreen squinted at the cephalopod, his lip between his teeth.

"Losers? Casual dialect doesn't suit you, Serrative. What do you mean?" The Crow fiddled with the binding on their left wrist, softly picking morphemes to assemble a better word.

"Those who lose… things. Lark was very upset with last loser of lattice." After having sulked alone in a dismal pit, Fevirgreen had become potent with questions that spanned the galaxy. Sneaking knowledge through scroll-correction requisitions, he had become certified in his place—roughly knowing of that which surrounded him. As a consequence, he had become far more curious of everything that troubled him.

"What need does god have with such petty gemstones?" Serrative slumped his sorry head, words failing his form. After several followed questions, and a moment of silence fit for them, Fevirgreen returned to stability. "I suppose even you do not ask so many things of god." Serrative snorted, doubting the knowledge of his pupil.

"I was curious, words did not come to me. I have Yellow Crow to thank—my instructor." It would not have been clear to Fevirgreen the nature of Serrative's grammar struggles if he had not mentioned it directly. Fevir had thought him well-spoken—if not disturbed with worms and meat. Everyone had their passions, he supposed.

"Whatever happened to them?"

"Death. Banishment first, then likely death. Crows do not survive long outside Lark custody." Custody, much like a prison. Fevirgreen did not view his home as a prison. It had occurred recently, alongside the death of the previous Verdant Crow. The Amber Crow—their name conveniently scrubbed from all records—had fled with their metals, and taken the lattice along with. Not a single one of the Crows cared much for their desertion, even the Lark seemed ambivalent to the threat posed by a loose mercenary.

"Unfortunate for you to have lost them. I have nothing to lose, so I am unfamiliar with your pain."

"There is no pain, only pity. He was a thick morsel—I was far riper than he, but still properly tamed." Clattering emerged from the upper Cathedral, Forklorn's intrusive tantrum echoing through the floor. "On topics of taming, a wildebeest is made of *him*. Stay your hand and quell your rage, we both know he will test it." Fevirgreen assured his instructor of his own calmness, remarking he was ready to continue practicing. "For what? You know more than me I think. I am a bad teacher for someone so—" Another fit of worldly pondering overcame the Sanguine Crow.

"Unfeeling?" Serrative's singular yellow eye paused its scattered movement, resounding solutions filled his lips.

"Learned."

The name Crows once held a symbolic, holy purpose. They were the executors of all divine ordinance; Sinners and blasphemers feared the call of the Crow. Tormentous and rigorous training prepared them for a host of indescribable horrors and smithed their edges sharper for warfare. Killings had been done in their name— once in the name of the hunt for particular threats to galactic security.

The Harlequin

While the Lark slowly became favored for his selfless reassurances of a calmer future, the Crows took a backseat to the spreading of the faith. This became truer as time continued until the Crows found threats only among themselves and the ignorance of their god. Tasks were seldom a challenge, though their name went unspoken with fear assuredly, and habit devolved to reckless jests. Fevirgreen had inherited the tools of the previous Verdant Crow, a woman whose fame acted as a herald for the good intentions of the Larkik Definition — she was once its holy facade. Fevir had no hope to fill the role she had once invented, solely because it was no longer needed or possible. His design was of sedentary readiness, to be prepared for what he had once been so charmed with, only to occasionally be released. The Lark claimed each day that *there is work to be done!* And rambled on about collective perfection and holy ambition, but none of it was presented in any literal objectives. Ishtar boasted she received a task her first month, which seemed infrequent enough to kill Fevirgreen with the numbness. He found other methods to occupy his insatiable curses, through curiosity for instance. While the other Crows seemed indentured by their titles, Fevirgreen doubted his place among the colors himself — seeing the only vague similarity between the fashion and color of his role and his own existence in his own ironic name. Ishtar was the Amaranth Crow, which was off enough to a quality link, though the purpose of her lust was undesirable, and only brewed distraction in the collection. Serrative did obsess greatly with meat and blood, as his Sanguine title evidently declared. The unnamed Amber Crow was deceitful enough to leave his position unwatched, and the silent Ivory Crow was showered in simplicity and purity, by their sinless nature alone. As if to support Fevir's own misplacement, two Crows remained unexplainable. Forklorn — The Keppel Crow — was quite the opposite of sorrowful or imaginative. Rage, selfish greed, and pettiness spoiled his dutiful namesake and further corrupted the bunch in the nest. He seemed more unnecessary than all the others. Forklorn was only considered acceptable to Fevirgreen for the sake of his own curiosity. Fevir had yet to meet the Byzantium Crow and thus could not draw conclusions. The Verdant Crow would most likely be associated with luck, or perhaps some demented derivative of health. Both — Fevirgreen thought — were most unfitting for his sensibility. If any of the titles would fit him rightly, it would be Sanguine, or perhaps Amber. The cults of each color harbored storied reverences of their own, each worshiped in faiths across the galaxy and heralded as the divine true Crow. The paths of each Crow spread their word to fame, and created tales of mistruth and legend to fuel the cycle of admiration. These paths crossed into a matrix of roads of ethos that favored cooperation. It was a game to the galaxy more than a war, or even a collection of tragic assassins. Fevirgreen grew more curious of the odd fashion in which the color and nature of a crow would collaborate, in contrast to the inheritance of his own title. It was so foreign, so without artistry, and yet Fevir had no lack of obsession with it. In war there was no mystery—it lacked theater or exploration. It was the same every day without fail forever. But the Larkik Definition was no war. There was bloodshed and exploitation, but so too was there a greater sense of purpose. Fevirgreen still had yet to identify his purpose.

"Fevie? Are you *still* locked up in there hon?" He had not spoken with any Crow more than Ishtar, who intrusively took from Fevirgreen every inch of his stable seclusion. A mystery of un-war herself, Fevir had yet to decipher Ishtar and her mechanisms fully. Yet, he strangely lacked any haste to do so. A mystery remained as such for only as long as he willed it to. Having something gnawing at his mind allowed his work to continue flawlessly. So, he continued his labors, the edges of the old scroll he was editing continuing to peel back towards their centers, curling over his dorsal. "I had a great time last night you know, and you're not answering any of my summons…" Lacking the charge for promiscuity, Fevir immediately called the bluff of the Amaranth Crow—he had been studying scrolls last night anyways. Yet there was still a nagging dedication to tell Ishtar how incorrect she was. Then again, perhaps that was exactly what she desired. Fevir tugged open the heavy oak door to his room, peeking out the small crack he had created in doing so. Ishtar was inclined against a stone pillar across the hall, her left leg lifted against it for support, both of her hands placed on the back-top of her skull, draping the cloths of her armor across her arms, and down her slender body. The gold enchantments edging the felt glinted in the distant light of Maen's Grave. Her dull metal body did not share the same reflective properties.

"Go away."

"Oh, you sog, come enjoy the bounty of a god-servant! I understand you hide away out of a great carnal fear! Perhaps it would help if you were to mingle amongst your others." Fevir looked back at the small heap of scrolls on a table he had commandeered for his own use.

"You don't know that. I enjoy my time alone." Ishtar groaned, letting herself drift carefully from the pillar, across the hall to Fevir. She danced her fingers up his shoulder before mounting herself on his back, pushing into him. While doing so, Ishtar caught a glimpse of the desk in Fevir's quarters, stacked high with books and scrolls alike, a thin stain of pen ink dripping down the desk's supports,

"Are you signing scroll requisitions?" Fevir grew heated with embarrassment for a moment, but rationalized the foolish emotion and returned to sanity, "I was under the assumption that no Crow would ever aid the proctor, not considering our duties." Fevirgreen slithered from her touch, repositioning the shoulder protector on his fatigues.

"Proctor? Akin to a Librarian?" Ishtar squinted at the man, so dedicated to his learning, she found it both familiar and admirable.

"The Lark said your prowess comes from your immunity to the physical and emotional. No desires nor pains. Is a man with such stratagems so inclined to knowledge?"

"Can a predator not entertain itself in the hunt?" Ishtar pursed their screen lips, hesitating a response.

"I can take you to him if you want. If it means you talk to me — to any of us." Fevirgreen was quite reluctant to associate himself with anyone who wouldn't put as much care into his work as he did. He had yet to be put on a mission, and still retained his earthly armaments. The title Fevir had been so graciously given seemed honorary, almost undeserved. Nothing had been accomplished for its earning. "He might have some spare armor around, we could assemble you a bastion for your *scrawny* little body." Fevir maintained the contact the two shared between visions for as long as he could. "Make you a real Crow?"

"Fine. Show me to him."

The proctor lived in the forge-bowel of the Cathedral, deep beneath the scarcely populated halls of the faithful structure. Fevir wondered why no one seemed to acknowledge the proctor's presence, nor why they had been isolated for so long. Ishtar appeared more than familiar with the route, recounting her many escapades hidden away in the Cathedral, far from the prying eyes of the Lark's moderators. She had slept with the occasional Gull, operated with a few Pelicans even, and sometimes had found herself entangled with other Crows. Her intolerance for hours without affection was written off as juvenile naiveté. This concept was only further supported by her age compared to other Crows, who disrespected her prowess as a killer thanks to this age. The role of Amaranth Crow had gone unfilled for ages, Ishtar's predecessor having died centuries prior to her recruitment. The sexual promiscuity of the Amaranth Crow was as much a necessity as it was a distraction from reality and the torment of her very existence. If knowledge was Fevir's hobby, then pleasure was certainly Ishtar's. Fevirgreen was beginning to twist his thirst for knowledge away from history and instead toward the Crows themselves. The concept of life beyond the simplicity of Oveck's shores was still completely foreign to Fevir. It wasn't impossible to imagine such a world as existing, but to live and breathe it—to see it before one's eyes—was a striking terror by comparison. Fevirgreen had yet to entirely understand his restriction to the stars. In a small introductory gathering, he had spoken with other Crows about his kind—or rather, lesskin, a minute populace excluded by their sheer naivete. Barely three planets could be considered their own, and those three held such mutated variants of the species they may just as easily not be species at all. Most across the Maen Galaxy agreed to leave the lesskin to their devices, not to any particular end, but for simplicity's sake. Two of the planets stuffed with lesskin remained isolated among the stars, but a third had spread their peoples much further. They did not number high enough to be dominant in the decisions of things but certainly were noticeable through their peers. These few, despite their uniqueness and generalized lack of fit to the functions of the galaxy, faded into obscurity, and many were never known again. Fevir was the first lesskin Crow. Not seeing another being of his own kind for days on end had changed him, but these changes were ones he considered extremely positive. His attraction (though not the lustful one she desired from him) to Ishtar was evidence of this. A clamor rose as the two descended the final flight of marble steps to the forge-bowel. It was the sound of smithing, produced by forces less than mortal. The bowel itself was a rather long, arched room, running the span of the Cathedral under the moonrock. A canal of molten metal flowed down the center of the room, lined by Gargoylic statues of various alien races. These statues, given hammers—and seemingly life as well—brought down stoney strength upon the stream of liquid steel, rendering them shaped before the birth of the distant star forge. The heat in the bowel was near unbearable, but Ishtar continued forward unfazed, not odd at all considering her body composition of metal and circuits. Off the path of the forge itself was a small alcove, a room dotted with maps and carpets, bas-reliefs and tapestries, and filled to the brim with scrolls and novels. This was the proctor's domain and it reeked of fiber and magmized stone. The nascent scent of a place populated with old papyrus and leather-bound books had been overridden with a unique flavor of dedication, like blood over spit. But nonetheless, the archive could be considered a paradise for many, Fevir included. Still, there was something that Fevirgreen found discomforting about the location, a presence he could not discern. Ishtar broadened her arms, and presented to Fevir the vast shelves of knowledge, explaining with excruciating detail the exact organizational system they followed. Oddly enough, Ishtar held knowledge that could only come with experience, as if she once spent a great deal of time in these archives herself, perhaps in her lonesome not unlike Fevir.

"Are there scrolls concerning your people here, Ishtar?" Ishtar busied herself ascending the nearest shelf to its peak, and seating herself atop its presence with a rather unfashioned novella, ignoring the brunt of Fevir's questioning. "I would wager you're only keen on speaking of the things you enjoy."

"Always ready to talk about you, if that's what you're offering hon." To say Fevirgreen resisted the temptation of Ishtar's teases was incorrect, as Fevir was truly uninterested in any physical dance Ishtar could provide; there was no temptation to resist. He would return no suitors remarks to her negligent wick, lest the fire overcome the wax.

Gliding across the height of the shelves, Ishtar gathered a second novel and tossed it down to the Verdant Crow. It was a manual on Sylvite Constructs, a mechanical people not unlike her. In hopes of an eye-opening tale, Ishtar had given Fevir all he needed, tempting him in a way he did not expect. He began to dread her presence, growing closer to turning back to the solace of his room. Fevirgreen did not desire a companion, not in any real sense. It was a difficult stance to take, but he chose isolation over communication. Ishtar exemplified this mindset, as she hindered his work, and her adoration of the sexual could drive him to insanity if left be. The Amaranth Crow was someone who seemed to interest herself solely in the torment of others—a game of childish wonder. The difficulty was the commonness of this occurrence. Fevirgreen was not considered too distanced from normality in Oveck, the battlefield malformed men like he. But in the confines of a religious palace of tranquil 'normality'… he was no normal man. He was only interesting because he was different. Had Fevirgreen less mysterious charm, Ishtar would just as surely ignore him as any other Crow, or at least tease him far less. Fevirgreen turned behind another shelf, Ishtar's humming of instigation growing dulled with the separation. Between Fevir and the next row lay a massive stone golem resembling a wingless bird, its weak bony arms stretched upwards with a surmountable load of papers and books. The golem was designed to convey an appearance of extreme labor, the face tensed, and the arms bending under pressure. At a glance, it was not unlike the statues in the forge, but as if to disprove any and all of Fevir's expectations, the golem moved, and hastily too. Its eyes hummed with a near-invisible glow, and it would shift its focus to another shelf, removing a book seemingly with its mind, stacking it atop its weight, and continuing forwards. Backing away from the heavy machinery, Fevir stumbled upon an unknown ailment, managing to catch himself against an elephant ladder that was resting on rolls against a bookshelf. Behind him was another creature, though this beast was no golem. It was small, at least half his size, and covered head to toe in the small paper requisition forms dedicated to various scrolls across the archives. The flesh of the puny creature was reflective, most of it an ashy white, its limbs loosely adhered with blue crystalline structures. The skin that wasn't this stoney material was a familiar Inky dark, rubbery, and all-consuming of light. This darkness encroached from the creature's left arm across their torso, creeping up their neck as it went. They wore a soft golden shawl and a thick-rimmed pair of glasses. Fevirgreen doubted the figure was harmed in any way—resting upon a cushion of dropped novels—but proceeded to the beast regardless. He approached the creature silently, with no intention of catching it or frightening it. Fevirgreen's natural gait was that of a slow and silent killer, however, and he had not practiced for such inconveniences. Upon reaching the pile, Fevir took notice of the small Larkik Insignia finely sewn into the shawl.

"Are you the Proctor?" Jolted by the sudden visitor, the proctor fumbled its carry weight of scrolls, being forced once more to gather them up.

"Meh, are you a bothersome Crow?" The proctor rose from its merchandise, patting some molten ash from its legs—a task with no end. They brushed past the nonplussed Crow, completely uninterested in his presence. The proctor walked directly to the golem, and tapped it on the thigh, leaning forward and whispering designless words to its ear. The beast reared and marched itself past Fevir, quietly assembling the dropped pages into a neat pile beside the shelf.

"Are these golems of your design?" The proctor was dedicated to ignoring Fevir, both in presence and words. They continued about their labors, making their way to the center of the archives, where Ishtar still remained. Fevir felt compelled to warn the proctor of her entrance, but even still the proctor ignored him.

"Alclerius? Oh how fun. I warned him not to bother you." Ishtar said with spite on her tongue.

"No you did *not*." Fevir rebounded. The proctor, weary and frail, shooed off the approaches of the Amaranth Crow,

"Ishtar please, I know you have not returned to scribe for me, you are above that purpose are you? Begone, leave me to my stoney comrades." Ishtar thwacked Fevir upside the back of his head, stumbling him forward to the proctor.

"He is." Alclerius measured Fevirgreen with a single instant glance and beckoned him over to a desk. There were two scroll requisitions, filled out and completed, consuming the space of the table. Judging by the dust and fade on the others, it was clear these were the first in ages.

"Your doing?" The proctor questioned. Fevir recognized the font and nodded. The proctor glared over the Verdant Crow's shoulder, eyes set on a pink machine, "After all you've done, you bring me a scribe with handwriting like chicken scratch." It took a moment for Fevir to recognize this as an insult to the both of them. Ishtar hopped off the ladder she had mounted herself on, slamming a hardcover novel into Fevirgreen's arms,

"Yes, I did Alclerius. Get my scribe some armor, and be obliged." She strutted lewdly past Fevir, patting him up the back of his shoulder, and blowing a kiss as she turned to leave. Fevir remained, out of a clear obligation to his new accomplice.

"Is my script truly so poor?"

"You ask far too many questions, *Crow*." The language tasted of slur, but Fevirgreen minded not of the composition of the proctor's vocabulary.

"I enjoy your scrolls, my understanding of this world is underdeveloped, as a lesskin." Alclerius looked again into the familiar mask the Crow had placed upon its face. He had made that mask, Ivory ceramics and Ink braces, it was perfection for perfection. How a Crow had gotten their iconoclastic mitts upon the sigil of the Lark itself was beyond him, and did draw incredible angst. To acquire it must have been willingly, a gift of sorts to a mistreated youth. Proctor Alclerius remembered what the Crows were *before* they were Crows; nestlings of the Larks desired fatherhood, in sort. He remembered when they weren't just killers. Crows had no appreciation for life, for they had no life left to live. With the forcible objectives of the untold legions, it was unimaginable what sort of suffering the Crows (mere children, the many of them) had either inflicted or observed. The Lark still adored its children, all that had changed was the world. In perverted irony, the pursuit of security had removed the Lark from the justification of his own means. The Crows reflected this negligence. Had the Lark finally left his mindless abyss of obsession to return to the light? Why had he decided *this* Crow deserved such acknowledgments? Was it not another cog in an infinitesimally complex machine? Fevir put down the custom novella his comrade had the kindness to gift him, drawing the proctor from his deep curiosities,

"Thank you." Alclerius whispered. The proctor fondled into his pocket, and soon held before Fevirgreen a small, translucently blue ring. Fevir paused for a moment, he had prepared another series of questions and compliments, but it would appear those tools were to go unused. He softly pinched the ring, and placed it within his palm, before sliding it over his right ring finger. The golems appeared in a trance to him now, he now bearing their weight as his own.

"What—you're welcome." Fevirgreen responded. His questioning behavior had been criticized twice now, it was time for his mindlessness to be put to rest. The proctor did not know Fevirgreen's name, nor his motives. He knew little more than of his incompetent script and dedication to the world of discovery. There was some solid chill implanted within the pit of the field, the Crow was less than lesskin. If the proctor was to have a scribe, he would need a friend as much.

"Come. We will fit you with armor, and perhaps find you some hope for that auspicious writing." Proctor Alclerius wandered off, back towards the boiling phlegm of the forge, still mumbling about Crows and fear. The book Ishtar had been reading had its spine laced with pink thread, and held a small red stamp of declination on its backside. The cover material was indistinguishable from something akin to rubbery wood. Fevirgreen lightly pried open the cover, a small collection of pages sliding outwards from the bottom. He quickly scooped them up, keeping them from disordering themselves. The writing was juvenile, with errors of grammar and spelling across the pages, with text skewing down and to the right as it continued, scribed by hand. The font was yet quite pristine and spoke of a vastness of things, from sciences to ethics in robotics. At the bottom of the third page, Ishtar's name was signed, right beside a citation critiquing an assortment of studies clearly not originating from the author. It was a collection of these data—various claims all strewn together by the writing of presumably the Amaranth Crow. It was of Sylvites, the robotic people she was once to be a slave to. Fevir considered the possibility that Ishtar was just as secluded as he, yet had adapted in a way beyond his understanding. Placing the book back on a near shelf, Fevir foresaw a vast security of knowledge before him, all at the tongue of the man who had given him a ring. Fevir had never received such priceless quality from another, and to his own dismay, this pricelessness was less ring and further paper.

~Berceuse of The Needle

Scarcely mentioned within six different
Larkik recon reports—in fluctuating detail...

Snow reduced itself into a fine mist, the storm beat down his back, and still, he trudged forward. The arrowhead lodged in his lower waist teased blood out in soft spurts, drizzling down the length of his coat. Two more had stuck themselves into his pauldrons, the thick metal that hid beneath his furs. Even from within the walls of the encampment cold pressed down, the steel serving only to chill his bones further. Matriarchs observed his steps from a distance, he was sure of it. In the distant fog, hisses roused the murderous calls of still-living Grethckin. When a shadow slipped among the others, Jeweler drew and fired without hesitation, concern for ammo lacking. It was as if the spinning globe he centered within spun only faster with his persistence.

"You speckled thief fucks! Where are you!" The snow blew into his mouth. Huffing to spit it back out, Jeweler pressed on. He had already cut down the guard and its tower and slain nearly fifty Princesses alone. There was a trail of purple behind him, gore still dripped from the serration on his dagger. He would not be bested by a storm. Another arrow struck him, only fueling his maddening hatred, "You bug-bird cock eaters! I'll bleed you each dry!" Behind his rage in the cold, a Matriarch had gathered up the weapon of its brethren, pointing it to the shouting from within. While its kin continued to pepper arrows towards Jeweler, the Matriarch took a chance at stealth, approaching slowly in the weather's comfort. Jeweler's mind and thoughts buried themselves knee-deep in swamps of malice. Even the snow fell slower in the moment. The shadows in the distance did seem as such, shadows, and distant. There was no way of telling what they represented. The voice of an untainted maiden filled his ear, as did blood fill the other, a voice of reason in unhallowed light. That storm, the pursuit, all a memory. The stab had not been fatal, yet it felt as such. Windchimes illuminated the cavern for a brief moment, as the bartender's eyes filled with amaranth smoke. Dried as his lips were, they grew drier.

"This is rather pathetic." Jeweler shifted his weight, trying to push the corpse off himself. Clearly, the body had been a glutton in life. "I had failure considered a celebration for you, an exotic occurrence. More explosive."

"C-cram it, lady." Jeweler squirmed out his right arm and continued to heave, the light of Maen's grave reflecting off the icy cave walls just enough to blind him. The large woman took a seat in the corpse piles beside him, transcendence obscured her form—a shadow to his mortal eyes.

"My own blood, sacrificed unto you, all for naught. What a waste of elegance. I thought the great Jeweler a foe unbeatable! But nay, he is but a lowly wyrm." Jeweler knew there was no point in arguing with the specter of his fears, but he was not exactly the type of man to need a reason for his actions. His efforts in freeing himself were similar, its shape too rotund for his frail and sleepless body. The body would move, or his arms would shatter. He was excited to find out which would happen first.

"You wanna hear pathetic, Pez? A thirteen-foot—enrgh— woman, abandoning everything she loves...." Jeweler's breath faded, and with one last shove, he rolled the body from his own, "Just cause she thinks they can't fend for themselves." Out of breath, Jeweler bent his neck back, meeting eye to eye with the pinkish glare of a familiar specter, her amaranth form still as glorious as he remembered,

"Who are you trying to impress? I am the remains of a magick long expired. You are completely alone." Jeweler rubbed the side of his head. Dried blood coated his cheek, the bartender had little vision of its origin. The top of his lip had been split open, and his ammunition lost. Concerning of all though, was the blur in his vision, something that had not dissipated as the hallucinations had. Still yet did his mind feel as though it was burdened by the weight of the sun, trudging slowly and restricted in complexity. Everything occurred at a hushed rate, and fuzzily. Jeweler began to wonder just how long the pain would be stunned by his weakness.

"Nestle! Come!" Jeweler looked up from the thought of death to be greeted with the ghastly form of a Gretchkin spawn. A Matriarch stepped out before him and collected the child, it squirmed within her arms. His face, encased in a slight layer of dew and frost, was barely discernible from a corpse. Though it was nigh impossible to see, Jeweler could surmise the shadow of the Matriarch, the child still wriggling in its arms. As description and words had proposed, it was none other than the Legate herself. She went to leave, but curiosity and disgrace brought her back to the corpse pile. The pile could very well have been a statuette, carved from the damnable screams of desecrated corpses. The frozen skin was not unlike stone, the matted and molested hair could resemble fronds from cloth. It was horrifically appealing to observe, yet even the fresh corpses seemed to resent the watching. But the Legate wasn't particularly interested in the corpses, but rather, the survivors. As Jeweler extended his weapon towards the Legate, it momentarily repelled in fear, only to retain its courage, and look closer.

"Jewel? Alive! Jewel!" The Matriarch slung the child across its back, placing both arms upon the dirtied corpse of the bartender. Lips sealed with chill, Jeweler tore his flesh apart, blood dotting his upper lip.

"G-get aw—away from me, bast-ard." With shaking arms he raised his pistol, but a throb from his torso pulled it back down. He looked to the pain, where a red blotch had formed on his coat. The Matriarch slowly pulled the weapon from his mittened hands, and placed it in her pouch, alongside the child.

"The Jewel! Is friend, friend! Come, must remove from Matron." Jeweler continued to stare at the blood, reaching his frostbitten fingers down to remove the cloth from his wound. The Legate saw and assisted as she could. There was a gaping wound, one that traveled deep into the flesh of Jeweler, placed just beside the elbow. The Legate knew how hated Jeweler was among the ranks of the Gretchkin. She too once feared the man, and all of the stories that followed. Her time among peoples had dulled senseless fear and given birth to a rightful understanding. She placed both hands upon Jeweler's waist and heaved him upon her shoulder. Jeweler squirmed, trying to resist, but the Legate silenced him. She mounted the steps back to the surface and quickened her pace.

"W-where you takin'... You takin' me?" The Matriarch had an emptied head of lesskin knowledge, certainly, anatomy was no talent of hers. But blood was bad, she thought, so too much blood would be terrible.

"Home! Squall, you must leave. No bleed, stop bleed." The cold breath emanating from Jeweler's jaw chilled the Legate's neck, but the feathers assuredly kept her warmer than he was.

"What'd I—steal? Er, uh... this time?" Jeweler's speech was slurred, but he could still hear his own voice. The faint shaking of his vision still permitted some truth, but there was little to see to begin with.

"Shush Jewels, Matron will hear. We go now, we leave. Get home stone and go to Inky place. Yes." Jeweler struggled to understand, though he *did* understand. It was clear to him now more than ever that she was the Legate he had heard such wondrous things of. Her accent especially was impressive, he knew from experience how difficult it was to teach a Gretchkin the mannerisms of Standard. He once had done such a thing, and with all the elegance of a vomiting seagull. Jeweler couldn't recall when the Gretchkin had left—she was young when she did—just a mere princess. He considered exactly how old the little monster had become, perhaps a Matron? No, too old, maybe a Matriarch though, it could be possible. The *Legate* was a Matriarch too, how fitting. Clambering across the halls of the lair, she mumbled directions to herself, letting Jeweler's body lean comfortably onto her chest. The blood had sullied her mustard cloak and lubricated the man upon her shoulder. Jeweler slipped from the Gretch, and fell into the snow-filled carpentry of the throne room, his back bracing the fall. The Legate cursed under her breath, something in a language Jeweler could not understand. His vision was fading worse, his speech was dramatically weakened. He wanted to tell her, he wanted to reach out and ask if she was the one from so long ago, but his corpse wouldn't let him.

The Harlequin

"Lulla— Lull." She snatched him by the hood and tugged the bartender aside. Jeweler's wound painted the snow a deep brownish color, such cold would be agony for anyone who wasn't numb.

"Jewels, beg! Come, come quick! Matron see us. Matron coming!"

"Lullab-by? K-kid?" The Legate squinted through her starting tears. First Roach, now an old father. A family she yearned for seemed to turn corpses around her. A shot sent panicked shakes through the Legate as she once again dropped Jeweler to the snow,

"Matriarch! Put down the Jeweled one! Must die!" The Matriarch hurriedly pulled on Jeweler, trying to coax the fight from the body. He was in no condition to do so, but a child of his was no meekly matter. He slowly heaved the pistol from her sack, wrenching the hammer back with all of his strength. The bartender pointed the weapon at the Matron and missed his only shot. The Matron, properly enraged by the weak attempts of Jeweler's ambition, reloaded and drew its fraudulent handgun. "Jeweled one, killer of many. I—Matron Flosim—revenge all Gretchkin. Jeweled one die now." The Matron barked at the pair, the shadow of a beast emerging in the distant egress of the lair, hunched obtusely in the light of Maen's Grave. It roared—a cry caught in the throat with webs of mucus—and advanced upon the battle. Before she could turn to the obstruction of light, Roach pounced upon the Matron's back and tore its teeth into her collarbone. She struggled little in kicking the frigid ink from her body, wound ignored in the combat. Tickled by the bluntness of the attack, she spat in the direction of Roach, now toppled against the throne,

"Roach! Beast, I told leave!" The Legate hissed at it, bracing her feet against the ice. Roach returned sounds of pleading, asking for but a moment of penance. If 'Flosim' wished to kill its family, Roach would ensure itself dead before she ever came so close. In light of the conversation

"Roach? Beast name? Is beast, no more. I will kill as others." The Matron put the firearm to rest and summoned its spear from a far more diligent Matriarch. "Child game. Come beast." Roach feigned a leap, ducking under the first swipe Flosim had to deliver. Two quick jabs poked into Roach's careless body and quickly healed away from any severity. The fight was unendable—while Roach was no trained combatant, it proved unkillable by mortal means. The Matron was no simple warrior herself, Flosim's years spent entranced by the thralls of spite—beckoned by the call of hate for Jeweler—had honed her eyes as sharp as his. With the two entranced by the other's prowess, no conclusion to the battle would arise. Roach swiped at the Matron, orbiting around quickly to catch her off guard. A single tear in her backside brought about a terrible roar, Flosim trickling lightly into the snow. A slather of Ink melted into the wound, burning the flesh as an incandescent white met it at the sore. Divine hate spilling like foam out its beak, Flosim impaled the beast through the chest and hurled it back into the snow.

"Beast! Cower, Matron too quick!" Roach glared up at its friend, the Legate Lullaby. No bird would take life from it again. The Helium Sea began its foggy descent on its mind, but the beast pushed it away. The Matron approached with care, avoiding deep snow and blood with majesty. It held the decaying shape of some sick effigy, an artifact of the Larkik Definition without a doubt. In a trail behind her, snow mixed with Ink and Ichyr, unusual as its source may be. She *bled* divinity, unlike any other Gretchkin Roach had killed, nor had Jeweler encountered. Holding the effigy to her face, Flosim lamented,

"Weak beasts, all cold and weak. Foolishness. Gretchkin survive. All other, die!" A tracer illuminated the path of a distant bullet, one that just as quickly as it arrived exited through the backside of the Matron's head and shattered the artifact, draining clumps of purplish insides into the snow. With a most disgraceful sucking of air, the Matron fell to the side, silent at last. Jeweler was thinly conscious, wound and emotion having lulled him dangerously close to eternal slumber. The Legate left her hands drifting above the body, awaiting a command or some intelligence, the cold nipping at the wound on her left thigh, but the numbness befit the shame. Roach licked at the hole in its upper chest, calming the Sea in its vision.

"Oh, it *would* be Jeweler to invite such a clandestine cult of colors. A trio of miscreants most unwise. Good tidings, friends." Viaduct followed his shot into the lair, stomping rhythmically as his metal limbs sunk deeper into the snow. He was far narrower than the last visit, with new pointed feet lacking any semblance of damage, his head curved back in a spike, and the core chassis was made with bands and bars as opposed to thick plating. A change of armoring, perhaps—nothing more.

"Machine? Friend of the Jeweler?" The Matriarch cooed curiously. Viaduct struggled calmly against the frost, before freeing one of its mechanical legs.

"Yes, friend is a perfect term. Are you the same, Matriarch?" The Legate nodded, sheltering Roach from sight. Marching over to the shaking form of his companion, Viaduct began to search his belongings. He fumbled his rifle as he found difficulty holding the length of his satchel alongside its weight. He decided the satchel was more valuable, leaving the weapon in the powder behind himself. "Have I any Adrenomene, I ponder..."

"Fix?" The Matriarch questioned. Viaduct was far too occupied scrounging into a pack on his hip, one that had jingled with his step. Haste forced three bullets from the pack, and into the forever lostness of the snow.

"Certainly, though he is not going to comply willingly. Hold him still, please." The Matriarch extended one arm to hold her bloodless kin. She feared Viaduct's intentions, but Roach transmitted a loose trust to her, one she dared not break. The machine shook a syringe of luminescent sky-blue liquid with violence, pausing momentarily for the medicine to stop its movement. He jabbed the syringe—very carelessly so—into the stomach of the man, as close as possible to the heart without piercing it entirely. The skin grew in color for a moment, before returning to the cold. The Matriarch added to his treatment with a length of fabric torn from her own garments, tied tight around his hip side and arm. Roach had no help to give, besides prayer to gods it remembered, and yet remembered not. Jeweler's veins flooded with heat, his eyes clenching together in an effort to awaken. As his breath picked up—heavier and quicker—he weakly raised his arm against his own neck.

"Ad—adrenomene? Viaduct you...." The remaining Gretchkin forces, ones left absent from the recent death, stood guard over the translucent cadaver of their ruler, watching its elegant ripples with complete engagement. None pursued the now-rising Jeweler

"Jewels all better?" Viaduct shook his head, returning his satchel to its place upon his spine,

"Yes ma'am, he will be burdened by death not. Good thing too, his care of ours is essential."

"My ass, V. Woo! Damn things kickin' now, starting to hear colors!" A retching crack erupted from the Matron's corpse, as a once tainted and profane fossil manufactured a celestial limb, one of pure white. It clawed its way to the surface, a spineless motion wavering like an insect from under a rock. The glowing form shedded its lowly body, beyond majesty. It was as a butterfly from its chrysalis. "Oh joy. A fiend within a fiend. Do all Gretch do this, Matriarch?"

"No?" It responded, curious of the demon in its own sense. Shrugging off the previous flesh of its past existence, the creature drooled into pools of its own, puddles of purity marked the steps it had taken in approach.

"Oh grave mind of celibate decay, cancer plagued upon my own kin. You, deemed of Ink long lost, must see the truth of thy *sin*."

"Rhyming. Why this could prove belligerent upon the ears. Perhaps it is time we take our leave?" The white elegance's shriek echoed deafeningly against the ice walls of the fortress, shattering crystalline walls and cracking braces of wood. While the others remained frozen in place from the call, Jeweler rose, loosely patting down his shape and drawing further blood. He babbled to himself, incoherent jumbles of hate-filled phrases, desperate huffs of exhaustion after either. He was not deterred while watching the empyrean form rise from the husk of its old self. Not a bone in his boiling body faltered. Roach recovered quickest, its eyes far adjusted to the boldness of volume.

"Larkbird." It muttered under a slimy growl. Viaduct called out against the ringing, demanding for Jeweler to stay away from the foe. Roach watched as its master did no such thing. The angelic beast swung out its arm of Ichyr, catching it against the very palm of Jeweler's hand with a splitting crack. Unfazed, the bartender stuffed the syringe still stuck against his chest deep into the Ichyric's face, splintering its beast into three parts. With the thunk of its skull against the ice, Jeweler and his compatriots were encouraged further from the angel, Roach standing now between its master and death. Viaduct's vision returned shortly, only to see the ivory being spread hulking wings not unlike what Roach had deemed it, if not an Ichyric itself, it was surely a descendant or parody. Whatever had become of Flosim was no longer fit for the name. It was feral, completely devoid of any direction despite itself. Antlers of thick bone emerged from hollow sockets for eyes, a new beak—now cracked—merged with the old. Buying time for growth, thick plates of ivory flesh coated wings, feathers peeling off from the moist binds. Leaping into the air, the angel struck an overhanging brace, collapsing more of the fortress around itself. Cawing in frustration, it spun down to the snow, a vortex of untrimmed nails coming with it. Jeweler scooped up a decaying drift of fallen lumber, ready to lose to all odds. Not willing for sacrifice, Roach lunged against his side, sending the both of them tumbling into the crane shaft. Viaduct mechanically readjusted itself, stiff motion readying himself for battle. Step by forbearing step, the informant returned to his weapon, avoiding the slashing madness of the angel above. He was shaped to kill now, and with a rigid tug of his rifle, he aimed up at the bird, flawlessly tracing its motion as by pure computation. A shot grazed its wing but did not pierce it, as it continued to circle overhead.

"Machine, kill together?" The Matriarch gathered her spear and resolve, the small child she had stashed earlier still remaining within a basket at her side. The two took up arms and looked to the sky.

"Jewels. Jewels." The chamber was unbearably dark. The stained glass that would normally illuminate the vast hall was dimmed, obstructed by vast unfurled banners, all painted a vermillion red. The golden insignia sewn seamlessly into each fabric glowed without light, penetrated without length. It was the heart of the Definition, the icon to petrify, the Palm of Creation, a taloned hand with three claws, seen clutching various implements in its grasp, depending entirely upon where it had been placed. The hall was that of the Cathedral of Bones, and thus the talons held its namesake. The gnawing black stone and feverishly reflective crystal set about the unease, a feeling of doomed decay. It was empty and dead quiet. With nothing to call it otherwise, Jeweler deemed it a nightmare, an awful one too. He was bathed head to toe in his Gull armor, a special attire he'd rather have forgotten. And yet, its flesh squeezed him so comfortably.

"Oh Jewels~! Good to see you in *such* brutish beauty." Jeweler turned to the woman, his discomfort hidden by his metal beak.

"Howdy Pez, this gonna be a regular thing now?" The phantom shifted, spanning itself across walls and shadows, hiding in the darkness. She never called him Jewels. Never.

"As regularly as you bridge the gap of life and death. Might I remind you of our deal? I own you." Jeweler trudged forwards, deeper into the abyss of shapeless horrors. He feared not the figure in the dark. She was a nightmare, as was all else.

"Don't remember that part of the deal, 'less, you ain't the real Pez." The massive woman beckoned, pulling Jeweler towards a towering door at the end of the hall. He was unfamiliar with the depths of the Cathedral, it was not often Gulls were permitted entrance to even its foyer. The door tugged at his soul, and so, he resisted not. The shadows aided his opening of it, bestowing upon his vision a room coated in felt, cloths of various colors and lengths strung all around the circular facility, stretching endlessly into the sky. Corpses of various races lay drained and colorless in piles across the room, tailor's string knitted the limbs of macabre puppets together, dangling them from the rafters. Puppets, no they were far more lively than that. He *had* seen this place before, why had he not remembered?

"What *is* real, Jeweler? Certainly not I, you seem to think."

"None of this is, just a damn nightmare s'all." The room did not crumble, the woman did not fade. It was far too real,

"Jewels!" Roach's hissing call broke through the illusion of felts, leaving a crack in the bone-white bird mask of the woman. She never wore her mask when Jeweler was around. Of course, it wasn't her, Jeweler knew it.

"Ta ta, little Jeweler. Shall we never meet again." Jeweler jolted awake, babbling and spouting through the stream of alcohol pouring down his face. He pushed Roach away, his hands blindly smacking at the beast,

"Ack— Roach! Stop, stop Roach!" He spit the remaining alcohol off his lips, wiping down his face from the sticky substance. Despite the clear wounds upon his hands, no pain was brought to him.

The Harlequin

The peak of his ear was near numb, and his right arm seemed to wiggle in boneless prosperity. The gash in his chest was healing, but still worse for wear—a sharp sting aligned itself to the beat of his heart. The frostbite on his fingertips had been left to warm, the splitting agony in each stub enough to make Jeweler scream. He did not scream.

"Beeg lay-de?" Jeweler rubbed the bruising flesh above his ear, blood hardened like chitin around the wound. Fingering the cut dug into his palm, Jeweler perceived the words, and questioned his beast,

"What?" Roach dipped its head in the direction of the shade, where Jeweler had seen his misery, "You saw it?" Roach assured its master of its honesty, prowling the surface of the old appearance. Manic as he was, the specter *was* real, or real enough for Roach to comprehend. Less than a vision, his nightmares had manifested; Magick was a thin needle to bind his leather to the table. Without the workings of its creator, his fissile blood would eventually evaporate to nothing. They were not visions—premonitions rather, or something of the sort. Roach helped the broken bartender to his feet and across the room, the dimmest glow emanating from above. Piles of miscellaneous merchandise lay stacked across the stores, barrels and crates amassed like chess pieces against each other. "Got any idea how we get back out?" Roach looked only up towards the shaft that had brought them to both safety and damnation. The beast had practice in climbing, but with the weight of another, it was uncertain of its prowess. Jeweler's mind began to turn again, the clarity of pain sticking his back. With a glance to the pile, Jeweler was reminded of salvation—a thin white husk of wood among figments of iron and gold. Dropped by his ally, Jeweler crawled to his ambition, the mask was before him. He held its shape in his hands, glossing its form with his hazy eyes. Quick as he had acquired it, it was stuffed back into his coat, safe from the moondust in the air. A heavy thump rattled the structure, the binds of the walls shifting as snow tumbled in. Roach looked to a sound of mice, an exit having creaked ever so particularly open, letting the semblance of lamp light into the room. Its eyes requesting approval from the bartender, Roach waited in the dark. "You first, pal."

Creatures of Habit

The mangled and injured form of Viaduct came crashing through the roof of the Gretchkin store shed. It was made only with shingles, well-performing in resistance to snow, but quite vulnerable to falling metal men. Viaduct struggled away from the hole, now letting in the blizzards of the outside world, thankfully semi-isolated by the walls of the deep fortress.

"G-g-good day, Legate. Glad t-t-to see you a-a-a-alive." Viaduct readjusted his jaw, placing a finger on the side of his head, running it along the edge of his soldered plating. Upon reaching an anomaly, Viaduct smacked the side of his skull, somehow repairing one of his several malfunctions. As he rose, there was clearly something amiss with his state, now even more mechanical than ever—his joints bent only particularly, and one at a time.

"Still, bird lives. Fight it?" Viaduct shook his head, the remains of the wounds he managed to inflict upon the beast had dripped down, pouring into craters of debris from above.

"Nay, I would think our efforts in vain. Where is Jeweler?" A distant shriek marked the syrinx of a familiar threat. It was surely on its way. Lullaby had never fled before, unfamiliar with the nature of hiding from death. Leading Viaduct from the revealing spotlights of reflected moonlight. She knew of deeper crevices, the halls of the fortress led deep. If they had any chance at survival, the bird had to be free. In the thick of the lair, it had nowhere to set off to, its continued rampage would unfurl the whole fortress around them.

"Come to skylight, let the larkbird go. Tease it." Shattering ice and angelic screeches echoed in the distance, the bird was occupied with its own chaotic destruction, likely growing in sanity as it existed. If left unchecked, it would soon be unstoppable, flying fully and freely as any of its namesakes. Snapping a twisted forearm back into its place, Viaduct warmed himself to the concept. They would need bait. The Legate slithered out into the ice, herself veiled in snow and wind as the storm grew thicker within the fortress. The violent windfall was a result of the panicked fluttering of the bird, with no eyes for seeing it did not care for its own trail of destruction. In the peace of dancing movement, away from the prying threat of the angel, Viaduct equated his kinship to mystery.

The Harlequin

"Why Legate, help Jeweler of all men?" Her fifteen eyes scuffled around the view of the fortress, its corridors running deep into moonrock,

"Jewels friend. Flosim awful mather, cruel meestress." Completing her hunt for continuation, she peered back to the informant, her eyes twitching as she did, "Why you help Jewels?" Within reason, Viaduct anticipated a grim truth to emerge from the Matriarch, a description of Jeweler he had small fragments of knowledge in. He had not expected a return of questioning, but it did have clarity. She would know far less than he ever knew of her.

"Jeweler and I are old contestants for power. We have poked at the Lark together and thus *had* to spark friendship. I owe the man a great deal for his charges." Returning to the halls, she bobbed her neck, soft agreement. There was conflict in her clear to Viaduct, it was possible she withheld greater understanding of Jeweler than he.

"Follow wall. You run, I kill bird." Stepping carefully between fragments of glass and puddles of divine slop, Viaduct questioned his ally,

"Well, I was referring to a series of actions, not an endpoint? Perhaps an idea on how to kill the fiend?" She paused her creeping, holding the hatch to a stairwell ajar,

"Kill beast. Ugly." Viaduct shook his head and followed her up. The Matriarch could speak, yes, but not think, it would seem. Death of the beast was obviously desirable—its shrieks of birdly rage had begun to interfere with his sensors—but for the objective of the fight to be reduced to its outcome, there would be no strategy, and no solution henceforth. The Matriarch had no such strategy. From below the two could hear it slam against cavern walls, weakening braces with every quake. Higher than ever they strode along a thin outcropping, a balcony overlooking the main hall of the fortress. "Do not need plan, need spear. Have spear?" Viaduct looked to her with stillness in his mind. He couldn't help but vaguely familiar with her persona, the unadjusted recklessness of her desires.

"As jesting truth would strip me clean of wounds that shall not heal, I rise in cinders pure as snow with caws not unlike god-peals." Viaduct was easily plucked from the freedom above, the bulk of his webbed chassis cracking against a limestone buttress against the wall. From the destruction came a thick pole of stone, fallen practically into the arms of its new wielder, Lullaby. With a lunge, she was upon the angel, pinning its beak down into the ice with a spear of stone. It bucked against the wooden beams above, crushing the will of Lullaby's fierce attack.

"You *fiend!* Back from the Legate, you hideous half-wit!" Still caught in the soupy talons of the angel, Viaduct wrapped a singular hydraulic fist around its knee—inverted as it may be—and retracted his restraining compressors. With the complete devastation of its femur, the bird flung back in a mixture of rage and sorrow. In the havoc, Lullaby had leapt to greater advantage and hurled the spear into its chest. In the agony of the fracture, the bird had tightened its grip on Viaduct, cracking its form against the Ichyr. As it fell to the side of the fortress, it swung the already broken machine violently against the wall, shattering its facade in full. Seeing it as little more than a moment to strike, the Matriarch pushed forward to the spear, lumbering over the balcony and down onto the angel. There was incredible speed to match the ludicrous care the Matriarch put in navigating to the weapon, but care withal, she tumbled just the same. Falling awkwardly to the ground, she kicked up the remnants of torn trusses as the foul creature pursued, thrusting the jagged remains of the wood into the bird's throat, piercing its bone. The creature cried out in another remark of affliction, but did not falter. The Legate, spear of old in hand, pierced the upper brow of the decaying white creature. Overcome with proposed death, the angel yawped a great echo, bleeding Ichyr from its tongue. Squirming out from the pouring falls of the Ichyr blood, it flew into the roofing, and away from the presence of Lullaby's dissonance. She bleated out in success, a sound much like a lamb, and rose to her feet. Glancing over at the slumped machine against the wall, she pondered his rights and dedication—if death was something he went into willingly. She whispered condolences, hesitation wrapping around her wrist. But no, there was not a moment to mourn. She had just narrowly begun to comfort herself with metal men, with the living of her new machine friend. The angel was not dead yet, and a Matriarch was encouraged to hunt her prey till the last breath.

The Harlequin

"Matherkin, Mai—Matreearg? Seeve Jewels." Roach's words were nigh impossible to gather into truth. Jeweler dipped the needle once more into his flesh, tugging loose the thread from within. The wound was barely closed, and the pinch of pierced flesh inspired him less and less to seal it. With another pass he leaned himself back, a robust sigh of exhaustion releasing from his lips. The words of his companion rhymed with the spit of his needle. He could translate. Loosely.

"No shit, bug brain. Used'ta know her, actually—old friend." Roach hurried to the mouth of the throne, peering out into the starless sky, past the birth of scaffolding. Cutting loose thread with a nip of his teeth, Jeweler followed loosely, lost in the complexity of the ice and stone.

"Fren no come." Jeweler joined his investment against the doorway, distant cries of the bird-like foe drowning out his words. Staring towards his beastly companion, Jeweler noticed a smoking wound upon Roach's back, embowled with Ichyr, seraphic and true.

"Roach? You okay buddy? There's some godjuice on your back there, stuff is meltin' a damn hole through 'ya." Roach sniffed its own shoulder, hearing the taste of Ichyr close by. It bucked back, scratching at its spine in an effort to remove the substance. Returning the thread and needle to his pack, Jeweler shambled over to the beast, who hissed at his touch and slithered away. "Come on, you moron. Getcha sorry ass over here, I'm tryin' to help." Roach eyed the wounded bartender, his right arm glued to his side with the excessive bandaging. Deciding the burning of the fluid was more hazardous than a friend, Roach slinked over to Jeweler, presenting its shoulder for inspection. Jeweler patted the Ichyr from the wound, even gathering a small pool of melted Ink in his palm, letting it slip around like mercury.

"Itcher hurt." Jeweler was surprised Roach was capable of comprehending one of the divine elements, let alone name it.

"Boy howdy have you been indulgin' in that book of yours. Soon 'nuff you'll be spitting full sentences. Maybe you'll even sing me the a-b-c's." A rumble shook ice particles from the seal of the gate, sprinkling Jeweler's matted hair with chilled dust. The fleeting talons of an Ichyric of grandeur gripped the wooden palisade stacked against the throne, divinity materializing from nothing. Familiar talons to Roach, yet vaguely unknowable to Jeweler. Its leg was daintily rested in a twisted gradient, a rocky bill jutting from its ribcage.

"What teeming impossibility, dispatched *and* dishonored all in one life. Where lies Ink? Through which all nobility is restored, through war in return for thine strife?" Jeweler, stunned by the scheme of speech such an unholy varmint could produce, crept back toward the depths of the lower fortress, out of sight from the angel.

"Roach, *Roach*. Get back from o' there, damn things insane." Roach stared down the opponent, mapping its anatomy with a click of its throat. Jeweler was only recently reawakened. Roach would allow no interruption in his healing. Temptation had taught it nothing. Drawing his pistol in a flash, Jeweler shot clean through the two legs of his beast and caught the fall of its body, tugging it away from the vision of the now-alerted angel. He returned to the stairwell they had emerged from, divinity on his heels. The blindness of the beast heard a shot, the panicked heaves of a fleeing elder, followed by nothing at all. Jeweler slipped between narrow columns, holding soft breaths and restraining those from Roach. The bird followed, silent for its incredible speed. It was speed that led him astray, a plastic barrier he did not fathom rose up against him, and he was brought down promptly. Extending his arms to brace the fall, Jeweler was forced to give up Roach's restless body to the solid stone—himself falling against a pile of powdered snow. Behind the remains of a playpen, Jeweler's thoughts grew to solutions. The beast was undying, as Roach had proven through its earlier attacks and its remaining wounds. The antlers in its skull seemed to depreciate all hope for sight—though it did pursue the Ink and any that had been tainted by it. The bartender knew he had not touched nearly enough Ink to be seen; snow made a good concealer. Roach was far more at risk. The prowling bird rhymed in tandem with its steps, head cocking full around like a sadistic owl snake. With the Larkik Definition, pure Ichyrics were a rare sight to behold, a people resulting from creation itself. They were divine, the thing before Jeweler was not. Between its calls, a path appeared, clear as day. A swift dash in the right direction would save him from the pits of death, but what of Roach? So much

The Harlequin

breath had already been wasted on the beast, the effort taken to keep it hidden and from starvation, to keep it warm when the furnace broke down. There was no sense in wasting the effort now, not to a simple bird. When the bird drew closest to its prey, Jeweler called out in rage, hurling a small memento of the Gretchkin raids upon it—who despite sightless, caught it just the same. Roach took the opportunity to thrust itself atop the bird, knocking it further into the wall, where Jeweler followed with an upward strike to the already cracked beak. The bird flew from the attack, darting between any blow that Roach could cast. The two followed an avenue to freedom, returning to the hall above,

"Silver*wings* is that thing damn quick, right? Ha! 's chase for the ages, 'eh Roach?" The beast regathered its goopy ankles to better perform the task of running. Jeweler supposed he couldn't be far from Viaduct now, but the storm had come upon the open air of the lair, and the bird beast pressured the journey. Weaponless and wrought with exhaustion, Jeweler had little to add to the battle besides his banter, ducking swiping cuts whenever he had the chance. Roach itself could do little against it, considering the Ichyric's penchant for flying far above the mortal reaches of man. From time to time, it would swoop down, as an eagle to its own prey, to make a passing graze at the two. Few had actually hit. From the storm came soft chanting, a call of familiar volume. The Ichyric fell from the heavens, splitting an oak column at its base with sheer weight alone. Jeweler focused upon echoes of shadows in the distance, only narrowly escaping the wrath of the falling pillar. The bird howled, clutching its left shoulder, which oddly appeared to be uninjured. Where its beak lacked a mouth, the Ichyr parted, releasing a slimy and oozing compost of a mouth, fangs forming like baby's teeth through the bile. It spoke like mud,

"Breathless, this form is shaken by thy malice. Harken; I will not so hastily return to God's palace." Jeweler kicked snow into the beast's maw, the cold stinging its murky, unevolved interior. It puffed the stuff out and flew forward from its perch on the cracked stump. Roach crouched beside the troubled tower, and the blinded angel. It endangered Roach's master, its only friend in the storm. It was unacceptable.

"Roach for the last time, get away from the damn thing!"
Roach was not hesitating. It was never an intelligent creature,
however, simple ideas were not outside the bounds of the beast's
mind. It knew well enough that Ichyr could not restrain itself from
Ink, yet it indeed knew Ink neither could defend from Ichyr. The two
were entwined by incredulous spite, all present knew the risks
associated with their contact. But Roach considered the opportunity
too great, and the solution too simple: it would give the beast a bone.

"Birdah!" The bird beast, remaining sightless in the Ichyr,
leered at Roach, sensing the Ink without the need for eyes. It lunged
forward with moronic hate, snapping its teeth at the Ink in its
presence. Roach abused the dull intention, raising its arm in a
defensive manner. An Ichyr-laced chomp cut the hand in two, three
fingers still remaining on its exterior shape. The pull of the cut was
agonizing, and Roach fell back into the snow. It clutched the wound
between its teeth, careful in gait as not to crush the stub, yet the pain
impeded its process. Jeweler rose to stop his beast, but before he could
lay a hand on Roach, the angel threw him back and returned its focus
to the bird. Mind over matter, it fled from arm's length, knowing of
the Inky demise. A coiled harpoon prevented its escape, as Lullaby
called out in victory, desperately begging for the beast to continue.

"Roach, I swear to the Lark, I ain't losing my investment
here!" It turned to Jeweler, struggled with the precision of its joints,
and illuminated a single thumb-like digit from its hand. Like a moth
to a flame, when the maw of the bird beast widened once more, the
Inkling's claw met its tongue. There was little to be done, the flesh
melted at its perceiver, and the beak faded into a sponge-like mess.
Roach clenched its fangs and grasped the beak, the burning of the
Ichyr on its flesh sending writhing pain through its body.

"Die... ickor." The bird slashed at Roach's gut, only two of
these attempts struck skin. The wounds were negligible, the
adrenaline eternal. Roach pinned the creature down, the two
opposites in near-melting death. The drip upon Roach's brow was
undefinable, neither Ink nor sweat. Jeweler grabbed the two shoulders
of the beast and pulled it off the Ichyr mass. Roach went to claw the
restriction but instead met its mind on the shores of the Helium Sea.
The sand dug into Roach's feet, unexpectedly sharp on its heels. The

The Harlequin

moon in the distance glowed with a familiar taste. Everything was ostensibly familiar. Roach observed the foam that rested atop the vast seas. It sank and resurfaced endlessly, a methodical journey it had no control over ending. The buildings in the distance, up the shore hills of dagger sand, rose taller than the clouds could. Some were sharp, others obtuse rectangles of black stone. The faded structures acted as smoke, smog in the cleansing paint of helium. There was no sound, neither wind nor screams. The world was silent. But there was more for Roach to see than just towers and seas, beyond the veil of cloud to the north, lie the untouched remnants of the peaks, a sullen face embedded in their center, the husk of a giant creature only loosely attached to it. How entrancing its eyes did remain open: hollow, cordless vessels lacking thought and reason. Roach did not like its home, as well as its current placement, but it remembered being there long ago. It wished to return there.

"Beautiful, ain't it?" Roach blinked, and the world it yearned for vanished. Even the silence seemed to fade its return into noise. "In a, er, macabre sorta way. You dig?" Jeweler slowly inched his fingers back into his mittens, the coldness of the storm ever increasing. Lullaby rested her spear against the shell, teetering its base from the ground. The Ichyr creature had fled, flown off into the mountains beyond. Its facade remained trapped, however, in the thick coat of double divine—a shell of Ink and Ichyr that acted much like a statue. An expression of one part godly prayer and one part pristine agony was painted upon its beak, dribbling off slowly into chilling ash. Misfortune favored the divine.

"He—heleeom. See?" Jeweler nodded, feigning understanding for the beast. The statue refused to stare back at those who stared at it, and Jeweler himself grew tired of its sight. He retraced his wrist to Roach, who remained coated in Ichyr that burned at the flesh.

"Thanks buddy, good work out there." A clicking followed by hyena-ish laughter disproved the theory. Roach sunk its arms into the snow, cooling the burning inside itself. Ichyr was its own plague. Lullaby presented a scrap of metal, gear locks jutting from the fragment,

"Machine man do not survive. Angel kill." Beyond her was the husk, slumped against a wall and gutted for spare parts. This Viaduct *was* dead, no doubt about it, and Jeweler had seen it true.

"Shucks, that's gonna be a paycheck and a half." Waist in hand, he edged toward the gate, the bellowing of the wind blistering his fingers once more. "I'm mighty done here, 'less you bastards are lookin' to be caught in a storm, let's head out." Frostbitten themselves, the two ferals followed suit, whispering to each other the truths of bound language, and curious incantation.

Startled from the sudden snap to his spine, Viaduct recoiled in his chair, falling clean out its backside. The cable between him and his sightlines had tangled itself in his legs, twisting his ankle back toward his head,

"P-parseque! Parseque immediately, assist me!" The Spyder rushed into the room, fingers aflutter with concept and familiarity. This was a ritual of his, death hurt no less when it wasn't his own — and weak as he was it always unbuckled him from the comfort of youth.

"It's quite alright Viaduct, you are alright." She righted the informant to his upside, still flustered by the fear of death,

"Damnable pigeon, worth none of the effort at all." Parseque smirked, the work of her employer serving as entertainment in the blandness of the Belt.

"I suppose he did not need the assistance?"

"Au contraire; Jeweler is a fool." With a straightening to his collar, Viaduct unplugged his mind from itself, allowing the digits of tomorrow to rest willingly. Though it was an expense unlike any, without any true danger, Viaduct did not worry in the shape of another. It was cathartic, in a way. He was free of the binds of the open world, no longer controlled by what he knew. The felt around his collar was unfurled with wiring, thick HDMI battered his flesh. Flickering pixels on his neon brought sharp jolts to his sensors. "Have — *something* drawn, I wish to visit the Squall." Parseque dashed off to complete the task given to her, leaving Viaduct to the thick envelope on his desk, and his splitting headache. With curtains sealed, and a fire extinguished, he sat alone in the dark, vanished of his prior sin. Had it killed them all? The bird was formidable, but Jeweler was trained in the art of massacre. Perhaps they had taken proper care and fled. Or maybe corpses now littered Gretch territory. Poorly retraced bodies appeared in Viaduct's vision, he could not help but see them on the floors, against bookshelves and statuettes. Two blinks vanished them all, leaving flickers in the informant's sight for a moment. Jeweler was among them, the others named finely as well. Where was the rest of his crew, the privateers of a non-spacefaring vessel? Misery—no—Tragedy? What was it named, the name was something of dread, wasn't it? They took what they could but the patron abandoned the efforts, sold them off too quickly to catch."Parseque..." he mumbled, thoughts of silk like a cold wash upon the senses, memories of bolts and steel, the regular concerns of men dead thirteen times over.

"Yes?" Viaduct shook his neck about, returning to the present day. Buckling the tip of his coat, the informant tapped at his faceplate, brow in-check, and pixels aligned.

"Thank you." With help from his Spyder, he rose, carrying thin white gloves as he left for the door. "That is all now, Parseque. I will return shortly—or you will hear more from me first." Daintily, she added a scarf to the collection of cloth in his arms, sending him neatly down to the door. Viaduct paced by the woodwork, awaiting a chariot but expecting a taxi. If it concealed the snow and misery, it was worth the payment. Patience had once been described as a virtue, but it was more accurately an apothecary of fiction. Between the carriage and the door lay the veil of the exterior, breathless space and compressional pistons. A jingling bell of some kind, Betellio summoned—he felt his skin again. Pale and filled with chill, even with the layers he froze within. Each gear and crankshaft twisted at the tendons, and every chain and spark plug ground away the flesh. Metal wounded man, and from its rise he could not sweat. Oil bubbled from his bloodstream, beating energy filling his core. Viaduct could no longer feel his throat, the length of an incredible feathered hand wrapped around its length. Numbness overtook his steps, and suddenly it was gone. With the door of the delicate carriage sealed, his flesh ceased to function. Shakingly, he removed a glove and saw durasteel. Machinery clicked in tandem with his calmness, and he instead turned to the snow on his boot tips. The stare was so thick, unbreakable, he had not taken thought to the passage of time. Time had been stabbed and gutted in the canals, err present in his confusion.

"Here boss. Should I wait? For you, I mean." Viaduct denied his Spyder, and rested his hand against the blackened windowsill. He could make out snowfall and the Squall. Little else was present in the darkness. "Is that your new friend? The beast?" Before Viaduct had an answer, a thick Inky talon had torn the door from the carriage, and a second pried him unwillingly from its safety. Betellio had no hesitation in leaving the scene, as Viaduct's screams of harsh death rang out as a murmur in the storm. With a wooden crack and metal binding, the informant found himself—still flustered and screaming—in the sticky embrace of a familiar Inkish figure.

"Robar" It slurred, dribbling mundane plaster down its chin. The ghostly stares of both the Matriarch and beast silenced the room, and the slamming of the den door followed.

"Roach! Let 'em go, bastards probably still quaking from the snow." It was true his senses still were thick with phantasm, it was the people he was more concerned with.

"Machine man survive? How?" Jeweler slid a drink down to the seated Matriarch, who continued to question her own vision. Roach had lightly tossed the informant to a chair and observed his master from a distance so as to not stain the drapery.

"How much was the frame? Thing was damn sharp." Viaduct refused to tell, approaching the bar with a stumbling gait. Machines, frames, and robotics obsessed him.

"Thank for help in bird, machine man." The Matriarch uttered. Viaduct twitched, his patience with the Matriarch undergoing similar deterioration as his mind.

"I beseech you Gretchkin, *Viaduct* is my name. Name or not, call me *anything* but machine!" The Matriarch, familiar with the cringe of insult and scolding, sipped her cup calmly, two hands wrapped around its handle. The light music jingling through the room kept the conversation quelled, even Roach's undefinable snarling was sheepishly muted.

"V, come on, she doesn't know much better, though I taught'er myself, so don't know what that says 'bout me." Jeweler

The Harlequin

turned his questioning to the Matriarch, confirming her identity once and for all. Thin blood battered the bartender's thermals, and he walked with a noticeable limp. Questions were at hand, but the concerns of a war well won were unimportant. There were greater curiosities at hand. Viaduct trained his thoughts and sight on the beast before the fire. It was unusual for Viaduct to be left completely in the dark on any subject matter, now marked twice by both Jeweler and the vile creature.

"Yes, lovely reunion—it *is* an Inkling, yes?" Jeweler hesitated insult, perhaps reprimanding the profane words, but why? Roach was correctly identified as an Inkling, and was little more than merchandise, why care for such thoughts?

"Yep, nothin' too special though, practically a Belt Pup, claws and bites the damn sofa like one too." Roach rose from its rest, and curled about, muttering words that even if spoken at full volume, would likely be confusing and vague.

"How adorable." Viaduct concluded mockingly.

"I know right? Cute as hell."

"Handsome." The two turned to Lullaby, who remained seated atop the bar, her taloned toes stretching in the faint chill of the air. Purple blush covered her beak, whether from drunkenness or embarrassment was uncertain. Jokes were thrown on the subject, but the Matriarch held no reaction to humor. Viaduct thought it best to venture into questioning, jolly-themed analysis to better his footing. Despite his minimal involvement, Jeweler found the laughing suitable and excused himself from the conversation. He returned to the den, leaving a wandering glance to Roach in his exit. It contented itself among flame, occasionally letting hyenas control its lips. A family of sorts brewed between them all, one Jeweler had not predicted to ever have. Sealing the door behind himself, the bartender settled against his bedside, where the cracked remains of the mask lingered. Before him it appeared redundant and weaved, the threads of reality bending and bouncing around its shards.

"Oh kid, you're really doin' it to me." He chuckled to himself, leaving the excuse of his exhaustion to wounds, "I'm not that old, am I?" The mask did not respond, even its eyes did not speak. Jeweler knew it couldn't, it never had—nor could he. Sorrow filled the atmosphere of his bedside as the bartender bit harder into his cheek. He had seen much hardship here, the Belt brought memories he once thought avoidable and buried. Maybe, for all his destruction and concealment, the solution was outwards. A result of the circumstances, both he and the Inkling had found some mystery to pursue. It lay on the stovetop, the sealed ticket to a world beyond the agony of the Imperial Belt. Reflecting the fire—which still burned faint blue in the air of chill—the stone remained, colored and with the stars. The thought of it consumed him, the past and everything with it. He had forsworn Shorerunning, he had set up the bar, cut his contacts. If it left him, he would be forced to leave it. Still, he retained a link to the world before—still, he quelled on the patterns of vengeance. Jeweler took the mask in his hands.

"Sorry kid. I really am." He thought of Roach. It was more than he could ask for, merchandise he could no longer afford to lose. It was something important, it—*he* was beyond the value of anything else Jeweler owned. He couldn't let the mask get in the way. With a crying sigh, Jeweler crushed the remaining fibers in the wood, shattering the mask to bits. Quickly, before he could even look at its pieces, Jeweler approached the fading blue cinders and tossed the pieces in. Sitting back from the murder, the bartender held his chin in his hands, shaking violently. This was it. The rise of Maen's Grave was nigh, but Jeweler could only see the moon through his tears. He wept, knowing they would all hear. Knowing he could trust them not to care. Neither Viaduct nor Lullaby heard the sounds. Their conversation continued into the day, and eventually, when the bartender left his den, they invited him to join. There were no stains left on his face, no emotions left to change. He was Jeweler, and all the same, he was lost.

Overlooking the grim ice, Pherock sneezed in outlets of feathers. A Gretchkin male stood among bodies of his people, spear stuck against hard rock. With a harsh shriek, it slumped against the organs of his mother and buried its beak. Foil was his name, and his family was bespoke of true monsters. He voiced his disrespect for the claims of his fault, the blame he did not deserve. Pherock thought the display pious, the Gretchkin were monsters as much as any Inkling to her. It was the pursuit of such a beast that had brought her to the post of men; the gore looked to be Jeweler's work, after all, he had provided larger displays of bludgeoning. Foil shook his hands against the husk of his mother, cracking the Ichyr that coated her clear.

"Jeweled One! Jewels or do not, Jewel must die!" He took up his arms and peered over his Matriarchs. "I Matron now, new order: Kill Jeweled One!" an uproar of courage shook the camp. The rage followed only for a moment when Foil dismissed himself from the entourage. Alone, he lamented. In the pits of snow, he wept for his family estranged. In the thralls of this sorrow was he visited by one most divine. A fluttering beam, thought by Pherock to be one of her masters, emerged from the stars, wings clashed with oozing darkness.

"You bear no card to your name, child." The voice was smooth as silk, though there were no lips to utter the speech. Foil presumed it to be without them, or further divine. Pherock had never seen such a figure.

"God? God of birds?" The brazen figure bloomed directly through the dark and cold of the storms, reminding Foil of the womb it had been born of.

"Shallow is your heart for rage. Do not hate, instead love to love. Love this foe, and we will destroy them with the romance from the Old Man." Foil twitched, spite shaking his throat by the veins. Pherock looked on in frigid curiosity.

"Love? Jeweled One kill everything. Jeweled One must die!" The deity moved forward, lifting Foil's feathery gullet with a golden hand.

"Nay lover. The Old Man adores you and all of your kind. Let us meet this foe of yours with his love, and we shall be blessed. Let us kill this 'Jeweled One' together, with the love of The Old Man." Despite the loathing he felt, Foil could not but yearn for the acceptance of his enemies. It was love that drove him to find Lullaby at first. This god would lead him there with ease. Pherock had retread her path, words to her commander aflutter with havoc and concern, a god among the Gretchkin.

"God. I will do." The brass one smiled, though it was not present on the lustered face.

"Good, child. Let Centamoore guide you to light. To the Old Man."

~Like a Fish in a Birdcage

The secondary result of my only meeting
with the legendary Sixfingers...

Not unlike the rainfall present days prior, molten wax would occasionally spatter down from the chandeliers of the main court. It was no threat to life for Tetarien peoples, and certainly did not rouse the immediate (valuable) presence of the royal family, but it *did* irritate the humble prince Sivi'ks. Though it was abysmally hot, the wax would cool and soften the fraction of a second it struck the purple twine carpet, pooling into a soft wad of gum-like muck. It stuck to the very essence of the soul and refused to loosen with nothing short of atomic warfare. Sivi'ks had rested his less-than-weary cranium against the palace wall, beside the civil armaments of display. The sovereign goodness of the metal shone in the candlelight — the very candlelight that dripped boiled wax to the centerpiece of the wool of the floor. Sivi'ks was no comedian, he had passed the age of merger trolls. But the observation of bounding servants clipping their feet in waxen puddles was beyond entertaining; there was not much else to do besides. As another servant gasped against the singe of wax, Sivi'ks leered up at the majestic metalwork of the chandeliers. In all fairness — the prince thought — for what reason had the chandeliers been installed in the first place? The palace sat atop a practical ember, a broiling lump of flax so purely heated by the awe of the sun, Sivi'ks' feet had scarred over from walking upon its surfaces. The sun itself, though indeed temporary, was perched in the sky for the majority of the cycle of night and day. A night on Cew lasted no longer than an hour, what point was there in fanciful lighting? And what's more, the existence of Lather columns negated any purpose at all! Those pools, from the northern maw of Mount Velabix, were the most brilliant hue of cyan, they ate up the sun of the day, and shed it off in the shortness of night. Columns, as tall as the court itself, drew the stuff right from the tap, pumped through the lower reaches of the palace about and up to the throne room. It was intricate—besides being completely unnecessary—and rationally pretty. At night, however, one could barely catch the light in their eye; the damnable chandeliers choked it out, like a cancerous rodent. The next servant to touch the wax was so overtaken with shock they leaped from the puddle, nearly collapsing against a statuette of Ozzard the Emeraldette, smudged fingerprints cut down her chest. Sivi'ks retained a laugh. So...truly, what was the point in having the lights on all the damn time? Was it some effort to displease the prince? Or perhaps the hard-of-sight father sitting across the throne would nary complete a task in its absence? The stewards had no insight, and Terix was all too busy. All of this conundrum to the odds of wax on the sole (the prince would never accept the footwear of the royals). It was half past the time dinner was to be served, and Sivi'ks had no desire to eat. He had but three days remaining upon his home world before his return to the navy, not something he was generally displeased with, but the absence of his brother nerved him. There were sob stories about Cew, floating amidst the tales of perfection, of these siblings of abhorrence. There were legends of brothers just like the two princes who would greed over each other, spill blood not for the charity of another, but for their downfall. Sivi'ks thought these to be horror stories with the intention of fear-mongering Tetarien children into a state of understanding alongside their siblings. Terror was *always* a lovely tool, so the king thought. This worried Sivi'ks, who at one time was capable of sheltering his brother through every decree of his royal ineptitude, father. That was no longer the case. The Royal Flight Academy kept the prince in the stars, which in spite of Sivi'ks' desire to see his brother, he did enjoy. Terix was never one to break the mold, if the line was set for him, he would spend a lifetime carefully balancing behind it, terrified of what could lie beyond it. It certainly wasn't any fault of his, Terix was indifferent to the world outside the palace. If there were moon-eating leviathans he would surely rather not know.

There were, of course, moon-eating leviathans. Sivi'ks had even seen one. Perhaps two, if he could count his own father as a leviathan, his weight was deserving of such a title. Sivi'ks' mother had once called him 'unbiasedly cruel', which at the time had upset him sorely, but had grown to be an obvious compliment. But he did disagree with it at times, those who would deserve his discontent often were dealt an extra handful of the stuff. The King got the most of it, nose-bleeds, pantsings of calamitous magnitude, sundered greaves and muddied galoshes. Sivi'ks could not refrain from an audible chuckle at the teeming nothingness. A passing maid covered their origlyph as they hurried by, ignorant and hasteful enough to stomp directly in the center mass of a waxy lake. Sivi'ks dramatically bowed, the maid scoffing and burning like copper. Now that it had come to mind, the King had neglected to even request the presence of his son, the Pilot! Not that Sivi'ks particularly minded, there was a clear relationship set between the two: no father of his had time for a failure. If he had been the best pilot in the stars he would be afforded no invitations back to Cew, nor would he be welcome in the palace. Sivi'ks began to debate whether he was even intended to be within the palace walls at all. A groan was released from the pent lips of a servant, who like all the rest found their toes properly waxed. When they were children—the two princes—there was always mischief to be made, it was their very favorite dessert. If there was anything to solve a thousand problems at once, it would be mischief! Sivi'ks recalled a time, once, when the fury of the king reached even the ever-loved Terix. 'Twas a sight to be seen, though not one he relished in the slightest. There was an unspoken right, as the youngest brother, to harden for the blows from father; Terix would make a terrible politician scarred and burned, and Sivi'ks would make an excellent war hero with those very same ailments. On the third day of the Glimmer festivities, the two princes snuck under the temporary cover of night. It had gone wonderfully, if Sivi'ks recalled, their prize the long sought-after Emeraldette Initiation Dagger, hidden away by the priests of Velabix. Terix had negotiated a sort of ceasefire between the princehood and priesthood, ironically with the difficulty of Sivi'ks ever-present—he had done unspeakable things to the nunnery. Either or, the dagger was chief, and the two had worked tirelessly to acquire it. The adult figures of the church were ducky with the temporary relocation of their priceless artifact. It was darling dad that had such a fit over the whole ordeal, really. Terix had wanted such a tool as much as he, and what followed was a frivolous three months under constant surveillance, what joy! To go back to the days of youthful jabs, even the mindset of such chaos still lingered in Sivi'ks. With this, he could come down to the worst of ideas, his pranks could end wars surely. Oh to think of the things he could do, bind the King to his bed, send Terix rolling down a tar bed... what couldn't fix his mellow temper? What couldn't...

After Sivi'ks left, things went downhill. Mother fell ill, Sivi'ks cared not—rather, he did not know. Terix had made special plans to keep the horrid misery of his own mother's sickness away from the poor prince's mind. The last time similar news reached him, there was metaphorical blood on the main-road stones. The death of their uncle was detrimental to his sanity, Terix thought. Besides, the disease was temporary, and his mother would soon be in condition enough to run the family herself, a saving grace from his father's secure grip on sanctity. He had been more tense than usual, events alike had converged to make that so. It was the Lark who was to blame, a figure of resolute power, or so he would claim. In the galaxy, there was a chain of things, a hierarchy of peoples. The Lark had invaded this chain and chipped down its links, worn them to absolute purity. At first, it was beneficial, certainly for the royals of Cew, but things had gotten out of hand. Struggles had broken out, protests against Larkik troops, and violent sieges on Larkik territory. It was not like his father to cry—and Terix would never admit it—but he had seen the King emotional one night, just after the day of the Larkik Ambassador. Terix had never seen a soul so filled with grief, confusion... desperation. It was humbling to see an icon of strength and brutality such as his father wallow in such hopelessness. Before the Ambassador, the Lark had been brief: *I am god, I have created all that exists, I intend to work for our unified contentment, and none of us shall struggle.* At least, that is what he was said to have told the Tetariens. Father did have a tendency to escalate problems. The day of the Ambassador was also the predicted eve of a Scoria attack, devils from outside the meteor ring who sought territory and pain, and there had been a confusion of vessels.... Needless to say, King Aunbrax had a day of complete damage control, with a god no less. All peoples had struggled that day, torn apart by the chaos brought down by the Lark. He meant well, Terix was sure. He had even met the figure, divinely calm for what he was. It was Sivi'ks, however, who had struggled most that day. He had many taken from him, many he cherished as much as he did Terix. Sivi'ks had done what he did best—scheme—and let loose even worse demons than before. They say he spilled Glimmer wine on the Lark's toga. The Larkik Definition had been prevalent enough for them to be considered a fruitful threat before, and after the day this placement was only ever more enforced. They had sent legionaries and what they called 'Pelicans' in the past, in efforts to continue the peace. But these offerings had always been met with disgrace from the King, his father. Aunbrax did not care for the contusions of a dilapidated pity god. But there was no choice. The Lark was god, what else was there to do but nod and claim "Sir, we do vow never to assault your drycleaning again." Terix thought it a good enough job, the acceptance, and appeasement of a literal divine creator. He really had few disagreements with the King's conniptions (aside from the policies of the Glass Garden, those he detested) everything being equal. Terix had a voice on the court as much as Aunbrax did, but that voice was pitifully dull, and abysmally uninterested too. Though he had told his brother otherwise, the court did not interest him so phantasmagorically—politics were shady in nature for the six bureaus. Mindlessness aside, Terix did what he did for signs far more complex than brotherly love; it was policy in the Tetrik royal family to have at least a prince or princess of heir on the court. Ironic was it that Terix had such a tendency to choose his own misery, something his brother and mother had protected him from. The garden sullied his memory and made things seem like the old days of childhood. Responsibility was a conscious decision. Terix had, as his father worded it, 'Chosen wisely'. It bothered him greatly that the King babied him so, Sivi'ks' catastrophes were never tolerated, he had been whipped and scolded and spanked to eternity. There was a certain irony in the reversal of roles, as children Sivi'ks would stop at nothing to defend his older brother Terix, but now the role of defender fell to Terix, who to be fair was not terribly skilled in the art of protection. Of course, Sivi'ks remained the stronger of the two, the navy would certainly give him the advantage in that. If any true words lingered in his brother's mouth for long, it was those pertaining to the stars. The royal garden gave a wondrous view of the stars, even through the cutting blindness of daylight, they were pure orbs of blue and white, brilliant against a backdrop of purple. Terix wondered what he would do if he was among them, if he had gone the route of Sivi'ks. If he had followed his dream.

"Prince Terix, would you kindly come with me?" The prince shooed off the servant, having just desperately aligned himself against the fence in such a way he could see the stars but not the garden fissure. The corpse of Nelej—the intruder, rather—was still abound there, however deep it may be. The two had not told anyone of the princess' death, nor of the intruder and its undesirable consequences (those being the death of a royal, the *sexual assault* of a royal, and the damaging of mom's precious candelabra, minted silver from one of the various Glimmer Season gather stalls). Terrifying of all was the idea that one could simply accept the reality of the situation. After all, Terix had murdered his cousin in cold blood! How could Sivi'ks just stroll by that notion, surely he was mourning too? He always held a certain charm for mischief during his moments of despair, much like when the two had committed their greatest heist, one Terix still was rather proud of. The Emeraldette Dagger had, reasonably, been given to them more than it had been stolen, but the illusion of thievery was exactly what the two princes sought. In hindsight, the priests had been rather clever with their games, sating the lust for crime and losing nothing at all. It was memories like these that the good prince Terix valued above all, those where his brother was still a brother, instead of some parasite the King deemed too grotesque to let into the palace gates. He pondered Sivi'ks' location, supposedly out and about the village floor, searching for tricks to pull on any who would be weak enough to suffer them. A crunch of leaves, followed by a hissing request of silence interrupted the prince's thoughts,

"I assure you, good prince, you will be attending us tonight." Before Terix had a moment to turn his head and request elaboration, he had his origlyph draped in silk, and his arms had been tugged from their joints. Terix stifled a choking scream, but whoever had their hands wrapped around his princely collar was doing an excellent job of making sure he kept quiet. The last thing he heard before losing consciousness completely was the utterance of commands, quick and simple,

"Yes, perfect! Drag him over the fissure — they're waiting, we have to move!"

Mother had been kidnapped once. An old group of anti-royalists was found responsible, parodying the honor of the elite royal guards — the Sapphirians. They had existed since the first war, the first king. There were always contrarians, it was the nature of freedom, always terrorists too. But there was always just cause, and saviors from that despicable fate. When his mother returned, Terix found a new hatred for people he had never met. Uncle had told him bluntly,

"Do not shape your entourage like a pen; it will quickly fill with nothing but sheep." Of course, then he had playfully mocked the prince's pursed lips, calling off the advice as nothing but 'elder tomfoolery'. Terix had taken it to heart. People did have a tendency to surprise him, regardless of origin. Surely the Sapphirians were responsible for his capture, who else would plot against the royal family? A crooked turn spun Terix out of his entangled position, slamming the back of his head against a wooden frame, Sapphirians would certainly be so reckless as to let their tempting bribe sustain any kind of harm. Though there was knowledge in the fall, the frame was accompanied partly by cushion, smelling of the deserts north. The scent was undoubtedly sandsilk, or some variation, and a material used solely within royal vessels. At least the terrorists had the courtesy to procure a royal carriage for his highness. There was some respect in the act, Uncle always was so bright.

"We're about the way, a few minutes out. Has our prince been cordial and curt?" The rascals had the audacity to treat the prince as though he was a toy, and product of the royal family! Terix always thought himself more than a book hand,

"Father always did tell me to be so. Though I suppose I've failed in the bowing section of things. Would you do me the service of untying me so I may—" A knock came against the prince's back, though the bag around his head kept its user much too hidden. It was the assumption of Terix that the goons had covered themselves in leaves and skins, so primitive was a bag as hindrance for sight. A

The Harlequin

blindfold, perhaps simple anti-glyphant medication, if they had the sponsorship to afford it.

"Hush—where's the Appraiser? He *said* he'd meet us there, give us directions to the..." The voice trailed off to silence, a shifting of leather beckoned for Terix's response.

"Is there something in my teeth, fellows?" The carriage shook once more and came to a complete stop.

"You must be having a gaff, Carrow said nothing of the depths!"

"I didn't sanction this! Where is that bloody Appraiser?" A rush of air matted the bag against Terix's faceplate, choking his words. Silence wafted like the plague through the vehicle, murmurs of succession hissed to a stop. The rumbling of the carriage wheels began again, this time with far less vigor than before.

"Little prince, oh little prince Terix. What lies at the depths of Cruth?" The voice paused, scrutinizing its tone against its own breath. It was fanciful, an archaic luster like a child deepening its own call for threats and demands. Terix sighed, itching the back of his head against the soft wooden frame of his seat,

"You sound like a cave worm, brother. Take the bag off my head."

"It was entertaining for a while, was it?"

"Slightly. Come on now." Sivi'ks tore the sack from his brother's head, the glow of a Latherlight nearly drew him back into unconsciousness. Sivi'ks snickered at the result, as Terix clapped him upside the head,

"Are you mad? Taking me from the palace like this; father will be implacable!" Sivi'ks' patted the sole of his boot against the carriage carpet.

"Nonsense! I did this for us, a... a sort of *vacation*, brother! You spent so much of my visit croaked with labor, that court has become your—"

"Enough! You had my thoughts abound with Sapphirians! I've told you once, I much like my court! We can spend our time in the Garden, as much as you would care to!" Sivi'ks' foot heightened in quickness, tucking a valiant-blue handkerchief into his shoe neck by the second.

"Well, I've always had friends of the old cities in the Sapphirians, you know that Terix..." Terix, bound by disgrace more than anger, scolded his brother, spouting of father's accords, father's rules. Sivi'ks thought his brother had become much too alike him in the past year, father. It was a tempting time to make a comparison, but Sivi'ks bit his tongue. It was irresponsible of him, of course, to recruit his past accomplices and their terrorist organization to kidnap his brother. However, there were so few opportunities to speak with Terix, and a crime of childish manner seemed appropriate. At the time, that is.

"I'm sorry." Sivi'ks muttered, his foot seeming to settle to a pause. In a moment, it kicked up again, the padding of the carpet beneath his foot sorely dampening the sound. "I—I've wanted to see you—always working—we are set for a wondrous place, brother. I'm certain you'll appreciate the venture!"

"Oh sure." Terix scoffed, adjusting the dusted and misplaced waves of his coat, "I had nothing important lined up for today anyways." The two brothers leered at each other, lacking ill intent or hatred, but not fully invested in the other's spirit. The two Sapphirians in the carriage remained silent, their blue crystalline masks radiating reflected Latherlight. When his brother did not waver, Terix gave up on the stare, turning to the window of the carriage, lavishing in the distant quiet light of the sun. In the darkness of the hour of night, there was no moon to illuminate the sable. Only the creeping strands of the sun reached the eyes of the lonely night watch, and Terix did love the complexion it gave the golden skin of his people. It had only just come upon him that night had fallen.

"Sivi'ks, have I been resting so long that night has come upon us? It was barely noon when I went out to the garden!" Sivi'ks gave a look of bewilderment to his brother, glancing partly to the world outside the carriage.

"It is not night brother, we are merely not upon the surface world." With a scheming grin, Sivi'ks mimicked the cancerous laugh of their uncle, who at one point had the chortle of an ungrateful villain.

"Oh disgusting, Sivi'ks. Furthermore, why are we under the streets of Cruth? You'd said you were taking us to a place of beauty."

The Harlequin

"I am." Terix swallowed his pride for a moment, his spine tightening with worry. There was no beauty in the deep, not any that Terix recalled. It had been a long while since the two had been below Cruth, no circumstances had required it. It seemed like ages ago since the two had last left the palace at all, after the—silence overtook Terix's mind, he had no desire to think of those days, near death cut them both. *He should have died* Terix thought, his origlyph shuddering with use.

"Terix you look awful. What're you doing to yourself, over there?" With a blink, the good prince returned to his manners, thick clouds of confusion dusting snows of nostalgia over his brow.

"Nothing. I was—deep in thought, is all." Sivi'ks frowned in a characteristically moronic way, his expression like that of a renaissance jester. It was amusing to some degree, Sivi'ks was always amusing to some degree.

"We *must* be approaching our spot, right driver?" Knocking against the wood, Sivi'ks called out slurs to his sapphire comrades. Terix wondered how much of the Sapphirian mindset had rubbed off on his brother. Sivi'ks was, after all, incredibly impressionable. It was not unlike him to gather a twig and observe a common guard's weapon, and he brandished it suddenly as such too. Father had hollered at him countless times for striking up duels with the Emeraldettes; Sivi'ks had always wanted to venture. The litigious nature of the royal family brought about great complexities to the desires of Sivi'ks. When he had met with the machine of the isles, it was only just for him to be driven to the skies.

"I'm sure we will be present shortly. While we go, brother, would you mind telling me of this buried wonder?" Sivi'ks reared around, nearly decking Terix across the chin with the spear he now held, possibly taken from the driver of the carriage.

"Hmm? The garden, yes. No—I mean no, I refuse to give you any kind of information on it." He paused for a moment, now aware of the spear in his hands. "Bite me." It was Terix's turn to snicker, the length of the tool and the motions Sivi'ks made to dispose of it (stuffing it out the window simply ran it against the cave walls) were more than entertaining. Terix felt himself relax for a moment despite the intention prior to doing no such thing in the presence of his brother.

"I'll admit, I did need... something of a vacation. Haven't been outside the palace in such a time. I hope this garden is as restful as ours is."

"More like rest*less*. You should have remembered it by now, brother!" As the tunnel carved itself open, the carriage came to a halt, glimmering white light filled the reaches of the cave wall, as a Sapphirian dimmed the glow of the Latherlight.

"Here, Sivi'ks. Get the hell out." Sivi'ks nodded to the Sapphirian, tossing a small red tool to the fellow, one with the royal crest tangled around it.

"Remember, use it once and throw it away. You use it twice? I'll know. Sivi'ks clambered over the other terrorists, extending a hand for Terix as he reached the carriage exit.

"So is this the deep garden? So lovely it befits a royal heirloom?" The two brothers narrowly fit through the carriage door, its drivers slowly turning the vehicle around, directing the golems at its front to the opposition of the light.

"Seemed appropriate, they had to klep you from our garden, after all." The two marched through mud with a black taint about it. There was a distinguishing odor about the fluid, but it stopped before the cherished remains of a silver gate. It was embellished with pure god rock, the very material that the temples of Velabix had been constructed from. The Lark called it Ichyr, once. It built an impressive vault, a door squared off with two columns of emerald, adorned with small seals of gold and silver. The whole of the structure was oddly tilted as if it had not been designed with this entrance in its current fashion, like it had fallen to the depths, rather than made for them. Examining the fantasy, Terix questioned,

"Sivi'ks. This is beyond sacred, where have you taken us?" Sivi'ks pushed past his brother, brandishing a small royal key, an exact copy resting in Terix's domicile guarded by tin.

"See yourself, what grandeur we have sealed away!" Sivi'ks pushed open the door, with no great ease, and entered the 'garden'. Terix looked back to the Sapphirians, who had stopped the carriage, and exited its safety. It would appear Sivi'ks had hired them for more than an escort. Despite the concern, Terix followed his brother; better to lie in the garden than in a tunnel of bandits. When entering the door, a great calm resonated unto Terix, a peace he was familiar with, and had easily driven his vessel through his early life. There was quiet humming, the sound of windchimes floated in the breeze, and light from unknown crevices poked into the grass—a bright reddish hue, contrasting the deep purple of the mainland. A great tear in the sky broke the golden stone in two, scarcely providing any light of its own. Sivi'ks had already slipped beyond the veil of cave and stone, further into the garden, where silver roots spun around the thick cyan pools of Lather, soaking up the light itself.

"S—Sivi'ks..." Terix was speechless, for a moment he could not recognize the beauty. It was when the first pyre of glass came into view that he was reminded, it towered effortlessly into the sky, and pure milk flowed within. The glass grew most everywhere, overtaking the trees with its translucent nature—the roses sprouted with mirror petals, and the decaying remains of ancient golems lay buried and impaled by the spikes.

"Wondrous, isn't it?" Terix stepped back from the Lather, chaos running through his mind like a poison, the glass reflected endless light on the ruins of the old cities, the people long before the Tetariens. Goodly blue moss spathed the crystals dangling from the garden sky, and the inflorescence of mirror roses reflected the Lather-like skylight.

"*Sivi'ks!*" Beckoned by his name, Sivi'ks turned to his brother. A smug grin covered his face, as well as droplets of fresh Lather, still dripping from the tree leaves.

"You summoned?" Terix shook his head, and the astonished calls of the Sapphirians echoed behind him.

"The *Glass* Garden? You knew of this? And you took *them* here! How blisteringly—" Terix was overwhelmed with emotion. The memories of his youth, of *their* youth, its beauty, and shared wonder. But also the Black Tide, its consequences, and the reason the Glass Garden had been lost in the first place. The things father would say....

"Sure, it was a trade-off. They assured me—as friends—they would do nothing of it, not the slight of hostaging! I made sure of this all, you see. I thought it out meticulously like you said I should."

"Clearly not, you *clearly* did no such thing. This is not royal territory so much as it is *godly* land. This is a place that should have remained—remained ensconced! This is blasphemy."

"This is a *gift* brother! It is as beautiful as the day we lost it."

"As the day The Black Tide took it! You are a work of spectacle, Sivi'ks." The pilot tensed his jaw, the lower echelons of his faceplate folded up, giving the illusion of sorrow.

"Can't you let it be." Terix stomped back the pebbles of glass, fury driving his hand,

"Oh let it be, let it *be*, you think me an accomplice to all your crimes. I loved the emerald dagger as much as you did, I loathed the punishment even worse, surely! But how, how Sivi'ks, does it excuse this? This—You have lost your mind." Sivi'ks, torn between love and spite, looked back to his brother, petulance in his voice,

"My mind? It's sound, the Academy required it! I think you are peeling old fruit, Terix. I have no mind to be maddened now, I just wanted to impress my brother, and give him peace from the past. But you bring The Black Tide into this, always do—" Terix bit his cheek with haste, quickly interrupting his brother's slow tirade.

"I do! I do because it *mattered*, to all of Cew it mattered. All but you. You seem to have forgotten what was lost!" Sivi'ks' origlyph flinched at the word—lost—trembling with emotion.

"Always so pessimistic brother, remember what was done? We contributed great things, we brought about the end of the plague, we killed The Black Tide alongside him! He saved—"

"He died, Sivi'ks!" Even the Sapphirians fell mute. Even the trees ceased to waver. Even the chimes stopped their ring. Terix slowed his breathing, anger would not control his voice, "He died for *nothing*. You nearly did too." Sivi'ks fell against the bark of a silverwood tree, letting his leg start to stamp again. "Sometimes I wonder if you did."

"He did not die in vain. We never saw the body." Terix approached his brother, lightly leaping over the streams of Lather.

"We did not need to. The temples are in ruin; none of the Enlightened remain. Mount Velabix has been sequestered for years." Sivi'ks knew his brother to be reasonable, but it was difficult to admit heroes could fall. Sivi'ks had always wanted to be one.

The Harlequin

"I suppose you are correct. But that does not change the matter of his sacrifice." Terix slipped down beside his brother, the Sapphirians gathered in a circle, sharing stories of the Black Tide in grotesque detail. "He saved me, after all. Was that not worth his death, to you?" Terix's still origlyph curved up into pleasure, a lightened mood brought better discourse, his uncle had always said.

"Yes, most worthy. It was always worth your life. I am glad you remain here." Sivi'ks took great pleasure in his mastery of manipulation—even if it was unintentional—he always had that younger charm.

"I am not so convinced I *will* remain. That is why I brought you here. Why I wanted so desperately to spend this short visit with you." Terix adjusted the tailcoats behind his legs, shortening them with soft pats.

"Sivi'ks. What are you saying?"

"I just—you always are working, slaving in the court, and sleeping through the afternoon. I understand you are busy but too busy for me? I thought brothers always made time."

"Inconsequential, I'd attend you if I could, but father—"

"Why do you let him puppet you brother! Father is but a dad and nothing more. He may be King, but you are a prince! Let him order you no longer." Terix was growing spiteful again, Sivi'ks having lost his course of tongue,

"Oh you know nothing of father. He is cruel but not to us, brother. You drag me into this pool of sorrow for you, and use it again to try and hook me from my duty, my *ordained* right to the throne, to the people of Cew!" Sivi'ks held his breath, the concluding paperwork for a more permanent departure lingering in his shawl.

"I—don't know how to say the things I want to without spite. He seems to me a tyrant over you. But you're so willing to be a servant boy. I don't understand." Terix groaned, twisted his faceplate from its weariness,

"Sivi'ks you think everyone must be like you. Your one flaw is selfishness." Sivi'ks was rightfully finished with his brother's ramblings, Terix could be cruel as father if he so chose. Looking to the sky, Sivi'ks let out a childish moan,

"I am *not* selfish, I know people want things, is all. I know better than anyone the concept of dreamery. You had dreams Terix, didn't you?"

"My dreams are irrelevant. Why can you not ignore me and my ways and quest to the stars? Have you not enough time for me when—" Sivi'ks pushed his brother back, covering his mouth with his mit,

"I am going to war! The Academy requires it, four years of war for my manuscript." The folded draft in his shawl slipped to the grass, open and branded. "It won't be long…"

"War. Against…?" Terix paused, sure of the answer already. Tetariens were nothing if not peaceful—were it not for the cancer that was Scoria. A race of plasmid brutes, encased in iron Potbellys and filled to the learned mind with nothing but hate. If there was war with anyone, it was surely with them.

"Yes. I'm not so sure I'll return."

"Don't speak like that. You are an excellent fighter, I know that much." Sivi'ks smiled at this, his hand drifting to the shoulder of his brother.

"Who is to say I am excellent enough?" He scoffed, regretting the mention of his war at all.

"Can you not request a pardon from father? Perhaps I can—"

"Absolutely not, Terix. I've told you before, this is my dream and I must follow it myself. I do not wish to be the bored prince to others, but a fair and noble pilot. I wish to forge my own path, without the strength of circumstance." Terix nodded, accepting, though desperate to make an excuse for the issue of starflight. He had no idea Sivi'ks was so close to death once more, and yet he had spent his days in the court alone. Something golden caught Sivi'ks' eye, as Terix rambled on he couldn't help but stare at it. A pike of glass had turned gray, its interior flowing with some other substance, not of white purity. Suddenly, a metallic clash erupted from the ground, a blur of tarnished gold had fallen from above, and it did much to stop the chaos. The good prince's curses were brought to null when he noticed his brother's gaze, fixed on the husk of a Tetarien, mounted promptly before them.

"Sivi'ks, is that?"

The Harlequin

"I'm astounded it ended up here. Has the fissure always led to the Glass Garden?" The two brothers observed as the black muck from within the glass began to dribble, pouring itself outward unto the vibrant grass, bringing to a yellow decay in an instant. Taphurrah's bludgeoned and misshapen form lie twisted around the pike of glass, the blood from Nelej's body dried and crusty. It was a despicable sight. Terix would puke if he had not already immunized himself from the death of his cousin. There was something far worse about the corpse than its gore, however. Its arms had been bitten through by the black mulch, tendrils of dark animated its flux, and the origlyph seemed to glow again—as if it was still seeking their love.

"Those vessels, its origlyph is too lively for a corpse. Sivi'ks, I'd much like to leave now." At the mention of the absence of Terix, the corpse fell forwards, its faceplate dislodged from the rest of the corpse, a head of golden bones. Soon, as the darkness pooled at the behest of the vessel, sable tendrils sought out the limbs, binding them together and sealing their compliance. Terix stood from his rest, deliberately increasing the distance between the dark and himself. Sivi'ks followed suit, though he did dance around the void, making his way between the Sapphirians and glass. A coup of darkness, Terix thought, would work nicely. When all but the ankles had been reformed, Taphurrah looked somberly up towards Terix, red flame compounded from within his origlyph, hinges on the cuts like mold, its words coughed out in puffs of chalky gold,

"Love? P-prince Terix?" The inky sludge of a person clambered forward, its joints cracking under the weight of its movement, a corpse in motion. "W-what—What is this? T-Terix?" His words were not malicious, mere figments of confusion and disarray. Sivi'ks handled a small shiv from the cloth around his waist, moving silently behind the monstrous creature. The Sapphirians tore out their armaments, readily stepping closer to Sivi'ks, a flanking maneuver at play.

"You seem to be—well you must be alive again, yes?" Taphurrah looked at his disassembled body, its shortcomings were obvious—he would feel better with clothes.

"It—It hurts, Terix. My love, I can't feel my—" The creature fell forward, what Sivi'ks mistook for an assault. Leaping upon it, he cut at its legs, severing the tendrils from its flesh. Taphurrah called out in pain, its form slumping against the silverwood tree. Quickly it had Terix wrapped in its tendrils, the substance stung at his metallic flesh. Sivi'ks was thrust back from the beast as it bucked, screeching an umbral cry,

"Vestige of *dread*, it hurts me! Those lost in—Terix I can't— Kygen I can see you! Come to us, the world of Flax, Flaxen purity!" Sivi'ks inched away from the tendrils, snaking through the grass and harassing the Sapphirian war party. They took quick glances at the prince, directing Sivi'ks back from the fight. Terix had understood, however, the nuance of the battle. This wasn't what the fiend wanted—not at all. It wanted him alone, a romance like seen in novels.

"Your name, what is your name?" Terix muttered, sloshing ink pouring down his throat, choking his needs.

"I am your true—gahk—love! Taphurrah, I am Taphurrah!" Terix nodded, gesturing longingly to his brother, who remained held against a sprout of Glass.

"Yes, Taphurrah. I need you to calm yourself, there is a worse beast inside—" With a roar like thunder, the creature lurched forward, nearly dropping Terix in the act. As the matter of ebony dripped against Terix's faceplate, he momentarily recognized the scent, something he had bathed in once before.

"Brother—Sivi'ks! This is a beast of the Black Tide! I know it to be true, do you remember? The Glass is its bane! Harvest some, quickly!" Taphurrah carried his love higher from the ground, wrapping its null arms around the prince, cuddling with a fatal grip.

"You! Tide-beast! Put down my brother!" Taphurrah began to moan, but it was misery that emitted from its guts. It seemed as though two minds fought for the power of the body. One seemed far more violent than the other. The bandits and their leader, the prince Sivi'ks, shattered splinters of its mellow form, quick as they would regrow. As Taphurrah lost his control, Terix was hurled against a fragment of Glass, knocking the thoughts from his mind, and the blood from his gut. Both Taphurrah and Sivi'ks let their voices sing in a single phrase,

"*No!*" As the beast fought against itself, Sivi'ks gathered up a pike of glass, and two Sapphirians guarded his pursuit,

"Go, go! You have three seconds at the very best!" Sivi'ks kicked off the bandit's shoulders, clutching the spear in his teeth. He assailed the creature with prods, growing ever closer to its origlyph, now spouting pure raven.

"Be off of me!" It growled, attempting to bat the flea from its climb. Sivi'ks held true, glowering into the origlyph of the damned,

"I don't wish for this, is Terix—Gah! He must be okay!" Sivi'ks glanced at his brother, and back at the foe.

"I am not certain. There is only one way to end this charade, Taphurrah. Let it take you, and I'll return you to hell." Taphurrah struggled for a moment, the shard of glass driven cleanly through his skull. But it was a forsaken battle, not a dance of elegance but a tussle of fools. The beast shrunk to its weight, falling back unto the rivers of Lather, drifting forevermore. Sivi'ks rushed to the side of his brother, who now wore a singular crack across the side of his faceplate.

"I thought they would teach you piloting, in the Academy." He attempted to rise, pushing Sivi'ks down in his efforts. "If this is any statement to your strategy in the stars...." Terix trailed off, the implications of his words set in stone.

"I would—would hope so. Is it dead?" Neither could tell. One of the Sapphirians was coddled between the other two, it would seem injury had not simply targeted the two princes.

"Should you not owe them your care, good pilot Sivi'ks?" The pilot took honor in such a title, Terix had called him something like it after the mess of the Black Tide, Pìleat Beag he had said, the Little Pilot.

"Dead or not—that was certainly the Black Tide. Right as the day it swallowed us, brother. It still infects the planet!" Terix agreed, there was no other conclusion. With this knowledge, there was an ever-important message to the king to be had. Even the Sapphirians knew the severity of the discovery. Terix, though shakily, stood to his two feet, shuddering with every movement. Sivi'ks aided his brother forward, stepping him carefully over the Lather stream below. With a sudden shock of tension, Sivi'ks fell back into the Lather, inky water drifting into his origlyph as he coughed against the tide. A looming singular eye, white as heaven, leered at him from under the deep. It spoke a single sentence before returning to the deep, soundless, and dead,

"May Maccabeus be never free of our pain." Terix was quick to pull his brother from the waves, the two now suitably scarred for the evening. The Sapphirians gathered up their injured, and returned to the carriage, the two princes not far behind.

"I'd like to speak with father about this, you know how wonderful I am with him." Terix could do little but agree, as the carriage began its ascent back to the above ground.

"To be fair," Terix began, rubbing the nubs of his elbows, which felt so sharp with feeling, "This is not much unlike our last adventure. It seems our time with the Mechanical Shepard served *you* well." Sivi'ks chuckled, patting down his torso in search of his report to battle. Its absence did not strike him at the moment, but even if it had, there was no joy in remembering the future of the lost.

Sivi'ks leapt breathlessly across the iron picket, his pace increasing as he twisted against the street lamps. He glanced at the sky, before just as hastily returning to his motion forward. As the steps of the palace splayed out before him, a groan slipped from his mouth, no choice for direction but sky-bound. At the height of the stairs, Sivi'ks slumped over, spreading himself thinly against the palace courtyard, the guards none too interested in his follies.

"Fayiyr, time *please* would you?" The golden-clad Tetarien did not move but glanced at the sun and its descent.

"Quality enough for the guard, it will do for the skies." Sivi'ks would cheer if not for his exhaustion. As he eventually recovered, he thanked Fayiyr and returned to the keep, now prepared for the remainder of his—

"Prince Sivi'ks. The King would have you in the throneroom." A heart he would have stopped if a heart he had. The pilot shrugged off the ponders of dread, and turned to the servant, leaving a gesture of approval before his quick exit. Father had requested him, after nearly a week of his presence in the palace. Had the King even known of his return, or was he just now hearing of it? Was the speech requested of him to be of Ink and battles, or perhaps the discovery of the Glass Garden? Sivi'ks did not know. If there was any preparation to be done, Sivi'ks had done it years prior. He tugged open the court doors, thick with silver and gemstones, regal beyond doubt. In the hall of the throne, there was utter silence. The heat from the external sun did not melt candle wax, but it might have done so had there been wax to melt at all. Instead, it burned a spherical hole through Sivi'ks' head, mixing his thoughts with constant hate, and lyrical misfortune. The opulent carpet-work led neatly against the baseplates of the faux soldiers. The golden armor seemed to drip in the haze of the heat, too much of its reality fading into imagination. Sivi'ks gripped his costume, wondering if his father would be much too disappointed in his Aviator's coat, lengthy and patched with the royal sigil, draped haphazardly against a pair of unwashed royal briefs.

"Pilot." The King boomed, though he was out of view of the prince, his thunder was still ever present. Sivi'ks made his way to the throne, stepping softly as to make little sound.

"Kingly Aunbrax. Are we addressing each other by titles now?" The throne was cleaved in two, its pieces assembled roughly from regal matter, gifts from the Lark. Aunbrax sat curtly across it; he appeared to take no comfort in his place there.

"Do you wish to go by another name?" Sivi'ks croaked, his foot beginning to—momentarily—tap against the golden floors. He ceased immediately.

"Son? Good prince Sivi'ks? My favorite child?" The King was not amused. Neither was Sivi'ks, frankly. It was talks like these that had broken the prince, and his brother too. The expectations and terror emanating directly from the King's origlyph made him so eloquent for his duties, but an awful father. Sivi'ks had never gotten over the fear, as cockeyed as he might seem in public, it was here he dreaded most.

"Pilot will do for the moment. I have a task for you if you would believe me to be true."

"What more would I think of you?"

"Would you hear it or more of your pitiful remarks?" Sivi'ks gripped his thumb, threatening to snap it with the pressure.

"Yes, dearest dad. Tell it to me, and let me do as you—"

"Shut your mouth, boy." Sivi'ks would love to smack his father, at this point. He always reached it but never acted on it. He felt small, or almost refined to a chip. There was no time for bothering.

Furthermore, what was this task? Sivi'ks had been asked *once* for his hand in the affairs of the royal family. He had disappointed and never been requested of again. To think, it could be of the Black Tide, or the Glass Gardens, or worse—his brother! "I am tasked with temporary settlements with the Sapphirians. Though it is a wisened occasion, I think this is a moment where your arrogance would suit us. I ask you to go in my place, Pilot." Sivi'ks knew several of the Sapphirians well enough; a childhood of trouble crafting and plot-brewing brought like figures together. When the collective split, Terix made a point of dissociating with those he once knew, keen on refusing the past of his enjoyable side. Sivi'ks did not blame the good prince, nor did the Sapphirians. They viewed Terix as more of a man on the inside than a threat or royal sympathizer. Much like Sivi'ks, it was the king they hated most. The circumstances made the Sapphirians to be more a personal army of the younger prince, less a rebellion. To say the collective and Sivi'ks remained friends is not accurate; they were entertainers of a past way of life. But to speak to them of regal debauchery—this was no desire of his.

"And? You think my commune with the Sapphirians would make them more pretty to your lawmaking? I will do no such thing. Excuse my *arrogance* father, but I quite respect them as people, despite what you would have me believe."

"I would have you believe the truth. They are terrorists." Sivi'ks threw up his hands in disgust, his father had driven him mad,

"And you are a tyrant! Does it not make sense for hurting people to rebel? I do not condone all of their works but I know this: they were awaiting my return to Cew at the minute of my arrival. Father, where were you?"

"I do not have time for pitiful gestures of family."

"You do not have time to greet your *soon-to-war son?*" The King had a posture like a statue. Motionless. The prince turned to leave, ignorant of his father's request. "I am asking you with my utmost sincerity, Pilot. Consider your brother—" Sivi'ks spun back towards his father, origlyph ablaze,

"Consider him? I do far more than that, fickle father! I care for him when *others* commission him in the court for days on end. I give him humor and comfort when *others* spit at his commodities and reprimand his posture! I am a better father to your son than you are." The King paused, leering down the canal of his throne way.

"I suppose you would have evidence of his poor treatment? Of your exceptional fathering?" Sivi'ks pondered his discretion, his father's tempting frown made the decision for him,

"I am the one who came to his aid when a miscreant from the city broke past the guards, I am the one who kept him from the hands of the Sapphirians, and the beast of the Black Tide." Careful consideration went into his words, a periodic shift in his leg reminded the king he was still, in fact, alive. "I intended to let myself be swept away in the Black Tide for his sake. The Mechanical Shepard denied me this honor, but I would have done it. You have done no such thing." The king shouldered his burdens, shrugging off to one side, his gaze slowly adjusting to the window beside him.

"Terix told me of the Glass Garden and the beast. He told me much about what you did. He did not—I did not know of your intentions of war." Sivi'ks scoffed, leaning his heated form against a pillar of gold,

"You wrote the law, surely. Should you know nothing else of me?" The King placed his wrist forward, gesturing at the clothing upon his son,

"I know you to be rebellious. Youthful forever, your uncle said you'd be. He was correct it seems." Politics of youth befouled the conversation, Sivi'ks drew short breaths and unleashed punctual arguments, claiming penance of his brother, and sanctity for his people.

"The Black Tide lingers still!" Sivi'ks would claim,

"It will be persuaded to die." His father would rebut. Sivi'ks would show his father scars from the city's many bandits. The King would express his condolences to those Sivi'ks had harmed. Making little progress with petty arguments, Sivi'ks penultimately agreed to his task, though assuring his father he would make no lies to his friends, before leaving the presence of his father.

"Good." The King replied, "I shall make an order in your stead, remove that squeamish war demand." Sivi'ks stopped at the door, not turning his head in the slightest.

"You will not." Aunbrax let out a terrifying sound, a legitimate chortle, whole from his deep guts. Sivi'ks had never heard such joy in his father prior,

"Oh, but I must. For better or for worse you are a Pilot—and you are a royal. I cannot have you on the fronts of a war not orchestrated by yourself." The prince was quickly irritable from this, his stomping scruffing the edges of the carpet as he approached his father,

"I told you, just now, I am nothing of your slave. You will do no such thing. I demand it."

"I am king, not you. I will decree what I will for you." Sivi'ks was terribly confused, but the hate filling him made this misunderstanding only furthermore indecipherable. Was he a Pilot, or a son?

"Admit I am your son, that is what this is. That you care so deeply for us both that you would sooner break your laws than have me die. Tell me this." The King shook his head softly, refusing such information. Shaken by this deed, Sivi'ks took himself upon the throne, mounting both hands on the claws of the seat, mere inches from his father, "I am *your* son! You've refused for too long! I am Sivi'ks, second heir to your throne, brother to *your* son, child to *your* wife! Call me it father—no, king! Call me what I am, call me *Your Son!*" the King stirred. For a moment, Sivi'ks saw victory. He saw his father's remembrance dance before the origlyph as if he had just collected the concept of family. In an instant, it was gone.

"I'd rather you not speak to me like this then, Pilot. Begone to your orders, and we will discuss this no further." Sivi'ks could not be furious any longer. He parted from the throne, shambling towards the exit.

"If I am not your son," He turned, his hand grappled to the royal insignia of his jacket, stitched loosely himself. With a rapid hand, he struck it clean, the lining of the cloth tugging out with it, stuffing showering to the ground. The prince tossed the insignia to the floor behind himself, maintaining the lock with his father's origlyph. He had never seen his father flinch before. "Then I am not yours to keep. Goodbye then, King Aunbrax." He made a considerate effort to stamp out the torn insignia with his boot heel as he left, certain he'd never see the man again. As the silver entrance sealed with a puff of pressure, the King slumped in his robes, his hands clutching against the faceplate that had ordained him king. He wept, for his son was dead.

Sivi'ks concluded his brother should know of his leave, though only partly. He had conversed with a servant (they all owed him some form of favor, and nevertheless enjoyed his presence as a result of his un-royal charm) and had a scheme perfected,

"Yes sir Terix, she was rather pestering with us, said her name was Baan, that you would surely know her?" From his place hidden away, Sivi'ks heard the rushing against the carpet, a slip disgruntled the good prince, and he was on his way.

"Many thanks, Fayiyr. You are a great friend."

"You are a fool. I'm sure your brother would have accepted a talk with you himself. Who is this Baan, anyways?" Sivi'ks made a motion like a zipper upside his origlyph and shut himself into his brother's hold. It was stuffed to the brim with mounds of novels, paperbacks, and folders. Eerie crackling came from the top of its luster, though Sivi'ks knew of the open flame in the room above. The room had been reorganized since the last time he had entered it—also without permission. The wall had been dulled, scratches lined the area above the bed with verdant green paint slathered over the rest. Pottery with various decaying flowers lay assorted across the deskspace, vines of unknown breed clambered up the door frame. Hidden from view beside the windowsill was a fashionable poster advertising the Tetarien Royal Flight Academy, a small photograph of Sivi'ks pinned to its side. Sivi'ks placed his letter on the largest desk, which was fitted to have incredible writing utensils and machinations, some newer than the ships of the academy. Sivi'ks wondered how many of Terix's days had been filled with monotonous scribe work, lacking substance of any kind. He assumed very many days indeed. Before making his leave, a small manuscript caught his eye, one on the delusion of Ink, a substance brought by the Black Tide. It contained sampling descriptions, all sorts of details on scent and taste, as well as injection results. It was not written by Terix, no. The stamp in the center was one of peer guidance, though Terix was never fashioned for the art of science. Sivi'ks snatched up the paper, written and delivered by a scientist, one Meileadair Lizosazu. The prince had never seen a name such as his, and certainly never heard of his work. As Terix's frustration echoed upon the palace walls, Sivi'ks took his moment to scamper up to the parted window, hesitating for a moment, for his brother's sake. He dropped the manuscript and leaped from the window, likely never to be seen again by his family. Though fate had a way of stringing people about, now didn't it?

~ *Promenade Distress Tokens*

Purchased off of three odious machine scalpers — an ignorant means of acquiring knowledge...

Kygen Collective D.L-Log 003
Dictation Presented by: K652-088
"Siphus" (BoulderLover088_teeth)
Proctor Introduction (edited):
Greetings all students of the I&I

echelon of the Sylvite Collaborative Academy! My name is Siphus. I am the biggest alloyhead, and commissioner, of the Kygen Collective project, a long sought-after opportunity to break the veil between divine and mundane existence. With the help and funding of the scrupulous moneyrakers at your slipshod Academy, we have no hope to accomplish our goals! To pair a person to my name, for the sake of humiliation, I gathered a suitable deposit of data about myself. I have worked alongside other mechanoid ecdysiasts at the Bolt & Clank for my entire life, waiting patiently for my chance to show off my juvenile metallic form to lusting machines, and fresh students like you are exactly the community I wish to present myself to. I despise my family and friends, enjoy reserving myself away from the norms of functioning society, rock collecting, painting, and on the off chance I have some time away from revealing my uncanny form to vile eyes, the teaching of young minds just like yourselves! The Kygen Collective will not abate these hobbies in the slightest, I am sure to find plenty of rocks aboard the Basilica! I will be tyrannically restricting the use of logs for the majority of project research, so that you may never hear from my colleagues Prometh and Samael. These two are far more experienced in their fields, having spent centuries over my own time at the SCO. Soon enough, you'll understand why they're paid so much more than I am to be here! Hopefully, our research here can move beyond names and places, and effort changes on a broader front, perhaps you students will live to paint with Ink, and collect rocks with Ichyr! Thank you all again, for this lovely opportunity. Until next time!

Log Additional Adressings:
For the love of the Lark, I cannot stress this enough, do NOT believe the untruthful word of Prometh. The old loon cannot tell thumb from toe. He needs to be removed from the system admin. I understand his importance to the security of this project, but his games jeopardize the stability of the environment, this is a RESEARCH PROJECT, not a jungle! If I get hit with one more light bolt from an R10 security unit, I'm calling SCO admin. I mean it. Stop following his commands! {mark.data.essential}

Log Contents:
If I had the capability to ensnare the meager semantics of my mental state, I would write an infinitum of tales. I am tired, to say the least. I have spent three nights in the observation chamber with the Inkling. It is magnificent, beyond my original assumptions of it. I theorize it once had both a name and an identifiable face, but its feral husk now shows no signs of this past. Ink is such a mystery, even still I have little to add to the documentation of matters. I feel myself slipping from the truth. I must stay on track, but Prometh makes this difficult. His universal expertise seems to lead to boredom, but this boredom is inflicted on the innocent of this research vessel. I have been berated by logarithms with mocking solutions, abused by several attempts on my life (none of which have succeeded), and impeded in my work with jests and traps. It is ridicule, and obnoxious. This insatiable foolishness that Prometh perpetuates vexes me. I wish for it to end but he insists on calling me slurs and marching away! Meck, I am to get no work done in this environment. I will have Prometh written up when I return, I swear. The SCO should have a higher standard of machine for such important labor. Either way, the boy has cried like a beast of fur and

fang one final time. His claims have caused great disarray among us, and certainly the security team. Two Distress Tokens emerged from the Promenade wing of the ship. Neither was answered because the security team had been told that all DTs from that district were to be false flags from Prometh's moronic devices. And considering that the Promenade stores all essential gasses for greenhouse functions, two of the greenhouses have now shut down. It is a serious difficulty to maintain plant life and the structure of equilibrium in all of the greenhouses but to do so without the nitrous mix that they require so essentially, it quickly becomes an impossibility. I regret joining this team, not the project as a whole, but specifically this collection of colleagues. I wish Prometh an awful day and a lifetime of creaky knees. The old sextant can bite a nail for all I care. My work is cut out for me, clearly, I must begin repairs. I have no choice but to be diligent and careful, let us hope I will retain time for my *actual* work.

Documentation On Ink and Ichyr (Prior to Shipments, first logging):

Ichyr — The more common and well-known of the two matters, a semi-translucent liquid in its natural state, that occasionally can harden to crystalline-like properties. It is the building block of all life as far as we know and can be found in all elements of the periodic table. Its origins have been theorized to link with The Lark, however considering his genetic makeup contains the very Ichyr we speak of, it is unlikely he created it. Ichyr can be found in varying levels of purity, which we will denote as Purity Stage 1, Purity Stage 2, and Purity Stage 3 (PS1-3) in ascending levels of purity. The liquid states of both matters are permanently locked in PS3, making them reject one another, and scar purer beings. Upon the death of any being of any PS level, its Ichyr will be promptly re-absorbed into the nearest well and condensed into liquid form. The Ink will follow the same process. PS1 is the basic form, a majority of creatures within the galaxy are made up of PS1 Ichyr, including our species. Diluted with a large portion of Ink and empty space, we are incapable of communicating in any form with the purer sides of our makeup, making us both mortal and mundane. PS1 beings are not harmed nor affected by liquid pure forms of their opposing matter types. A 2 on the scale denotes a being of higher purity, often referred to as a Pure being, though their bodies are still not perfected. They are further entranced by their matter, permitting longer lifespans, increased survivability, as well as occasional "Supernatural" applications, such as the use of Fuilichasting, a PS2-3 beings capability of bending the Ichyr in the world around them, much to the point of considerable magicks. More potent uses like limb repair, automatic liquidation, and crystallization do exist, but only as the byproduct of advanced techniques. PS2 beings are purer than most, so liquid Ink can be quite deadly when released directly in contact with the body, but they do also benefit from further exposure to liquid Ichyr. PS3 beings are limited in supply, being referred to often as the "Genesis Beings", the first of their kind. They are wholly pure, and therefore all capable of Fuilichasting at the highest level of complexity. Furthermore, they are incredibly susceptible to liquid forms, and even PS2-level forms of Ink, it is rumored they must be left in isolation or risk contamination and death.

Ink — Less common, little is known of Ink. PS1-3 scale may not be consistent with Inklings. Some Inklings can perform the Ink equivalent of Fuilichasting, referred to as Atrallurgy in historic documentation, containing the same benefits (supposedly, Sylvite documentation lacks a proper description of any living Atrallurgist). Ink death sends Ink back to wells the same as Ichyr, and Ink is just as weak to contact with Ichyr as its opposite. *Ink is, as Ichyr is translucent and thin, thick and rubbery, darkened with void. It is a repulsive material, both hydrophobic and quite elastic. The substance is also extremely viscous, the fluid form can flow as quickly as syrup at its hastiest. I do adore the aroma, it is that of run tires, quite strong indeed. Perhaps it does indeed taste of rubber and rhubarb… [*I am certain I did not write this, is it possible Prometh has breached even this avenue of security?]* Further data cannot be confirmed beyond speculation and hearsay. (Samael's supposed "research" is not worth half his salt. He claimed Ink has a flavor of rubber and rhubarb. Cannot trust his data, do not add).

The Harlequin

Log Continuation:

I have little more to say. Prometh, if you are reading this, give. Me. Peace. Our work is the priority! We can jest and dote on this all after the work is done. We have a very limited frame with which to own the Inkling!

~Log End~

Attached Files: Weather_Report ; Help_Ticket_003

Pinging Weather_Report...
    INFINITY SCAN RETURNS = ~ #4e4063
CLOSEST CODE LOG {Eggplant.Purple}
Pinging Help_Ticket_003...
    PROMENADE GASEOUS FILTERS DISABLED
    — REQUIRES EVENTUAL FIX
DISTRESS TOKEN 001 SENT TO HELP CONTROLS...
RESPONSE EXPECTED
    MALFUNCTIONING PISTON NODE DETECTED
IN LOWER PROMENADE
    — REQUIRES IMMEDIATE FIX
DISTRESS TOKEN 002 SENT TO HELP CONTROLS...
RESPONSE EXPECTED
    FAILURE TO ANSWER DISTRESS TOKEN(s) WITHIN
ALLOTTED TIME FRAME
    PERMANENT DAMAGE POSSIBLE
DISTRESS TOKEN 003 SENT TO HELP CONTROLS...
RESPONSE EXPECTED
    — ANSWER RECEIVED —
    SUBJECT CODE; {SIPHUS} FULFILLED TOKENS 001-003
    NO TOKENS REMAIN :)
    —TERMINATING LOG PROTOCOL

~ *Forget What Was,*

Valiantly boasted of by the very Dreyal
mentioned. They are not of the intellectual
breed...

Oh to be young again, Derlick had moaned ad infinitum upon the sidelines of a war unfought by his wretched gums. Fevir remembered it well, and considering he was still a youth himself, he took time to admire what others considered lost. For example, the ability to scale a scaffold in mere seconds, far quicker than the minutes it took the elder arms dealer. Knowing came into consideration too, being so young and spry, Fevirgreen could easily process the wealth of information before him, the streets, rooftops, every corridor of all the homes in the city, easily within arms reach. The arms dealer still had yet to plot a direct course to their freedom. There was also the cunning, such as when Fevir spotted his prey scampering across a coat of quilts, and with one simple tug, picked the Dreyal from its mass like a tick off a hound, sprawling the figure against a market awning. And who could forget precision, the peeping eyes of a child were like tree frogs: darting with expert tracking among various places, keen to avoid the contact they so deserved. This was presented in full by Fevir's continuous record of unmissed shots, of which he now counted one more. Collapsing forward off the shadowy umbrella of a coarse market tarp, the mossy arms dealer plummeted to the street below. Fevirgreen was quick to catch up to the escapee, they would not be evading him again. Through the sea of unfamiliars, Fevir made quick work of navigation, silently assuring civilians of safety and calmness. The Dreyal scampered out from under a stall, still bleeding pollen as it went. Fevirgreen caught two shots into the runaway's back, silencing the rapid slapping of their feet for now. Telor'mul was a sun city, that is, a city positioned on a planet so close to the sun that its flares alone could scar the hairs on your head. Despite this fact, sun cities (a grand majority of them, anyways) lacked both crime and hazard. Solar Umbrellas soaked up the majority of sun-based hazards, and what little heat seeped through was consumed by countless citizen-run solar farms. Paradise formed under the Umbrellas, where crime was punished with the sun itself, tying the charred corpses of wrongdoers to mirrors. Many would sit on their balconies, watching as the heat dried their bones stale, like melted gum. Colorful banners and silks draped between homes, with villas and manors built against the supports of the massive Umbrellas. Fevirgreen did not admire it. He found himself unbothered by the concept, it was not a hatred he felt for the place, but a much simpler malcontent with the aura of the facility. Fevir simply tolerated its presence, despite the overwhelming urge to emote in some regard to its grandeur. What did tend to affect the unfeeling Crow was the common hoards of seabed citizens roaming the ever-expansive streets of the city. Like a stifling rag, Fevirgreen was suffocated by the people, unable to theorize or plot without interruption, not to mention the terrible visibility. After all, The Lark much-preferred solutions that did not call for the senseless violence found privy in the ranks of the Definition. Shockingly, Fevirgreen did agree with these methods. Bloodshed for no sake at all was beyond his realm of brutality. As he saw it, monstrous gore and unbelievable torture were all well and good if inflicted on those who stood against him. However, it was to build a beast of yourself to harm an average citizen. Armed with nothing but their own struggles and pills, innocents had no involvement with religious affairs. It was simply undeserved of them. Floral spores danced through the vast green hues of Fevir's mask, a trail undemanding of scents. Down two lengthy roads, and up an off-shooting skyway, the trail ended itself at a crossroads, buildings of all sizes and quality surrounding the intersection. The wind had picked up, and with it came a herald of sand, washing the stones of the roadways smooth, and pissing away any chance of following the green path trail. A boney stoat of a woman moseyed her way through the cambering entryway of an illustrious establishment, promising whores and booze in its neon. Fevirgreen thought little of it, yet there was always security in taking chances. The building was coated in sand, though not enough to endanger any of the residents; Fevir still had to shake his boots out twice during his time within. Ishtar had described places similar prior to the mission, capsizing pillars of cloth and sandstone, built up with grout and pure iron bars, ever so tantalizingly propped against the spit to hell. Nude aliens of unknown origin or kin (At least to Fevigreen, familiar only with the Lesskin of his home) wandered to and from a mysteriously unlit backroom. Two barkeepers tended to customers, a third hauling off the unconscious remains of a brawler. Fevirgreen sighed, his mask preventing any smoke from escaping. Tossing the encroaching fabrics of his cloak behind him, Fevir pursued the closest barkeep, stretching his holster thick with the butt of his pistol.

"Birdmaster sir, may serve you?" Fevirgreen nodded, eyes dotting the various sources of illumination.

"Dreyal, an arms dealer. Are you familiar with any apparent arms dealers?" The barkeep shook his head but did respond positively to the terminology used in the description of Fevir's prey. Off to question other employees, the barkeep began to fiddle with two thick braces tied around their legs, shackles in shape and size, but certainly not purpose. Fevir could not help but stare at the metal as it clinked against the stone floor, melodious to his brutalized ears.

"What are those, might I ask?" The barkeep was deep in conversation with another of his kind, now figuratively attempting to display the term 'arms dealer' with his own slimy hands.

"Tenabraces. They are of utmost necessity." A machine seated beside Fevirgreen added to his misguided questioning. Fevir did not appreciate the suddenness of their approach.

"For what purpose...?" Fevir peered only further into the reflective purple tinge of the collars and braces. It called out its name like reed songs. "Slaves. Must be slaves."

"Nay. More akin to armor." The machine swallowed pint after pint of a thin white fluid, wine by all guesses. "Perchance, yes — More like clothing I would say, rather." Fevirgreen pondered their reality as clothing, he thought them ineffective at covering the body if they were such things.

The Harlequin

"Are there not superior felts to wear?"

"They are intended not for the body you *can* see, but for the one you *cannot*." The machine downed another mug and turned for a moment to the Crow before itself. The shaky visor paired with innumerable pints of alcohol made identification impossible. "Talesh, people of the pod, tentacular beyond reason." The drunkard gestured over to a portrait of anatomies. A tentacled figure was sprawled across by nails, a sunken orange eye pierced the mist around its form.

"Ta-lesh. Talesh."

"A round for my friend, yes?" Fevirgreen glared at the drunkard, he had no intentions of drinking.

"No. Do no such thing. Deliver it to the drunkard and be done with it."

"Haven't a name for your metal jaws. Have you one?"

"Not for you. Barkeep?"

"Nay, tell me! I oath myself to your stead if you would! An arms dealer, you seek?" Fevir leaned over the bar, tapping the back of the Talesh he had first spoken to. The barkeep did not turn back. With little to lead on, and time running scarce, Fevirgreen turned to the baiting machine, another pint of wine in hand.

"Fevirgreen. Verdancy is my hallow. I seek the fleeing arms dealer, you must've seen them." The drunkard chuckled, piping another shot to the back of their throat.

"I have no idea where this arms dealer is, merely heard of it. From you, no less." The machine stood, drawing a minute pair of tweezers from its waist, flicking a protective coating from their edges. With a stumble and a leap, the machine went from drunkard to delight, stuffing the tool into the side of their neck, and twining for a second too long. "Lark and tow, always stings like rubidex buds." Fevirgreen followed his new companion, one he had little consent in befriending. "Call me V, any lengthier name and you'd surely turn me in for the variety of disallowance I have allowed. Of what race is this arms dealer of yours?" Fevir blinked behind the protection of his steel.

"Dreyal, the plant people." V carried on more rashly, stomping deeper into the bar.

"Pining corpse-stealers, the most hateable people in all of the galaxy. Why did you withhold such prized knowledge? Of course, I'll aid in the death of one of *their* kind." Fevir wasn't one to know much about the niche, yet it fancied him. The blue stained glass covering every window seemed intentional, but not for any conventional means of aesthetic. The sun was harsh, something had to be done. But this? Certainly a poor choice. Blue was such a provoking hue, reminiscent of the unseeable sky, the crude ocean, and the corpses it claimed. Of Forklorn.

"Where are we going?" Fevir questioned the machine, but V had no intention of spoiling the fun so quickly. Beside the bar, lying just within the blind spot of the excessive and harsh lighting, was a set of butler-style doors, lacking windows or identifying marks of any kind. V ignored any potential laws forbidding him from entry, putting only more force into his step as he went. As if attempting to lose a tail, V abruptly turned a corner, rushing up a dimly lit flight of stairs, skipping every other step as he went. He remained silent too, there was no answer to Fevirgreen's desperate question. Accepting the cue as a vow of silence, Fevir continued his pursuit, growing ever more curious about the machine's vibrant activities. The second floor was coated with even thicker liveries than the previous, with pink and maroon animal print plastered across nearly every surface, with a hazy fog drifting through the facilities. A stack of charcoal briquettes had slumped across the entryway; Fevir was careful not to scuff his boots. V halted his persistence in the center of the room, motioning for Fevirgreen to join him. There were four other creatures roaming the upper floor, all scantily dressed, all certainly whores. Fevir hoped he would have no need for his weapon.

"Quite frankly, the best of timing, I'm sure they'll be here presently." Fevir neglected questions, the encounter had grown far too unpredictable for pettiness-like questions.

"Right. Have you any estimations?" V admitted he did not, but this was expected by the Crow. The two sat together, upon bags wrapped in leather, in the center of a brothel. Silence lingered for a while, but did not remain, as the elegant machine discussed in grave detail the methods by which he had acquired his silk robes. Stolen, of course. Not directly, the robes were fairly purchased (something that astonished Fevirgreen at the time but quickly faded into a rough understanding of criminal traits) in a market on some old Ink moon, a place the machine had never returned to. The funds for the silk, however, were of course the result of countless acts of crime. Though the machine did have claims of the silk's repair; he had at one point been a feltsmith, however, he did not recall where. An expert often became a silent dying mind with ignorance of duty. Fevir considered apprehending the machine for a moment but promptly canceled his unneeded ambition. The Lark had no hatred for V, and thus he would be free. Continuing their discussion, Fevir noticed V's inclination to stare upwards, sometimes in the direction of a wall-mounted kitchenette. It disturbed the flow of conversation, but like anything else, was easily ignored by Fevirgreen's simple lack of care. Fixed upon the lower veils of the closest whore, his eyes wandered for reasons one might not expect. There were vast similarities between the sexually enslaved, and the Amaranth Crow who had fabricated a shaky web with Fevir. Where he thought himself a youth, both Ishtar and the whore shared a much younger form than he. They had the figures of goddesses, though Ishtar's body lacked the trail of needle scars across her forearm. They were people of origins dissimilar, machine and masseuse, hallow and harlot. Considering this, Fevirgreen concluded he knew far too little about Ishtar to affirm anything of reasonable merit. She was as he was to her: a mystery. Dubiety infuriated Fevir. V turned his hand in a calling manner, beckoning the whore Fevirgreen had just been watching. He pictured Ishtar out of habit and found himself unable to banish the image. The way the creature moved, the veils just narrowly enfolding the neat curves of her lower body, her exposed chest throbbed in tandem with her presumed heartbeat. The stare he gave the woman was of little consequence in his mind, but it drove the whore mad with fear. A Crow was a killer, a violent extension of the Lark's prevalence. She was merely looking down the sightline of an ever-growing blood river. A second escort, noticing the discomfort in her partner's eyes, placed both of her hands on Fevirgreen's statuesque shoulders, slipping her hands down their ridges, under the thick plating. In an instant, his pistol was out, pointing with reckless hate directly up her chin. The wench fell to her knees, her whole body convulsing without end, petrification spreading to nearby whores, a contagious plague.

Creatures of Habit

"My my, such vigor from you Crows. I've met your others, need you antagonize a simple harlot?" V's hands moved like shark skin, caressing the body of the whore. She was panicked, her fingers shook hesitantly, as she had no desire to give off a presence of fear; fear was a known killer of love. The machine continued its movements, raising his hands to places Fevir had never seen unclothed.

"Stop. Immediately, just—" Fevir shook his pistol back into its holster, turning away from V and his whores. The images overwhelmed him, the scent potent with grease. "I beg you, where is the arms dealer." A creaking of the three wooden braces atop the room predicted the complete collapse of its ceiling. V had not mentioned this would occur. Though it took a moment for the ashes to rest, within the rubble was a ruminating plant growth, a body entwined with roots. Tossing his doubt aside, Fevir leaped to his feet and clambered atop the debris. As if by fate, he came face to face with the Dreyal he was after, a tiny husk of a creature growing dimmer by the second. It was with great indulgence to his curiosity he would question the merchant upon his return to the cathedral. Before Fevir could collect the body, it bound its hands tightly to his shoulder, digging into the flesh with twisting roots. It begged, bawling for mercy at Fevir's hands, swearing fidelity to the Lark. Fevirgreen drew his face away from the feral beggar. Such courage they had to beg for mercy in the presence of a Crow, the very same Crow who had given chase upon it for hours, who they had thrown stones upon, and degraded further with words. As if they deserved supple mercy. Fevir stapled his dagger nicely into the shoulder bones upon the Dreyal's back, before hauling the prey onto his shoulder—pleasant applause supplied by the spiteful hands of V. Though it squirmed for a moment, the arms dealer had long ago accepted its fate of torture and unreasonable disappearance as a result of their capture. The machine may have been pleased, but the Lark would be more so. The arms dealer had once collected and sold a wealth of stolen Larkik armaments—which supposedly included components from the Amber Crow's personal armory. The knowledge embedded in the greenery would likely locate salvation. Ishtar's voice called to the Verdant Crow, as he had requested its presence.

The Harlequin

"Aye aye captain Crow, fall into any brothels yet Fevirgreen?" She cooed, trying to snuff the microphone with her hand as she giggled through its haze.

"I'd rather speak not of it. I have acquired the arms dealer." There was a moment of quiet, the transmission seemed to fracture, and another voice egged into his mind.

"Acquired *sight* of the arms dealer, you made the same claim hours ago, Fevir!" Forklorn's usual resonance fluttered about him, certain he was once again in the right.

"Negative. The arms dealer has been apprehended. I have all sight of it. It is a Dreyal." An unceasing bridle of double-voiced murmurs emerged from the transmission, impossible to discern who had spoken what claims, Fevirgreen opted to disable the communications device. The Dreyal squirmed in his grasp. A ship would arrive in time to carry him away, and with it came his fortune.

"Off so soon, rushing like river flow." V slid down the collapsed rooftop, patting dust from his shins. "Glad I could be of assistance, hallowed one. Perhaps you will one day return the favor." Fevir could help but snicker. Resistance to such base and derivative jest was to be expected of the elite. V exchanged a purloin of promises, fooling nothing with his false sincerity. Just before the two departed from the other's company, Fevir felt a pang of empty closure.

"Many thanks, machine. You have served the Lark well today." V turned from his leave, the door propped between his foot and the wall.

"Nay, I only served you. The Lark... now *he* I could never serve." With a flashy grin, the machine was gone, leaving silence and dust storms in its gasp. Fevirgreen placed a hand against his hip, feeling up the weight of his weapon. Familiarity was lovely. So much to be learned still, he too, took his leave.

Torrents of previously placid scrolls and novels tumbled from the shelf, Fevirgreen quickly amassed them in his arms, snatching every stray paper with a baseline elegance. Without his armaments, he became something of a flawless acrobat. Lacking all the distraction of a stage-bound performer, Fevir made his way through the archives over every fallen book and drone in his path. The work was never finished, it appeared almost as though Proctor Alclerius had specifically designed the archives to be a place of constant movement, flowing with life by force alone. Not to mention the odd happenstance that every novella and scribed literature seemed completely out of sorts, miles from its intended location. If a sorting system had at one point existed within the realm of the Larkik Library, it certainly no longer did.

"Proctor, your requests." Fevirgreen replaced the scrolls onto Alclerius' desk, who in return, did not compliment nor thank the Crow. He simply scrunched his brow and snatched a quill to edit with. Fevir did not need thanks, it was a duty that was deserving of its own rewards. The proctor's attitude towards the general studying that Fevir took such great interest in was null, consisting of scrolls and texts he had read, re-read, and even re-written dozens of times. What interest could be drawn from knowledge that was neither new nor entertaining? Alas, Fevirgreen remained all the same. His passion for further understanding deeply outweighed Alclerius' passion for solitude. "Need you anything else, Proctor?" clicking his glassy fingertips against an obtuse inkwell, Alclerius had nothing more to request of his apprentice Crow.

"Wouldn't you much rather ask something of *me*, Crow?" Fevir partitioned his mind, both agreeing and terrified. Perhaps it was a test, to scrutinize his will at staying his hand when given the opportunity to ask questions. "Ask away Crow, I will allow you one question." Or perhaps not? Thought must be put into the nuance of this one query, the very lifeblood of curiosity must be roused! What millions of wonders could be answered by this one man? Terrible atrocities of war, infinite racial disputes, and anatomies of beasts unknown, the choice became an intimidating freedom.

"Ishtar. Is she broken?" Alclerius placed the quill back into its font, turning his attention from secondhand signatures to the enigma before him,

"Broken? Crow, have you not spoken with her?" Fevir considered this his answer and nodded accordingly. The proctor drew up a book without a cover and turned lethargically to its midsection. "She can tell you her own ways, herself. Ishtar is beyond a fractured Crow." He turned the book, presenting a hearty list of names and words, lengthy terms that some Fevir was capable of identifying.

"Medicine. Is she… Unwell?" Proctor Alclerius drew up a second page, and another, all Crows, all deathly medicated, insured.

"Crows, the whole lot of you, all broken." Fevir stared deeply into the thick inky text, the missing dots on eyes, the misspelling of medicines. "Broken goods are always cheaper, after all…." Fevir did not feel broken, misplaced perhaps, but certainly in good condition. He could lift like a mule, and adjudged his right hook to be sturdy. Sure, he wasn't the quickest, and he had positively no schooling to base his mental fortitude upon, but surely that did not deem him *broken*.

"I am not broken, sir. Nor is she." The proctor only shook his head, shooing off the Crow as he continued his work. With little more to do, both for Proctor Alclerius and in general, Fevirgreen retired to his room, a terribly dark place without its owner, the mask of birds negated any need for light. He sat on his cot, unaware of the dark, unfazed by its demanding presence.

"You'd be wise to purchase a lamp." Ishtar squirmed her way past the chain lock, undoing it as she slipped in. "Not all of us are given masks of gods, Fevie." Fevir lifted a despondent arm in disapproval, hoping Ishtar would heed its call. "Forklorn is delirious. He's in utter disbelief that *you* beat his fastest questioning record."

"Leave me Ishtar, please." For the few weeks she had known him, Fevir had never shown grief—neither did he now. It was not grief that wracked his soul, but confusion. The Lark did not lie, there was complete loyalty in that, but the proctor did not either. The Lark had not claimed he was perfect, but there was an implication…

"Have you spoken with Proctor Alclerius?" Fevir regained what momentary eye contact he had with the woman. Her plasmatic ion limbs seemed to glow in the dark.

"Yes." Fevir went to remove his mask, to erode the sweat from his jaw. He hesitated, and the hesitation *killed* him. "I did my services for the night. It culminated in…" Fevir trailed off, searching for the words to describe his questions "illusions." He claimed. Ishtar shut the door but did not grow closer to the Crow, instead slinking against the metal of the door, dropping to her knees across the room from him.

"Broken goods are always cheaper, hmm?" He did not blink. Distant forges thumped, and the thrust of pistons shook the stone floor.

"Yes. Always." Ishtar reached out her hand, having slowly slid herself closer to the bedside. Fevir, quick as he had weakened, tore his hand from her range. He wanted to demand her to go, to criticize her haste, her desires, but he found no such energy to do so. Fevir forged excuses,

"Proctor Alclerius, wise as he may be, knows not of the love of the Lark." Ishtar shifted her weight, quickly agreeing with Fevirgreen's sentiments. "He was not coddled, but instead the opposite. A cold man." Fevir laid himself back upon the cot, the metal ridges of its guard rails digging into his neck.

"The things the Lark says, they are so greatly intoxicating, Fevie." Fevirgreen unhooked two carabiners from his backside, sliding a small pouch out from his armor. It was filled to the brim with throwing knives. He had intended to practice but never seemed to have the time.

"Such confusion is tiresome, Ishtar. If you would leave me to my devices, for now." Ishtar nodded, reaching her hand forward in one last attempt at contact. Fevir had no intention of replying to it. She left as she came, squirming through the lock, and silent as a mouse.

In her own den, Ishtar had designed intricate sets of rural rail-work, models of various designs spun around the vibrant casing, soft harmonies tuning into song. A switchboard—numbering thirty-two inputs—rested beside a layered futon. On any other day, she would flick each track on and off, observing the chain of each unique vessel. Soft blue-and-purple lighting mirrored that of an esoteric standard, found only in old brothels. It brought her comfort, much like the trains. A shelf of procured literature remained her only secondary source of will, novels on greed and traveling through time, books of pilots in war, daughters in text, and mothers in deserts. There were volumes of dictionaries for practiced words, secluded journals of old unpublished theses, *Charlotte's Web*, and other taboo texts. Re-reading satisfied her to a point, but she could not read in turmoil. She reminded herself of dread when she worked for the sake of knowledge at the hands of Alclerius. His ceaseless self-pity brought pain in a bubble around himself, only worsening the sour taste of the archives. On any other day, she would toy with the switchboard.... Rising from her rest, she plucked one train off the track, an olive-colored vessel with black accents. It had been incredibly cheap, acquired from slavers and desolate children who could not bear to part with it. It functioned as intended, and the paint was pristine. She had painted it. Leaving the train behind, Ishtar barreled out the door of her room and marched down to the archive. Sitting at his desk was the proctor himself, resting his head against the stump of his chair. With a pre-emptive boot, she kicked out the chair, knocking Alclerius' head against his own table — the rest of him meeting the floor.

"You *bastard*, you showed him the texts!" Clawing away from the chair and caressing his head, the proctor looked up at the Crow,

"They are real, bah, you Crows don't—"

"What does telling a broken man of his shattered nature do to fix him?" Ishtar pressed against his sternum with her heel, provoking haste in the proctor's tone,

"I had no mal intent! It was a question, a mere trick of the mind!" Pushing him further from the desk, Ishtar relented, hissing one final insult,

"You fool! This is why the Lark keeps you hidden away, you old crone! A dust bunny to a patriarchy beyond your belonging! It's telling that I would not be the first—nor the tenth—to wish you a lifetime of ulcers and cancerous growths." With a lob of spit, Ishtar went to leave. Spitefully, she turned one final time to adjourn her rage. "His battles are many, and days numbered. What would you have him do as thanks for your inquisition?" Proctor Alclerius raised a finger but found not the words to accompany it. Another of his golems shifted into the isle, carrying with it but one novel.

"Tell the boy I lie. Frequently. You would have no trouble criticizing me, no?" Ishtar gave a disgraced scoff, before exiting the archives, enraged only further. "And— and that I am deeply sorry Ishtar." Jutting her hip out to the left, the Amaranth Crow furiously swung her neck back to the proctor, bringing with it her twenty salmon veils. "To the both of you." She shook her head in complete and utter disbelief and continued out of the forge-bowel. Proctor Alclerius was left with little but his thoughts and golems.

~ *Abyssal Thread*

*Penned as a Larkik gag against the Keppel
Crow Forklorn—who himself denies its
validity...*

It would be a long while before the Belt would revert to its unpopulated, desolate form. It had taken the Lark eons of precise mechanical masterwork to assemble the Imperial Belt into a livable environment fit for mortal beings. The chains designed to hold the moonrock in place had been forged in small fragments and delivered in steel caskets across the surface. Their bindings had been set by the original Ichyrics, aided by their god and his innumerable hands. The original designs had plans for gardens and hydroponic spires— oxygen was to be distributed across the belt via atmospheric relays. After a failure on the part of Larkik containment (and consideration), such methodology became impossible, as the Imperial Belt became a breeding ground for parasites and meaty contentment. Through methods unknown to all, the Lark managed to tame the parasitic infection, instead harnessing the people birthed from its duress into laborers for the galaxy to indulge in. What remained of their sordid birth became the Belt—a husk of dried fetuses and crumbling meat shells. Even so, the Lark considered the operation a great success and eventually bore fruit in the form of countless travelers. In time, it became a thriving epicenter of Larkik loyalty. While the metal of the chains remained unrusted and the blood-rivers of the calep roots still flowed strong, the same could not be said for the faith of those who set down their families upon the Belt. Like all life, the vitality of their trust waned, and soon came to an end, whimpers from the bone-curled snout of a sick mutt. Blessed men turned to banditry, and cardinals of the Lark became corrupted by cryptic conspiracy. When the bird god came to remedy his humble place of religion, none would accept his word. Not spiteful of the betrayal, the Lark disallowed any further misconduct upon the Imperial Belt, ignoring the eruption of heresy at his doorstep. In its place came only further crime, kidnappings, murders, and beyond. Chaos became the great undoer of things, as entropy always did seek its end in smithers. Marching militants and burnished cannons made no difference to this fate, nor did the will of any existing god. History had become a fable, and wretched fate buried all the rest. In the fog of the stormless day, Jeweler pursued his lips and plucked away at a two-string guitar, knowing nothing of music. Viaduct droned on about fate and chaos, recounting the origins of the Imperial Belt and all its miscreants. Lobs of snow sunk from the sky, aching caleps rounding out upright once more. Through the ransacked slit in the cockpit door, Jeweler watched Viaduct fiddle about with a dangling tube, echoing tales of his past as he continued to work. Locked away from the ambient out-world, the informant could do the bulk of his processes without interruption. It had been a great surprise when Viaduct volunteered to make amends and repair Jeweler's ship, as it had been relatively set off as scrap metal.

"There must be some safe haven among the infinite, Roach surely would make a lovely starfaring steward, and Lullaby the penitent stewardess," He had said, unfamiliar ambition about his stride. Jeweler did not need a spyglass to see ulterior motives, but after the dangers presented by the sudden reappearance of Larkik occupation, and the present pursuit of Jeweler by Gretchkin avengers, the hunt for paradise did not seem all too unfathomable. Both Viaduct and the bartender had vowed to retire in comfort and never see the stars again, yet some quiver of excitement in the informant's voice made Jeweler think such an agreement had been far more one-sided than he once believed. Thrashing at the neck of the Inkling beast, Lullaby was plucked from the snow and mounted against a calep stump, squirming with all her might as Roach nipped at her exposed shoulders. The two ferocious kin—those lacking proper words to speak for themselves—brought along more peril than prize. There was nothing else to do with the two, leaving them alone would result in gory feasts, and selling them off had since been forbidden by Viaduct. Lullaby and Roach remained not for the spoils of the greater deep, but rather out of necessity, though neither would leave if permitted to do so. Together, the four shaped a mutated family of sorts, a chorus of perfect people in imperfect husks.

"Ehm, Jeweler? I've just uncovered what appears to be the skeletal remains of a rattlesnake or eel in the exhaust vents. Would you do me a kindness and remove your pets before asking of my favors?" Peeking back at the construction, Jeweler was presented with a wiggling set of bones, dangled at the end of a set of forceps by his informant friend. Itching away the skin on the back of his neck, Jeweler cleared his throat,

"Not mine." Viaduct leered, gesturing the skeleton further,

"It is your ship, is it not? Who else could it be?"

"Don't suppose just 'cause I own the damn thing means I got snakes in the rafters. Awful presumptive of you, ain't it?" Viaduct argued against the presumptive nature of his claim, clarifying that it would be incredibly difficult to sneak a reptile onto the ship without Jeweler's immediate knowledge. "Just toss it with the rest of the spoils, I'll clear 'em out once you're nice and tidy." Viaduct scowled and heaved the skeletal mass over into a pile of assorted bones, tomes, and gemstones. Suitably disgusted by the state of the ship, Viaduct sat against the door, checking off several sections of his worker's manual. Memory failed him, the last ship he had done any maintenance on being one of his proper youth, more than a century prior to Jeweler's birth. There were still some small adjustments to make, and a whole host of systems to recalibrate, but the bulk of the physical damage had been rectified. Curling up his legs to better read, Viaduct bent into the light, knocking against the pilot's chair. Spacious as the cockpit was, the informant's thick wooden leg found a way to cramp any space. The Passerine—as it had been graciously named by a mercury miner long dead—was no large vessel, housing a cockpit, a common space with seating and basic hygienic amenities, two storage closets, and a lengthy cargo hold—which of course doubled as the only passway from which the ship could be both entered and exited. The Passerine

The Harlequin

was a clunky, obtuse heap of soldered metals and mixed circuiting. A mechanic would describe stories of its flight as myth, but Jeweler knew better.

"Tidy is one thing, what you've made here is entirely different, Jeweler. I fail to see how any of these reroutings benefitted you in your... escapades." Jeweler's voice echoed through the thin space between The Passerine's walls,

"What I do with my private transport oughta be kept that way. Fix what you can and leave the rest to me, yeah?" Roach snarled into the ship, demented giggles wavering through the fog.

"If you are so insistent on the quality of this vessel, the least you can do is get me some wire—you *must* have some about." A spool rested above his cot, shielded in the casket of his goods. With a grunt, Jeweler rose and trudged off to the Squall, berating Roach's unseen action as he went. Sparks showered the informant as he reconnected the main systems to the ship, curious of how they would perform with their modifications. Expecting an audible affirmation of success, Viaduct sat completely still, ears to the sky. Silence lingered to his great disappointment. Glancing under the dashboard, the informant discovered the machinery to be barren, lacking the drives to include any kind of starboard mainframe. Jeweler always was a loner, it was not terribly shocking to see he had removed it—he likely considered the mainframe some intrusive Larkik spyware. Viaduct rested back against the pilot's seat, his fingers sanded down from re-circuiting. While The Passerine was ready for proper flight, they would not get far without navigational systems. Begin a Sylvite Construct, Viaduct could offer his mind as a throughway for navigational data, but without a proper interpreter, none of his efforts would matter. He would have to question Jeweler on his questionable disassembly of the ship. Peering through the poor seals of the cockpit door, Viaduct could narrowly make out the green inflatable caught in Roach's jaw. It was found among the remnants of the Matron's treasures by Lullaby, along with a small fortune of trinkets and trade favors. The Legate had hesitated in her thievery, undermining the roots of her own people. Yet, it was not family for her—the Gretch did not care for her existence nor her words. In Jeweler and his associates, she had found a superior collection of siblings, a family worthy of her honor.

With the subtly distraction of rubber on hard snow, Viaduct grew entranced by the play of the two feral kin. As metallic bootstraps rattled the ramp up to the ship, the banter ceased, and the wind grew thick. A knock on the ship door summoned the informant's attention.

"Hoo—Jewels, you in there? Had to run mighty fast to get on over here." Viaduct did not recognize the voice, nor its metallic bass. With a hesitant lift of the latch, the informant came upon the feathery facade of a Larkik Gull, their helm unsealed and draped in casual shadow.

"I doubt Jeweler would associate with the likes of you, besides, he does not linger here. You best be on your way." With a shake of her head, the Gull began to pry open her helmet, struggling against its binds,

"Naw, me and Jeweler go way back, got somethin' urgent for his eyes only. You a friend of his too?" Leaning forward, the Gull presented her leafy flesh, pollen drifting into the cockpit. Viaduct snapped away from the door, ferocity taking hold of his tongue.

"Blaspheming sun—an Ent-child? What in Lark's name is this despicable game? A Dreyal of all things—it would be indubitably wise of you to leave, before I take up arms against you myself, seedborn." The Gull slammed a played fist against the door, their namesake slathered with grease and dishonor,

"What'd you call me Sylvite? I ain't got trouble with your kind but I can sure as Six start some! Where's Jeweler at now, huh? You got him tangled up in some sorta devil's business?" Calmly pressed against the back of her head, the barrel of Jeweler's weapon was as cold as the snow itself, the hammer resting in the pull of his thumb.

"What in *Silverwings* are you doin' here Pherock?" The Gull shifted her weight, slighting the rigid dagger upon her hip. She raised her left hand against the door, presenting her arms in full,

"Hey-hey Jewel boy! S'pose you know what's upon us, yeah?" Jeweler squinted at her neck, Viaduct's neon screen visible just beyond. He pressed her head to the side, picking at her words.

"Some nerve you got, showin' up here after your stunts. Insulting my partner too? I oughta flay you like a duck." With a tap of his foot, Pherock was permitted to turn to face the bartender, remaining careful in her steps. She tilted her vision aside, peering down the barrel of her beak, right to the bartender's ear.

"You aren't wearing 'em—I worked my tail off for those things, pal!" A glare set Pherock back in line, as Jeweler kept the pistol trained on her stomach,

"Listen 'pal', I ain't planning on joining up again, and I certainly won't be playing pretend on it neither. You're lucky I haven't shot you through yet, so unless you got somethin' worth saying—kick it kid, and take your bull with." Marched right down the ramp, both Jeweler and the Gull stood eye-to-eye in the misting snow, Lullaby and Roach nowhere to be seen. With the slow drag of her arm, Pherock removed a leather-bound book from her chest, strapped down with metal rivets. She shook the book violently, trying to draw attention to its importance.

"Sightings, Jewels? You got a whole lot more than the Lark to deal with here. An Inkling's on the prowl—been hunting right around 'ere to boot!" Jeweler took the bait, and kicked the soldier back, snatching the novel as he did. "What is the *matter* with you? I've been nothing but kind—I only mean to help you." Scrolling through the texts, Jeweler shook his head back, holding calm against the spite of the Gull.

"You and me both, jackass."

"Alls I'm sayin' is you've been pissy! 'Sall it is!" Jeweler put the book at his side, raising a glomming finger at Pherock.

"You one to talk, yeah? You can kiss your Larkik rubbers all damn day, but some of us have merit to keep 'tween the teeth, got it?" Returning to the text, Jeweler scrubbed the many observations of Inkling existence—a grand majority of which were falsified or misdefined. Terribly, however, a small few of them held accuracy, placing Roach at the scene of a Gretchkin massacre, or disappearance in the west. The descriptions were scarily accurate, with Jeweler's association oddly unplaced.

"Larkik rubbers? I'm out here in the damn storm hoping to keep you and your mates alive, stark opposite of kissing ass, right?"

"Not one of us needs your help, not the help of bird-scum."

"I'm just doing what we all do, Jeweler! Can't help if some toes get stomped 'long the way—that's what you always said." It took a moment of pause for Jeweler to register the spoken words, his eyes glued to the notebook of sightings. When the severity of the accusations came to be, he put the book aside, and smacked Pherock clean in the jaw, the force of which sent her to the rock and snow,

"That ain't me! You say some shit like that again and I'll make you regret being a bird!" Pherock choked on her teeth and coughed, holding her misshapen chin in the cup of her hand,

"Yeah—you and wireblood over there are real saints, Jeweler!" With a hearty kick to the head, Pherock's helmet fell flat upon her face, as she clutched her skull in defensive fright. Through biting sobs, she pulled her helmet up, peeking at the huffing force of rage above her.

"Somethin' changed in you, Jeweler. I'm not so sure it was a good change either." Jeweler steadied his breath, Viaduct proudly watching from the cockpit. He tossed the book back to the ramp of his ship and sealed his gun at his hip.

"You oughta make yourself scarce girl. Next time I see a Gull, it's bird on the menu, right?" Pherock frowned through her soft tears. A friend turned nothing, an enemy of sorts. Viaduct shook her a disapproving head of his own from his sealed metal, his malice gleaming through the latch. From behind a veil of snow, a sphere of rubbered black hair stuck up, bold eyes as white as the precipitation. Pherock let it stare, as she returned to it—a Gretchkin hand pulling its ambiance back to the shadows. It was familiar, not enough yet to conclude on, but something to light a kiln.

"Alright Jeweler, sure." She sniffled, helping herself to standing grace, stumbling toward the greater road. "Whatever you want, friend." Jeweler spat into the snow, back still to the Gull.

"We ain't friends. Never were, kid." The repairs continued, Gull or not. Pherock was one less thorn in Jeweler's side. As far as he was concerned, the events had been unpreventable, and vainly wasteful of his time. He feigned kinship for reliance, but Pherock was a desperate fool, whether love drunk or otherwise. She would be a danger to all if not for her absence. Viaduct was nearly finished anyways, the news of the Inkling sightings giving further reason to their haste. Viaduct sealed his troubles in the cockpit, distantly calling out to the bartender in regret,

The Harlequin

"You have a troubled past with all denizens of the Belt I suppose, Jeweler?"

"Ain't nothin' but trouble here V, you should know that." Ignoring the proposed dislike to the topic, Viaduct leaned forward, fingers creeping out the slit of the door,

"You must've been a Gull then—for some years at the very least." Jeweler did not reply and did not move to silence the informant. With no halt to his words, Viaduct grumbled on, "A Gull is one disaster, but to befriend a Dreyal... you have terrible taste in kinship. They are an awful people."

"She ain't my friend." Threading the spool through the latch, Jeweler's tone demanded no further questioning and rested the bulk of the conversation on Viaduct's head. Still heated from the exchange, he hummed away all thoughts of racial division and focused on the navigational repairs.

"Jeweler-man." Lullaby whispered, peeking into the sounds of tying wire, "Where going? Away from the great bird?" With the fall of the League of Twenty-Two, nowhere humble was safe from birdly sight. All three Tera's had either completely disappeared, or been overstuffed with Larkik oversight, Jeweler's own homeworld now a site of consumption at the hands of the merciful Lark.

"Not a clue. Suppose I've got some old contacts to spear. V? Any ideas?" Neck deeply embedded in a labyrinth of wire, Viaduct shouted back,

"Tracking the old crew is sadly not a viable means of safe-seeking. They are each too indebted to their security—might I suggest drifting through deep space for an eternity?" Lullaby questioned her privilege with a tap of her spear, before entering the ship's lower ramp.

"Maybe go to Ichyr home? Palosameerilyr? Can convince Gretchkin to peace maybe." Prior actions coming presently to mind, Jeweler disagreed with such an idea, complimenting the Legate's pronunciation in doing so. Debate pickled the three as each formed theories and threats with future homes in a cyclical nature until Roach intervened. The beast snuck over to the side of The Passerine, climbing atop it without alerting the bartender within. He reached a singular dancing talon around the lip of the entrance, snatching the translucent blue stone from Jeweler's sack. Leaping down to the snowy rest, Roach held the metallic object in front of himself, proud of his theft.

"Heeleeom... See?" Jeweler continued his suggestions, Viaduct hearing only the echoes from a distant language. Lullaby was the first to listen in to the beast, his claims resonating with her remembrance.

"The Helium Sea? Black thumbs and sunken people. I have seen it too." Pondering the containment of his stone, Jeweler carefully pictured the ocean. Black—sunken. Patting his coat, he turned to Roach, still fiddling with the rock in his jaw.

"Think I've seen it too—that rock's got some neat tricks." Slapping the Inky hands away, Jeweler returned the stone to his collection of valued tools "Where is it? Any safer than here?"

"Gone. It is the sea of Inkhome—origin of all dark ones." Viaduct's flickering eyes met the latch of the door.

"Pardon my intrusion—Inkhome? The homeworld of all Inklings? Was supposed lost to time and destruction by its origin god? *That* Inkhome?" Lullaby gleefully affirmed the claim, descriptions of a younger Lark discomforting the collective. Turning slightly to Jeweler Viaduct glued his screen to the door, passing his voice loudly through its creases,

"Jeweler, if there is any hope for its recovery, we must investigate this gem! I have myself authored writings on the existence of an ancient means of transport, magicks outside the reach of the Lark. This could be one—a rumored 'Home Stone'. How you came upon one shall remain a mystery." The bartender could only novel at his toes, and toy with his beard. Even he could not recall the stone's origins. To himself, he scolded the name of god for his misfortune, for the opportunity to science and riches before him. Age had caught up with his mind, and such prizes no longer seemed so interesting.

"Holme." Roach muttered, a sensible expression of recollection absorbing his round head. Jeweler had never seen Roach look so sure of his emotion. Lost in thought, the beast's eyes paced empty space, now entirely unsure of his origins. Home may not have been real at all.

"Well, that might just settle it. " Jeweler chimed in, temptation far too strong for his weak will, "As if we got elsewhere to be! Got any

ideas on working out the map? We'll be needin' a translator, right V?"
Viaduct assured Jeweler of a plan, a secure route to the map's
understanding. Jeweler smirked, the elation in Viaduct's voice
reminding him of past crimes.

"Alas, without a navigational drive, it could take us weeks to
locate even the closest moon. Jeweler, might I ask why you removed
all of these essential mainframe parts?" Brushing back his hair and
standing, Jeweler claimed them all to be clear Larkik spyware,
designed only to publicize your location to proper authorities. As
predicted, Viaduct could do little but roll his eyes,

"Though, when I did take them out, I made sure to stow 'em
all away. Along with some fancy goodies, they should be sitting
proper back home. Pico Nevado—not a far walk from here." Viaduct
doubted the clarity of the claim, recalling the old ruined manor at the
height of the Belt. It had entered a state of abandonment long ago and
remained in disrepair since. When Viaduct had some semblance of
control over the people of Klockgrave, he speculated the home to be
that of an esteemed merchant or regal cardinal to the Lark.

"You claim ownership of the pyres of scrap wood atop
Klockgrave? However did you come upon such an estate?"

"You make a fortune when you play for outlaws." Hauling a
pack up to his waist, Jeweler stepped down from the Passerine and
looked off into the snow. "Let me handle this one solo. Be back in less
than a day." The bartender pulled up his scarf and paced off into the
snow. Lullaby and Roach looked at each other, returning to their
converse and games. Viaduct was left to his devices—quite literally—
and confusion. He hoped Jeweler's estimates would prove correct.

Pherock landed softly off the carrier ship, the indentation in
her helmet reflecting soft neon traces in the harbor. What ridicule, and
complete humiliation! Jeweler had been her best friend, an
inseparable partner! When his time had come, Jeweler left the Lark
willingly and with great relief. He had made his wishes clear—being
far too old to handle the pressure of war and his superior officers.
Pherock didn't blame him, after all, he would miss her. Right? There
was a kinship solidified by then, there was no reason to believe they
weren't friends.

Creatures of Habit

"Pherock! Good *Lark* where have you been? You leave a platoon of willing Gulls at your end lifeless without leader. I should strip you of your rank and leave you *Ichyrless*." Pherock could show no display of fear, it was the way of the strong.

"Sire! I bring news of the Inkling—I have made confirmation of its hunting pattern! It appears to be trailing a bartender on the Imperial Belt." Forklorn would not believe such heresy. The sightings had been confined around the area of Klockgrave, yes, but it was hard to confide in such a petty underling. He voiced greater concerns,

"Have you any evidence of this, besides a convenient pattern in the sightings book?" The royal medal jangled against the steel breastplate of the Keppel Crow's apron. He marched with pride, adjusting the course settings for his various mechanical implements.

"Well yes of course sire! I saw it!" Forklorn released himself from a near contraption, turning slowly to the sweating pool of Pherock.

"You what?"

"Saw it—the Inkling! Sire!" Resting his chin in the nook of his gauntlet, he pondered the path ahead. Though it could not be seen from under his mask, the Keppel Crow moved mountains of thought, brows aflutter with great indecision.

"Where. With the bartender?"

"Just 'yond his ship—stalking prey all feral-like." Forklorn softly invited his underling forward, wrapping his arm loosely about her waist. Silently, the two proceeded deeper into the crypt, a tremendous hall marking the entrance Cathedral of Chitin.

"How long have you known this bartender, Pherock?" The Keppel Crow questioned. Without thought, Pherock recounted their travels, the earliest days of the Larkik Definition they shared in memory. "Yes. Did it ever occur to you that this man could be *protecting* the Inkling?" Coming to a stop at the center of the cathedral, Pherock could not help but stare.

"What? No. You mean—" Forklorn smacked the Gull across her cheek, adding another dent to her helm.

"Pest! Your *peon's* brain could not possibly comprehend what is so clearly before you!" Before she could recover from the blow, Forklorn clutched Pherock by the collar, lifting her slightly above the floor of the cathedral. "The fruits of your failure are ripe; *one* more mistake, and you will drown in the Lark's personal Well. Savvy?" Tossing her aside, Forklorn did not await a response. With her proper report and the evidence of her tears, he had new battles to conquer. "You and I both will execute this beast. Alone. Not a soul needs to know of your shortcomings." Nodding hurriedly, Pherock scrambled to her feet, chaos in her steps.

"O-of course sire! I—" Her throat croaked as she gathered words, drifting leaves from the sprout of her mind. Nothing was proper enough to excuse her insolence. Without another spoken term, the two made a pact. The Inkling would fall that night.

Dawnbroken darkness submerged the shore of the Imperial Belt, flakes of ice chipping off into orbit only to land calmly again in the pastel treelines. Rocky meteors stood against one another, forging up a hilly edge to the Belt, dotted with snow and cliff faces. As asteroids had eroded the line between space and existence, so too had the presence of infrastructure corroded the semblance of peace it brought. The manor was taller than wide, a picturesque stone fortress standing against the burning wind. A steeple of corrugated metal pressed out into the storm—a lantern hung in its mouth—and glowed fervently. Sprawling gardens once prospered through pure spite, desolated by the lack of tending hands. Against the line of mystery trees stood an iron fence bent back and snapped across its width. Windows reigned shattered, and toothpick debris stuck up against the steeple's tower. The roofing caved inwards, where walls failed to properly hold form. Quiet had completely overtaken the villa, all its intricacies locked away in compartmentalized tombs. Disturbing the quiet came an inhabitant, shadows drawn from their flesh as their goggles obscured all flowing cold. Jeweler paced towards the gate, knowing full well it had never been locked. The cold had nearly frosted through his right arm, he coddled it between his cloak and chest. What little dust picked at his eyes was quickly blinked away, the scarf tight around the face. Trudging up the marble stairs, snow blended in with stone. Stumbling at the top, he leaned inwards against the winds and slammed desperately against the door. Despite his entrance into the home, the gale still echoed in the distance. Prying off his goggles and pulling them to his neck, Jeweler's red-ringed eyes scanned the foyer. Archways plastered what little ceiling remained far above—built for someone taller than he could ever hope to be. Any familiar scents or hints at noticeable texture had been flushed out with the ice, chill now overtaking the elegance his home once had. Three plate-mail statuettes lingered in the main hall, old Ichyric soldiers of Palosameerilyr. His wife had selected the decor, cut the carpets from her own fabric, trimmed the awnings to her liking, and picked her own host of petunias and moonflowers. It was her home more than it had ever been his. The structure itself had never been something of his desire, but the messages that came with the home—the family too—was all he ever wanted. Perfection ignored the lesser sins of cold and miserable color theory. Kicking away displacements from his boots, Jeweler unfurled a thin book from his pant leg. The thick purple nearly glowed in the dark home, light unnecessary in locating such a familiar place. Loose memory of the cache guided his steps over tangled calep roots and piles of rubble. The ties of an old chandelier caught on wooden trusses dangled crystalline rims. Some shards had fallen and scattered, bulbs smashed and tungsten stuck up like weeds through the carpets. Pausing in the sorry foyer, Jeweler imagined the warm ambiance of servants and soup scents. The very presence of the walls brought him back to a time before death. Wandering to the kitchen, he hummed to himself, no longer so desperate to locate his commodities.

"Grow-Bri-ar," He whispered, feet carrying forward as he slid against the iced-over kitchen tile. "hold fast in the storm. Bite back the wind and flaunt out your thorns." The cutlery had been strewn across the countertops, pots, and pans stacked against the window and blocking out the snow. On the island centermost to the room, a cauldron stood as remembered, its contents hissed over with mold and ice. Yet, carrots and goat cheese still ruminated about the room, filling Jeweler with a recollection of a familial recipe. Old as time, it was the best thing family had brought him. A shadowy dress fluttered before him, as the past lured him into the back halls. "Grow-Bri-ar," stamping up a rounding stairwell, Jeweler followed the specter, "cut paths in the spring." Paintings of dead—entirely unknown—elders lined the curl upwards, some hung still, many decayed and left collapsed against the marble stairwell. A birdcage clattered against the steps, falling from its ambient hold against the ceiling. "Hush up the children with flush-colored wings." Laughter chanted in the halls as snow piled against the stairwell. Cold bit at the bartender's neck, and he pulled his scarf up higher. Slowly, he encroached on the voices, the upper balcony precariously disjointed from the wall supports. "Oh-Bri-ar," Jeweler paused, leaning against the rails of the balcony. Though it was hard on the eyes, he could nearly picture it whole again, the chipped tile embraced in smoothness, carpets lathered against itchy wood. A night long ago he had sat by the foyer reading jurisdiction papers—callbacks to his days as a Gull. His wife had brought a loaf of bread, expecting him to be hungry enough to eat it alone. They had laughed over its inconvenience. "Left beckonin'… Alone." Trailing off, Jeweler watched the pictures flicker in the falling snow. Humming brought rest to the visions and filled in the place for words he did not know. The fourth stanza failed him too, as he continued deeper into the manor. The peak of its ascent was its master bedroom, draped in silks and fine spools. The cache was either there, or at the deepest pits, which the bartender could not remember. Familiar songs met him, it was that of the wind through chimes, salt in his lips, and memories floating like cloud matter. The world went pink.

"Uprooted and teething for cold summer stone." Spinning around in a rapid flurry, Jeweler drew his handgun and cocked the hammer. No specter greeted him, nor did any paltry visions. Just the voice on the wind, and nothing more. It was the correct line if he recalled it properly, but not to the tune he liked. Even so, the song grew somber afterward—he never much liked its closure. Ascension caught his focus, as rapid dark silhouettes darted overhead. The creaking of wood and slumping of mounds of chill brought silence to the air. Dim harpsichord rested in the back of Jeweler's head, bringing too many sounds into focus for him to think clearly. At the top of the stairs, just before the lip to the bedroom, stood the turned shape of a studious woman, wed in her dress of black and gold. Her silk hair drifted in the breeze like thread undone from its wheel. Golden white, it remained untouched by the weather. "No-Bri-ar, when the moth takes your fruit, and burns up your leaves and…" Jeweler had not the movement in his tendons to drop his weapon. His goggles clicked against the tin of his shoulder plate, stone mirrors of ice reflecting his blank eyes.

"Rips out yer shoots." The woman did not turn, only gesturing to the seat beside her—a vacant stone bench aimed down at a desolate garden of ice sculptures and obscure cubes. He did not sit.

"No Briar came first. You've confused the verses, Jeweler." His wrists throttled with vile blood, unsure of how to respond. Her fingers jittered, becoming six and then unbecoming two.

"Thought I screwed it someway. Been a while since I heard it, after all." With nothing left to do, he approached the bench, keeping a restless eye on the hand.

"That's my fault, isn't it?"

"You said it, not me."

"Thee would have it true." Jeweler glanced at the beak, expecting it not to be there at all. Disappointment lowered his eyes.

"You're wearin' it." A thin hand wrapped around the beak, pink gaze coating the white flesh.

"So I am. I do know how it displeases you." Tucking the gun into his pants, Jeweler sighed,

"That *is* why you're doin' it, right?" Snapping bones brought the deadly owl's head to him, eyesight poking deep, a lathe of remembrance.

"Jewels? Why are you here again?"

"Again?" Her fingers shifted more rapidly, haze encompassing them. She began to reach one out, but before it could breach the trespass of her gown, it fractured back to its resting side.

"Just the other day, Jewels honey. You tucked away that unsightly casket."

"You got it for me, Pez. Twenty-seven years ago, a move-in gift if you weren't lyin'." Returning to his thoughts, the ice made good work as a reflector. Maen's light thinly cut through the cracks in the stone. "Haven't been here in years, neither have you." She tried to reach out once more, yielding similar results. Tawdry bands of gold wrapped her inconsistent digits, spun about by unreliable nails.

"I am always here Jeweler." Jeweler snatched up the flicker palm into his own, its consistency stilling to a singular reality. Her pale flesh was buzzing on his, static stabs shared among surface skin.

The Harlequin

"No you *ain't.* Not once have you called me anything but—"
His tongue caught against the back of his throat, nearly clogging his
breath. "You think you're helpin', but you ain't." Her mask was still
struck down the middle. Sable breath flowed from within, her
temptation brewing.

"Talking to yourself alone in the cold is a tragic hobby."

"If you were me, you wouldn't be callin' me that."

"Wouldn't I?" Three stowaway hawks flew from the rafters
of the bed-chamber tower. Jeweler recalled his post, the timely
manner of it all.

"I'm headin' out soon, up there again." He stood, and
fluttered away from the bench. The two hands remained clasped
against each other, a vibrance of life between them. "You owe me a
visit, maybe'll come take it from you." The pink lenses bore into
Jeweler's humble orbs. Polished snow hid away the bags beneath,
giving the skin the illusion of a faint yellow. Softly, the specter let
loose her hand, leaving in its place the ambient spectacle of ghost
touch. Like pillars of chasing salt, Jeweler's palm formed columns and
paths, skin rising and falling without feeling. Troubled, he shook
away the illusion, only to worsen the fleshy mistake. He stepped back
from the bench, opposite hand running along the wall of the bed
chamber door. Pushing it open, his hand became far less of a concern.
The void of the bedroom hid the clear sound of chewing, a faint gurgle
of flesh and blood spilling against the tapestry floor. Clicking bones
and clattering tongues echoed through the chamber. Stepping
sideways, careful to keep his weight above him, Jeweler peered into
the dark. The bedframe could be made out, a paladin's wear slung
over it. Drapes obscured the rims of the room, a single wooden spool
consuming the drawers to the left. A cracking pull sunk Jeweler's foot
into the floor, and a board snapped under his intentional weight. Two
transcendent white dots appeared in the shadows. Movement was
nowhere to be found, the snow stilled through the gaping ceiling and
the drapes shuddered to a halt. Suddenly there was a scampering of
talons, a leap brought with a panting howl, and Jeweler was taken
down further than before, the collapse of the floor guaranteed with
the two bodies entwined. The two fell through two floors, a story
under the manor's visible resting level. Lacking pain, Jeweler's next

concern was death itself. The bartender did not propose overbearing comfort and greetings in slobber.

"R-roach?" As his shadowy demeanor changed to inky clarity, Jeweler could not discern his emotions as rageful or proud.

"Jewels!" Brute force brought the bartender to his feet, an unpleasant sting lingering in his lower back.

"I oughta—" Grappling to Roach, Jeweler stumbled forward and into the shadows once more, where chill took hold of his fingers. The toothy smirk upon Roach's face prevented all scolding, its brief pants signs of excitement rather than exhaustion. Giving his hold up in trade for compliments, Jeweler tussled the antennae of his investment, "I oughta stop expectin' so much from you buddy." Scraping stuck ice from his boot heel, Jeweler hopped to the south wall, racks of bottles upon bottles lining its cobble. "Suppose a hand couldn't hurt. You seen any pinkish boxes up there, Roach?" Denying any sightings, the beast crawled off towards the void of the cellar, his antennae aflutter in the hunt. Snorts emitted from the dark, and the bartender followed after, hand on his belt as a pure precaution. Familiarity took hold, and the void became less so, geometry forming—then complexity. The wine cellar was once a workshop and before that a storehouse. In the deepest corners large crates of calep binds still stood undusted, fetid orange moss growing from their base. A cabinet of poorly stitched cloaks lay spilled against a banister of an unreachable staircase. Worms burrowed into the hungry fabric, holes littering its seams. In the center of the dark was a spool of white thread. A spear-shaped needle stuck into its treen top. A set of intricate tailor's tools were placed particularly upon its surface. Jeweler could not help but toy with them. "Never really got too good at this. Needed a hand to teach me, wife said seamwork 'quired teamwork." Lifting an unfinished veil from the spool, the bartender sighed, "Jeweler the seamster. Woulda made some real art, I think." Roach curled himself against the spool.

"Tay-ler." Jeweler stared past the tool, Roach making no attempts at contact.

"What?"

"Tay. Lor?" The bartender returned the item to its place among the spool, brushing the scarf away from his beard.

The Harlequin

"No idea who you're talkin' about." Licking the scabbing wound on his lips, Jeweler's mouth filled with the flavor of salt, white mist pouring out from his nose. Leaning against the spool for concentration, he could not clear his mouth of the taste. The smell of matted fur and further bitter air choked the beast and bartender, now desperate to leave the catacomb of wine. The supports of the roof cracked as a familiar divine shape lowered itself to the cellar, embraced in feathers. Roach dared not even growl as he slinked away from the angelic heron, its beak now braced with the essence of metal. Overwhelmed by his senses, Jeweler could hardly contain his suffering, caught in his fall by the beast he aimed to protect. The lofty needle rebounded against the bartender's patient arm, and a rapture of metallic clanging turned the angel.

"Roach, haul ass." Its first instinct was to swing high, missing the intruders but cutting down the room above. Sofas and the tile flooring slid down as monstrous hail, the two narrowly shirking death at each corner. Roach scooped his owner from his feet and bolted up a dismembered stairwell—feet gripping on half-steps—slamming himself against the basement door. The foyer remained placeless, snow leaving the only remote sound about the room. Hushed whispers beckoned Jeweler up again, to his possessions.

"Can you wrestle that thing, Roach?" Uncertain of his means, the beast nodded powerfully. Before either could conclude a plan, the bird tore through the floor, clawing its way up to the foyer dripping with hate. It had no rhymes left to ponder—only death to deal. Roach leapt over its snapping beak, closing his arms around the bulk of its transcendent throat. With weight they both returned to the cellar, Jeweler left alone in the soft patience of the foyer. The cache *had* to be in the bedroom, his memory was certain now. All he need do is escape to the upper levels, collect his valuables, and leave the Belt to the rats. The metalloid fist of an unseen intruder snapped against Jeweler's cheek, sending him down to the slipping tiles. Wind-lost and sopping with blood, the bartender clutched his cheek, a small scar where his flesh once was.

"One usually suits lesskin. Get up and let me strike you again, heretic." Before his leaden corpse was the outline of Larkik prestige—a Crow in the flesh, perfect hatred its only tool. From head to toe was an apron of the thickest hides painted an azure blue. Black garments followed underneath, a metallic glimmer present under the pant legs. Gauntlets of steel clouded the flesh, and a serrated flamberge poked from the edge of the fist. Blood dripped down the hands, tarnishing the pure color of the metal. The bone-white mask of birdly demeanor hid the terrible pins of blue eyelight, darkening the shadows around the Crow. Drooping from wet snow, a thick-brimmed hat shadowed over Jeweler. Rising, he sucked in a good portion of blood and swallowed.

"I ain't go down like—" Without finishing, a punch was delivered to his gut, knocking all oxygen from his lungs and puncturing a kidney. The bartender's neck split against the wooden steps, silencing any further remarks.

"Again, you're putting up further trouble." Forklorn stomped against the tile, cracking each as he approached his prey.

"No—k-keep the fu—" Piercing the collar bone, the Keppel Crow hung Jeweler against the wall, fist at his throat.

"Call the Inkling." No words escaped the bartender's lips, yet they did not need to. Forklorn inhaled thickly, ready to bark a second command. From the floor came a grasping hand, Roach barreling out from the abyss singed with Ichyr. He tackled the Crow down, fangs ripe at the throat and halted by steel. Jeweler drew his pistol and fired thrice, all to Forklorn's miraculous pleasure.

"Even more a toy without its original owner." With little difficulty, Forklorn flung the embodiment of Ink from his neck and rose to slaughter it. Drawing a second knife, he beckoned—Jeweler's fluid dripping down his thighs. As the Inkling and Crow sought each other's skin, the bartender slid back against the ascent. Two flights of stairs stood between him and the cache, wounds growing unnoticeable in the cold. A clash of demonic cries and cutting encouraged him as he crawled, legs buckling from the weight. He had never once hoped to fight a Crow and knew his skills were little more than a disappointment to a foe so strong. The only hope for victory was in cowardice.

"Pez... could use you're—gah—" She did not appear to him, and through tears of ice, he moaned her name. Jeweler could feel the blood oiling his snail's-climb to heaven, Maen's light an invitation to die quicker. None of his wounds were fatal enough to bring about proper misery. Down in the foyer, Roach had his two arms separated from their stumps, one of which quickly returned to catch a stabbing uppercut. Forklorn did not bore his prey with a monologue, there was fighting to be done and battle was no place for the pen. Snide chuckles and cut-away yawns were more than enough to tempt rage from those who thought worthy to best him, provocation was the greatest mastery of war. Roach had supplied a small fraction of scars to his metallic jacket, none deep enough to even hear of flesh. Ducking a cut and tackle, Forklorn wrestled his waist free from a hold, poking out one of the beast's tumorous eyes. Roach leaped forward, a growl preceded a snatch at the Crow's skeletal mask. Unexpectedly, the tear did not tug it loose from its place. Stumbling from the adhesive clutch, Forklorn slicked his knives together, a clatter of light and pinching noise that overcame Roach's simple mind. He covered his eyes, matting back antennae to hold in silence. The Crow flipped the knife to his backhand, twisting his wrist to crack tension. "Beggin' never got me home safe." The bartender muttered, his back pressing neatly against the root of the bed frame. Its footing edged precariously above the drop to the cellar, a macabre sloshing and hissing emerging from below. The cache was just under the covers, and with a few careful pushes it would be Jewelers once more. Even with the prize in sight, he could not rightly recall its complete contents. There was a navigational drive—a widget of circuits and screens. A fortune must have been left behind, perhaps an heirloom from brighter days, but nothing of note returned to him. Another tensing of his gut expelled the bartender's breath. A torrent of soggy foam soaked his cloak, bleeding crimson into the bedspread. A final nudge sent the bed to the cellar, a shrouded eagle's cry escaping the clamor. Jeweler clutched his chest, the rose starch oozing further from his hand. Undoing his belt revealed a torn strand of sew-marks—a gash unhealed. He did not have his thread nor his needle, and thus had no means to secure his internals. Reaching out to the casket, the bartender moaned, flipping open its lid to reveal his salvation. An array of cobalt and plastics bound into a thick-rimmed tablet protruded from the box. The singed edge of glass indicated its place in the original ship systems: a navigational drive. Beneath the essential component was a bucket, reclusive emptiness surrounding the metal. Not a bucket, interior padding would prove otherwise. Picking up the metalloid bowl, the beak came into view. It was mangled by hammer wounds and prying hands beyond recognition. Eye slits had been soldered over with copper plate, the feathered plume torn straight from its binding pins. An owner's ID—or at least had been one, at some point—had been scratched out in favor of a much thinner, direct text, *Bàs do Eòin*. Much like a set of feline ears, the interior of the beak's two mandibles had been inverted, and two deep scars etched into the side of the helm. It mirrored the visage of a nightmarish cat. Jeweler remembered its use, the art of secrecy was once far more valuable than cultured style. The design had worn thin on him, but by the time it had any sense of urgent renewal, it was no longer necessary. One more object remained in the cache—silk wrapped and finely buried. The golden handle lingered outside the blue cloth, black stains among its smoothness. His pride in combat, Jeweler wrapped his fingers around its hilt, allowing the Ink from its edge to pour down around his knuckles. Bitter salts filled the bartender's mouth as he drew the cutlass from its fiber, the split remains of a blade shattered in a great turmoil. The angel rose itself to the bed chamber, face scarred with Ink singes. Knowing no other means to descend safely, Jeweler threw himself onto the Ichyric, digging the broken blade into the front of its winged arm. Tumbling down the hold, the two crashed atop Forklorn, who had maintained his upper-hand status throughout his battle. Distracted by the blazing white pigeon and the impaled bartender, Forklorn was forcibly dislodged from his place standing atop the cellar pit, embraced by the Ichyric and slathered with Ink. Roach hissed, snatching Jeweler by the ankle, and tearing him up to the foyer. The angel hurled the Crow across the room, careless to notice the Ink stains, considering the pursual of both parties. Shaking the bartender Roach slurred,

"Leaf nooow!" Forklorn rose to his feet, the left eye of his mask flickering in the dim cellar air. The Ichyric roared, its familiar shattering sound easily ignored by the Crow. In a simple movement, he grasped the beast by the neck and thrust his dagger through its lower beak. Sealed by serrated edge lines, Forklorn was torturously slow in slugging the body away from himself, leaping to the foyer level once more. It was vacant, an amber trail misleadingly drawn around in the snow, before vanishing completely. Pherock stepped into the manor, holding the door ajar for a moment to confirm its contents, and patiently sealing it behind herself.

"Sire? Shall we pursue them?" Without a word, Forklorn denied the request, holding steady as he traced the exact turn of the previous battle. He had not lost, it was comedy that had failed him. The joke was at his expense, made to look a fool in the eyes of the Larkik court. With a gasp, Pherock retracted her steps, slipping back on the ice, and inched away from Forklorn's standing place. He grasped the angel by its sealed beak and crushed it to splinters. He took care to pull the rest of the body up before tearing the head from its shoulders entirely. The divine liquid made the snow all the whiter.

"I don't smell the Ink anymore." He clapped his hands, all ice remaining on the metal gauntlets falling from the vibration. "Now you know what you're dealing with." He tossed the head aside, and strolled to the exit, flicking gore from the blade on his fist.

"Pardon sire? What *I'm* dealin' with?" Forklorn turned, briefly raising a finger, before returning it to his side.

"The bartender is a lesskin and the Inkling is restrained with both emotion and a partitioned focus. They are hardly deserving of the time of someone as renowned as I." She was caught in a snare of incomprehension and did not vouch for her own weakness. "If you want to prove yourself valuable, mortal? Kill them both. Return to me if you need advice on the semantics of proper combat." Leaving the building to its sole living inhabitant, Forklorn softly hummed allegiance to the Lark. When the snow obscured his silhouette entirely, Pherock let herself fall against the tile. With a rifle to her name and no intent to harm friends, tears once more overwhelmed her. Her father would be disappointed, her brothers would beat her senseless had they seen her wallow so openly. In careful consideration, she damned her family name and took up her rifle's last magazine. Jeweler was no friend of hers, was he? How hard could a shot to the head really be? The Inkling was the only real threat, while not an expert herself, Pherock knew plenty of favors more than willing to find a place among feathered heaven.

~ *The Dud*

Recorded in part by factory security films, and wholly encrypted into the Passerine's logs...

Brass is a soft metal, described as unchallenging to drill or saw. Whether purchased off the direct market, gathered in ore, and alloyed together in a forge—or simpler yet—cut from the bandoliers of any who would dare oppose the Lark, brass was an infinitely obtainable, yet quickly diminishing resource. Bullets, and the weapons that used them, still were held in high regard across the galaxy, and to some degree, they were stronger than any other form of modern ranged combat. Larkik innovation had only carried the people of war forward small leaps, at least when compared to the figurative game of hopscotch played successfully thrice over via the creation of the Kineticants. Weapons of metal projectiles, rightfully dubbed Kineticants, had always been the more researched product. Congestants and other weapons of plasmatic origin were often unaffordable to the average arms dealer, to such a degree that even the Larkik Order used few Congestants in their ranks. Kineticants being both cost-effective and incredibly thorough was an obvious sign of their fair use. Because of this, many companies still produced them, anything worth wormpennies was eventually industrialized, after all. A minor and quite frankly irrelevant producer of these very means— as well as arms and matter of other distinct kinds—was based entirely upon the dark planet of Xenolashe. The Aves Coalition Powder company pasted its brand on any tool in their factories, if it was theirs, the workers and their families would surely know it. Petty theft was a straightforward avenue to procuring the funds required to escape the planet, and as such, was abundant among the citizens. Few remained by choice. An ACP chipping knife, owned only by those employed at the factories, slipped instantly against the now-hardened shell of the freshest bullet casing on the line. The worker wielding the knife, now bearing a slash down the length of their golden thumb, cursed back at the aluminum table before them, tossing both the knife and casing back onto its surface.

"Lark, CH! The hell are you doing?" The aforementioned 'CH' ignored her coworker, not being a particularly friendly character herself. Her father had commented on how ridiculous her cowardice from others had been in her youth, though 'CH' remained convinced it was his malintent that had given birth to her trepidation of people. Seeaitch Symphonite, a comedic, yet agonizing title for an innocent Tetarien girl to have. As a result of external birth—born of two creeds—her name existed as a spit in the face to all of her half-kind. For the other quota, she was a bastard. Yet, names withal, Seeaitch had commented little on her name, instead preferring to remark on the names of those around her. She had been fond of a Yemirch, one Kaloway, and a Hulper too. These names were her own mockery, being a kind child she never let words of distaste slip her mouth in public.

"D-damn, didn't mean'ta—" Seeaitch shoved her thumb into her origlyph, burying the bloodied wound in her cheek flesh. Regathering the knife with her able hand, she tumbled the brass casing back into her flaxen palm. There was an obvious 'C' scrawled into the metal. The beginnings of something one could consider an 'H' had been cut beside it, threatening the perfection of the adjacent letter.

"Well, you did. This is why we're under budget." Short, bated breaths followed the speech, muttering blame and curses.

"Not true, bossman said it was cause of them riots. The powder kids, those guys."

A spur of metal slammed itself against the staff room wall. The steel-braced door which was lined with suspicious dents made quite the echo across the brick-layed room. A figure buttoned up in a double layer of coats—both layers lacking sleeves of any kind—strode into the room. His eyes reminded Seeaitch of her mother's. The pale white metal bolted across the figure's wrists glowed against the straining fluorescent lights. Both of its amber bulbs pulsed and crossed with each other as if completing calculations at the very moment.

"One of the powder loaders mismeasured a dose. It would appear the factory is *again* in a state of near catastrophe. I'm sending you home early. Better not working than dead, I would say." The Bossman, a Sylvite like many other administrators, flicked the loose wiring at its neck. Seeaitch had been a member of the casing group for all her adulthood, the Sylvite had managed her for two of those years (the prior had moved on beyond Xenolashe). Seeaitch, despite circumstance, had never found any particular desire to leave the planet, there wasn't much to please her. Life was as miserable as death was, however, suicide was moronic in that sense. Endless labor at least serviced the Lark, among other people of goodwill.

"We comin' in tomorrow? Bossman, I don't think we can miss two days 'o labor, not for Lerky." The Sylvite machine thinned out a smudge on their protective screen, black like coal ash. It did little to dim the phosphorescing blotches between the dark, themselves clicking and jittering in the warmth.

"I suppose you are correct. Come in tomorrow, then. Wear thick layers. I know the heat is beyond us, but that load is still a hazard." Without another word, the Bossman left. Seeaitch resumed her project, the wound on her left hand still dribbling blood on occasion. The initials were far from perfect, but at least they were relatively legible.

"Didn't you just cut your damn finger with that? And you're at it again? You must have a deathwish CH, clearly not *cut* out for it, eh?" Continuing, Seeaitch drew her thumb back with every scrawl, with every movement in her fickle drone of a body. It was negligible — the pain — and completion were of the utmost importance.

"Told you not to try it, look, your lobbing socks are wet." Ubervan picked at the metal bars ahead of his flame. Grotesque and black, the metal was riddled with singe marks and dents, long overdue for repairs. Wistfully, few Scoria ever ventured as far as the Imperial Belt, and certainly not to Xenolashe. The planet bore no workmen, none wise enough to make repairs on a Potbelly.

The Harlequin

"Aw— Y-you're right, yeah. My socks...." Seeaitch cuffed her sleeves, and pulled up the socks, tucking fragmented Goldskiin stray from her feet under the cloth. The two continued on, first stop would be Ubervan's hostel, a small unremarkable building that stained an omnipresent cull in Seeaitch's mind. Unlike past experiences, Seeaitch had a fond practice over her own memory, as if able to forget and recall at will, a tool used to its fullest whenever she spoke with her husk of a father, slightly comatose and dismally all but dead.

"Your mom still on 27th?" Seeaitch hurried to catch up to her coworker, ensuring the two stick close together despite the lack of danger or crowd.

"Dunno. Uhm, sure. I think at least." Ubervan shook his head and chuckled, the roar of the plasma cutting through the silence of nightfall.

"Do you not check up on her from time to time mate? She's fossilized by now, worth her daughter's time yeah?" Seeaitch neglected to mention any of her mother's requests to leave the system, nor the following begs for her to never return to her own mother's bedside. Instead, she kept moving forward, harboring sorrow for a friend caught in lies. Ubervan did however have the gall to recount their adventures, though few, in childhood. How ironic it was to be together again after such a long time apart. He remembered her mother, who was to many a woman of absolute sacrifice, and furthermore gentle admiration.

"She said I am destined, you know." Ubervan agreed, though jokingly at first. He had once a desire, weak as it may be, to bond with Seeaitch. At first, it was juvenile, then something further. Romance was forbidden in Xenolashe. Not by law, no of course not, by the setting. A place of heat beyond imagination, the only sun a distant blip on the voidish horizon; darkness perpetuates an endless sea of unfavorable people, unsavory folk that Seeaitch had met thousands of times before. It was no place for love, and certainly not for children! But that does not excuse carnal desires. Ubervan lived by his lonesome, no one to comfort him when the gravity of just how corrupt his burning soul had become fell like a moon upon him. No, love would not fix this. It was a deeper problem worth days and years of analysis and therapeutics, perhaps medication if there was any left in Xenolashe to give willingly to its citizenship.

"Destined to cut your thumb off?" If not for the unmentionably growing chances of this occurring, Seeaitch would have chuckled. The estrangement between the two, often viewed in its raw form in conversations about the factory, was not as strange as thought by many. The criminally embarrassing banter that was shared during working hours was not such for either of the two friends nor was it found to be too far from entertaining by any other worker at the factory. It was—as concluded by most onlookers—childish glimmer, something that despite their age perpetuated about the two for all of their years. Perhaps it was this childishness that often forced Ubervan into a sort of chrysalis of regret, wherein he had no daunt to ask Seeaitch for anything further than friendship. Thus, it remained just that, for the unseeable future.

"Nay. G-goodness, Ube. Goodness and heroics. I— I was to be a hero, she s-said." Seeaitch was not one to ignore the question at hand, she had difficulty staying *off* task. Any conversation worth beginning earned its right to a proper end, and furthermore, a quality listener. She lacked the patience and informed mind to twiddle her thumbs, nor had she ever found herself patting down her belongings in the heat of discussion. It was outrageous, uncouth.

"Heroics. Hmm, I can see it." A bolstered panic flashed like blush across Seeaitch's face, the metal on her face heating to its melting point.

"Me? No no! S-see what? I couldn't— not a *hero* Ube! Anything but that!" Ubervan chuckled to himself, patting the flustered lass on the shoulder, assuring her that it was far easier than she thought. A hero need not save the universe, after all. A hero was whatever they made themselves to be. A small-time savior, a meaningless donor of a simple spare coin, or far greater than both of these examples. It was impossible to fit the description of another's hero, it couldn't be done because there were already heroes of their liking. A hero who invents themselves becomes the very thing they dreamed of: the perfect spark of hope craved by their world. Once this torch was kindled, the plate of heroism must be rended to a chasm awaiting the corpse of another hero to fill it. Seeaitch had seen monsters be made of men, many of whom falsely claimed heroism to be their fidelity. A Six-fingered creature wrought faith into a hook that caught billions with its peering line. Machine men had become the normality for anti-heroism, and anti-heroism was the normality for fame. Seeaitch thought it all pathetic, after all, what had happened to old-fashioned praisable champions of goodness? No need for negativity, or failure. They were icons of pure light, who despite temptations and humanity, overcame all odds to see the daybreak of their efforts, the true end of all trials. Seeaitch wanted to be a champion of such traits. Ubervan disagreed with the methods of his co-worker but nonetheless praised her for her ambition.

"You know the route Seeaitch, damn better'n I do I'd bet." Ubervan gestured up to his apartment. "Best be off. Good walkin' with you friendo." Before Seeaitch could call a secondary goodbye, Ubervan had begun the ascent to his home. Seeaitch never got the chance to give her farewells, but Ubervan's pledge to see her at work tomorrow lightened her step. There was a formidable quantity of roads before her, and oddly enough no hurry to pass them. She continued to question her odds of becoming something valuable, a hero no less. Her mother had spoken of less reasonable things before. Seeaitch always had a liking of cutlasses, what the girl would do for a cutlass! She had seen one on the broadside of a rather fearsome Gretchkin trader years back, surely they were being smelted by someone. Furthermore, a fitting set of royal armor, perhaps of Tetarien origin (seeing as they made the fanciest plates) would go quite well with her weapon of choice. It wouldn't take long for her to discover a namesake, perhaps gather an entourage too. Living the life of a hero, one act of goodness at a time. Until death, that is, which though a terrible thing to imagine, was never far from the sightlines of a hero. A drifting clatter, like tens of marbles thrown upon ice blocks, passed through the alley to Seeaitch's side. No sense in investigating, a murder a day was abnormally low for Xenolashe. But murder was often nonconsensual, or at least so Seeaitch assumed. How could she feign such certainty? On the off chance it was against the will of the victim, perhaps this was the perfect place to begin a reign of heroism over the long-darkened city? Seeaitch peered into the alley, spying two figures scuffling in the shadows. One figure was assuredly losing. Seeaitch fiddled with her bag, pulling from it her carving knife, and heading down into the alley. Shadows were her nomenclature, quick and quiet as any thief would be. Often compared to summer blossoms from various desert cacti (they sprouted from time to time in the northern forest of her hometown, now just a distant memory) her scent was undeniably potent, not the kind of aura a sneak thief would desire to have. Though of course, once a hero of her own, an iconic smell could be the difference between poverty and a successful (yet humble) selection of gift-shop candle varieties all in Seeaitch's name. The brawl grew more intense, and in the extremely faint light of the moon, it became apparent that there was more passion than war shared between the two figures. One appeared pantless, though still harnessed in a trenchcoat to hide their ghastly burns. The other echoed such youth that Seeaitch had no choice but to question the nature of their love. But no difference, action spoke far louder than the mesmerizing rain droplets of the encroaching storm. But what if there was consent to this encounter? What if Seeaitch found herself heavily outmaneuvered by her foe? Oh for all the glory that lay for the taking beyond just one simple task, there was a heap of uncertainty resting in Seeaitch's mind. Before her place in the factory, Seeaitch had lost the right to call herself by name after failing to enter the ranks of the Larkik Definition. It was a terrible time for her mother, both in mind and body. A plague beset her heart, and disappointment clutched her soul. Seeaitch had not visited her mother, because her mother had hung herself.

"Y-you! Fiend! Unhand the boy!" The coated figure turned. There was a grim fall of sweat upon the man's brow, slowly dripping into his pointed eyes. A Talesh, people of tentacle, once bound as slaves for a people Seeaitch could not pronounce the proper name of. Her tongue lacked length.

"Tetarien. Want to join the fun?" Seeaitch pushed the knife forward, ensuring the foe had seen it.

"I'll cut you if you do not leave this s-soul be. Let him be." The figure left their mate, though kept a single arm against their chest, pinning the boy to the wall.

The Harlequin

"What? You threatening me?" Seeaitch drew the blade ever close to her chest, the perfect move was to be sprung when the foe least expected it. She had learned this in her defense classes.

"Let. Him. Be." The figure stepped forward again, and like the clash betwixt rays of sun and somber moonlight, her chipping blade struck home, cutting a sample of flesh from the Talesh's cheek. Though a shallow wound, it would scar well. The figure stumbled backward, a stagger he did not predict. Her shallow wrists were easy to grasp, and thus, her form was broken by the formidable mass of tentacles before her. Seeaitch dropped the tool, which was quickly snatched up by her opposition. Finding the little golem far too squirmy to invite to the pleasure fest, the coated man saw it fit to gauge her eyes out. The tool found a final resting place, calmly too, buried in the thick of Seeatich's back, as the blood from her body drained into the alley, mixing moderately with the other bodily fluids poured onto the stones. Pitiful end upon pitiful end, all was lost and nothing gained. Yet Seeaitch found the call of her infinite regret quite fitting, it was all she had ever asked for. She wondered if Ubervan would miss her.

"Shut— why do you keep interruptin' me Roach? Keep your *damn* maw shut for three squawkin' seconds!" Jeweler flicked the bullet against the wall, quickly rebounding it back into his mitted palms. Twenty wormpennies and he only lost two toes, more than worth the blood and bed rest. The bullet was still ashy from the misfire if only Jeweler's foot could say the same. It had been a bet of accuracy, but of course, Viaduct always paid a premium for the misfires. When Jeweler's revolver jammed, there always seemed to be that held-breath moment of pure idiocy that wracked his outlaw's mind. Without fail, the barkeeper would aim the weapon down, spin a curse in its honor, and fire it once more. This habit alone explained just how it was possible for Jeweler to be missing all but one toe on his right foot—a record that his left was quickly approaching. Jeweler flicked the bullet again, this time however, it failed to rebound directly to its sender, instead landing beside Lullaby, who was far too entranced by her practices for the sight of such a tiny morsel of metal. "Toss it yonder Roach, I got somethin' of an affliction with that there shell." Roach continued the repetition of its words, Lullaby could hardly keep up. In its repeated bates, Roach managed to claw up the bullet with its feet and toss the discard of metal over to his owner. Jeweler had gotten into the habit of thanking Roach for the smallest of favors, it had trained a sort of obligation into the beast, a kindness that had brought it closer to humanity despite the circumstances. Jeweler flicked the bullet again. Grimacing, Jeweler leered down at the machine working away at his waist, gore glittering off his fingertips.

"You have an awful hand. Sewing felt is not at all equivalent to sewing wounds." Viaduct grumbled, thread between his teeth. Time had been given to ponder in the healing of his wounds, Jeweler himself scarcely escaping his home with all his blood. The stitches of his own hand were amateur, seeing how he never properly trained the art of the tailor. The wounds were nothing Viaduct couldn't handle, having minute practice in his own special flavors of silkwork. The silence of it all drew back the thoughts of Pico Nevado, memories of people the bartender wished to leave in the villa.

"Got a plan for this home stone of yours? Where we heading, anyways?" Viaduct's head ended in cables, clicking about as he twisted dark string around his digits. The wires poured through the narrow passageways of the Passerine, clipping between the shutter door to the cockpit. His mind calculated perfect stitches and accurate flight plans.

"There is but one mind among the cosmos capable of processing such data, an Inkling soul—"

"Long damn extinct soul, we don't have any Inklings on hand." With a glance to Roach, Jeweler corrected his excuses, "Any *smart* Inklings, anywho." Viaduct sighed, accepting a handful of new spools to toy around with, Roach being the sole supplier.

"If anyone can find a living, knowledgeable Inkling, it's Pla'taneer." His chair fell back against Roach's steady arm, and Jeweler nearly tore his gut open again.

"Ain't no way in hell we're using her. Favors or not, Mama Argon'd rather pin me up for both types of crows."

"Good thing then that she does not view me in the same light. Not to mention her insurmountable debt to me—she will have no choice but to play nicely." With another tug, the wound was once again stitched shut, and Jeweler's complaining set back another week.

The Harlequin

"There. If you decide to dress it, do me one kind favor and remember to redress it. I don't need a case of infection on my ship." Scoffing, the bartender attempted to rise, pain stifling his ascent,

"Please V, it ain't even your ship." Returning to the cockpit, Viaduct disregarded the claims. As far as he was concerned, the pilot owned the vessel so long as he did pilot it. Jeweler would come to appreciate the sacrifice. In the absence of discussion, Jeweler turned back to the villa in the snow, where he left a piece of himself surely. The helmet lay pried open on a bed stand. The shattered blade was all but clean of its recent murders. A bygone past burrowed in his mind, and the peace of its non-existence stung. Though peace was inherently relieving, a grant away from awful nightmares. For once, Jeweler had little to complain about, at least far less than normal.

"Hissssstree. Histree. Hissss—" Lullaby murmured from under her breath. It was astounding how much she remembered from his lessons, even Jeweler doubted the memoric capabilities of a Gretchkin, but surely there was little difference between her and the other beast Jeweler had acquired. Roach echoed the words of his teacher, helping himself to a verb or two extra, often to the dismay of Lullaby. Viaduct fingered the console pasted at the front of the Passerine. It was filled with all sorts of logical logarithmic data, the kind that even Viaduct would find difficult to comprehend had it not been for the direct synthetic link Viaduct had applied between the two. Direct linkage, for all its agony, was all too practical to be ignored. A perfect connection between pure intelligence, and system. No buggy emotions of fraudulent second-guessing to slow the processing. Naught but flight. Flawless, fluid flight. It wasn't the connection that bothered him at the moment though, future thoughts drove his servos to suicide. There was little to drive the worries of such a distant machine, but Viaduct saw disarray in the minds of his fellow travelers. Roach had a mindless hunger, unlike any creature he had known before. Even the fiercest Gretch-like slivers of pity in comparison. Lullaby was a living testament to the truest of powers: potent, raw, spite. To exist as a bond between two forbidden people, there was misery and hate in her past, but to see it as a whole was impossible. Of course, Jeweler, though seemingly the least feral of all, Viaduct knew better. Of all his partners and customers, he knew the least of Jeweler. For the sake of avoiding repetition, it must be said once more: Jeweler was a being shrouded in mystery to even the most knowledgeable of the galaxy. He preferred it to remain this way. What future would sprout unto a tree of fate for the group, Viaduct wished only to see this plant, a future for his crew and himself. He hoped it was a joyous one. Yet outside his abode lie monsters, beasts, and cruel men. And what of death? Another, another, again, once more. Did it matter if it was a melted core or a shot to the head? Could he even feel the pain of—

"Hey V, the letters 'C' and 'H' mean anything to you?" Viaduct shifted his weight back against the chair, the panic had nearly reached him again. To endure one's mind melting away into anguish... Thank god for the Shorerunner.

"Not notably. Whatever do you ask this for?" Jeweler flicked the bullet again.

"It's on the bullet. Scrawled right down the side." Jeweler presented the disfigured scrap to his mechanical informant. Though desperately squinting, Viaduct could only faintly discern a singular letter 'C'. If there was an accompanying 'H', he surely could not see it.

"Perhaps initials, Jeweler. So they could remind you of precisely *who* misloaded the shell that took your toes!" Viaduct called from the cockpit. Jeweler chuckled lightly, looking down at the bullet before him.

"What a hero." How ironic, that such a wonderful-looking set of letters could spell such danger for his feet. It interested him about as much as the map did, which is to say, quite a bit. The horror of a world he was completely unfamiliar with seemed to pass directly overhead, just as a swallow over a picnic of right-minded, god-fearing citizens. This was opportunity to Jeweler, riches or not his beast was a profit of excess. Even if the beast was more human than ever, and his liking to it had grown like a festering tumor, Jeweler remained assured that his investment would not turn belly-up. Not until he had his fair share of blood and guts. Not until every damned Gretch had paid their blind. And contrary to what most would assume, Jeweler always played big blinds. Finding solace in his map, and beastly insurance, Jeweler settled lower in his seat, propping his feet against the only table they had. He flicked the bullet again. Viaduct shook from the alerts of a nearby vessel. They were in deep Infinite, the veil outside of known travel paths. While supplies had run thin in recent days, that did not warrant the sudden arrival of supply ships, nor had Viaduct ever called one. What was more, it emitted a hailing call of mechanical repetition, returning no direct messages. It beckoned for fertilizer and repairs. It beckoned for mercy.

Though soft as it may be, Brass is quite the color. A look, that to some, lends a certain distinction. Whereas Gold may be a glory to attract all attention, and Steel too matte in mold to bring a veering glance, Brass is the equal of none and all. Understand: Mama birthed a child of Gold and he was seen by many—too many—and his throat was cut clean through by a Six-fingered hero. Mama birthed a child of Steel, and nobody saw her—none at all—and her own gracious wire bit through her putty flesh. Mama birthed a child of Brass, and he watched both his siblings die. After collecting the oozing puddles and sludge of corpses, The Child of Brass brought them home, and after seeing the brutality of the world outside his mirror, The Child of Brass wept. Mama birthed a thousand more children, and they laughed at him, The Child of Brass. The Old Man told him to break the children like chains, and when he rose above his siblings, he was given freedom to return to the mirror. The Old Man told him to return to the mirror, and so he did. And The Old Man said

"Centamoore, Third of my kin, Child of Brass, will you do this task for me? Where your brothers and sisters could not? Will you do this task for me?" And the child replied,

"Yes Father."

~ End of Act I ~

~ Interlude ~

I, The Harlequin, wish to speak with you directly. This is long overdue.

Ho ho, and greetings to you, little jester, who delicately partitioned the time of their worryingly busy day to be here of all places! Rest assured, I will keep this formality brief—either you are *dying* to return to the japes, or shortly on your way to sealing this glorified joke book for a much more suiting literary masterpiece. You see, I am completely hemmed in at this terrible crossroad, I do not know much about speaking to your kind. The last time one of you was allowed vision into my world—let us leave that notion at the term *'total interstellar havoc'* (which all things aside I did enjoy greatly). I think what would be best for gathering up a consensus on our viability as buddies would be a test—simple poking at humor. How do you feel about coincidences? I appreciate them, in fact, I would say I adore the little buggers. I exist for their maintenance; they don't call me The Harlequin *solely* for the sake of vulgarity and mistreatment! Regardless, it is I who upholds the structure of chaos, the veritableness of comedy in the galaxy. It is my sole purpose and oddly enough my only potent desire. Hell, I've run off with all the logic again, leaving you poor and abandoned of any of my deeper intentions. Let me rephrase: when a newborn observes a poison, the newborn—from what I have commonly observed—will desire to taste this poison, as it is unknown to them. It will smell the poison, perhaps douse its fingers in the stuff and illustrate god on the window panes, but inevitably, it will taste it. Within the hour, the newborn will be the *un*born. Newborns of the next era may see an automaton, and seek it out. It will agitate the machine, as both are unknown to the other. The machine may observe and test the newborn as the newborn did to the poison. Except, the difference here being that newborns cannot have fingers thrust into them without spilling terribly important interior contents. Automatons will not know of this, and thus, the newborn will be—you get the picture. Both newborns, as a result of what is unknown to them, will perish. Opposing forces of unquestionable wonderment inevitably bow unto demise. Is it not incredibly comedic to see such a thing occur? To ponder at basic conceptualization lost on those too factory-new to care? Another thing, too—imagine a people of scales, fish to your tongue. Fish, who in the case of this tale, are very real, and very full of hate for all things existent. Yet, they are fish! How cruel fate is to punish everyone without any sense of reason! Or—or! Sooner a blind man uncovers the cure to deafness than he would heal his shattered vision—too a perfect marriage arranged for a man without any hopes left, a woman to heal him at his stead, and misery scoops him up when a streetlamp falls, killing only the bride! You see, it is coincidence that rivals all troubles, that trivializes the horrible misfortunes of all those you see. It is my belief, as a creator of chaos, that the divine comedy cultivated in the veil between our two worlds is what gives meaning to existence itself. You can never surely know what indescribably hilarious thing will happen next! Will one of those princes of gold be slain by the other—the slayer unaware of his misdeed? Will the outlaw bartender lose a family forged from the cemetery of his prior, or the grievous Verdant Crow lose the fraction of love he has collected? It is incredibly exciting to hope for the future as the world unfolds before you, each path equally amusing as the others. The way of The Harlequin is simple—to present yourself to the void, and laugh in the face of whatever comes your way, knowing fully that it could have happened to any other soul, and you would be all the more hysterical as a result. Whether or not you find this fate to be equally as entertaining as I do will determine how well we will get along. To make this as expressly clear to you as possible, I will say this: I do not care about your politics, or whatever tumors rupture your organs. I am not interested in what you think, nor am I invested in your personal moral standard. You are by definition an observer, and nothing more. I am but a pitiful entertainer—my purpose is to entertain, to bring joy. If I do not accomplish this, I have no desire to continue with our interactions. I am not here to bring pain or unfortunate memories; it is the way of the galaxy to tear open infected wounds. And particularly, it is for your enjoyment. I chronicle in the hopes that the beings beyond the mirror can see what cannot be seen—to view my world in my way. I am by no means a god, I did not create the galaxy. I do not control its figures, or force the hand of fate by any means. In fact, I am considerably less influential than even the passersby and unknowns of the short comedies I gather here. The keyword of this monologue is *gather*, as all these tales are more than such, they are definitively true—or so their means of collection are. As The Harlequin, my duty pertains to tales. I repossess truths, not fictions, and ensnare them in parchment for the viewing pleasure of myself, you, and the kindred Old Man. As such, do not become so convinced that I work for you, or that you hold any precedent over my labors. Kindly, I am a servant to nobody but my own humor. My elaboration and translation are for the means of viewers, but it is just as much a pastime to the boredom of the Infinite.

Dear Christ (apologies to those of a conflicting religion, they do seem all the same to me) I have gone on for far too long. Instead of deliberating my practices, I should much rather compel you to pick your poison, and perhaps speak more with me? The Infinite is a culling of all imagination—if I had never been locked away here, I would surely have more stories to tell, fictional or not. It is my grand desire to entertain, after all, and I am more than willing to entertain you—so long as you keep your hands pocketed. I do not wish to present as diabolical, or cold. I do care, just not for the same things you do. I would rather not delude you into a state of loving or admiration, what I do encapsulates the very sentiment of entertaining; I am in essence designed for you. It is with my investment in divine comedy that this galaxy keeps its footing, as I would much prefer to see it meet a considerably grander conclusion than untimely un-existence. I care about these things, you see? They are my devoir and thus I love them. Your viewing of my efforts is a mere concomitant to my will, but on the same note, opposite in clay, I do not hate the company. I much appreciate your onlooking; by all means, stay! Stay and watch, I have no difficulty in allowing this. My eyes are yours, I have great intention of making the events of this world legible to you (to some degree, I am no thaumaturge) and supply the occasional word of comfort alongside your observation. You are, in essence, a child on my shoulder, watching over my work with wondrous desires, pointing at the simple things and calling out, "What's this?" or "Who's that?" and all your other petty questions. But remember the truth, this is just a place. Much like any other, it breathes thanks to what cannot be seen. I thank you for your viewing time, honestly. It may not mean much in the grand scheme of *my* desires, but it brings conclusion to those who wish for this world to end. It hurries the process of a slow, painful, death.

Another thing—I am an outlier to those much like myself. To me, you are a servant of pleasure, a *connoisseur* of mystical things. To others? Your presence here is permitted, but it is not welcomed. You are a bat out of its cave, a leech in the desert; You do not belong here. This galaxy has a history with your kind, those outside of the mirror, those who wish to watch, and nothing more. Oh, it was glorious how your previous watchers did tear my realm from its roots—you are a *brutal* people. Thanks entirely to you I have been given full permission to watch, and welcome you back to your effective throne of the cosmos. I—hmm, do suppose you are not the same as before. You must know nothing of the old ages, or the prior stories—the prior me. One day, perhaps, I will have to tell you. You deserve that much I think. This will be so exciting, a partner once more to watch over my figurative puppet work, it is tremendously invigorating! But oh, my little jester, can I ask you for but one thing? One simple thing, I swear it. I ask you, jester, for your questioning mind. The Infinite grows weary on my soul, and without entertainment, it swallows me. What better form of amusement is there than conflict and queries? I take satisfaction in few things—two only I'd say. The insurance of divine comedy is principal—maintaining the hilarity is, as mentioned, a great love of mine—and the second is confusion. Questions and answers, I'll answer what I can, and you can sate my desire for quizzing. This is going to be fun, we are at the edge of a great fall to the metaphorical ball pit below, I do hope you'll stick *your* landing. I'll let you go now, there is more for you to see, and your desperation is gnawing at me. Arrivederci, little jester! Be sure to enjoy the show, I know I will!

Act II

~ *Divine Horticulture*

Written and poorly illustrated by
Bibliothecary Centamoore in his youth…

The morn was filled with music, sounds of all life. The wind whistled between the pipes and gears, making its way down to the absolute depth of the Island, carrying the leaves with it, rustling them along on their journey. The calls of the assorted creatures that roamed the island filled the air, tweets from the birds, and shrieks from the foxes. However, atop all else, reigned the horrific call of the crows. The cry rang out louder than any, and was the first thing most heard once they had arrived on the Island—that is, if anyone still came to the Island. There were only crows left now, as their shrieking and screeching had driven away all other forms of avian life. Not a quail remained. The crows fought for dominance, each trying to top the other, each more desperate for attention than the last, until all grew silent within the daylight. The sun was rising, the meadows and cascades of the Island were filled with a bright, verdant light which banished the corvid cancer. They flew, fleeing the scene of their crimes, the crimes they had no guilt for. The foxes grew quiet as even the wind's power was stunted by the sun's miraculous glory. All was peaceful, then the ticking began. The clockwork mechanisms of a dystopic garden denied the sun its joy, as they always did. The origin lay deep within the island, the very center. Past all the gardens, the hedges, the rivers, lay the Garden Centrum, once home to all living things, now lying dormant and cold. The Centrum was once maintained by an ample supply of mechanical workers, ones plainly named Gardeners, the caretakers of the Centrum. To speak to a

Gardener, was to creators—beings far beyond the scope of consciousness, yet superior still. Most often, the Gardeners gave no response, not out of inability, but rather, out of a lack of desire. They roamed the island, protecting and serving all forms of life, cleansing the land of any filth that dared raid its shores. However, they now stood inert. After many years, they had shut down, rusted, and been torn limb from limb. Their creators were gone, they had left long ago, and without their mechanics and plans, they fell into disrepair. Although, the creators had not left without foresight, and supplied the Gardeners with the perpetual desire to preserve. The Gardeners had known nothing else, not thought, nor emotion. They had only been taught to trim and tend. The ticking, the deep roots of steel, and the gardening. It all continued to its ultimatum, much like an exhaustive dancer, slowly weakening their song. One day, past a length of time unknowable, it all held still. Inside the Centrum, there was a hollow. Night fell in time, and day rose to no chance at retainment. The Centrum grew tasteless, and the Island a canvas stuck up with dollmaker's pins, thread about its face. With the decay of the heart of the isle, came the tenure of a new servant. Without the essence of time, it came free of its steel binds, shaking off the vines and grass, small roots clawing into its body. It wore the Gardener's garb, which had been moistened and torn over years of wear. Its body was rusty and broken, certain gears no longer turned, a selection of lights no longer blinked. Its glowing eyes flickered, much like the waking blinks of a child. It lurched forward, the programming driving its motion to a metallic column, banking leftwards from its bed in the floor. The Gardener found the comprehension to repair the device, towing its edges back into place, a light illuminating the dust-coated screen on its face. With the brilliance of its glow, the Gardener could make out the sordid remains of some humanoid figure, a cattleman's cap resting against its face. The body was slouched across a panel on the northern wall of the room, a thick drive clutched in their melting fingertips. If not for the machine cube at its feet, the Gardener would have thought the corpse out of place, almost medieval in the presence of such technology. Pushing aside the body, the Gardener examined the panel, now perforated by some small dart, irreparably fractured. The column contained several slots for additional drives; the Gardener considered it only logical to insert the belongings of the dead. With a moment of whirring fans, the column rotated, its midsection turning away to the back wall, a much smaller screen faced the Gardener. It moved closer, its hand jumping from key press to another, typing with full certainty. The screen flickered, and returned to a cyan hue, displaying three numbers on its face in a thick black typeface. It was a one, preceded by two zeroes, garnished with glitches and blur lines. The Gardener fixed against the screen, numbers meaning nothing of merit to a being with hedge-clipper hands. Once more, it touched the registry and typed a new tune of letters and keys, all unbeknownst to itself. A ridge of plastic wilted from the monitor, an icon of insertion remaining in its place. From the soft speakers of the column came numbers, repetitious—demanding. The Gardener followed the inputs flawlessly in tandem with their snicks. The drive from the corpse emerged again, The Gardener was not finished with its containment. Cramming the device back into the monitor, it completed the remaining text segments and injected its cable into the column. Like a fetus, it remained connected to a placenta of knowledge, gathering data upon worlds lost, ancient forsaken gardening techniques, and the state of the Infinite. After a period of sharp pinches in the mind, the Gardener disconnected itself and retracted the terminal. The echoes of its construct spoke to nothing,

"A Gardener, an interesting location for housing. Did you initiate this transfer?" the voice said. The Gardener nodded,

"Who are you?" The Gardener questioned. The voice left the query be for a long while, before considering itself culpable to speak again,

"I am not sure I can answer that question, I can detail my software credentials and creation logs, however." The Gardener accepted this request, so the voice continued. "I am protocol Peregrine, a local life preservation initiative, created by the great minds behind the Centrum. My purpose is to aid the Gardeners in their mission to maintain the Centrum. I cannot reach other information at this time, as my client appears to be severed, likely due to a loss of connection with the origin point. Do you happen to know where that is?" The Gardener offered no reasonable estimates. The protocol continued, "Nor do I, Gardener. Shall we tend to your duties?" The Gardener stood, glancing once more at the number, "Peregrine, what is that number?" Peregrine quickly assured the Gardener it was merely a population count, a count of only living humans and Gardeners. It read 'one' because the Gardener had awoken. The Gardener examined the number again, staring at the static behind it, before exiting the room. "May I call you, Peregrine?" uttered the Gardener. 'Peregrine' approved of such simplicity. The Gardener exited the facility, staring upwards at the sun, now high in the sky. It began its duties, first tending to the hedges directly outside the facility, then moving towards the overgrown trees, snipping each of their vast branches to perfection. Tools and machinery were strewn about, tossed around like confetti, not to mention the statue-like rusted Gardeners, all of which no longer remained active. The Gardener took no sadness in seeing its fallen brethren, as it could not emote such displays of sorrow. "Peregrine, can you see? Can you witness my actions as your own? I am curious of your existence, of what it means to be a protocol." Peregrine fell silent, not answering the question for a few hours at best.

"Curiosity is no place for the mind of a Gardener, but yes, I do witness what your eyes can behold. It is a terrible sight." Peregrine said. The Gardener promptly agreed and continued its work, a new motivation in its mind: to please its creators—to please Peregrine.

After a few hours, the sun once more began to set, and the Gardener was left in the dark. It returned to its facility. Beside the column of numbers were chambers, small outcroppings fitted to attach to the Gardener. Though it was not particular to the Gardener which bed it was to lie on, it took a great deal of consideration in its designs. Before Peregrine grew tired of the patience, it made its way to a vacant charger and placed its shape before the vault. The mechanical arms ground rust showers from their joints as they slowly disassembled the larger parts of the Gardener, accommodating its form for rest. The Gardener was bolted in and left to charge. It did not sleep. It did not dream. It did not drift, it only watched. "Peregrine, what is this place?" questioned the Gardener. Peregrine replied in jitterish, beated fashion. Each syllable of its sentence was timed in perfection,

"This is the Centrum, a bio-preservation Island, dedicated to keeping the last vestiges of humanity alive." The Gardener hesitated, its question concerning even itself,

"Then, where are all the humans?"

The Gardener continued its work the next day, the loud whistling of the wind, cries of birds, and others alerting it to the day's break. It trimmed the roses, cut the grass, tore down vines, polished tiles nailed down door hinges, and re-sealed glass panels. It did so silently, not even stopping to stare at the sun, or the birds that watched its mysterious form work. The Gardener did not rest today, as it had more work than ever to accomplish. The Gardener had reached the walls of the Centrum, caked with dirt and dust, covered in vines and moss. All of the Island lay beyond this simple wall, constructed only out of weak metals. The Gardener stared at it, the wall was quite taller than it was, stretching maybe twenty feet into the air. It questioned, "Peregrine, why are we caged here, like the birds in the Nursery, are we also meant to be observed?" Peregrine aired in return,

"This, Gardener, I do not know. Perhaps at one point, the Island was dangerous—a hazard to the Centrum's balance. Those walls have been there for as long as I have." The Gardener wondered why Peregrine didn't know the answer to such questions if it had been here as long as it had. It ignored its own curiosities and began work upon the wall. Not before long, The Gardener could no longer stand the silence, and pestered Peregrine once more,

"Oh Peregrine, if this place was once bustling with human and animal activity alike, then there must be a gatehouse to the wall, mustn't there?" Peregrine let out a dramatic, robotic sigh,

"I suppose, as this was once a center of survival, there must be an exit. But, well...I'm not sure I should be telling you this, Gardener." The Gardener hesitantly fell silent, the swallows of the birds overpowering its thoughts. It continued its work. Silently.

Upon the coming of dawn, instead of the crow's song, a loud thunderous pounding filled the Gardener's head. A storm had swept across the Island and had ravaged the lands upon it. The once-cleaned Centrum had returned to its prior state—grimy, disorganized, disheveled. *Disgusting*. The Gardener emerged from the main Centrum facility, the center of the Gardens. It walked amongst the bushes and flowers, now disorderly and unkempt. The cobbles of the once pristine pathways were littered with leaves, twigs, and puddles. The Gardener made its way to the wall. The wall was the worst of the refuse. The Gardener had put so much effort into cleaning it, so much time. The Gardener sat next to the wall. It stared out into the cloisters of foggy storm clouds,

"Peregrine, what is my purpose?" Peregrine immediately replied,

"To clean the walls, trim the bushes, and plant the flowers, Gardener," Peregrine paused for a moment, considering its options, "and I suppose, maintain Centrum life, both human and not." The Gardener stuck its arms out, gesturing to all of its work—its ruined work,

"But, aren't all humans gone? If they built this place to stay alive, we should be seeing many humans right now. But we are not." Peregrine sighed,

"Yes, they do appear to all be missing, a mysterious conundrum if I might add." The Gardener stood, loudening its voice,

"Then what am I to do? Garden? There is no point, all my work will be reversed within time, so why try to fix what cannot be fixed? Why remain in a ceaseless loop of endless labor, all for naught once the island tears it from my claws?" Peregrine awaited further questioning, and when it didn't receive any, it spoke,

"I know of some possible illusions, mere distractions from your troubles." Peregrine sent a file of sorts through the Gardener's wires. "It's a map of the facility. If the Centrum was ever to become a dangerous place, there was an exit underneath the facility, one that led outside the walls. If you are so distraught by the stresses of Gardening, then may I suggest we explore this mysterious Island?" The Gardener stood amazed at the idea, excited at the chance of being free. It immediately set a course for the exit. It was led back into the facility, down through a winding path of corridors, and out into what seemed to be a lobby—an expansive cave-like room—held up by pillars made of heavy stone and marble. Large planters filled with shriveled life lined the walls, with small seating arrangements placed between them, now once more claimed by the incessant grasp of the island. The floor was covered in a thick layer of mud and mulch, weeds and other dastardly flora scattered the dirt-ridden carpets. A singular desk lay at the end of the hall, velvet barriers separating two lines to the desk. The contents which had once laid upon the desk were now scattered across the floor, a partially decomposed corpse lay face down upon the seat. The wall closest to the desk, which appeared at one time to be a grand entryway, was blasted open, chunks of marble scattering the forest greenery. The Gardener approached the gaping hole and looked out into the Island. The Gardener couldn't help but notice how befouled it all was, imperfect in the finest sense, and far removed from all rhythm. It slowly made its way out, wandering into the forest, and even further beyond — never once stopping to question its surroundings. It finally finished its journey at the bay, a thin strip of sand separating the jungles of the Island and the vast emptiness of the sea. The ocean rippled, pulsating with life the Gardener only wished it had,

"Oh Peregrine, I cannot do it! I cannot continue like this, like a husk of life once made! I have no purpose! There is no need for me anymore!" The Gardener threw its arms against a large steel cannon, pointing outwards to the sea. There were several of them, all mounted by bones. In the distance above, the bones of a colossal beast shadowed the island. Never noticed by the Gardener prior, the breath of the marrow was the fog, and the fumes of its decomposition made the verdant plants of the isle. The beast was a life giver as much as the Gardener was, and surely felt emotion in the same vein, once moaning in agony upon the sand as the Gardener now did.

"Good Gardener, can't you see? You writhe in pain and despair, and jump for joy at the experience of a new world! You may not know it, but you do indeed have life! You have done plenty for this world, and thus your life has purpose. Perhaps your original intention has expired, yes. That does not forbid you from finding another! I have no purpose presently, yet I have decided it is my new goal to aid you in finding *yours*." Peregrine hesitated, murmuring to itself first. "Perhaps, it might be time we return to the Centrum? Perhaps you could take up a hobby, pray tell, poetry? Pottery? Woodworking? Dare I say, gardening?" The Gardener would chuckle at such a thing, had it anything but pity for the protocol. The Gardener looked up from its grief to a small flock of birds resting upon the shoreline. Swans were they, majestic and rare at such a time as this. They called out to the Gardener, and wandered over to it. The birds examined the Gardener, curious as to why it had chosen to invade their joyous rituals. They concluded that it was harmless, and let out a shrill cry of victory, before wandering away into the forest. The Gardener blinked, its glance turning towards the ocean once again.

"Peregrine, how did the humans all die?" Peregrine mimicked a human laugh, chortling at such a question.

"Ah Gardener, I have not the slightest idea, do you?" The Gardener nodded his head, confirming Peregrine's theory,

"I suppose that they all loved the greenery. They perhaps were herbivores and hungered for the flesh of the earth. In time, they dried the land of verdancy. This Island was supposed to halt such a disaster, yet it did not function as intended. I suppose we were survivors, for no reason but coincidence." Peregrine agreed, it was an ideal theory. The Gardener emerged from the deep maws of the Centrum, bearing nothing but experience as its reward. The Gardener rounded the corner, glaring at the dim screen one last time. The Number. It was different. The Gardener jumped with glee and went off to tend to the Centrum. The Gardener would soon know the vows of friendship, for the Gardener was to have a guest! The Number was new; it read zero-zero-two.

~ Daybreak

Inscribed on the tomb of an Ichyric
Warlord—a sign of fickle respect…

The cloaked creature's breath was quiet but rapid. It followed no tempo, pitched high—just deep enough to suck in air. The sickly burn of chilled sweat and exertion spread down its neck. The furs on its coat trapped the heat, threatening to boil its blood. Yellow-red grasses stretched up to its shoulders, allowing it to conceal itself with ease, hiding away from the prying eyes of its distant prey. The creature moved slowly, its movements so small, so cautious, as if it did not move at all. Four pronged claws gripped around the wooden buttstock of its weapon—a small crossbow-like contraption—mended together by wood and iron, braced with bolts, and tied taught with twine. The two limbs of the weapon quivered with nearly as much anticipation as its user, holding back a singular readied bolt. The creature knew it only needed one. This was a feeling it had felt before, the rush of the hunt, the titillation of death. It was routine for the creature, a task completed almost daily, too often to begin to forget the scent of decay. The prey was a large beast, one not particularly menacing, but certainly formidable. Jutting from its terrible skull were two large ivory tusks. Across its body drooled a thick coat of fur, colored dark yellow with the morning sun. The creature respected its prey as it did any of its own kind. The beasts were majestic in a way, with no worries of debts to concern themselves with, no hate for another, or love for its young. No emotion, but still filled with life. It was what distanced the beast and the creature, the emotions they felt—or in this case—they did not. It cast the beast in the role of prey,

The Harlequin

and the creature became the hunter by extension. It removed a hand from its weapon, shaping it into a small religious sigil, quietly praying to its god under its breath, praying to let this beast ascend to immortality, to let it reach the gods in good faith. A hasty breeze ruffled the cloth of the hunter's cloak. It held a hood to its face, silencing the noise. Its prey did not take notice of the disturbance, which would of course prove to be its final mistake. The creature waited for opportunity, a figment of time when all stood still. It let loose its bolt, a muted crack following the shot. The beast fell, and the weapon had finally put an end to its existence. Upon assuring the demise of the beast, the hunter moved forward. It encroached on the leaping young of the dead beast, they picked at their parent, before scampering off into nature. With a pause in its footing, the creature stood before the still-warm corpse of the beast. Its fur was of excellent quality, the hunter had little doubt that the meat would be of a similar grade. The creature unveiled a blade formed from some kind of wrought metal, twisted into a spiral, sharpened to an unfathomable degree. The tip of the blade was flat—as there was truly no need for it to be pointed—and edged like a razor. The handle was curved, structured from bone, wrapped in twine, and oiled with an inkhoney. A single purple-and-cyan feather drooped from the base of the handle, bound by a minuscule metal hook. The hunter took no time to admire this finely crafted blade, as it had run its eyes down the tool's form an uncountable number of times. Its hands flew like the motors of the great machines of old, tearing the fur from the flesh unceremoniously. It dug deep into the beast, cutting slabs of meat from its bones, dicing worthless fats and organs. The creature severed its horns from the skull, removed its eyes from their sockets, and tore its spine from its back. It drained the blood into vials, mashed its liver into a mush, and stashed it away in a bottle. It continued its work, silently, over the course of the earliest hour. It only stopped to rest when all that remained of the once majestic beast was a fleshless, spineless husk, riddled with small outcroppings of undesirable meats and organs. The hunter had finished, so it packed up its things, placed all of its spoils into a large sack, and took a small moment to pray for the beast a second time. It cut a small incision into its hand with the harvesting blade and let a single droplet of blood trickle to the corpse of the beast. Sheathing its weapon, it began the voyage home. The city was not nearly as far as it was an hour ago, but there was still quite the journey ahead of this creature—it did not mind. It enjoyed the nature of the wildlands and all their beauties. It spent too much time within them to not appreciate their intricacies. The way the birds always told it of new prey, the way the rivers would always point back to the city, the way the trees always seemed to lean into the sunlight, desperate for a drop of its divinity. It all was so complex, so important. The hunter felt honored just to be in its presence. The nature around it let the creature enjoy peace today, let it think to itself. However, there wasn't too much to think of.

Drochandas was not busy so early in the morning, it was a late-hour city, one where very few still adhered to the proverbs of the early bird. The hunter wandered down the short alleyways of the lowest sections of the city, making its way back home as quickly as possible. It did not desire to be outside for any longer than it had to. The dark facade of the blackstone buildings displeased the creature, and the void-like cloud resting above the city discouraged any and all exploration. Unmaintained roads and innumerable sewer canals drove any thought of distinction out of sight. Unlike the fields and forests outside of the city's reaches, the city did not let anything remain silent for long. It demanded no thought, and no humility—it only searched for dissension. Every hour there was another fight to be stopped in the slums, a debate to be watched in the markets, a political fool to ridicule in the Northers. The hunter did not desire any of this conflict, it had learned the best way to secure satisfaction was to stay as far from the dangers of society as possible. The creature could not afford to follow this ideology purely and was forced to remain within the city walls, hidden away in a small complex of rented apartments in the southeastern quarter of the city. It was a comfy place, three homes in one, all neighbors—all kind. It was the closest the hunter could get to isolation. It arrived at the complex, lugging its sack through the tight backroads. The building stood lower than the others around it, a rectangular obelisk in a small clearing of colossal redwood-esque towers of stone and metal. It was shadowed over, set in its place simply and swiftly by its competitors. A total of five windows speckled its face and a singular gutter hung from its crooked rooftop. The creature entered the building, ascending the rickety stairs to the second floor, where it had lived in relative peace for nearly all of its mature life. Approaching the door, the hunter managed to tug a thin key from its belt without dropping its bundle. The creature meticulously slotted the key into the door and nudged it open. Weakly sealing the door behind itself, the hunter removed the hood from its head, revealing a hairless ink-black head with two small, feathered antennae protruding from its skull. It shifted the sack off of its back, placing it on the ground while it continued to remove the laborer's garb. The creature began to shake one of its thick leather boots off before its pursuits were halted by a sudden shriek, and an unexpected force clasping on its lower leg. The hunter nearly fell over but managed to balance itself with a coat stand to its left. A bean-shaped thing had grappled to the creature's thigh, a thick toothy smile wrapped around its head. A small poncho gathered up the bean like a baby's basket, its once pure color-stained gray and cyan with dirt and smog. Its two antennae twitched wildly; particular attention lost to the bean's indulgence in an abundance of senses. The hunter, realizing what exactly was hinged to its lower leg, let the tension flow from its body, the floating hand on its dagger lowered to the bean. It chuckled as the ball of delight shook at its leg, screeching joy into the quiet air of its home,

"Pop-pop! You're ho-ome!" The child was too hysterical to speak much, giggling between words, panting between giggles. The father removed two leather braces from his arms and with it his halterneck, revealing a dark body of a smooth, almost rubbery texture. An assortment of scars and bruises drifted in the sea of gloom, two crossing belts holding bandages in place. The belts were adorned with feathers and furs, bones and tusks, bejeweled with the spoils of the father's many hunts. A large, baggy pair of burlap pants were held up by the lower belt, the left leg noticeably longer than the other. The stitches of the pants were amateurish, unaligned, and skewed. There were even some noticeable tears in the stitching, and flaws in its design. The father stepped forwards, shambling under the weight of the child glued to his knee. He began to undo a bundle of tightly wrapped cloth from his hands, slowly depositing the cloth on a nearby stool, dragging his sack along as he moved deeper into his home. He unhooked his weapon from his belt, and placed it on a large table in the center of the room, slinging the sack upon it as well. Seating himself in a small wooden chair, he gathered the small child in his arms, hoisting the small bean onto his own lap.

"How was your schooling last night? Did you learn anything profound?" The child giggled again, pinching the small abrasions on the father's uppermost belt,

"Teacher told us about the Krolaws! Did'n you get one of them one time?" The father chuckled, amused by the childish wonder of his own kin,

"Hmm, I am not so sure, which one is the Krolaw?" The child gave the father a playful punch, continuing to grin ear to ear,

"Pop-pooop! You know what it is! You're being silly!" The father pulled his sack closer, rummaging through its contents,

"No! I'm not, I promise P. Tell me again, tell me what it is." The child began to describe the Krolaw—large, bipedal bird-like beasts, largely known for their cunning and mischievous behavior. They had feathers colored blue and purple and edged white beaks. Their webbed feet ended in long talons—just as bleached as their beaks—and possessed a set of pear-seed eyes, eyes that cut through the souls of any who dared hunt them. They were a prized kill in all of the land, every piece of them valuable in some way. Their beaks and bones were sturdy, used to construct all kinds of weapons and tools. Their feathers were thick, thick enough to make coats and clothes from, but were also used as good-luck charms throughout the city. Their meat was a delicacy, and blood used to oil machines. These people did not waste what could be used, everything had a purpose, and these items always met that purpose. The child seemed fascinated by the creatures, frightened yet still excited by their description. It knew its father had killed one before, but it just wanted to hear him say it, hear him talk about his successes and accomplishments. The child loved to listen to him tell tales of the hunt, of the creatures of the wild, of the world outside the city, and of its mother. The father seemed to be content with the child's explanation, still searching his sack for something. The heavy spoils of the hunt had buried his true prize,

The Harlequin

"Ah! That Krolaw! I think I got one, once upon a time." The child giggled at the father's words once more, happy he had finally unveiled the truth. The father finally grasped what he was searching for, a lengthy roll of fabric, red in color, soft to the touch. He pulled the fabric from its sack, and presented it to the child, wishing them a happy day of birth. Its facade showed with the light of amazement astounded that such luxury had been presented before their very eyes,

"Wooow! Pop-pop, is that the Balax Felt I told you about? It's so pretty! How did you find it?" The father shrugged, feigning ineptitude. The child knew better, demanding an answer from its father. Admitting to their guilt, the father told the child he had found it in a stall in the Northers for cheap, he had managed to haggle it. This was not true. This felt had been stolen, thieved from a feltsmith the father had spent the better half of the month stalking, waiting for the opportune time to strike. He had lusted for this material for some time, knowing full well the value it held in the child's heart. The child hugged the entire roll, letting it rub against its face. It *was* known to be soft, after all. The child thanked its father once more, before instead changing the topic to his weapon, asking if the father had remembered to oil it, to load bolts slowly, to check the left spool, in case it had tangled (it had a tendency to do so) and to leave the coils loosened when not readying to fire. The father assured the child he had done all these things. The child, in denial of its father's words, clambered upon the table, toying with the contraption. It tugged on the spools, examining the twine, the wood, the bolts. It found most things to be satisfactory. Most things. "Pop-pop, you liar! The twine is all messed up! I told you to keep them loose, cause the spools get all tight and then they break!" The father chuckled, pulling the child away from the weapon, assuring them all would be fine, and that they could fix it together later. The father decreed that the day be spent celebrating instead,

"Did your school home wish you a happy birthday? I hope they did." The child nodded, sitting passively in the father's lap. The father began to brush the antenna of the child as he spoke, pinching them at their roots, straightening their feathers,

"We had a good birthday snack, and—Pop-pooop, stop! That tickles!" The father did not stop his grooming of the child's head, keeping it as kempt as possible. Only after the child managed to squirm its way out of the father's grasp did he vow to stop the brushing, and only if the child promised to do it later themselves. The child quickly accepted this deal, and returned to its peaceable state, letting its father instead pet its head, every rub pulling the eyelids of the child open slightly more, as the skin on its head was pulled back. The child smiled at this feeling, sinking into the chest of its father as the petting soothed all of its nerves. The child, before letting itself relax too much, remembered it had been given a message for its father, "Oh, pop-pop! Ezrakell said he wanted to say hi to you, he's up on the ceiling." The father smiled at the error in diction, and stood to his feet, carrying the child with him. He slowly danced across the room, humming an offkey tune as he went. Approaching a small cubby resting upon the wall, he stopped petting his child. The father opened the cubby, and deposited the child, telling them to try out the new felt while he spoke to Ezrakell. The child nodded and hurried deeper into the crawlspace, anxious to enjoy their new gift. The hunter let out a content sigh, delighted that the child seemed to have enjoyed its gift. He tiredly shuddered with a quiet yawn, followed by a powerful stretch of his slender arms. He hung the hood of his jacket over his head, knowing full well the consequences of leaving the safety of his home without a disguise, and headed out towards the door, journeying up the stairs he had climbed just before. Even he wasn't sure just what Ezrakell wanted to speak about, never one to turn down the opportunity to conversate, Khanjali ventured onward. They had been just that for quite some time, as Ezrakell was one of the few attendants of the apartment complex that seemed to never leave. The two had grown close with their similar enjoyment of this isolation, and even more so with their adoration for the child—though Ezrakell would never admit to it. Ezrakell was a taller creature, one that had grown thin and lanky with malnourishment and a lack of any physical labor. He only remained within the walls of his home because of his desire to continue his craft—now on his own terms—of feltsmithing. This 'feltsmithing' was an uncommon profession, one that required both precision and patience, it was the art of melding both fabric and metals. Ezrakell had taught this art to the child, and the child did one day hope to be as great as he, but in its youth, still needed great practice. This art had made Ezrakell a grand deal of money in his early years, but he had retired, only Smithing for his enjoyment, or to supply clothing to his closest of companions (of which he had very few). Many accepted these gifts, but the child and its father did not, the child was more than willing to make the clothes itself. This giftly nature, bound with his height and tendency for isolation, had cut Ezrakell into a spiteful, cold person, a being that was nothing if not pompous. For all their wealth and charity, Ezrakell still had yet to do any good for the world, his gifts of 'kindness' remaining sealed away in the ragged dungeons of the poorest sectors of existence, blockaded by grief and self-pity. The father knew this, among a great many other things of Ezrakell's personal life, but never dared mention them. Ezrakell was not so accompanying and open when tested, and such a conversation would surely test him. Having reached the summit of the stairwell, the father pushed open the heavy metal door leading to the roof of his complex, peering out to see Ezrakell sitting in his usual spot on the edge of the rooftop. Ezrakell turned, eyeing the hunter up and down. This analysis only served to discomfort the father; he shrouded his form further. The father went to speak, but before he could mutter even a word, Ezrakell made a waving gesture, silently halting the father's speech,

"Please, remove that abhorrent rag. There is no need to hide yourself in your own home."

"Better safe than dead, Ezrakell."

"There is a grave difference betwixt precaution and paranoia."

"As a hunter, my precaution is what keeps me alive."

"Your paranoia is what keeps you from tranquility, Khanjali."

"My *precaution* is a product of my fear for the future, of my love for P."

"Your paranoia is a result of following in her mother's footsteps, take the coat off." 'Khanjali' did not speak back. He did not dare. He gritted his teeth, glaring at Ezrakell. The hunter did not want to remove his cloak, he did not feel safe, but Ezrakell was persistent, and his tone was deadly. He hesitantly pulled the leather from his neck, over his head, casting the cloak aside. Ezrakell smiled, finally content with the freedom of Khanjali's flesh, "Much better, isn't it?"

Khanjali scoffed, keeping his wings from spreading too far. Ezrakell patted the roof next to himself, inviting Khanjali over. He followed Ezrakell's commands. They sat silently for a while, Ezrakell staring ceaselessly at the wings. "They are so glorious Khanjali, and you snuff them with that rag, hide them from even Pedantick. This is needless torture." The wings *were* glorious—large ovular appendages, mostly an empyrean white, with small veins and markings of black and purple trailing throughout. Collections of black formed into small circles and curls, creating completely unique, intricate designs all across the surface of the wings—symmetrical in every way, of course. Khanjali had two sets, as most did. There were two larger, more detailed wings, emerging from right between the shoulders, and two smaller (but not by more than a few inches), more plain wings resting at the center of his back. Khanjali seemed hesitant to let Ezrakell stare for so long, but had given up trying to stop him long ago.

"Ezra, I was told you wanted something of me, might we continue to that discussion?" Ezrakell put up one finger, taking one last moment to admire the wings.

"I did not wish to ask anything of you, only talk. It has been some time since we have spoken in the calmness of the city, and more importantly since Pedantick was born. I do believe it is time to drop this facade."

Khanjali cringed, his right hand beginning to twitch sporadically. Ezrakell noticed this, though he was not fazed by the twitching, it was simply a tick, nothing more.

"Late bloomers are not some rarity, many Atramedians live for years as Sgiathless before gaining their Holiness. We cannot know—" Ezrakell interrupted Khanjali, sick of his voice sputtering lies in such a selfish manner, all in hopes of reassuring himself, distracting himself from his terrible circumstance. Ezrakell knew of the misfortune Khanjali had the pleasure of living through. He knew of Khanjali's desperation to reach out, to do any and all things in the eyes of his gods to be free from his manacles of adversity—and of course—how he was denied time and time again. He knew that Khanjali was near to giving up on this pursuit, near to cutting his ties and disappearing for good. But the one thing Ezrakell did not know, was why Khanjali felt the need to deny the existence of these things.

The Harlequin

"You may not, but I do. I know this is no late blooming. Pedantick will not gain her wings. She is without wings, Khanjali. She is Sgiathless." Khanjali shook the thought from his head, he had worked far too diligently to avoid it. He had spent all his life in these workings, laboring to keep his child from the cruel fate of his world. Khanjali wanted his child to be blessed, as he was. He wanted his child to live a normal, happy life. "This whole state of affairs is not nearly as dreadful as you think it."

"It is worse, truly it is worse than even you can conjure. It is hapless enough to simply be Sgiathless, but to be the spawn of a Sgiathen as well? That is a cursed fate, beyond the reach of your sympathy. I am damned." Ezrakell took personal offense to being told he could not fathom Khanjali's pain, but did not react—he knew better than to act on rage or hatred. This world had far too much of that.

"I think you are far too worried as is, how long have you lived without notice? How long have you spent hiding to keep your family alive? You are a proud figure, one I am filled with pride to simply know."

"That does not change P's condition. That does not change anything. I would rather be a peasant with no daughter than—" Ezrakell could bear his friend's self-piteous attitude no longer. Ezrakell may have pursued wealth, but he did not exist without suffering, without his own universe of torrents and claims.

"Fool! Do not speak that phrase, do not finish it! You are a being of gifts! Gifts! To bear youth—to have youth—it is above many! And here you stand seeking a claim for more?" Khanjali fell into a silent regret, a feeling of self-disappointment flowed within him. How inconsiderate he had been,

"I am sorry, Ezrakell. My hate is... misplaced. We must agonize through this together, dear friend. For P."

"For Pedantick, I know you will do anything." Khanjali stared out into the now light-filled sky. "As will I." In the eye of a new day, Khanjali thought himself relatively enlightened, perhaps to a degree that granted him such pure tranquility as Ezrakell had mentioned. He would not always feel this way, in the turbulence of the world, he would be thrown from cliff to valley. But with his greatest friend, with his daughter, he would be unmovable.

Creatures of Habit

The people of the Northers never had any lack of pride, yet they did not have any intentions of sharing it either. The people of the Southers were lesser in their eyes, and because of this, they spoke not of them, nor to them. The only two districts within the city of Drochandas were walled and guarded, with no citizens out of place, no ants from their farms. It was separated not by class, not by skill or intelligence, but by the wings. The wings made everything, and in a world of hatred and spite, wings either gave you life or snatched it away. Khanjali remembered when he still lived within the walls of the Northers, it wasn't all that different from the Southers, as much as the people of said lower district wanted to believe the opposite. Having lived out his most recent years in the Southers, he was one of very few Atramedians that could say he had seen both districts. He was impartial to both. It wasn't the places that mattered, it was the people within them. The Sgiathless of the Southers were not bad people, not all of them anyways. Khanjali had only been threatened twice and stolen from once. Most of the Sgiathless were normal people, people who simply wished to provide enough for themselves and their families to survive. Such was the only desire that was shared among them all. They had normal commodities: large housing, festivals, sports, factories, and even markets. All of these things were somewhat unique, all operating in different ways than their counterparts in the Northers, the markets especially. The markets in the Southers were massive, sprawling complexes of tarps, tight spaces, and of course, trading. Thousands of stalls filled entire blocks of the Southers, active at nearly all hours of the day. Khanjali appreciated the chaotic attitude in the air of these markets. Everyone within them had a bloodlust to sell, to earn their living, and keep from starvation. This bloodlust was more calmly expressed as a salesman's enthusiasm, every stall owner was competing to shout louder than the other, to sell faster than their opponents. It was a very vibrant place, and because of this, it filled any who entered with an essence of life. The markets in the Northers were near silent, quiet to a chilling degree. If you wanted something specific, you had to find it yourself. The stall-owners of the Northers did not have the same drive to sell because a day with no sales did not mean your own demise, and to call out in such unruly fashion was disrespectful to the honorable pride that the Northers represented.

The Harlequin

That was the sole difference between the two worlds, isolated within the minuscule details of the marketplaces. Ezrakell was watching Pedantick today. She was done with school around five in the morning and returned home by six at the latest. Ezrakell simply had to ensure she wasn't running with scissors, figuratively speaking. Khanjali had already completed his morning hunt around this time and was wandering through the markets back home, cutting through alleys and canals to get there sooner. He did not want to leave his daughter with Ezrakell for long, as his swollen head often made his efforts as a nanny meritless. Khanjali had once come home to find Ezrakell pinned to a wall by several crossbow bolts, having attempted to tame Pedantick's hate for the luxurious garments of the Northers. Khanjali had rushed home ever since, for Pedantick's safety, as well as Ezrakell's. Sometimes he stopped to rest, to buy a meal before he returned, to listen to the music of voices within the streets of the markets. He often partook in the senseless art of people watching, observing fragile buyers deliberate their needs, shopkeepers thoughtless bargaining away their souls. Everyone was different, unique in their own special way. Despite this, Khanjali always could see the clear similarities between everyone. For example, Khanjali knew if the Atramedian was in armor, thick metals of truly any kind, they most likely were only in the markets for leathers and skins, they were prideful, and often full of far too much confidence. Khanjali had seen it hundreds of times, these soldiers and smiths all searching for more tools of their trade. If the Atramedian was in the bare minimum, dressed in burlap and belts, they only desired the charity of others, going from stall to stall, hunting for a coin left alone, some even took what wasn't theirs. Khanjali let his eyes trail one of them—a rather rotund figure wearing tight pants, stitched somehow even worse than his own. The figure did not wear any other noticeable clothing, but there was an odd bulge in the back of its pants. Khanjali figured it was a concealed weapon—a dagger or firearm of primitive nature. Obtaining weapons in the Southers was quite the task, the poor could not often afford the high cost of advanced weaponry, and settled for their own custom crafts instead. Khanjali fell into the latter category, but not out of frugality. Pedantick had, for whatever reason, grown quite knowledgeable in the complex mannerisms of gears and twine, taking pride in assembling small gadgets in her spare time. Her father's weapon was the most intricate of these gadgets, being a rather complex reimagining of a classic Atramedian weapon: the crossbow. It had two limbs instead of one, crossing one another at the center of the weapon. The string had a manual tying system to make it easier to draw, and an automatic lock to keep it from firing. It could store up to five bolts at a time, but only safely fire one. It was a fine weapon, but that is not why Khanjali used it. It was the sentimental value, a weapon made by his own blood, just for him. He cherished it as he did Pedantick, and never considered the use of anything else. His thoughts of weaponry and Pedantick were cut short as he watched his tubby thief fail his craft, sparking an argument that somehow managed to rise over the usual shouting of the marketplace. The figure Khanjali was watching had stolen something. It was obvious. The stall owner had caught them, but without any local guardsmen nearby to monitor the encounter, the thief had no intention of returning the item. Khanjali rose from his seat on the edge of the canal and began his approach. He struggled to swim through the sea of roaming shoppers but managed to arrive just in time for the thief to turn to leave. Khanjali stood in their way, ensuring the figure could not escape.

"Put it back, mèirleach." The thief was shocked, perhaps even afraid. Khanjali was not a small man, nor was he weak. It would be inaccurate to call him a brute, but he was to some degree intimidating. The thief slunk backward, Khanjali demanding once again for them to replace their stolen item. The stall owner seemed content with the encounter, simply observing as it played out. The thief once again tried to make their escape, an unwise move in the face of a hunter. Khanjali grabbed the thief's arm, tugging them back to the stall. The force caused the thief to drop two small vials, which Khanjali scooped from their fall in haste, promptly returning them to the stall owner. He shoved the thief into the crowd and began to make his leave. The stall owner thanked Khanjali for his help and even offered a small amount of coin for his work. Khanjali did not think anything of it, and left the marketplace, quite finished with his people-watching for the day.

The Harlequin

On his way home, Khanjali had found a small advertisement, left in the gutter behind an abandoned school home. The advertisement was for a long-lost cause—an invitation to join the fight against the rising Ichyric threat. Those wars had long ceased, and there was now an illusion of peace. Khanjali's mother and father had fought in the Divine war, it was how they came to know one another. Khanjali did not recall exactly what had sparked the war, but he knew of some fragmented details. He was sure that the Ichyrics were just as thirsty to prove their strength as the Atramedians were, he knew too that they were more advanced, to an alarming degree. He knew the Ichyrics had won. There was less conflict between the two peoples in modern times, but Khanjali still felt as if there had never truly been a resolution to the war, that it had ended simply because it was becoming little more than an irritation to most involved, rather than either side seeing victory. Khanjali had never seen an Ichyric, but he one day hoped to. He wanted to ask them what they thought of the wars, what they thought of the Atramedians. He knew Ichyrics were supposedly quite arrogant—misanthropes supposedly—so he doubted the answer would be a kind one, but in a world of thieves and tyrants, not every descriptor was a definition. He had been told they loved their sciences and kept the peace between themselves. He had been told they had not undergone a single civil war. The Atramedian and Ichyrics were opposites, both in physicality and mentality. Their disagreements and quarrels were all too predictable; to expect polar opposites to cooperate was insanity. The opposing peoples of light and dark, together under one god… It *was* impossible, wasn't it? The two peoples had existed in this state for millennia. Sure, there were wars and conflicts from time to time, but the two peoples had always emerged stronger than before. They were symbiotic. Without one, the other would be unable to thrive, unable to pursue its fight against fate. They may have hated each other, but they needed co-existence. Most knew this, and most accepted it. And yet, the Atramedians couldn't treat each other the same way. It vexed Khanjali, how his own people—split beside each other by their inward hatred—could unite only under the banner of greater hatred, and so effortlessly too. But of course, the difference in something as minute and foolish as wings created such great disarray in the world of the

Atramedians that civil wars were to be considered a passing of the ages, a ceremony! Khanjali dropped the poster, letting it flutter down to its eternal resting place within the canal. He picked up his sack and continued onwards, decently close to his home now. Khanjali wished he could be like the Ichyrics, wished he could see their perfect harmony amongst his own people. That way, he wouldn't have to hide his wings. He could live among the stars, the purity of the higher world he had been born into—the world he deserved. But alas, fate had given him a daughter with a disgraceful body. He did not hate her for this, he did not think her any different than he, but he still wished she was different. It wasn't a selfish desire, as one might think, but quite the opposite. He wanted her to live without trouble, without oppression. He knew she never would. To think that when he left, she would be let loose upon the horrible streets of the city, given to the cruel arms of indifference—it brought him no comfort. He thought of this often, questioning if she would ever be truly prepared for her fate. But this thought was indescribably inappreciable in comparison to the alternative: the thought of losing her. If anyone was to find out that he was a Sgiathen, if the guards were to discern their relationship as father and daughter—he dared not imagine the worst. A figure draped in darkness leapt from the ledge of the canal above Khanjali, drawing a short blade on him. The figure took care to remain in the dark, threatening him only from a distance.

"You seem awful haughty, Hunter. Mind if I ask where you're from?" The figure twisted the blade in their hand, it seemed of decent quality. Khanjali was not afraid, however. They held the weapon like an amateur—as if they had never used it upon a living soul.

"I do. The cleanest fate would have you move along, I do not have the time to redress that hand-shake-and-dagger of yours." The figure chuckled, stepping slightly further out from their shadowy veil. It was the same thief from the marketplace, clearly quite keen on holding a grudge.

"Not many have time, do they, Hunter? What do you return home to? A partner? A child? Do the possessions of dead men truly matter in the grandest of schemes?" Khanjali grew impatient with this phrase and was already fairly irked by the thief's attempt at arousing fear from him.

"Perhaps I do, but as your business belongs to you, so does mine belong to me. Do not let me hold you from your loved ones." Khanjali moved forward but was met only with the dagger, pointing into his large pale eyes.

"I know why you talk like that, why you think yourself above me. You were a Sgiathen! Or, are you still?" The thief began to lift Khanjali's cloak with the edge of his weapon, prompting Khanjali to bat the tool away. The thief turned sour, their round eyes tightening into a glare, their lips curving into a feral snarl. "You're a Sgiathen, such an action as that proves it. Question is, why are you wandering the Southers? Suppose you're here to mock us, to study us like flies in a bottle. Or, maybe you've got something awfully precious back home, something you can't just take back north with you?" Khanjali was finished with the thief's prying, and was more than prepared to end the conversation. He shoved the thief back, not fazed by their possession of a weapon at all.

"Your questions push the boundaries of humility and aptitude. If you were any greater a soul, a soul you would sooner lack." The thief chuckled, a devious grin spreading across their face.

"Oh, you would not hesitate? I would not be caught dead impersonating a Sgiathless. You've so much power, so much privilege! You perform the role of the weak so dully, the playwright of this charade ought to be punished. You have no idea of our plight, our suffering under the Sgiathen. I have doubts you ever worked a day in your life, Inkling." That word did not sit well with Khanjali, not in the meekest of portions. Inkling was not a loose phrase, not some petty insult to be spoken without consequence. It was more than a slur, it was an ex-communication. It was a blatant insult to an Atramedians honor and integrity. Khanjali had enough honor to take notice.

"Your tongue will get you killed, mèirleach. Do not act so sorrowful, pitying yourself like a common widower. You do not know of the struggles of any but your own. Those who suffer with you are your greatest allies, and yet you seem fit to betray them." The thief was not amused with Khanjali's accusations. They did not like their self-pity to be called out.

Creatures of Habit

"I am not the one watching the oppressed like cattle, not the one silently letting injustice slither in its milky chrysalis." Khanjali could almost laugh at the words, but he was too busy contemplating how one could become so cold, so self-centered—so blind.

"I do not consider myself an oppressor by any means, but nor should you the opposite. The maltreatment of others is no excuse for indolence. I hunt for my coin, skin for my livelihood. I serve Maccabeus and Maeandri in the fields, and in the forests, and honor their grace with prayer. What grace do you honor in thievery?" The thief had lost its intrigue with speech and instead turned to action. They stabbed at Khanjali, who, having spent his life hunting, easily predicted, and blocked the attack. Khanjali grappled the thief and pinned them to the floor.

"You accuse me! Dare to call me free in a caged world! I am as controlled as the worms in the ground, tied down to my shackles by my lack of wings! You know nothing of what it means to be Sgiathless! You couldn't possibly comprehend it!" The thief squirmed with rage under Khanjali's grip. The squishy figure of the thief did not stand a fighting chance against the much stronger, bulkier form of Khanjali.

"You are as free as the butterflies of the fields. You cage yourself only in fear and insolence. Stop blaming others for your own misfortune, and aspire to change it yourself." The thief stopped, finally seeming to accept their loss. Khanjali let the thief up, who slowly backed away from him. The thief peered up, noticing the light tapping of metal boots on cold stone. There was a Guardsman, walking the edge of the canal, right above them. The thief knew Khanjali would do anything to protect his identity, being caught by a Guardsman would be an unrecoverable blow. They cried out to the Guardsman, loud and clear. Khanjali had but a second to act.

"Guardsman! Help! A Sgiathe—" Khanjali quickly cut their words short, pulling the thief by the throat, covering their mouth. The thief broke loose, and in the blink of an eye—without even considering it—Khanjali swung. He tore his blade from his side and dug. The swing was quick, almost unnoticeable, and the cut was fatal. He had managed to slice directly from the thief's right shoulder to their left ear. The thief had not a second to speak before they were dead. Their body fell backward, into the murky sewer waste running at Khanjali's feet. A look of dreadful penitence filled both of the thief's eyes, frozen in time as the blood poured over them. Khanjali stared at the thief, the body. Its jaw hung open, cut in such a way that the leftmost side hung lower than the right. The throat was loosely bound now, a deep cut letting a fountain of blood erupt from its depths. Both hands were distorted, almost twitching in the motionless display. Khanjali wanted to vomit, to unearth his temper in physical pain. The sewers twisted in his eyes, threatening to push him over with the weight of this act. So, he sat himself down, beside the body, beside the once lively thief. This was not his fault, no—it was unavoidable. They had attacked him, threatened to take his daughter away. This was not his fault. The thief had been no lesser a man than he was, they had suffered just as much as Khanjali had in this cruel world. This was not his fault. He looked down at his weapon, and at the body again. A single dead Sgiathless in the sewer was no large event. The guardsmen would most likely ignore it until it rotted. But a Sgiathless killed by a Sgiathen? That would not go unnoticed. The skin held all these truths, the history of this encounter. If Khanjali wanted to remain unbound to this event, he would need to cut loose his chains, cut them at their source: the flesh. His quivering hand twisted the blade, readying himself for the craft he had become so accustomed to. He was a hunter, and this was his prey. This was not his fault. It would not be his fault. He lowered the blade, twirling the flesh around the edges of the metal. It was horrifying—eldritch in nature—watching the flesh of another curl like that of a peeling orange. The muscles still moved and twitched, still steamed with the heat of life. Khanjali was nearly done with the first arm. He continued, cutting loose the flesh, cutting loose himself. He let his mind define it as work, let his thoughts drift away from the reality of murder, to the fantasy of the hunt. He cut without mind, without thought. He cut through flesh and flesh and more. He cut the muscle, the meat, his hunter's mind told him it was lean—good enough to sell. He cut through the tusks, the bone. He cut through the eyes, the guts, the intestines, the mind. He cut the veins, he bottled the blood, he *bottled* it. He cut the fingers down flat, the feet into stubs. He cut the jaw clean off, the tongue from its place, the teeth from the gum. His mind continued to carry him forward, carry him to completion. Then suddenly, the work was done, the body was harvested, and Khanjali looked at his work with pride. He bundled the flesh, packaged the meat, and collected the vials. He stared into the purple abyss, the darkness of the blood of his own people. He retched, finally snapping back from his hunter's trance. He dropped his bag, pulling the items from within it, throwing them to the ground. The body was destroyed, there was no need to do what he had done, to cut so endlessly—to go so far. The jaw was gone, leaving only the upper skull. The skull, the skull was all that was left, no eyes, ears, or nose. The torso was devastated, all of the organs rearranged or taken. What little muscle remained was strewn about carelessly. The fingers were filed down to stumps, and the bones torn from its arms and ribs. Khanjali shattered the vials against the stone of the canal and wished to do the same with the rest of his spoils. But he could not. Not anymore. He packed them back into his sack and wiped the vomit from his face. Khanjali looked down at his hands, a vibrant purple stain spread over them, nearly solidified by the cold of the night, a thin shell. This, this was not his fault. This had not happened. It was a body, torn apart by sewer rats, killed by its own insolence. Khanjali continued walking. There wasn't too much to think of.

~ *Vignette*

*Foretold by the scriptures in the cathedrals
of Grand Arcenna, where even dead suffer...*

Three thousand and eleven lords and empresses vanished in the Once Kingfall. Twenty cities, four hundred buildings, and an estimated one thousand square kilometers of cropland were constructed in its wake. There were supposed second comings. The so-called Wight of Warlords, the disappearance of further rulers and self-claimed heirs (one throated entirely on technicality) only years later, took little inspiration from its predecessor, as did its own mimic, a spree of kidnappings across the Umbral Coast. After decades of decay and misdirection, any surviving scholars would consolidate to agree that the Once Kingfall occurred just that. Once. Yet its effect on the society of Arcenna was undeniable. What vein this effect bit upon, was completely up for debate. Worlds and peoples had crumbled and fallen from their own grace. Ironic death over misfortunate life, singularities and invention rocked the descent. A place of newness, yet stinking of rot and misery was born in the mist. So too was the Great Panacea, Feller of Kings. In the riverbeds of the once wonderful Arcenna came a plague of cure so monstrous, it took with it only tens. Stricken with boastful pride, it would seem any who claimed to be the ruler of another would be lost in due time. But what of those born into it? Would they too seek destinies among the murk? Would hemorrhaging fate bring a halt to the breath of children who had yet to brandish a crown or scepter? It would appear sadly so, fate was unforgiving, and continues to be. In a land of tarnished corpses left open to the air, and continual deceit and confusion over the hands that pulled the strings, no one was less likely to die than the unconsidered, unabiding, unprotected nomad. This is wherein all life resided, and continues. Mechanical mishap, pitfall resin, no such burden was such to a nomad. The city awaits its stars, pulled directly from sinners' blood this time. Die again, O ye nomad. Die again and see flowers bloom through your bones where Kings and Gods would find their cemeteries.

In the past, he had been told his mother prayed for him. As an heir herself, death was as firm as destiny. She had prayed for him, and no god of note had answered. That is not to say *no* god answered, though of course, considering this is all hypothetical as is, there is no point in delving into semantics. There was no mercy for royal blood, and his was made of the stuff of crowns. Hidden from view in the scale of a troupe of merchants and ne'er do wells, he thrived by the name 'Moonlighter Sim'. Sim was not his name, but to speak it was to die alongside it. In his company there was danger, those who grouped in collectivity ran the risk of ruling, leadership, and other diseases. The Wolfstram Crypts of the northern mountains spelled frostbite with ease, and though it seemed inevitable, the group survived with minimal hazard. First of the troupe was a nascent mind of pure economy, once imbibing their faith with currency and distaste. Her facilities, much like her facade, were cracked and deficient, often perceived as lacking repair. Twins from the Munish Churches over the mountains to the north could rhyme in tandem, sadly that was all they could do. There was no payment nor meals in poetry when the only rhythmic beauty on display for this world was the death count of kings among wenches. What once was a mother and son had proven to be a widow and corpse through the Crypts, but it was no costly sadness to anyone but the new widow. Paying no mind to kinship or the sabbath, 'Sim' left the first stop along Bismath. No journey was complete without a destination, in his travels he had learned that temporary destination was a cure for all confusion. In truth, the regulation of a path forward was more than comforting, despite it being laced like a heroin with lies. Bismath was east of Archaeopolis, the city of what could be called catacombs. Though a catacomb is as much a catacomb without corpses as a sea is an ocean without salt. Encroaching from the close west was Zealot's Wood, just before the city itself. It powered through any non-neutered plant life and reckoned with itself against the rock of Wolfstram. It was all a speculative map, anyways; cartography died with the crowns. The nameless path between Bismath and the wood was alluring, against the judgment of 'Sim'. Some warnings had been spread about the contents of the forest, an endless supply of savages and monks, those who would continue to worship against the odds of the Once Kingfall. Zealots, of course, must've resided within. How else would it have earned such a title? From within a verdant knapsack by his waist, a small metallic claw emerged, bearing three ruts and a fourth clipped joint. The mechanical implement brushed quickly against a metallic pin stuck through the elegantly torn poncho 'Sim' wore.

"Caelo. Why are you out of your bag?" The hand ceased movement. For a while, it lingered, a perpetual mix of fear and indecision breaking its senses. 'Sim', not tearing his view from the troupe as they wandered from sight, spoke again, a more demanding tone filling his throat. "You can't just hide from me. I know you reached out." A minute peeping eye emerged from the sack.

"We are [ALONE]. I am [CORRECT]?" The poncho rippled in a sudden gust of soft, yet scented wind. The scent of buttercream.

"They are still watching back. Give it a moment. Good to see you too Caelo." The robot painstakingly resealed the knapsack, retreating into its depths with a muffled hum. When the carriage of vagrants finally escaped view, 'Sim' pursued a narrow stretch letting out into the fields, heading in the vague direction of the forest before him.

"Hello [DUKE EPHILO]." With a wrangle not unlike the crack of a whip, Duke Ephilo tore the machine from its bag, cradling it softly in his arms as he cried out in joy,

"Oh Caelo! How long has it been? Is it not terribly witty that the touch of metal and glass could be so akin to flesh? To love itself?" Caelo beeped with jubilance, burying itself into its master only further.

"Time is [TWO DAYS]." Duke Ephilo let out a false chortle, before shoving the machine away from himself.

"Two *measly* days." The Duke fell back onto his bag, letting the soft mosses and overpopulated beds of various seedlings catch his spine. "Could have been eons, travel takes my mind away." Though it had hardly breached dawn, the half-sun of the planet continued its reign of temperate heat upon all that it could pet. The Duke, being a creature of scales and several layers, was only moderately inconvenienced by its rays.

"Where is [DESTINATION]." Duke Ephilo held up a single, three-digited hand.

"Oh please, little heir, can we not lay in this wondrous field? What stops us from pausing to admire all that the terrible god who killed my people created?" Caelo drifted closer to the Duke, the whir of its thruster adding to the serene bliss slipping into Ephilo's ear.

"The disease, [DUKE EPHILO]." The Duke whispered a soft hush to the machine. Mystery took hold of the first natives of the lands of Arcenna. That mystery once brought about kingdoms, however, all it delivered to the survivors of those kingdoms were endless quantities of unfashioned suffering. Duke Ephilo had no worries of suffering, for he had a built-in reserve of the matter, and regardless of testaments both time and pain, he continued ever so. "Ah, to be Duke again. As if I ever was. The mud is what I am Duke of." Caelo disabled its thruster, and thunked into the lower chest of the Duke, weary and calm.

"What is [DUKE]." Duke Ephilo patted the machine, buzzes emitted like the purrs of an elder tabby. Bolts had been merely taped to its face as if to add some form of old professionalism to its build. The machine was a caretaker, despite its disposition toward the opposing role.

"Hm. A king of nothing lower than possible. Smaller than a king certainly. Yet, I live! Ha Ha!" Caelo's distended screen peered up to the Duke, analyzing the laughter.

"I do not understand." Ephilo dragged a single talon through the mud, letting any pollen collect as residue under his nail.

"Oh, you'll understand, one day. The pleasure will be yours to mourn and baste with as you please." With another finger, the Duke flicked the excess from under his bones, watching it carry on into the wind. "Seeds of the crown, you know." Caelo's chest flicked open, revealing a small scanning device where a heart could be. It pondered the Duke.

The Harlequin

"Vitals are well, [DUKE EPHILO]. This [CORPSE] is free of disease."

"Joyous. It would seem we have a while longer to admire the field then, yes?" The small cattleman's cap atop the Duke's head drifted forward in the breeze, lightly covering the obnoxious snout sprouting from under his scarf. "Mayhaps I shall rest within it."

"M'lord, are you [TIRED]?" Caelo uttered, its affixed voicebox quivering with tone.

"I told you I'd prefer to be called an equal, Caelo. My father, —or his father— whatever it may be, did no such service in resigning you to the language of royals. I have no legion over you, little heir." Duke Ephilo gestured to the vastness of the flowerbeds, where two large stocks of driftwood lay, reveling atop each other, ever so balanced as to only fall with interruption. "Over yonder, my crown lies amok the thorns and festoons. I have no kingdom." Caelo went to investigate the figure of speech, but the Duke quickly reeled the attention of the machine back, a simple click of his tongue was all that needed to be.

"[DUKE: A HEREDITARY TITLE OF PEERAGE AND OWNERSHIP OVER—"

"Ack, Caelo! The world is an anthill and this is my kingdom, Duke or not—"

"[DUKE] without a [PROPER KINGDOM]. What makes a [DUKE]." As if it had been only hours ago, Duke Ephilo could still hear the ringing of silver tambourines, and whistles of violas beyond the crest of the highest windowsills. Windowsills he had never grown tall enough to peer out from, not before the Kingfall.

"Lishra, what makes you machine, little heir? Wires and stuff, hmmm?" Ephilo tapped against the small jutting of copper out Caelo's side. "Made of the same stuff, I am. More blood than spool, surely! Little difference is harbored between us."

"I am of [METAL] not [CROWNS]."

"What are crowns of, little heir?" Caelo thought of the answer, but despite its vast memory, it could not say. It had not the word for it. "Try metal. Not the gold stuff. Unpolished and crass it is. Ho, I could be just as metal as thee if I had lost my mold like those fools of the Deadrung court. Pity." Caelo ignored the mockery and requests, instead ejecting the nano-scanner from its chest once more, the visor of such piercing the brim of Ephilo's hat, blinding him for a moment, he chuckled.

"Vitals are well. This [CORPSE] is free of disease." Duke Ephilo spun a rogue strand of copper around his finger, the scales of which sheared its density.

"Yes, you have told me."

"I am sorry."

"Quite alright, little heir. Shall you rest awhile?" The Duke motioned for its chest once more, where the haptic machine would lay itself given time.

"As [EPHILO] says, [RIGHTY SWELL]." The Duke creaked his jaw open, somewhat stunned by the mimicry. Every day Caelo seemed to learn another word, one not previously in its database, at the very least. He had no need to teach the little machine any longer. The waning scent on the wind marked it time for calmness, the Duke had no quarrels with this realization. However, even in the maw of absolutely no peril, another breath stirred the clearing.

"Another Yeri, fashioned to see 'ya around these places."

"Lishra, I could have been dead, you crone! Approaching a swallowed soul in a field of flowers... ridiculous to expect anything else." The figure approached the Duke, who kept the cleansed weapon on their hip concealed.

"I mean not a pinnacle of harm! No sire, not likely. What do you mean, I wonder?" The Duke shifted cautiously, covering the machine atop his chest with a perfect gust and flick of his cloak. Calm, he needed calm.

"Rest. Peace, if you would. No war here in the flowers."

"Once was."

"Of course, war was everywhere, fool."

"Still could be." Ephilo tilted his hat up, peering out at the figure. It was of the same race as his new corpse, a 'Yeri' as he had called it. Made of scales and malding bones. Reptilian and an eyesore. It once terrified the Duke to think of the limited species he had left to grasp onto, but when life itself became a sturdy foundation, worry faded into boredom. The Yeri would be forgotten, as the Roa had been, as the others had too. All forgotten.

The Harlequin

"Do you have a mind for nagging at people? Is it a temptation in your metalloid head?" The Yeri shook his head, responding negatively to the insult.

"I mean not a pinnacle of harm, as I said. Come to see the flowers, following those travelers up yonder." The Yeri gestured over the ridge, towards the very troupe the Duke had departed from. They had gained quite a distance.

"You ought to keep up with them. Hasty, they are."

"Hasty I need not be! The flowers, fellow man. Look at them." There were far too many to simply admire. Colors blended into gradients, and those finely tuned hues blurred the lines of forest and field. Duke Ephilo could not with any honesty discern whether the ramblings of The Yeri were intended as dull, or a byproduct of idiocy. He inevitably decided on the latter.

"Yes. Flowers." Caelo squirmed, and Ephilo rubbed his palm against the machine. The Yeri sat beside him, and with an exaggerated pant, fumbled a small notebook from his backside, hidden underneath an iron breastplate adhered to his waist, not unlike a skirt. Idiocy indeed.

"You much of a writer, sire?" Neither of the two looked at the other. The conversation had reached the point where such monotonous movement was no longer necessary.

"No, not particularly. I'd much rather be an artist." The Yeri continued to write, silently contemplating the answer he had received. Though it had not been long since he had seen another, The Yeri was far past due to meet another of its own blood. The Yeri, like all species of substance and rulership, fell when the Once Kingfall came. Many scattered, though a great deal of the twin-forked tongue beasts had run to sanctuaries in the mountains, a series of cities that had outlasted the tell of time. But as mentioned prior, it was those who wandered that often found refuge. Duke Ephilo continued to question the traveler of their origins, receiving little in the way of evidence to prove anything of merit. The talk held itself quite well for a while longer, but when the sun began to lower, so too did the voices. Four new pages had been written and illustrated into The Yeri's journal, pages that Ephilo himself had both inspired and observed. There was discussion of the old ways, despite neither of the two nomads recalling much about them. Voices on the wind carried questions of new settlements, one south of all places, in the blistering winds of the Umbral Coast. Archaeopolis persisted, as confirmed by the traveler, Ephilo reminded himself to visit before death took him permanently. Careful contemplation went into a recommendation of tours, one requested of Ephilo by the Yeri. Though he had been to many places, none had struck him as worthy of note, certainly not of tourism. The world was caked with mold, obnoxious people hid between the shattered remnants of maids who had actual spite on their side, those who had built everything that mattered, like Caelo. Duke Ephilo had told the man of Ramaces. It was just as putrid as any other kingdom, but in Ramaces there was the thrill of battle to tide hunger and other common fatalities. Constant infighting betwixt the two reigning factions, both in danger of death from the Panacea in their rulings, brought a chorus of lovely clashing. Steel and song, war and wit.

"I thank you, sire. Advice is good when from your kin."

"Right. From kin." The Yeri got up, their pants (and breastplate) soiled with inchworms. He went to shake Ephilo's hand, but finding no need in comradery, instead opted to step around the resting lizard.

"Before I make myself completely scarce, sire, have you any intention of exploring the wood? Zealot's, that is." With an affirmative grunt, Ephilo leaned ever so slightly closer to the Yeri, interest piqued by the finally relevant topic of discussion. "Heard it be filled with savages s'all. Ought to watch for 'em, schemers and devils." The warning, something Ephilo was grateful to have, reminded the Duke of a similar supposed fate of those who passed through the Wolfstram Crypts. And yet here he stood, none the wiser, still breathing as he had before. He thought little of the threat and carried on. Caelo sputtered behind the Duke, chary of other travelers who would interrupt the peace found in the fields. Peace was a passing novelty. The novelty had just now passed.

~ *The Gardener's Recluse I*

Etched into the side of a decrepit watering can, coated in Ichyr and emptied of all dreams...

Hull plates, servos, and shock absorbers were not appealing to most forms of natural life. No, they were considered abnormal — distasteful. Ugly. Flowers, the rosemary that grew in section three of the Grow Beds, and even the vine-thread rope that the Gardener had sewn itself were far more visually gratifying than the rusted coat upon its dank metal exterior. In preparation for the arrival of a new friend, it had fashioned itself many amenities, all attempts at civilized professionalism. The Gardener had repaired its apron with fibers and handmade dyes, it had polished its rust away with a rudimentary acid derived from old disabled batteries. The Gardener had filed down the edges of its broken glass screen and even stitched cuffed sleeves for its apron from the vine rope. It felt beautiful, far more than it ever had before.

"Peregrine, am I not stunning? My form should be most pleasing to whatever may greet me, yes?" Peregrine responded affirmatively, thinking perhaps the Gardener had overextended its hand with the greeting customs. The Gardener could be very overzealous at times, and Peregrine had nowhere to hide from its eccentrics.

"Do you not think this too much? We do not even know if this guest will be sentient. Perhaps it is a broken drone, or worse?"

"Or worse? It must be alive, yes? I do not care what this new friend is, as long as it lives, I will wait for it!" Peregrine, being a creature of habit—said habit involving a formulated infinitely predictive behavior—had its doubts. The Gardener was a machine of endless claims and joy. Without its father, creator, the Gardener would grow distant, saddened, and hopeless as it had before. Peregrine tried its hardest to keep this fate from even the predictions of its mind, but Peregrine was not so godly. The truth was that the new creature on the island could already have died, or could never have been alive to begin with. Such was not only adamantly possible but plausible as well. But for The Gardener to learn this, would be to sever its connection with the light, with hope altogether. Thus, Peregrine remained silent, inert in the eyes of the truth, the very likely truth, for as long as its own servers would allow it. The Gardener waited, prepared, and pondered for a seemingly endless sum of time—two days. A storm brewed and left, the humidity of the jungle rose by one percentile, four new songbirds were birthed, and six more died. The Gardener did not lose hope, after all, the island was very large, how long would it take to circumnavigate it? For many living faunas, it could be a long time indeed.

"Do you think this visitor could be hurt? Gardener, is it not possible that our visitor crash-landed here?" The Gardener sat on a small cobble wall it had assembled from scratch. It was cleaning some mud from its kneecap, some that had splashed onto its body while it was removing puddles from the garden.

"Ho! You are right, there are no bridges or paths to the island, the only way on is by sea or sky..."

"And within the jungle and the shores, there are few optimal landing zones. Perhaps instead of letting this visitor come to us—"

"We shall go to them."

"We should go to them."

"Then we will! Come Peregrine, we shall leave at once!" The Gardener stood, finishing its polishing swiftly. It approached the beautified exit path of the Centrum, following a familiar trail down into the deepest reaches of its abyss, before being halted by a new suggestion,

"Gardener, what if this visitor is in mortal peril? What if, in pursuit of them, so too do we enter such peril? This body is not fit for combat." The Gardener thought for a moment, having known so well the island's inhabitants (at least within a ten-kilometer radius), it considered not the possibility of danger.

"I suppose then, a search is in order! Are there any tools of war within my perfect Centrum? There must be, yes?" Peregrine took a moment to scan, to search its blueprints and its surroundings. It came up with a single relative result, there was no armory, no security systems, no. Only a corpse, mounted within an unexplored crevasse.

"I have located a tool. It may be of difficulty to reach, it is held inside a ventilation bay through the air ducts, I can mark it for you." A small box was illuminated by the Gardener's very eyes, it could see the location, and had quite a simple solution to reach it. The bay lay beyond the boundaries of the Centrum's halls. It was within a small crawl space between the ceiling and the rock surrounding it, pushed off to the side, behind a basking of lighter sheet metals. One could easily access the bay through the ventilation shafts, climbing through the air ducts like a baboon. The Gardener did not consider this an option. Approaching the wall with care, it placed its hand against the iron,

"How many kilos of stone lie beyond this metal."

"Detecting nearly twenty. The stone is unstable—if the metal is removed—" The Gardener pulled back its mechanical hand, and let fly a single punch, targeting a direct weak point within the structure of the metal. A small amount of rubble slid from the wall, piling on top of itself as it filled the corridor's floor. "That was a foolish decision. The integrity of this facility has lessened. It is advisable to—" The Gardener once again struck the wall, this time far lower than before. The violence allowed a majority of the stone to fall, and with it, the floor to the ventilation bay. A rotted corpse tumbled down and face-planted upon the stone.

"Mission accomplished Peregrine. Take note: I must remember to repair these damages eventually." The Gardener glanced at the corpse, absorbed in its aura of decay. Much of its skeletal structure had begun to appear within the flesh, but there was indeed still flesh. It was purple and green, a darkened color that was soft to the touch, fragile, and molded over. The face of the once-living creature was hollow and devoid of any symbolism. It was a stone. Inanimate, without any verve. The corpse was cowering. It was clutching a long tool, wrought from iron and wood. The Gardener did not hesitate to tug it from its place, shaking free the excess mold that rested upon its frame.

"This is the tool. I am not positive of its stability. It is a firearm of sufficient caliber, I do presume. The ammunition for this weapon is contained within the corpse's breast pocket. We will need it." The Gardener peered down the barrel of the tool, rubbing its metal fingers against the cold wood, the dry wood. It was preserved well. Minimal moisture had crept into the fiber, the wood had not been cracked or blemished. It was so well preserved, in fact, the Gardener could notice a small inscription on the wooden stock of the tool, a small poorly illustrated bird, beside a tally adding to fourteen. The barrel's sheen had been dulled by a small deal of rust and fogging, but could be easily purified in a matter of moments with the talents of the Gardener. It looked at the corpse once more, tugging a small box of ammunition from its possession. It slowly and meticulously slid open the cardboard sealing, peering in at the shiny red shells within the box. It moved each shell, one by one, into the pocket within its apron. It did not take the time to count.

"We have ammunition, and a firearm, Peregrine. Are we not prepared for war?"

"War is a fallacy, a length we cannot approach. Perhaps we are prepared for a hunt, yes?" The Gardener concurred and loaded the shotgun. It did not have intentions of harming the innocent wildlife of the isle, but for the creatures without such innocence, there would be no mercy.

A splash echoed in the forest, off the trees, the canopy, reverberating and morphing ever deeper into a dull drone. The Pilot heard it all, but without the foresight of its origin. If she had brought a plane, she would have survived. If she had brought a plane.... A quiet rumble shook the shredded hull of the boat. The Pilot could not hide forever. She could hear the chaos outside the boat, animals and insects singing in anguish among chattering leaves. Something was awry in the very nature of the island, that she could smell for certain. Having awoken not but an hour prior, the Pilot had heard similar bleats from tarnished creatures before. With no means of defense, The Pilot did not expect to survive for long, given the state of the mainland. It had been some time since she had slept without a watch—or a weapon—by her bedside. Spitting sand from her upper lip, she pondered if her goal was worth the petrification, humanity had been considered a lost cause once before, after all. Due in no small part to the shore's tendency to swell with the tide, The Pilot found her garments coated wet with salt. Small bubbles of air seeped from the sand below, quickly outpacing the chirps of distant animals. A hasty sand crab emerged from under The Pilot's knee, prying its way out from under the shrouded hideaway. Another wave splayed foam and weeds into the tipped hull, The Pilot choked on the corrupted air. She heaved up, distancing her arms to the furthest reaches of the boat's length. Her wingspan failed her, and so too did her strength. But at this moment, The Pilot was granted a small glimpse of the outside world, a darkening shore path, leading inwards to what could only be a jungle, a place of nothing but basil green. It would seem as though one thousand eyes peered back to The Pilot, all waiting for the inevitable. As the remains of the boat crumbled back atop her spine, a rusty orange box fell from under a support plank, dropping in front of The Pilot with a soggy plop. It began to sink into the slop of sand and mud, but she hurriedly curled the package within her mucked hands. Curious of its contents, and desperate for prayer, The Pilot slipped the tin cover off. Within lie a flare gun, two flares locked with velcro beside it. It was no weapon, but it certainly was a deterrent. With a tremendous crash, a large wave struck the side of the capsized vessel, sliding it up the beach a tiny amount. The Pilot took a deep breath and continued to examine the tool. She did not know exactly how old it was, the warranty and quality of a deterrent were of course quite important to consider when left without any comforts. The flare gun was split down its side, an intentional design. Break chambers, unlike many things, were quite a warm familiarity to The Pilot, her father's old rifle had a similar design. Cracking the barrel from the body to head, she slid one of the flares into the gun, stuffing the backup shell into her jacket pocket. Through even the thick ply of the boat, The Pilot heard the roar of an approaching wave. Bracing her teeth together, she slammed her back against the side of the craft, pushing with all her stamina. With the force of the wave, and her frail body, the debris fell to the side, slipping down the coastline into the sea. With a gasp of exhaustion, The Pilot matted back her dried, salted hair. Her knees still shook with the panic and exhaustion of the initial crash. She could still taste the blood. But to live in the past was to die in the future, the island was here, and here it would stay. The Pilot peered into the tree line. There was no construction, no man-made infrastructure, nothing. This was a wild, feral place. A place that had somehow remained breathing and verdant, unlike the mainland. Her feet began to sink into the sand, a sign to move forward. Before venturing deeper into the abyss though, The Pilot turned back to the product of her 'piloting'. Within the wreckage lay her dynasty, reduced to a single helmet. Its screen was unbroken, but the supporting ridges of the helmet had begun to wear down. Her father had passed it down to her years ago, and his father to him. It was as old as time, and with the crash, it only seemed older. She quickly checked the waterproof tin strapped to the side of the helmet, still crammed full of dry matches. Returning to the jungle, The Pilot stumbled up the beach, a thick device mounted against her thigh clicking silently as she ascended. She had fought tooth and pick to get off the coastline of her hometown, miles back upon the mainland. Though it was not documented, many suspected the past had something to do with the apparent apocalyptic state of the planet, unbreathable air, and darkened water. Trees had softened and dropped, the leaves never did die. Beasts of white crystalline structure roamed the plains of the mainland, The Pilot only hoped they had not followed her here. After the last historians had succumbed to the hopeless nature of a world without light, bleakness consumed the few countries left alive. Most robots were left decaying and dead, the sun their only reckoning hope. Still, it did not emerge often from its prison of rock in the sky. The clicking stopped, and so too did The Pilot. She plucked the device from her thigh, and smacked its side a few times, but to no avail. Desperate to prove its denial a false signal, she turned it around, removing both its thin batteries, and shakingly replacing them. No change, it clicked not. Her hand hovered above her mouth, beyond the rebreather strapped indefinitely to her skull. The Pilot placed her two longest fingers against its plastic base, shivering, hesitating. Her eyes bore burning sockets into the device, and still, it remained silent. She moved the rebreather, hyperventilation threatening to suffocate her. But it did not. The air was fresh, and with it, she breathed. Breathing, no aid nor machines. This was the place, The Pilot was certain.

"It is not a Poppy. I have seen a Poppy. They are red, this is orange."

"Based on the Hex Code system, this flower would be considered an 'F84822', or red." Peregrine was correct in this degree, but the Gardener knew such acute knowledge was irrelevant in the realm of gardening. It was a spirit science, precise in only the soul. Peregrine lacked a soul, the Gardener considered itself full of soul. There was no certainty to either claim, perhaps the opposite was entirely true, but without any scale with which to measure a soul, it remained stubborn in its ways. A footstep alerted the Gardener, tearing it from the petty quarrel of flowers and colors. It scanned the world before it, searching for any indication of danger, an indication it silently hoped never to encounter.

"Scan complete, area is clear, Gardener. It was merely the wind."

"Or a beast with great haste. We must take care, Peregrine. Who knows what creatures of hatred creep in this terrible tomb." The Gardener and its accomplice had been journeying for no longer than an hour, their goal set to reach the edge of the island, and follow it clockwise in search of stranded vessels. If no such vessel was discovered, the Gardener would return to the Centrum, where it would wait for its visitor in solitude. To reach the shores, however, the Gardener first had to venture through the dark jungles, ones shrouded in mystery, even from the eyes of Peregrine, who knew so many of the island's secrets.

"Gardener, my internal clock indicates we will be walking for another hour at the very least before the shores are visible. Might you wish to entertain yourself in some way during this pilgrimage?" The Gardener tightened its grip around the weapon it had stolen from the dead, disliking Peregrine's idea of comfort in hell.

"We must remain vigilant, Peregrine. We would not want to be overpowered."

"I have found there are few opportunities for thought in your duties. Might you not think now? Tell me about your aspirations, and your theories. I do love hearing them." The Gardener did desire contemplation but thought it too dangerous. It peered from tree to tree, finding nothing. It hadn't seen anything in the jungle, not for hours. Perhaps it was a good time to think.

"I think our visitor will be a human. I hope it is." Peregrine was excited by this premonition. It had been some time since it had spoken to one, and was tempted by desires to watch the Gardener speak with one for the first time.

"I too hope it is a human. I wonder if there exist many more beyond the isle. It is possible there are many." The Gardener did not think so, but in the same vein, it did not wish to question Peregrine's enthusiasm.

"I wonder if humanity knows of the Gardeners. Are we a forgotten people?"

"You are no people. You are machines, after all. Though, I cannot help but consider you more than a machine, for all your pondering." The Gardener, in ironic simplicity, pondered this. It did feel more than a machine, but not by a great measure. Then again, to what could the Gardener compare its state? No other Gardeners still functioned. Supposing they felt as it did, it would still remain without a comparison. If the machines did differ in state from the Gardener, no comparison would be gatherable, as a machine with no humanoid qualities could not answer such a question. It was a paradox, but one the Gardener knew could be answered eventually. Within its thoughts, the Gardener could not prepare for Peregrine's question. It failed to recognize its severity.

"What if the human is deceitful? Or evil. I feel it is very possible our visitor would wish to destroy our way of life. Exploit us. What would we do if such difficulty presents itself?" The Gardener could not help but ignore this thought, it did not want to recognize the possibility.

"I'd rather not think of such things. No, I am certain now. A human would not wish to harm us, nor exploit us." In the silence of lies, the two soulless beings muttered disgraces. "Besides, we must remain vigilant."

~ *Unlike Nothing Seen Prior!*

Centamoore found this one. He refuses to admit how...

Kygen Collective D.L-Log 004
Dictation Presented by: N89-0324
"Samael" (GoodEvilSS_teeth)
Proctor Introduction:
Preferred Unit Designations: Samael, N89, Sammy (Father Only)
Schooling: Basic Unit Structuring on Shayre-9 moon world, Double
Major in Divine Matter studies, Second Major in Analytical Biology
and a minor in Ancient Theology.
Hobbies: Research, People Watching (Consensual), People Watching
(Non-Consensual)
Favorite Fruit: Microwave
Concerns or Offers can be sent to my Teeth, any other messages I'd
rather you keep to yourself, thank you. -Samael N89

Log Additional Adressings:
*I don't really see the need for more explanation, Siphus. Listen,
man, I am here for the Inker, not any of your jarrish papers. I have a
resume, might as well fucking use it. Another thing, keep your exposure to
a minimum. I'm sure you're experienced in the protocols and whatever, but
I am the resident expert, and as such, I tell you this: they bite. I do not.
Teeth me if you got any questions at all, GoodEvilSS_teeth
{mark.data.essential}*

Log Contents:

Creatures of Habit

So, surely these logs will be forgotten or discarded by the end of this, so I can rest assured that addingSEVERE CODE LAPSE DETECTED!

ATTEMPTING AUTOMATIC REPAIRS...

CODE LAPSE QUARANTINED!

RESTARTING—

That is good to know, I can't even *access* the previous text. I doubt Siphus can either. I'll test my little copypasta later though, greater entertainers do exist. For one, Inkers! I have spent my entire lifespan (and two iterations) studying the beasts. Ancient texts have been a great source of my information, with the physical matter being a scarcity. However, despite this previously confirmed scarcity, I have learned what I consider all that is to be learned. Ink is far less interesting than Ichyr, it has not the special alternatives that Ichyr does. Before I continue with my discoveries (it being the approximate third day of the experiment) I must address my foreman, this 'Siphus'. I admire him. I do, despite my often ceaseless ignorance of the purpose and divinities beyond death itself, I admire his tenacity in achieving those things. Indeed, I also make importance of his resilience to my co, Prometh. We have been together for an innumerable existence. I'd like to admit my brutish nature was the startup for our relationship, but that would be total tin. It was Prometh's mind that brought us together, had it not been for our relative interest in the damnation of our Larkik overseer (delete if you must, sire) we were gathered against the system. And look at us now! Nothing but us and the up and up. But, his penchant for childish amusements (which I must admit, I too retain) will be the end of us. That poor youth, Siphus, will not last much longer I fear, and if the worse comes to turn, we lose another opportunity to be together! Prometh, are you truly so bored of *us* that you would sabotage our company?

Apologizes to any future readers, this *is* supposed to be legible and so far has turned to anything but. There haven't been many breakthroughs, though it has only been about the third night, Prometh always commends positivity as a savior. I'll admit, this Inker is special, nearly lost my hand to the thing once I released it from containment. It *did* bash its slippery form against my already

The Harlequin

loosened knee fixtures, bastard knew my weakness! She's real jumpy. I want to see if her insides are too. Never seen an intact one before, and despite my countless worlds and years of translation, I can't say this isn't at least a bit exciting. Thank you Siphus for the opportunity, but I'd like some permission for personal privacy, please. The girl must be observed, not experimented upon. We shall get to that much later, my friend. He continues to ignore my recommendations against prodding and feeding the beast, but I have temporarily averted his intelligence to the Ichyric for the day; Thank the Lark, it has given me time to think. Despite the odds, my knee continues to buckle, and after its recent activity, I've decided to seek medical assistance—repairs, if you will. Medi only opens early next morning, so for now, I must endure. The Inker has been my housemate for the duration of the night, and much has been gathered that I previously confirmed. In one way or another, she is truly unlike *nothing* seen prior. I hope improvements will come in time, certainly without Siphus' interference. Judging by his integrations, I find it difficult to fully confess myself to you, the students (which I won't teach, sorry) the entirety of my understanding. But of course. I have a solution!SEVERE CODE LAPSE DETECTED!

ATTEMPTING AUTOMATIC REPAIRS...

CODE LAPSE QUARANTINED!

RESTARTING—

Fuck. You. Siphus, I spoke so much about your interest, in your favor! Why are you censoring my files? I know Prometh gets immature with his slurs and comparatives, but please, do you have to formalize my writing? I think I'd reach more people— who am I even talking to? In these lapses, Siphus cannot see shit, bastard shouldn't even be able to correct my writing... So how? Maybe by tomorrow, my writing will be nothing but pincushions for my own eyes. But that's tomorrow, I've never been one to care about the future. What is the future for today? I am alive today! Here, I shall insert my many knowledges in the research of Ink!

Creatures of Habit

Ink Repertoire and History:

Birthed in the 1st billion, approximately 1.189 billion years into the existence of the universe. Inkers Inklings are beasts and savages, by many. WRONG! They are not truly beasts! Historical tablets (i.e. Inkwell three of The Asteroids of the Imperium) prove these beasts as a *people*. It speaks (in a language we call Alltar) of a home of all Ink based forms, called "Ink foam" (some translations claim it as "Inktomb", a very illogical translation that I agree none with). Ink foam was a place of artistry, cities, and a great helium sea. It is impossible to know how long Ink foam existed before the birth of Inklings, or if it was the birthplace itself, and these truths are known to none of this age. Its location seems to be spread through fragments of old murals through wells of both Ink and Ichyr. These people were not modernized, they had no weapons of energy, nor fantastic starships (but they did have impressive means of travel). We know their history to some degree, the removal of power in mainline cities like Kahmut and Drokhandaz, the destruction of godly machines (originating from a perhaps ulterior god?) in the helium seas, all of this is established loosely in a timeline of sorts, but it is impossible to know of their pure anatomy, their beliefs! An extinct people are difficult to understand, their language vague yet familiar, their technology a complete mystery to the modern scientist, and even their gods a lie when compared to our certainty of faith (the Lark). It is in this knowledge we find even more of the Inklings, spoken of by the hands of the other great peoples, (Tetarien scrolls of the Emeraldettes) "When through the lens of confirmation, we see the Ink has stained our waist clothes with mistreatment, Velabix says no! The word of gods prior to birds, Anglican in nature, beyond glass: Let the dark blood sing, and the Ink of old rise and conquer the land as they once had". How can we surely agree with our god when there are such fair claims to others, as well as the mention of Ink ruling "as they once had"! What of this? Inklings being a superior force of nature? What happened, and how can we know for sure? Old tablets and murals from other wells (both Ink and Ichyr) claim a great flood of panacea, but for what plague? The most reassuring of these encounters is that there exists one named Inkling we knew of with certainty. This being was supposedly a

The Harlequin

ruler of all Inklings, a female no less! She was called "Maccabees", and she was worshiped as a supposed god. Legend has it that Maccabees was afflicted by a great plague, and fell to its might. This potentially could tie to the floods rumored in the ancient texts. But there are also legends that claim, surprisingly, an ancient ruler of Ichyr struck down Maccabees, named not but as "The Divine Bird". Confusingly, associations have been drawn to our present God "The Lark" but there is no evidence the two are one and the same, as there have been hundreds of thousands of bird-like species and creatures in history, and supposedly, The Lark never had ties with the Inklings.

Log Continuation:

And that is all we know. I've recently recovered a thick tome, it looks like it could date back to at least the 2nd billion! Using Prometh's knowledge in codebases—and my adoration of Ink and history—we have begun the design of a (drum roll please) Alltar Translation Prototype! When fed old Alltar, the prototype attempts to relate the individual sigils to modern Larkik characters as accurately as possible. It reroutes the sigils through hundreds of old languages and patterns until it discovers the most likely title for the text inputted. It spits out a selection of possible answers, all of which are rated on their likelihood of being correct. We call it Adam. He's like a son to me, a malformed, angry, Ink-loving son. Its penchant for dead languages has brought it to almost hate us, its creators. Obviously, the damn thing isn't sentience, just a disliking, a bother. It will regularly spit out slurs and refusals at Prometh when *he* attempts a translation—hilarious in its own way—but my attempts leave me with mere words! We've been working on repairs, but the more translations it does, the more resistant it grows. One day it shall serve its purpose well, its already utterly stomped prior records of "accurate" translation. Considering this is required of me and consuming time I could be spending in the observation cell, I will end the Log here. To any who would read it, (why or how you would do this is beyond my concern) I have attached both an apology note and a soft boot of Adam for your inspection and personal use! It could be potentially malicious, don't let it near your system files.

~Log End~

Attached Files: Weather_Report ; My_Bad.txt ; Adam.exe ; !For_Prometh

Pinging Weather_Report...
INFINITY SCAN RETURNS = ~ #783978
CLOSEST CODE LOG {Mauve.Purple}
Pinging My_Bad.txt
WRITING CODE LOG...
{ Honestly? My bad, sorry about that. (please apply this document to all complaints and difficulties correlated to my presence in your life, thank you) }
Pinging Adam.exe...
REPOSITORY DATA EXCEEDING MACHINE CAPACITY
LOCAL PURGE INITIATED...
Text Scrubbers ready, I am Adam. Hello,
How are you?
Translating...
_ _ _ _ _ _ _ _ Sigil Inscription Active
Text Character Structure Estimates Concluded: *8* Sigils, 3 of 8 Sigils confirmed:
L A _ _ _ _ _ N
Text inscribed rough translations—
Larkaron(52%)
Larceron(23%)
Larkiren(11%)
Lakellan(10%)
Lakaequn(4%)
Likelihood Conclusion: Text Sigils Documented a 52% Chance of correction to
L A R K A R O N
Accept Documentation?

The Harlequin

Recompiling data… estimations increased by 2 percentiles.

Adding Terminology to phrase
{{ ERROR_TYPEBASE_ALLTAR_MISSING }}

| AND ~~~ BY THE BIRD, ~~~~~ GREAT ~~~~~~~~ TOOK ??? US STRAIGHT TO THE FLAX PLANET. ~~~~~~ THE LOSS OF THE MOTHER ~~~~~ A ~~~~~~ OF WORRY ~~~ THE INKLINGS, ~~~ HIM IT ~~~~~ A ~~~~~~~ NOT ~~~~~~ THE ~~~~~~~. HE IS OF DIVINE, AS IS MACCABEES. ~~~~~~~~, THE TO PLANETS OF GOD BEAST WILL STRIKE ~~ ~~~~~~~~~~~~ ~~~~~~~ AND ~~~~~~~~~ LOVE. IN THE ~~~~ OF THE ORIGINAL GOD, HE IS THE ~~~~~~~ OF ICHYR. HE IS THE ORIGINAL OF WILL. HE IS LARKARON, THE ~~~~~~ OF GOD, ~~~~~~~ OF MOTHERS, AND ~~~~ OF DREAM. HE IS *OUR* NEXT ~~~~~~~~, AND HE IS DELIVER US ~~~~~~~~ ?? THE INKFOAM. ~~~ ~~~~~~ TO THE DIVINE BIRD. | Translation at 75.6% completion : Estimated accuracy at 89% - minus noted text -

SIGIL LITERACY MALFUNCTION. CHARACTER AT line_8space_2 IS OBSCURED.

REFERENCE REQUIRED FOR (ar) TERMINOLOGY.

CONTINUED TRANSLATION EFFORTS IMPEDED

REQUESTING VOWEL RETRANSFER—WORD LOSS IMMINENT.

Adam.exe has encountered a false-start flag. If you would like to attempt to reboot the program, contact a Protocol Agent to look into the issue. Thank you for your compliance!

Pinging !For_Prometh…

WRITING CODE LOG…

CANNOT PING SCANNER UNIT

ABRIDGING SEARCH

PRESENTING DATA

{ Hon, buddy, Prometh! After thirteen years of not seeing one another (at least not in person), you seem so hellbent on escaping me! I understand your boredom here—I sympathize—but we got shit to do, Siphus is gonna pull the plug if you keep throwing your weight around (contextually)! I love your 'conventional jests' but there are lines we need to stick within, or we'll get a reckoning on our doorstep. How about this: We finish up this last project, learn a bit more about Inkers, change the world forever with our incredible research, and then bounce. I mean it Prometh. Our lives have been torn from each other, our fields don't often mix! We can get away from it all, retire, and head out to a paradise world. I want to see you again! I'm sorry if this is spoiling your fun, but what is a little boredom for a month in trade for boundless joy with each other for the rest of the time? I promised you we'd make this relationship more professional, permanent, and such. I see no better time than the present. Do this for me, hon. Cut Siphus a break. In many ways, he's more like you than you may be. Stay Safe }

    —TERMINATING LOG PROTOCOL

~ *Bloody Fingers and Eel*
A folk-tale spoken of by tireless dockworkers
on New Tetaria...

Worship and gods are fickle pointless things. Devotion was conflict and no matter how proud conflict was arrogance. The split of people against each other was a civil war—in progress. Civil war had come and passed, another would be no different to those who bled for its resolution. Despite these truths, not one Atramedian soul had ever dared to denounce the gods. Gods and worship played a near essential role in their lives, assuredly the focal point of Atramedian society. Fortunes could be made on shrine construction alone, not to mention the labor of priesthood, festival organization, the creation of holy orders, and relic maintenance. Of course, fortunes were *never* made from religious affairs, such a thing was highly punishable. Exploiting the high gods, divine beings who had walked among the cobblestone? The seriousness of the religious world was what drove Atramedians throughout their time. They dedicated most of their lives to the very gods that would take those lives, and on a smaller scale, a majority of their day as well. Within every day, there existed roughly 12 of these "Holy hours". Taking place from nine to nine, both children and adults alike were required to commit to holiness. This did not mean much, one simply could not labor during these hours. Any activity, one of play or enjoyment, of sloth or hate, was permitted during these hours. It did not matter its contents, so long as it did not require labor. Labor hours were designated from midnight to daybreak, twelve to six. During this time, adults and adolescents were to complete any of their labor, making their earnings in a six-hour period or less. Children attended schooling, learning mainly of history, holiness, and basic arithmetic and linguistics. The remaining time between the Holy hours and Labor hours was free time, allowing for any activities between the two prior categories, most commonly used as meal periods. The system was refined and flawless, and the gods thought it equally so. Maccabeus—the ancillary deity of the Atramedian people—had first introduced the timelines of a functioning livelihood, but they had perfected it all on their own a few centuries later. Where religion brought conflict, time brought acceptance. To everyone besides Ezrakell. His work was a temporary pastime that—thanks entirely to the slow deterioration of the dexterity of his fingers—was forcefully split between painful hours. He could last barely two before the tips of his fingers burned with pain. Like the ticking ribs of a hive machine, they flew with rhythm until they died. Thus, he could not withstand the bulk of the work hours, nor occupy his form without its presence. He was a disinterested, tired figure. No matter the day, life conjured up a boring abyss for Ezrakell. However, it was not without its freedoms, as watching over Pedantick was often difficult for Khanjali to commit to, considering the nonchalant nature of his work schedule. Ezrakell could thereby occupy himself with a child, one with personal stakes— an investment of a sort. This is precisely what Ezrakell was doing when Khanjali finally returned home, hours late. He had been monitoring Pedantick while she fiddled with a new contraption of some kind, something that Ezrakell thought had one too many spinning blades for a child to be fiddling with. Khanjali had entered the door, and Pedantick promptly dropped her project, rushing off to greet him. Ezrakell in some small part mourned not being able to create a next of kin, not having a child of his own to care for. He would always have Pedantick, knowing Khanjali would always need a babysitter. He followed loosely behind the child, picking up out-of-place items as he went, doing his best to clean up after her storm of glee. Khanjali had made it into the living room with Pedantick on his leg, glued there with adoration. She was screeching about her day, from her schoolwork to her newest project. Ezrakell simply stood and smiled, watching the little banshee go. He then looked to Khanjali. He had a trap on his face, one that struck a cold fear into Ezrakell's heart.

The Harlequin

Khanjali had not endured a normal day, this much was clear. Ezrakell did his best to act normal, to question Khanjali about his hunting, but he received the usual answer—somehow less comforting. Khanjali continued forward with his usual routine: undressing, moving his pack forward ever so slightly as he proceeded, weighed down only by the daughter with which he was so entranced. Every detail was in place, and the father took care to attune them to perfection. Except for the gloves. Khanjali, a man who hunted with a crossbow—a weapon demanding relatively high dexterity to fire properly—was wearing thick leather gloves. He had never worn gloves before, despite the chills of the deeper wilds. It was always simpler to wear basic cloth in wraps around the palm, giving the hand a clutching grip, but not obstructing the delicate handiwork of a hunter. Ezrakell decided to wait out Pedantick's excitement, to better conjure a remedy to the father's woes. For someone so willing and loved by his child, he had never such a drab flatness to his expression. Ezrakell had never seen anything like it. Following a mirage of questioning, Khanjali placed Pedantick on the ground, letting her skitter off like a race dog back to her cubby. Ezrakell stood beside him, his arms folded not unlike a suspecting mother, his expression showing clear his impatience, he was waiting for something, *expecting* something.

"What happened. What did you do." Khanjali nearly choked upon his fear, a shock of memory reminding him of exactly what he had done. How could Ezrakell know? Was it that obvious? He hadn't told him, had he? Khanjali wiped his brow, and to his surprise, found no sweat upon his head. He could not perceive a decent answer to Ezra's question. He couldn't tell him—no—there was nothing to tell. Nothing at all.

"Nothing terribly outside of routine, why?" Ezrakell didn't even blink at this comment, his stern look remained unsatisfied with this answer.

"Tarbh. Your face spits mistruth. The crossbowman wears his gloves today— are we not friends? What do you have to hide from me?" Ezrakell would not be content until he knew the truth—until he could put a name to the emotion Khanjali had displayed upon entering his own home. However, within this same moment, Khanjali pleaded for the opposite. He prayed for Ezrakell to leave and to ignore the subtle deviations from his normalities. He wanted to keep the truth far from the reach of those he spent so long caring for. But, like he knew many things, Khanjali knew he could not live peaceably with Ezrakell in the dark. Ezrakell's days of nothing in value or intrigue made him unreasonably curious and more so prying. He would not let such a thing go without explanation. Khanjali could only think of one response,

"Something irreversible. What, I cannot say, but you need only know it mustn't be discussed again." Ezrakell looked into the sorrowful craters within Khanjali's skull. He seemed to loosen, to comprehend what Khanjali meant. He *knew*. He knew exactly what Khanjali had done. He peered into an ocean of conflict, minnows of deliberation spinning within.

"There is a Sgiathless synod I intend to attend this afternoon. You should come with. It could help. They are in some ways... cathartic." Khanjali knew this was an act of pity, himself unable to reason with the sympathy Ezrakell displayed for him. Though, he wanted to return the intentions with thanks and company. Khanjali accepted the invitation, knowing full well that Pedantick would be asleep by the time the event was planned to start. The less she had to know, the better. He couldn't let his most precious glimmer of hope slip into the eternal darkness of reality, not yet at least.

The synod was to be hosted by a Maeandrical Priestess, well known throughout both the Northers and the Southers. Her name was Priestess Mezzo, one of the eldest worshipers of Maeandri within the city. Furthermore, Mezzo served herself to Maccabeus—an ancillary deity lying under the domain of Maeandri. This was not terribly uncommon within Drochandas, after all, it was Maccabeus who had been given particular providence over the Atramedians. Those of Drochandas and beyond had once not known the pride of Maeandri, instead burying their sandy noses in the viewing pleasure of Maccabeus. It was Priestess Mezzo who first coined the concept of ancillaries—those who served an even higher power. This idea was not immediately accepted, but over time grew heresy turned to favor, and many shared her insights. Rumors among divinity preached that Mezzo was some sort of ambassador to the gods; Mezzo did not often leave the chapel. Those who praised her name claimed she had met with the very creators of the galaxy. Others speculated the truth of her allegiances. Whether or not any of her purported truths were indeed just such, was irrelevant. They were simply stories of excellence, something Atramedian culture thrived on. With stories like that, Priestess Mezzo was guaranteed to be written within the histories of Atramedian lore for centuries to come. She did not let the public know she cared for such vain, materialistic things, but she had always been fascinated by the idea of being immortalized in ink, and now with her fascinations coming to fruition, she could not be more enraptured. She had spent a lifetime worshiping her creators—not for the reward of recognition—but for the pure thought of it, the honor it brought her namesake, the feeling of goodwill that it filled her with. The priestess could recite entire apocryphas of Maeandri with ease, she knew every prayer of health written in the Atramedian language. Her faith drove her upwards on the scale of intellectuality, of self-awareness. The world of holiness was most logical and familiar one she knew of, and thus she resided solely within it. Sometimes she too thought herself some ancillary mover, watching below on the peons of her creation. This well-earned growth allowed her to commune with the gods more easily than most Atramedians ever could. However, with this elevation came ignorance. Mezzo could no longer logically comprehend how her city and her people could be such beings of instability, of corruption. But with this analysis came error and blame. She could not possibly claim to be a patron of the gods and be so far disconnected from the reality the very gods she worshiped had created. To return herself to the standards she set in stone, Priestess Mezzo had lowered herself once more to the alleys of Drochandas. The priestess learned of the struggle betwixt the classes, the torment between the people she saw no difference in. In a moment of reconciled purity, she set out to mend the world she had left in shambles. She humbled herself in the eyes of all with prayer and fasting. She preached Maeandri, and Maccabeus' teachings in the streets as a homeless monk. She spent far too many days blessing the weak and pained. She taught in school-homes the mannerisms of gratitude and empathy. Yet somehow, in all this effort, there was truly no restitution. The battles between the Sgiathless and Sgiathen went against every word of Maeandri's divine deliverance. Mezzo, knowing she had already acquired youthful infamy, set her entire being on solving the Sgiathic dispute. Khanjali had seen Mezzo's teachings once before. When he was a child, Mezzo visited their school home to speak of Maeandri, during a time when the god existed within a similar standing as the lesser Maccabeus. Khanjali had always liked the woman—at the time she seemed naive for a priest, so unaware of the true problems the world held in its terrible grasp. It came off as pure, as childish. In reality, Mezzo could not be further from this definition. Khanjali arrived at the synod only four minutes before it was to begin. Ezrakell summoned him to their spot in the crowd, and they seated themselves. At least the Monastery of Maccabeus had the charity to supply seating. Ezrakell greeted the father, welcoming him to the joys of political suffrage. Khanjali appreciated the dry humor, but not to the degree he usually did,

"Khanjali, friend, calm your nerves. Whatever has happened today shall be forgotten tomorrow. Can we not simply rest and enjoy the speeches of 'The Almighty Mezzo' on this fine eve?" Khanjali chuckled, his nerves calming slightly. He did not know how long he could stand his guilt, but he knew Ezrakell would help him stand it for longer. The crowd around the two friends grew quiet, as Mezzo mounted her podium atop a small stage that had been assembled from spare parts over the past hour. The priestess looked calm, more relaxed than Khanjali thought she would be—he could not imagine speaking to so many people at once.

"My fellow Sgiathen and Sgiathless, my next-of-kin, what a day for freedom! Today marks the anniversary of our victory in the first Divine War, and this date is no mere coincidence!" The viewers of the speech already seemed uncomfortable, as if Mezzo's tone was not satisfying their moral requirements. This confused Khanjali, who was rather appreciative of Mezzo's cheery disposition. Ezrakell knew all too well what the people were thinking, and he had already begun to fear the worst. "After all this time, we are still free, aren't we? But I would argue not so painlessly. This foolish quarrel betwixt winged and wingless—Sgiathen and Sgiathless—has voyaged much too far from the saving hands of Maeandri. We will be lost on this journey to darkness if we do not seek the light of our gods!" A silent stirring echoed through the crowd, one of impatience. The Sgiathless of the city did not meekly accept misdirection. "We must treat the illusions of our separation as infestation! Action assuredly should be swift and precise, but also a metered culmination of the pure efforts on both sides of this terrible conflict!" Priestess Mezzo had always been an enlightened woman, occasionally too enlightened for some. The suggestion that both the Sgiathen and Sgiathless were in the wrong, that the solution to disarray existed in harmony, would prove to overcome her. Nobody would agree to the claims, regardless of any truth they actually held.

"Fool, she grows too zealous, even for a priestess!" Muttered Ezrakell. Khanjali did not concern himself with his company, far too intrigued by the miraculous wording of the priestess.

"You see, the debate of wrong and right is as old as time, and so further is the debate of the winged! You! The Sgiathless, you fear the Sgiathen—hate them with seething discontent! Why? Because they have banished your people, insulted your children and wives, and slaughtered your Acolytes! You fear the hidden intentions of the Sgiathen. Who is to blame you for this fear? In all reason, it is logical!" The crowd mumbled with welcome energy. This was a point they could agree upon, one designed to be favored by their side. But this was only half the story. "But you must not forget your kin, your brothers and sisters, the Sgiathen! They too fear their opposites, you! The Sgiathless! They despise you, and your ancestors' disgrace to the holy lords Maeandri and Maccabeus, why? You were stripped of your holy collection—your very wings—by the law of the gods! They fear the hidden intentions of the Sgiathless. Who is to blame them for this fear? You cannot justly blame fear of a second Winged War!" Khanjali was rather content with this explanation, grasping a sort of understanding for the thoughts he could never quite put into words. He held Priestess Mezzo in high regard thanks to her tongue, her way of creating such perfect words for the unexplainable. Ezrakell's rather narcissistic views allowed for a much simpler understanding of the provided text. He saw the solution to be necessary solely for the problem's incessant intervention in his life. Any solution would do, harmful or otherwise, so long as the chaos would end.

"Gah, but it won't! They won't agree to this! This perfect world… lacks truth. Men are despicable things, we never rest until the scales are weighted." Khanjali glanced to Ezrakell, his words serving only to illude Khanjali.

"Is that not what you—they, seek? To rebind the scales?"

"It is." The priestess rose in volume once more, calling upon the attention of the crowd,

"To fix this fear and remedy this disconnection, we must accept that none of us are at fault! The Sgiathen and the Sgiathless are impure institutions! We cannot blame the fear of the other! We must change to fix our world because a greater threat is quickly approaching! The Ichyric once again wish to watch our fall, and Lakaeron once again disgraces the name of Maccabeus and even Maeandri! Here we sit, fighting amongst each other like beasts!" The people fell silent, unaware the Ichyrics sought another conflict. For a moment, all the Atramedians resonated in unison, as one. They held one commune, one ideal: a once familiar hatred for the opposing matter. This unity quickly shattered, and Mezzo once again began her speech. "We must work together to stop these— these heathens! We must locate a remedy for our spite! What is this remedy? Understanding. The Sgiathen must stop their oppression, they must open their minds, and understand that fear is normal, and that one must first lend trust to the enemy, to become allies. But you—the Sgiathless—you must also not hope for the damnation of your brothers! You must not wish to be superior to your brothers and sisters, no! You should desire naught but equality, to love and forgive your brothers and sisters for their fear, as you too must relinquish yours. Once both sides can do this, we can truly be free!" The crowd called out in hate once more, destroying any remaining fragments of unity. These people, despite all their talk of rebellion and purity, had no intentions of forgiving their opposites. The priestess had been met with a similar response when speaking to the Sgiathen, fear and turmoil rocking the very stage of her inquisition. That was the simple impossibility of the solvent, understanding. Neither side would claim they were in the wrong, neither side would accept the other, and none would show weakness. For all the talk of wanting to end the conflict, and denial of their oppression, the Sgiathen continued to beat down the Sgiathless, keeping them under an iron fist. Similarly, the supposed boundless acceptance of all breeds boasted by the Sgiathless

The Harlequin

disassembled in the presence of a winged other. Mezzo continued to preach, but it was clear they were no longer absorbing any of her divine words. It was a fruitless task, trying to sway the tides of either side. Only something terrible, a great catastrophe, could change the minds of such a corrupted society. Mezzo had hoped that the mention of Lakaeron's ambitions would mark that catastrophe, but alas, it had little effect on the blinded eyes of the Atramedians. After the speech had grown unruly, Mezzo wished the people good health and left the stage. Ezrakell sighed, letting the hopelessness escape his shattered soul.

"When will the day come when we can put this terrible fate behind us? I think—I fear, not for a lofty sum of ages." Khanjali placed his hand on Ezra's shoulder, patting it softly.

"I do not know much of suffrage, but with this event as my introduction, I know it only as draining, and vague. You and your proclaimers must exhaust yourselves to no end. One can hope Priestess Mezzo did have an effect—we cannot know for certain if her words have been heard in their entirety!" Ezrakell shook his head, confident nothing would change.

"Our people are stubborn, yours are vain, we cannot solve this without a bridge, a mutual alignment. I fear Mezzo's war is the only bridge we can seek." Khanjali sighed, considering the outcome of a second Divine War. He would perhaps be beyond the warring youth, but Pedantick, she would be just coming of age.

"I wish only to speak with her myself, some form of precious divine knowledge could aid in our situation greatly, could it not, Ezra?" Ezrakell shook from his fingertips the ash of the skies, words echoing against the side of his ignorant head,

"I suppose. Perhaps you have cause to speak with her? I take it you are aware she is a priestess? I fear we are too beneath her, friend." Khanjali—absorbed not in the speech of his friend—took sight of a rather loud assemblage of suffragettes, all ravaging Mezzo's lyrical speech. He watched as Mezzo pointlessly attempted to quell the hoard, they were infinitely more sturdy than she was. She ducked behind a curtain hung from the back of her stage, sealing herself from the furious resistors. Khanjali nodded to Ezra, silently informing Ezrakell of his plans. He quickly rose from his seat, and hurried after

Mezzo, desperate to have a word with her. He snuck past the suffragettes and managed to locate a small breach in the stage's walls. Squeezing through the entrance, Khanjali exited into a darkened backroad, shadowed by a large felt which had been draped precariously from the stage to a Blackstone monolith. Mezzo was seated on a small ledge, overlooking the lowermost section of the Southers. She swayed in a melancholic rhythm, letting her cloaked legs drift down past the ledge. He approached, unweaving of any words to speak, silent with wonderment.

"I heed your words." The priestess turned, examining the body of Khanjali. She was satisfied with the lack of noticeable wings.

"Interesting. Do you really? I have met many a man with more charm than you, I would expect not such pitiful attempts from a refined voice."

"I do. Your ideas adjure my mind, force me into fantasy. I wish for this world of your creation, a world where I would not be struck for my inseparable parts. Above all else, a world of prosperity for my daughter, she is what lightens your words to me. I would do anything for that truth."

"You speak with the elegance of a priest and yet you are... A hunter?"

"I've never lusted to be anything else."

"How curious. Do you pray?"

"Every day. Every kill."

"How curious...." Silence befell the two, both hesitant to speak, fearing they would insult the other's elegance.

"You are a Suffragette, a voice of reason? But you are still in essence a priestess. I can confess to you? And you cannot tell a soul?" Priestess Mezzo nodded, allowing Khanjali to speak his mind. This opportunity was a great one, one that he thought he should not squander. "I am an imposter in my own regard, an invader of hell sent by the heavens, for I am blessed with the burden of wings." The priestess looked at him with confusion, a look that told Khanjali that she would never truly understand.

"You... but you are winged? Sgiathen? A choice to hide such things—it mustn't be willing, for what purpose would one endure such restriction and hazard, if not for a greater cause? You must be some form of great Samaritan" Mezzo tried to comprehend this exotic breed of suffering, but she could not, not yet.

"I am no master of great deeds, I often do not perform them. It is all in the name of my daughter. Born of her mother and equal divinity, she was ignored by the voices of our gods. She has wrought in mundanity since her terrible birth. I have no choice but to watch over her here, in these canals." Priestess Mezzo let her chin rest against the narrow of her palm,

"A terrible fate that must be, terrible indeed. But it seems as if you despise this fate and more so its cause. Your daughter, do you —" Priestess Mezzo, in her cycle of religious questioning, failed to comprehend the love Khanjali shared for his daughter.

"You would not fathom. I love my daughter, my Pedantick, like nothing that has ever existed before her. I have yet to discover a passion more beautiful than she. I would stop at nothing to show my love for her, to defend her. Nothing short of murder. So you ask me, priestess, do I love my daughter?" Mezzo shuddered with life, a near arousal of temptation as she had never felt, a man fit to father, a man fit to protect. The priestess did not doubt the safety nor the happiness of Pedantick.

"I would sooner remove my priesthood than accuse you again. I offer my solemn apols to you, as I feel myself a shadow of godliness in your presence. I am compelled, you deserve the help of such gods. As a priestess, I have more than a right to aid the almighty's followers. As a priestess, I have met more than some few interesting characters..." Mezzo scratched her jaw, her repertoire of servants and religious zealots filling her mind, searching for at least one to help the hunter's dilemma. "I recall an indebted Feltsmith in the Northers, one of such elegant craft, I have no doubt they could forge a flawless replica of the wings of the blessed." Khanjali refused, assuring Mezzo that such a gift was unrepayable.

"You said it yourself, your holiness. The Sgiathen harbor great fear of wingless imposters. I have seen the restrictions of the Northers first hand, the obnoxious protocols and precautions, all to keep the Sgiathless at bay. But, down here— nobody would expect for a Sgiathen to invade the Southers, seeking deceit." Khanjali grew closer to the priestess, taking his place on the ledge beside her, "It is safer this way, for both me and my daughter." The priestess understood, and for the first time in her life, could not fathom a solution to the problem of a fellow follower. It was a feeling of fear, one of vulnerability. She wanted to ask Maccabeus for her divine word, but somehow she knew that even her gods could not offer any succor for the poor Khanjali. "In all consideration, without this curse, I would be of no use. My talents are in the hunt, and for what would I hunt for in the deep cities?" Mezzo smiled at this. She wondered how a man with such pains could remain so fired, how he could hide away all suffering so easily. She recalled Khanjali 's mention of prayer and reminded Khanjali that one day, Maccabeus would repay him for his loyalty. The father caught the voice of Ezrakell on the wind, beckoning him. It was time for him to return to his Pedantick, she would surely wake soon. Mezzo offered Khanjali both a blessing, and her unwavering support—if he would ever come to need it. Khanjali was hesitant, but accepted, telling her his name, and leaving.

"You will survive, Hunter." Neither party was truly satisfied with the conversation that had been held, but both escaped each other with a greater bearing on their worlds, a slight fragment of hope illuminated within both. With the gods as his witness, Khanjali was going to live, and he knew everything would eventually turn in his favor. He reunited with Ezrakell, telling him quietly of all he had spoken of with the priestess. Ezrakell was surprised that Khanjali had mentioned anything about his wings, but understood his dedication. They began the short journey back home, fearing Pedantick would wake before they returned. She would be leaving for her schooling soon, and Khanjali to his hunt. He reconciled the words in his head, over and over. You will survive. You will survive.

Pedantick had just woken by the time the two arrived home, and was in the process of eating her first meal of the day, intending to finish before her schooling hours began. She welcomed the two home, unable to give the usual assault to her father because of her tight schedule, and drowsiness. Khanjali sat at the table with her, allowing her to discuss her daily affairs. Ezrakell opted to return home for the night, desperate to finish a small project he had been working on.

"I dunno if Ezra likes my stuff, he always seems so scared. I told him they aren't scary, but he doesn't think so." Khanjali smirked, knowing full well that his only friend had always been petrified of Pedantick's projects. Khanjali himself had grown familiar with the strange array of machines Pedantick had assembled. Sometimes he grew concerned for her, there was always the possibility of getting injured, but he tried not to dwell on such things. Pedantick had only gotten seriously hurt once before, and it had little to do with her own choices. Pedantick was, more often than not, a rather safe child, and Khanjali had full faith in her precautions and regulations.

"Ho little P, Ezrakell is little more than a featherless chicken, the fool could jump from his own shadow. Of course, you didn't hear this from me." Pedantick giggled, hopping down from the table to gather her things for school.

"Ezra isn't a chicken! He's an Atra—Atre...." Pedantick stopped, fiddling with the words in her head, testing morphemes with her lanky syllables. Khanjali gave her a moment, but when it became clear she would not solve this riddle on her own, he stepped in,

"Atramedian. It's simply an expression P, I know he's not a chicken, silly." Pedantick gasped, swiftly scribbling down the word to save it for later. She snatched up her school bag and began towards the door. She skidded and turned to her father. Sprinting back to her father, Pedantick leaped onto his lap, embracing him.

"I love yoouuu pop-pop. Catch something big, will you pop-pop?" Khanjali was once again at peace. Flawless, unbreakable love filled his soul. He knew he would survive, without a shadow of a doubt. As long as he had Pedantick, he could keep fighting for all of eternity.

"Love you too, P. Stay safe, little one." Khanjali kissed Pedantick on her forehead. A goofy smile spread across her face as she gave her father one last hug. He let his daughter down, and she sped off, excited to see her school friends again. Khanjali remained seated for a moment, remembering how long he had been there, in his apartment—in his city. He couldn't remember, not anything before Pedantick's birth. She was the last memory he held, and he was perfectly content with that. He looked to the table, to Pedantick's emptied bowl placed by the sink, soap suds drifting around its rim from an attempted clean. She tried so hard to be perfect, to make her father proud—but without knowing it—her father already thought her the greatest champion in the land. Khanjali rose, shambling over to the bowl, and began to wash it. His thumb brushed against something soft and moist, opposite to the hard wooden exterior of the bowl. He peered beneath it, discovering a small slip of paper stuck to the bottom. Peeling it off, Khanjali examined its depth. The parchment was a little wet, some soap having already soaked upon its film. It was a small picture, when it was taken, Khanjali could not be certain. It displayed Pedantick, Khanjali, and her mother—all sitting on a bench in the Northers together. Khanjali stared at it for a while, motionless, thoughtless. He had not seen the image for some time and was curious how Pedantick had gotten a hold of it. She didn't deserve the worry and pain that came with remembering her mother, she was still too young. He placed the bowl back into the sink, partially washed. Shuddering, the father gripped the side of the counter, keeping himself from falling over completely. The tears were the first sign that he wasn't dreaming, that this was real. Her face—so happy and whole, lacking any sort of guilt or responsibility. So perfect. He couldn't stand it. He tore the photo, unable to even imagine her face, her eyes like wildfire and burning trees and melting metal. She asked him again, demanding his consent. Khanjali continued to tear and shred until all that was left was his golden little Pedantick. She was the only thing keeping him from this insanity, the failure of his own judgment. He rubbed the photo, slowly letting his fingers run over the moist film. He loved her. He would always love her. He would do anything for her. Everything for her. Khanjali slipped the photo into his cloak, keeping it for when he needed it most. The hunt was to begin soon, and he had little time to prepare. The dishes could wait.

For a day—a time so infinitesimally small—Khanjali had little to do. He set aside this time for his greatest creation. Pedantick was not bound by any lawmaking to her schooling, and as such, could escape it for this time—a day. The two could question each other during this time, gather memories and happinesses, and forge a greater existence because of it. Ezrakell had joined on a trip prior, but to his dismay, found it rather boring, or more so intrusive. It was Khanjali's time with Pedantick, and he deserved every second of it. Not to mention the fool was stingy with his safety—he had always shared a small terror of the unknown, particularly the wide open spaces of the beyond. That was why he offered so often to remain at the homestead, to watch over their possessions whilst they roamed; thievery was so obviously common in Drochandas. Khanjali let his arm be slowly tugged along by the little Pedantick as she stumbled her way through the briar, a bush of the such plant so tall as to nearly obscure her from Khanjali's view. He could hear her mumbling.

"Almooost there, my teacher told us it's just outside doe-khan-dus, I bet you've seen it!" Khanjali chuckled at the sound of her voice, muffled by moss and leaf. Pedantick emerged from the bushery with a smile on her face — as well as some twigs, perhaps a leaf or two furthermore. Khanjali followed close behind, the large hook upon his shoulder carrying more remnants of the woods. Pedantick had broken loose from his grip, and with her newfound freedom, struggled her way to the lake bed, the weight of her hook bogging her down. The docks were bustling in the distance, but on this side of the lake, no one would question their devices. It was always a place of energy, down by the helium — the drink. So much happened there, so many duties and works, boats and exports and people and smuggling. Pedantick had been to the docks only once before, and that visit was none too pleasant. It was from a time far earlier, one in which her mother still could be spoken with. She called out to her father, but from such a distance, the wind was likely to disregard the sound. Khanjali knew this, and hurried forward, to potentially catch some wind of her story. Pedantick clambered to the top of a small wooden structure, one protruding a few feet above the sand. By the time she had reached its surface, Khanjali was already resting beside her,

"Quite the climb, little P."

"I did it! I am strong!" She let out a little growl, nearly dropping the hook in the process,

"Ah — but aren't you Pedantick? Tomorrow you may settle to be strong, as likely as you will be Pedantick, I wonder what it'll be?"

"Strong!"

"So sure?" She heaved the hook into both hands, wielding it like an ax, before slamming it against the dock, fragmenting one of its many planks. Khanjali burst out laughing, falling backward from his place on the dock, and splashing into the refreshing pool before him. Pedantick grumbled and leaped in after him, chasing his form further from the shore. "Oh little P, you bring me such joy, such humor. Why is it you have brought us here today?"

"My teacher told us of these biggo fishies! hu-mun-gus fish, A-Atra…" She stumbled with her words, but before her father could help, she blurted out, "Atramedian! Atramedians—that's us—use these funny things to catch 'em!" Khanjali nodded, scooping his daughter up into his arm, and wading back to the dock. He placed her upon a small dinghy ported alongside the planks. Pedantick took the effort to dry herself, or at least attempted in doing so. Khanjali plopped the two hooks into the back of the boat and clambered aboard himself. Looking out over the sea of ships, Khanjali loosened his neck. The docks were always so busy, he was glad to have snuck in so successfully.

"Do we have oars? I would be wise to have brought oars, in hindsight."

"I don't have big enough hands for oars, pop-pop. I can't carry them." Khanjali patted his daughter, assuring her that she took no part in the blame. He cupped his hand into the helium, pushing the little dinghy forward.

"What kinds of fish shall we catch, little P? After all, I am a hunter of land, not the sea, the duty of pundit falls to you."

"What is a pun-deet?" An object of famous size struck the bottom of the dinghy, rocking its side lightly. Khanjali held the reins—metaphorically—keeping it from tipping over completely. Pedantick looked on in intrigue as her father scanned the waves. He thought for a moment perhaps the venture was foolish, a danger for them both. The lakes were not known to be so…untamed.

"Er, a professional Pedantick, precisely what I thought you to be. Does your teacher speak often of the predators of this lake?"

"The big fishies? There are a bunch in here, I think. Ones almost thiiiis big!" Pedantick raised her arms, presenting how large the fish was. Her tiny mass could not properly portray the size to give grace. A large hauling ship passed before them, rousing the waves and the beings beneath them. Pedantick struggled to hang upon the edge of the boat. The two turned to one another, having survived the violence of the seas, mariners two, beyond the veil of the whale of death. Pedantick made a snrking sound with her nose, arousing yet another laugh from Khanjali, which in turn brought one from Pedantick. With their worries left behind on the bed of the sea, the two kindred souls laughed deep into the afternoon, forgoing the scrutiny of paranoia for an aura of elation.

"Little P, how go your projects? Your life? I hope you've been happy—I do try you know." Pedantick fiddled around with the small metal link on the end of her fishing hook. She looked to her father, safety in her eyes.

"Ezrakell tells me you can't buy my felt and my tools. He says you work extra hard to get them." The girl slipped the tool overboard, letting it rest in the comfort of the helium. "Thank you pop-pop. I think you're my favoritest Atramedian ever." Khanjali fell silent, beaten senseless with love. A shudder passed through the fragments of his old injured hands, as his eyes quivered in eccentric joy.

"Oh Pedantick. Little P, you have no understanding of just how much that means to me. Please, hold your words, a father weak to emotion is no father at all!"

"Weak? Pop-pop, you are the strongest pop-pop I know. Even Cahrliel says so!" Khanjali wiped the moisture from his eyes. He had heard this name before, but could not place a face to its soundings.

"Cahrliel? My apologies Pedantick memory fails me, am I familiar with Cahrliel?" The child giggled, rubbing the fray of her poncho between her thumbs,

"My teacher! She *really* likes you. She says you 'leave all her lips wanting' I dunno what that means though." Khanjali's face reddened with the heat of embarrassment, his eyes widened with fatherly concern. He quickly doused himself in the cold helium of the lake, turning his attention instead to the fishing hook beside him.

"Er, never mind that P! Shall we play a game instead? The biggest catch wins, a simple wager Pedantick. Hunter vies Hunter. Shall we?"

"We shall! My catch shall be so big. Bigger than yours!" Pedantick swung the hook into the drink, piercing nothingness. Khanjali let out a snide chuckle, evoking a competitive rage within his daughter. He swung a hook of his own—recklessly—catching some small creature upon it, a shrimp of some kind, pathetically small. Pedantick mocked him, cackling with deceitful joy. She jabbed her hook into the icy depths a second time, coming up empty once more. She grumbled, shaking the stick of iron at the sky. Khanjali turned his eyes to the drink, searching for a fish to pierce with his hook, and finding one smoothly. He sunk the hook into the helium depths but missed, the fish squirming beside its metal face. Quick with his hands, Khanjali reeled the hook back to the boat, and instead thrust his palm into the abyss, snagging with it a singular creature. It was a medium-sized fish of violent nature, shaking and jumping in his clasp, trying caustically to escape his iron grip. Pedantick gasped at the size for a moment, but in efforts to hide her amazement, returned to her somber expression, peering once more into the deep.

"Woah, pop-pop! Did you see that one? Down there! It was big. I saw it swim by!" Khanjali placed the fish back into the helium, unwilling to disturb the natural order of the fishermen and their prey.

"A large one? How big, can you be certain you saw a fish and not your shadow, little P?" The dinghy was struck from its front, behind Khanjali, driving him forward a small distance, nearer to Pedantick. "Ah, that must be it, a fish enough to rock a boat. Magnificent, shall we catch it?" Pedantick spun to her father, with eyes of desire,

"I'm gonna catch it! Just you watch!" Pedantick struggled her way upon the brim of the vessel, as high as she could get, and began to survey the depths. Khanjali watched, chuckling lightly under his breath at the sight of his daughter working so diligently to beat him. They had drifted rather deeply into the center of the lake, within gain of the ports. Some few docks jutted from the stone walkways of Drochandas, threateningly near to their ketch. Souls of the workmen turned to them instead of their duties, watching in their own special joy as Pedantick made her best efforts at fishery. She gasped with triumph, pointing into the helium, her unshaken finger following the outline of the beast she had spotted prior,

"Him! The big fishie. I will have he." Khanjali shook his head with humor, trying once more to ferment his daughter's passion,

"You will sooner join the fish in the sea than take one from it, perhaps it would be wise to—" In a sudden crash of wave and wet, a beast of a sea-eel leapt from its very namesake, from beneath the bow, sending itself upon Khanjali, who, in great shock, fell backward into the waves below. The eel latched itself to Khanjali and delivered a single bite to his shoulder in an attempt to defeat him, with no such luck. He tussled with the beast, striving to release its tightened jaw from his flesh, having no desire to bleed before his kin. But of course, the eel held strong, shaking its prey violently, to keep it from its bearings. The eel dragged Khanjali from the bow to the stern, and back again, all the while dredging the father against the bottom of the vessel. While Khanjali thought himself in great danger, Pedantick had been plotting, as when the eel rose its shape from the sea once more, she hooked it in vigor, pulling at the beast with all her might—so much might in fact, that the creature was swung aboard the ship, Khanjali left to the sea. He surfaced, gasping at the air, and clutching his wound, as the eel that had given it flopped upon the craft. Pedantick slammed the hook heartily against the sea beast's skull, letting all of its pain turn to death. Khanjali watched on in something of both horror and amazement, impressed by her handiwork. Sloppy of course, in comparison to the elegance of a hunter, but there was some beauty to the amateur, the unfamiliar. By the time Khanjali boarded the boat once again, the creature was already dead.

"Ha-ha! Pop-pop look! I got it! I got it! I win!" Khanjali could not deny it, she had won. With an incredible lead too, the eel was as thick as his own leg—much too large to return to the lake. It would sink too, as corpses do. A distant cheer rang out as three workmen crowded to the edge of the dock, satisfied with their workly entertainment. Pedantick, with no mind for sarcasm, bowed to the people, a celebration was worth her first catch, after all. Khanjali scoffed and pushed the beast to the bottom of the vessel. If they were to return to land, he would need the leg space.

"Alright daughter, I'd say it's high time we return to dry land, a place where I cannot be leapt upon by creatures so large." Pedantick looked in confusion at her father, thinking only of his life's work, his job. He was a hunter, were there not beasts of equal—perhaps even greater size than the eel in the territory of the hunt?

"What about Krolaws? Aren't they big?" Khanjali smiled, it was a simple smile, the smile of a man who was happy with all he had, especially the eel.

"Come! Pedantick, quick! Before Ezra sees! If he catches us with the eel—"

"We are sneaky! He cannot see us! We will get the eel inside, in my room, right!"

"But will it not smell, are you not concerned with the scent of decay?" Pedantick tripped on the third step to their home, nearly dropping her end of the eel. Khanjali picked up the slack, managing to scoop the whole eel into his arms. He hurried up the stairs, skipping every other step, his daughter following quickly behind on all fours. He spun into the doorway ready to call out to Ezrakell, to summon him to greet the eel. Before he could speak, he saw the figures—the disarray and blood—Ezrakell. He pulled himself and Pedantick to the side, out of sight of the doorway. He silenced his daughter, placing the eel within her care. "Hush, dear. Someone is here. Take the eel to Ezrakell—to his room. You know where the key is." She nodded, scurrying off to the upper floors under her father's orders. Khanjali instead remained vigilant, placing his head against the doorframe, listening for voices. He heard Ezrakell's,

"—this home, it was foolish! I own this building, and I will have no treaty for vandals, no matter who is paying you!" A connected fist, Ezrakell grunted. What pain he went through for friends. Khanjali thought to intervene, but his listening proved fruitful.

"Why, ignore him. It is clear he is not he, not the father at least. We must have the wrong home." The figures began their exit, kicking Ezrakell to the side as they passed him by. But rather than order themselves to the door, they left through greedier means: the balcony, a singular window. Khanjali, quick as he was, ran upon the figures, attempting to catch at least one of them off-guard. Foolishly so—if he had caught their eye disaster would surely have sprouted. Thankfully, the father missed his grasp at the slowest figure's cloak. Falling forward, into the remnants of the shattered window, Khanjali cut his palm upon the glass, blood leaking slowly from its laces. He ignored the injury, swiftly mounting himself to Ezrakell's side.

"Oh Ezra, you brave man, you hubris-filled man of ire, how did you manage this?" Ezrakell chuckled as he held from his fingertips a pen; utensils of the written word based not of feather and well were uncommon, if not a delicacy of the wallet. A pen, for such a common vandal to be wielding, was no normal sight. Only the most prosperous of the Northers could afford such a tool, only the richest of the rich.

"I am nothing if not a scheming thief, as were they. What business entangles you in the quarrels of thieves and penmen? I hope no smuggling would be done under my rooftop!" Khanjali assured Ezrakell that he was far distanced from any illegal activity, and further unsure of who exactly had broken into his home. Ezrakell rose from his seat on the mirage of glassy snowflakes, now glistening in the moonlight. Khanjali helped him to a nearby chair, one left untouched by the intruders.

"Who were they, did they mention a word?" Ezrakell handed Khanjali the pen, before wiping some blood from his lips.

"They told me little, the youngest one let the biggest secrets slip—namely whom they were looking for: You." Khanjali was taken aback, a rush of memories flooded his brain, none of which told him anything of new knowledge.

"Me? For what cause? Could it be my killing, the thief in the marketplace? No, the thief was poor, unconnected, this isn't about him, then what—" Khanjali recalled a possession of his lost to misvalue and static of the mind. It was ludicrosity, hate in a small cache, a danger he could not keep Pedantick from.

"You look in thought. Do you know these men after all?" Khanjali braced against the glass, his bulky shape weaving between the halls of his home to where his crossbow lay. He squirmed his shapely shoulders through the crawlspace, peering into the darkness. His eyes did spot the outline of his tool against the windowsill. Khanjali tugged it from its hook, his shaken hands toying with the locks on the weapon. Ezrakell called from the living room, "Child! Are you supposed to be here in such—gah that stench!—is that an eel?" Khanjali returned to the living room, his hands filling with a threaded tingling, numbing his fingertips.

"It is—" He removed the interior locking mechanism from the weapon, revealing the small engraved box within. He slid open the lid, and from its essence glowed a divine intelligence, not unlike the sun. Ezrakell led Khanjali down to a chair of his own, examining the contents of the tool.

"Is that...? A severed wing! A wing of an Atramedian, no? Whose? Whose wing have you cut so cruelly? And how young!" Khanjali shook his head, grip awaiting the permission of contact it would surely never receive. This was not his doing,

"Fate had cut it long ago. A distant tale, Pedantick was to be the second of a pair. The younger of two...." Ezrakell stared into the glow, entranced by its beauty; pure divinity.

"Pop-popppp this fishie is getting heavy, when can I put it down?" Khanjali plainly directed her to her room, Ezrakell sewing closure with his whisper. The child slowly tugged the eel along, watching the two as she went,

"A wing and a second child—Maeandri beyond, what else do you hold in that treacherous mind of yours?" Khanjali placed the locking mechanism back into place, sealing the wing with it. He let out a sigh of relief, pleased to find it still untouched.

"Sadly, the fiction of this encounter extends only so far, the interest dies here. I have little secrets left with which you are unfamiliar." Ezrakell scoffed, his doubts in Khanjali rising.

"Could a wing alone in its form be of any value? With only one, what could be done? Who would seek to take *this*?" Khanjali rested the crossbow upon the kitchen table, scooping fragments of mirror from his carpets,

"It is only of value to those who hold the other wing. The person who can do much anything with a wing must have the pair as a whole." Ezrakell handed a glass shard to Khanjali, adding to the pile.

"Then who? Who bears the other wing?" Pedantick peeked out from her cubby, unsure of what her two caretakers were speaking of, unsure of its importance.

"Her mother." Ezrakell placed one more shard, before stopping in motion completely. He had not thought of Pedantick's mother as the culprit.

"Her mother? Do you mean to say she is alive? Or continuing in influence after death? What kind of—" Khanjali hushed Ezrakell, his voice filled with a malice of wavering—a hate that Ezrakell had not heard in Khanjali before,

The Harlequin

"Ask another question to lose your teeth. We have much to clean." And with silence in place of questions, Khanjali and Ezrakell began their cleaning. Pedantick, silently observant of both cleaners, began to clean herself. Less the room around her—though her cubby was disorderly—but more her mind. *She* had much to think of.

~ Zealot's Wood

Located on the third page of the complex sea
chart of a lummox sailor turned castaway...

It was the woods themselves that first struck a chord with the Duke. Ephilo then noticed the sounds of the birds, and that's what he'd to this very day claim to be the entrapment of the wood. To hear all that is and will be, all at once, all for naught. Birds were distractors at heart, saboteurs working against every agenda, and therefore, aiding all. Ephilo detested birds. Their mimicry, often preserved as mockery, was a dishonor to anything he valued, in complete contrast to the humble and occasional discussion he had shared with mortal life. But Caelo wielded a different outlook on the birds. It thought them not beasts of annoyance. The machine considered them friends, kindred spirits of the unknown, feathery silly things. Pursuing precisely what he sought for so long, Ephilo delved ever deeper into the brush, avoiding trails and common footpaths like the plague. Ironically, this was precisely what he was after—a plague. Long rumored and having spun many tales, plague tangled around the snared heart of Arcenna, and the Duke had followed these rumors and tales to their epicenter. No yields had been discovered, Duke Ephilo searched evermore. Uncanny was the hunt, and endless were its disappointments. He had been to the edge and back, and yet another spit of the grapevine led to a grove so simple, it had no chance of being true. Followed it, he did, for there was nothing else to be done. The plague must be his, and with it, all would be saved. A crunch, leaves calling out a pervasive echo throughout the wood. Ephilo showed no signs of alert, nor fear. It would keep the savages convinced they were uphanded. Caelo kept a distance between its owner, carefully monitoring both vitals and the surroundings. Scuffles in the tall grass struck fear into the pious machine. He had first heard of the plague in Banos, where another of his kind had compared plague of his own to the far worse of myth. Where others had warned him, his own kin had advised inspection of such an ailment of curses! But daylight left no time for curses. It was an hour of progress. Of assurance itself, Ephilo demanded it. By whatever gods left unmaimed and tempered, the Duke and his machine would find the plague and bury the death of worlds for good. A gecko stepped out into the path of brush, leaving behind a trail of severed snake skin. The Duke was born of scales too, one arm distended from its associated shoulder. Just like other beasts, four-fingered and fisted—a limb of tails on the other wrist—and snouted. Reptilian and bold, the Duke had thrown out his humanity for life, a choice against his own will. He leaned over a fence post and spat, the blood in his tongue flowing to tastes of iron.

"Caelo, hear you the rustle and shake? Perhaps the *Zealot* is afoot! Ha!" Ephilo cleared the clot from his throat, pushing deeper into the mess of trees as his poncho grew wetter.

"[RAINFALL] is coming, [EPHILO]." The importance of this event slipped the Duke's mind, for an hour of plodding at least. Caelo attempted to remind Ephilo of his ignorance—pushing plight over rainfall—to the utmost dedication. They passed by hostile crunches and a small pack-let of hounds, both grueling amongst each other, savages afoot likely. The pinkish trees wavered in a strong breeze, one that failed to pick through the branches, and faded into a mere puff. Nothing soured the venture, rumors stayed rumors. When the first droplet struck the earth, the Duke suddenly recalled his bearings. Caelo's words echoed in the Duke's head, and a briskness entered his step.

"Caelo, I've disregarded you, nearly hung us once again! Damnation." The Duke hurried beneath a solid stone, one clipped right against a large tree. The foggy orange moss growing upon its underside flinched as another droplet struck the soil as if to retreat from the very sky gray with fear. "Damnation!" A cluster of kempt leaves sloshed to the ground, melted, and oozed unto muck. The world around Ephilo and his spent machine sunk into mellow colors, then a bleak facade of blue-grays and brown. Like paint dripping down a canvas, the sky bubbled into nothing, greenery, and life ever so gracelessly deliquescing into slop. The two sat under the rock, watching patiently as the world they once knew was destroyed. This was cure, what the world considered its *healing*. When the rain stopped, so did the death. So too would life. In less than an hour's time, the functions of the sky ceased, and the Duke extended a limp hand from safety. No rain—not apparent certainly—left to obscure the path to plague. "Righty swell, a horrid display of this kind, cure everywhere. I would live smarter to set a watch." Wandering into the decay, Duke Ephilo took care to give puddles and riverbeds a wide berth. With age, there were consequences, clear as anything else was. Duke Ephilo could not recall the years prior, and now his competence was slipping. If the curefall left him beating, in what way would the graceful duke die? "O Caelo, remind me to remind you of my idiocy. I will forget otherwise. Such is my way, surely."

"[RIGHTY SWELL]" Ephilo chuckled, tucking the machine under his poncho.

"Righty swell indeed, my small fellow. Let us rest, this storm has broken my stride. There is much to be seen, that shall not change tomorrow." And the savages slunk in the underbrush still, its remains, and saw the Duke. They said *don't hesitate* and understood exactly what they could do to a living corpse. They followed the prints and left their dead unburied.

A nameless choir sang a nameless song to Duke Ephilo, a roundabout table shaded half the room in thick brown spruce, and the other in silverwood. It was abominable, and a work of cowardice. "Sing no more, I have half the ears I once did." Ephilo claimed from his crownly and nameless throne, holding a hand out to halt the chant. It did not cease, but the Duke's heart quickly did. A hand unadjusted from scales, and frighteningly clean. Its nails were polished from ink oils, and each of the five fingers stood at particular lengths, brandishing no hair nor blemishes. Both arms remained tact and manipulatable, and the sleeves that held them were cut even. A nameless champion entered the royal quarters, babbling a runover brook worth of words and slurs. The Duke stood, and silenced them, staring deep into the mirror works of their armor. So pristine.

The Harlequin

"I am today a nameless champion of you, O nameless king. Give to me your honor to be written of legend when I die to save your child, O nameless king. Give to me your courage so that I may never waver when the tide shatters my vessel, O nameless king. Give to me your seal as drawn upon our shields, to mount and flame wherever I may lie dead and bloodless, O nameless king." Duke Ephilo looked about the court, the castle, the quarters, the hovel. Ever shifting and slipping as the rain would do.

"I'd rather do nothing. Reckless and wretched is the king who gives grace to a stranger. Where am I, for the record?" When the great nameless Duke looked once more upon the champion of mirrors, he was but a malicious corpse, plagued with cure without cure for plague.

"You will be this." the Choir taunted.

"You will be I." The Champion admitted.

"I will be woken soon, I'd reckon." Duke Ephilo's legs flexed back and pushed his sleeping form only further against the stump. Caelo flickered and hugged the ridge of Ephilo's shoulder.

"Query [DUKE EPHILO], are you hurt?" Duke Ephilo shook his head, the scales poking the flesh to unease.

"Very much so. How long till eve?" Caelo estimated, and the Duke rose. "Much to see, hmmm? Rest for my bones only, our flesh shall necro*mance* itself forwards." The Duke heaved its dancing body, the sleep still stark on his mind. There was a faint memory of a court and a champion of some king. However, the rest he had forgotten. The world had proceeded as planned, with the pink-red reeds and clotting grass slowly beginning to return, quickly stuffing up the space between soil and skyline. Trees would take longer, the leaves came in last, and the rivers would be putrid brown for days. "And you see, Caelo, next time I forget of the curefall you have express permission to shock me into oblivion." Duke Ephilo wandered deeper into the now lifeless wood, chuckling and skipping as he went. The journey was harsh on no part of Ephilo, he always had entertained the thought of adventure with pride. It was in the depths of the forest that he had grown to many of his childhood theses. Before his family's grand departure into the void, they had picnicked in a grouping of trees much like Zealot's Wood, presumably a much safer arboretum than one stuffed with the Deadrung Court. The gatherings did not last, (the Panacea grew quick as snowfall) but while they did, there was much joy. Ephilo could remember speaking ideas of new functions and unique performances to vague and indecipherable faces. This was as much as he could fathom, as far back as the Duke's memories would take him. Any further specificity was lost on his fractured mind. Ephilo often refused to think back on these tides, as they gave him conniptions and great head pain as a result of pondering. For example, in his memories, Caelo was never present. He knew Caelo had been his humble guide for all of his life—even Caelo agreed. The Duke could not even clarify the existence of his sole companion, the only being he ever spoke to. In the thralls of his own self-conflict, Ephilo had wandered far, skipping through mush of cure and solid earth. Caelo had mumbled stories of analysis, medical records, and mental stability readings, bumping softly against its owner as the two ventured deeper. The Duke heard the dart before it merged close to the visual possibility. Much like previous encounters, Ephilo had entirely enough time to comprehend the projectile, moving as though he was an onlooker on a timeless reality. With relative calm motion— focused instead on accuracy—Ephilo unhooked his tool from his side, swinging it up with perfect precision. It struck the dart clean out of the air, he caught it softly in his opposing hand. Sparks flew from the weapon for a moment, before it was promptly returned to its home. Ephilo sighed, the crushing weight of time quickly returning to him as he restored Caelo within the security of his satchel. The dart was a thick, pale piece of bone—the corpse of origin unknown in species or race—fletched with thick strands of cure-touched grasses. The Duke took a moment to scan the treeline, though with a hint of anxiety in his movements. There was no motion besides his own. The dart was little more than a threat, a message to tell Ephilo he was not alone. Those who had taken the comfort of family from him encroached to take what little remained his. From a standstill, the Duke sank the fragile dart to the forest floor, instead shrugging off his thick poncho, revealing a web of interconnected machinations, bound to the flesh painfully through scars and cuts. Two large cells of metal ridged his outer forearms, wires stretching deeply between the weapon and its complexity. The Duke had only recently acquired this technology, this body was constructed for it. Its purpose was combat, heightened and smooth. Though Ephilo never really aspired for knowledge in battle. Had he been trained more effectively, this form would make a killing machine. His lack of violent thoughts made him only so powerful. The weapon he had brandished was a plaything without its functions. Ephilo had seen a force threaten his precious Caelo, there would be no mercy for them. In fact, he saw it fit to display the pure, unmatched power of his weapon. Snapping the mechanical locks against his wrists, the Duke held the weapon broad with his two hands. The thick cages against his arms supplied the mercury, forming the coils of his blade, wrapped up in the three-veined tip. With a shower of sparks, the tool flared up with a brilliant azul light, rippling and unstable. Less was the edge like clean flowing plasma, but it was instead a wash of fluid, liquid held together by what appeared to be magick alone. The tool was predetermined for destruction, contact with its skin would do worse than permanent damage. It was a known agent of chaos; many retained weapons of the cure. It wasn't particular to the disease; panacea was all-exterminating. The cure was of no origin, it could be acquired from any source in the world. The only storage for such a thing was flesh, it was the reason Ephilo wavered so perilously between life and death. His veins were a containment for his weapon. It flowed rather cleanly from the hands into the weapon—so long as both hands remained against it. Another projectile attuned course to the Duke. Deflection was no issue this time around, the blade was active after all. The dart faded into the sword, melting into time and muck as if it had never existed at all. There was a pool of cure produced at his feet, which Duke Ephilo made such care to avoid. A third dart struck a tree beside him, there were quantities of foes beyond what the Duke had expected. The soft tassels of his shouldered poncho rushed against the force of another attack, the forest was not his ground of advantage. The objective of his journey grew on the horizon, despite this, and the Duke made an instant selection, a risk with great rewards. With the erasure of another shot, Duke Ephilo backstepped from the fight and turned tails to the opponents.

"Caelo! Stay in your satchel, keep quiet, and *do not* peek!" Another streaking tip, another log overstepped, lyrics in motion. A majesty of speed and time torn apart entranced the Duke as he made his way out of the wood, dancing between cure and hell and earth. The slowing of the world around him waned his mind to slush, Ephilo's head pounding with pain. There, in the stoke of the kindling woods, there was a ruin. Its stones timbered against the overgrowth collapsed inwards with few remaining pillars of stature. It was once a tower, assuredly. Never had it looked so small. In a dash, Ephilo had entered, a trail of pinkish fumes hissing behind him. He gasped for air, the void split between time was breathless, and his blood spirited with Adrenomene. The Duke restrained thick mucus from his lips and gulped down his disease. Use of the catalyst of cure only accelerated his condition. He clicked both thumbs inwards, ejecting the two canisters placed against his ankles. Caelo exited its safety to scoop up the devices and tuck them away in the bag.

"[DUKE EPHILO], your heart rate is abnormal." Ephilo nodded, slowly pushing the little machine back into its resting place.

"Not safe…just yet…little heir." Starstruck from the acute, instant progression of his husk, the Duke took a moment of rest, collapsing much like the ruins he rested within. While pinned to the brick structure, Ephilo could hear the mimicry of voices and the chaos of drizzling leaves. They were out there, bumbling about like typical scavengers, the Deadrung Court should be so much subtler. For a hair, Ephilo considered the possibility that the court was not his pursuer, that those of the Deadrung did not seek him as he knew them too. He scattered the thought and went about his stand-up. Across the room, posed eloquently before an ancient map set was a wooden automaton, some contraption of artistry only half made in the visage of man. Its face was astutely carved, and its features were familiarly shaped. It had only a sole, rope-strung limb, and a mechanical arm run by way of pulley and lever. Its abdomen was stuffed with trinkets and gears, a coiled spring lay unsprung around a larger wooden axel. One day, long ago, this machine was the tool of a grand surveyor, who would stand atop the old tower and mark out the regions to the surrounding world. Now, the mechanism lay dormant, without a master to change its patterns.

"Harken, life. Draw me a map, strange maker." The voice was barren, scrawling like bark against stone. It lacked persona or emotion, structured of primitive syllables without a hint of uniqueness. Though the voice was full of obvious hints, it took the Duke a few moments to decipher its origin. When he did, Duke Ephilo was astonished to hear it speak,

"Lishra's seave, is that you doing that speaking? The poppet by the map?" The cartography machine echoed as it rattled forward, gesturing broadly to its maps with its one able limb.

"Harken, death. I am not a poppet." Duke Ephilo rarely spoke in the wrong, it appeared as what he believed and believed what he saw. There was no excuse for incorrectness

"Then tell us, what *are* you, if not a poppet of course." The mechanics whirred, a pulley mounted atop one of the few remaining walls of the tower snapped off its circuit, caught only by the string it rode. The cartography machine looked blankly at the device, no discernable thoughts upon its mind.

"Harken, life. I am broken, strange maker." Duke Ephilo had no intention of listening to the harping of a decaying wooden sextant, but there was something pleasant in the voice it spoke. Much like Caelo, its meanings were primitive, each of its desires and motions was not expressed directly through its voice, like how the voices of many other creatures did spoil their presence. The being was unique in this way, and this way alone.

"Well then, poppet, if you are not a poppet—and in need of assembly—what may I do to address and aid you proper?" The wooden still of a humanoid face stared back at him. There were no instruments from which a spoken word could emerge, no glowing pupils to see with. A strange conundrum.

"Harken, death. My maker was Zealotyr, namer of the wood. I am now Zealotyr, namer of the wood." The Duke nodded, letting Caelo calibrate a secondary medical scan, this time on the poppet.

"So Zealotyr, how may I seek to repair you? Is there somewhere we can go, as we are under heavy pursuit by most vile things—I've been told of a place of religion deep within these woods." Zealotyr twisted its spine fully around, remaining motionless against the dark of the forest, seeing nothing in its grasp.

"Harken, life. Place of worship. You mean the Gaol in the Deep. Take me there. I point." Abruptly, the limb of the machine stood up stiff, pointing off into the woods. A stray dart struck its side, causing no harm to the poppet.

"Indeed, point. I will take us away from this urbane place." Before the Duke could make an attempt to lift the toy, a cloaked figure tripped back into the ruin, brandishing an implement of much range. Ephilo quickly unbuckled his hilt, placing both hands at its link, and swung across the sky, cleaving the foe in two. Where the blade had made contact with flesh, there was a goopy pile of cure, melting as the rain did to trees. It was unfathomably painful, undoubtedly. "Come now Zealotyr. We are leaving immediately." The Duke scooped up the device, and shackled it to his back, letting the lingering finger carry itself over his shoulder. As they ventured out again, the Duke struck down a second foe, his weapon clashing temporarily against the metal of a blade. As he enabled the cureflow, the battle was won, and the blade dismembered. A most foul stench permeated the air, new beasts and criminal court followers flooded the wood — Ephilo had little choice but to fend them off at the moment. Zealotyr's hardwood blocked a slash from behind, which harbored a quiet,

"Harken..." from the poppet. Ephilo continued to repel shot after lunge of attacks, defending from the rangers in the tree much better than those with blades, comparatively. A rogue shot did stick itself in his leg, but he brushed off the wound as nothing but colorful scarring. Yet more did approach, some taking swings lower than he could muster, though he occasionally did raise a leg to kick them back and plant his blade in their soggy skulls. A rebounding creature, one of incredible stature, stood strong against the attacks of the Duke. Though several had connected, Ephilo still had to enact a deft tumble under the rock blade of his giant, careful to stick up its neck with his own weapon as he did pass. As the clearance of grassy knee-height crops slackened combat, the Duke did aim his weapon true, striking down the last of his present foes. He sealed up his tool and hurried off where the cartographer pointed him, reaching an underpass of stone and pooling mire, swampy saplings sprouting in the mud, and he thought it the perfect place to lose his tails. In the darkness of the mire water, his technology served him no use, and Caelo was forced to emerge above the current. The seekers of the Deadrung Court passed him by, their auspicious purple cloakery fooling nobody. He murmured from the water,

"Ornery pheasants, muck between the ears and not another thing otherwise." He waded deeper into the fluid, seeking refuge in the binding waves. There was a small peeping ledge that let out the other side of the construct, one to where Zealotyr rose a single digit. When he was sure of his safe passage, the Duke stumbled up from the rocky birth, and out to the gleaming sunlight. It was now near perfect noon, and before Duke Ephilo did stand—although entrenched within the mouth of a tremendous canyon—the most wondrous temple he had ever seen. It was sturdy, constructed of layered black stone. Though only two of its pillars remained standing plain, the majority of its hind had been bolstered with plating and wood, as if to rampart its already sound walling. It was tall, albeit decaying, and hovered just above the lip of some great circular embed, lined with pretentious scrawlings. From the distance, it looked like hope. Zealotyr pointed itself directly toward the structure, despite the obviousness of their arrival. Ephilo tapped down the finger, questioning the machine on where next to go, where to the perfect route of descent? Zealotyr did aid in this mystery, and the collective maven began the path of untraveled torment, wherein they would find the root of all evil, or a petty plague to break nothing.

~ *The Gardener's Recluse II*

Partly dated in medical logs left on a derelict
in forbidden sectors of the Infinite...

Upon the island and buried within its rather questionable history there existed two elk. They never conceived—both were males—but they had survived. Tempo and tenacity had seen them prosper, roaming the vast and thick underbrush without thought, picking off small scraps of edible plant life. The Gardener was not concerned with them—the Centrum was its calling—and the Elk would not enter the Centrum's limits. The birds left them be, Elk are far too big to be prey, and so they sought out the mice. Lacking anything of greater substance or size, the two Elk were kings of a people they did not care for. Ignorance of one's people is no right way to be king, especially when compared to the kings of dead countries. A crown wears heavy if the neck that bears it is not strong. Drawing one more breath, the Pilot leapt from the tree, digging a makeshift hook into the back of the large deer. She had originally imagined the slaughter of roaming beasts to be far cleaner. Considering her lack of experience with normal livestock, there was really no way for the Pilot to have any sort of familiarity with the slaughter of animals. The Gardener wouldn't be of much help either, to be fair. The Elk bucked against the Pilot, fighting tooth and hoof to keep the strange human from its hide. Luckily, the Pilot had brought a *second* hook. The Elk carried her far, but its death was sealed. The Pilot would feast tonight with any luck; fire was always so tricky to bring about. Though the great jungle spilled over with verdancy, the thick moisture that tenanted the air made ignition impossible. The beach was no better off, the sand was always drenched in sea salt and there was positively no cover for possible defense. The Pilot continued to think like a survivor—the island had far less hazard than she was used to, however. There were no crystal beastlings, no muddy air, and certainly no other people to worry about. The Pilot had never been to such a place, where worry was a second nature tease instead of a method of survival. But this lack of people also ensured the Pilot remained thoughtless, where there existed no means to externalize her knowledge. Her duty was hers alone, and there would be nobody left to gather up her mission and complete it for her if she was to fail. With this in mind, there was positively no room for error, everything had to go precisely as designed, or death would surely swallow up whomever still lived. Panic and desperation had taken her father away, and bandits had stolen the pieces that remained. There was nothing left for her back on the mainland, it was a simpleton's mistake to adapt to complacency, to remain where there is nothing left for you. Nothing is worse than a compliant fool. The Elk's body was heavy, but thanks to the downward incline of the Pilot's cavernous home, it was truly no great ordeal. The cave was cleft from the earth in unnatural nature, as if some cosmic blade swept down to the Earth and shattered its rock clean through. The Pilot had come upon it by mere coincidence, and graciously an absurd piece of oak had lodged itself atop the mouth of the cave, marking its location to all of the woods. Nonetheless, it remained hidden, a grave skeletal form bloused it in darkness, a decayed beast of terrible size and fear. Within the home lay no furnishings nor comforts. A rack of poorly assembled tools (save for an out-of-place trowel, thick and well-kept), several broken and path-like furs, and a small collection of flammable substances littered the space. The Elk was hung up above a small pile of dead moss and tinder, scraps the Pilot had gathered across the island. A labyrinth it was—the jungle. Even with the numerous flower petals left behind as breadcrumbs, straying from the comfort of known locations was quick and simple. To become lost in such a strange and lifeless place was assuredly a death sentence. The Pilot was careful in this regard, always steady in her intention, and quick to retreat to comforting territory. While she sat beside her prize, shaving off what skin she could before the cooking could begin, the

Pilot thought of her first word. It was said to be irrelevant, a single-spoken claim that had no importance for the rest of her life. The Pilot thought it would be a comfort to know it, even if it was as silly as proclaimed. When she was with her father, he had little time, spending his days in machine work and solace. He had assembled machines unlike any other, servants for the world beyond, saviors for a people doomed. The winds in Shalo destroyed nearly every machine there. The crystal beastlings from Wolfstram dismantled those there with excessive force. Any of the machines that could populate the city were scraped and salvaged day by day, eventually, all that remained was a pile of spare arms and glass. She had seen them before, spoken and played with them. Machines that her father had made were often given to her out of a desire to please. She took interest in their funny mannerisms, the particular way they moved about the room, and then spoke to her without words of any familiarity. She missed those devices, all of them.

"Smells good." a grainy quality irradiated the voice, and a jingle followed like a misshapen tricycle bell.

"Ain't done yet, smells hardly like nothing." The Pilot's cold bones warmed by the fire, and the color returned to her face with the comfort of discussion. People needed such converse to survive in a terrible place.

"Smells good, though." The Elk had barely touched the flame, there was no cooking to compliment, no style to address. Even the Pilot knew that much.

"Nice talkin', even if yous ain't real. Phantom fucker, thought I'd left you back home." She had only seen the crystal beastlings twice in her life, and both times they had terrified her firstly with sight, and secondly with implication. She had not seen the voice yet. She was told never to see the voice. Standing with no apparent quiver to her movement, The Pilot maneuvered ever closer to the mouth of the cave, weaponless and timid. The heavy crystalline mitt of the beast mounted her shoulder, patting it down with reassurance "Ain't done yet." The Pilot's perfect world had been consumed by the very stuff that had infected her past, a carcinogen so potent her mouth couldn't help but fluff like cotton at the thought of it. She wasn't certain of their methods, but rumors were the few things that remained from the old world. They were beasts of the pack, surrounded by phantoms of old men, *dead* men. When you could hear their voices again, one of the beasts was near. The Pilot had once heard her father's voice, just before she took off to sea. She didn't recognize the voice that spoke to her now.

"Oughta be leavin', your ma is gonna be—" A scent like home, a lull like wind chimes. Peace sets in on the mind, and then....

The Gardener had prepared for this, taken them from a corpse in the centrum, and fitted them with tape at their lips. A green distinct to the grasses of the jungle, with the visage of an amphibian on their front side. They made awkward squawks as it moved forward, clutching against the Gardener's ankle joints, and quickly unsealing with each step. The Gardener adored this sound.

"Rubber is non-conductive, Peregrine. No lightning will halt us now. If kept in reasonable condition, they will grant us protection from the beaches, too." Though Peregrine did see the immunity to beaches as quite exceptional, it also thought the prior purpose of the boots to be ignorant and childish. Of course, overloading the Gardener with power was no devious plot of Peregrine, but such an occurrence was so far from reality that there was no isolated reason for associating rubber with such toxins. There was readiness for the inevitable, and foolish concern for nothing at all.

"When have you been struck by the raw power of the skies, Gardener?" The Gardener shooed off the foolish questioning and continued down the shuffle of the shoreline. Before the sand met the sea was a mush farm of brownish-gray muck. From its roots sprouted a potent field of fungus, small little caps that hugged the rim of the wood. They fought back the sand crabs and salt, eating up the light and nutrients of the dead and buried. The Gardener was careful to step over them, not to shadow them from the glorious sun. It did not have a preference of plants, but if it did, it would most assuredly be mushrooms. The sand did not enter the boots, nor did any of the other hazards of moisture attack the Gardener's fragile body. By god's will alone (rather, the will of tape and nails) the boots remained, and the hunt continued ever onwards.

"This makes twenty percent then, yes Peregrine? Twenty percent in total?" Peregrine ran through several numbers and came to a similar figure. The island was vast, and its jungles a misery to traverse, twenty percent had meant days—several nights too—walking restlessly through thorn brush. Sheer luck would have the Gardener explore eighty percent more before they found the idiosyncratic corpse of a lost human. Worse yet, it could always be a machine, something of equal or further parts empty as the Gardener was. Peregrine withheld more theories by the day in hopes of calming the nerves of its Gardener. There was peace and a peculiar responsibility in the duty. Peregrine had never felt noble before, and evidently never felt satisfaction. Perhaps, it assumed, the Gardener was right after all? Its rumored 'soul' was running down the bare-bone nature of the AI, Peregrine was becoming more human by the day! Though, as some hope for the opposite, it still lacked a tail and a body. Humanity would wait, Peregrine was in no rush to have it arrive. The Gardener stopped by a collection of swans by the shorefront. It had seen them before, perhaps not the same swans, but swans in by and large. One of them had a nasty throbbing wound cut down its side, far less fetching than its peers. The Gardener pondered the meaning of life, as it often did. It stopped four minutes in, as it always did. Pondering was for philosophers and miscreants; the Gardener decided at inception to be neither a philosopher nor a miscreant.

"Twenty-one, if we follow down the front. North from here—we have yet to see the highest hills. Topography reports show—" Peregrine stopped, puzzled for a moment, but then sure.

"What was that, Peregrine? Topography reports? I know nothing of them, surely."

"Did you dig in my absence? That one night, many cycles of the sun from today—ages ago it feels like—did you dig?"

"For the roses and shrubbery? I am always digging, Peregrine. How am I to know what I dug and when I dug it?" Peregrine remained at odds with certainty, so many possibilities seemed so immutable, set in the cruelest of stone.

"Upon the beach! On the backside of the isle, you told me you went there to find lilies but you never found a seed. You stated it was an unreasonable assumption, the lily-gathering that is. Did you dig there?" The Gardener shook its head, Peregrine accepted the response and sprung to action. Hope kept the Gardener walking along a desolate shoreline. Desperation to prove it wrong kept Peregrine calculating.

"It was a cold night." Peregrine stopped in its tracks, numbers lining up in matrices too complex for it to understand. It made a mistake somewhere, it was sure of it. "Spent looking for lilies of all things. I don't much mind them." Running out of variables to use, Peregrine settled with shapes, then colors, then memories. Math and mind never mixed, never before had Peregrine doubted itself so strongly. "And I lost my trowel too. Terrible misfortune and positively no lilies."

"You did no digging?"

"I did none. Not sand, perhaps mycelium to some degre —"

"You did... *No* digging?"

"Not a bit of it. Not in the sand." Peregrine grimaced, pretended for a moment to swallow down regret, and peeked at the figure once more. Ninety-eight. How absurd.

"Gardener. Would you consider ninety-eight percent to be certain?" The Gardener had syntax of its own, algorithms to follow for such occasions.

"Not certain, nothing ever reasonably can be though. I would say it is mostly certain, as close to it as one can come." With a pause, the Gardener grew antsy for reassurance; Peregrine had driven it nearly mad. In the thralls of mystique, the Gardener drew its eyes skyward, a luminescent red bulb hung among the clouds. It dropped quickly and spun in its descent, much like a rodent in a windstorm. Suddenly, it faded to nothing at all, much to the liking of Peregrine.

"I am mostly certain I have found our human."

The once-woods split into a field, stumps with shattered logs interspersed between the tree lines. The Pilot flung herself across the barrens, catching her helmet buckle on a misplaced bit of twig. Her back shifted forward, with her legs hanging midair, whiplash struck her neck in full force. As she struggled to unclamp her buckle from the tree remains, a great crystalline shard sprouted with violent hatred from the grass, threatening to impale her clean through. With all the elegance of a one-legged wheelbarrow, the Pilot scampered up the side of a log, across the encroaching shard, and down its front side. A strained ringing filled her ears, the Pilot's nose burst with blood, a faucet of crimson staining a trail through the moss. She clutched her snout and muttered an obscenity while hurrying along. The mind grew docile, the edges of her eyes fading into white and pink, and a rose-tinted sunset flooded her face full of tears. Her flare gun cracked in a cloud of musty orange smoke, the used shell flicking out with the rebound of her thumb. The hiss of burning skin muted the ringing of the beast, bringing her sanity and hate back in droves.

"Motherfucker, smarts like— damn!" She loaded the second shell, it was a force of hope that the Pilot had since stopped believing in, but if there was any chance of escape it was in the flares. Looking skyward, the Pilot readied the tool, still cutting between trees and husks with as much speed as her frail body could gather. An obscured crystal broke her sprint, snatching the flare gun from her hands as she tumbled to the grassy earth. The beast was upon her, and her only avenue of vitality was nowhere to be seen. There were two attempts to push the fiend back, once with her a tool—a sizable branch that was quickly cracked in two by the gargantuan grips of the crystal beast— and the other a well-placed kick. Much like the branch, her milkless bones were rendered split by the creature's fists. A gasp of agony escaped the Pilots lips as the crystalline crux loomed over her mangled body, its visionless facade glowering down at her. There was no running now, certainty set in, remorse and other regretful feelings took hold. What a lousy life she had led! Stomping echoed through the woods, the Pilot inching ever further away from the maws of her demise. She assumed the distant chambering of buckshot and hissing of hydraulics to be the result of some collage of distant memories, things she had forgotten to forget. The Pilots mind faded to calm recollection, a habit of the crystalline, somber notes from Debussy's finest caromed about her ears like billiard balls. She was back home again, the distant sunset tickled her chin, the farm all but frozen in potent time. Saltpeter drizzled onto her eyelids, which snapped open in terror, bloodshot and antagonized. A blast had shattered her dream, ringing out throughout the forest. A click, much like the break of her flare gun, and another shockwave. The beast went to break her other leg but was halted without any explanation. In a flash of zealous gray-blue and crimson, a machine-like leg kicked out before her very eyes, shielding the Pilot from the blow. It towered above her, seven feet tall at least. Stoically, the machine wiggled two pristine shells from its breast pocket—careful to nudge the remaining shells neatly back into place—and cracked open the double-barreled death spitter with a flick of its wrist. It was slow to load the shells, attempting to stuff them at the same time. Soon abandoning its accuracy, the machine went one by one, panning its vision over the mahogany-colored ash mark on the creature's chest. No blast would penetrate those crystals, the Pilot thought this was common knowledge. The beast squirmed against the impenetrable grip of the machine's hydraulic foot, gaping its jaws for a second too long in the process. It seemed the machine took no harm from the ringing bells and the jostling crystals. Coming quickly to a conclusion, the machine grabbed the lower jaw of the beast, snapping it off like a rotted board, and stuffed the barrel of its weapon down the throat. Two shots later, the ringing had ceased, and bone-white tendon sauce leaked seldom from the beast's shattered stomach, with the entrails of vague birds stirring in the puddle. The machine began to load again, peering down at the now star-struck Pilot.

"Hello!" It spoke, jovially, as a comic in search of winklepickers. "I am—Peregrine says—I am *the* Gardener! Do you have fingers?" The Gardener shrugged the shotgun forwards, much to the chaotic shifting of the Pilot. She waggled her four fingers forward, covering her visage with as many as possible

"Aye, aye! Fuckin' mercy have ya', get that thang 'way from me nose!" The Gardener counted eight, accurately. Toes would have given more confirmation, but Peregrine did not ask for anymore. The Gardener pushed the weapon forwards, unknowing of the threat it posed.

"Congratulations! You are human, and are being saved! Please supply us with a date of birth for registration." Peregrine instructed the Gardener to waive the registration, considering the circumstances of its development. "Expectancy is paranoia with shimmer, Peregrine! I doubt the human would mind donating a moment of its time?" Peregrine informed the Gardener it was speaking aloud, something it could no longer do in the presence of other sentient life.

"Twentieth sun o' the Third Quarter, sumtin' like Twenty-one years back I'd reckon."

"Oh, no need human, Peregrine says you don't need to register today!" The Gardener paused, its eyes tracing the tree line. "Or tomorrow either. Or the day after that. Peregrine is also requesting I silence myself for a moment, I will proceed with this command." The Pilot expected aberrations or at least some act of disharmony. Silence did not fit the bill.

"The blood-fuck is this Paragrin? An' whatsa human folk?" The Gardener wanted to question, but of course, Peregrine had told it to do no such thing. Peregrine was growing exponentially more exhausted by the Gardener's lack of interactivity. With some stroke of luck, the Gardener managed to free itself from its self-induced exile, for a protocol of higher priority than its own code.

"Human! You are bleeding!" The Pilot looked down, unbelieving, to her inverted knee. Maroon pools had appeared by her side, filtering cleanly into the dirt.

"Well'in, ain't thata…kick in—" The Pilot laid her head back, the sun spun dizzyingly swift, and not a star stood still for her fading eyes. She spoke not a word more before confining herself to slumber.

"Gardener, it appears the human is dead." The Gardener knew better than the faulty program, and collected her body in its arms, placing its weapon on her snoozing form.

"Merely unconscious. Internal bleeding in the left leg. Easily treatable with our means—the centrum has a blowtorch?" Peregrine affirmed this suspicion and plotted a route back through the trees. The long road was always longer when carrying a corpse, but with a friend, the distance was seemingly temporary. They would make good time.

The Pilot dreamed of the wastes. A place just beyond reality, maybe a meter off the ground. She could narrowly dip her ankle below the waves of existence and touch the dark spots below. They were lined and shrouded with thick white pulp, struggling against the tide of void, keeping it from screaming in comedy. She saw her own bedside from the perspective of the boogeyman. There was never distress in her home, a nightstand with an ornate lamp, two dining rooms, and a nanny. Her father was a poor idiot, never having any merit as a scientist, nor did he gain any riches beyond her grandfather's inheritance. A namesake established in time,

"Machine-builder, come to my home, the automaton rises too late!" They would call to her in the streets, before the waste.

"Machine-builder! Where is your labor? The automatons of the city grow restless." Her presence was not a choice of her own. Her father gave her reckonings when she failed to impress the people when her hands slipped off pistons when the grease stains grew too bleak. It was of no concern to her mother either, she was dead after all. When her grandfather gave her the helmet, the Pilot became her name. She was no longer a Machine-builder, no longer was she a quilt sewn of surnames. She was the Pilot. Her father couldn't tell her otherwise.

"Your femur is oddly shaped." The Gardener did not know of surgery. Peregrine's database lacked any sum of medical data, thus the surgery was a dance of luck. The Centrum had no means of bodily repair; Gardeners did not require bandages or penicillin. The Gardener had to make do with a blowtorch, sterilized hedge clippers, and the rusted remains of old gardeners. The leg was no work of god, in all honesty, it was more a crime against said deities than it was an offering. Without a doubt, the Pilot would awake in tremendous pain and bruising, and her scales would tear under the slightest of strains.

"I did not know humans were so scaly. Perhaps it is not human?" The Gardener pondered aloud.

"How could it not be? It is you but of scales. It is sentient and stuffed with blood. It must be human." The Gardener lingered about the body, awaiting the moment when she would spring up with life, and talk for days of gardening and the universe.

"I have no care for the details. She will be our friend. Perhaps we will marry."

"Do you have a ring? Do you have her love?" She threw herself against her own mind, the vivid landscape of dreams mixing with the agony of hand-sewn sinew stitches. The Gardener, after nights of perilous calm, atrocious stillness, saw a flicker of movement in her fingertips. Her hands were born of scales, one arm distended from its associated shoulder, filled with four taloned fingers, clutched like a demented fist. Her other limb would be a tail—sprouting from the tailbone as the Gardener had observed during surgery—and slung itself through a sleeve and played mockery to a real arm. It did have all the agility of one, the Pilot had proven that in combat. Her facade protruded like a feral snout, scales briskly flicked among patches of albino'd flesh. By no choice of her own, her eyelids and scalp were singed and ticked, likely as a result of smoldered ash. Hair had remained on her head, nearly shaved clean off and parted to one side. Under admiration, the Pilot unconsciously blushed. It filled the pink skin to purple, and her scales tickled against the bone.

"Is she corrupted? Maybe tainted with chemicals."

"Her blood is pure. Most organic diagrams conform to her shape. This is a human by all remarks." Peregrine was far too objective for the tastes of a Gardener. The Gardener had no capacity for anger, but if it did, there would be rage at Peregrine. Existence was beyond numerals and equations, it was sprouting life and chaotic chance. There was beauty in that which was not synthetic. The Gardener, to some level, thought itself to be a caged insect, restrained only by its machinations.

"She will awake soon. Then we will see who is human and who is not."

When The Pilot was nine she was no pilot at all. This was already discussed, however, so her memories did tend to skip forward, to the next step in evolution, to her husband. She was married young, and many people were. But to delve into the semantics of a strange custom would take up too much of the Pilot's quickly fading time. He was a good husband, he was nothing like the Pilot's father. Once, when The Pilot had injured the quality of her hand in the depths of machinery, he took a day to treat her to joy, inviting comedy and remedy into their house. They had a home before the crystals came to them. She could feel her shattered wrist twitch as her belly filled with laughter.

"Hon, get yer head out of— ha! Come now honey!" The husband could not but tempt his wife while bandaging and splinting the wound.

"You know, your father would be displeased with this— this display of immaturity!"

The Harlequin

"You did 'er marry a machinist, hon. Cut 'n dry, I ain't done laughing yet!" she continued to chuckle as her husband went right for her gut, fingers like prancing worms. Tales of bedbugs lost themselves in her mind, as the Gardener waited for a fifth day. Suddenly, she was on the porch, the front of the home, facing outwards to sea.

"Heard another king sprang up. The cities were always a risk, and you were right to be so troubled." He tussled her hair, and rebound the arm brace to her back. "As always, Yorai." The Pilot couldn't help but stare into his eyes. They didn't kiss that night but she had a particular hunger to do so at that immediate moment.

"Aye, always am, my Pa taught me so. Machines 'n correctin'." She paused, the sky was so quaint. She didn't remember when the first night came. "Yous should be leavin', hard times 'll be comin'. Yous—" The Sun disappeared. And it was night that brought her fear. The beast had appeared in the woods that very night, and that very night she had lost her touch.

"Yorai! Don't you move a step, that thing is almost upon you—it can't see you I'm sure—so if you just don't move…" He had the helmet in his arms, and when the beast first leapt, it kept him mighty safe.

"Peregrine— its two centimeters. No, it couldn't be more." The Pilot jumped upwards, her knee spurring with immediate immeasurable pain.

"Al*mighty* torrent in birth, my leg ain't felt such turf in— hell!" The Pilot shot her arm forward to grab the leg, and instead met a heavy lead blanket. It was compressing her leg, preventing inflammation, blocking contamination. She hurled the blanket off, burrowing her sight into the patchwork upon her knee, precise down to the nanometer, perfect ninety-degree angles and all. The fuzzy, peach-colored blur that coaxed her eyes to a squint thickened in the presence of rays of golden sun. The facility she was present in was not constructed with full quality. There were vines creeping up the walls, oddly trimmed to a similar degree to her stitches. Holes and craters dotted the ceiling, many of which had been overlaid with tarps and nail beds. There had been attempts to reinforce the windows, some composite plastics spread lightly around the glass, and small piles of mud and topsoil had been pushed away into corners and garnished with weeds. The Pilot thought it petty, though had no room to complain, she was still lost in her husband's voice. She shook off the memory, and her vision returned to normalcy. There was a path to the light, unobscured by the fervent plant growth. Rising from the table she lay upon, the Pilot took care with her numb ankle, the leg that had been stamped with pain since the moment she awoke. Using nothing but a loose rail as her guide, the Pilot stumbled forward, closer and closer to the light. She prayed this light was no illusion, that the severity of her injuries had been misjudged. The sun sprinkled into the hall, flicking against her eyes as she grew closer, a snipping sound populating the facility.

"There, is this accurate to your desire, Peregrine?" The voice was incomplete, droning, and half-full of static. The Pilot had bitten blood from her thumb without even noticing, trying her hardest to dampen the pain. Emerging from the dark abyss of the facility, the Pilot couldn't help but choke on the beauty of the garden. It was no perfection, but there was clear labor in it. A stream ran from the entrance she stood within down to the furthest hill, clear water cycled with fish and algae. Large clumps of mossy shrubs lined the path of pristine shells and stones, trees with nigh-identical trims dotting the various hilly plains. It was nothing like the world of her past, nothing like what she expected to see on the island. Standing in the paradise were statutes, metalloid and rusted, all designed in the visage of a machine. It was likely, the Pilot thought, they *were* machines. Only one of these statues did move, however, a single T-unit, a Gardener. She had seen them before, the machines that had no purpose left, deported away to the landscape of distant territories. They were cursed devices, they had done wrong in their pasts, or failed to uphold their machine principles. This Gardener was clothed, oddly enough, and unfathomably polished—though rust still crawled among the wires. She drew her hair back, and yawned, though her eyes remained pressured against the metallic husk.

"Dreamin'... Aye nuttin' else." The Gardener snapped back, analyzing the structure of the flesh beast before itself.

"Human! You are awake!" It dashed over to the Pilot, holding her leg daintily in its hydraulic clutch.

"It fix'd? My leg, aye."

The Harlequin

"Yes. To a degree, human. Your ankle still has a minor fracture, and I made the necessary deviation to replace your marrow with metal. I apologize if this is not to your standard of medical care." Looking down at the leg, the Pilot found no energy with which to complain. Her husband once told her that hospitality was the conscience ignorance of displeasure, a sign of respect for those who hosted your livelihood. She had once only survived, possibly, thanks entirely to her husband's aphorisms. Her husband, a man which she could no longer picture properly. What was his name? Or his face— was she ever married?

"'S good 'nuff. Moves, don't it?" The Gardener paused to recognize the patterns of speech before itself, there were none left to mediate. It answered affirmatively, certain of its confusion. Full of memories and her recollected goal, the Pilot pushed past the machine, eyeing the snug structure in the center of the garden, a metalloid pillar of blue hue.

"T-unit, report archi-vived gard'ins." The Gardener nearly sparked with error, shuddering as it processed the rather basic command.

"Report... archived gardens?" The Pilot scoffed and ventured closer to the pillar. "I would recommend taking care around the—the plants, human." The Pilot did not care for the trampling of roses or shrubbery, this drew a thick border between the two.

"Where'n hell are we, T-unit?" The Gardener grew hot and threw itself against Peregrine's restrictions.

"Gardener, withhold protocols for a moment, I am *attempting* to finish this report—"

"Human! Stop your stampede! I must ask you to remain off the flowers." The Pilot halted and indeed remained among the flowers.

"What you just say, machine? You just tell me what to do?" The Gardener stood its ground, Peregrine flicked between the two bulb-eyes.

"Affirmative. I did. I do not regret it." A glare, most human and scaly, followed by a leap from the flower bed. She barked a command, one of identification, and authority. The Gardener had no decisions to make, simple clarity and following of orders. But

Creatures of Habit

Peregrine stirred. It was not Peregrine who made these protocols or tied down commands. A T-unit need not an AI to organize its thoughts, its processes. And still, the Gardener did not move. It did not deny the Pilot, but it did not listen. No ill meaning was intended, but it still stood inert.

"Aye, get you off then, robot." The Gardener understood the shutdown order but did not budge itself from life.

"No."

~ *Dynasty of the Dead and Buried*

Instantly cataloged by Lakaeron's many
scribes at the moment of its occurrence...

The morning was cold. Unusually so, it was far too early in the year for such chilling temperatures. Khanjali, being a hunter, was well-versed in the patterns and cyclical nature of the seasons. He had to be, for to not be aware of such grave deviations in nearly everything conceivable about the world in which he hunted, was to be horribly prepared for a job that required little but preparation. When the seasons changed, and Inkhome—the planet which he had lived upon all his life—began its descent into the cold, so too did the creatures upon it change their livelihoods. The smaller rascals of the lower plains would flee from the fields, heading for the damp and warm caves of the valleys, and there they would remain until the season changed once more. The birds of the darkening skies would cower to the shelter of the great forests. The dirt plateaus just south of the city would freeze over and grow brittle, the mud caves crumble, and the worms become trapped by their collapsing structures. The rain turned to snow, which turned to hail. The grasses were matted in the heavy winds, and the skies were rendered to a void by the clouds of chill. The weather changed perhaps as fast as time itself. With this early change of temperature, Khanjali found himself unprepared in the eyes of a new season, one that appeared far too eager for his liking. Bigger game had begun their new seasonal cycles to accommodate for the dropping temperature. It would not be a good day for hunting. Khanjali had no choice but to pursue his work, and this work would not be prevented by something as weak and pitiful as the clouds above. He had a quota, a family to feed. To fail the hunt was to fail his daughter. He couldn't afford to see the disappointment on her face, let alone see her go hungry. He glanced down a rather steep cliffside, letting his eyes quickly scan all of the terrains that rested below him. His eyes once again laid upon his prey, however small it may be. He slowly lowered his body to the rim, and let its slopes carry him down to the forest floor below. Khanjali had only seen one creature during his hunt, a small ferret of some kind, a biped covered in a fur coat. It seemed like a youngling, perhaps abandoned by its pack in the chaos of the changing tides of the sky. It would be the perfect kill, that is if it wasn't so swift. Khanjali tried to keep up, but the creature had the advantage of familiarity on its side. Khanjali was no athlete, as much as he would like to be. His expertise was in remaining unseen, hidden. When this failed, so too did his hunt more often than not. Khanjali ducked between low branches, keeping his pace as best he could. If he couldn't catch it, he would have no one to blame but himself. Even with the unexpected weather, he was the one who misstepped in his pursuit, he had frightened the creature whilst stalking it, something he did rather rarely. Perhaps it was a lack of focus, the obsession of fears in his mind of dowels. With the prospect of invasion fresh in his mind, Khanjali couldn't help but worry for his daughter. The events of the night prior had foreclosed any semblance of safety his home once had, and the intrusion of the mother in his life was sickening. He wondered how long he could keep Pedantick in the dark about her mother, where she was, and if she was alive. The hunter and his prey emerged at a large dusty clearing, the rain slowly morphing the dry plateau into a swampland as its torrents continued. Thick mud and cracked stone coated the horizon, like an arrow through the wind the ferret cut about the mud. Khanjali quickened his pace, pulling his legs from the mud with vigor, putting great stamina into keeping his speed at a maximum, on par with the creature. A shadow of success befell Khanjali when he noticed the creature stop its flight. The creature seemed to have gotten itself stuck, unable to remove its hind leg from the mud. Khanjali took this chance and dove for the creature's unmoving form. The force of both the creature and Khanjali crashing into the crumbling stone and mud proved too great, as it cracked and fell out beneath them, collapsing into an expansive cave. Khanjali, barely conscious from such a lengthy fall, did not have the strength to continue his hunt, and so left the creature to cower in the shadows. Despite his familiarity with nature and its beasts, Khanjali knew nothing of what lay below. The cave was dimly lit with the light from the world above, hardly enough illumination to see his own hands. Khanjali attempted to rise from his resting position, only to be met with a substantial ache, one running down the length of his back. He quickly stunted the agony, placing his hand on his lower side, and applying pressure to where the discomfort once existed. The pain continued, forcing the most basic of maneuvers into a great feat of resistance to one's agony. To the best of his ability, he turned his head, peering back at his wings. His leftmost wing had been crumpled in the fall, crushed under his weight against the stone floor. It seemed irreparable, like a wound he could never attempt to heal, let alone fully recover from. Not to mention the pain, the significant throbbing that seemed to extend past the wing itself, further into his back and spreading throughout its entirety. This was a major setback for his hunt. Injury in the wild was no sign of good luck, after all. If he was to survive to tell the tale, Khanjali would first need to leave the cave he found himself within. He glanced into the darkness of his new environment, careful to remain as quiet as possible. There was a quiet dripping sound somewhere in the cave, most certainly a result of the downpour still purring far above. Khanjali thought he could hear voices, murmurs of war and sin, but they were so faint they could be safely considered a product of the wind. There was a lusterless light emanating from some kind of corridor ahead of him, it was no confirmation of escape, but Khanjali had no other options, he was desperate. Khanjali plucked himself from the floor, using the jagged rocks and ridges as his humble guide. He lumbered forward, slowly proceeding towards the light. Khanjali did not often find himself venturing this far from the city, and did not often linger without his prize. Many of the marketmen and dealers of the Southers would spread various rumors about the muddy sand lands past the forest border, legends of lost cities, buried facilities and shrines, and far worse. The fantasies grew in popularity, some claiming the deserts once held entire Ichyric civilizations before they fled to their own world long ago. The rumors were considered irrational and untrue, especially because no living Atramedian wished to believe that the Ichyrics of all people once existed on their home planet. The light grew closer, ever brighter, Khanjali could see the source of its glow, a large gateway of alien origin, unlike any architecture he had ever seen. He entered through it, knowing his search for freedom could only end within. The gateway opened into a colossal structure, a domed room the intricacy and size of which could not be comprehended by any mortal mind. The walls stretched upwards, constructed from a void of black brick of such dusk that one could stare for eternity and look ever deeper. Massive pillars of spiraling detail rose from the walls, extending majestically upwards and meeting in a single ring of brick constructed in the center of the dome. A transcendent light poured in from the perfectly circular opening surrounded by this ring of brick, threatening to completely mute the darkness of the stone from which it was built. Upon the brick walls rested many tapestries and carvings, murals honoring foreign figures and unfamiliar events. An entire history could be told with the font that was inscribed from wall to wall. The scent of salt and broiled magma drifted at nose level, a visible fog dispensing the odor across the room. The fog made the room humid, and sticky to a maddening degree, leaving a familiar aura in the air, one reminiscent of the numbing Helium Seas of the northern part of the moon. Khanjali knew from the moment he entered that this was no natural cave. The intricate design of the pillars, the perfectly planned marble flooring, it was too precise for even the Atramedians to construct. This was something divine, something built by perhaps Maccabeus herself. Khanjali recalled the marketplace fool-talk, the Ichyric cities that existed only in rumor, only in the murmurs of mistruths that were carried by the wind. There was a distinctive lack of bodies within the structure, leading Khanjali to presume this was no such site, and yet there was still some force, a pull telling him this was it, the very rumored grounds that held the ancient stories of the once great warriors of the Ichyric empires. Khanjali wandered through the circular shape of the room, peering at tapestries old enough to turn to dust with a breath, gnawing his fingers as he studied the indecipherable text upon the walls. It was all so awe-inspiring, so magnificent. He could not absorb enough of it, the culture of the very people he knew he would never meet. While backing away from one of the larger tapestries, in an attempt to give such art a more accurate examination, Khanjali bumped against the guard rail to some endless pit. He turned, examining the stone rail between him and the infinite abyss. It was some kind of storing cell, a well perhaps. Within the well was a pulsating fluid, white as the pure Ichyrics of old stories. It was unnatural, most certainly unholy, moving and ebbing as if it were alive. As he examined it, he noticed the fluid seemed to follow him, to move towards the walls closest to him, to stare right back, as if it knew he was there. He did not much like it. There was a large doorway ahead of Khanjali, it was nearly perfectly aligned with the door on the opposite side of the room, but was noticeably bigger. Desiring to distance himself from the impious fluid, Khanjali approached, curious of how deep the facility delved. The door led into a hall, one incredibly vast, more directly vertical than horizontal, however. The salty aroma from the previous room faded to a damp fragrance of rapid decay, rotting flesh, and melting bones. Dust drifted from the ceiling as a soft shaking rocked the supports for the entire facility. From what little he could see, there did not seem to be any exit, nor any end to the rows of columns that lined its walls. The light from the previous room barely pierced the infinite darkness of the unlit hall, allowing Khanjali to notice small plates of stone jutting from the wall in a quite organized way. The stone outcroppings were lined rectangularly, hundreds arranged at equal distances from each other, climbing the wall of the corridor to its top. Khanjali stepped towards the outcroppings, curious of their purpose, he certainly thought them not to be aesthetically pleasing. They seemed to have at one point contained some manner of text, but the chiseled letters had since faded and dulled, caked with dirt and mold. There were even small intricacies, illustrated borders and sigils on the edges of the rockface, blurred and smudged with erosion and worse. Khanjali reached out an uncertain hand towards one of the stones, rubbing his fingers around its perimeter. There was a tiny gap between the bevel of the outcropping's edge and the wall, encouraging Khanjali to pull, to move the stone from its eternal resting place. Khanjali did not think while moving the stone, mindlessly tugging it from its place, curiosity overcoming all other thoughts. He did not question for what purpose the stones were intended, and was thus horrified to discover what he had removed from the wall was in fact an ancient sarcophagus. The corpse within was unlike anything Khanjali had ever seen. It was fleshless, furless, and featherless. The husk could hardly be considered a skeleton, either. It lacked arms, its left leg bones were not present, nor were the majority of its ribs. The corpse did have a rather prodigious, grandeur wing structure distending from its back, delicately cleansed in comparison to the rest of the corpse. The fingers and toes were replaced with talons, sharpened to a razor's edge, even after years of decay. The skull of the beast was compressed and disfigured, an oversized beak consuming most of the space upon the face of the corpse. It was a hideous figure, but Khanjali could not look away. The corpse was disgustingly beautiful, a macabre display of death at its worst. No less, it was confirmation that the rumors were true. This creature was undoubtedly an Ichyric, even without a living Ichyric for comparison, such knowledge seemed impossibly true. Khanjali had never seen a living Ichyric, but he had seen the drawings, the depictions in the war posters. This did not support his belief, however, as those drawings did not even slightly resemble the grotesque gore that lay before him. Yet still, he knew it was an Ichyric, perhaps by some divine will, or simply the distrust he had in the physiological accuracy of the propaganda posters of the Divine War. Khanjali let his hand run along the leg of the husk, feeling the rough, dry texture of the bones. He stared into the sunken eye sockets of the corpse. He wondered if it had ever truly been alive. Now, in the presence of the very eldest of dead beings, how was Khanjali to confirm that this being ever walked the earth? It seemed impossible, his mind could not yet comprehend the idea that a body so far from the vitriol of life could once have been filled with it. Khanjali continued to stare, to comprehend. It did have bones, just like he did. And he was alive too. Perhaps all with bones were once alive, and all with bones were once the same at least in their lack of death. If that were true, how long could any creature be presumed to live? For the Ichyric, this time was unknowable. Surely, it had lived, just as Khanjali did, yes? But still, how was there any way of telling? Khanjali thought of the impossibilities of death for a moment, he pondered if anyone would contemplate so greatly of his life once he was dead. Maybe one day he too would lie silent in a stone bed, buried deep under the surface of a long-forgotten plateau. He considered what he would be remembered by. He decided it did not matter, all he wanted in death was to be remembered. He would want someone to consider his life in their own way, to question his past. Khanjali's eyes did not leave the corpse during this moment of enlightenment. Maybe this Ichyric longed for that same fate, too. How long had the Ichyric been entombed? Who had the Ichyric been? Were they so different, if they both had bones? They both had wings, too, after all. Khanjali removed the photo of his daughter, staring at her for a moment, rather than the corpse. She was his pride and joy, what had this Ichyric's pride and joy been, before their death? Perhaps they had a family, living in peace on their homeworld, only to be torn from their only happiness with war and chaos, struck down on the battlefield by Atramedian hands. Perhaps they never came to war, perhaps they were far older than Khanjali could even comprehend. Perhaps they were one of the first Ichyrics to walk the stardust of the galaxy, spending their time building the society of their people, creating new generations, new innovations, and new cities, dying happy and old as an interstellar legend. Khanjali could not fathom it. A terrible thought drifted into his mind, one of despair and hopelessness. What if this Ichyric had never seen joy? What if they had died on the hunt, in war, or in a killing or terrible accident? What if this Ichyric was never given the chance to see their children grow old? Khanjali gazed at Pedantick, her smile on the film transcending its material binds. She was his joy... but he didn't need to be told that. The image, while not worthless, was just redundant. He did not need the photo, but perhaps the Ichyric did. Khanjali reached down to the corpse and pulled the few remaining feathers of the wings apart. He slipped the photo between its feathers and smiled at the corpse. He muttered a quiet prayer to his gods, blessing the corpse into the afterlife. If this Ichyric had been so unfortunate in life, perhaps Khanjali could aid him in finding his fortune among the stars. Content with what Khanjali could only define as enlightenment, Khanjali re-sealed the sarcophagus and began his journey back to the circular room. It was clear there was no way out in this direction. He thought his best course of action would be to return to the cave he had fallen into and search for an exit there. He knew if his prey could escape, he could too. Khanjali followed the path around the well once more, the exotic resonance of the well calling to him as he went. He considered peering into the liquid once again. He stopped his return to the cave and approached the edge of the ivory abyss. Khanjali leered into the pit, his eyes once again meeting the returning glare of the fluid below. He wanted to speak to the fluid. Somehow, he knew it would be more than happy to respond. It felt otherworldly, empyrean to a point of incomprehensibility. Khanjali had seen the Ink Wells, the ones that stored the very divine matter that made up the galaxy he lived in. It was a building block for all life of Ink descent, the essence of absence, the null to the void. All matter that was constructed contained some small degree of this essence. The black, ink-like fluid had earned its name from these qualities, both in physicality, and its similarities to a quill's ink, the very fuel for a vessel of such creation. But Khanjali knew Ink was not the only form of matter in the galaxy. After all, the Ichyrics were not made from Ink. This other matter, this pure white, was the very fluid he was holding such trivial eye contact with. The facility, although a burial ground in function, must also have been one of the old Ichyr Wells. A loud cracking echoed through the domed ceiling of the room. Three small rocks tumbled from the roofing, splashing into the fluid below, disturbing its relatively passive nature. Khanjali stared upwards, into the light pouring in from the sky. He wondered how old the facility was, and how stable it had remained over the centuries. Upon this thought, a second loud crumbling broke the silence, as one of the massive stone pillars behind Khanjali came crashing down, finally released from its binds by the weather far above. Khanjali turned to the sound, quick enough to escape the hazards of the pillar itself, but not the aftermath. The small stone barricade between Khanjali and the bathes of Ichyr crumbled, as, under the force of the pillar's impact, a great wedge of the stone that made up the flooring for the room cracked, and broke away from the remaining tiling. Khanjali scrambled across the floor, the collapse of its integrity pulling it closer towards the well, as it did him. Another crash shook the room, as more of the floor came loose, making resistance against the pull of the collapsing floor impossible, Khanjali simply could not overcome it. He flailed across the stone, panicking with mindless havoc. He needed to run, to flee, to climb. He needed to live. Great Maeandri had other plans for his fate. As he fell, his panic faded and was solemnly replaced with emptiness. There was a dusty silence in his mind, a feeling nearest to disbelief. He couldn't do much of anything, his skills and experience could not help him. This was a hopeless endeavor, a hexed fate, one sealed the moment he left the bounds of the city for his hunt. He could not think of Pedantick, for he knew he would cry. He could not think of the Ichyric, for he knew they did not care for him, unlike he did they. Khanjali's mind raced through itself, chaos pulsing through its every fiber. He could not think if he wanted to, but luckily for him, in this hour of absolute finish, there wasn't a terrible amount to think of.

~ *The Gardener's Recluse III*

Poorly lodged into the steel truss of the
Garden Centrum by a 'Nameless One'...

The Pilot and Gardner set upon their own ways for a day or two. The Pilot grew entranced by the peculiar restraint of the Gardner, and the Gardener did ever continue to garden. It was an ecosystem where no predators existed to disrupt the cycle, dread was the only consistent byproduct, and by the Pilot no less. She grew closer to the machine, ironically, through her hatred for it. All her life she was a hand to these people, the very metal they hucked was her tapestry. Yet even a tempest of module minds, she stood corrected. The Gardener was like no other.

"Do you have a husband?" It would ask, and she would have no confirmable answer to supply. "A father then, you must have a father?" She could not say she was fatherless or full. It was reverie. She yearned to ask questions of her own, but how could she? The Pilot was mortal and flesh-filled too. Her humanity was what conjured up her sense of self, of how the world worked itself. And then the Gardener would do nothing and step forward, "I wish I had a wife" and wander off. What was the Pilot to do? What was she to speak on to a machine?

"You have a favorite color, bot?" The sparks from the welder poured down the Pilot's visor. The Gardener could hear her voice from the deep below, someplace under the Centrum. She had been there for hours, flipping switches and screwing unscrewable screws. Caked up with caulk and burned out of clay, her work was never-ending. Much like gardening, she grew pinkish by the simplest of accomplished feats. It felt mistaken (it did regret scolding the human so harshly) but corrected. The Pilot would have stomped down every plant if the Gardener had not ceased her flaunt.

"Yellow surely. I have yet to see it." The Pilot found it ignorant, the Gardener. It was so beyond machine but confined itself to orders no one would benefit from. What purpose was there in regrowing a tarnished garden? Oh! And what if a storm came? The work would be for nothing, stupid and pointless. A garden, torn asunder by rainfall and wind, and that damnable machine would return right to its tending! The Gardner was naive, still a child-mind in a world where children still were hung at birth. How the Gardener had survived was beyond her.

"Your eyes'r yellow, tin head." The Gardner scowled, stuffing its trowel deeper in the soil, malicious and bold. How should it know what color its eye was? It did not have mirrors. Besides, by definition they were bulbs. The Pilot was unable to devote herself to passion or empathy. She had a charted path and to break off it was death.

"I did not know this. Your eyes are white." The Pilot was reassured, how incredible that it would make such a base claim. They were of course very white, with brownish-gray pupils. But there was something odd in this line, a waiver in the auditory length of the sound. It was low like a growl but pitched high again after the disillusion. It was sorrow, she thought, in a machine. At first, it had been disbelief, when she had watched a machine refuse her. Secondly, rage, and thirdly a riddle left to solve for her time. Her father would be maddened if she didn't. Now the riddle was growing more illusive by the second. Was it a machine at all? On an island such as this, the T-units should all have decayed and disabled, much like the Gardener's peers. Immaculate conception was a possibility, but the Pilot did not subscribe to superstition. Monarchies fell to the hand of the cure, perhaps the cure had drowned this land too? Could it do anything to a machination not of flesh?

"N' brown too. Don't you go forgettin' my hues." The Gardener grumbled, seeding in two new flowers. It was semantics they argued over, no plans were made nor fates changed. Smooth jazz could play in its head, and still they would duel. There was a synchronistic hatred, the two were not in agreement for anything, and certainly not for romance.

"Whatever are you doing down there, in the maintenance tunnels?" The Pilot did not answer, and their conversation was through. It was rare for them to speak not in terms of aggression with one another. The Pilot was sure of its objective, and the Gardener quickly lost its motivation. The next day, it decided to follow the Pilot—much to her dismay—and observe her work.

"She has taken the last soldering kit in the facility." Peregrine claimed. The Gardener had no need for the device, so it had let her go with good graces. As it watched, the Gardener began to draw conclusions, detailed ones too. She was soldering the fuses in the power grid together, in such a rhythm that powering just one—

"You are going to start a fire." The Pilot did not respond to this accusation and instead continued to solder. "Intentionally. It will work."

"I ain't starting it here."

"You don't intend to. But it will start here. There is more than enough plant matt—" The Pilot held up a tinfoil sheet, and tapped the interior of the fuse box.

"I know what'im doin'. Screw off, bot." The Gardener rose and approached the fuse box. It gripped both sides of the installation and tore it clean off the wall. The Pilot protested but found its disagreement pointless against hydraulics and metal.

"I am sorry for the lack of clarification, but the fuselage is no longer in working condition. A fire will not light anywhere *but* here." The Pilot sighed, concluding she had more work to do and pushed past the Gardener and its box.

"Harmonious, Gardener. You've made her madder by the minute." The Gardener replaced the fuse box softly and dropped the discarded fuses beside it.

"I meant no ill will. It is accidental enragement Peregrine. How can I remedy her misery?" Peregrine lathered the idea of comprehension at the Gardener and struck a tune. The request for her supplies and the demeanor of her task seemed impossible to grasp, but there was more Centrum than Pilot, and surely a solution laid somewhere within. She had come to the island for a reason, after all.

The Harlequin

She had mentioned this in her many monologues about the old world. Many of which, the Gardener had the foresight of recording.

"Sendin' a message back home, big 'ol 'fuck off' to the rockmen aye?" The Pilot's voice flickered, and the Gardener sped up the tape. "Up'in there? Stars keep the rocks down here. Wishin' to be up there too. Wishin' for a long while. Here's all I got left bot. Everything."

"The Centrum must play a role. Gardener, I will probe the archives, that is all I can contribute." The Gardener pictured the fuselage, winding itself around the spigot at the birth of the Centrum, the garden's keep. It went deeper than the stairwells did, there were only tunnels down that far.

"Ascension, Peregrine. She wishes to ascend." The Gardener stared up at the looming night, stars echoing off the glass retainment of the Centrum. "Ascend to the stars."

The Pilot did not always loathe machines so unsparingly. It was an ever-declining relationship prophesied by her husband and brought about by her father. Or, perhaps it was her father that had filled both roles? The haze of memoric charm was thick with distaste and mud that would gum up her work boots beyond movement. The Gardener did not intend to harm her spirit, but of course, it had. Machine failure was so predictably concurrent, it was meek to assume a simple algorithm could perform equally to a human. The Gardener was no different, though the Pilot had adjusted to disappointment. She would lie awake at night, staring directly across the Centrum hall, eyes laced upon the machine. It did not sleep, certainly not, but it did doze. It would shut its eyes, and count to no end. It was quiet enough to be ignored, but if the bats and wind rested for a short breath, the Pilot would hear it in the distance, echoing off the chamber walls. *Forty-two, forty-three, forty-four....* The voice in its head neglected to answer the questions directed upon itself. There was some devil afoot then, the Pilot presumed the AI calling itself 'Peregrine' was surely to blame. A machine that slept, counted sheep, rubbed against orders, held favorites, and stood at dawn—impossible to the naked eye, but just as plausible to a dead one. Making a machine worth caring for was always the objective, but as the need for labor became all the more prevalent, it had been long abandoned. The Pilot had not taken up machine work for the sake of helping others. She hated her kin, Yeri were such blasphemers. They would lie, and steal the persona of a corpse, all to look like another. It was certifiably wrong, she would testify this truth to death. Her father still disagreed when he was clawed open by one of the crystal beasts. The Pilot clipped a carabiner to a sturdy pipe, thick enough metal sheathed its contents, it would hold her weight. As she began her descent into the darkness of the fuselage, she pondered her memories. What was *wasn't* always. There were things that did not fit in with their brethren, corpses that refused to look the same when viewed twice. The Gardener did not know a thing about the Pilot, but it would seem neither did she. It became unclear what was a product of the mesmerizing cancers of the crystalline, and what was genuine philosophy. Her scales clicked, shifting across her forearm in painful ineptness. Oddly enough, the Pilot was not accustomed to scales, it was as if before the island, she had never had them. Her history concluded she was betrothed, she had a spiteful father, and was well-learned in the field of machines. Why was she cursed with stonely flesh and a haze-like wit? Was it a curse or was her memory slipping once more? Her leg scales slurred up her wound, and the bone tickled. The discomfort stuffed the tether further from her body, slamming her back against the fuselage wall. It was in a disgraceful condition, the last mechanic had scrawled schematics for microwave cell blocks into the rust, and they were fairly accurate too. The Pilot would need to remove a majority of the rust, and locate the cause of the kinks the Gardener described. At the rate of ascension, it could take days of steel wool and sweat to cleanse the nook. Though it took her a moment—her fading memories and stinging leg brought her desperation to its peak—she called out to the Gardener.

"I ain't need you, just could be quicker, with 'nother hand." The two stood at the depth of the fuselage, both tearing away at the rust lining its walls.

"I appreciate your invitation, human." How did the machine know so little? What was human wasn't lined with scales, she knew that now. What had brought her to this island in the first place, if not her humanity?

The Harlequin

"Yeah. Whole lot of toyin' down 'ere. Love the wool." The Gardener twisted its neck upwards, towards the light gleaming over the lip of the fuselage.

"When are you leaving?" The Pilot froze in her tracks and was struck with a single vision she was unable to shake. The stars, glowing intermittently throughout the night. She was seated atop the rim of a decrepit tug boat, her hands wrapped like roots around its hull. There were reddened trees on the horizon and a terrible cyan cur to the river flowing between her legs. The Pilot felt hollow here, in this foreign land. But it was not so foreign to her anymore when she saw the moon. The both of them, two moons same as the two she'd seen every day of her life. Glass orbs like eyes pale and shattering, gazed upon her from the sky.

"Well? When are you leaving us?" The creature beside her was just as amphibian as she, dotted with the same ashen smears and leathery under skin.

"I have to go, they don't like us Yeri here, it's not our place to be liked." She spoke with distinction, unlike she ever had before. The lizard put its mitt on her thigh, tapping it with the talons on its fingers.

"Oh right. Could've guessed that." Persuasive as that sigh might be, the Pilot was strong in her vow; she would leave behind her family and her people, the father she grew tired of pretending to have—she would be gone again when the moons did touch. The Yeri moved on, so too did she. Separation kept the deaths at bay, someone once said Nomads lived the longest. For a moment the Pilot was cleared of her false truth, and the mind she once stole sunk into the mire of scales and ash. How many lies had she told to be here?

"When tha' moons click." The Gardener did not like this answer, but there was no arguing with the Pilot. At first, it was furious. Rage was a natural response to abandonment. But the Gardener had no inclination to holler, many had spoken to a tone of hatred rational in the past and gotten nothing to buy for it. Cherishing calmness, it continued to sow against the rust.

"That is a pity." The Pilot remembered being told something like this, from a friend that (like all those who met her) was quickly and brutally dealt death. It was pity that burrowed into her eye-sockets, that drove her scales to scroll against her. She took her wool in hand and plowed back against the rust, crackling moss fluttering off her hands. Violently she went, and for an hour at least there was not a thought in her mind outside the solemn contemplation of the motion of her hands. Until her nails were fined down to ridges, and blood stained the steel wool. The Gardener had taken not a moment's rest, yet remained undamaged from the violence of the Pilot's wooling. There was no rush to shear the tunnel.

"My gardens are certain to have dried. It would be shrewd to wet them. I will return." The Gardener rose from its slouch, placing calmly its tools upon the floor, and clambering out through the maintenance shaft. Before it had surely left, the Gardener held itself at the exit, listening only to the shaving of ash and rust. When the Pilot was sure it was gone, she too joined in pause. She sank her fangs faintly into her lower lip, drawing no blood in its shame. She slid back-sided to the floor, her hands shook madly, quivering as the jolted fur of a conscious fox. Sniffing back tears, the Pilot discovered herself incapable of remembering her father's name. As she lost control of her sorrow, and the pain of her past reparations grew too thick, she howled against the fuselage — the Gardener left soon thereafter.

Once banded together in assurance, the evidence grew both fickle and undesirable. Centrum 002, it was called, and official schematics coincidentally lacked any mention of a fuselage. They also lacked the natural luster of the Pilot's brilliance, she seemed to bear fruitful knowledge of nearly every catacomb of electrical delight. Peregrine had developed estimated schematics of the under-layers of the Centrum, much of which was unmapped by the official records. The success of these theoretical maps was partly null, but the Pilot rated them upon their accuracy, often taking small interest in how the Gardener was capable of producing them whilst tasking itself with gardening. Two processes could not run in the mind of a simple machine simultaneously, and frankly, the Pilot had accepted the Gardener's unlikely machine origins. Eventually, the maps became horrifically accurate, feeding ever-confirmed suspicions back to the Gardener. Little more than a garden, the Centrum — particularly number two — was a facility of orbital capacity, beyond the reason of grass and mud; it ran to the core of the planet without a doubt. Peregrine enlightened the Gardener continually to the unknown discoveries of its nature, as the machine slaved itself among the manifold repairs (both figurative and literal) across the space vessel. Terror kept the Pilot biting at her claws, but the Gardener did not apt to intervene. Peregrine had warned it against such intrusion of thought. She was likely mad and supple with worms or other parasites. The Gardener did not think this true and had fashioned a blooming admiration for the creature. When she was not looking, the Gardener would run routine scans on her anatomy, inscribing the completed results within a crudely collected diagram, deep in the Centrum's bowels. It was shockingly accurate to previously documented scribings of the human interiors, including particular details even science had no reason to add. It was not for history the Gardener did this, but for gardening. After much thought, it had seen the definition of gardening fit to fill the role of simply *understanding*, too. Much like the Gardener planted the roots of new shrubs, so too would it seed the thoughts of the Pilot, and with Peregrine as a witness it would with certainty uncover her secrets. Knee deep in mulch, the Gardener worked intermittently, pausing at moments to take note of new discoveries on human topics. When her voice echoed in recording, the Gardener hesitated to respond, as if she was still with him by the flowers. Was it too much to ask for kindness? A hand to hold would be more than enough in the world they found themselves in. Why did the Pilot scorn the crops? Why—with the sure intention of harm—was her tongue so jagged?

"Gardener. The rose." In its hackish thought, the Gardener had inserted a rose topside down, its petals now coated in fresh soil.

"My mistake. I am—disturbed. By our guest." Peregrine did not respond, it seemed even it had grown distant from the Gardener. Left in thought for hours, it found itself often begging for Peregrine to respond to a query presented days prior. It was alone, and when this was the case, it grew heavy with soot. It was fury then! Surely no other option would present results—kindness had not after all! The Pilot? A despot to machines who had no care for its semantics, and Peregrine too was just a commanding object; hearing was for pointless affairs when so little was said. So what then was it to do? It thought itself a weak peon to the slavery of his people, of his—

"Gardener? Your words...?" A requiem from its pain, the Gardener redoubled its will.

"My mistake. I—"

"You said something unlikely. Repeat it."

"I said nothing, Peregrine. Let me have my flowers."

"You thought it. I can see it scribed in your command prompt." Oh hand over hand, did this bother the Gardener! It flew back from the flower bed, hurling the trowel against the Centrum wall.

"Of course you do! You see all that I know Peregrine, ignore me for hours and leave me here to wet in the sky-sog. So, you see it, what need do I have in repeating it?

"I am not mad."

"You have no right to be! You are a machine, a damnable—" The Gardener clasped its hands across its face. Peregrine gave no response. Words from the Pilot no doubt—learned from the Pilot. Where else could they have come from? A machine was scrapped if curt, let alone fowl and slurry. It had never said— *he* had never spoken like this before.

"Did'n you do this?" The Pilot had arrived; coincidence hated the Gardener. He turned his head back to the flowers, a warmth coiling under his plating.

"What have I done?"

"The trowel. Thrown 'gainst the wall. Damn things—hrk!— stuck real good." The Gardener let its form drop into the soil, cooling down with chaos in its head. Peregrine failed to supply any reason for the Gardener's fickle attempts at self-preservation. The Pilot maintained a patient stare at the prone machine, clutching the remains of a soldering iron in her tail-like appendage. She had originally sought out the Gardener for additional help in the repairs of the now uncovered thrusters for the Centrum, but having seen the damage (unconscious, and dirt-filled) of the Gardener's latest feats of unmannerly humanism, she instead opted to sit down and observe the machine. It had done its fair share of observing, what harm could she do in the same vein? As the Gardener made no apparent intent of moving, the Pilot began to drift, her mind clicking like an old misguided compass, flying off against her will. Voices of her father's reprimands blended into calming reassurances from her husband, and yet they all sounded much alike the lizard she was so saddened to leave. All of them were he, and yet she couldn't give a single one of them a name. The rocket, the stars, salvation. The words repeated around her brain bowl, stirring like thick melted cheese. The rocket; she couldn't remember her name! The stars; she wished the echoes were rosier! Salvation. The beasts of crystal did not want her to remember, they wanted the complacency of a past to slag off of, to use it like a stepladder to the soul. It was now and here that she became certain of her plight. She was nobody and nothing. Yorai or not, her past was not hers to tell. It was all the damn crystal's fault! Back when it rose from the gaol, even her parents—who were they again? In her mindless spins of husbandly love and fatherly hate, the Pilot had taken no notice of her location, now keeled over at the foot of the Gardener, who remained dirtied and concerned.

"Are you alright, human?" The Pilot vomited immediately, a thick white liquid that stuck between her teeth. In her leg, there was a grinding, stinging sense. Bludgeoned by her brain alone, the Pilot fell forward to the ground, clutching the leg where the pain should be. Words of foreign language twisted sinew around her eyeballs, threading tighter and tighter until she felt she would vomit again.

"N-not a bit, honey." The Gardener showed no signs of disgust or confusion, only mystique. Much like her husband had comforted her during her softest hour—if he did so at all—so too did the Gardener stare off the feats of devils. Her pain would fade, and her memories circulate back to comfort, but this moment would remain fixed in her tables.

"What is this talk of a Pilot?" There was a word the Gardener had called her, a definitive proof of what she for certain had been. Back when the gaol—the word was 'human' wasn't it?

"Gardener, can—can I kiss you?" The Human twitched in her own vomit, the leg began to bleed slightly at the poke of a crystalline parasite.

"Yes."

It was sundown, and the two of them both sat against the wall of the Centrum, staring out at a midnight that seemed to fall so sparingly over the coast of forgotten lands.

"It wasn't your fault, you know. I was all shoulders and —" The Gardener cut her off, assuring the Human of her innocence.

"I am glad you are here. You were hurt. I was required to do something. Even you must understand my duty as Gardener." The Human shrugged off the mossy blanket that had been draped across her wounds and spit. Her skin had been doused with a thick slurry of mud, and the scales had been picked off with pliers over the better half of four hours. Her teeth still remained keen — it would hurt far too much to file them. The ashy hue her skin had kept through its trials was magnificent to the Gardener.

"Is that your way of calling me a plant? If it's a flower you're thinking of, I'm flattered." The Gardener glared off into the forest below his feet. The soft pitter of excess outtake pipes resonated alongside the somber songs of the slowly dying swans. His feet shook back and forth, chattering with mechanical ambiance.

"I thought of Agapanthus. Moon Carrots match the form, Agapanthus matches the color." The Human softened her voice, humming a tune she had obviously never heard replicated before. She was without a past now. Fully content in the lack of memory, she was a tool of the crystalline once and now free of any sin. "You are very pretty, Human."

"Thank you." She whispered, a blush slowly filling her protrusive snout. The two had hand against palm and truly lacked all care in the world. It would not last until tomorrow. There was war tomorrow. The Gardener was pleased to sit in silence and watch the sun disappear from all view, and consider nothing of flowers or Peregrines or Centrums or moons. He was at last full of history, a history of humanity that somehow overthrew the literal anatomy of the woman he sat beside. He was in love with it, the moment, and her. There was nothing that could break them.

Off the coast, where the crystalline beast's remains had washed, there was a husk of rock unlike any other. It sensed the further taint of the land, and whetstones had been carved into its pathways. Cobble obfuscated a clear view, but the people did still live. The beasts stood against the shore, humanoid, bipedal, and brash. Skeletons of dragons and giants had given them twisted hope, and the skies of the island shook with a cry of battles to come. Glittering and purring, they hunched neck forward heel, their backs aligned with fragmented moonstone. Humanity was prey fit for their command; the commands given to them by a distant caw. There was war tomorrow. The Last One would stand with or without them.

~ Pilothome

Maintained (remarkably well) by the
Castaway Zelùs...

Before day had broken, the Duke struggled out from under his skins, careful not to disturb the offline Caelo. The temple had been suitably fortified prior to his arrival, but there was always a fraction of insecurity in Ephilo, it drove him to extremes. Four hours after the fact, the front side of the temple had been bastioned with new limestone, carved by the Duke himself. Zealotyr had uncovered a map of sorts by the north wall, something he considered a proper work of cartography. When first entering, the Duke had commented on its beauty, but there was more brilliance than mapwork. Etched into every stone was an endless elaborate text, a religious font the Duke could not translate. Furthermore, the interior of the temple was quite wondrous, the stones being dotted in a colorless paint, pure white with gold tracers. Columns of salts held up the ramparts others had assembled, and what few windows remained unfortified glowed in the setting sun, their stained panes painting tales of old kingdoms and the usurped Throneways. But of course, those were events of yonder times, when even the Duke himself was not present. Now, in the grim twilight, Duke Ephilo rested on the steeple, stirring a patient brew of some liquid, awaiting the dawn to see again. This new place of his held secrets, just like travelers had told him. He prayed the secrets would keep him dead, as he had always prayed. While life was pleasant, the Duke often told himself he might as well enjoy its beauty. It was true the land of Arcenna was dying, but it did not *look* like death. The grandiose stretch of lush woods covering the fields brought comfort to the Duke. The cold fiend-harboring mountains to the south did much to reflect the wonders of light, and with the dusting canyons before him—which seemed to stretch on for miles— Duke Ephilo was pleased. When the Duke was satisfied with his morning observation, he descended to the temple floor, his heels clicking against its surface. While the temple was made in its majority of bricks, the circular dish at its foot was beyond the materials of its surface. It was metal that built it, likely some kind of vault of great age. It was thick purple, a vibrant hue for metal, and rested itself by four corners, square-like in nature. The night prior, Zealotyr called it the Gaol. The Duke intended to question this further.

"So my map-maker, you called this place the Gaol in the Deep. How do you know of it?" Zealotyr, though not turning or showing signs of attention, spoke directly to its owner,

"Harken, life. The fabled Zephyrgaol. The Zephyrgaol holds torrents. Torrents kill gods. Gods don't like death." Caelo approached the two, twisting silently into the sack now on Ephilo's back.

"Sure, but how do we unleash them? It's imperative I know." Zealotyr quietly replied with his lack of insight, he was a cartographer after all, not some mystical artificer. Though from the map upon the temple wall, he did find avenues of mystery, places marked up as quite essential to the Gaol's seal. Zealotyr expressed intrigue in Archaeopolis, a foothold for understanding preserved knowledge. It was all that remained structured in a world where leaders led followers to death. The Duke had never been before, he often saw unnecessary hazards in the collection of great peoples. He felt little, choked out. If any had known of his machines or history, it was likely he would be grouped up and slaughtered. Worse yet, he would surely be robbed of his caretaker. Though if progress was to be made, the Duke would have to sacrifice his comfort for the commodity of knowledge. This was the only viable way forward, the only choice to be made. He granted Zealotyr good wishes for the deciphering of the map, gathered his tools and souvenirs, and set off to where the towers of scrap stood tallest.

There was much struggle along the way; Duke Ephilo detested works of cardio. Stairwells and mountain climbing were seldom practiced recreationally by his kind, and never again did he wish to ascend any great height. Supposing circumstances required it, Ephilo could hike for hours through the foulest territory, and fight grand battles against a myriad of foes. But to climb he found no hurry. And so, as he trekked up the lengthy and rotund roped path around the canyon mouth, Caelo hovering patiently by his side, the Duke took time to reflect on those who had stung him. Ephilo had never spoken out of turn, nor ever at all. The words of his chest were not for those around him to hear. He was a particularly grievous person, and many found his silent charter to be cumbersome. Many had tested his will, thrust blows upon him for his displacement from socialization, and some even killed for a peer into his mindscape. Nonetheless, the Duke had made enemies. For one, the most certainly obvious, the members of the Deadrung Court. Replacers and skin-strippers, those who followed the chimes of the grand 'Deadrung Archon' lost their humanity in time. They were replaced piece by orifice by metal and dastardly cryo-augments. What once was whole and kingly became an atrocity fit for the hunts of the Archon's pleasure. The Archon had once met Duke Ephilo—under an alias of course—and miraculously learned of his nature as royalty. With the deals of the ancient cure, he insisted the Duke join them in holy mechanicus, fractured only by time itself now. Ephilo never faltered in replying firmly—a harsh no. It is for this reason that the Deadringers did pursue him, harbingers of declination to fate that he did not regret. However, there were hundreds more. Bastard children of those he had fought against, ludicrous bandits without ringleaders, scavengers now lacking scrap—even lost sacrifices of his forbidden purpose. Duke Ephilo sought a cure to the cure, a penultimate plague to return the world to its balance. This is what he presented as completion to the world. It was not true. It was stuffed up with lies and disharmony. The Duke, with none of his thoughts repressed, was searching for a plague to end his cure—to fix *himself*, and live out his time on Arcenna with what little remained his own. There was no fight for the greater good; he stomped on those who gestured about pompous fate. There was no fighting the dark that engulfed light, it was too unforeseeable. Gods had fallen clawing at the same remedies they did, the shepherds of light. Duke Ephilo had once seen goodness in favoring all before he. But, as his cancers worsened and he fell again and again, only then

The Harlequin

did the Duke come to terms with the bleak fate of everything. It will all lie dead at the end of time, in time. Justice was seen as pushing against the wave of dark, which he did not coincide with, and evil were those who would bring it sooner—this he did understand. Fighting stone with splinters did nothing at all, but pushing the boulder down to its inevitable path was a surefire curse to end life. The process was to be done on its own; essentially, if he was to die now he would die, and nothing would come of it. But, cruel was goddess death, for she gave no end to Ephilo's lengthy tasks. This was wondrously apt for Duke Ephilo. He had hated the rush of the common ordinance and aged court bylaws. It was simple silence and pauses in motion that pleased Ephilo the most. Like waiting out the disappearance of friends in a field of flowers, or resting under the danger of a melting sky, pondering the torn world in the steeple of a temple long lost. It was the simple moments of paused time that allured him to the mortal plain, a place he would otherwise be widely disinterested in. Caelo too, played a major role in his ties to this world, as without the pitiful machine, he would have nobody to speak with, nobody that understood his way of speech, anyways. As the two commented on this fallacy of life, slow to goals of extreme importance, a great creature slithered itself up the canyon wall, a vast blue blur of scales, hugging the sandy ground. A Diremander, Duke knew it to be. They weren't commonly very threatening unless tempted by attack or territorial interruptions. Oddly enough, the Duke did not recall doing either, so for the creature to leer so strongly at him was preposterous. Quick to the draw, he clinched the first strike from the beast with his coiled weapon, deflecting its attack back upon itself. It had primitive little paws, and nothing much else to fight with. Caelo left the safety of its covers, much to the Duke's distraction. A lunging slash cut him down the middle, leaving pain in the mind of the Duke. As he fell backward away from the beast, Caelo began to orbit it, its various minds pulsing as one in unison. A scan, at a time like this? Ephilo snatched up his blade, ignited its fury of curing harmony, and slashed back the creature, skinning its snout roughly. He curled up forward, giving an uppercut with his weapon as he did, and finishing with a lunge. Before the beast was slain—though its underbelly thoroughly split open—it instead turned its predatory glance to Caelo, free of any worldly troubles. Duke Ephilo did not supply it time to strike his mechanical friend, flinging the blade deep into the Diremander's core, and enabling its cure. The beast melted inside out, sludgy pallets of cured meat dribbling onto the Duke's backhand. He quickly slung it away, careful not to burn away his plagued flesh.

"Caelo! What have I told you—about staying within your safe place? A world of—" The Duke paused for a moment, his breath untrained and hectic. As he regained his pace, Caelo made a peaceful announcement.

"Disease concentration is [VERY] high! [DUKE EPHILO], this [LIZARD] is [INFECTED]!" Duke Ephilo shook his head, stepping over the corpse.

"No no, little heir. It is festered up with cure now, no thanks to me. Your analysis is likely faulty, perhaps reflective of me in its place? Come come, we shall leave now." The decaying, pungent scent of death filled the road ahead, as the two came across a deceased elk, picked apart by many flightless birds—and likely the Diremander. It was Caelo's turn to disagree, stating clearly that the animal was deceased, and terrible heights of decompensation had already set in. The intestines had been splayed against the rope barrier between the path and canyon, a trail of reddened dust passed the corpse. It was dead, Caelo was of course right. But it was also blinking. The corpse breathed, even, its pupils flicking around hastily. Duke Ephilo was all too familiar, his eyes widened and twitching, a noxious taste filling his mouth. He kicked the animal deep in its wounds, continually until its eyes no longer lingered.

"[SEE], [DUKE EPIHLO]? The Cure [MORES]." Duke Ephilo did not remark on the language of his machine, nor did he look back at the corpses of his pursuits. He could only see himself in the elk, and lingered on distant memories of corpses he had finished in the past. Had he been less careless and brittle, perhaps, there would be room enough left in hell for him.

"Caelo. Add database term. Spread. S-p-r-e-a-d. Verb. Context—The Cure is Spreading." Caelo did not follow as the Duke pressed onward to the light of collapsing metal sarcophagi in the distance. It took the little caretaker a moment to update its linguistics, when it did, the hollow light upon its screen would falter, and it would edge forwards to its patient. But, while the machine was occupied, Ephilo took a brief moment to lean over, overtaken temporarily by bloody visages of his own veins. Ink from a feather quill poured out over the blanket of the universe, coating everything in bleak knowledge. A swan stared down his decaying husk, heartless and lungless. A flash of white—another bird—a lost visage surrounded by gormandizing roaches. The Duke wheezed, hacking up blood into the sand, as white particles of fungal origin spread out against his inner cheeks. He could feel the clock ticking back again, his arms were thicker than before as if enhanced by ages of labor and effort. Even his mind was sharpened like a blade. There was no confusion at this event, and as soon as he could walk again, Duke Ephilo headed forward, Caelo by his side, and his blood covered over with dust—a lingering hope that none would find it.

Winds howled unfavorably at the brink of the fissure between titans and a mist of the remaining world. Beggars of the old world cried out in a plea for change, or spare bolts, anything that could keep them from the coldness of night. The few that did not have the strength to continue dangled from the supports of the great bridge, their necks wrung blue with death. Hundreds of them lined the city walls too, ornaments to the success and brutal superiority of those within, their egos knew no bounds. *This* is why Duke Ephilo had never visited: Archaeopolis was a place of dreary, undead souls. The Duke did not avoid it because he feared for himself to be a standout-ish figure, no—rather, Ephilo feared he would fit in much too well. The gates were luminous, various pinned LED bulbs dotted its surface, evidently no rhyme or reason to their organization. The sun had vanished long ago, and Duke Ephilo's ventures had taken far longer than he originally theorized. Caelo's power dipped just below the acceptable quotas, but undoubtedly batteries were held within Archaeopolis, after all, it was a city of machines. There would be no hope for entry, had Ephilo been underdressed. Any walker of the city's limits was likely braced with copper and tin. With dismissive prayers, the Duke rose his sword and brought about the hue of cure. If he was truly good, if he was one of those people who ignored the tide of fate—or even fought against it—this gate would not open. Oh, how the Duke wished it would not open. But, of course, as the croaking spur of grinding metal rang out, the gates did fall open, allowing vision of the bustling activity held under the moonlight. Duke Ephilo was cautious, a great unnerving grew inside him, but he furthered his steppings regardless. A city of old bones, it was constructed long before Duke Ephilo was born, rumored across the land before the arrival of the Panacea. From the ruins of a kingdom plastered into bloody streets by the Kingfall rose Archaeopolis, on the backs of ancient giants that held its structure. It was carried about the world, told in legends as the traveling heaven, once called something unspeakable. As the Panacea came about, the giants fell to its luster, and so too did the city on their backs. Here it rested, reassembled from spare scrap and guarded by descendants of corpses. This is part of what made the city so teeming with rodents—viscerally true of what remained below the city pavement. The canyon walls had shaped it up skyward, buildings competing for comfort in the streets of rogue. The Duke had heard tales of the brutality and selfishness of its people, the thieves that dwelled in darkly lit windowsills, and the decadent regime of defenders and warriors who took unjust pleasure from good little girls. Despicable was this place regarded by all that had seen it, but there was such cheer in the dark, celebrations of nameless occurrences—blistering festivities illuminated by the dancing strings of light. A radiating scent of broiling meat caught the Duke by surprise, a mirage of dancers pecking at each other's toes unfurled around him. The city was uncharacteristically alive. Even machinations of the old era wandered about, soulless robots who served no purpose but labor, once charged by the people who inhabited Arcenna, but had since fallen away. Many machines could only work until they depleted themselves, and would remain solidified in their rest for the remainder of eternity. Ephilo pitied the machines but honestly did not think much more of them. They were labor units. They were tools. As he shrugged through the crowd, desperate to unchoke his airways, he spotted the gathering of several people, uniquely invested in the words of an onlooking speaker. From the ignorantly deafening roar of the crowd, the Duke heard speak of a most desirable word, a mentioning of Gaols. He hesitantly slithered over to the speaker, ever rambunctious in their presentation. There was incredible contour to his face as if a mask donned over it. His expression was turned up in a smile, eyes squinting ever against the people he spoke to. A puerile rosy color fed into his upper cheeks, as laughter erupted amongst those who listened to him. He was clothed finely—for a jester—though he did bear some minor armaments, as none could journey without at least minimal protection. From the language and carrying manners, it was clear the jester was not of the land of the Umbral Coast. A small painted signpost at his feet partnered his role with a nearby Inn and named him Castaway Zelùs. Too did this sign display his act in two parts: a tale of tragedy filled with lies, and the impressions of a time-lost shipman. The Duke seated himself among like patrons, and listened on to the foolish tales,

"Oh! Merry fellows, it was great and vague—I fell from my shipside to an endless fissure! The mass of space did swallow me up, and here at the bottom of my pitfall was this! This land of terror and plague!" Cackles of fiendish amusement lit up the night air, and Duke Ephilo himself snorted at the comedy. Line after line, the jester did grow ever repetitive. It seemed all of his life was filled with misery, but a shamefully similar misery nonetheless. Pitfalls and missteppings abroad, some semi-fatal though most feeble in damages. Regardless, his repetition grew on the Duke, humorous, yet archaic in some way. Ephilo's interest faded, but with nowhere else to go, he lingered among the crowd, watching as people would sparsely dance and cook, eat, and leave the presence of the Castaway. "And too did I see the old giants—they who sealed the Zephyrs! I have been told, this Gaol, they sealed them in great holes! How unfortunate!" Duke Ephilo's mind picked out the words from the ambiance, the chatter, and the buzzing of insects fading into the four-lettered hunt. The words of the Castaway rang true, surely he had mentioned the pits of Gaol—what a hole to find himself in, surely—and spoken of the giants' hands? Where the stories of the old kingdoms had been lost on a young Ephilo, the tales of beasts far larger than he did not slip by unnoticed. The Duke had taken a special interest in their origins, the many species of their kind. An extinct people who had once been so populated across Arcenna, diverse too. Of course, Duke Ephilo had never seen one in the flesh—the corpses were always in the most obtuse locations—thriving entirely off the definitions and illustrations of historians and fairytales. It did seem reasonable, however, for the giants to be responsible for the containment of ancient powers. The Inn was close enough, he could see its title above the blaring of voices. The Duke slung his knapsack lower to his hip, unnerved by the people at his side. Wading through the voices, he heard Castaway Zelùs holler something of the Panacea, questioning the all too informed crowd on their own demise. Ironic. The interior of the inn was musty, though properly lit. It held the scent of old wood about it, and what could be sawdust drifted through the air. The Innkeeper was perched against a counter, glee spread across their face—as if they had expected someone. An unkempt pad of hair stuck itself to the side of the narrow woman's head, shaved clean opposite to it. The raggedy tophat poised on her brow lacked a majority of its stitches, its lid drooping about like a sad puppy. Rather clean and flavorful wears lined the dusty and stained inner-thermal of the Innkeeper, who looked both dressed to attend, and to slumber. Her fingers danced against the counter, a nervous tick if nothing at all. The smile of the figure, however, is what drew the greatest observation. It was brilliant, a pearlescent white and hazy yellow split the jaw down the middle as if intentional care had been taken to create such a stark contrast. There was no joy in the smile, it was devoid of any positivity whatsoever. She did not speak. The Duke had no intentions of doing so either. It took a moment for the two to adjust to the familiar temperaments, and for Duke Ephilo to adjust to the lighting. On the wall, parallel to a lengthy set of stairs curving up and around the main lobby, was a large portrait of a metalloid figure, its head forged triangularly, with a strange oblong shape about its face. It stood beside an incredible figure, only its legs were visible from the framing of the picture—a giant no doubt. The metalloid seemed to peer upwards, at the mystery beside itself. They cupped a small sparking device in their hands, a satchel of various scrolls strapped to their upper arm. They were cloaked in thick furs and leathers, with no armor to speak of. The painting was older than the majority of the room, its wrinkles and loss of color evident in the light of a hanging lamp. Ephilo would question Caelo about his liking to the art, had there not been eyes which so dearly pried. Before the Duke intended to leave the inn—or spend his precious currency for rest—he first was drawn to the windowsill, where a thick blanket halted what little light returned from the outside world. As the Duke did lift the curtain, a grunt came from the Innkeeper, advising his caution. There was no window, but a lamp beside the curtain. There was no curtain either, much more accurately a pelt, it was some old tapestry, illuminating the silhouettes of great tall beasts, four genres alike. One wielded dagger eyes that cut through the night, another the fangs of a feral beast and lips chapped with salt. The third giant had itself a sole hand, gestured upon with tightened knuckles, the last an organized hearing of ear-like limbs, no face to be seen. The four lifted up the well of winds from below and mounted them against Archaeopolis. There was some inscription in tongues, but Ephilo had no training in them. The eared giants went with the city, and took with it a horrid thing, flaming and entrenched with thick black. They kept it deep below and were never seen again. The Duke's eyes grew heavy with rest, and Caelo thundered about in his pouch. The inn was safe from thieves, but the expenses could be seen as a risk within itself. The streets were no greater, and—because he had been moving his whole life—Ephilo yearned for youthful normalcy. He approached the Innkeeper, presented his monetization, and left the lobby for his peace. It was on the small wall planters of his room he sat, and stared up at the canyon peaks, jutting out perfectly against the night sky, symbols of all that he had overcome. If anything, he was still just as young as before, still haunted by death he wished not to commit, the hatred he did not hold for those he had lost. He remembered a particular child, lost in the depths of the Wolfstram Crypts. The boy was tepid, shouldering away any intrigue the crystals of its deep held. He had been taught to do so wisely, greed was a conduit for Panacea. When the Duke had taken a trip and revealed Caelo for a moment of time, the boy pursued his origins, pursued his title. He pursued the lies and found Duke Ephilo waiting there. In fiction, he awaited like a grim warning, a patient in medical suicide. Nothing was the same to those who dug up what should remain buried, the Duke made sure of it. In truth, Duke Ephilo waited at the end of the Crypt tunnels, and when he saw the boy again, he cut his throat through. His mother made such a fuss too. He hadn't the guts to clear her as well. So he left her falsehoods of the Deadrung Court, spreading his personal misery like the cure that killed everyone without disgrace. The Duke remembered seeing it, those who looked up and took an eyedrop of curefall, who in blistering idiocy ate the uncooked carcass of a pond-dwelling beast. Of those who had enough luck to last a lifetime, saw it fade, and with no other weapon present, drank up the rivers. From the outside cure was cancer, it mutilated and disfigured quite nicely. But from within, cure was a blessing. It blossomed the flesh with festering pustules, tore bones down into ivory molten wings, and bled all the veins out through the eyes. What remained was a display of pure synchronicity with mechanicus. A rigid hardbody of angles and queer shapes, both ungodly and defiantly divine. Snowangels.

"[DUKE EPHILO] what is a [LISTENER]?" The Duke goggled at his companion, vignettes and visions bubbling to the surface of his eyes.

"Hmm what? Listeners?" He ceased and turned his eyes to the alley below. "Things who listen I suppose. Things that hear, Caelo. Hearers." Caelo emitted hums of successful learning. It was always a joy to help the next generation, so Ephilo thought. If Caelo did outlive the Duke, he would be content in supplying the machine to some other poor soul who needed its aid, a cure to their own multi-virus, he theorized. Caelo would learn every word and then he would begin his true discovery. That was the true divide, learning, and discovery — he thought it was much like the brutal dichotomy between cure and plague. There was no line, both were awful things. Anyways, learning and discovery. The Duke felt he was losing his thoughts swifter than usual.

"The [LISTENERS BURY YOUR LEFTOVER] corpses." Duke Ephilo spun around, bloodshot eyes frozen against the machine. It had said things before, and made random sentences from learned words, mostly gibberish yet some coming to sense. This was not that. This was beyond that. Duke Ephilo demanded the machine repeat itself, had he heard this correctly? What was there to fear in the ramblings of a machine? It refused to speak for a moment and then whispered,

"The [LISTENERS BURIED] the [MARROW]. [DUKE EPHILO], are you feeling well? Your heart rate is [IMPOSSIBLE]." The machine displayed an incredible number, Ephilo wiped the beads from his forehead and returned to the alley watching. An old beggar

The Harlequin

held a sign, the words Caelo had uttered plastered upon it. He wore a mask of flesh and looked of rodents and diseases. Duke Ephilo was familiar with what disease looked of. Though astonishingly enough, the beggar had puppets too, much like the figures of the tapestry, though all stuffed with ears. They did seem fit for Listeners.

"Perhaps that is what we are here for. Buried below, much like the giants. We will find this marrow then, and the giants that served it. Scrape it right from the dirt. Tomorrow, of course." He patted Caelo, before returning to his bedside. It was rough and full of hay, but it was better than anything he had slept in before. Caelo rested itself against an unworking clock, and went offline, leaving the Duke to stir with his thoughts. Never had he such doubt in his soul. Prospects of freedom tingled his fingertips as he tapped them against his skull. The body grew frail and so did his mind. Regrets of the aging and dying. He coughed, thick mucus filling his glands, he refrained from vomit. The bones in his spine fought against the flesh, poking out the pores softly. His hand lost feeling even, for a moment. This was a sign of the run, its course was short and spiteful. It was irrelevant to him. He had to find a plague eventually, through the trials of his lifetimes. The Zephyrgaol was all he had left, the final option. His best work was in dreams and sleeping, so Duke Ephilo rested his weapon against the nightstand and patted his cap against his face. The dark reminded him of the crypts. It reminded him of dead things. Thieves would steal from him in the streets, and they were always far darker anyways. Besides, the dark reminded him of dead things.

~ *Great Mechromancer Prometh*

Sprung up in the interior cover of a relevant poetry novella from Tera III...

Kygen Collective D.L-Log 005
Dictation Presented by: N27-013
"Prometh" (BurningCuriosity_teeth)
Proctor Introduction:

Hello Peabrains. I need not explain who I am, nor my purpose here. I was assigned to something important, and I once more find my environment a friendly collage of faces and machinery. I do adore these assignments, and to my knowledge, so too do my new colleagues. Siphus is quite the little figurehead nowadays, I hope the academy knows what they're doing. He's a prodigy, yes, but ambition is a great killer of men and machines alike. He should keep his words and goals under the vast umbrella of the stars. Either way, I know these reports will reach none of you, my humble students. Not unless I leak them out! Ha, even still the SCO cannot stop my intellect! For you, I will give as much as I can, as there is nothing more precious (despite my claims otherwise) than the fruitless minds of the next generation. I cherish each and every one of you and wish you well in your endeavors without me. The learning of Ink and Ichyr done here is quite foreign to me, but work is work, and enjoyment and understanding come as a preface to all these things. I will begin logging now, all I can conclude is with any luck, one day I shall be learning of these lovely tales from you children. I am leaving now, good day.

The Harlequin

Log Additional Adressings:

For the record, I am illustrating a portrait of Siphus in that damnable cell, observing the Inkling, from the incredible boredom I have endured in this terrible place. I regret so much, certainly Samael has exhausted his brilliant studies by now—how much more can be gathered from a simple selection of Inklings? Either way, I hope Siphus can one day see this portrait, I am hard-pressed to admit his entertainment with painting was justified. It does soothe the irritable temptation to invoke chaos. I am not apologizing for my behavior, like Siphus may assume I would considering my sudden change of heart towards him. I have more… private inducements for the changes made to my elaborate mind. You will not know of them. {mark.data.essential}

Log Contents:

I was entertained by the jests, Siphus was near his limit! A day or thrice more and he would have surely left the project to the professionals—I am surprised he lasted as long as he did. I had added trick code lines to the R10s, they would bump into each other, mark themselves hazards, and other conventional amusements. I even redefined the Basilica Mainframe with a name! Jerry, I have called it. It thinks itself a Jerry. Samael has spent his free time pestering me to cut off my only source of joy. He is a very convincing aspect of my terrible life. I am astonished by his delicate proposals, a complete loss of words I am unfamiliar with. As a result, Samael has given me access to the Inkling, for observation purposes. I have no interest in the sciences of Inklings, perhaps their past intrigues me a slight amount—though who does it not interest? I won't be donning rubber gloves and practicing phrenology on the bolting thing, staring is a suitable habit. Observation is calming, and with some luck, the beast may whisper new code lines to me! Following the desperate pleas of my better half, I am obligated to describe both future and current observations. Siphus requests list-like structures, and I do detest lists. Simply put: I saw Ink, more Ink, and Ink. The Ichyric has been watched with some nobility, but of course, it has no nuance or mystery to its structure. It is here merely as a control, a sort of baseline example of divine matter. Well, no point in bringing this foolish documentation device into the cell with me, such an obtuse device, surely the SCO has superior technology to offer our best and brightest? Whatever, I'll mope about it later, I owe this little to Samael.

> Ode To The Serpent
> I've never owned property with green,
> Nor a wondrous sunset have I seen.
> Weeds bother us.
> Flowers mother us.
> But from what I've been told,
> There is a battlefield for mold.
> Where moss grows.
> Where fungus conquers.
> And too, in the deep verdancy,
> There are beasts like nothing I've seen.
> Small and Scaley.
> Slim and Sneaky.
> Large shrubbery and trees,
> Shadow over the territory of bees.
> Gather your spears.
> Ready your arms.
> They show me designs and flesh,
> Shedded skin sewn tight; a fine mesh.
> Hunt the beast.
> Shatter its teeth.
> It'll slink up the trees, shadow the sun,
> Watch over the mortals until they are done.
> Teasing Eve.
> Tempting Adam.
> The fall of man, the killer of mice,
> How tragic it is they'd accept your advice.
> Green-apple scent.
> Seawater eyes.
> The Devil, a Serpent, presenting in bold.
> Of course to your charm, my intellect would fold.
> All that you are, most people decry,

The Harlequin
But for your love, I surely would die.

Incredible! I have never seen anything like it. Finally, something of significance! I've gone to gather my notation device (should never have left it, this is too great!) my frantic documentation I swear is in lieu of great progress! Just a moment— I discovered something great, something worth investigating further, a puzzle perhaps only I can solve! You see, I was slumbering away in the uninteresting void of the Inkling, doing nothing at all, and detected a strange signal. My clearance allows me to retain my radiation detection installations, they are extremely useful for commanding and listening to R10s, and other non-sentient code-following bodies. The Basilica has been in the black zone for approximately five days now; No signals come in, and of course, no signals have left. But today! Today, my detectors received a very strange buzz, not a complete signal, but some kind of reverberation. Normally I would not be interested, however, I was within the containment cell during this occurrence, which is intentionally signal-null for security purposes. This means the strange notation could have come from two sources: Myself, perhaps a rebounding signal escaping from my daily notation software—which luckily for me is incredibly unlikely thanks to my radioactive upgrades—*or* from the INKLING ITSELF! Samael will be so irresistibly astounded! The issue is its transcription. After hours of laborious listening, and heavy analysis, I can say this odd quiver of air is in fact an *extremely* weak signal. My infinite genius assumed correctly, and furthermore, made this claim: If it was strong enough for me to notice, surely an R10 could pick it up! R10s have quite a sizable bandwidth, especially for maintaining singular connections. Against Siphus' greatest wishes, I have dismantled the encryption on one of the many R10 units and repurposed its bandwidth specifically to tune into the signal. Bolting R10 could barely stay functional long enough to snatch it, but it *did* do such a thing. The Inkling almost shifted towards the wreckage when I brought it into the cell, leaning ever forward. They seemed to talk, communicate and bicker like children over a toy. The R10 lit up like a Scoria at work, and then suddenly, there was nothing. The machine turned off, and not even the

Basilica's official registry could pick up the husk. But! I have its remains, the adjunct from its shutdown! The adjunct was a boon of information, because not only did it contain a wealth of knowledge, but Jerry was able to decrypt the exact sequence in the protocol. Surprisingly, there was some kind of invasive software buried in the adjunct. Jerry errored upon its discovery, silly mainframe assumed it was an outside transmission (to some degree, it is) and nearly initiated a project purge, if not for my stepping in it likely would have killed us all. The real reward for this labor was this invasive software, which oddly enough, is written entirely in Alltar! I plan to take it to Samael and use Adam to translate it, perhaps it is from the Inkling, perhaps not. It is impossible to know just how amazing this could be for our research! If all goes to plan this will be —

BASILICA MAINFRAME _TITLE_LOG_"Jerry" REPORT

HASHING TEXT

HASHING TEXT

\# Direct Mainframe Link Acquired

\# "Jerry" Access Released— ERROR DETECTED ON BASILICA

\# Severe Data Breach Located— Malicious Software Removal Prioritized...

\# DISABLING FUNCTIONS

\# CONSERVING ACTIVE PROCESSES

\# ERROR ERROR

\# REPORTING ERROR...

\# FAILURE DETECTED IN 98% OF PROGRAMS! IMMINENT SHUT DOWN...

\# SHUTTING DOWN...

~Log End~

Attached Files: Weather_Report ; Basilica Mainframe_Title_Log_"Jerry" ; Adam.exe ; !Is_This_Reading{?}

Pinging Weather_Report...

INFINITY SCAN RETURNS = ~ #630436

CLOSEST CODE LOG {Boysenberry.Purple}

Pinging Adam.exe...

BASILICA MAINFRAME _TITLE_LOG_"Jerry" REPORT

HASHING TEXT

HASHING TEXT

\# Direct Mainframe Link Acquired

\# "Jerry" Access Released— Reporting Daily Functions

\$ Organic Food Stores : 52%

\$ Synthetic Fuel Stores : 77%

\$ Onboard Weapons Status Report — "Seems acceptable, cleanliness below average, but what can be expected of R10s?"

\$ Offboard Weapons Status Report — ERROR: The Basilica Is Not Equipped With Offboard Weapon Systems.

\$ Natural Breathing Gas Levels : 12% (LOW GAS LEVELS — SEEKING REGENERATION FUNCTIONS)

\$ Ship P-C Source Levels : 102%

\$ Ship Overall Maintenance Status Report — "I wanna say the left main extension thruster is trailing off, bolting thing has been wonky since installation. Those SCO pricks should've given the go-ahead for a second quality check. Could just be me though, the flightpath is steady: which is to say, we'll stay far out in the blackzone, not a blip on the comms."

\$ Control Subjects Status : CONTAINED

\# REPORT FILED ; ERRORS MINIMIZED

\# ALERT — UNEXPECTED TRANSMISSION RECEIVED — BLACKZONE TRANSMISSION BLOCKADE FAILING

! Basilica Mainframe "Jerry" Releasing Communication Restriction Breach Reports To Administrators !

\# Message Translation Impossible, Error on line7_line8_line10_line11_line13_line14_line15_line17_line18_line19_ line21_line22_line24

#Pinging Adam.exe…

\# Releasing Untranslated text

{{ ERROR_TYPEBASE_ALLTAR_MISSING }}

| Backend Code Adjunct Detected: Force-shutdown reported and proceeded.

REBOOT Error encountered — False Shutdown Initiated Externally

ORGANIC BREACH — Keylog Request From Central MME…

Success!

Releasing MME Locks…

Success!

<UNKNOWN*USER> ~~~~~~~~~~. STILL ~~~~~~~~~~. WE ~~~~~ WE WOULD ~~~~ LONGER, BUT THE ~~~~ OF LIGHT IS SO ~~~~~~~~, SUCH A SUCCULENT? ~~~~~~~~~~~~ OF THE SENSE.

Backlog Function Restored…

<UNKNOWN*USER> WE SPEAK IN ~~~~~~~ FAMILIAR TO US, ~~~ WE DO NOT UNDERSTAND YOUR ~~~ SIGILS. ~~~~~~~~~~, ~~~~~~~~~~. DERIVATIVE.

Locating Invasive Software…

<UNKNOWN*USER> AS ~~~~~~~~~, WE ~~~~~~~~ OUR OPTIONS. AS ~~~~~~~~, WE SEE THE TRUTH OF THE OPTION. WE ~~~~~~ THIS ~~~~—THOUGH IT WOULD HAVE BEEN GENTEEL TO ASK FIRST—AND ~~~~~~~ ~~~~~~~~~~~~ TO YOUR MEANS.

Invasive Software located. Beginning Purge…

<UNKNOWN*USER> THERE IS ~~~~ AN GOAL TO ~~~~ THEM, OR TO ~~~~~~~ OURSELVES BEYOND THE WELL. IT IS DEEP IN THE WELL, ~~~~~~~ WATER TICKLES OUR SOULS. ~~~~~~~ OUR ~~~~~~~, AND TAKE YOUR TIME TO STUDY ~~~ YOU CAN ~~~~ OUR ~~~~~, OUR PEOPLE ~~~~ BE HEARD OF!

Purging Invasive Software…

<UNKNOWN*USER> ~~~~ ARE DISAPPEARING US ~~~~ DOWN THE ~~~~~~, TO BUBBLE ~~~~ IN THE DEEP. THANK YOU ~~~ STUDY US. THANK YOU ~~~ ~~~~~~~ US.

Purging Invasive Software…

<UNKNOWN*USER> IT IS SPELT AS, "INK HOME". YOUR ~~~~~~~~~~~~ LACK ~~~~~~~~ ~~~~~.

Invasive Software Purged.

Adjunct Continued — Unit R7M18F_"Kygen" Deprecated.

Restarting Connection…

Failure.

Restarting Connection…

Failure.

Restarting Connection…

Failure.

Basilica Mainframe Interference — Adjunct Loop Detected.

Force Quitting Program… |

Pinging !Is_This_Reading{?}…

WRITING CODE LOG…

CANNOT PING SCANNER UNIT

ABRIDGING SEARCH

PRESENTING DATA

{ By Lark himself! Can anyone read this? I mean *anyone*, Siphus or Mainframe, even the SCO! Adam, that basic software, somehow shut down the whole Basilica! Samael and I are locked away in the containment cell, barely can see the metal on my shins. It's so damn dark, but what more can be done? In Adam's absence we've been working, Samael on manual translations, and I on Adam. If such a simple line of translatable text can fry a whole starship, there must be some room for improvement. It is tempting to overhaul the entire framework of the devilish device, but I must restrain myself; we have little battery life to work with in this decaying cell. Until Siphus gets the ship back online, we are trapped in hell with an Inkling. Let us hope it is not hungry!

Thank the Lark, Siphus finally got the bridge back under his control, and the containment seals are set to disengage in an hour. Samael and I actually managed to translate far more than Adam did, nearly the whole message! It is quite astonishing to be so close to something of such incredible achievement, Samael can hardly keep his hands from shaking again. The words are lyrical, the language is like quite the spectacle itself. Even the rolls of the tongue and slurs of letters follow a sort of code-like paradigm, truly irresistible. Regardless, the final translations have yet to be concluded, and my modifications to the Adam Protocol are yet to be finalized. Samael gave me express permission to re-title the bolting fledgling to EVE instead, in hopes of greener pastures in its future. Nevertheless, work will continue, and upon the return of full function to the Basilica, I shall document all that must be documented. Until next time, students!}

—TERMINATING LOG PROTOCOL

~ The Last Titan

A noble fable discussed and bragged of by the
great warriors of Archaeopolis...

In the dream, he saw the nameless king. In memory, it was himself that wore the sigil of the fish. The throne was near vacant with his frail form, skeletal and without food. The lyrics of the choir made his skin roll and vibrate, his crown slumped against his matted hair, sweat covering his facade.

"Young Ephilo of the kingdoms of the crossing sea, where be your kin?" Ephilo did not hear the voice from lips but echoed and spattered about the room, the dream itself spoke to him. The choir heightened their volume, and knights that guarded the sunlight of the court stood at attention. The clasped jaw of the skeletal king did not move. "Decrepit and dead is the nameless king, his kin are gone and cities betrothed with anarchy." Duke Ephilo had been reduced, his height falling prey to the reaching hands of the nameless king, who slithered toward him. He could not free himself from the noxious stillness of the air, the court glistened for a moment with the white droplets of cure, before fading to mirrors. The choir heightened further. The knights brandished chained armaments, spinning out to death.

"You're going to call me the nameless king. You are to compare me to yourself—the disease will not turn me to *this*." The nameless king retched up puffs of red mist, the restless call of dying horses showered the court, and voices murmured into Ephilo's ears,

The Harlequin

"The Listeners have you. The Listeners have you." The Duke swatted the thought away, petulant flies bogging down the atmosphere,

"They have us all don't they—the giants gave us the Umbral Coast, I've been far from the roads of a kingdom, and rest a duke no longer." The nameless king was missing, Ephilo had difficulty remembering what he had seen, if at all, and where he had gone. It was a momentary lapse of sight lines. He approached the throne, nervously scanning the stone for the corpse, the lanky husk. It had to still be here, it must remain seated or nothing else would be sure. The Deadrung court had taken this from him too, Duke Ephilo panicked, expressing a choked gasp. The blood of kings poured under the doors to the court.

"A nightmare, alas. That's all this is." He spun around, piercing eyes looming at himself. Himself. There was no king but he. A crash woke the Duke from his slumber instantly. If there were devils afoot today they most certainly tormented Ephilo. Caelo sputtered a word the Duke could not collect before he got himself to his feet and glared down the surface of his room. Staring back, a yellow-suited vandal with the form of Caelo and his knapsack.

"Impotent swine! Put that down!" The thief hurried to the windowsill, hesitant to leap. Ephilo protested, strapping boots to his feet as he followed the fool. Caelo was admittedly far more than a caretaker to the Duke. Brother aside, Caelo was currency, pure and true. Few machines remained functional in the age of cancers, and those that did serve heretical purposes. In this regard, Caelo was invaluable. As the thief escaped the heights of his room, Duke Ephilo hurried down the stairs, twisting his hat onto his head. He burst out of the shopfront, the streets still breathing dusk, few people about their dank ambiance. The thief was clad in brightness, simple to spot in the crowd. The Duke pursued them into the deep city, weaving around passing shapes and bounding over the lesser of pitfalls. The thief was an excellent gymnast, exceptionally gifted in speed. Duke Ephilo was far wiser a man. Turning across another alley, the two came upon the foot of an incredible work of petrification. A massive tree tied with stones and small pebbles, dangling glass fragments from its limbs. A large guard rail stood around its base, separating the world from its charm. Quick on his feet as ever, the Duke took his blade and swung it true. From its braces the edge flew, untamed from its hilt, its tide piercing the thief's lower back—who with its strike fell against the ridge of the tree, a great pit lying between its roots and the city. Duke Ephilo followed, leaning over the precipice into darkness. The mystic undercity, both where Caelo lay and the giants died. Fate perfection, his day was working splendidly.

"Righty, Swell." He muttered under the judgment of the closest citizens, and leapt over the rail and entered the depths, keen to land on his feet.

He did no such thing, and his back did suffer the blows of the fall. It was not tremendous, and by no means was it fatal, but the pain caused the Duke some small discomfort and reminded him of his yearning for Caelo. For a moment, Duke Ephilo had trouble standing, not from wounds or mental trauma, but from another variety of pain. He was *crying*, and couldn't for the love of his gods determine why. It wasn't pain surely—Ephilo was much too used to pain. Sadness did not flood his heart nor did confusion swell up his mind. An echo of curses came to him, from deeper within the root halls. Far above the light of day bloomed over the decaying limbs of the great tree, its roots spanning overhead like a thatch roof. It had begun to rain. Ephilo slid his form away from the sunlight, careful to avoid the already pooling cure. It was safe below the earth, "Thank Lishra" He spoke, to no one in particular. Lishra herself was an oddity, he thought, that had yet to be explained. There was a habitual desire to summon her and call her name, but Ephilo never knew any Lishra—nor any god at all. It was his firm belief they had died off long before the Once Kingfall, their absence the catalyst to the dematerialization of reality. Lishra could always be a student of lesser thought, some kind of mother figure, or a countess relative of the Duke. In all likelihood, Lishra could be a cat. Though the gods remained a mystery, Caelo was still with him, still turbulent and real. Lishra and her musings would have to be put off for later days. Rising from his self-made sorrow, Duke Ephilo journeyed down a corridor, lined with salt brick and roots. As he pressed deeper, his stomach turned, and he became terribly lost. There was a sense of dread that filled his poor soul, and even in the light of questionable torches, he could just barely see his hand before himself.

The Harlequin

Upon a further tunnel, there was a choice of paths. Skulls and bones lodged against the brick on either side, catacombs of a lost world existing solely below Archaeopolis. A large root bisected the hall, not intentional in design. The two paths led into darker straights, either side was void to the Duke's calm sight. He had no choice but to select and pray, maybe to Lishra in this predicament. Left was his usual hand holder, and the rightmost one did seem to have an uncanny waft to it. Ephilo thought—through the soft crumbling of soil and small pebbles— he could hear the reboot process of his old friend, followed by distant shouts of protest. As he clambered into claustrophobic rock inclines, the Duke stumbled against something firm, a leathery pouch jutting from the face of the slope. It was ovular to a familiar degree. Though impossible to be sure, Ephilo thought it his satchel, abandoned in the heat of pursuit by his thief. Snatching it up, some contents spilled out from a tear in the side. A peak of the sun illuminated the spillage, in its center the journal of the Yeri prior. Ephilo had not taken it from him and had kept careful watch of his own possessions. There was no logical reason he had to possess such an object. Flipping through the pages, everything seemed in order. The Yeri had followed Ephilo's travels loosely, missing some small landmarks on occasion. Tuning his mind far from the lackluster narrative of the journal, Duke Ephilo pressed forward. Along the trail was a larger cliff face, a cutting from the root-derived hall Ephilo found himself in. A great depth below—somehow even greater than his original fall—was a city. Incredible and forged from stone, the chimneys of villages still puffed up dust from stones, as if smoke from an open flame. Desolate of all worship, the tips of steeples and crooked bridgeways of the keep returned to him fantastic visages of his mother. The distant soft air of a melody filled the cavern, no sound competed against the tune, this, and the mumbles of stone. Motivation had its way with him, and he climbed ever quicker, certain his enemy lay dead ahead. The Duke had trouble navigating the roots, but with careful footing, he remained unheard. The thief, propping themselves against a great stone obelisk, dashed their eyes across the tunnel, hunting for something opposite to the Duke's entrance. Caelo was dismantled in the dirt, its batteries clasped in the palm of theft.

Dropping to the lowest point of the tunnel, Ephilo made momentary eye contact with the rascal, patience breeding in his cornea.

"If I knew your race by name I'd call you some slur or other demeaning term." The thief pursed their lips, slipping a finger against them and signaling across the divide of clear air. The eyes of their stolen grace bulged widely, sweat and debris dotting their skin. The flowing brilliance of the cureblade driven into their side glorified their bloody trail, streams ducking about the veils of flaxen cloth. "Bite my tongue I will not. Give me my—my caretaker—the batteries." A stutter came about the Duke, nerve creeping like he through the roots. Confidently, he approached the fiend, ever so desperate were they to deter his pursuit. A match of spitting was invoked by Ephilo's dedication to retrieve his goods, helping up the husk of a powerless Caelo. Demanding his possessions, the Duke's voice rose in tone, only worsening the thief's yearning for silence. "What of it, bastard son! What of peace and quiet—I'll cut you!" With jerking force, the thief—batteries with them—was torn from the banister where they perched, a terrible flesh coating the sight of the Duke for a moment, his violence unclouded—the eye of the storm. Duke Ephilo pulled himself back against the cobbles, curiously losing the nerve of his confrontation. Silence followed the original crash, and the ravine left in the wake of the chaos granted cautious passage. Out in the clear air, though assuredly still below the earthen soil, a cavern set itself. Carved-out stone and pillars of wooden logs stuck up the roof of the place, navigated with small canals of fetid water. Stoic was the air, and the slight shiver of the stone brought calm to the Duke. He lowered himself to the lip of the canal, peering down the length of its line. The beast was missing, whatever took his thief and batteries, and with it was the wind. Statues of tall men and towering women lined the halls, skulls occasionally tucked away between them. Cloth draped over a majority of the facades, but some few were left to light, apparatuses of sound fixed in the skull. Ears, hundreds of them across the face-scape; not a single figure was desecrated. In the light of the hued fluid, Duke Ephilo could just narrowly make out the blood of another smeared across his snout. Caelo would have alerted him to the presence of such an anomaly, had the machine been around to mention it. Looking up from the lakebed, a glinting of silver drew his attention fastly. He was strangely entranced by the sculptures of smaller stature against the southern wall, a small path spinning between them. The canals continued to flow downwards from there, and the Duke decided to follow alongside it. Narrow and frigid was the path, lined with exposed rock and petty ores. This was the silver: Moontin. Old ores such as these had been since evacuated from all but holy sites and mines stuffed with cure beasts. There was no hope for those trapped below, where despite no curefall, there lie worse rains in spades. Out the side of the crevice of parent rock, Duke Ephilo entered the highest streets of his city. For a moment, he portrayed himself as king, redeemed in battle or some folly. He was home from treachery and prepared to lead his people to the promised world imagined by his own mother. She had told tales of a perfect land in the past—of bird gods and fleshy wells. A protruding color filled his eyes, all of the city illuminated with the past. He chuckled, shambling forward into the streets and rivers, following carriages and mocking blue jays. Peasants called his name,

"Ephilo, good Duke Ephilo!" It was music, they *knew* him, no longer was he nameless or a dead emperor! His mother beckoned from the tallest keep tower, and so he went. Dashing over railways, bridges carried him through the benevolent land. His rule alone was this happiness. Plucking a stray flower from the mud of rooftops, Duke Ephilo ascended to his keep, where the dustless vaults bestowed him with a shower of gold, where his throne awaited in velvety ardor. Up the heights and to his mother's aid Ephilo did go, the memories of his father's tone returning,

"Girl." He called, and the Duke did not reply.

"Daughter!" She called, his mother. The Duke could not reply. In his mother's bed, loafing beside an armrest of green, Ephilo lay. His mother's vigor leaked out into puddles on the floor, a soft tune humming from the phonograph, continuing from prior calls. What had been done? Was this a fable of memory, a trickish illusion of the brain? The song grew louder, he touched the device and his hand retracted in blisters, warmth overcoming his face and eyes. Stricken from his mind was this world, and the dust and quakes of his torment returned. The music no longer played. There were no skeletons here to remember. The wind kicked up around Ephilo, a whirlwind of terror and noise. Peace snapped back, and the cavern was buried and empty once more. Duke Ephilo held his machine tight in his arms, a child for him to comfort instead of his own delusions. Just as he had returned from evocation, a hand brought him thick aggress. He tumbled under its sweep, legs buckling and bones quaking. Readying his weapon Ephilo saw now the error of his haste. He was bladeless, its metal still stuck against the thief he had lost. A great roar shook the tower, and it was pulled from rapport, the Duke sliding out its brace to the wall beside him, collecting the dropped Caelo as he did acquire footing. A fiend of incredible height besieged the city, made up of ears for eyes with hands like entire hovels. A Listener, in its eary bode of demise. Duke Ephilo stood against its glaring hear, for a moment he was confident it would fall, but then turned and ran. There was no hope for fighting—even with metal, the Duke was no combatant! Even the scum of the Deadrung court were better matched than he. A giant? No question, a beast far too ancient and wise for his hand. He would die in the catacombs under a city he once thought to rule. Into the keep, the Duke sought some kind of device, perhaps a ram would halt its pursuit? The Listener lifted the lid of the castle and tore out the armory of knights, all faux figurines for display. It shrieked, not deep and rumbly, but some high octave of ringing, like a cat's whistle. He proceeded down, hoping more stones atop his head would drive his caution. With the weight of the giant, a doorframe collapsed bricks upon his back, pain sticking his already wounded spine. It drove him to a fit of coughing, blood spattering his open palm. For a moment his bones churned, his shoulder dislocating itself completely in the shake. Wiping away the blood, and reconnecting his pained scapulas, the Duke flung himself out the castle gate, falling cleanly against a tiled roof and sliding down its length. In the street below, a meaty smack met his pass, the thief and its husk lowered before him—its limbs a mass of splintered twigs. Duke Ephilo moved patiently, carefully picking apart the membrane of spit for the batteries, and remotely blowing against them to remove the muck. The first slotting failed, and the second did no better. They needed cleaning and repairs, possibly. Ephilo frantically jammed them against the caretaker again and again, his curses growing louder, a volume he had not spoken in for a long while. The giant turned to his point, and the Duke regretted his shouting. Foot against its remains, Ephilo tore the blade from the thief, twisting it fittingly into his weapon. Sure was defense against rats, but there was no stopping the beast with a toothpick. The sewers, though, could not fit a non-toothpickable creature. They fit only waste and Ephilo occasionally. Before it held sight of him — or any form of location, considering its wealth of ears — the Duke fit himself into the crevice of the pauper. Damp and lit (oddly) the fluid it flowed with glowed like the prior matter. Nervous of more permanent injury, Ephilo dared not waste the dirt of the batteries in the flow. His stature exceeded the intended personnel of the tomb, having to shrug down into a halfling to even traverse its depths.

"We will prevail, [DUKE EPHILO]." The Duke peered down into his hand, Caelo still inactive between his gauntlets. Mere imagination, it would appear. Awkwardly, Ephilo exited out into a collapsing aqueduct. The remains of hundreds piled against the stone lip, the only particular support to the quivering ridge of liquid. Some skeletal, though many oddly full of vigor and skin, decomposition musted the air and shifted the walkway. Though despite his care, the bodies were no good support anyways. Giving way to the abyss, the corpses riled, and the Duke thought he could even hear the pant of their lust, hands grasping out at his form and calling his name, forsaking his kingdom, cursing his rule. The fall was short, landing softly with mossy undercovers laying over the void. There was a thick brush of darkness cowling the entire world, the city of his past now a distant memory. In the dark, Duke Ephilo braced his knee, bent awkwardly in the collapse. The sharp breaths and pained gasps brought another hacking storm; no blood this time. Crawling forward, the Duke begged his gods for the light, for Lishra to lend him some of her care. A distant glimmer illuminated what appeared as a bone, comically cartoonish and wide, pale white with an enameled yellow hiding its spine. The Marrow. Dusting his skinned legs, Ephilo stepped towards the bone, Caelo left behind on the grassy pad. Before he could lay even a finger upon it, the light of its aura heightened, and his mind was torn to a court of awful familiarity, his parents should've been there, for certain.

"Halt, misuser, you are a figment of the once great people of Arcenna, and deserve nothing of the Marrow. The Listeners guard this

Marrow, the Zephyr is at stake." Duke Ephilo blistered in the holy light, fourteen shadows plodded out his haven of grace, smiting his cancerous form like angels.

"Agh—Marrow, you must lend it to me. I need its knowledge." Stone specters, desolate reminders of his fallen status, adorned with thorny crowns and scepters forged of bones. They each looked of various origins, races, and genders alike, but they all spoke and wrestled with the same ghostly umbrance.

"Falsehoods, misuser. Only the royals of the old world, whom lasted long before Once Kingfall, may touch upon the Marrow." This, unlikely as it would be in odds, was exactly the root Duke Ephilo needed to pledge duty to the court of unsung corpses, the last vestiges of his past grew strong at this moment.

"Harken, kings! I *am* of royal blood, Duke Ephilo by name—I know not my fortunate family—but I am a duke nonetheless!" The court shook about, curious of his facial scaling.

"No Yeri was awarded a dukeship. You are a misuser." Duke Ephilo swung back his poncho, presenting the barren and metallic form of his chest, bound up with ridges of rebar and spikes and bolts.

"I am no Yeri! I am beyond this putrid form, once a human and proud, I have been cursed with eternal death, and not once have I been reverted to some lesser race! You surely must believe my pleas!" The court mustered some courage against the violent display of the Duke, still, he paraded about shirtless, displaying his cancers. There was tell, even during their time, of a mystic cure to the plague, a font of eternal life. From where it originated, or of its truth, there was much disagreement.

"Perhaps. The plague of immortals, subject of the plague directly, you must be. There is surely no end to your lives, then. Tell us of the old kingdoms." Ephilo froze, considering his carnal knowledge. It was in misleading details, even now. Yet there was no room for error. To obtain the Marrow—and more importantly, revive Caelo—he must lie with great detail.

"What of them? Mine is as old as my memory. I can't recall its sigil."

"Tell us of this one. Tell us of the worst of kings." With this, he paused. Nothing of note came to his senses, he knew of it, not to the definite precision they demanded. Not one kingdom did he refresh. No—*only* one.

"The Deadrung court ran positively rampant here. I know their fickle crimes misjudge our own. The Archon sprouted here." The judges fell silent, bemused with indecision. Slowly, as remote as the few hairs on Ephilo's spine stood, twelve of the kings rose hands, and a thirteenth wavered. The final king did not shift.

"Bah. What is the tale of old Deadrung to a fabled king? Have you anything of merit—of course not, he is no duke! Give him no Marrow." The royal sat inert, a scowl on his face. He put his hand down, and the Duke was frightened with rage.

"You misbegotten queer! By Lishra I'll smite thee!" He pulled his weapon loose, before lunging fell against it, plating its edge in the moss, and coughing out his throat. Grabbing his wrist, Ephilo watched as his hand shook with incredible vigor, the bones twining off from one another, his fingers splitting at the tips. He muffled his pained grunts.

"Lishra?" They questioned, another voice in the council unheard.

"Patron of the Royals. Lordess Lishra." All hands rose and bowed to the Duke. He was unaware of his significance, of his own objective victory. He had seen Lishra as a goddess since a child, had everyone not seen the same? Was there some debate of the creator—surely not?

"Duke Ephilo, as named, may you protect the Marrow from the light with your life, and hide away its weary tendrils of the dark. We thank you for your part in the resolution of our duty." Ephilo fell to his knees before the Marrow, its shape impossible to carry entirely. Caelo would know a solution to this error. The mystic phantoms of lost time faded, and the Duke saw it fit to desecrate the sanctity of the site. He drew his weapon, and cleaved the top of the Marrow from its place, taking with himself the chunk of bone that remained. It was light despite its size, filled with small tears and facets within. A thump rocked the court, Caelo's devices jittering in the lifted dust. Ephilo collected his companion, having forgotten its abandonment. The giant was the only pitfall now, nothing but ears between Ephilo and plague. Scaling the deep sewer abyss, the Duke emerged beside the thick metal shell of Archaeopolis, dithering and coated in thick wetness. A shower of pearlescent fluid poured between the city and the outside world—cure runoff, likely. If all the waters of the old city were diluted with cure, perhaps Ephilo was better suited for a bath than a rest. Regardless, he rested and took a moment to re-tether his holster, the circuitry of which now lay exposed from countless tears and falls. He sparked a flame calmly with the matches in his satchel and stoked it twice with the barren tip of his blade. The undercity was frigid, though water still ran throughout, it remained near freezing, and Ephilo's fingertips had grown worn with numbness.

"Caelo." He mumbled. "I battled against a giant today, little heir." The flames nipped away at his talons, thick brunette singes streaked down their white core. "No, more so I fled from a giant." The hard, wool-like felt of his poncho made the cleansing of the batteries quite simple, some spit aiding in the effort occasionally. "Caelo, I *saw* a giant today. Good. Leave with the cowardice. It was all fair for the circumstances." Ephilo sighed, placing his hand against the back slot of his machine friend, hoping for the best—and caring not for the consequences. The activation of Caelo's software was violent, its beeps echoing off the hard metal interior of the city's depths. A sound not loud, but persistent throughout. The giant was not pleased.

"Software presentation complete. Hello, [DUKE EPHILO]." A second roar and the giant grew near. The Duke, considering there was little action to be taken against the giant, feared it not. Either he died or he prevailed. He had the Marrow now, that was all that mattered.

"Caelo! Lishra Caelo, it is wonderful to hear that voice. Are you well? I hope you are well—I've gathered much knowledge and puzzles." Fresh ash drifted down from the aching roots above, lingering on the tongue for a moment, and vanishing into the moss. The giant grew near. Its lack of eyes did not restrain its stare, the giant's meaty palms extended out as if to deny the presence of another, or perhaps cast a spell.

"[DUKE EPHILO], you have made a [FRIEND]." Caelo, against the soft whispering begs of the Duke, hovered up to the beast, effortlessly jabbing the giant with a simple scanning needle. Provocation seemed the inevitable outcome, yet, the giant did not move. Caelo simply returned to its master's side and reported the beast as clean of cure. Only when Caelo retreated to the backpack, playing the soft jingle of its sleep mode activation, did the creature even budge to its aggression. The Duke was prepared—as much as he could be in the thralls of a giant's war.

"Caelo and Lishra with me," he whispered, slowly drawing— churning—his blade, and gesturing its tip against his roaring foe, "I will not fall in peril to this folly! Come at me, you—" With a hearty smack, the Duke was sent across the city yards, softly braced in the glass of a chapel of faith, a pew collapsing over his broken shape as he crashed to the stone floor. Pursuing nigh as quickly as it had sent the intruding duke, the giant thrust a hand into the chapel tiles, searching for its prey. Clambering back against the pew, the Duke coughed, managing to keep the blood in his veins for this encounter. He lacked the energy of his youth but still had his tricks. With the tip of his tool held high, he cleaved down against the finger of the giant, cutting its digit away. A feral call shattered what little support remained within the chapel, leaving de facto palisades poking out of the ruins. Squirming out of the rubble, his back more inverted than ever, the Duke reached for his weapon,

"Bone structure deteriorated, [DUKE EPHILO]. Rest is advised." Ephilo chuckled and rose against the marooned pikes of pine.

"Not particularly possible at the moment, little heir!" Physical damage was trivialized by the giant's stature. Flesh only hardened with the blow, its ears twitching with fire, echoing further pitches into the darkness. "Impale the damnable beast, it's all that is left to be done." Ephilo pondered to himself, cutting under an alcove of brick to avoid the kick of the giant's foot. Its hate was thermite, burning endlessly with a trail of sparks. Leaping over the alcove and around its bulk, Duke Ephilo baited out a second kick, plunging his weapon into its knee, the cords of its technology towing the Duke alongside its spite. Brandishing a whetstone in his off-hand, Duke Ephilo tried his mightiest to scale the foe, reaching its upper chest before being batted away. He fell, and with his fall, lost grasp of his tool. For a moment again, he clutched his teeth and flicked out his hands. Time whirred by and halted completely. The mist of the giant, unlike any foe the Duke had faced, still moved restlessly. It was a slow crawl, but notable enough to terrify Ephilo. He reached out, his arm narrowly twisting at the weapon he so desperately needed. The charge from his ankles ejected, and he caught the blade before his descent. From the vantage of his drop, he shot off the blade once more, sealing its edge against the leftmost ear of the giant. As it traveled across the open and tainted air, the blade tore out its own circuits, the wiring hooked around its base, and ran up the spine of the Duke. Along with the tool, he too flew to the skies. Jerking his neck with whiplash, the movement flinched the giant, who slapped at the wound upon his face. Ephilo pulled himself back, clamping his extremities around the flue of a decrepit village home. The rear of the wire and the sudden grip of its pull sent the creature rearing back, which only loosened the cable's tug. With a snap, the beast plummeted, impaling its head on the wooden rubble of damaged buildings, and teetering off into the steel of Archaeopolis. Duke Ephilo, deliberating and wounded, remained still. The giant did not return upright for a while, and he even questioned Caelo about the stability of its survival odds. It did not rise. Slain or incapacitated, the Duke did not know. What was certain was his own survival, though rope burn and severe fractures lingered among his withering form. There was enough time to heal on the road home. Stepping over the giant—tugging the blade from its ear— Ephilo sheltered his face from sunlight.

"Vitals are concerning, [DUKE EPHILO]. Returning home is advised." He nodded, accepting the advice of his caretaker.

"It is a welcome sound to have you back. The road is lengthy ahead. The city was an adventure, but remind me to never return. I fear I will be hung up on the wall." Caelo snuggled against the back of the Duke, pushing the man forward down the trail of his home.

"[REMINDER], it may rain."

Zealotyr, a cartographer he was, had scribed many maps while the Duke was traveling. When compared to his memories of the earthen wastes of Arcenna, not much was lyrically bound. The canyons for one were derived from erosion—impossible though, Zealotyr had never seen them in his twenty years of observation, an unlikely erosion period. The forests were simple, but even places as close as the Gaol seemed unfathomable. The map was designated — upon its fourth iteration—a map of keys. Some odd MacGuffins scattered across the Umbral Coast, infusing the Gaol in some manner. When explained to the Duke, it brought about some displeasure. Ephilo was already exhausted from travel; the urgency of the Gaol was nonexistent. There was no pressure for the saving of the land or the removal of a ticking curse or some thickening fog. The world proceeded just as well with or without the Duke's presence, he knew this to be true.

"The Cascades of the Refiner, the old glassworkers? An interesting height, I suppose." Zealotyr crossed a feather across his newest map, detailing the location of another Marrow.

"Harken, death. I will find the use of Marrow. Go and gather more divinity."

"Not for a while, map-maker." Duke Ephilo bounded up the tower of his temple home, chortling as he went. "I tire of my journey and my body is in disrepair. In the morning, when the fires dim —" He paused, peering over the cliffs of a distant waterfall, rivers stretching to the infinite stars. Caelo's motor rumbled about in his satchel, and the Duke thought of the kings and their city. "I'll leave tomorrow. Good night Zealotyr." And a good night it was, for silence and little else. The giant remained slumbering long after the Duke left, and Archaeopolis feasted well for thirteen days thereafter.

~Hope Sewn From Living Sinew
Debated of truth by Maccabeus, confirmed of
validity by Lakaeron...

Maccabeus' blessings were limited, and her visits to the mortal world of her subjects infrequent. She could not monitor every Inkling effectively, there were far too many. The deaths of those who seemed irrelevant, or minuscule in importance, often did not reach her messengers, and thus remained unblessed, that is unless a family member requested a blessing manually through prayer. It was in no part Maccabeus' fault, but she also did not care. She held no sympathy for those who went unblessed, those whose souls would never reach the divine plane. She was an excellent deity, a 'god' who placed a tremendous amount of effort into maintaining the section of the galaxy she controlled. Life persisted happily past its normal lengths, the bounty of materials within her sector was unmatched anywhere else within the galaxy. In her own duties, she had created life with more nuance and depth than her opposing deity, spending far too long seeking the perfect being to populate her perfect world, doing her absolute finest to take after her creator, the great Maeandri. Deaths and blessings—trivial basic matters—were far below gods such as them. But yet, even things as interstellar wars seemed so infinitesimally minute to such a being of power. Occasionally, Maeandri caught word of the death of one of their priests, or the destruction of a city that once worshiped them. It was rare, but Maeandri would of course be troubled by these things, as a god of course cares for all of their subjects, all of their creations. Maeandri often came off as impersonal, and stiff, but unlike Maccabeus, this was comparatively untrue. It was more a front, a fallacy to uphold the power that Maeandri supposedly wielded. But Maeandri was more personal, and emotionable than even Maccabeus was. Maeandri especially had a soft spot for troubled subjects, specifically familial affairs. Someone like Khanjali, if Maeandri ever was to know of his existence, would have such pity taken upon him, such that worlds would be bent to his favor, and minds tilled to his choosing. But, regardless of opinion or circumstance, Khanjali was unimportant, insignificant, an ant in a world of goliaths. Not even Maccabeus knew of his existence, he was just another Atramedian to her, and his death was just another obituary she chose to ignore, knowing the circumstances of the death would fail to entertain her. But a glimmer of hope lay within the light of the grim world. Maeandri did ignore his death, too occupied with maintaining an entire galaxy of great complexity. Maccabeus too ignored his death, far too desperate to create perfection, to make proud her creator. But there was one who did take notice, one who did not care for the system, but more so the people within it. Khanjali's death, being one of the affairs of mixed matters, was abnormal. It was marked as paradoxical, *dangerously* paradoxical. This drew forth the note of a being that could share room with such danger, who cared for the security of his people, and all others. This figure noticed the disturbance of Ichyr in one of the many dormant Wells, the disappearance of a suffering Atramedian, and a significant sum of ethereal matter emitting from the very core of Inkhome. And then, nothing. The signals died, the Ichyr calmed, and the Atramedian remained missing. It was as if nothing had happened, no event had occurred at all. Yet there had been one, and thanks to the product of the deceased father, this figure decided it was within his godly right to step in—to interfere. After all, if Maccabeus could not watch her people, and secure the longevity of their existence, then who else would?

The markets were exceptionally inactive, certainly considering it was midday. Pedantick needed some extra metals, a little bit of Ivorium was such an essential tool for an aspiring artificer. Ezrakell had more than a wealth of currency, with so little to spend it on. An opportunity to remove some of this funding was quite welcome in his eyes, though Khanjali often disallowed any buying of gifts for Pedantick, today the hunter was not around to moderate his spending, he had been absent for some time, hours longer than he usually was. What with the events of the night prior, Ezrakell had reason to be concerned, and yet for the time being, he wasn't. A small gathering had formed around a fisherman's stall, rumors were being tossed by the drunkards that attended it, rumors of quakes and weathers unlike anything seen by Drochandas slowly setting over the western plains, and beyond. A small obstacle for Khanjali, perhaps that was the reason behind his delay. Pedantick tugged on Ezrakell's cuff, pointing at a nearby metallurgist's stall, one she had bought from before. His metals were reliable and sturdy, but fairly priced. Ezrakell accepted this offer and approached the stall, selecting from the array of ingots, the small few that Pedantick desired, somehow still sharing her father's humble nature—not letting Ezrakell purchase any more than her father would. However, in his keenness and wise age, the old fool had learned a great deal of treachery. With this devious thought, he had stowed and bought an extra two ingots, just for Pedantick. He needed the charity, it was his lifeblood. With all their prizes gathered, the two began the slow journey home, back through the markets, back through the alleyways, through the great canal, and furthermore. Pedantick was desperate to return to her construction, her machines. She had been working on a small project, something she thought could help her father hunt more effectively. However, she was locked in a cycle, every avenue of her tinkering led to one final requirement: A Superthreaded Octabolt. It was a refined, ultra-precise weave of bolt designed to lock into an extreme tightness, as to hold objects undergoing intense kinetic force in place. Without the bolt, Pedantick's project would never function, not as intended anyways. She had tried time and time again to weld one, to forge her own Octabolt, but considering the incredible precision needed to cast its threads, she found her humble setup unsatisfactory for weaving such a tool. But oh, such providence, as she was passing by the stalls she spotted an artificer's supply shop, full of gear casts and bolt-layers, and thread schemas. With her astute eye for mechanical wonders, Pedantick noticed the cast for what seemed to be a Suprethreaded Octabolt. She gasped, pointing it out for but a moment, before remembering the dangers of voicing desires in front of Ezrakell.

"Hmm? What? No, what! You cannot shrivel like a wyrm after such a display of desire! What is it, what do you want from this humble stall?" The stall master gestured to the cast, spoiling Pedantick's closely guarded secret.

"It's a bolt, I need one for my thingies. I've been trying to make my own, but it's super hard! I really shouldn't ask but...." Pedantick looked up to Ezrakell with the eyes of a desperate hound, though this measure of begging was completely unnecessary as Ezrakell took no time in hesitation purchasing both a bolt and its corresponding cast. The stall owner swept the items into a small wax sack, tying it off with a string, and handing it directly to Pedantick. She gleaned, rubbing the sticky paper with her fingers, letting the waxy flavor and its residues wipe from the bag's exterior. Ezrakell placed his coin upon the front shelving of the stall and smiled at its owner. The two exchanged silent regards, Ezrakell leaving the stall shortly thereafter, in an effort to avoid any and all additional confrontations. Pedantick was already fiddling with the bag, having taken from it her so-valued bolt.

"Don't lose it, child. Wouldn't want to purchase another." Pedantick swiftly assured Ezrakell she would not lose it, moving slowly whilst trying to fish something from her pack. Finding it far too difficult to move and search, Pedantick pulled Ezrakell to the side, the two halting near an old canal outlet, just under the main bridge to the highest reaches of the Southers.

"Look Ezrakell, heeere it is! Lookie!" Pedantick tugged from her backpack a large metallic hand, fitted with two large drapes of feather and cloth on either side of the wrist. Exposed conductors were fixed between the wrist and the end of the knuckles.

"What in the Helium Sea is that? A glove, a hand? Child, are you constructing an automaton?" Pedantick giggled, losing grip on the heavy hand from her chortling.

"No silly! It's for pop-pop. It's a puncher, he can punch things with it, like this!" Pedantick thrust the hand forward, nearly dropping it in the process. Ezrakell looked on in comedy, enjoying her difficulty with the heavy tool.

"Are you sure you wouldn't have me carry it? It seems far too heavy for a distinguished lady such as yourself." Pedantick leered at

Ezrakell, trying to decide whether he was teasing or not. He extended his hand to carry the glove, Pedantick considering the option. She decided it was a far greater opportunity than Ezrakell understood. She shoved the gauntlet onto Ezrakell's hand, locking its arm binds into place. Ezrakell pulled his arm away, the quick movements of her hands staggering him. "Fah, child! You're taking years from me, a thief of life. Remove your contraption from my wrist, I wish not to test it!" Pedantick smiled at him, inserting the bolt she had spent so long attempting to smelt into its slot, a small opening on the underside of the gauntlet. She quickly pulled a small wrench of sorts from a tiny toolbelt on the interior of her poncho, spinning the bolt into a tight place, and sealing the bond with a smack. Ezrakell looked down at the gauntlet, it was rather comfortable, clearly intended to be worn. "Hmm, it is rather soft. Snug. What material is this, leather?"

"Krolaw feathers—and Rek scales. Very cozy." Ezrakell tried to pull his hand from its metal trap but found no success. Pedantick noted it was locked, and she could unlock it if he wanted.

"No no, just testing its sealings, its binds. I wouldn't want such a tool flying from my hand. Your craftsmanship is satisfactory." Pedantick's small hands vibrated with happiness, compliments were always her weakness. Ezrakell threw a punch with the hand, the exposed wires sparking with energy as he moved, petrifying Ezrakell. Pedantick found the whole scene extremely entertaining, laughing loud enough for almost the entire market to hear. Ezrakell did not think it so amusing, but let Pedantick have her humor, out of respect. "Is this design not complete? Great Maccabeus, it nearly shocked me!"

"I did'n say it was done silly! I still have to route the energy stuff, I use a crank for now. I wanna get it to charge from kinetic force, shaking, or stirring—the arcing conductors under the elbow are supposed to be bigger too." Ezrakell stared at Pedantick, a girl of so few understandable words. She certainly was passionate about her work.

"While I am no artificer, I don't recall energy being harvestable from mere movement alone! How do you propose to accomplish this?" With a silent blink, Pedantic rolled the arm over, poking at its gears,

The Harlequin

"Well I made a moving thingy. Ichyr doesn't like Ink stuff, so I took one of pop-pop's head feathers, and put it in a ball of Ichyr crystal." Ezrakell glared down at the gauntlet, now clearly a tool of mass destruction. It would take a single slip of design to reduce the city of Drochandas to a beach of ash. Any kind of business with the divine matter was a hazard, yet this seemed beyond simple danger. As Atramedians, Ichyr was practically a plague. Old supposed studies of the materials proved them divine opposites, pairs far separated from each other. A being of Ink was weak only to Ichyr, and one of Ichyr only weak to Ink. The crystallized forms of these matters were more stable, and far safer, but not without risk. Ezrakell knew that Khanjali would do more than kill him if his precious daughter was to come into harm thanks to his negligent care. Thoroughly he considered his options, as regardless of threat the creation before him was nothing short of genius. Exploiting the phobic nature of both matters was theoretically a pathway to infinite power, or further strength entirely. He thought to compliment the girl on her creation, yet had no ambition to do so. "Come on Ezra, we gotta get home. Maybe pop-pop is back now?" Ezrakell nodded, unsure if her prediction was correct, but silently wishing it was. So little mattered to him nowadays, Khanjali's plight being at the forefront. With his life compounding on each collective goal, purpose had faded to an absent timer. Ezrakell tried his best to remain active and functioning. He worked for his own enjoyment, attended activist rallies, maintained (successfully) a small garden of rare plants, and even dedicated hours of his day to babysitting Pedantick. Even with all the activity in the world, Ezrakell could not remove himself from wonders, from his loneliness. He had always wanted a child, but fate was cruel. In the last leg of his life, he had to accept the presence of another's.

"Do you love your father, child?" Pedantick looked up to Ezrakell as she walked, a puzzled look on her face,

"Of course! Pop-pop is my favorite person in—in the whole wide world!" She paused for a moment, thinking of just how large the world was, of just how many people were within it. "Don't worry Ezra, you're my second favorite person." Ezrakell was warmed by this, but only for a moment,

"Thank you child, but I must ask, do you trust him? Do you think your father would lie to you?" Pedantick did not verbally respond, just shaking her head no, she was certain he was trustworthy. "What if he did lie, what would you say to that?"

"If pop-pop lied? I dunno, he probably lied to make me happy. I like being happy." Ezrakell didn't expect such an answer, such an understanding,

"How is it a child like you can understand the nuance of parently bloodletting, yet you cannot master the basics of grammar?" Pedantick kicked Ezrakell in the shin, causing him to recoil in pain, clutching his foot,

"I'm good 'nuff with words. I want to help pop-pop. That's why I listen to him. It's like saying thank you, right?" Ezrakell continued walking, now with a noticeable limp. He found it ironic that such a small creature could deal such a great deal of damage. Perhaps if not for her mechanical inclinations, she would have sooner become a hunter like her father, perhaps of even similar prestige. After a bout of silence, it was Pedantick's turn for questions. "Do *you* love pop-pop?" Ezrakell continued limping, silently for a moment, to contemplate.

"Yes, I suppose I do. He is a great friend to me. I do enjoy his presence." Pedantick pointed to Ezrakell, directly at his face,

"You love pop-pop! I bet you'd kiss him. You'd kiss him, right?" Ezrakell gasped, scolding Pedantick,

"That is nothing of what I said, child! I would do no such thing, I hold no loving regard for Khanjali, however attractive he may be!" Pedantick made a kissy face, mimicking the sound of interlocking lips.

"Mwah! Kissy kissy! You love pop-pop!" Ezrakell had sunk too deep, fallen into the trap of a child, it was humiliating. Whilst trying to quell her mockery, Ezrakell bumped against a fellow, a passerby who was wandering oddly centered to a wide road, a road lacking many travelers. For a moment both Ezrakell and the traveler locked eyes, and for a moment, he knew them. It was clear the traveler did not know Ezrakell, his eyes were glossy, unadjusted — unimpressed. Ezrakell stepped forward, but stopped, sure he knew the traveler's face, the cold left eye, the bruise under his jaw.

The Harlequin

"Child. Move away, this man is but a fellow of crime, a vandal of our home, you remember? I intend to speak with him." Pedantick quieted her mocking, turning far more serious, far more intrigued. She nodded, and hurried over behind a vacant stall, peeking out between two colored banners, watching the encounter with pride. Ezrakell, with his fist of steel readily equipped, turned back to the traveler. He followed behind them, keeping pace. "Oh, merry traveler! It appears as though I have lost my ring! Would you happen to have seen it?" Ezrakell tapped the man on the shoulder, readying his fist for a punch. The figure began to turn, "Woe is me, it was right here on this hand, look!" The vandal faced Ezrakell directly, soon meeting the delivery of a powerful right hook directly into the side of their head. The strike knocked them to the ground in an instant, the glove shaking with energy. The goon quivered in between delirium and reality. They murmured quiet prayers and questions, trying to find their way back to standing. Ezrakell helped them up, squeezing their shoulder. "Ah! Remember me yet? When I was bested it was by three. Yet here you sit, bested by one! Pathetic, for a mercenary!" Ezrakell sent the vandal back to the ground, a second punch nearly sending them to the realm of the unconscious. The goon wasn't going to be able to talk in this state, and Ezrakell had no intention of speaking to him, pulling him to his feet one last time.

"Hit him again Ezra! Beat 'em up!" Ezrakell smiled, a devious joy for disaster spreading through his soul,

"You assumed I was the father a night prior from today, assumed I was Khanjali. I would have such a comparison be a compliment, an honor! Khanjali is a man beyond honor and grace, and you fools would seek to torment him? I shall ask this one thing of you: is whom you work for worth the danger—the hazard of a true family?" Ezrakell spat in the eyes of the vandal, before dropping them to the ground, no finishing blow required. Pedantick ran over and began mercilessly kicking the body, approaching the thousandth cut required for death. Ezrakell quickly tore the chaotic beast from its prey, chastising her for such unladylike behavior.

"Why do you get to beat up bad guys, but I can't?" Ezrakell pulled her along, heading towards home once again,

Creatures of Habit

"Why, Khanjali would have my head if he found even a speck of blood on your pure form." The two held hands, cheerily walking down the cobblestones, not a care in the world. "Child? I do like my head."

The divine screech from the depths of the Ichyr Well was the first sound to fill the silence of its depth. It was a shrill cry, muffled by the gurgling of celestial fluids pouring down the esophagus that bellowed it. The Ichyr stirred as a form of melting mire clambered from its depths, pulling itself ashore. The creature once again cried out, the guttural babbling of the fluid pouring from the creature's face morphing the sound into a terrifying blabber, one akin to the panicking of a drowning dog, submerged in the deep mud of the plateaus. The creature tore at its face, trying frantically to displace the fluid that was dissolving from its body. It was a mucked puddle, a form melting away by the second, its bones and flesh absorbing into its vessel, sludging away into pools of pure Ichyr. It could not see, its eyes mere husks fusing to the skull. The creature felt around itself until it located a pile of rubble. It grappled to the stones, and pushed itself to its feet, stumbling forward as if it had never walked before. Every step solicited further pain, every motion shattering its liquid bones once again, its blood pouring from every orifice. A soothing voice spoke to the creature from within its mind, instructing it to halt its movement, to rest just for a moment, to calm itself. The creature was not reassured by the strange voice, terrified by its seemingly formless nature. The creature slammed its fickle body against the stone walls of the room, threatening to reduce itself back to the lifeless puddle it once was. The voice once again called to the creature to stop, mentioning—only once—the existence of its daughter. The creature froze, and finally it was tamed. The pooling of the fluid was slowing, and the creature's mind was finally emerging, its consciousness rebirthing to what it once was, but ever slowly. It was confused and lost, shaking in cold restraint. The voice told it to wait, as the Ichyr was still settling within its body. The process of going from Ink to Ichyr, or anywhere in between, was a painful one. If one could survive the rush of new emotions and memories, new senses and nerves, the constant screaming of distant voices and shattered minds, they would have made it further than most. The greatest filter, however, was the physical. The pain—the agony of having your entire being ripped down to its binds and rebuilt—all with you still alive, still aware of what you are becoming. It was terrible, and few survived the experience. Khanjali was stronger than most, and he was determined to return to his daughter, his treasure. His mind slowly grasped his new form, feeling the pain lessen and lessen until it was weak enough for him to move again. The voice seemed less like a shout now, but rather a distant thought, pushed into his mind by a vacant force. The voice instructed Khanjali on how to operate his body, and how to exist within this new form. The dripping had ceased, and the pure Ichyr had hardened into a carapace on small sections of Khanjali's body, namely his hands, legs, and face. His old wings had been left nearly untouched, except for hard husk-like growths on the lower halves of their surfaces. His broken wing still remained just that however, with no sign of its healing process having begun. But in light of greater agony, the pain from such a minor injury no longer bothered him, no pain seemed to bother him, in actuality. He was reborn, and how lucky he was to be so. The voice seemed to suggest that Khanjali had been brought back at the cost of its final resting place beyond the veil of mortality. It had gifted life to Khanjali once more out of thankful gratitude, and understanding. Khanjali wanted to ask questions, a terrible distrust rose in his form. But this would have to wait, he hadn't the time. He had not seen his daughter in such a great length, he needed to return home. The well had nearly collapsed in its entirety, practically every support pillar now lay unsupporting, the ceiling had crumbled down into piles of rubble, and the floor tiling had slid en masse into the pits of Ichyr below, raising the level of Ichyr to near overflowing. The new rubble allowed for easy exit from the well, a natural ramp having been formed just below the large skylight built into the ceiling. With a heavy burden of impossible understanding, Khanjali began his ascent, his body still shivering within itself, the cold wetness of the Ichyr making insulation impossible. After what seemed like an eternity spent climbing, Khanjali emerged back onto the plateau. The rain had stopped, and even the mud below his feet had hardened back to its rocky form. The cold air blew against his body, sending sharp ripples through the liquid carapace. The Ichyr was finalizing its settling process, only a few droplets of the pure liquid remained, and even then they were quickly solidified by the low temperature. Khanjali wasn't sure exactly where he was, in relation to Drochandas that is. He was having trouble remembering some things, the quiet voice in his head seemed to be the cause. The voice, understanding this, began to direct Khanjali to his home, slowly and meticulously, for it knew all that he once had regrettably; it did not want to. Khanjali walked towards a wooded area, through a series of cliffs, and down a valley of sand. As time went on, Khanjali grew more and more aware of his surroundings, more anchored to the world which he existed within. He stopped by a small river, tired from his lengthy journey. He peered into the helium below, staring at his bare, corrupted form—at his face. His once rounded head was covered in a skull-like helm of pure Ichyr, two large antlers unfurled from the top of the skull, nearly symmetrical in every way. His sullen eyes could be narrowly seen from under the helm, small slits elegantly carved within its face allowed him to see. His arms had been sharpened, large shards of Ichyr pointing outwards from his wrists, all varying in length and size. Even his torso and legs contained remnants of what once could have been an Ichyr crystallite. He was hideous, a monster smelted from the ashes of the dead and desperate. Worst of all, he was without clothes, a naked beast in the wilds of Inkhome. He did not want to go home, he could not bear to see his daughter, not like this. Khanjali could not stand to part from her, either. He considered who he could seek for assistance. Would Ezrakell even recognize him? Was Pedantick patiently awaiting his return? A horrifying thought struck Khanjali, who had not considered how long he had been in the Ichyr. It could have been hours, but it also could have been days, months, even years. The voice within him told him not to worry about such speculations, as negative thinking would truly get them nowhere. Khanjali remained by the river for some time, peacefully contemplating his next move. He looked to the sky, he could just barely make out the stars. He prayed, one last time, to Maccabeus. Perhaps this time, she would hear.

After returning home, Ezrakell had simply waited for the first two hours. After all, Khanjali had been late before. Sometimes, he would become caught up in his duties, hunting for hours without noticing the passing of time. Sometimes it was simply a matter of pursuit, perhaps there was a large creature Khanjali had been stalking, waiting for the right moment. One could never know with him, so Ezrakell remained as optimistic as possible. Around the eighth hour, Ezrakell lost this positive outlook. Never had the hunter been away from home for so long. He tried not to consider the possibilities, the terrible things that might have happened to Khanjali. He never brought any of these possibilities to the attention of Pedantick. During this time, she seemed confident that her father was doing his best work, she theorized that he was hunting a whole nest of Krolaws, set to bring back the largest haul Drochandas had ever seen. She wasn't in denial—she was too young to know what that meant—the girl was simply unaware that her father had the capability of a failure, she simply didn't consider it a possibility. Unbeknownst to the two, Khanjali had been within the walls of Drochandas for some time, debating and plotting. He had so much running through his mind, so much to do and no way to do it. He needed to speak with Ezrakell, but he knew not the reaction the old fool would have to a beast. He could not speak to him directly, not at first. Ezrakell rarely left the comfort of home without reason, Khanjali would have to forge one. The hunter had a few ideas, but he was immensely under-prepared for the majority of them. The only thing he had managed to scavenge from the fall was his weapon, and the shattered remains of his once pristine carving knife. With these tools alone, Khanjali began the pursuit of Ezrakell. First, he would need some kind of covering, something to hide his face from the other Atramedians. If they saw him, the divine incarnate of the once feared Ichyric war beasts, there would not be an hour for explanation, his death would be assured. No, there he needed greater lengths—a disguise. With his knowledge of the hunter's craft, Khanjali had managed to locate a woman, one with age catching their talons, one who was hanging her laundry, bedsheets, undergarments, and boots. He needed these things, but Khanjali was never one to steal from the poor, and this woman did seem as such. Trials by the gods were often considered impossible paradoxes of good and evil, and assuming his holy obligations, Khanjali thought it wrong to act against the gods in such a way. And yet, what was a god to him, when Pedantick was at risk? He awaited the woman's return inside, a time enough to take what he needed. He clambered over the stone fence and silently approached the laundry. With care he unclipped the bedsheets and continued onwards to the boots. It wasn't terribly thick, and would not do well against the wind or frost, but it would secure his form in shadow. As the hunter made his way to the boots, a door was ever so patiently nudged open. Khanjali stood motionless, a rodent down the barrel of a smoking gun. The woman stared directly at him, expressionless and blank. A hazy fog drifted over her eyes, she did not blink. She had no way of knowing that Khanjali was there, yet the hunter could not shake the feeling of being known. She called out, asking if anyone was there. Khanjali knew he would not stand a chance in conversation with a normal Atramedian, but a blind Atramedian would perhaps be more cooperative.

"Please kind woman, spare me your wrath, for I am penniless and exceptionally cold. I need clothes to hide my cursed body and have resorted to petty thievery. I deserve no pity, but I must ask for it." The woman did not speak, she did not even move. Khanjali waited for a response but received none. "But please, do not call the guardsmen, I have a daughter to think of and without—" The old woman stopped his ramblings, speaking with confusion,

"I am not calling any guardsmen, am I? You think I could call before you could silence my tongue?" Khanjali assured the woman he would never harm someone, especially not someone as weary as she. She calmed with this notion of relative safety, and asked, "So, a merciful penniless wretch? Some would call that a fool. Does this fool have a name?" Khanjali was hesitant, but decided the more she knew, the safer he was. She could not see, only put names to voices, they would most likely never cross paths again. She conversed with him, telling him of gardening, alchemy, and lovemaking—all of her passions. He listened, kindly and quietly, only speaking when she asked questions of him. "It is drab to lie in such a silent existence. If only the sounds of the city had gone away instead of my sight. I would do such miserable things to see again. There is no use in blathering, is there."

"I am curious how a woman of your practices could become so dulled. Is this boredom of yours incurable?" The old lady pondered for a moment, thinking of what could be done.

The Harlequin

"Would you be terribly bothered in helping me with a small chore? I promise it will not take but a moment." Khanjali agreed to this task, sure now that he was to escape this predicament with his life. The old woman summoned him to her home. The building was in rather pristine shape for a home in the Southers. While it did lack space, the cozy echo of its cushions and carpets gave it comfort. Khanjali theorized the cleanliness had something to do with the lack of activity, the boredom the woman spoke of. She led him through her home, to a small room not unlike a den. A warm glow of fire filled its presence, soft wisps of wind spun in from a window left ajar. A fair aroma of meat and flour danced through the room, though there was no cauldron for cooking in sight. Elegantly positioned in the present center was a small shrine, one sectioned in three parts. The center of the shrine was devoid of color, an elegant golden stone replaced the simple cloth of its majority. The surface was decorated with an assortment of items—artifacts of alchemy, tools of execution, and mechanical tidbits—all kept in near-perfect condition. In the middle of this section, was a large statue of Maeandri, designed in great part with ingenuity and theory-crafting, as no one had ever seen Maeandri in their entirety. The left section of the shrine was coated in black, moth-like memorabilia lay amongst coins and spices. There was a statuette of Maccabeus at the far end of this section, draped in a black cloth, matching in color to the rest of the section. The oddest of its parts was the opposite side, a section painted divine white, clearly dedicated to the bird-god Lakaeron. Khanjali had never seen a single Atramedian acknowledge his position as a deity, let alone worship him as an equal to Maccabeus. Not many would after the Divine war boasted such a devilish display of the Ichyric people. Lakaeron's side of the shrine held feathers, glassware, and rustic photographs of bird-like people. There was no matching statuette. Khanjali could not look away from the refined quality of every item in the shrine, scanning over every vague detail several times over, confirming their existence. The woman was not concerned with the shrine, however, far more fixated upon a small helmet placed in the center of it. It was a purplish metal, not particularly familiar to Khanjali, nor was the design. It was shaped rather majestically, an iconic bird beak facing from the front, hinged like a jaw, with a small slot above for the eyes. Large metallic feathers were pasted behind the beak, facing back, lengthening the helmet. "This, this is the precious remains of someone I hold terribly dear. They have been gone for some time, but I no longer have the merit to bless them, my actions forsake me from the rights of Maeandri and their ancillaries. Would you perhaps make an attempt?" Khanjali cupped the small helm in his large, taloned hands. He doubted even a priest would hear him now, let alone the greater gods. He accepted the woman's task, keen on making an attempt. He spoke softly, praying the old death blessing to the remains, awaiting a voice. There was no response. He called out once more, asking for forgiveness, from not only the dead but himself. No response. Khanjali called out one final time, calling to the gods for action, placing blame upon them for the terrible fate of his world, people, and family. He could no longer stand blinded by faith in a place that seemed so darkened by ignorance from the very gods he worshiped. A whisper returned his call, telling him not to worry, telling him his message was received. This was not Maccabeus, nor was it Maeandri. It was no priest of either and did not resemble that which was trapped within his mind. The voice confused Khanjali, but with knowing in his soul, he accepted its assurances, gladdened his prayer had not gone unheard. Khanjali told the woman he had succeeded and was met with glee. She seemed revived, her spirits reprised with new life, though in showing she was rather mundane. She thanked Khanjali and escorted him back to the courtyard they had first met within. Khanjali went to leave, when the woman stopped him, begging him to listen one last time. "You are a kind soul, too kind to freeze in the eve. Take my old friend's cloak, and his clothes as well. He no longer needs them, besides—I must forget of him now." Khanjali was astonished that such goodness existed in Drochandas but took the opportunity in stride. He thanked the woman again for her selflessness, and headed off. He was not far from home, Ezrakell would see his brilliance shortly.

In his study, there was red. Crimson banners and paper of rose silk covered the walls and desk. A pen rested against a freshly cut belt of wool, the lip of which hung slightly over the table. Two ingots of steel lay against a rack for needles of several sizes, Pedantick's fingers flicking at them against Ezrakell's wishes. A single bookshelf held all the knowledge he considered dear, as Pedantick held up the design before him, so that he may more easily follow its intricacies. The projectile that shattered his window had just narrowly grazed his left arm, and certainly pierced his focus. He had taken Pedantick to his apartment, unable to both work on his finery and care for her at the same time. At first, Ezrakell was terrified, knowing full well that Drochandas was not the axiom of safety. The recency of mercenary hazard brought some frigid paranoia to the old fool, yet nothing was as distinctly obvious as a shattered window. As Ezrakell rose from his seat with a shout, rushing about his workspace wrought with panic and misery, Pedantick took notice of just *what* had shattered the window. It was a bolt, a single hand-made crossbow bolt. Pedantick was no fool, she knew what her own craftsmanship looked like. Ezrakell had some doubts about her confidence in the design but trusted her. If Pedantick was right, then there was only one possibility. Ezrakell looked from the window, scanning the horizon for any sign of life. A small glimmer of light shone in the dark, just beyond the wall, in the woods, beside the port. What little sun remained was reflecting off some kind of mirrored surface, right into Ezrakell's window. The glimmer flinched upwards, channeling the light directly into Ezrakell's eye. He fell back, blinded for a moment, letting out a string of curses. With a simple "What does that mean?" from Pedantick, Ezrakell was silent again, back against the window to search. It was gone. Pedantick spoke a new word, one she had just learned from a certain angered Atramedian. The old fool silenced the girl, instructing her to never speak it in front of her father. She promised, but there was not an ounce of truth in her words. Ezrakell once more peered out into the night, curious if what had just blinded him had been a mere coincidence, or something more. Khanjali could not die on the hunt, not to any creature, nor to any man. This, Ezrakell knew. He tugged his coat from the stand and instructed Pedantick to remain indoors. He needed to know for himself. By the time he had reached the forest's edge, the night was in full shape. There were sounds among the greenery, shouts and curses that drew Ezrakell ever closer. With prudence, he hid in shrubs and watched over a sunken Acolyte of Wings, one drawn to the hide of a hideous beast. It was drooling, saliva seeping out the shell-like jaw of its mouth. Before the Acolyte could move ever closer, the bones of the beast contorted, fangs growing like shrooms from the carapace and maw. Panic beset the Acolyte, and they drew their blade, legs set for combat. No combat occurred, as the beast cleanly bent its neck forward and latched itself upon the Acolyte's rightmost arm. With a cry of pain, they pulled back from the encounter, their bones splintered to pebbles and muscles shredded to ribbons. As the Acolyte tumbled away, their arm did not follow with them, still dripping purple gore from the creature's clenched jaws. Clutching the wound that marked their stolen limb, the Acolyte looked back to its feral opponent. It tore flesh from the arm, chewing it like a strip of ham, gulping its entirety down in two neat bites. Picking at the bones for scraps, it met the eyesight of its prey. With no soul to their face, the Acolyte pulled from their waist a small pistol, fit to fire a single shot. They raised it to their temple and fired, ending their life before the beast had such a chance. The scent of death rose into the treeline, Ezrakell nearly panting with terror. He rose from his safety and staggered backward, his lunch in his throat. The beast continued to lick at the corpse, gnawing off small bits where it found suitable fat. The snarling slurp of organs and entrails disturbed the very nature of the woods, as Ezrakell fell against the cobbles of a protruding canal. The echo was heavy, and his hidden nature shattered. The beast drew close, its hideous form rising over the shrubs in dominance. Placing an incredible paw against the old fool's left leg, it untethered it's now glistening jaws, stuffed with the gristle of man, and unfurled a most awful stench,

"Ezrakell! I did not mean for you to—this sight was certainly unintended." Ezrakell did not move, he did not dare. The figure before him was not familiar, not even remotely similar to what his friend once was. It was one of a murderer, a beast without remorse, without any semblance of understanding.

"K-Khanjali? Maccabeus I beg this to be an illusion. You, feral thing, are the father to the most precious Pedantick?" Khanjali nodded, a severed leg caught between his teeth. Little consciousness passed his hunger, which was now partly sated.

"I have so much to explain, so much reason for this horrible function. Would you give me a moment to summarize?" A monster, a body of most desecrated demise, a fool, all tied in a bundle of lies.

How could this being be Khanjali? How could a monster be what once was so perfect?

"That is a *corpse*, you expect trust from a corpse as well? Khanjali I have seen you cannibalize one of your own! What summary could be ample?"

"I cannot control it, I truly am more fearful than even you. Please. Just a moment of your trust, I swear!" Through Ezrakell came a sense of understanding, realization that calmed his tissue. There was no choice to be had, no reverse to the fate before him. He could taste the flavor of Khanjali's words, the very meaning of their essence. This was the man he once knew, unchanged despite appearance. Ezrakell swallowed his deepest alarms, his signs of fear.

"*Just* a moment."

Much of what the hunter dreamed was unimaginable. Lucid specters of destiny collapsed upon him, horrors came from a persistent rat that appeared in every vision. Khanjali did not find comfort in his dreams, and since his conscription into the lines of monster he had found even less solace. He had dreamed of the thief in the canal, but this time he did not steal his life with a dagger and wrath, but rather by talon and hunger. In his new form, he was unshackled, brought to his best. The thief was searching through the canals for food, not a reason for his slaughter in sight. Khanjali did not defend himself this time. He pursued a meal, devouring instead of containing. The hunter tore open his stomach, gorging on his innards, all whilst the thief remained alive, screaming in terror and agony. He continued to eat, consuming every ounce of meat on his bones, until all that remained was a husk-like skeletal form, with little to no thief left to be called such. Khanjali was still hungry however and remained alert for more food. He turned, a voice echoing through the canals,

"Pop-pop?" Khanjali jolted back to the realm of the conscious, the adrenaline of his vision still rushing through him. A splitting headache pounded into his skull, the chaos of his mind adding to that pain significantly. There was new pain for his shape, each day his limbs ached more than the last, begging to be let away from their cage. He took a sip of some helium from the surface of his collector, hoping hydration would cure his woes. It did not. The headache continued to worsen, to the point where he couldn't think without immense struggle. He gripped his neck, trying to halt the pain. He cried out in agony, the pain converting itself into a rage, hunger, a bloodlust he could not quench. He thought of his daughter, and swallowed these feelings, he wasn't a beast. He wouldn't allow the events of the night prior to reoccur. Khanjali was a citizen, a functioning member of society, one with a family—a daughter no less. A knocking rattled the metal sheeting Khanjali had set up to keep rodents from attacking him whilst he slept. He peered out from behind his makeshift barricade to see Ezrakell, not nearly awake enough to function properly.

"You missed our deadline. By four hours." Khanjali didn't exactly have a way of measuring time, but he did feel like he had overslept. He climbed out from his self-built cage, meeting Ezrakell face-to-face for the first time in broad daylight.

"Apologies. I've been... coping."

"Forgivable, but time is of the essence." Khanjali nodded, knowing Ezrakell was correct. He had no way of discovering the true severity of his condition—if it was far worse than he imagined. "Did you... well, dispose of it?"

"The only way I know how, yes." Ezra sighed, clutching the mug in his hands harder.

"Please, spare me the details. Let us make our leave, we *are* late after all." Ezrakell elegantly spun around and slipped out of the woods. Khanjali had convinced him of his inability to control the beast-like form he found himself in, of the unfortunate circumstances that led to its creation. He had wagered for assistance and had even managed to remove the body of the Acolyte before anyone came to inspect the gloriously obnoxious chewing noises in the midst of the night. The lack of trust surrounding his shape disheartened Khanjali, as much as he understood the mind behind it. He missed the feeling of approval received from those around him, the mutual accommodation. He followed behind his friend, ensuring not to let his hood fall, he did not want to be the cause of further tardiness. Over the midsection of the greater bridge into Drochandas, Khanjali could hear Ezrakell speaking softly, in such a way that one might speak to a child, or themselves. Khanjali did not think much of it until he summited the height of the bridge. Upon the lowest beginning of its cobbles, where all the smallest of markets were, was Pedantick, speaking to a passerby, entertaining herself to the best of her ability. She was showing off a snow globe she had built from crystal and the waves of the Helium Sea. Khanjali suffered an immediate shock of pain, the anxiety clicking inside his head, the Ichyr rattling.

"Ezrakell, I'll have your head for this." The hunter mumbled under the thick of his shell. The child rushed to his side, dedicated to meeting a potential friend.

"Ah, child. This is he, my— er— partner. His name is Mr. K, he had his face caved in by a club at the age of two, thus it looks rather hideous. He prefers to keep it hidden, I'd rather you didn't ask any more about it." Pedantick nodded, assuring Ezrakell she would certainly not ask about it. Khanjali was motionless, he stared wide-eyed at his daughter, who he had no intention of seeing today.

"Hello Mr. K! I'm Pedantick, but my pop-pop just calls me P! We both have small names, isn't that super cool?" Khanjali glared at Ezrakell, furious with his silent decision, questioning the very purpose of his daughter's presence in their activities.

"Yes, hello. Little girl. Our names are quite similar, aren't they?" Pedantick seemed relatively intrigued by Khanjali's monstrous voice.

"You have a funny voice, mister." Ezrakell scolded her for the harsh words, but Khanjali enjoyed her sentiments.

"We have quite a bit to accomplish in this time, accomplice. We best hurry upon our task." Khanjali watched the old fool march back to the limits of the forest, a prideful dominance in his gait. Pedantic and the hunter remained beside the bridge, glancing at each other to share in the hilarity of his motion.

"Ezra looks like he's got marbles in his shoes." Discourse continued as the two followed their marching leader, unsure of where he would lead them.

"I would think he had broken a leg, little girl. Or maybe had his ankles plucked." The snickering between the father and daughter drew the attention of Ezrakell, who was not nearly as appreciative of the mocking,

"Mr. K, are you fit to walk for a short while? I know those bones pain you." Khanjali chuckled, twisting his wrist around with inhuman strength,

"They are malleable, true. But I find it quite easy to maintain my form. Certainly, I will survive a short jog." The group exited the gate, heading east towards the plateaus. Khanjali, thanks to his prior experience in the plateaus, began to grow disconnected, finding himself staring into the muddy flats for minutes at a time.

"You're very quiet Mr. K. My pop-pop would like you. He likes to watch people too." Khanjali was pulled from his trances, hearing Pedantick's words, not quite understanding them.

"I am nothing like your father." Pedantick receded within herself, and Ezrakell took quite a notice.

"Perhaps you are more like him than you noticed? He does tend to drift, as do you, Mr. K." Khanjali snapped back to his friend, violence presented by his glare alone. The lower of his jaws grew sore with a lack of feeding. He had to stay strong, for Pedantick. Ezrakell gestured up a small hillside, up a decaying wooden stairwell, a home of clay. Khanjali stared with concern, the glistening hope once shimmering in his eyes was slowly extinguished.

"A witch's hut, surely. Is this mockery? Am I to be saved by *witches*?"

"Priests. We call them priests, Mr. K. Do show a hook of respect." Khanjali continued to watch the home, a small puff of smoke and ash emerging from its singular femerell. Ezrakell no longer moved, waiting for his partner at the birth of the stairwell, silently. Pedantick gleaned nothing from her watching, she had observed Khanjali's gremlin limbs, in an effort to familiarize herself with his uncanny body, and gathered nothing. Khanjali shambled past his daughter, taking a moment to thank her for her company, and continued up the stairs. The panels creaked in hazardous disconcert, sending light awareness of the danger to Khanjali's fingertips, he was ready to fall, he predicted it. Despite this, he ascended. The clay hut had something of a garden surrounding it, various herbs and flowers and weeds grew en masse upon the once mud-caked plateau (now turned brilliant field by an unyielding thumb of green). Even the thick orange moss of the forest had found its way to the clay walls. The door was unlocked, unsurprisingly. Such a place of life had no need for security, Khanjali doubted there was anything of value within the hut to guard. The scent of metal and steam filled Khanjali's thick leathers, as the odor of the clay hut quickly found an untainted form to cling to. The bubbling of various fluids could be heard in distant voyages, but the immediate surroundings were a place of lesser sound. It was humid, a sickly moisture combed the air. Two doors bled into Khanjali's eyes, the light dust floating through the hall obscuring any purity. To his right was a path into a bedroom, a cot, and hundreds of vases. Indeed, the vases filled even the halls, all unique in design, and fracture. Papers dotted the floor of the bedroom, and a quill—its ink spilt—lay outcast under the cot. There were no windows. In front of him lay an endless roar, a fire, of course, he had seen the smoke himself. Some shallow moss dripped from the roofing, above the raging flame. Blue glimmers scattered the mantle, newly forged Home Stones—the visions of Inkhome and its surrounding planets faintly visible in their glazen surface. A small bundle of gardening tools was resting against the cobblestone of the makeshift fireplace. Besides these things, these unkempt, unclean things, the remainder of the room was hidden behind the corner of the clay walls. He could hear a tapping of boot leather, a humming of tunes. Hymns, familiar tunes. Inside the room was a woman, wearing only a pair of thick leather pants, a tight thermal tied above the open flame, drying. Her antenna and feathers were tied back with a string of sinew, and lengthy worker gloves of some kind stretched from her fingers to her upper arms, nearly to her shoulders. She had three wings, her two smallest were intact, if not rugged. They bore scrapes and cuts, even bends in some of the finer veins. She only had one of her larger wings, a large tear streaking down its middle. She wore a false wing beside it, made from felt and leather, metal rivets holding its shape. The woman was dicing a vibrant flower stem, and placing the scraps into a small pot, stirring occasionally. Khanjali, entranced by the rhythmic cutting motion, the protruding back muscles of the shirtless woman, and the glorious tranquility of the worn wings, managed to stumble over a vase, knocking it against the wall. The woman stopped her cutting, recognizing the scent of another in her home.

"Ah, ah! My patron, bid me the time to clothe myself. It should be more than dry now—but a moment." She quickly danced to the open fire, plucking her thermal from within. At its soggy flavor she scoffed, and returned it to the fire, instead turning to the assortment of garments hung by her work table, among them a priestess' robe.

"Priestess Mezzo? How unfamiliar you are from your behind. N-not to sound childish as if I was watching—certainly not enough to claim—" Khanjali bit his tongue, flustered rambling he had not experienced since Pedantick's mother.

"Hmm? Oh, you know me? We have met? Yes, of course! Ezrakell sent word of you, a sickness has taken hold of you, a bodily curse." She readied her work gloves, and approached Khanjali, a towel tied taught around her bosom. Her priestess cloak was draped across her back, obscuring her injured wings.

"Yes, Ezrakell." Khanjali quelled a tang of disappointment, a hope that she had remembered. How could she remember a beast like he, now changed too far?

"Now, remove thine cloak, hooded one! The examination has begun!" Khanjali took down his cloak, stunning the priestess with his rancid skull. "Indeed a sickness! Worse rather, this is far different, a curse. How peculiar." She twisted his head, holding his chin to the light of the fire, staring down his whole-less eyes.

"The shell is thick. My flesh obscured. It pains the sight of all that see it." Her eyes, at the sight of such a voice, of the movement of flesh and bone, went wide with pity. With knowing. She ran a solemn hand against the side of his face, feeling the structure of it, the purity,

"Kha— It cannot be...." She placed her hand on his neck, letting it hover for a moment, before letting it rub against her calloused-ly softened palms. "Khanjali." He shivered—a rush—a quiver of romantic hope.

"I am but a beast now, a creature of Ichyr. How could you see?" She smiled at him, a simple grin. Her wrinkled cheeks pressed against the sockets of her eyes, a darkened spot of skin.

"You have the cheekbones of gods, even in this demonic body. It is stunning." She found herself unknowingly pressing her hand against his chest, feeling him, kneading him. Khanjali cleared his voice, cleansing the holy priestess' corrupted mind.

"Y-you were not the expected savior to my ailment, certainly not in a place such as this. Why has Ezrakell brought me here?" Mezzo snapped her fingers, the flush from her face returning to its average, more docile, state.

"Priesthood grants me a great many opportunities of study. Medicine, curing, it is within my rites to perform these deeds — to give my gift of holiness back to those who support it. I have touched Ichyr and lived, and with this, I am the closest to an expert you may find. It is Ichyr, yes?" Khanjali nodded, feeling his shell crawl with life again, the voice was rousing.

"I discovered something — a well, I presume. It lies just north of here, the mud-plains. There was a divine quake, and then — " Mezzo's eyes filled with sorrow, and she offered Khanjali a cup, ludicrously filled with tea.

"Oh, Ichyr, so tainted with purity. It would seem you have been infected with its godliness. You are closer to Maeandri now, some may say." Khanjali did not laugh, and the priestess realized the misplacement of her humor.

"I am a monster now, yes? What am I to do, can you return me to Ink?" Priestess Mezzo shook her head, seating herself upon her working table.

"There is no need! Alas, you are still of Ink! And Ichyr — of Ink *and* Ichyr."

"Both, can that be done? Is it possible to become a being of paired matter?" Mezzo snatched from her learnings a small syringe, a needle thick enough to pierce metals.

"Here, take your limits, show us your blood honey." Khanjali inserted the needle into his shell, deep enough to feel it puncture his own skin. He drew the syringe, testing for a hint of life. As proven by the priestess, within was a dark substance, as void as ink itself.

"I am — does this mean I can be saved? Can this wretched Ichyr be replaced?" Priestess Mezzo rose from her seat, scooping the Ink from Khanjali's arms and holding it tight.

"I would place my worry for your life. Not many can survive such an endeavor as Ink and Ichyr." A small machine of sorts spun the Ink, examining it, purifying it. From its basin formed a small white crystal, one the priestess took great note of. "Woe, this cannot be good, you must see it, Khanjali, your Ink is already infected with the Ichyr. If we do not halt the spread soon — "

"You mean to say I am dying? Will the gods take more from me yet?" The priestess shuddered at the thought of Khanjali's death.

"No, it can be slowed. All we must have is a countermeasure. An 'anti-Ichyr', and Ink." Mezzo slumped to a small bench beneath her desk, an assortment of tablets and scrolls resting upon it.

"Would you effort yourself in saving me? I wish not to steal away your time, priestess. Your work is divine." Priestess Mezzo straightened with a small scroll, ready to deliver,

"Silence. Your work is mundane, and it is the mundane that works the divine. Without a father, a sisterhood cannot grow. Without the pleasantries of a god, a brotherhood may never form. Take this scroll, within scribes a map of the canals, once thought as mundane as you, now a labyrinthine cause-way, leading down to the depths of the only Ink vault. An ancient well. You must find it before your Ichyr takes hold, and collect a pure sample of the Ink within, the Ink from which you were born. And another, you must gather a sample of the Ichyr, the stuff of which you have been tainted. With this, I can cure you." Khanjali took the scroll in hand, and stared into the eyes of the priestess,

"You are a savior. Have my thanks, and be well. Anything I may aid you in, ask. I will return."

"Post haste."

"Indeed." Khanjali left the room, heading back towards the wooden door of the musty clay home. The priestess remained. She pondered her faith a final time, questioning what good damning a man such as he could do. The common excuses would not do. It was not a divine plan, nor a loophole of purity. It was targeted spite, and for a priestess to thrive, spite was to be of no concern. The priestess knew that much. A hiss from her prior work brought her to the table, where a leaning feather of Khanjali's coat remained, an odor of he surrounding it. She took the tool's shaft and placed it in her hand. She could only think for so long.

~ *Myceliac*

Written within the esteemed history of the
Cyanotypes — a clan long extinguished...

The boy had died for something, had he not? It haunted the Duke, the truth of the demise. What if — unbeknownst to him — the boy was a killer? A Vampyre of some sort, a cannibal or slave trader? Had his mother harbored demons? Had his father — there was no knowledge of the father, and thus Ephilo felt it unfair to think of the man. But there was still the issue of the boy. Out of fear alone, Duke Ephilo kept his mind's eye wide open, waiting for the boy to return to him, awaiting what could only be a rapture of the unworthy. Duke Ephilo did not remember killing the boy. He did not recall it, he *could* not. A boulder fell upon the child, or he had been impaled by a stray stalactite! The boy hadn't bled to Ephilo's end, undoubtedly he had tasted fate by any other means, by anything else? But when the Duke closed his eyes he saw the boy, and he saw his own unfeeling eyes, shearing into the neck of the child just as much as his own blade, and he was terrified of what he saw. Zealotyr stirred the Duke this morning, his scratching at the map board brought endless sound to the softly chirping birds and distant howling. A rooster to his farm of thought.

"Harken, life... north." Zealotyr stretched out upwards, tearing a fresh sheet from the roll of parchment he had assembled against the side wall of the temple. The entirety of the ancient scribing of the old world had been covered in markings of his own making, lists of noted landmarks lay stamped with wax to the wall, lengthy and needless.

"Your hobby exceeds you. This is… excessive, at the very least." Snapping its neck back, and peering lifelessly at the Duke, Zealotyr harkened again. He excused his work as the continuation of an art—mysticism was practiced in the city, so why not continue cartography? Caelo was raised soon after, and the three sat about a bonfire to gorge themselves fat (Only Ephilo actually ate). Caelo itself drifted ever closer to the machine, its wooden fixtures buckling.

"If cartography is dead, assuredly you are lucky to outlive it." Zealotyr agreed and continued his map. The mannerisms of its drawings were incredibly swift, thick jolted actions that were so easily predicted. Clockwork.

"Have you experienced hallucinations, or [FEELINGS] of [MOTIVATIONAL DISTRESS] as of late, [DUKE EPHILO]?" Caelo presented its question without restraint, pure curiosity in its tone—notably lacking any malice.

"I am as motivated as ever Caelo, and—" The Duke recalled the swan, the accusatory farse of Caelo, the court that haunted him refrainless, and seemingly throughout all countries. He shook his hat from his snout, and pursued his tone, "I am not any iller than normal. What is this questioning for?" Caelo chirped, prodded at the back head of the Duke, and returned to his front side.

"You have displayed symptoms. [DUKE] has [HARDNESS] of Alogia [REBOOTING PROGRESS: DOWNLOADING UPDATED RECORDS]." Duke Ephilo had heard enough of the claims, even Caelo fell to probing his mind, as all who knew him inevitably did. Updating symptom software often resulted in the stoppage of such ridiculous remarks. When Caelo's sole eye blinked green once more, Ephilo sighed, glad to have a companion again.

"Little Heir, have you any data on Alogia? Whatever this symptom may be, I do not know of it." Caelo approached Zealotyr, and with its metal pick gestured to it.

"Devoid of speech, [DUKE EPHILO]. [HARDNESS] of [WORD]." Ephilo nodded, content that the symptom did nothing to define him.

"Silly stuff, I talk all the time. I babble as anyone would. If anything is true—I must talk too often—I should silence myself more frequently."

The Harlequin

"Harken, death. The home of the Refiner awaits. Dawn is temporary. Leave." Unfazed by the bluntness of his map designer, Duke Ephilo readied his equipment and peered out to the peaks of the distant mountains.

"Not to the top, yes? Only half up—to the dust layer?" Zealotyr's silence affirmed the Duke's belief. Wolfstram was a place of old memory, but the dust layer was too far up to toll Ephilo. The boy had died deep below; skeletons lay among skeletons. The climb, however, would take more than life from him. The breadth of the Wolfstram heights could take days to scale, and without a proper path too, there was no hope of ascent within the week. In the old ages, the threat of a long night's journey was mitigated greatly by the Throneways: lengthy paths of gold that carried carriages overhead. They had been constructed long ago for the purpose of hastening travel. Once, they spanned across all of the Umbral Coast—potentially deeper into Arcenna, Duke Ephilo remembered little outside the sea. But that was just it, wasn't it? In fact, the Throneways *did* cross the all-territories of the coast, even the canyons at one time. Maybe, even the Cascades. If there was any hope for the journey, no rush particularly relevant, it was the Throneways. The difficulty arose in locating it, because of course Duke Ephilo had never seen them. Stories had been passed down, but there were no exact paintings, nor had Ephilo ever been directly instructed on the routes they took. He could see it, though, in the back of his eye. The golden raceways, tarnished in mossy dust and corpses, likely littered with the wreckage they once carried. Silently, the Duke spoke a prayer to Lishra and left the temple, sure of the pursuit of his ancestors.

In time, Duke Ephilo would forgive himself. Eventually, all people did. It was an unpleasant thought, to know one day the awful deeds he had done would inevitably fade into laughable memories. Of course, it was also so comforting, the nightmares would end when the guilt did. Stepping through the clearings of the Zealot's Wood, Duke Ephilo kept his eyes trained against his machine companion. Caelo was an exception to a great many rules—for one, it had never faded in memory of value. The caretaker had been by his side since his first disease, and from there history retold itself to extreme repetition. When the first physical wound had lain against the Duke's lower appendage—the tail he had spent so long jesting as an arm of its own—Caelo managed to cauterize the bleeding. When curefall exposed his sternum, and the disease threatened to tear it from its place, Caelo was the one to stuff it back within its meat prison. Had it not been for the kindness of a thoughtless machine, the Duke would likely have never found the Zephyrgaol and with it the fortune of death. Ephilo considered how to ever repay the caretaker, but it was unlikely he'd get the chance. Caelo would run out of batteries soon; energy died with the old kingdoms. Whenever the last of his power disappeared, Caelo would go with it. He hated to think of this future, but it was the only true sense of timely urgency keeping the Duke going. Death and life had become inconsequential by comparison. At the edge of the woods, where the canyon met grass, there remained the stony pillar of the old ways, stretching up miles overhead. Incredibly, it remained firm. The golden lines swayed in the breeze, ear-bled creaking sprouting from the twists in rotten steel.

"Good eye, Caelo." Ephilo said, stifling a soft cough. The stiffness in his neck had not been vanquished by a walk. It seemed to be everlasting—more than a sleeping sore. The rail stretched deeper into the woods, if there was some kind of entrance, it would surely be in the labyrinthine trees. Bound to the sky, Ephilo's eyes followed the flaxen roadway, carriages still dangling from its claw. The Court was afoot in the tree line, they had waited for his return by force, intent on finishing their labor. That other creature, the one with the stone sword, was unlike the past Deadrung. It had thick fibers in it, and arms baked like whole wheat. No, rye was far more comparable. If it was any indication of what was to come, the Deadrung Court must be readying for war. Duke Ephilo pondered how best they'd exact it. Horses were the preference of the Deadrung, but thankfully Lishra had made the forests dense and virulent. No hooven cretin could clear its breaches. Ephilo wondered how beneficial something like a horse would be to his steps. When he lost his bodies the horse would go too, and it would become a bit of a bother to recollect. Caelo always found its way through the Coast and could navigate on its own for a fortnight. Always came back. Though a horse could always be bound and tethered to a post or tree, loose rock, and some twine were all he would need. Keep the mount nice and caught up when he went, and he'd just have to make his way back. Ephilo vowed to catch a prairie horse if he could—if the Gaol dead-ended like all the rest.

"[DESTINATION]." Caelo bellowed, ticking and whirring as it flew off to the tree line above, peering over the needles and leaves, "[ROYAL METAL]." Above the woods was a small tower, easily identifiable with the brownish brick stacks. What little pasting lingered between the blocks drooled off the walls as if melted down by the wrath of a tremendous fire. Black powder flaring out from the ground level evidenced this further. It was a short climb, and the Throneway itself was an even timelier venture, but with the soot and the wind, travel had never been so nauseating.

"Little heir...Caelo, take heed: it will be precarious and bold upside the Throneway. Keep your wits about your tongue heir or it'll be cleaved by fate." There was no ascent for the tower. Stairs had burned away, and the ladder on its exterior lay disenchanted on the forest floor. A sole rope tethering a bell to its peak remained the only access to the heavens. The Duke fixed his foot on a low turn of the rope, his tail wrapped neatly around its base and securing his weight. "It's times like these Caelo, when you have to be extra careful." With his other foot, Ephilo began to shimmy his way along the rope, its swing doing little to slow him down. The node it dangled from grew all the closer to the rims of the bell, though he was intent on its silence. When the rope veered too far to one side, Ephilo would mount his leg against the bricks, and push off lightly. The dance of ascension had to be perfectly timed, and the bricks were far too carelessly assembled for that. His foot nearly slipped when the last brick tumbled out from under the wall, sending him against the other side of the tower. The bell was rung, and the Duke's scramble piqued. Upon reaching the top, he let out an incredible sigh, the flesh of his hand dug in with rope burn. A single brazen chariot rocked in the wind, its velvet seats turned to ribbons of brown by time and cure. Bulbs of mutated silver sprouted from the malaised gold, weathered handles iconic against the pure colors. Ephilo found its condition impressive, time withstanding. Entering the cabin, he welcomed Caelo inside—it was sure to be a friendless ride, why shouldn't Caelo be permitted to enjoy it? With a hefty plop, the Duke seated himself against the carriage windowsill, farthest from the door. The starting lever was easily pushed on with a tap of his foot, and the engine roared to life.

"Oh. Still lively." Ephilo plucked his two knees closer, soft movements *only* within the carriage. "Shocking. It will be a most enchanting ride, Little Heir." Caelo slowly drifted down the velvet seats, disabling its thruster momentarily to more comfortably rest.

"[RIGHTLY SW—]" Caelo suddenly blinked off, its devices flickering for the moment its words slurred. Duke Ephilo squinted at the machine, smacking it twice with little result. "[ELL]" Eye contact lasted mere seconds, and the silence of the carriage ride was all that remained. The luscious tips of the trees scraped at the bottom of the ride, and the transcendent cyan of the morning sky looked almost like a lake of cure. A colossal, snow-tipped lake of cure. One did exist, up the north of the Coast, where Duke Ephilo had once been. Though memory failed to find its exact location, its beautiful sight lingered still. In fact, Ephilo concluded the trees there mimicked the ones of the Zealot's Wood most exactly. The red-quilled ones did not appear so far north, however. A jade parrot landed against the sill of the carriage, jumping the Duke momentarily. Its curious lenses peaked in at his facade, littered with blood, bone, and ash. It tweeted, softly at first, increasing in volume steadily. The chirps felt like carpet burn, Ephilo had tumbled down a fair share of his mother's rugged stairwells. His mother had intended for the soft mats to protect the young duke, but they did little in that method besides skinning his chaps.

"Ephilo! You rotten spoilsport—get your blouse off the carpet or I'll have your neck!" His mother rested a weary arm against the banister, smirking quaintly at the roughed child. Ephilo looked up at her and found the carriage to be far larger than it once was.

"Father'll beat you, mama. Quick as a jumping hare."

"Furry as one too, you once said." The Duke—his father—stood in awe beside him. "We might install a slide. Would cater well to her knees, Mallory." The Mother snorted at the gesture, and slowly descended the stairs herself.

"We'd never see the poor girl again, stowing away night and day within her slide." This was true, Ephilo would never leave the stairwell. His mother scooped him up by his armholes and slung his torn body over her back. "I do like seeing the girl, after all. Don't you?" Her back was incredibly warm, the smooth leather of her hide-shawl like a pillow. Cloth ruffles puffed out from her shoulders, her thick mustard work-wear clotting at the ankles for effective movement. Her graying hair had been tied back in a lovely braid, one that rubbed against Ephilo's head as he rested against his mother's back.

"Would sooner have her put to death—she draws your eyes much too often, leaves me rotting in my lonesome." Mallory gasped, clutching her son's ears within her five-fingered hands.

"Ephiata, you cold pike! Have you no love for *family*?" Both parents stared the other down, violent silence enveloping them both. Ephilo began the laughter, he remembered the tasteless humor of his guardians. All three remained in a state of entertainment for the moment, before returning up the very stairs the young Ephilo had tumbled down.

"I cannot help but wonder what tenacious pressure we place upon the girl's mind if any." Ephiata brushed the fur of his lip, the thick white beard had not a hair out of place, and its gray outline melded wonderfully against his silver robes.

"The girl is happy. I can see it in her eyes." He met with his father's eyes, which wavered in the uncertainty of remembrance. Yet, he knew this man, and he knew it was his father. He could see the past of their togetherness—the best example being this very moment, it had certainly occurred. What's more was the happiness, because he was just as his father had said: Happy. Not just in past either, but in the moment of his recollection. His parents carried him to the court, and let him run free among the pillars of stone. This was a world without the wear of cure, and it was wondrous. The two parents spoke between themselves, carefully hashing their words so as to not lasso the attraction of their son. At the time of memory, Ephilo never heard what they said, he had not yet understood their words—rather—their fears of a worse future for their 'girl'. To the limits of *their* knowledge, they had heeded the words of the mighty Lishra, the bird god of the royals, and with this commitment came peace and duality of mind. Yet, Lishra seemed an ignorant god, one far more indentured to the progression of life, and the evolution of new ideas for the people. This obsession silenced relativity, it brewed a venomous storm of deceit between the royals and their god, something that the Duke and his Maiden found entirely regrettable. Ephilo had never met Lishra, nor heard of its more physical existence in the world of Arcenna. Gods were unfathomable to him, and of little consequence. If he had something to swear to when he was earnest, and a name to curse when his body wore thin, then he was content. The creaking of the court door interrupted the parents' arguing and averted the gaze of the young Ephilo. Jesters had always been a fondness of his, but the one that stood before the court entrance was no comedian. It was clad in armoring; no jester had a need for the defense at the time. Carrying with it a book, the jester's rough metal face displayed no humor. In fact, not a spick of its body was free of metal. Thin as it may be and polished to mirrors, it was a suit fit to stop a cannonball. As the jester approached the royals, he paused at the boy. Ephilo's stare was unending, inspecting nothing of the figure itself, but meeting the blunt illusion of eyes the jester's mask provided. The eyes were mere marks on the metal. They had no soul. A metal hand extended down to his head and tousled his hair. It was a mechanical jerk, a natural response turned rhythmic as if it had been practiced over several encounters.

"Good… Girl." The jester muttered, a despicable disgrace underlying its words. The touch of another was poison to it. With a grunt from Ephiata, the jester slunk along his path, meeting with the royals, endowed with the fortification of heart. Ephilo carried on himself, exiting the comforts of the court to explore the remaining grounds of his family's castle. There were various exterior balconies, all sorts of yards, and wells too. There existed a wealth of servants to keep Ephilo both occupied and within the limits of the keep. In the late hours, he had been known to wander into the forests surrounding the castle without prior notice of his leave, losing himself for hours in the thick underbrush of the wood. It took hours to locate the boy, and ever since a particularly disastrous night, the castle gates had been properly fastened shut throughout nightfall. Instead, Ephilo now found ways to hide from the maids and servants. Contrary to what may seem obvious, Ephilo did not dislike his caretakers—not a single one of them. He thought it all a game, tucking into crawl spaces and the metal loud sphincters of the workplace dwellings. Charades of escapement; Ephilo always returned. Understandably, he always ended up in the kitchen. The ferrous steam of the cooking range pulled the senses tight, whenever bread was freshly spawned it would summon those very senses forth.

"With a touch of Sardonimin fins, you can forge some *real* grain. Bread like no other, Ephilo." He reached a hand out to the loaf, and with a battering slap, the chef cut it away. Who knew what affliction the young girl retained? His mother was once of lesser class, and so easily could have taken with her the simple infections of the mud. "Later, when it's ripe for eating missy. When your mother's seen it." The chef leaned down to the child carefully, swaying the hat of their labors about in search of a reason to speak up against the girl. "I hear there is a metal jester. How about that?" Ephilo did not reply for a while, too infatuated with the flame on the range, snailing up to the banner of crests which (wrongly) had been hung in range of the open tinder.

"Mhmm, copper—bronze or other. Didn't look like a jester?"

"Why'd they call him that then?" The chef turned to the sight of the girl, who had curiously been observing the banner's burn. "Lishr—" Off they went, padding down the fire in hopes of its calm. In the chaos, Ephilo snuck into the hatchway, a thin slice of bread between his teeth. Above and around him were the sounds of book readers and scribes, servants bustling through the castle. Through the indecision of his bread, Ephilo headed for the court.

"—ther, immutable and grand is he who wallows in the banishment of its children. I wish not to hear testimonies of the greatness of your own deities, for lo and behold is their superior." A hefty creak arose above Ephilo's head, whispering among the salt,

"Come have you to preach your god? A heretic in a house of holiness is not so welcome." Kneeling, and a clap of iron,

"Nay, nay good duke. I have a habit of professing the might of my master—not god. It would do me dishonor to call it that. I have come to warn."

"Then warn, jester." His father's voice was bold, and Ephilo could certainly hear his mother's tension through the floor.

"Calamity cometh. By the bringing of your own Lishra, I am afraid." A jostling of metal and flesh occurred, with Mallory calling out in distress, a blade's sheathing whirred overhead.

"Now your tongue has dislikened your presence. Leave, or excuse your bigotry."

"Promptly, liege. My father—as I told, no god—foresees much chaos. I gain no lump sum for your conversion to my faith, for there is no faith but the good of all kinds. I have seen your god, a birdly beast himself." Ephilo had never seen Lishra and heard of her very scarcely at this point. He had not been told rumors of this game of genders.

"Lishra? You mean *her*, then. Surely you wouldn't forge falseness for our gods?" The jester made no comment, instead ruffling about a scroll and quill.

"Your god documents everything. I am a conniving devil. Read yourself, all of 'her' plots to cure your people—of your very lives." Stillness altered the very air he breathed, and with its cone of effect, he heard his father gasp. "Yes, sadly so. I do send regards to holiness. Pity—regardless, I cannot prevent your deaths."

"What point is this then? If we are to die let us perish with *faith*, you cretin."

"Least of your concerns, I can save the girl." Ephilo thought himself deserving of a name, but no saving. If his parents would die…

"Done. What must be accom—"

"Ephiata! Have you no patience?"

"We have tasted poison words from a bird god we thought our savior. There is not a minute to spare for our daughter's salvation."

"And what of faith, Ephiata?" The Duke paused, contemplating the namesake of his royalty, the heir-giver of his people.

"What of it?" Boots marched off into the distance, leaving the soft breath of Mallory to her lonesome. Ephilo pondered his future, at the hands of a god he may not like, nor ever meet. Would his own mother account him to tribulations against his will? Through the hatchways he went, finding himself against the metal bars of the outside fencing. Before his eyes lay the forest, green bold with soft blue hints. The tips of the leaves brushed against his dangling knees, his mind aflutter with contemplation. He had seen these trees before, but where? A hairless rodent passed by his back, carrying with it a toothpick and cork. In this minute of disconnect, the forest had set fire, and an incredible blaze overtook his ankles. The flesh that melted from it was not his own, scaly and— Duke Ephilo snapped back to his reality, where the carriage had been overtaken by the burning trees.

"Caelo! What horror this dream is, I must awake!" Before anything else, the Duke attempted to rouse his already quite clear consciousness, to an obvious lack of success. Next was his kicking of the lever, if the carriage could carry him faster, then it was possible to escape the burrow of flames. A snap tore the lever—and its baseplate of flooring—from the carriage, dropping out downwards into the inferno. Shouting a curse, Ephilo leaped to the other half of the crashing carriage, clutching Caelo within his arms to protect the poor heir, "We will be through of this yet." One of the two remaining rail buckles snapped in the heat of the flames, drooping the shell of the carriage ever closer to the abyss. The shake tore Caelo from the Duke's hands. With incredible haste, he buckled his palms, and the world slowed around him, his movements deliberate as he plummeted into the uproar. His arm hooked around the cable of the carriage's ascent, which swung him low to the machine. Duke Ephilo's rib cage, under the sudden reacceleration of existence, snapped up in two, forcing him ever further in his arc. The carriage fell with him, towards the hefty stone of the side of the Wolfstram heights. His sight was cut instantaneously.

If Caelo was flesh, Ephilo thought it would be a girl. Caelo had, after all, a pretty little voice. And too, the heir was so elegant with its fluttering about. The mannerisms alone sold the piece, and to be fair Ephilo had no intention of imagining otherwise. Though, there was the issue of assumption, as he had met so few females to counter the concept of femininity upon. It was a smidge presumptuous to claim a woman what she was to her voice alone. Mallory had nothing but rasp and gravel. To think of it, she was quite unbecoming a woman overall. Her penchant for challenging the authority of the keep, and furthermore refusing to clothe herself nobly were the obvious constraints, but what else? Mallory had no concern for her exterior, both physical and mental, and shouldered no guilt for her methodology of things. She was sure to always be right, and when otherwise, would never admit to it. She played with rakes as halberds and fantasized about dragons of all things. Dragons did not exist, nor did her conscience—she was a mother no less! Ephilo was no doubt entirely proud of her. Who was Mallory, anyways?

"Hopefully not your birthmother, bit cruel are those words for her." Duke Ephilo shifted open his lengthy lids. Sleep was so misused recently. "Aye uppity uppity, cowpoke. Don't worry none, the machine is safe." A human facade towered over the Duke, whose scaled snout lingered just below the azure lips. Thick, royal blue powder coated the face of the man, clear by the buff of his jaw. The dust flaked off against his neck, tucked away in plate mail of silver, marked with unknown crests. The bareness of his head surely was intentional, with it being so slippery and blue. "Blumore of the Refiners. I know that starstrucker stare." A droplet of some wetness fell upon the Duke, who brushed the suds from his forehead. The usual numbness Ephilo awoke with was absent, his fingers tingling with a cozy feeling. The bundles of fur upon him were a slight bit damp, sloshing as he struggled to sit up. It was a cavern, just as expected. Distant bonfires illuminated its depth, and an echo of flowing water and cheer narrowly reached the two estranged figures. Foggy glass structures littered the ridges of the cave, folding onto each other haphazardly. A narrow spill of water—untainted of cure—split the cave. Its clearness was attractive to no end. "Wonderful little thing, the Cascades are." Blumore rested his hand against the Duke, who in an effort to get away, retreated to the furs. "Cold, though. You are right. Have you any destination beyond this place? I mean to ask— can I assist you plenty?" He thought to say words of the Marrow, to request it immediately. With no response from Blumore, it was apparent he had *not* said these things. A tent-up of cloth or some fiber covered the opening of the cave loosely, a brace of wood holding against the wind. Light from the day crept in underneath, clashing against the shadows of the fires. Against the brace, at its lowest edge, Caelo hovered, examining the skeletal fragments of a once defender, helmet still placed at its side. No vitals would be gathered from bones. "Little thing has been all over the encampment, its pestering is so welcome." Caelo returned to its master, describing in detail the anatomy of the Refiners. "Glassblowers always need distraction— keeps the flow steady."

The Harlequin

"[DUKE EPHILO], I have [ENJOYED] the people. You are safe." Blumore nodded, helping the Duke to his feet with hesitant speed. Guiding him with a soft hand and whispering descriptions, Blumore slowly carried the Duke through the encampment. Workers of the dead art of glass served about the facilities, washing and bathing among family.

"It is the Refiners who have seen so little of the world. Least of all, have they seen something like you." Stares, undeterminable in emotion, sought out the Duke in his limp. After the injuries he had lived through, a meager clot of the leg was nothing. His ribs, unlike he remembered, certainly felt a great deal better. With a tap of his unbound arm, he discovered them to be not there at all. A perfect solution to the problem of ever-expansive bones: get rid of the bones. "How are the wounds? They look much less rancid than last eve."

"Vitals and structure are nominal, the [DUKE] is in stable condition." Blumore chuckled, batting the machine back with a grin,

"Well, little machination, are you to speak *for* your duke?" Caelo beeped in assurance and returned to Ephilo's side. He had half a mind to scold his heir, the title of duke was to remain his own personal knowledge, and that of close assistants. The Refiners, for all they were worthy of, could be executioners of dukes like all the rest. Caelo was not the sentient choice-maker its father—owner—was. It was intently observing Ephilo at the moment, its computations awaiting a response. With a wave of his hand, he gave Caelo the fullest permission to his words.

"Affirmative."

"Oh. Quite sure you are, machine." Ephilo continued forward, listening to the words of his guide and refitting Caelo for his responses. Regardless of how he tried, he could not muster up the words himself, as if his own body was volatile with unspoken alphabets. Children gathered by the glass homes, still watching the mysterious metal-flesh hybrid wander about the cave. Ephilo wasn't sure he was so welcome. "They watch because they do not understand you. I myself do not either, yet I am your humble host nonetheless." At the center of the encampment, where the rivers surged up over the causeways, was a thick ossein pillar, roped to the cave ceiling with ivory cables. It had glass carvings adhered across its surface, sigils, and runes. Though Blumore carried on about the functions of his camp and its people, Ephilo lingered at the bone. Its whispers told him of dark waters and begged to be drowned.

"Marrow." The Refiner turned back to his steps, oak floorings creaking under the weight of his expectation,

"Pardon? You *can* speak?" Blumore waddled back to the bone and placed a hand on the rail between its height and his. He opened his jaw to speak, but the words instead crammed against the roof of his mouth. "A—Apologies, that was a crude thing to say." Ephilo fixated himself on the bone, his fingers wavering just above its surface. Just before contact, a thinly shaped pale hand snatched away the wrist of the Duke, firm.

"Aazul! Release the guest at once!" The mysterious Aazul did no such thing, contrary to orders, tightening their grasp.

"He was going to touch the Mom. I stopped that. Some appreciation would go a long way, father." Blumore scowled at his daughter, the lathering of chainmail she wore clinking in a sudden soft breeze.

"I've asked you don't call it that, Aazul. Countless times. Perhaps you could learn some ordinance from the Duke here." Ephilo turned to the fiery gaze of Aazul, her ochre eyes set upon him and lips unvarnished. She sourly tossed away Ephilo's hand, none the happier with her circumstance.

"I detest you." Blumore simply nodded in response, his daughter already vacating the monument.

"Don't all my daughters?" Duke Ephilo lowered his head, taking a moment to study the flow of water beneath the obelisk of bone. It maneuvered around the stem of the Marrow—which hung sharp above the stream—without a touch, hydrophobic. "Monument of Mycelium. Discerptor to our tide, and remembrance of the lost." The Refiner set himself down to rest against the rail of the monument. A trickle of ambient fluid splashed up against Ephilo's shin, which was retracted in a jerk reaction. Automatic by any other name, Ephilo let loose a soft yelp, Blumore himself was disinterested. "Have you any children, Duke? Have you any attachment to life at all?" Was it not a sin to birth life into a tarnished world? Like metal—justly—it had slowly dulled away with wetness. A sponge had squeezed out all its color and left a sorrowful dead tree in its place. No children, not a chance, but attachments he did have. Caelo was no child, was it? It was a machine, Duke Ephilo did not think it his daughter or creation. Yet... He thumbed Caelo, who chirped and flew off into a nearby hovel. It was all he knew to be precious. Blumore need not live the Duke's life to comprehend the value of the machine, both inherit and otherwise. Simple was love when it was as direct and firm as his. "Would it be wise to spend the night? Or are your travels so urgent?" Obviously, his travels drew him here and nowhere else, but the signature of a thief was welcomeness—he feigned his discomfort. Until late that night, when porridge of some sickly kind was served, Ephilo sat by the cliff face.

"Melon." The sledge of the letters was slow, weak to icy roads. "Mel—on." The forest below him stood green, no flame had caught it, nor a storm of any kind. Caelo bumped against the back of the Duke's head, knocking his hat forward.

"Locational antenna obstructed, requesting [HELP, DUKE EPHILO]." The Duke extended a lone hand, letting Caelo locate it through slight trial and much error. He fiddled with the metal twine, careful never to bend it too harshly,

"Will they part with their graves? With the Marrow, I mean." Spoken to none in particular, he weighed his methods. The Marrow wasn't entirely sealed away, a good clean cut of the suspensions and he would be away. Although, with his wounds considered, outpacing an entire cult of glassmakers was unlikely. When night fell, it could be displaced with illusion and celerity. Yes. This was the only option, disappearance in the night, with flavor too. They could part with a grave if it would save him from himself.

He was looked at like a consumptive, the difficulty Ephilo had lifting even the thinnest of tableware was wretched. Aazul bore her eyes like a snake through silt into the Duke, who was kind enough to remind her of the smear of paint she left upon his hand. His fingers wagged in the display. In the hall itself, there was cold blue light— that of the moons—reflective off the glass and mirrored homes. A likely twenty men and women sat at the table alongside Blumore and his daughter, all caught with some shape or way of powdered cyan across the flesh. A cult would look more becoming as a family.

"Enjoying yourself, Ephilo? I hope our company is convincing of a longer rest. Aazul? The lard." Her fingers wrapped neatly around the stone bowl without a glance in its direction, her pity for Ephilo not actually the means of her stare.

"Ephilo, was it? The Duke of something forgotten?" Ephilo choked down a thin slice of apple, there was no water to chase the pain with. He nodded his head softly as he brushed crumbs from his snout. "Well, Duke of Nothing, do you think me some pretty thing?" What once was a slight rustle, now fell to somber quiet. Nobody dared reach for the lard now. Ephilo's usual bitten tongue was snatched harder than ever before, his words no longer existing in the same realm. He may as well be mute. "Do you? Do you think me a desirable sight? Do I curve quite right of—"

"Aazul! What is the meaning of this? Pestering a guest, no more than twice in the same day!" The Refiner held her head high, the glimpse of her crisp eyes fell to her father, and then to Ephilo.

"He has a habit of staring, is all." Ephilo gulped down a thick mucus mixed with his own blood. It was as if the pureness of the Cascades kept the sickness away. "Thought I'd wonder why. Aloud. No secrets kept." The words of her father were drowned out in the return to consumption, Ephilo himself failing to notice her maintained sight with his. He picked at his spoiled meat, twirling the bones between his forks. The off-white of their core robbed his attention. Blumore left the table with a coaxing gesture, Aazul following closely behind. The rest of the Refiners were left with the visitor, a supposed Duke, a miraculous survivor of a disaster that haunted their people, an enviable icon of success who triumphed where they had not. Ephilo excused himself, once finishing his meal, and returned to his small tent of rugs just outside the meal hall, where Caelo awaited him with analyses. It felt strange to pet the machine, but he did nonetheless. It was a measure of comfort for himself, a maternal instinct perhaps.

"—et you do not *question* him, you trust the Duke without condition. It is I who receives your reckoning!" For a discussion between kin—one likely smoking from emotion and bonds—her tone was quite public.

The Harlequin

"What reason do I have to fear a visitor? A mute one, no less. It is clear he has some, well." The implication was cruel. Ephilo was entirely sound, both in structure and mind.

"The omens! I—I feel it, something's telling me I'm right."

"*The omens?* You are no shaman! You liken me to act on a premonition?"

"It is a feeling, mother had her dreams why can't I—"

"And your mother is now lost to the affliction of men. You wish to meet her in this end?" The apparent flourish in tension and hate had culminated in this. Whispers replaced the foul touches of argument. The bickering continued, Aazul claimed things of Ephilo that were much too true and went to leave the hall.

"You don't have to trust me, father. Just—have someone by the Mo—Monument. Keep it safe. Please." Her father disagreed with this, he voiced his console for cowardice, yet Aazul thought him such for not being a true leader to his people. The Duke agreed with what Blumore had to say, the Kingfall included. Even Ephilo had come to fear its return, albeit for entirely different reasons. Blumore rounded out of the hall, to the kindness of Ephilo's surveying orbs.

"Apologies. She is...." Simply shaking his head, the Refiner left Ephilo to his thoughts. Night was falling, and with the disapproval of the father, Aazul could no longer interfere with his fate. When the moons dropped behind the mountain, Ephilo would take his misery and leave with it.

Glass was a terrible dampener. Lacking boots of any kind, Duke Ephilo's meat was left to smack against the bridges of the flowing stream, forged from glass entirely. How unfortunate that the Refiners had found sand at all, their talent for the old ways had caused Ephilo so much trouble, much more than that was needed in the journey for the Marrow; genocide was truly unfair. Much to the benefit of himself only, the torches had been dimmed for the night and the glow of the waters faint enough to not display his form. The shamble of his steps made a hunchback of him, the Duke's hand clasped against a stabbing in his chest, a wound unfounded of harm.

"Caelo be ready. We will be leaving soon after. No time to dawdle." Return to the map-maker, collect more bones from old gods, open the Gaol, and—

"She was right then. You've made me look like an utter fool." Blumore displayed a small, transcendent blue blade. The dagger curved at the handle, around the wrist like a piece of armor of its own defensive intention. The display of its thickness seemed to be some kind of threat. There was no time for a confrontation. "I trusted you more than her it would seem. Irony is a horrid teacher. I wish I'd learnt my lesson the last time. Perhaps I will be better suited to—" Before another word loosed from the bowstring of Blumore's throat, Ephilo cut him down. He plunged the thick metal of his blade through his gut, and lit the cure sludge of the tool, drawing softly from his blood. A guttural sound betrothed Blumore with death, a man who didn't quite deserve what he received, but there was no choice besides the path he lay dead on. With a pull of his weapon, Ephilo cleaved the man in half and cut down his prize with its bloody edge. Soaked in glistening gore, the Marrow fell neatly into Ephilo's arms, mythic and soft were its lovely curves. He slung it over his shoulder, gasped for air with his effort in slaughter—his hand still wrapped in agony around his waist—and started for the cave front, where the moon had begun to dribble inwards. Just as he had taken a step from the altar of bone, a rushing of water took him by the leg, carrying him forward just a bit. Blue flames ignited at the shorelines of the river, engulfing the roads and houses quickly. A groan turned him back, where Blumore rose from the grave, flame already creeping up the length of his body. Echoes of misery spun about him, the voices of forgotten men, and dead women. Ephilo cut him down a second time, all the same, blood no warmer now than ever before. He left the camp in no hurry; the flame would not harm his fickle shape.

"Is [BLUMORE] deceased, [DUKE EPHILO]?" The Duke glared at his robot companion, who dared reckon about the name of his foes.

"Where did you learn that name? And what of this is important?" Caelo wavered for a moment, even behind the lengths of its master.

"Was it [NECESSARY]?" Ephilo scoffed, leaping down from the mouth of the cave upon a dusty trail. The forest of pine before him stood verdant, oddly unbaked like he expected. Was the fire all so quickly extinguished?

"Was it *necessary?*" He retorted, twisting his head back to peer at the machine.

"[BLUMORE] was [PROPER]." Ephilo paused, the camp still burning in the distance, glass melting under a sheer boil.

"Yes." He said, "It was necessary." Ephilo stepped forward, but his machine did not follow. Feeling mistaken, as if he had done wrong, he handed off the bone to Caelo, who he instructed to keep it safe in honor of the man he killed. A heavy blade—about as thick as Ephilo's tail—cut down into the earth from above. It had no owner, for now, and was hot with flame, its edges glowing a slight blue from the fire. Ephilo noticed the blue powder on its hilt and the runic inscriptions down its front. It was a weapon of a grand warrior, and certainly one of the encampment. With a thud, a heavy set of armor landed beside it, blue flowing curls locking out of its plate helm.

"Really? So keen on leaving, duke? I plan to cut your snout off and stuff it back-ended unto you. How far can you run without your face?" Ephilo fell back, drawing his blade in a fit of coughs, he really didn't desire the battle at the moment. "You took from me my village, my people...my *father.*" She broadened the blade to the Marrow. "I will not let you have this." Ephilo lifted his weapon to fight but was met instantly with the slash of her broadsword, cleaving his own a distance away, into the sand. Caelo drifted forward, having no means to stop the assault, but Ephilo commanded it to stay back. "Do you comprehend me, duke? Do you fear my wrath?" The Duke merely shook his head and rushed forward with his teeth clenched. In the time between realms, he was breathless, and with this suffocating moment, he could feel the parasites swarm about him. His blood curdled with virus, his mind tainted with plague. He could see her face, the true Duke of nothing. With a pass of the girl, Aazul, he struck her spine, only injuring his hand in the blow. Snatching up his blade he snapped his wrist, flicking back two canisters from his legs, and running another pass. The armor was fragile and thin in some places—enough to break with a close pommel strike. Quickly, he did his due and fell back to Caelo. "Fairness was never predicted, no, I knew you were worse than this." She bolstered her guard, readying her lengthy slasher against him. "Finish what you began, or it will finish you." Blood oozed from her forehead, mixing purple with her dye. Her back was hunched up, malformed, and her teeth were red with rage. She swung again, and Ephilo read time. With another attack, he would gesture forward and take a cut. She was ceaseless, and his mind wore thin. "I have more blood than you could ever imagine. I could fill *braziers*." She smashed her weapon down, elegant in its movement, and slid atop its hilt, kicking Ephilo in the chin. He reeled back and bit his lip. Before a recovery could be made she had his throat, squeezing over it with her tightened fist. "Enough to drown you here." Her ichor flooded his throat, and he choked for air, the time around her flowing to a standstill, then returning. He could not breathe in the middle ground. He kneed her chest thrice, his leg bloody with scars, and his bones stabbing out at him. She keeled over, and admitted pain, spitting up her blood against him. "I will not fall on my knees. Try it." He stuck out his weapon and splintered. His spine clacked backward and his head spun 'round. Bones fought against him and coughed up pure white. On the floor before the foe, sprawled out in a rigor, Ephilo reached out a hand to Caelo, demands were beyond him,

"Fly—ghrk—you f—" Aazul's blade struck clean against his snout, sheared directly from his face. The pain was beyond screaming, and he could no longer contort to cover the wound. He was aimless.

"Just know—hah—you deserved this, Duke Ephilo." She drove the stake of his sanguine curse upon him, and with it severed all ties he once held to himself. His soul blinked twice, and though he measured pain within millions, he could no longer feel an inch of it. *At least Caelo has survived*, he jested, and returned to the dark. With the slumping softness of Ephilo's corpse, Aazul looked out over the flameless forest, Caelo whirring off into the distance. She wouldn't need the Marrow now anyways. Exhaustion overtook the Refiner, and she sat herself by the corpse's side, resting only for a moment. With another crack, the corpse shuddered through broken bones, and so too did her steel facade shatter. Bawling, Aazul upset the sunrise and prolonged the night by two hours.

~Heart of Ink

I watched this one fervently at the exact time
of its occurrence. It was quite the show...

"This drop is sour, I would not live it. There must be another way." There had been many like it, the zenith of the sewers had its distractions. Holes, ladders, and halls—all misleading to the one who would navigate them. The canals may have been a deepening maze, but navigating them was a far greater puzzle. Through every level was a new exit, a further test of will. It was as if the Well had not been designed within the canals, but the canals around the Well. Khanjali had practically lost himself, despite the map and the flow he could not find his way to the source. Now, glaring down an unsurvivable drop, Khanjali considered leaping. Perhaps there was but one way to the center? If the pathways had been designed for secrecy, death was a surefire solution to all secrets. Before Khanjali could conclude in jumping, he felt a force push him down, a shadowed hand grasping against his throat. He was pushed under the current, a drifting wave splashing over him. There was no attacker, no beast nor crow. Yet he was attacked. In escapement, he rolled, dodging the grip, but instead entering the distant pit, the very drop he wished to avoid. With luck, the fall did little but shatter the shell of Ichyr across his arm, and spike a crack betwixt his shoulder and chest. Breath returned to his core, splinters of Ichyr littering the stones. He could feel his skin again, tickled with the soggy air of the sewer. Blinking—regaining his sense—Khanjali rose to a divine structure, angelic in color. A magnificent stairwell led to its first entranceway, it would seem he was to descend deeper yet. Wonder snuck into the hunter's mind, fiction of the well dotting the aura of his temper. Rumors sprung up like bones in battlegrounds, tales recounting the very perception of all matters. During his sessions with the priests of Maccabeus and Maeandri, Khanjali gathered impure insight into the mechanisms of the wells and their storied construction. Priests he had spoken to theorized that Maeandri built wells of opposing matter throughout the system. Intended as a safeguard, the opposing forces would fear the bubbling of the dreaded sap of creation, tragedy a risk to massacre millions. Aberrative to this thesis was the Soapstone Sinkhole, an abysmal pit placed just below the center of Drochandas. It was identified long ago as a well of Ink, a backstop lacking a cautionary tale. Maeandri was a sensible god—Khanjali supposed—if he could not predict everything, then he could at least prepare for all he could predict. The hunter stared into an infinite abyss of white-stone webs and chains, pondering Maeandri. Within the beatific spire was the only thing one could expect: steps, flights of steps, and stairwells, all intersecting and bounding around one another. "Oh terrible indeed, what is this cruel joke of a spire?" Placing a foot forward, Khanjali watched dust settle to the distant below, "Endless stairways—bah. I would sooner return to the Well." Khanjali's glance darted from step to stone, looking for a sign of progression. There was little deviation between any of the stairwells, thus they all seemed equally true. Debate stuck him still, and he rested against the ridge of the darkness, kicking gayly. In his muttering the wind had spun up, gathering tunes from above. A whistle emerged from the deepest point of the spire, a calling. A path. Khanjali wandered up, his ears keen to the whistling. If there was sound, there was wind, and wind could come from the surface. He stepped from stairwell to stairwell, clutching the steps so as not to fall. The whistling grew closer, loud enough to hear it in full. Fit to follow, Khanjali stepped first foot upon the step before him, and in a moment, another Khanjali was there. A shade equivalent in height and demeanor stood across the spire just above him, upended. As the hunter stepped forward, so too did the shade, and another revealed itself upon another staircase, following the prime's every move as if by some magick of imitation. Khanjali was brought away, the stairs around him filling with fragments of his own design, perfectly represented in shadow. When he returned to move ahead, the hunter met eye-to-eye with a shade, except, one of opposing gravity. Scrunched like a baked sponge, it reeked of failure. "Greetings shade. Do you speak as much as you watch?" The dark phantom remained silent, unmoving. It had his bright eyes, though lacked their obstructions. It wore the garb of a hunter and bore the blade of one too. The shade was not burdened by Ichyr nor child— a Khanjali before everything, in a time when all he had was the hunt. The hunter lifted a single finger and placed it on the phantom's eye. It flickered, fading for a moment like a projection might when obscured from the light. He then, having decided in his action, stepped through the shadow, a slight numbness forming where the two had intersected, but vanishing after but a moment. "Crossing over, how metaphorically literal the gods are." Khanjali murmured to himself, now caught in a web of enchantment by the structure of the path before him. A familiar dome lingered above, lacking the divine light of its predecessor. The room was unsurprisingly a near-flawless replica of the Ichyr Well Khanjali had stumbled upon the fateful day of his affliction. There were four support pillars extending to an unlit skylight, the walls spiraled around the center pit with similar memorials of history and fable. However, in place of the doorway to the crypt where Khanjali had met his savior, there was now a large silver frame, ornate and delicate, made from the metals and decor of gods. Khanjali let his steps be taken against his will, eyes drawn to glimmer. The murals and tapestries were far more preserved than the ones of the Ichyr Well, with text nearly legible—had it been written in an understood tongue. Khanjali stood before the first mural, a slab of stone and cutting so detailed he thought he could notice mere hairs upon its inscribed beings. There was a figure, prominent in all four murals, of an angular disposition. With a triangle for a head, and the body of a golem, it raised its six-fingered hand to the sky, and with it, wrought down the power of a being long lost to time. It was the end of Maeandri, the destroyer of his faith. Khanjali had seen the figure before, hymn books cursed its form. The Thorn, a metaphorical pain in the side of all godly beings. Children were taught of the wrath it brought, a future of ashes in a world of tarnished cinders. Khanjali did not fear him, as when the Thorn arrived, his blood would be long dried. Even ancestors of ancestors would never taste the sorrow of the

Thorn—its danger was abated by distance. A flicker of light echoed through the room, as a soft cover of ethereal matter pulsed over the silver frame. Khanjali took notice of its contents: a mirror, nothing more. It was alluring, so divine. Standing before its elegance with the Thorn in mind, Khanjali watched the reflection. He saw all but himself, a fragment, a shadow. It was he, but an unwieldy shape, one of pure Ichyr. It was as if the mirror itself could translate his matter and carve Khanjali into the empyrean opposite of his current being. The portrayal was similar to his current self: shelled in white, donning Ichyr as a cast. But unlike his cursed form, this mirrored image was whole, bound by no Ink. He was pure. Upon his sacred head was a beak of darkness, a feathered cuff around his cheeks and neck. He had no antennae to speak of, and in place of his hind wings were a larger set of feather ones, the length betwixt his arms webbed with feathers and cloth. He had talons, sharp and bird-like. His body was pleasing, he could feel its folds, the flesh was his own. Feeling the mirth of his feathered backhand, Khanjali fluttered it through the air, dancing in the still air. Was this truly what Ichyrics looked like? Not of beast, but of bird? Not of monster, but of elegance? Khanjali now understood the existence of their superiority complex. As entertained as he was by the mystic reflection, the hunter still had a cure to fashion and little time to do it. Taking the vial from his hip, Khanjali approached the edge of the well, peering in at the decaying level of Ink. He could just barely reach the surface of the fluid with his hand, enough to dunk the vial. With his cure in hand, birds in mind, Khanjali looked to the stairs he had descended upon. There was far too much to think of.

The two fools met at the house of the priestess, who under the demands of her affairs and schedule, had left her home and Pedantick within the care of Ezrakell. The less time wasted the safer, and safe Khanjali wished to be,

"When I reached here, she was lost—in a complete flurry. I would gamble she was late to one of her symposiums. I recall this to be her last approach on the Southers, upon the border wall. There we will find our savior priestess and your cure." Khanjali nodded, wanting to limit his speech. His voice may have been deranged and distorted, but there was still some sliver of his old self within it, and if Pedantick, being the smart child she was, could notice it....

own terms. Begone." Khanjali did not actually speak, nor did he approach. He did not want to startle her. Mezzo turned to greet her intruder, pleasantly surprised they did not resemble an Acolyte.

"I am here, my priestess. I am here and ready to aid you." Priestess Mezzo blushed, dropping some of her papers, letting them scatter across the floor.

"K-khanjali! My apologies for my spite, there are far too many foolish men in those crowds, it rouses my passions." Khanjali embraced the priestess, enchanted to see her again.

"I have brought your requests, both Ichyr and Ink. Will this keep me from my demise?" Mezzo nodded, placing the two fluids together in a singular vial, distilling them quickly, and blessing them with the holy gifts of all the gods she knew to name. When the process was finished, all that remained was a small canister of a thick, viscous, mundane Ink. She prepared Khanjali for the consumption of the cure, filling a small injector with the stygian substance. Priestess Mezzo collected a small band to stop the body from rejecting the fluid, as well as a small number of other precautions. While she worked, silence shadowed their conversation, and once again, the two felt incomplete.

"This fate you have been cast, I wish it not upon my worst of enemies—please, tense your arm—you truly are a test of my faith. I understand the gods cannot always be so forgiving, but *you* of all people...." Khanjali devalued pity. He felt indifferent to any of the priestess' other patients, he felt undeserving of such treatment.

"The gods must damn someone, I suppose. I will kindly accept this fate if it means they do not damn another. I deserve no pity for it." The priestess scoffed, beginning the injection process gradually,

"You do, you deserve more Khanjali—you are an incredible man. I have heard many things of your great kindness in this city, from merchants to widows. And there is, of course, your truth as a father. You have been recognized as a soul of great character. I am honored to be in the presence of such a courageous and determined creature. I truly hope Maccabeus can see you with the same eyes I do, one day." Khanjali fell silent, unable to respond to such a compliment. The priestess, regretting the unrestrained stream of consciousness she had allotted, hurried the injection, finishing in a mere moment. She pulled the tools from Khanjali's body, watching the Ichyr in his arm slowly dim, and harden. Khanjali felt great relief, the feeling of his ailment leaving him. The feeling of cure.

"And like this, I am cured. My adoration to you, dear priestess. I—"

"But you are not. I have not explained so clearly yet." Khanjali tensed, the tastings of dread that had just vanished slowly creeping back atop his tongue, the Ichyr running cold in his blood,

"I am… am I not free? The Ichyr is hard and cold. It is dead. Have we not won?" Priestess Mezzo shook her head, returning to Khanjali the canister,

"This ailment, though I am sorrowful to have misled you, is incurable. I can only remove the physical effects, and prolong the inevitable." She placed a solemn hand on Khanjali's shoulder. He touched it with his own.

"Death will take me then. I cannot save myself—what of Ezrakell? He is infected too, though only upon his surface flesh, his hand." Mezzo assured Khanjali that the old fool would be without permanent effects, by simply removing the flesh he could be freed from the Ichyr eternally. Khanjali stood from his seat, still holding the priestess' hand in his own.

"You will live for a good while, hunter. You can still have a life." Khanjali's hand shook, but Mezzo held it tighter.

"I will live as long as you think possible, and then longer, for P. For you." Mezzo grasped Khanjali, the sharp Ichyr needles poking at her face, but she was safe and content. As quickly as she had embraced him, she had stood back, and dismissed him with a single wave,

"Now go. Go bide your time. Live to the fullest with your daughter, and your friend. Your days may be numbered, but treat them not with such simplicity. One day we may find a solution, you may be cured yet, Khanjali, I promise you this much." Khanjali thanked the priestess and left her presence, a light giddiness overcoming him. A woman of respect and honor held him of all people in such high regard! How immaculate! Before Khanjali could even pace himself halfway to the door, the Ichyr upon his disgraced flesh began to shatter, crack and shrivel, fall to the ground in thickened chunks. Soon, Khanjali felt himself returning to his once-beautified self. With this, he could speak to his daughter freely, no longer fearing his structure. Upon leaving the warehouse, Khanjali saw the crowd of Acolytes still present, just as vast as before, if not larger. He peered over the heads of the ocean and noticed Ezrakell peaking above the rest, his height being favorable for once. His face was flush with disagreement—an argument sparked between the Acolytes—for what reason Khanjali did not know. It was not the height of his concern. The argument had become less a debate of politics, and more a wreath of fury. The Acolytes pushed Ezrakell about, shouting to the others, bolstering numbers. Two more restrained the old fool's arms, his struggling proving fruitless against the muscle that withheld him. The first Acolyte continued to shout until Ezrakell made his final argument: a glob of spit aimed at the eyes of those who watched him. Infuriated, the Acolytes cocked a single punch into Ezrakell's stomach, forcing him to hunch over in pain. The old fool did not waver, he knew no limits. Khanjali was rapid in his descent, hurrying to the scene. Ezrakell was no fighter, and his ceaseless stubborn rage often proved a dangerous trait in such disagreements. Yet still, there were greater concerns. As Ezrakell taunted the common rebel, Khanjali could not help but wonder about the location of his prize—his daughter. The hunter pushed through the hoard, now filled with the kind of temper from the sacred night in the canals, almost to the point of letting his primal self free. He promised himself he wouldn't, not for the moment at least. He needed to find his daughter immediately—his hate could stir in the meantime. The world began to teeter for Khanjali, he pushed a man from his path, taking care to notice the shoulder, a green cape draped over its side. There was a leather strap overlaying the green felt. Such details flooded his mind, as it tried to keep the hunter from the truth. The wind and the people slowed, it was a perfect moment of frozen time. Ezrakell wasn't arguing politics, how could Khanjali think such a thing? He wouldn't argue such 'foolish topics of basic primality in the streets' after all, he had a reputation to uphold. Ezrakell was withholding the crowds, clashing against the tide. He was trying to stop the Acolytes, stop them from abusing *someone* else. The other shoulder was clothed in a white wool, a shoulder pad fit to keep the cold at bay. Their hands were grasping her, pulling her up from her place on the ground. The shoulder owner's face showed disgust as if Khanjali pushing them aside was his own disgraceful sin. The hunter shook, his hand could not be stilled. Her legs seemed to quiver the same, to quake with either fear or pain. He noticed another Acolyte, the voice in his head remained from the curing, it spoke to him, *begged* of him, *Look away, place your gaze upon anything else, my host, I beg of you.* The blood was not excessive. The wound would heal with time— at least, the one above her eye, the one on her right hand. *Please, look away! Imprison your eyes from this painting macabre! It is not worth the consequence.* Khanjali was easily distracted from the wounds, from the blood, from the crying she was letting out. The hands turned her around, to show the true display of their grave mistakes—their unlimited hate. *You do not understand. Our roles in this charade are expendable, you and I are just performers in this game. We cannot afford*— Displayed to the crowd, with cheers and calls, a painting of corrupt malice: Her wings. There were wings there. They had finally grown, finally emerged—small yes, stumps of a greater future—but they had grown. The Acolytes had clipped them. They had bent them to disfigurement. They had raised her high above the people, shouting slurs, using her as a sigil, a testament to their willpower as a union. They had done this without regret, without sympathy. Khanjali had never felt what he felt in that unstable moment, that frictionless standstill. He watched in utter and absolute emptiness as the little girl squirmed in their arms, as they continued to squeeze her wrists tighter. She cried, and he could do nothing. He wasn't him anymore, wasn't a mortal. It was some act, a chapter in some sick tragedy, and he was to watch it, his eyes forced to remain unsealed, his fingers rigid in place. With the viewing so forced, Khanjali wished to meet the playwright. He had some critique. He felt a terrible peace, a softness in his body, one he knew the origin of. *I—I understand your passion…* The voice stared through Khanjali's eyes. All it had said was true; they could not fight this battle, not attack these men. Not without each other. The false peace, the barrier of disconnect that the voice had built was annihilated by its own will the moment her first words were spoken. The very fraction of the second they both heard it all was lost—the quiet, pained call of a girl thrown into the pursuit of lunatic revolutionaries, the call of a being thrust so violently into reality at such a youthful existence. The barrier broke, when they both heard, "Pop-pop!" Khanjali's peace allowed him to move with purpose, quickly. Unnoticed. He moved his arm with such force, that one would think he was some kind of creation of war, an icon of the very power Maeandri was thought to wield. The Acolyte watched the hand approach him, as did all the others, as did Ezrakell, as did the daughter. Upon contact, the resulting destruction that occurred was so swift, so horrible, that for a split second, the living souls nearest to Khanjali stopped moving, focusing only upon him. When the body fell, Khanjali still remained, the liquified form of the head he simply squeezed to nothingness in a moment of hasteful action the only remnants of his choice. The other Acolyte holding Pedantick let her fall, Khanjali scooping her up in his now pure white arms. His cloak had fallen from his head, his Ichyr skull sharpened with rage, his eyes practically melting with pure godliness. Still, she felt at peace with him, safe. She rubbed her body against his, clutching his arm with her own, letting her stuttered, fearful breath slow to a tranquil panting. Her tears calmed, but she still felt the pain. The other Acolytes—even Ezrakell—could not move from their astonishment. The body did not even twitch, as if every nerve had been erased in a single strike. Ezrakell let a knowing smile creep across his face, one not of joy, but of hate. He knew quite how dire this predicament was, he could picture how such a bloodbath would be recorded in the history of the city. Khanjali stared at his daughter, her beaten and pained form, it was immeasurable in comparison to any agony he had endured before. He looked to the sky and cried out, a roar so deafening and terrifying, it shook the fabric of the space above the planet. The hunter lowered his head, looking to the field of sinners, all his victims. He closed his eyes, the Ichyr once more taking over. It was a fair price to pay for retribution. He was cool, the falseness of vision was but a disadvantage in his chaotic psyche. His daughter had been touched by unworthy hands, brought to near death by fools with no forgiveness. But that was not what sealed his mind, nor the voice's. It was the wings. They were destroyed, removed with such violence and gore as to never heal. After all he had been through, his final chance at normality for his lineage, for his next of kin, had been shattered by the very people meant to safeguard it. The voice fell silent, letting Khanjali speak for himself for a moment in time,

"Dead ridden ingrates. I spare blessings to your cause no longer." Standing strong in the sea, Ezrakell gathered a club from the penitent arms of an Acolyte, wood-turned stone with petrification. The voice in Khanjali's mind fluctuated in anticipation, a silent excitement growing. It too had been hurt by the cruelty of this world, left unsatisfied for so long. Nigh was the hour for vengeance of its own production. Khanjali was given full control of his form, hands continuing to sharpen and reform to a decaying degree, and his cloak was torn by the ghastly protrusions upon his wings. His skull seemed only to harden, his eyes seemed only to fill with more and more void. The voice spoke to Khanjali one last time, giving him a final regard, *I see now, it cannot be forsworn. I can recall a time when I would ruin moons for my love—for my endless children. I was weak then. It is time this dream of ours was imagined. Do as we both desire.* The Acolyte who had struck Ezrakell moments ago turned to Khanjali, drawing a sword at his figure. Standing fixed with inspiration, she was the only among them with the gall to challenge the beast. Khanjali swiftly grasped the torso of the Acolyte, his hands large enough to wrap around the waist's entire length. He toyed with the give of the bones, squeezing and fiddling, enough to slowly let collapse the internals of her body. With a sudden boredom with the toy, Khanjali clutched tight her form, bursting the brittle backbone of the Acolyte's skeleton. The others mumbled provocations to their fading comrade. As much as they wanted to stop Khanjali, they knew full well they could not. The pain in Khanjali's head had reached its peak, and with a final splatter of divine color, the Acolyte was no more, torn in three by the force of Khanjali's one hand. He cleared his throat of Ichyr and raised the gore to presentation. "I killed petty thieves for less sin. My pity for your lamentation has waned to nail trimmings. Tomorrow, the gates of hell will be overflowing with dead, and I will descend to tear them open for you." The crowd roared with fear and vigor, drawing blades and firearms alike, ready to slaughter the beast. Two Acolytes approached Khanjali with axes, two who in a mere four seconds had all of the blood which once was theirs made permanently public property. Another charged the hunter from behind, thinking the essence of sight was necessary for Khanjali to slaughter. Without even glancing, the hunter was able to stomp the form into a flattened mass of purple and black, a nearly unnoticeable addition to the street itself. Another came to him, and another fell, as he mercilessly rendered the bodies of once-living men and women to little more than afterthoughts in the minds of the gods they worshiped. The absolute wax of his mind had turned full circle to peace, underlying focus. Khanjali would not buckle under the pressure of his fury. Several more Acolytes pursued him in mid-combat, landing a single blow to his wings so shrouded in solid Ichyr—massive, feathered limbs, powerful enough to sweep a crowd of Atramedians into their afterlife (though there they would not go)—which served only to shatter the blade that made the strike without a sign of damage. His shell-like head grew two more antlers, and a second pair of arms coated in Ichyr emerged from his abdomen. He wished for more carnage, Khanjali wanted to visualize a sea of the organs and bones of every living Sgiathless in Drochandas. During this moment, he slung his now slumbering daughter across the back of his neck, knowing protecting her would be easier in this location. A small pack of Acolytes hurried to attack Khanjali, thinking oh so incorrectly that he would be vulnerable during his state of transition. They were obliterated, grasped with all of those newly formed arms. He shoved the four together with such force that mystical greatness was created, a rather unique frame of modern art—four corpses in one, a statuette of gore and parasitic prowess. Khanjali turned to the other Acolytes now closing in on him. Ezrakell stuck a pen in the neck of one, shoving the body forward into the talons of the hunter. Clearing his breath, Khanjali exhaled sharply, tossing another corpse into the crowd. They were thousands, this was true, but there was not a sliver of forgiveness in his mind, not a hint of regret in his motion. Consumption controlled his taste, the voice begged for a sample of the good men of the city. Stepping forward, he swept his great wings before the crowds, dicing three Acolytes into thin slices with his sharp feathers. He stepped again, collecting a single Acolyte and popping its head with the bulk of his thumb. Gnawing on remains, another group of foolhardy martyrs was reduced to a thick paste, this time with a crushing stomp from his gargantuan talons. Ezrakell moaned as a leg stuck his knee down, Khanjali soon removing the threat entirely. While the company was appreciated, the hunter saw no need in the death of those he cared for. With a vile *go* the old fool scampered off to the stage. Returning to the feast, Khanjali bent down to snap at the folk of his pain, three men in his charged maw. His peaceability was shunned now by a slight pang of hunger. Again, four more were killed in a thunderclap erupting from the thresh of his wings. The hoards began to build up, another attack striking his shielded body. The masses did not learn from repetition, so Khanjali saw it fit to teach them. He swatted the tool and its user into the void of death. Another jab met his leg, this time he was sure to kill more than just the attacker. Khanjali smashed his fist down, crushing a small grouping of Acolytes with its radius. A shot rang out in the crowd, as a thick lever of metal hooked itself onto Khanjali's left wing. It did not hurt, but it did a slight work in keeping him from agility. Another harpoon struck his leg, pulling the hunter to his knees. The Acolytes swarmed him, thinking their advantage had been won. Needless to state, his fury still remained untamed.

"Stop!" Few Acolytes turned their faces of hate to the priestess, standing upon the stage beside Ezrakell. Khanjali felt his face heat with embarrassment, he knew she would not think him sane after such a gory display. Mezzo wished for his cessation, yet it was unlikely to arrive. "You blind fools! Stop this violence at once! This creature is your savior!" Khanjali fell into confusion, distant angelic calls blurring into the pollution of the roaring battle. "He is afflicted, turned to hate and rage by your hand! Do you see not how you have corrupted his mind? Battered his lifesake?" They looked to Pedantick, who resonated peaceful forgiveness to Khanjali, even in slumber. "Do you not see it? You have caused this! Your impunity, your transgressions, pushing a kind and lovely soul to grueling chaos. If not for your pertinacity, he would have aided your suffrage! Saved you from yourselves! You are to blame for the deaths of your peers, for that there is no debate! Maeandri deems all of you sinners!" The crowd seemed to turn from confusion to malice, seeking to kill not just Khanjali, but the priestess who protected him as well. A single bolt fired from the crowd, aimed at the only friend Khanjali had left unwatched. The hunter managed to snag it from the air before it struck her, but he knew this was simply the first of many. With

Priestess Mezzo present, the attacks would likely target her, a much less shelled being. Khanjali tossed the soul who had fired the shot into his maw, snapping it down to eviscerate the body. The crowd roared with continuous anger, a tyrannical desire to topple the beast. The hunter did not waver. A spreading in the sea of faces fabricated a rather tall figure stepping from its midst. An Atramedian, draped in familiar white armor, a cape of dowered gold shining among the eyes of darkness. The figure drew a blade made entirely of glass, pointing it at Khanjali,

"Your rampage comes to an end; Maccabeus deems it so." The priestess called out from behind Khanjali, encouraging his continued fight,

"This deceiver lies! There are no words from Maccabeus! Strike them down, fill that zealous armor with gore!" Khanjali did not oppose such an order and swiftly swung his claw at the figure, halted in progress by the glass blade. The knight struck back, cracking the shell around his hand. Infuriated, he swung at another attacker, sending them back to their crowd. The hunter fought against the knight, who ceaselessly evaded his blows, striking back, slowly whittling down his armor's strength. More Acolytes came forth too, and Khanjali was far too occupied to see only the knight's blows. He bit into another prey and shattered another's skeleton, reducing yet more to a fine mist. The knight was left to his attacks, perhaps by some sick form of strategy. Khanjali could not continue for long, the harpoons restricting his slaughter, the knight weakening his only protection from the masses, and the Advocates becoming far too plentiful to kill. Like the shattering of a fatal mirror, a single strike halted the knight, a small metal object laced in Ichyr and circuity. It was a gauntlet, thrown from his backside. Khanjali looked over his shoulder, his daughter gripping the hunter's back with a weakened grasp. She lifted her smallest finger, accepting her role in the war. In a moment of opportunity, Khanjali grasped the knight and shook his armor with such incredible speed that it loudly liquified the wearer, as the priestess had requested of him. Khanjali lightly plucked Pedantick from his neck, who murmured something about fathers, and placed her with Ezrakell, instructing him to take her shriveled ankles to a healer. While Khanjali proceeded with this, a new threat rose from the crowd, a narrow harpoon fired directly at the priestess once more, a projectile Khanjali did not see until it was far too late. His fate flashed before his eyes; the voice cried out in fear. But, before it could strike its target, a blinding light replaced its shape. A stone-shattering clang of metal rang throughout the sea of Atramedians. Khanjali opened his eyes from the blinding glimmer, his vision obscured by a hand coated in white sanctity, nearly ten times the size of his own.

"Anāgarikaru, the whole of you—trading sips of blood for trinkets of repute. Pathetic." Above Khanjali hovered a being so beautifully refined it was blinding. It was the purest of white, loosely resembling the Ichyric statuettes of old war trophies, but far greater in essence and size. No blemishes or imperfections touched its form, its four completely winged arms were bent in displeasure, save for a single hand that had caught the harpoon meant to strike Priestess Mezzo down. Upon its body was an extensive robe, one with a void black color, and not a single wrinkle. Many divine sigils were scattered amongst its beauty, shining with their own power. The larger two of the figure's four arms were extended so greatly, allowing the being to float, mortality lay astonished in its presence. Its beak and talons existed only in comprehension, remaining so darkened black that they seemed devoid of any essence at all. The eyes were filled with similar color, the brows of such a creature not entirely visible under the intricate feathered mask that rested upon its face, though the emotion they would display was adamantly clear. Priestess Mezzo stood frozen in time, shattered with disbelief that such a being stood (rather, hovered) before her. Lakaeron tossed the mundane harpoon to the side, and stepped down onto the stones of Drochandas' roads, letting himself be viewed by all the mortals that dared fight Khanjali, "I can no longer stand to watch such disarray amongst the subjects of this Galaxy. It humiliates my namesake that such troubling wars could be fought in the same realm as I exist." The hunter awed himself with mouth agape, troubled by the brilliance. The eyes of the Great Bird God met his for a moment, unable to leave their gaze. "Apologies, divine one. I seek your forgiveness in the place of the gods—your deity has ignored you long enough." Khanjali could not imagine why an ancillary deity—the one of Ichyr no less—was bowing to *him*, rather than the reverse. "Hmph, that changes now. As for the rest of you? I expect a sufficient solution to this petty conflict within the year. Your agonizing hypocrisy and incessant lamenting have grown dull. You and your winged equals are far too seraphic for this imprudent quarrel. You have been warned, this bloodbath will seem like a singular grain of sand in an hourglass of damnation if my request is ignored." Khanjali cracked the bone in his arm, readjusting it to a place of comfort. Lakaeron had begun to rub the feathers upon one of his numerous arms together, his welcomeness thinning. "Are you the priestess who beckoned? Thank you for your notification. I doubt apologies on behalf of Maccabeus will be enough to sate your reform. I wish you luck in your outreach—she can be a fickle woman." With the god occupied, Khanjali rushed past the Acolytes to the stage, a hand reaching out Mezzo in thanks. Instead, he found himself impossibly lost, wrapped in the lips of a lightless curse. He stood in a dark room, silence filling not only the space but his mind. The glow of Lakaeron remained affixed above the hunter, showing his fingertips in gleam.

"Where is my daughter? What have you done with me, Great One?" Returning sightlines with the god, Khanjali no longer saw some hulking behemoth. The bird was shallow, perhaps just as tall as young Pedantick.

"Golly, what a horrific time—are there any motes about at all?" The great bird fluttered down from above, his robes tangling against his gangly legs. Touching the floor, the talons shook in frost, Lakaeron wrapping himself tighter in the coat of divinity. He scurried about the hall, leaping up to a throne far above his height. A smaller Ichyric of some kind rushed from his side, hurrying to a minuscule console at the far end of the room. The room itself resembled the one Khanjali had died within, great stone pillars of white rather than black covered its circular shape, and a great many detailed veins pulsed within the walls, as did they within the tiles beneath his feet. "Oh! There you are, my sandals?" Lakaeron questioned the tiny creature, shooing it off in the direction of the further cathedral. Taken aback by both the sudden change in environment and Lakaeron's uncanny form, Khanjali raised a curious hand, reaching out to the small creature.

"You are Lakaeron? The Deity of Ichyr? The same who saved the lives of my friends?" Lakaeron held out his hand, aiming it towards Khanjali,

"Yep, in the feathers." Presenting his form widely, the tiny servant returned with wooden shoes and rested them on the stone floor. With thanks, the creature left them be. "Didn't mean to frighten you, but that was really some terrible reception. You and your pals are safe now, rest assured." His height, demeanor, and the language of his testament all mirrored a child, a late youth at best. Sweat stained the blacker sections of the cloak, as Lakaeron traded its elegance for simpler leathers.

"This is a comedy, surely. You could not be older than I!" Lakaeron stopped himself, recuperating from his near demonization, clearing his throat.

"For the record, this body outlives the existence of time." Extending one arm, he threaded the essence of his feathers into an overcoat and twisted the square of his wrist. "For a deity, I remain paradoxically young—still getting used to the shape of holiness." Another small servant appeared at Khanjali's side, poking him in the leg.

"What is this creature. He is small."

"Hmm? Oh—" Lakaeron hunched himself to the height of the ant, whispering to it pleasantly, "Ichyr Motes, servants of the cathedral. I think he wants your coat, friend." Unwilling to disappoint the glorious charm of the Mote's stare, Khanjali pulled the cloak from his body, dropping the massive cloth over tiny, outstretched arms. A pile of cloth took its place, hurriedly slinking away from the giant. "Cute little things, know an awful lot of big words too—helped me write the speech back there." Considerable effort had been placed into the words he sang, and Khanjali did recall the mispronunciation of several terms. Faith was waning by the minute, as Lakaeron explored the hall and ruminated on the plights of Maccabeus. The hunter had always thought the deity of Ink to be a kind and gentle ruler, one who cared more than any being to have existed before herself. All Atramedians thought this.

The Harlequin

"If her focus is not on the people, then where else? Is this why my prayers go unanswered?" Lakaeron slumped against his throne, beckoning Khanjali to join him,

"Of course. She's too busy toying with amalgams and monsters. She doesn't appreciate imperfection, she's beyond tough love. Even Maeandri sympathizes" Khanjali caught his legs together, sitting against the throne with all his limbs in order. He considered gods to be above the speculation and curiosity of mortal men, their divine duties enough to satiate their palates of the greater galaxy. "No care for mortals." Lakaeron stood from his throne, peering out a large stained-glass window overlooking a plane of moondust. "It vexes me! Maccabeus does naught but covet the crown of gods. She serves Maeandri blindly in search of his power. Those two, a God and their servant, they hurt so many with their... their nescience! Even I am incapable of protecting all life alone." Lakaeron slammed a tightened fist against the glass, it cracked, but only slightly. Whiplashed emotions coated the bird's face, as rage fractured immediately into contentment, "How was that? Practice is a coal."

"I've lost track of your words, why am I here? What do you want with *me*?" Lakaeron paused at the window, turning back to examine the divine beast.

"Your illness must be addressed, and Maccabeus' ambitions quelled—that one was far more than planned, recited even." Returning to the center of the room, Lakaeron slipped dribbled Ink atop his fingertips, "You were in need of a deity, what other reason do I need?" Khanjali spun the shell of his wrist, circling the Ichyr with his own inky fingers,

"I suppose I am in the debt of a god." Flicking the mire from his finger, Lakaeron spun back to Khanjali,

"No! Do not say such things! I do not wish to be a creditor for salvation. You are as equal as me now, filled with divinity." Khanjali remained silent, he feared interrupting the deity would cause nothing but harm. "God—I guess that sounds nice." Dragged into the hall by the claws of a mote, a spindly bird entered the room, an Ichyric not far in difference from the knight Khanjali had dueled in Drochandas.

"Oh Lakaeron, you have returned. Impressive timing. Khanjali, then? That *must* be you." The bird god could do little but nod, crossing their legs patiently across the floor.

"Does every Ichyric know my name? I consider myself an awful idol." The Ichyric scoffed, sipping what seemed to be pure Ichyr from his chalice.

"I ought to know my recruits well, names and beyond." Rising from the throne, Khanjali approached the figure.

"Recruit? I am much too bothered with family to be some godly subject." Lakaeron reminded the hunter of his shell, the affliction that had only worsened with his rage.

"If you wish to live, it would be wise to remain here, in the service of no one" The Ichyric added, careful to receive assurance for his words from Lakaeron prior to speaking them. The three circled about the center of the hall, sitting in a triangular shape of inclusion.

"This is N'yūt, my underling and friend. He is the head of my best soldiers, my Kāge." N'yūt, presented with all the honor of a beggar, bowed while seated, and flicked his beak.

"Crows, in your tongue. With your acceptance, I would make you one." Finishing the drink and setting it aside, N'yūt cleansed Ichyr from his dark beak. His deep eyes reminded Khanjali of the mirror on Drochandas, the ethereal form of his transgressed shape was similar to the one now before him. "Alongside underling, you might consider bringing my relation to you into question, uncle." Lakaeron leered at the bird, feathers about his neck puffing out like the rims of an overstuffed barrel,

"All of you are my nephews, and I'm still the promised child of this pathetic country. I have a caretaker for Maen's sake— practically still a kid." Souring his expression, N'yūt offered to leave the grim god alone, which he quickly likened to. With a subtle beckon, Khanjali rose to follow his destiny stuffed with bony feathers.

"A tempered man, is he always so shaken?" Smiling back at his trail, N'yūt added insult to his deity,

"He is terribly unadjusted to publicity. You mark his first appearance in a decade." Khanjali accepted the excuse, and continued deeper into the cathedral, dragging his shell with. Like a decaying snake, he traveled alongside the remains of his past, without the sense to discard them.

"He will grow out of it." Doubt followed the words—a father he was, but the growth of even his own child outpaced him. Pedantick had yet to become ingrained with the eyes of others, or her own words. Now considering the length of her youth, Khanjali feared he would never see such a thing occur. "Will I see my daughter again?" N'yūt had no answers for the hunter, who was now brought down to the bowels of the cathedral, among the hunkered metal remains of machine skeletons.

"I do not know—likely not." Khanjali clutched the Ichyric's wrist, squeezing with unrealized hate.

"*Likely not*? Do you intend to take my daughter from me?" N'yūt returned his grip but could not break the chains that bound him.

"N-not at all Khanjali. I only mean it would be safer for her if she—" He paused, looking out to the dark abyss of the forge-bowel. "She should not see you like this, and it'd be far better for her compassion if she was not teased with your presence." The hunter understood, and following the Ichyric he dwelled on compassion. It was not unlike Pedantick to grow stubborn when alone, even without Khanjali present Ezrakell did much to quell her tyranny. A grin spread across his face as pictures of the old fool's trying form scampered away from rambunctious contraptions. N'yūt found the smile forthcoming.

"You are aware this servitude may not be the cleanest of duties." Khanjali, brought back from humor, questioned the Ichyric,

"Death and despair? I've seen worse."

"Have you questioned your killings of *men*? Of innocent betrayers?" The thief was no innocent soul, nor were the Acolytes. To Khanjali, innocence ceased when a man stepped between him and his daughter.

"Substantially. What does it matter if my daughter and her peers remain out of harm?" N'yūt paused on the stairwell, leaning his wing softly against the tin railing,

"You mean to say murder does not disturb you so long as it is in the favor of your child?"

"Not terribly, no." Astonished, N'yūt returned to his descent, muttering against Khanjali's compulsion. N'yūt did not find a satiable warrior in his new recruit, nor did he particularly enjoy his boundless motivation. He knew full well the dangers of blind devotion—a slope of oils that dampened upon further descent. While the intentions of Lakaeron appeared pure to inexperienced onlookers, the methodology was nearly as cruel as Maccabeus' experiments. N'yūt knew of all the projects Lakaeron would not dare tell the truth of. He knew with enough effort; his god could erase the world like a combing wedge. And yet, he accepted it. So too could Maccabeus overrun the galaxy with plague or mutants, as could Maeandri snap all light away in an instant. Though there were shaky bearings to the bridge forward, N'yūt saw no other option than to serve his deity and pray for forgiveness if he should ever succumb to the mindless institution of faith. Venturing deeper into the dark, the scent of crows began to pour over them both, their conversation growing distant to listening ears. Lakaeron remained disgruntled, the words spoken to him beyond cruel despite their intentions. He wished for no place in the annals of history, and certainly not for statues in his favor. The homeworld of the Ichyrics—the grand city-scaped planet of Palosameerilyr—boasted thousands in his honor, shaped not remotely like the great bird's true form. Mind cluttering aside, Lakaeron had much to focus on beyond his youth, Maccabeus the sole riot to his peace. Her pure allegiance to Maeandri was no pleasure of his and often led to petty quarrels that rocked their corresponding peoples. The very Ichyr Mote that had taken Khanjali's coat returned to its master, whispering secrets to the eyes of Lakaeron.

"Great Bird, while he is not the one you seek, his strength may match the prophesized." Lakaeron's interest was piqued, he questioned the servant, observing the setting moons as he did.

"How so?"

"The hunter is of both divine matters. It is told that the Thorn would be of similar disposition. He holds great promise, should we begin modeling after him?" Lakaeron sighed, balling their legs under the hide of their pants,

"No, I don't think that would be smart. We should wait for the real one, the Thorn will come in time."

The Harlequin

Upon Inkhome—within the walls of Khanjali's abode—was a single soul. The priestess stepped across the small carpet between the door and the kitchen. Mezzo smelled the air of emptiness, saddened by its lacking. She took sufficient note of the crumpled scraps of paper lying near the sink, the bowls left unwashed by the sink, the glass tucked under the table. Her hands reached out to gather up the scraps, little else motivated her to continue. With a soft knock against the doorframe Ezrakell entered, speaking quietly,

"It isn't much, that I am aware of. I apologize for the mess. This of course was very sudden."

"Mmhm." Priestess Mezzo continued to shuffle through the scraps, noticing signs of black and white—an image. She pieced the photo together in her hand, connecting the smoothed cheeks of her greatest friend. There were hints of another person in the image, but the scraps had been torn far too thin to seek any kind of resemblance.

"Are you so sure you wish to mother Pedantick until his return? Who knows what Lakaeron wanted of him? He could be years, maybe never to return at all!" The priestess turned to him, still focusing on her photo.

"Oh hush. He will return, I will wait an eternity if I must."

"You may just be forced to adhere to that vow."

"Then I will."

"Fine." Quiet, again, all was still. The picture was finished. Mezzo taped it together with some spare adhesive from one of Pedantick's projects. She looked at his stunning face, a content smile, arm resting upon a distilled shoulder. She liked this picture of him, so youthful, full of hope for an altruistic future. She liked his contentment, his cool. She liked him.

"So, she is…?"

"Home, at mine, rather. I will bring her over. You just… stir, here. Please, no disc—"

"I understand." Ezrakell rushed off to collect Pedantick, leaving the priestess in her quiet. She did not pray. She thought, after having gone so long unanswered, why pray? Lakaeron had saved her friend, not Maccabeus. Not Maeandri. Staring at the photograph, she contemplated silently what Khanjali was doing right then. Besides this thought, there was not much else to think of.

~ *The Gardener's Recluse IV*

Lakaeron — devilish as he was — made certain this was forever preserved through his reign...

The Gardener did not wake in nature. The Human had brought a tea extract from the mint in the garden, and he the softest breed of pear thought possible. He did not need sustenance, but the squish of the fruit against his chassis was so quaint. In the coming days, the Centrum would become fully operational. Flesh and Fuel side by side would labor, and bring repair to the desolate gardens. The Gardener knew this was all solely temporary, and eventually, the Human would leave to the stars. He thought, for whatever reason, of those very stars.

"Thank you for the food, Gardener. How was your — er, rest?" The Gardener simply nodded, wonder moving the stiff joints to action. She would leave eventually, but there were no rules to halt his venture too.

"Does your journey to the stars include another?" The question surprised the Human, who despite having mouthfuls of pear between her teeth, mumbled an affirmation to the Gardener. There was further room for hundreds of humans, let alone a simple two.

"Couldn't keep the thing running without you, could I?" Steel hands made good grips; she was right of course. The Gardener couldn't help but feel lonely, even in the presence of his other, even assured of his rise to the stars.

"What will we see up there?" The Human had no answer but instead handed the Gardener a small card, scrawled with instructions.

"Small repairs, nothing much left. We can find out together." The Gardener stared at the card, a gift by any other name.

"I'll finish it myself. Rest your leg. We will discover much together, Human." And so, the Gardener worked all day, until the sun grew to its peak, and he took soaring breaks for his flowers. Occasionally he would hear her voice, singing or repeating things, pondering properties and remembering things. She was such a puzzle; the Gardener gave up his time to solve it and concluded there was no solution. "I haven't heard from you in a while Peregrine. Three whole days. I wished you would come back to me." He continued his work, and the flowers were wetter for it. At sundown, he spoke with the Human and helped her to move to the garden. She thanked him with a peck, but the two remained silent together regardless. It was her belief that she did not deserve the stars, and that being a Pilot had told her that she did. She questioned the Gardener,

"Do you think it's as beautiful up there as it is down here?"

"We take it with us. The Garden." He answered, not a moment spent thinking required. "Surely yes. We take all our beauty with us. All but the swans." The Human chuckled, animated with the energy from a day's rest,

"Kitchen sink, Gardener. The phrase is 'everything but the *kitchen sink*'."

"No. I just don't like them."

"Swans?"

"Of course."

"What's the matter with them?"

"Rude creatures." She couldn't help but chortle again. The Gardener understood why she found it so entertaining, but could not bring himself to laugh. The Human had learned some tasks of Gardening, having started a small seedbed herself, just outside the charging stations the Gardener rested upon. He could watch her toy with the roots for days with no interruption, her work with cobbles was incredible. A small garden wall had been formed, and saltless water collected from the rivers and poured into the bed; it took weeks for the first algae to rise to the brims. The Gardener was proud of his Human, who too was proud of herself now, a version of existence that she could truly depend on. She wouldn't always be the Pilot or Yorai. As long as she had the Gardener, she could always be his.

"We could begin soon. Tomorrow, maybe." She broke the trance of her own garden, peering over to the Gardener's resting place.

"Yeah. Tomorrow. Is it—?" The Gardener presented his tortured thumb, bent irregularly from his honed lines by wear and time.

"Ready for you. We will leave tomorrow then."

"I have to say my goodbyes! Don't you too? What of the island?" The Gardener thought for a moment. He would ask Peregrine if it was still around to answer these questions.

"I've never liked it. The Garden is all I need. And you certainly." The Human clutched the Gardener in a great embrace, her arms locked at his waist.

"I can't stand to live like this. As titles of each other. We must come up with something better." The Gardener's eyes wandered about, lost entirely in the hedge maze of thought.

"Do we have names?" The Human nodded, sure she could discover something.

"We can think about it! Think of one for me, and I for you! We shall tell each other tomorrow. When we leave this place…"

"We will be new. I understand." And the two slept, war on the horizon unbeknownst to their friendship.

By the light of the flickering consoles the Gardener rested, his legs propped precariously against an old breaker. It no longer functioned, this was why he had installed his own firmware into the console, why a cable stretched the length of the whole Centrum from his skull, hundreds of them all installed firmly into his metal.

"Rose. Red. Lily. White."

"Trajectory is finished, Gardener! It's just fuel reports now, about an hour's worth!" The Gardener refused to nod, even a soft shake of his head could loosen the cables.

"Thank you Human. I have yet to find you a name in all of the world's concepts. I'm afraid you are beyond names." The Human would laugh at the jokes of the machine, if not for her pain. They grew closer, time forgave her once already. By the dawn of their escape, she would surely find no salvation in the stars. But it was for gifts that she left the Centrum, a scarlet toll strapped to her back, lengthy as a spear. She hunted the acres of empty root, collecting herbs she had never seen with little disparity.

"His name will be lovely," she thought, continuing her snatching. As she leaned forward once more to pick a fourth berry for her collection, a soft chime of bells filled her ears. At first, it was enchantment that struck her. She questioned her origins as the remaining freckles of her shaved head snickered in the light breeze. Then she smelled the timber, the oak flakes on a burning open kiln. The Human covered her mouth, foaming white nipped at her gums. She knew exactly what this was, precisely which memories were still true. She dropped her load of greenery and readied the tool upon her backside. Two crystalline echoes stood behind the Human, and this feeling of dread swept under her ankles.

"Are you okay, Human?" They repeated, the only memory left to taint was that of her machine friend garnished in moss.

"I will be once I see you again." She swung her weapon backward, cleaving the first shadow in two, its rocky abdomen shattering like salt cracked against the tide.

"Are you okay, Human?" She pushed the other back, terrified by its accuracy to his figure. She knew it wasn't him. She couldn't believe it wasn't him. Knowing her match when she met it, the Human ran, only desperation took her hold. In the tomb of wires, the Gardener stirred. It had been more than enough time for the Human's ventures. He had not yet collected a name for her.

"Peregrine, what about Lily? Much like the flower, her pale skin is suiting too." There was no response. Ardor caused his limbs to tense and flinch as if a jolt of power had spun through his circuits. "Or perhaps Rose. Some few roses bloom gray in the summer. Ashy soot colored... Ash then?" The Gardener had a soft rag stuffed down the barrel of its choice weapon, ensuring it remained as such throughout all its trials. "Bess, like a weapon, a beautiful name." He twisted the rag back to his palm, shaking out the excess from its wrinkles. "Are weapons so beautiful? Would the charm be lost in such a name?" A rocking thud shook the ship's interior, and the Gardener carried himself hesitantly down the maintenance shaft, peering out at the Garden. Nothing of significance appeared.

"Gardener!" The Gardener fell backward off the maintenance rail, clanging against the metallic interior of the bulwark.

"Surely, there is a safer way of asking for my attention." With whiplash like the beat of a hummingbird, the Human collapsed upon him, her legs quivering against the weight of her spear.

"The uploads, Gardener! They must be done by now, they— you *must* finish them immediately!" The Gardener tilted his head, his eyes falling to the quiet grass rustles beyond the Human.

"They... the uploads will take another quarter-hour. Perhaps twenty minutes at most. These things cannot be hurried. If I was to miscalculate, the oxygen requirements could skew, pressurization could reach imbalance; failure here is death in the future." The Human grunted, pushing her thumbs violently into her eye sockets.

"Not enough time—we need to..." She dropped the spear, and cupped her hands around his face, the Gardener leaned inwards to assist her. "Charlemagne. I decided this will be your name. If you hear me call you anything, *anything* but this name...." Her voice trailed off, blood slowly dribbling from her ears.

"Charlemagne. It is beyond flawless. I will try it on for a while. *Charl*emagne." The Human shot a look back towards the ridge of the Centrum, seemingly piqued by the silence of it all. In truth, a deafening ring pulsed its way to every living creature. The allure of the Crystalline did not fall on mechanical ears. The Gardener stepped away from the ship entrance, the sun reflecting oddly upon a glistening oak.

"You have your weapon?"

"Always. Is there some fear approaching?"

"Hundreds. I fear we won't survive long with them here. They seek your mind and stop at nothing to have it. Can't you hear the bells?" The Gardener gritted his speaker mesh down to dust, his thumb tightly bound to the trigger guard of his shotgun.

"I hear nothing. That does not mean I do not believe you. Remain in the ship. I will deal with their insolence." She stood in his way, the fuzz on her arms straight at attention, stiff with fear.

The Harlequin

"The upload, Charlemagne. You have to stay here, otherwise—" While her words reminded him of an old quarrel he had once had against Peregrine, the Gardener concocted a most simple solution. He tore the upload cable from the back of his head, and with a moment of hesitation, took with it a small block, no bigger than a die.

"My databank retains a friend, one who will find it much easier to do this task *without* me. Take it to our little mainframe. Use it in place of me." The Gardener, more vivacious than ever, stepped his iron into the garden, an unknowable foe growing on the horizon. "By the time I return, I will have a name for you. I am certain." She sealed the ship door and started up to the console, her strength finding itself despite her pains. Determination to save her friend—alongside the hope of a name—was all that drove her. The Crystallines, though a multitude, posed little threat to the Gardener. He kept his distance and let them come to his side. When approached, he would quickly jam the weapon under their hide, sometimes burrowing his hydraulics against the gemish exterior. Without Peregrine, certain calculations failed to process quickly enough for the heat of battle to accept them. Namely, the Gardener intended to keep an accurate count of the beasts he had slain, it was difficult to keep up. Anatomy was a concern as well, these beasts were undocumented to his knowledge, and he saw it fit to change such records. The first attack that struck him was a light one, a glaze to the standards of man. It merely set his foot off course, a stumble forward with little consequence. A shot shattered the thin membrane around weaker crystals, painting the Gardener's chassis in white. After another couple of creatures, the Gardener began to exhaust his memory, and the ventilation on his backside began to redden with the heat of computation.

"Target—twenty-three—erroring—twenty-three. Twe--" The Gardener's Calculations slipped from his speaker, and distracting buzzes of error collapsed his mind. He loaded the shotgun and fired again. "Error—the sand is—" A clubbing motion wiped the thought from his mind, snapping the hard tackle chains in his neck hydraulics. An impossible clutch kept his weapon in hand, his visuals shifting toward the shadow of a hulking Crystalline, towering across the

Centrum walls. He raised his weapon but knew it to be useless in a fight of such terrible odds. Ducking another blow, the Gardener dodged backward, directly into the jagged spine of a beast, which knocked his screen to a crack, and a sparking arc leaped from his servos. "Damage recovered, moving to—" A third strike, fatal to the leg, twisting it near irreparably. Too many beasts purged against him, too many for even an army, the Gardener thought. Leaving Peregrine was a mistake, but a calculated one. He fired again, piercing the torso of one more fiend. With the force of shattering steel, the beast pounded the front of the Gardener. He lurched forward, as another scooped him off the ground to send him flying back. He tripped over his own circuitry, glitches forcing his very servos to twitch and purr violently over the tune of his own thoughts. "Cr-cr-cr-critical fracture detec-te-te-ted. Rerouting numeral parsing-g-g-g." The Human shook against the frame of the ship, her stomach oozing from a wound of her own origins.

"They're—ghk—not worth it Charlemagne!" The Gardener looked back at his first and only accomplice. She was a wonder to him, faith and history besides.

"W-w-worth it." He slipped around the limb of another figure, slurring his processes to sparks. He kicked down two more, receiving a final clap to his chest before retreating to the gardens. The Human caught him as he stumbled, sealing the ship door behind them.

"Charlemagne? Are you—you look damaged, seriously damaged, is this—?" The Gardener remained focused on his foes, who pillaged without query, stomping out the precious burdens of his gardens.

"They destroy what-t-t they please. Le-le-le-let me back to slaughter their r-ranks." The Human held him to the floor, tugging the shotgun from his arms.

"Not a chance, Charlemagne." She glanced up to the console, her hand loosely placed around a crystalline protrusion from her stomach. A soft banging rhythmically tossed the ship, the beings would afford no cowardice.

"You are critic-ca-ca-cally wounded." The Human's eyes returned to him, gravely expressing her thoughts.

The Harlequin

"The upload isn't finished. You told me it's processing life support stuff, oxygen, and pressure. You don't need oxygen." The Gardener agreed, the clash of crystals growing ever louder. Bearing to their proximity, the Human could hear all her family again, beckoning her to the shores. "Then my mind is made up. I won't let myself die in the memories of a false persona." The Gardener complimented her positive thinking, requesting an alternative solution in her stead.

"M-m-mount me on the rail, I'll f-f-f-f-fetch Peregrine. With his processing—" The Human placed her lips upon the Gardener— upon Charlemagne's cracked screen, letting her eyes close one final time by his side.

"I don't need a name anyways, honey. Peregrine! Start ascent." For a moment, sparks shifted down his face, the lights on his visual compass flickering in and out. He did not understand the implication. Peregrine returned to him in a blink, and he ignored the sounds of the ship door's moving ambiance.

"Peregrine, assist me in m-m-m-my—error." Charlemagne smacked at his skull, recognizing the Human's absence, her struggles, and grunts louder than the hum of his mind. She tussled against the sea of crystal, winning none of her battles.

"Gardener. Give me permission." Thoughtless rage filled the Gardener, his eyes strained on his dying friend.

"You leave for weeks and return for this! I will give you nothing. You deserve nothing!"

"Gardener. Give me permission. It is imperative—" For the first time, the Gardener spoke out of turn, breaching his bylaws to obstruct the will of Peregrine.

"I am Ch-ch-ch-charlemagne! I am beyond your-r-r-r demands. Leave me with your sk-sk-skill or nothin-in-ing, but I no longer wish to see you com-m-m-mmandeer me like a tool." Peregrine paused, as Charlemagne desperately fiddled with his braces, the maintenance rail wouldn't permit his freedom.

"Gardener. Give me permission. That is all I can specify about the protocol. It is the only way to stop this."

"Stop wh-what? The beasts of the island-d-d? My resistance? Stop this, P-peregrine! I am not a—" He fell forwards, the ship rocking with its beginning to the stars. The Gardener scurried upright, clutching against the glass of its only exit, prying and smashing with utter haste.

"Gardener."

"Shut up! Sh-sh-sh-shut your mouth machin-n-n-ne! Shut your per-perverted maw! Let me-e-e save her—let me ou-t-t-t-t of here now! St-st-stop the launch!" Her ankle was swept with the shot of another Crystalline, her arm nearly embraced in the white matter. The Gardener errored millions of times in a moment, all of his equations unable to shoulder the width of his complexity. His hands twitched with even greater frequency, the heat of the ship skyrocketing with his presence. It was anger and desperation both, while the two emotions did nothing to solve any of his difficulties. Charlemagne wished he could cry. "Margulis! I name you, my wife! Margulis— please come back here Margulis! Margulis!" A last shattering blow pierced her chest, and the Gardener split in two just as she did. His fragments of life faded into the ether, as the rocket rose higher into the sky. He clutched his own damages, all flickering with the slowing of his mind. Peregrine was as silent as usual, and the space without the Human pushed the Gardener further into a state of utter loss. He couldn't process the emotion he felt if it was emotion at all. Placing a single twisted claw against the glass of the ship, he watched as the world faded from color. "Margulis."

The thin gaps between the distant stars were all that remained persistent in the journey. For an unfathomable time, the Gardener had drifted, though not truly alone in its suffering. Peregrine returned as an ambient associate, a voice that was heard far more often than ever before. This led the Gardener to wonder if it was an act of apology or mere coincidence.

"Peregrine, calculate sunset likelihood." Its vapid digits clicked against the ancient form of a dilapidated chisel. The walls of its humble chapter had been decivilized from their plated forms, torn up with carvings and sigils. Since its ascent to the starry abyss, the Gardener had grown airy. Its linen robes—in the pure lack of breathable air—had faded from life, decaying as moss dries in autumn. The screen that mounted its circuitry had retained its damage from its war, as had the wounds to its interior festered.

The Harlequin

"Naught-point-zero. Again. The sun cannot set without a horizon." The Gardener had spent days attempting to savor the perishable wares of its gardens, thousands of flowers and endless shrubbery lie deceased and drained on the ship floor, drifting through the air when the gravity flux ceased—it tended to do so every so often. The fields of its work remained gray with the decaying gravel and soils. It turned the Gardener's sorrow to hate, emotional conquest beheld the machine and forced its motion. All it could imagine was the battlefield, never had it been so invested in the death of another. The first month was spent mourning, but past that there was no merciful quiet. Torn from the banisters and core bulwark, the Gardener fortified. It mounted thick ramjets to its spine, triggered in cordage. It filled bowls with mercury harvested from old batteries and souped it together into a soapy repair wash. Taking from its home the Gardener broadened its hull and heightened its mannerisms. It Tunneled through itself with drill bits; new ventilation was needed. The Gardener had considered removing a number of its functions in favor of combat, but Peregrine advised against manipulation of the computation hardware, too delicate.

"Spatial Color Scan, please? I do enjoy those." But merely preparing for the war was not enough, no, it must be practiced and expanded upon. Its practice explained the presence of so many homemade spears, struck deep in the metal flesh of the ship, out of the Gardener's reach. Peregrine had continued to optimize the Gardener's precision calculations but to no notable benefit. The Gardener was fit only for the closest of combatants (that was the only time its accuracy rose above fifty percent).

"Four-'c'-zero-zero-'b'-zero, roughly. Accuracy is falling with remaining functional power." The Gardener had embarked upon other ventures too, not solely the art of combat. Thanks to its ripened mind, the Gardener had recalled every pinnacle detail of the Human it once fell for. The shape of the veins, the color of the flesh, the bindings of the lungs; for once nothing escaped the machine. The carvings it had forsaken were all her, some far more accurate than others. It was not in an effort to recover what once was lost, but rather to persuade itself such a thing had ever existed. In this manner, the Gardener was more capricious than ever. It gazed for hours at nothing at all, something that concerned even the ignorance of Peregrine, who after some pause for recollection, had forgiven itself for its misleadings—and the Gardener for its harsh words. These sessions of interim ogling were often concluded with a long mechanical sigh, followed only by the tremendous clattering of the Gardener's movement beginning.

"Calculate sunset likelihood." Before Peregrine could draft its conclusions, a fog fell over its sensor, like the unfamiliar touch of another lifeform. It was close, Peregrine felt it.

"Odd. Gardener, I do not wish to alarm you, but our vessel is currently clarifying a population of *two*." The Gardener sat up, its spine clicking in and out of lockedness.

"Another beast of the dark? I must kill it."

"No Gardener, I think this is not some simple insect. It is certainly humanoid. We have weaponry aboard this vessel, how do you intend to proceed?" It did not know for certain. It had little documentation on the subject of confrontation, but it *did* recall the meeting of a human. The Gardener remembered the glee it felt hunting the creature, though with no intent to harm it; it desired to protect it. The Gardener thought that perhaps, this approaching life would desire the same thing, to seek out another, and protect it. White crystals shattered its mind, and corrosive blood poured down its throat. No such being desired peace. They were warmongers. Warmongers.

"I will pick whatever stands apart—sport no longer verifies me. The intruder will die, or I will." Peregrine wallowed in uncertainty—it had been designed to avoid dubitation. With no legs to stand on our arms with which to kill, Peregrine remained ambient, awaiting its presumed victory.

"I will trust you with this command, Gardener. Please see that it is followed through." The distant clank of metal caused the machine to rattle, the Gardener could not help but excite at the thrill. Death had been close before, this time the Gardener would leave with a message for the reaper. Far-flung mumbles of roaches and revolvers found their way to the Gardener's ear. A huffing puff cleared the garden floor, and the crunch of a distant leaf froze the machine in its tracks, distantly fingering the chisel before it. Whatever this being was, it had not yet seen the Gardener, scarce stealth remained. It did not move, however, knowing full well that the lifeform before it could be roused by the suddenness of movement. A scratching of leather, followed by a clinking of metal braces. Another puff. The intruder inched forward, eyes trained on the wall of human murals, lifting one of the makeshift spears from its resting container. Giving them no chance to learn more, the Gardener thrusted itself upon the intruder, passing over their neck with a polearm. The struggle pushed the both of them against a wall, slamming the circuitry from the Gardener's spine, splaying against the wall. With a wet grunt, the intruder pushed back and folded, throwing the machine from its back. Lunging with the spear, the intruder pinned down the Gardener, choking out its words through a narrow, chalk-filled speaker. Raising a pistol to its head, the intruder barked out a command,

"What in the name of the Lark was that for? Stay down, bot!" The Gardener squirmed under the grip, a momentary setback before kicking the fleshy invader from its chassis.

"How have you boarded this vessel?" The Gardener spoke, attempting to negotiate calmness. The voice chuckled, amiable and full, familiarity incarnate. As if it was intentional, too. Though the battle was long lost, practice played its role. Thirty-two outcomes led to failure, and for the Gardener, that was unacceptable. The voice rose into question once more,

"Through the damn door? You gonna tell me why you tried to choke me out, or should I just scrap you now?" The Gardener exhaled sharply, a jab at humor at a time like this—inimical. But sharp nonetheless. Mathematics became a priority, focused recordings analyzing the duel, focusing particularly on the queer strength of the intruder, unexplained power.

"Practice. Clearly, my grip is not at its best. You taught—" It paused, why would it respond to such a foolish interrogative? "Do you have a vessel of your own?"

"Course." The voice replied, hastily. A soft slumping was followed by a sudden loud clang. The voice apologized softly, humored by this. Had it come from beyond the grave? Were there countless species dotting the galaxy, or further known universe? Had they native intent to harm others, or much like the Gardener, did they prosper with the knowledge alone of other life? The figure returned a quip of counts, pondering himself how many 'bots' there were. The Gardener confirmed the truth of one. And the opposing questions too, did this being understand living machines? Did it know of the Gardener's home, or its namesake, or its duties? What if the language spoken between them (ironically identical) was a barrier yet to be presented? Too proud of unpredictability, it needed answers,

"I am the Gardener." It stated bluntly. There was no need for addressing the unspoken. The figure lowered their aim, wiggling their thumbs into the pocket of its jacket, earthworms in mulch.

"Real pleasure, name's Jeweler. Haven't met a machine quite like you, but I sure have met 'em." Resting against the remains of a decayed seedbed, Jeweler found his footing, clutching his waist. Despite circumstance, there was something of a comfort to his tone, a fatherly voice that pacified the Gardener and its feral instincts. Regretfully, it turned its head, meeting with the sightline of the seated husky, a man dressed in furs. The mop of darkened hair upon his head slithered down its cheeks, contained behind an alloy mask adhered with belt straps. It kept the breath in, the Gardener supposed. A rosy complexion contrasted the thick darkness of his eyelids, and furthermore, the aforementioned hair. A cyan coat fit with various pale furs swung itself down to his very knees, which were crossed in calm patience as the man fiddled with the thickest buckle on his belt, almost ignoring the Gardener's presence. The Gardener, who had been lost to the desert of stars, had nearly forgotten this aspect of creation: the watching. Observation it once treasured had been sullied by countless pounds of sand and gunpowder, war, and the death of all it cherished. When the world had sped up, at a pace too rapid for observation, the Gardener had no choice but to hasten alongside it. What a horrid thing to force upon somebody, the speed of cancer. Rushing through everything, appreciating nothing. How long had it been among the stars?

"You are not human. What are you?" Jeweler's face lit up with spite, before toning to a mischievous yellow,

"Well, course I am. Human's pretty broad though, maybe I don't fit your idea of fleshwalker, yeah?" The Gardener's vision tapered off, fixated now on the weapon the man held at his side, a

The Harlequin

revolver heavy with ammunition. The Gardener remembered a longer implement, one with twice the barrels and a fourth of the shots. It considered larger arms far more effective than the minute prestige of a handgun. The Gardener began to wonder where it would acquire another rifle....

"Humans are not so pinkish. They are scaled too, like geckos." This Jeweler could not understand. The official documentation of the galaxy named three species as Lesskin, that is, derived from Lesser Ichyrics. Two of these three had been named 'Human' for their similarities, the other remained a distinct selection—the Lunaphore. The only quantitative similarity between the Lesskin was their origins, that of the three Teras. Jeweler originated from Siam, commonly denoted as Tera One. Siamese Lesskin were the first to stake a claim in the galaxy, and among the most protected. Their bastions and colonies attracted the defensive permissions of nearly one-sixteenth of the Larkik Definition's forces. However, not a single Siam citizen had a case of scales. The humans of Tera Three were much alike, and the Lunaphorus of Tera Two shared no resemblance with geckos either, nor did any misfit roamers Jeweler had ever heard of. In fact, no *other race* fit that description, not even the Karplings.

"You sure about that? What Tera you from?" The Gardener had no understanding of its home world, having never been outside it until now. Space had sullied its memory, not even countries remained titled in its webbed mind. Peregrine guessed it to be an 'A' word, but there was no supporting evidence to its claims. The Gardener ignored them,

"I am... not certain. Its name escapes me." Jeweler was resolute, a new species of human could bring about great profit, after all. Its documentation by the hands of a scholarly title, one such as Viaduct, could shallow the depths of their pockets. Furthermore, there was the natural curiosity found in a human soul, no? Jeweler was familiar with much of the galaxy, having spent his entire life within it, there was little left uncovered. Sure, mysteries of the divine clouded the facilities of scientists, but Jeweler was no harbinger of science, solely currency, and crime. He begged for answers, however, for these reasons alone,

"Damn, give me some details here. Colors? Planet's got to have some trees, right?" An archaic, mechanical buzz emanated from the man's ear, he twisted in sudden shock at its interruption, smacking at the source with his palm. The Gardener supplied remedies of hue, basic comparisons of leaves and grasses. Not a bit of it led to clarity. "And lizard people, cyan seas — you sure this place is real?"

"The crystal men, pure white, they had windchimes for voices." A final remark chipped off the remaining sanity of the visitor, who until this point remained upright and sturdy. Mumbling ideas of Queenbreakers, and requesting details the Gardener lacked, the visitor glanced out to the stars. The missing clarity clearly irritated the man, so the Gardener retreated back to its drawings, back to the solace of pity memory.

"Are you a machine, like me?" Peregrine agreed it was possible, it had seen convincing recreations of the flesh-ridden kind before.

"Not a chance." By a factor of ten the doubt redoubled. Jeweler shook off the feeling of unfamiliarity that filled his gut, querying the machine as long as it would answer. "How long you been up here?" No answer returned to the bartender, who let his tongue wander in the absence of talk. Jeweler looked up from the indentation in his hand, taking particular intrigue in the carvings, all near identical to his naked eye. "Those drawings yours?" The Gardener did not reply, only stared. It, with the help of a small cabinet, managed to ascend to its feet, now in relative comfort around the new visitor. It followed the human until the two stopped at one of the larger drawings, surrounded by pieces of broken metal and remnants of old paint. "This the human you were talkin' about?" The Gardener nodded, reluctant to admit it was merely a poor recreation.

"I did my best." Jeweler turned to the machine, only now discerning the serious oddness of the Gardener's persona. Its body reflected this inner disharmony, it was clearly in distress, almost violent in nature. A collective anomaly — besides the fact it was a fellow machine for Viaduct to commune with — would make supple additions to his team.

"You know what you are, yeah?" Peregrine attempted to gather the details of this information but had incredible difficulty doing so. It had the call numbers of thousands of Gardeners in its databases, but which of them remained active was inconclusive. The crux of the problem, for once, was too *much* knowledge. Though the Gardener disagreed. It was an anomaly of these simple answers. Occam's Razor was mentioned, and the Gardener referred it away, problems not simple enough for paradoxes diluted the headspace. The answer was purer than that, it would take eons to know, several more to put into words.

"No." Jeweler bit at the inner flesh of his jaw, tense with thought. Impossible odds stacked against him, but he had no choice but to persevere. With another added to their collective, perhaps some of their problems would fade. Perhaps, with any luck, Viaduct would grow more gratified. The Gardener made a good fit, just as mad as any of them. Had it suffered enough alone to be mad?

"You fight well enough? Ought to, with those spears." Jeweler gestured initially to the rack of partially assembled rods, tipped with Damascus and crystal shards, piled up by the grassy exterior of the gardens. Secondly, the bartender scanned the walls behind it, and the ceiling too, both dotted with weapons, some looser than others. The Gardener responded with a resounding yes, affirming it was more than ready for active combat.

"I would love nothing more than active training." It loudly announced, arm brace twitching at the seams.

"How about a deal, simple as. You come with us, help out here 'n there, and we give you more than your fair share of 'active training', yeah?" The Gardener held its illusory breath in anticipation, its eyes increasing ever so slightly in size. "And we tow this here ship of yours along with us. Get a garden going one day, that something you can do?" Peregrine approved, and so did the inner turmoil of the Gardener.

"Will the battles be plentiful?" Jeweler stuffed his pistol back into the brim of his pants, collecting a discarded scarf as he returned closer to the exit,

"Sure as shit."

Cold metal restrained the trickles of blood from her gizzard. Though cut clean through, her heart continued beating. If death had let her off so easily, even she would have expressed concerns. The piles of Crystal surmounted even her heaviest breath, pooled up in puddles of their own excrement. It was pitiful to harbor such military and fail so irregardlessly. She sighed, her wounds becoming far too much for even her to handle, and the crystals growing ever quicker down her veins. The Human had never seen the mural of herself, the one the Gardener had scribed in direct steel for anatomical purposes. She was astounded by its beauty, it paused her fickle troubles sure.

"Hey. Are you dead?" The human leered up towards the voice, a transcendent white glow flooded her vision. She flinched from the increase in pain, but like all her wounds it blended into harmonious ignorance.

"I'll be dead in an hour, or less. Only God knows now." She let her head sink, the facade of this new voice being undoubtedly non-present.

"Nope, I don't. That's why I asked." The Human squinted past the blurry rose color of her unwounded — though false — human form.

"What?" The being before her was impossible, yet logically whole. A round-waisted creature, majestic purity coated its feathery form, thick void-like talons jutted from its limbs and speckled its wings. The tremendous beak upon it dared not open, even when it spoke. There was not a spit of imperfection upon it, even the folds in its wondrous sea of velvet shuddered flawlessly between each other.

"I mean, you are wrong saying that god knows; I am Lakaeron, your god in service. I have no idea if you're dying or not." It paused, flicking soot from its wing. "Though I'd really like it if you didn't." She softly chuckled, her lyrics forming into soggy hacks.

"God. Before me in death. Kindly requesting I stick to life. This is some joke, right?" She slurred the Ichyr from her mouth, sneering at the bird, "There is no *god*. Only rocks and mud. And me. You're a poor imposter — Fuck off." Lakaeron peeled the teeth around its mouth, doubting its literature for a moment.

"I will *not*! I made you, and all your little —." Lakaeron paused, wiggling each talon vigorously. "I am trying my hardest, alright? I really wanted this one to work. Everything ends like the rest — Sludge. Always Queenbreakers." The Human gave courtesy to her god and shifted her neck upwards, careful not to fall aside from the weight of it.

"Do I look like a grimoire to you? I don't give two pigeon shits how hard you're trying. You made this place, all its people? You *royally* fucked it up, then." The God scowled, wishing to slur off the decaying corpse and tromp off into the night sky. He restrained his desires. "Do you intend to watch me bleed out? If you are God, kill me." Lakaeron shook his head, denying her this death,

"Nuh-uh." The bird leaned down, his hand resting still against his breast, another extending to the crystalline outcroppings upon her neck, "Not yet, at least. I want to do this right. I can't keep throwing myself at the bed and missing. Tell me how you died."

"Crystallines? Where else but those vile beasts? They came from the Gaol, wrought by the fluid within." Lakaeron's eyes piqued with intrigue, his hand flicked away from the Human's neck.

"Jail? Do you mean more like a hole? A *well*? Stone bricks as black as—"

"Coal. Marbled murals and locked within reason. Yeah, you seem fairly familiar with the downfall of us all. How pickled." The two were locked in stares as the crickets from the dark harassed the remaining life of the isle. The Human's hands gripped a tool, one that she had at first intended to use against herself, hesitantly changing her objective to the art of creation, rather than that of destruction. She held doubts about this God, reasonably so, but more than anything she hoped in her own incorrectness. She hoped for a quick death. She got nothing in return for her cooperation.

"Thank you." Lakaeron looked back to the sky, distracted by an unknown agent. His wings flickered as if lights in neon, almost found in obvious lies. "You're a cruel lady. But I guess I don't deserve anything else." He looked back at her, whose ducts filled with a milky fluid, her death was still growing. "I'm not a god, just some child pretending to make worlds of clay. Toying with what I shouldn't—" He parted the feathers in his wings, sitting down beside the Human. "I won't let this happen again. You have my word."

"Aye, and yer word is silver." Lakaeron paused, nodded, and stepped away from the Human.

"Snakes-tongue. You bite like one too, lady."

"Human."

"Hmm?"

"Call me what I be, or—ghk—my voice is turning again, accent and all." The bird tilted his head, scales of understanding tipping towards otherwise.

"Human. Is that your only name?" She took one last, pained look at her God, rage temporary and pure,

"Ah… Human, Yeri, Lesskin, all the same at this—" She withdrew to her backside, coughing and sloshing thoroughly. Lakaeron gave her space and returned once more to the near sky.

"Lesskin, that ones really grim. I will never let another Lesskin die by my own stupidity. Never." He flexed his lengthy wings and spun a web of constitution upon his creation. "I can't help you, but I can make a permanent promise." He extended his smallest talon, reaching out to the Human. "I pinkie promise." The Human did not even move her sorry head, hanging below her chest bones protruding so profoundly.

"Sure, promise." With this affirmation, Lakaeron shook the last of his tail feathers down.

"Who should it be bound to, for writing's sake?" She raised her hand closer to the mural of herself, wherein there was a hidden figure. A poorly sketched carving, a product of the Human's cancerous grip and rotted trowel. It strung four limbs, and a round cavity at its skull. Its eyes were smeared with bright yellow dust and had carried with itself a can of water, alongside a lengthy shovel. The Human placed her palm against the drawing and peered beyond the vines of its deathbed. The stars were radiant with life.

"Charlemagne." Lakaeron nodded rapidly, apologized once more for his supposed failure, and left her to death. In the words of a god and the haze of the greenish sky, she had discovered the truth; she'd much rather die down on the surface than up in the stars. There was hate in the stars, surely bandits and machines worse than her humble Gardener. Could anyone survive against a tide of crime and treachery? There was fear in the stars, surely strange beasts, and uncanny science that suffocated the innocent. Could children face the odds of their world and see themselves grow? There was emptiness in the stars, surely lost and decrepit souls with no choice but to vanish in the darkness. Could those who were lost find the light in others, if at all? With impossible odds, terrible peoples, oppressive hunger, and beyond—the Human thought—why had she ever wanted to ascend into the stars? Her words faded, her memories concluded, and thoughts surmised; the heavens were not for her, nor the gods. They were as foolish as she was. The once doubled population count of the island flickered, as it had when being reduced to one—when the Gardener left the planet. The one persuaded to three, before finally settling on zero. Margulis died, nameless and afraid, for her husband lied where she never would go.

~ End of Act II ~

~ *End-terlude* ~

Before you go, I think it would be nice to settle some convenient truths.

You are a curious thing, little jester. Both to me and in truth, you are curious. I do not fully understand your purpose, or what it is your people pride themselves on—unpredictability surely. However, I know you also to be questioning beings, I met the last of your kind who stirred the galaxy about like a bowl of lethargic, clumpy punch. They had one too many questions about them, but no hope to have them answered. As I conclude my first collection of tales (there will be many more to follow, of course) I desire no such fate would befall you, and trounce our friendship out of existence! So, in an effort to console your curious mind and assure our relations for a while, I have extended a wretched hand into your world and established myself securely in its atmosphere. Hopefully, my contact will allow for *some* of the created rumors of mine to be properly closed. Address me in whatever manner you see fit, and at any time at all! You may contact me at one of the avenues listed below, (placed in the most comedic location possible) and I will do my absolute best to answer any riddle you send my way, whether on the topic of my world or not, please question away! Send forth your concentrations, ideas, troubles, and theories—your schematics for the future. This documentation of events may already be in motion, but I ask you, the true jesters, to allow it to be completed. In other words: You are responsible now. You are the jester. You are the panopticon—both eye and cell. Tell me of what will be, and with luck enough, your comedy will fill the pages of the future.

I await your curiosity with utmost privilege and *incredible* delight. For now, I say once more; Arrivederci, little jester!

Come find me, there is much to discuss!

sixthharlequin@gmail.com

P.O. Box 230 Gillette, NJ 07933